Chapter O1

<u>Five weeks later</u>

"Why is it always so difficult to find a dress that I like and feel comfortable in?" Kirstie sighed, glancing at Louise who was sitting on the chair opposite her, watching Kirstie stare at herself in the mirror.

"I have no idea, maybe you are just being too picky." Louise said thoughtfully.

"Yeah maybe, I just want to find something that I look really good in." Kirstie admitted, sighing as she scanned the rails and picked up another selection of dresses.

"What did you wear to the reunion last year?" Louise said, trying to prompt her into finding a suitable dress.

"Just a simple black dress I think, but it's different this year because I'm taking Ben with me." Kirstie pointed out.

"I want to make sure his eyes stay on me." she added.

"I'm sure he will regardless of what you wear." Louise said.

"I'm kind of sad that I don't get to go." Louise said sadly, feeling slightly left out that she was the only one of the group that didn't get to go to the reunion, since she wasn't part of their university.

"Maybe Matt will take you as his plus one?" Kirstie suggested.

"Apparently he's already taking someone." Louise told her.

"Oooh really?!" Kirstie said, frowning to herself that maybe Matt was secretly seeing someone and hadn't told her.

"I think I've finally nailed it!" Michelle said excitedly as she burst out of the dressing room next door. Michelle smiled to herself as she stood in front of the mirror and twirled around.

"Wow, that looks amazing!" Louise breathed as she stared at Michelle in a knee length flowing red dress.

"Who are you taking Michelle?" Kirstie asked.

"I'm still trying to convince Mark to come with me." Michelle replied. Louise and Kirstie glanced at each other awkwardly.

"Does Kathleen know?" Kirstie frowned.

"Yeah, we've spoken about it and although she doesn't like him, she understands. She knows how I feel about him." Michelle admitted, her cheeks colouring slightly as she stared at the ground. Ever since everything that had happened she still felt on the outside of the group and as a result she'd relied on Mark far more than she'd intended too, causing her feelings for him to intensify.

"This is driving me mad." Kathleen said, appearing beside them, her jaw set in frustration.

"What's wrong?" Louise asked her.

"I just feel so frumpy in everything, I still haven't managed to lose the weight I put on when I was pregnant with Daisy. I don't feel good in any of them." Kathleen explained, sighing in frustration.

"That's not true, you look great, you just need to have more confidence in yourself." Michelle told her sweetly.

"That's what David keeps saying." Kathleen sighed.

"I'm so happy things are back on track with you and David." Michelle said, wrapping her arms around Kathleen's waist and hugging her tightly.

"Speaking of men, I heard that you have one in your life now Louise?" Kathleen asked, wiggling her eyebrows at her.

"Yeah Peter, he's amazing." Louise said dreamily, her eyes twinkling as she thought about him.

"Unfortunately we don't get to see each other as often as we'd like because of our hectic schedules, but I got to spend Christmas with him which was amazing." Louise told them.

"Aww I'm so happy for you." Kirstie smiled at her.

"I'm so excited for the reunion, it's going to be amazing for everyone to be together again!" Michelle said excitedly.

"Speaking of which, does anyone know if Chloe is going?" Kathleen asked. Michelle's smile slowly faded from her face as soon as Chloe's name was mentioned.

"After working on her for the past couple of weeks, I've finally convinced her to come along." Kirstie smiled.

"Great." Michelle muttered under her breath.

"Don't even think about starting on her, she's been through enough the past few weeks!" Kirstie warned her quickly.

The four of them instantly stopped talking when they noticed Chloe walking towards them, her cheeks colouring in embarrassment when she noticed them staring at her.

"Hello." she said shyly, when she reached them.

"Oh my god Chloe, it's so good to see you." Louise said, quickly pulling her into a hug. Chloe smiled at her when she eventually let go of her. Kirstie hurried over and quickly hugged Chloe, squeezing her tightly when she suddenly realised how much she'd missed her best friend.

"How are you doing?" Kirstie whispered in Chloe's ear.

"I'm okay." Chloe replied.

"So, have you guys found your dresses?" Chloe asked them.

"I definitely have." Michelle said, twirling proudly.

"Kathleen and I haven't yet." Kirstie told her.

"Do you know what kind of dress you want Chloe?" Kathleen asked her kindly, feeling slightly sorry for her because of everything she'd been through with the media.

"Amy said I should go for something as short and fitted as possible, since Andy will probably be there." Chloe said smiling slightly.

"To rub the little bastards nose in it." Kirstie laughed. Chloe nodded slowly.

"Who's Amy?" Michelle frowned. Chloe sighed quietly to herself as she turned to face Michelle. Even though she knew that she would never forgive Michelle or forget what she'd done to her and Lee all those months ago, Chloe didn't have the energy to continue the conflict, so she made the conscious decision to make the effort to get along with Michelle all the time she was being nice.

"My cousin that I've been staying with, she's a little bit wild." Chloe said, smiling slightly.

"You'll get to meet her later, she's catching us up." she added.

"She came down with you?" Louise asked.

"Yes, we got a hotel because she wants to see the sights of London." Chloe told her.

"Why don't you bring her to the reunion as your plus one?" Kathleen suggested.

"She has a theatre show booked that night." Chloe told them.

"You could always bring Lee?" Michelle said, a small smile playing on the corner of her lips.

"Do you ever hear from him?" Kathleen asked, before Chloe could respond.

"No, not since the day I left. I sent him a text and asked him not to keep calling me and he hasn't since." Chloe explained, swallowing the lump that was rising in her throat. She knew how difficult it would have been for Lee to resist the urge to keep calling her, to try and win her back, but she knew that he cared about her more than he cared about himself and would have wanted to respect her wishes.

"Okay, that subject is off the table!" Kirstie said sternly, when she noticed Chloe's eyes filling with tears.

"Besides we need to find you the hottest dress we can." Louise smiled, quickly standing up and scanning the rails.

"I'm kind of nervous about the reunion." Chloe admitted quietly.

"Why?" Kathleen frowned.

"Because I haven't seen or spoken to Matt since I quit my job quite abruptly, and I kind of let him down at the last minute." Chloe explained.

"I just hope he's not offended." she continued thoughtfully.

"I think he would understand why you left." Kirstie told her.

"Hopefully he managed to find a replacement quickly, especially since there was still a lot to organise for the tour." Chloe sighed.

"The tour got cancelled though didn't it, so it should be fine." Louise told her.

"What?" Chloe frowned. Louise nodded slowly.

"But it's meant to start next week isn't it?" Chloe asked, frowning in confusion.

"It's been rescheduled to next year." Louise said.

"Why?" Chloe asked nervously. Kirstie and Louise glanced at each other awkwardly, the two of them not entirely sure what to say. Chloe glanced between the two of them, suddenly feeling slightly nervous about what they were going to say.

"Actually never mind, I don't want to know." Chloe said quickly, trying to steer her mind away from thinking about the Eclipse boys. The last thing she wanted was to be reminded of how she'd broken Lee's heart.

"This one is perfect!" Louise exclaimed, quickly pulling a dress off the rails. Chloe gasped as she stared at a black bodycon lace dress with a corset bodice that laced up at the front.

"It looks a bit fitted." Chloe said nervously.

"And short." she added.

"Exactly, perfect for you!" Louise said excitedly.

"I think we all know that you can pull it off." Kirstie smiled at her. Chloe smiled back as she tentatively took the dress from Louise, starting down at it, still not entirely sure if she could pull it off or not.

"Oh what the hell." Chloe giggled, finally deciding to throw caution to the wind.

"That looks sick, you'll look amazing in that." Chloe heard Amy's voice from behind her. Chloe quickly turned to face her, smiling slightly at her infectious excitement.

"Guys this is Amy. Amy this is Kathleen, Michelle, Kirstie and Louise." Chloe said, quickly making the introductions.

"It's nice to meet everyone." Amy smiled at the group.

"You've literally found the perfect dress to make that twat's eyes pop out of his head." Amy said quietly to Chloe. Chloe rolled her eyes playfully, not quite able to bring herself to tell the group that it wouldn't make a difference anyway, Andy hadn't wanted her even when they were dating. Before Chloe could talk herself out of it, she quickly walked over to the till to purchase the dress.

"She seems so much better than when she left." Kirstie said, smiling happily as she watched her friend.

"I think she just needed some time out from everything." Amy agreed, sighing quietly to herself when she remembered how broken Chloe was when she'd arrived in Nottingham.

"After a couple of days, she started to feel a little bit better, even though her heart was broken, the pressure from the media was finally gone." Amy explained.

"It did get very out of hand." Michelle said thoughtfully.

"It almost destroyed her." Amy told them.

"The things they were saying were disgusting though, I think it would be difficult for anyone to cope with." Kathleen agreed.

"And she's self-conscious anyway." Kirstie pointed out.

"It was a build-up of things I think." Amy said carefully, not entirely sure which of Chloe's friends, if any, knew about her losing her baby.

"I've been keeping her busy though." Amy added, trying to steer the subject slightly.

"Aww that's really sweet, I'm so happy she finally has some family in her life." Kirstie smiled.

The five of them fell silent as Chloe hurried over to them.

"I've just noticed the time, we're going to be late!" Chloe told Amy, sounding slightly flustered.

"Where are you going?" Kathleen frowned.

"We're meeting Nathan for lunch." Chloe told them.

"I'm so excited!" Amy squealed.

"I used to have posters of Eclipse on my wall when I was a kid!" she quickly added.

"God that makes me feel old." Kathleen laughed.

"We have to go." Chloe said sternly, quickly linking her arm through Amy's and leading her out of the store.

Chapter Two

"Your friends seem really nice." Amy smiled at Chloe as they walked towards the cafe.

"Some of them are." Chloe said shortly.

"Is Michelle the one you told me about?" Amy asked. Chloe nodded slowly, her heart fluttering nervously when she spotted Nathan sitting at a table in the back. As soon as she laid eyes on him, her thoughts wandered to Lee, like Nathan was a constant reminder of him.

"Hey Chlo Bo." Nathan said happily as soon as they reached him. Chloe smiled and quickly hugged him tightly, suddenly realising how much she'd missed him.

"How are things?" Chloe asked him.

"Fine, nothing exciting going on." he replied. Nathan turned to glance at Amy when he felt her watching him. She let out a small squeal of excitement and quickly threw herself into his arms. Nathan raised his eyebrow questioningly at Chloe, smiling slightly when Chloe rolled her eyes and smiled.

"This is my cousin Amy by the way." Chloe chuckled, quickly sitting down at the table, smiling to herself when she noticed that Amy was still holding onto Nathan tightly. Nathan breathed a sigh of relief when Amy finally let go of him and sat beside Chloe.

"I can't believe you worked with them for three years and I didn't get to meet them." Amy pouted.

"We've been over this, we weren't in touch!" Chloe laughed.

"I still don't know if I can forgive you." Amy teased.

"I'm an Eclipse fan, in case you haven't already guessed." Amy laughed, turning to face Nathan when he sat opposite them.

"I had guessed." he laughed.

"Thankfully not one of the fans that hate me." Chloe said, smiling slightly. Nathan smiled slightly, a warm feeling spreading in his chest when he realised how much better Chloe was than when he last saw her.

"If you want, I could arrange for you to meet Adrian and Steven at some point?" Nathan offered, smiling slightly when Amy's eyes lit up.

"What about Lee?" Amy frowned, when she suddenly realised that Nathan hadn't mentioned him.

"He's not in the best place at the moment." Nathan said, glancing at Chloe nervously.

"Why, what's wrong with him?" Chloe blurted before she could stop herself.

"Didn't you read about it in the papers?" Nathan frowned. Chloe shook her head slowly.

"I stay away from the media now for obvious reasons." Chloe told him.

"Not long after you left he ended up in rehab." Nathan said quietly.

"What?" Chloe whispered, swallowing the lump that was rising in her throat.

"His drinking got really bad." Nathan told her, trying to downplay just how much Lee was struggling. The last thing he wanted was to cause Chloe more anguish.

"Is that why the tour got cancelled?" Chloe asked. Nathan nodded sadly. Chloe swallowed the bile that was rising in her throat, her eyes filling with tears as she thought about the man that she loved struggling so much to get through each day that he'd had to find a way to drown his sorrows.

"I'm so sorry, this is all my fault." Chloe whispered, gently wiping away her tears.

"You can't blame yourself, you were struggling. It's not your fault, it's the media's." Nathan told her, quickly reaching over and squeezing her hand reassuringly.

"Is *he* still in rehab?" Chloe asked, not quite able to bring herself to say Lee's name.

"No, he got out about a week ago." Nathan replied, realising instantly who she meant. Chloe nodded slowly and fell silent, her brain working overtime. She knew that she was the reason that Lee was struggling and she needed to see if there was something that she could do to help him, to be able to reach out to him as a friend, to try and repair what she had accidentally broken.

"Maybe I should go and see him." Chloe said thoughtfully.

"If that's what you want." Nathan said, feeling a small glimmer of hope that one day Chloe and Lee would finally get back together. Chloe glanced at Amy, smiling slightly when she saw her nodding enthusiastically.

"Let's go then." Chloe said firmly, quickly standing up before she changed her mind.

"Don't you want to go alone?" Nathan asked.

"No, I'll be tempted to do something I shouldn't if I go alone." Chloe said shortly, staring at Nathan as she waited for him to come with her. Nathan smiled slightly, his heart swelling with pride when he realised that Chloe's confidence was slowly returning to where it had been before the media had interfered in her life.

Chloe's heart pounded against her chest as she followed Nathan into Lee's house, Amy following closely behind them.

"Wow." Amy breathed, as she stared around the house in wonder.

"It feels so weird being back here." Chloe whispered, her stomach churning as she gazed around the house that had been her home for a few months. Her brain was a mist of thoughts, swirling with a mixture of good and bad memories that this house held.

"Maybe this was a bad idea." Chloe whispered thoughtfully. Amy smiled at her sympathetically and took her hand, squeezing it gently, trying to provide some reassurance. Amy knew how difficult it was going to be for Chloe to see Lee again, but she knew how much Chloe still loved him, even though she wouldn't admit it to anyone, even herself. Chloe followed Nathan into the living room, gasping quietly when she noticed that Lee was asleep on the sofa. She walked over to him and carefully perched on the sofa beside him, unable to tear her eyes away from him, almost like she was in a trance.

"He looks awful." Chloe whispered sadly when she suddenly realised how dishevelled Lee looked. She felt another pang of guilt when she noticed the large dark circles under his eyes.

"I think he looks handsome." Amy giggled, trying to lighten the atmosphere. Chloe's eyes filled with tears as she reached out and slowly stroked his face with her fingertips.

"I'm really sorry." Chloe whispered, wishing with all her heart that she hadn't been forced to break Lee's heart in order to protect her own sanity. Her heart sunk even further when she noticed that despite it being late afternoon, Lee was still in his pyjamas. Nathan's words from earlier swirled around her head, she couldn't help but feel concerned that Lee felt like he had nothing to fight for anymore. Chloe quickly pulled her hand back when she noticed Lee's eyelids flickering open. He glanced up at her for a moment and sighed quietly, not quite able to believe that Chloe was sitting beside him on the sofa. He'd dreamt about her so many times since she'd been gone that he couldn't help but feel like he was still dreaming. He opened his eyes further, his heart pounding against his chest when he realised that Chloe was still beside him. Lee rubbed his eyes and slowly sat up, unable to tear his eyes away from her.

"Chlo?" he asked, not even daring to hope that she'd finally returned to him.

"Hey." Chloe said awkwardly, suddenly feeling slightly nervous about how he might react. Before Chloe could react, Lee shuffled along the sofa and threw himself into her arms. Chloe gasped, losing her balance and falling back onto the sofa. She wrapped her arms around Lee's neck as he lay on top of her, holding her tightly. Despite the fact that Lee was crushing her under his large frame, in that moment, she didn't care.

"You finally came back." he whispered in her ear, his voice breaking with emotion. Lee held her tighter than he'd ever held her before, afraid that if he let her go, she would leave him again. Nothing had been the same since she'd left, he had no purpose and nothing to live for. There seemed to be no point in struggling to get through each day when he knew that Chloe was no longer in his life. Time had stood still from the moment that he'd read her note, he didn't even know how long she'd been gone, all he knew was that it felt like they'd been apart for a lifetime.

"Lee, you're crushing me a bit." Chloe said breathlessly. As soon as she said those words, Lee quickly sat up, pulling Chloe with him, burying his head in her shoulder and sighing in contentment.

"I missed you so much." he whispered impulsively, trying to hold back the tears that were slowly filling his eyes. Chloe closed her eyes, her heart pounding against her chest as she desperately tried to fight her feelings. In a few short weeks, she'd forgotten how it felt to be in his arms, how loved and safe she felt. After a few moments Chloe sighed to herself when she realised that Lee was never going to want to let go of her. She slowly sat back, watching him closely as he quickly wiped the tears from his eyes. Chloe glanced down at his lips, as he leaned towards her.

"Wait!" Chloe said, quickly turning her face away from him. Lee frowned at her and raised his eyebrow questioningly.

"I have a boyfriend." she told him tentatively, slightly nervous about how he was going to react. Lee stared at her, in numb shock as he tried to process her words. He couldn't quite process the idea of Chloe with someone else. Another man who got to hold her tightly in his arms as she fell asleep. To tell her that he loved her and comfort her when she was upset. He felt sick to his stomach at the thought that he could have lost her for good.

"Why did you come back then?" Lee snapped defensively, trying in vain to hide how hurt he was feeling.

"I'm here for the University reunion and I heard that you were struggling so I wanted to reach out to you as a friend." Chloe quickly explained, suddenly feeling really guilty when she noticed how sad he looked.

"But I can go if it's easier?" Chloe offered when Lee remained silent. Lee shook his head slowly, not quite ready to say goodbye to her again yet.

"I didn't realise you had met someone." Nathan said quietly, glancing at Lee and feeling a sudden pang of guilt when he saw his expression.

"We went speed dating didn't we." Amy said, trying to lighten the atmosphere. Chloe nodded slowly, trying not to look at Lee as she felt him staring at her intensely.

"And out of eight men, five of them called her." Amy continued, trying to fill the awkward silence.

"I'm not surprised." Nathan said, smiling at Chloe.

"She got the beautiful genes." Amy grinned.

"No I didn't." Chloe protested.

"Yeah you did.....you lucky bitch." Amy teased. Nathan and Chloe burst out laughing, watching Amy as she pouted at Chloe, pretending to be angry. Even Lee couldn't help but smile at her.

"This is my cousin Amy by the way." Chloe said, finally glancing at Lee when she'd eventually stopped laughing. Lee nodded slowly.

"I'm the fun one in the family." Amy beamed.

"You mean the wild one." Chloe smiled. Amy shrugged.

"So tell me about this boyfriend then?" Lee asked, his mouth feeling slightly dry.

"There's not much to tell really." Chloe said quietly.

"He's great, his name is Martin and he's a builder.....and he's very good looking." Amy piped up.

"I think he's really into you as well." Amy added, frowning slightly when Chloe glared at her across the room. The last thing Chloe wanted to do was to hurt Lee any more than she already had, and she knew from his body language that he was struggling to listen to Amy's words. The four of them fell silent, clearly picking up on the tense atmosphere. Chloe couldn't help but squirm slightly as she felt Lee watching her closely, he'd barely been able to tear his eyes away from her since the moment that he'd seen her.

"Is this where you used to live?" Amy asked Chloe. Chloe nodded slowly.

"That must have been *terrible*." Amy teased.

"It has a pool and a gym too." Nathan said, rolling his eyes.

"Ooh, can I go in the pool?" Amy asked Lee.

"If you want." Lee said, smiling slightly at her.

"I'll show you where it is." Nathan said, quickly standing up. Chloe's heart pounded against her chest as she watched Nathan and Amy walking out of the room. She couldn't help but feel slightly nervous about spending time alone with Lee, she knew that when she was alone with him, it was more difficult for her to fight her feelings for him.

"She's a bit intense isn't she." Lee said as soon as Nathan and Amy had left the room.

"She's only eighteen, so she's just young." Chloe said, still not quite able to bring herself to look at Lee.

"I think she secretly looks up to you." he told her.

"Probably. She's just got her first boyfriend so she keeps asking my advice on things, I keep telling her that she's asking the wrong person." she said, smiling slightly.

"Speaking of boyfriends, what's going on with you and this Martin guy?" he asked quickly.

"What do you mean?" she frowned.

"Have you slept with him yet?" he blurted, his stomach churning as he waited to hear her response.

"What?" she muttered, thinking that she must have misheard him.

"Have you slept with him yet?" he repeated.

"I'm not answering that." she said quickly, her cheeks colouring.

"But I need to know." he insisted.

"Why, what difference does it make?" she asked, feeling slightly confused as to why he was acting so strangely.

"Because you only sleep with someone if you love them, and I need to know if there is still hope or if I've lost you for good." he admitted.

"Well my relationship is my personal business. I didn't come back for us to get back together, I was just trying to do the right thing." she explained. Lee opened his mouth to ask her again, but quickly closed it when he realised that she wasn't going to answer his question. His brain was spinning, feeling slightly sick to his stomach that Chloe might have fallen in love with someone else. He desperately needed to know if there was still a chance that he could win her back.

"Can we change the subject please?" Chloe asked, snapping Lee out of his thoughts.

"You seem a lot better than when I last saw you." Lee said sadly, reluctantly changing the subject like she'd asked. Chloe nodded slowly, turning on the sofa to face him. She quickly tucked her legs underneath her and rested her elbow on the back of the sofa.

"I just needed to get away from the pressure of the media, it was too much." she admitted.

"I know, it did get really intense didn't it." he agreed.

"I'm just really sorry that I had to hurt you in the process." she said softly, finally looking him in the eyes. As soon as she locked eyes with him, she felt goosebumps rise on her arms, her legs feeling slightly weak under his intense gaze.

"It's okay, I understand why you did it." he told her.

"It was slowly tearing me apart, and then when Andy's article came out and the fans were telling me to kill myself....I knew I couldn't take it anymore." she explained.

"I know, when I saw the sleeping tablets on the counter, I was so afraid that you had tried to take your own life." he said sadly.

"I didn't, I just thought about it." she said.

"That's why when you asked me to stop calling you, even though it was killing me not too, I did, because I knew that you needed to get away from everything." he explained, his heart breaking a little when he remembered how broken Chloe had been, as a result of his lifestyle. Chloe nodded slowly.

"My aunt has been helping a lot though, she convinced me to go to counselling to help with my confidence." she told him. He smiled at her, feeling a warm sense of pride in his heart when he realised how much happier she was now that she finally had some family in her life.

"They gave me counselling in rehab too." he told her. Chloe raised her eyebrow and waited for him to continue.

"Once you finally come down from being on the drink, they try and help with the root cause, so that you don't end up relapsing." he explained, sighing quietly to himself when he remembered how alone he'd felt when Chloe left.

"Did it help?" she asked. He nodded slowly.

"I made a promise that I wouldn't drink again, and I haven't touched a drop since." he said quietly, his eyes flicking to the window as he remembered how he'd sworn on Riley's grave that he would never relapse.

"I heard that the tour has been cancelled." Chloe asked, snapping him out of his thoughts.

"Yeah I can't bring myself to go." he admitted.

"Why not?" she frowned.

"Because why should I stand on that stage, pretending to be happy so that the fans that destroyed our relationship have a nice time." he said bitterly.

"You can't give up what you love doing though." she pointed out sadly, her heart sinking slightly as she thought about him no longer doing what he loved to do.

"I'm just taking a break." he told her.

"My voice isn't great anyway, because I was drinking too much, so I have to rest it." he added.

"I thought you sounded a bit hoarse." she said quietly. Lee nodded slowly. He sighed deeply as he watched her closely, desperately trying to resist the temptation to pull her into his arms and kiss her deeply. Before Lee could stop himself, he slowly reached out and gently stroked her arm with his fingertips, smiling slightly she shivered involuntarily.

"Your neck looks so bare without your necklace." he said sadly.

"Please don't." she whispered, squirming away from him slightly as his fingers trailed along her collarbone. Chloe closed her eyes, trying to focus her mind away from the intense desire that she was feeling for him.

"Why not?" he whispered, smiling slightly when he noticed the effect that he was having on her.

"Because I have a boyfriend and it's not appropriate." she said quickly, her eyes snapping open.

Lee sighed and reluctantly moved his hand away from her. Chloe jumped as her phone began to ring. She glanced down at the display, her heart plummeting when she saw that Martin was calling her. She stared at the phone on her lap, feeling slightly uncomfortable as it continued to ring. Lee couldn't help but feel a small glimmer of hope when he suddenly realised that Chloe still had *Broken* as her ringtone.

"Is that *him?*" Lee asked sadly, staring at the screen, his heart plummeting when he read Martin's name. Chloe nodded slowly.

"I'll call him back later." she muttered, her cheeks colouring as Lee stared at her.

"I should go and check on Amy." she said, quickly standing up and leaving the room, safely placing her phone on the coffee table.

Chloe smiled to herself as she walked into the swimming pool room and perched on one of the loungers, glancing up at Lee as he sat on the floor, quickly rolling up his pyjama trousers and placing his legs into the pool.

"This house is epic by the way!" Amy called as she swam over to them.

"Thanks." Lee said, smiling slightly at how excited she was. Chloe burst out laughing as she glanced over at the hot tub and saw Nathan waving at them happily.

"Are you coming in Chloe?" Amy asked her. Chloe shook her head slowly.

"Just strip down to your underwear, you'll be fine." Amy insisted.

"I don't want too." Chloe sighed.

"Why not, he's gay...so he won't be looking at you." Amy said pointing at Nathan.

"And he's seen your body before." she continued, pointing at Lee.

"That's not the point, we're meant to be going to the theatre, and I don't want to be in wet underwear." Chloe said quickly.

"Oh shit, I forgot about that." Amy said, quickly climbing out of the pool.

"And yet you are the one who wants to go." Chloe chuckled. Amy shrugged and quickly pulled her clothes on, cursing as she struggled to pull her jeans onto her wet skin. Chloe stood up and hovered awkwardly as she waited for Amy.

"Wait, are you leaving?!" Lee exclaimed, starting to panic slightly. Chloe nodded slowly, glancing at him as he quickly stood up and walked over to her.

"When do you go back to Nottingham?" Lee asked.

"Monday." Chloe said quietly.

"What day is it today?" Lee frowned.

"Today is Saturday." Chloe told him, smiling slightly.

"Will I see you again before you go back?" Lee asked nervously.

"I don't know, we have quite a hectic schedule." Chloe said, trying to remain firm in her need to stay away from him. Despite the fact that she longed to spend as much time with him as possible, she knew that she would be tempted to get back with him and she couldn't allow that to happen. Lee nodded slowly, his heart breaking all over again as he watched Chloe walk away from him.

Chapter Three

Kirstie smiled to herself as she gazed around the table at her friends, not quite able to believe how much things had changed for them all over the past year. She couldn't believe that Kathleen was now a mother and her and David had finally found a way to make things work. She smiled at them as David picked up a peanut from the bowl on the table and gently fed it to Kathleen. Kirstie frowned to herself as she watched Michelle sitting silently beside Mark. Despite everything that Michelle had done, Kirstie couldn't help but feel slightly sorry for her friend when she noticed the way that Michelle was gazing at Mark. She clearly had strong feelings for him, but Mark seemed completely disinterested, his eyes wandering the room as he gazed around at other women.

"I wonder where Matt has got too." Chloe frowned, gazing at her watch.
"I know, he's never late to anything is he. I hope he's okay." Kirstie said thoughtfully. Chloe gasped, her glass of wine slipping out of her hand and smashing loudly on the floor as she stared across the room at the doorway. Kirstie frowned and quickly followed Chloe's eyeline, gasping when she saw Matt crossing the room, his arm draped casually around Nathan's waist.
"Did you know about them?" Chloe asked Kirstie quietly. Kirstie shook her head slowly, trying to ignore the feeling of hurt that she felt.
"Hey guys." Matt said casually, as he and Nathan sat down at the table. The group stared at them in shock, not entirely sure what to say.
"Are you guys a thing?!" Ben exclaimed, glancing between Matt and Nathan.
"Yeah." Nathan said awkwardly.
"Oh my god, since when?!" Kathleen exclaimed.
"A few months I think." Matt said, glancing at Nathan who nodded in agreement.
"We didn't want to mention it until we knew that things were going well, because we didn't want it to be awkward at the studio." Matt explained, glancing at Chloe who sighed quietly when she was reminded once again of her own situation.
"That studio is a hive of secret relationships." Michelle laughed.
"I'm surprised you didn't tell me." Kirstie said quietly, slightly confused as to why one of her best friends, hadn't felt that he'd been able to confide in her.

"We literally didn't tell anyone." Matt said, feeling slightly guilty when he noticed the hurt expression on Kirstie's face.
"I bet he told Lee though." Kirstie pointed out, pointing at Nathan.
"I only told him earlier when we decided it was time to make it an official thing." Nathan told her. Kirstie nodded slowly. Ben smiled at her and wrapped his arm around her shoulders, squeezing her slightly to try and reassure her.

"Oh my god, I've just noticed there's a pole over there!" Kathleen laughed as her eyes wandered across the hall.

"If Amy was here right now, she'd be straight on that." Chloe giggled.

"I would love to learn how to do pole fitness and dancing and stuff." Kirstie said, taking a sip of her wine.

"I think you'd be quite good at it." Ben winked at her, a wide smile on his face that caused everyone to burst out laughing.

"Amy and I have been having lessons, it's actually quite easy." Chloe told them.

"Yeah it probably is for you, but not everyone has a really strong core like you do." Kirstie laughed.

"True, I hadn't thought about it like that." Chloe giggled.

"You could totally teach us how to do it!" Kirstie said excitedly.

"No, everyone will stare at me!" Chloe protested.

"Everyone keeps staring at you in that dress anyway." Kathleen laughed.

"No they don't." Chloe argued, as she quickly stood up and walked over to the bar, finally deciding that she needed some alcohol. Kirstie smiled as she watched Chloe walk through the hall, almost every man in the building turning to stare at her as she walked past them.

"She just doesn't get it does she." Kathleen said, smiling when she followed Kirstie's eyeline.

"Can you put your eyes back in your head please?!" Michelle snapped at Mark, when she noticed him watching Chloe closely. Mark shook his head at her and sighed deeply.

"I think I need a drink." Michelle said shortly, quickly picking up the bottle of wine on the table and downing it.

"Slow down Michelle, you know what you're like when you are drunk." Matt told her. Michelle rolled her eyes at him and continued to drink. Kirstie smiled at Chloe as she returned to the table, slowly pulling down the dress and wincing slightly.

"You okay Chloe?" Kirstie asked worriedly.

"This dress is like a second skin." Chloe smiled slightly.

"You look amazing in it though." Kirstie told her.

"You almost turned me straight when I saw you wearing it." Nathan chuckled. Chloe glanced at him for a moment, before bursting out laughing, her cheeks colouring slightly.

"Oh god." Chloe mumbled, her heart sinking when she noticed Andy walking into the hall. She squirmed lower in her seat, trying to hide herself behind Ben. Ben followed Chloe's eyeline, sighing quietly when he noticed Andy.

"I think I need to go home." Chloe admitted, swallowing the lump that was rising in her throat. As soon as she'd laid eyes on him, she couldn't help but remember what he'd done to her all those weeks ago, how the lies that he'd made up about her, had finally been the last straw. A few lies that had been printed in ink, that had caused

Chloe's life to almost be destroyed. She still couldn't understand what she had done to him to make him hate her so much.

"Don't let him push you out Chloe, he's the one that was in the wrong not you." Ben pointed out.

"You have nothing to hide from." Kirstie agreed, feeling slightly sorry for Chloe when she noticed her squirming. Chloe slowly picked up her drink and downed it, trying to escape from the flashbacks that were swirling around her head.

"You should go the opposite, show him that he hasn't affected you." Kathleen suggested.

"What do you mean?" Chloe frowned.

"Like for example, get up on that pole and dance, show him what he's missing." Kathleen explained.

"That's a really good idea." Kirstie giggled.

"No, I can't." Chloe said quietly.

"C'mon, you can do this." Kirstie said, quickly taking Chloe's hand and standing up, trying to pull Chloe up. Kathleen laughed and quickly stood up, taking Chloe's other hand.

"Okay fine." Chloe giggled, finally giving in and standing up. Her eyes flickered to Andy nervously as she quickly walked past him, her cheeks colouring in embarrassment when she was reminded once again of all the repulsive things he'd made up about her.

"Okay so, you need to climb halfway up the pole, keeping your right leg straight, bend your left leg at the knee, engage your core and then slowly lean backwards." Chloe said, quickly demonstrating to Kirstie and Kathleen.

"And then if you want too, you can let go and do something pretty with your arms, but it depends on how strong your core is." Chloe told them as she quickly let go of the pole. Kathleen and Kirstie stared at her in amazement. Chloe quickly slid down the pole and removed her heels.

"There's another one you can do, you need to walk around the pole, then throw yourself onto it and spin around, doing something pretty with your legs." Chloe demonstrated, smiling slightly as she spun around, eventually coming to a stop and jumping off the pole.

"Your turn." Chloe smiled at them.

"There is no way I can follow that." Kirstie laughed.

"And I just wanted to get you up there to prove a point." Kathleen whispered to Chloe, smiling slightly when she glanced behind herself and saw that Andy was standing close by, staring at Chloe. Kirstie jumped as she felt someone place their hand on her rear. She quickly turned around, frowning when she realised that it was Andy.

"Maybe you should have a go beautiful, and then we can dance?" Andy asked, glancing up at Chloe as he said those words, a small smirk playing on his lips.

"I'd rather not, especially after what you did to my friend." Kirstie snapped.

"Yeah well she had it coming." Andy said shortly. Before Kirstie realised what she was doing she reached out and quickly slapped Andy hard across the cheek, all the anger that she'd felt over what he did to Chloe, finally bubbling to the surface.

"You like to get people to fight your battles for you don't you." Andy sneered at Chloe.

"I don't know what you're talking about." Chloe said dismissively, quickly pulling her heels back on and climbing down from the platform.

"How about the fact that you set your boyfriend on me like some sort of attack dog." Andy said smugly.

"What?" Chloe frowned.

"Oh.....you mean he didn't tell you he came to my house and beat me up." Andy sneered.

"You're just making up more lies....Martin doesn't even know you exist." Chloe said shortly, quickly walking away from him. She froze to the spot as she heard Andy calling after her:

"I meant Lee." he called.

"Lee beat you up?" Chloe frowned, slowly turning to face him.

"Yep, his friend had to stop him." Andy said, smirking slightly when he saw how shocked Chloe looked. She remained frozen to the spot, trying to decide whether she believed him or not. She knew that he was prone to making up lies, but she also knew how angry Lee got when anyone did anything to hurt her.

"Also, stop pretending to be a tart when we both know that you don't like to give up the goods." Andy told her, smiling slightly as he slowly looked her up and down.

"You always try and blame me for everything, but it's not my fault that you didn't want me." Chloe snapped defensively.

"Why would I, who wants to be with someone who doesn't know what they are doing?!" Andy said smugly. Chloe felt like someone had stabbed her in the chest as he said those words, her cheeks colouring when she locked eyes with Kirstie and quickly realised that she'd heard what Andy had said. She'd never felt so mortified in her life. Andy stared at Chloe, smirking slightly when he realised how embarrassed she was. Before Chloe realised what she was doing, she quickly slapped Andy hard across the cheek, her hurt quickly turning into anger.

"What's going on?" Chloe heard Lee's voice from behind her. Chloe quickly whirled around, frowning to herself when she locked eyes with Lee.

"What are you doing here?!" Chloe exclaimed.

"I wanted to see you again before you go back to Nottingham." he told her. Chloe nodded slowly, glancing at Andy and smiling to herself when she noticed him squirming nervously, his eyes fixed on Lee. Lee glared at him, smiling in satisfaction when he eventually turned and scurried away.

"I can't believe he said that about you." Kirstie said quietly.

"Please don't tell anyone that I lied about doing things with him." Chloe said quickly, wishing that the ground would swallow her up. She glanced around nervously, searching for Kathleen, sighing in relief when she saw her walking out of the bathroom. As mortified as Chloe was, she couldn't help but feel a sense of relief that at least only Kirstie knew the truth and she could be trusted to keep it to herself.

"Of course I won't say anything." Kirstie reassured Chloe, snapping her out of her thoughts. Chloe nodded slowly, falling silent as Andy's words swirled around her head.

"I think I'm going to call it a night." Chloe said quietly.

"Do you want Ben to give you a lift back to the hotel?" Kirstie offered.

"No, it's okay, I can walk." Chloe said shortly, before quickly walking away from them.

"I'll make sure she gets back safely." Lee reassured her, before hurrying after Chloe. Chloe gasped as she walked out of the hall and was hit by a cold blast of winter air. She huddled her arms across her chest, desperately wishing that she'd brought a jacket.

"Chlo, my car is in the car park if you want a lift?" Lee offered as he hurried after her. Chloe stopped and turned to face him, watching as he quickly caught up with her.

"Besides you can't walk the streets of London in the dark, wearing that dress. You're like bait for all the creeps." he said, smiling slightly.

"You can't say stuff like that." she laughed. Lee shrugged, smiling at her. He gestured for her to walk in front of him, quickly bringing up the rear as the two of them walked to the carpark. As soon as Lee unlocked the car, Chloe quickly climbed into the passenger seat, sighing in relief when she closed the door and was finally out of the cold wind.

"Are you cold?" Lee asked as he climbed into the car and noticed Chloe shivering. She nodded slowly, watching Lee as he quickly switched on the heater. She sighed and snuggled into the seat, smiling slightly when she felt the seat warmer kick in.

"I bet you've missed my seat warmers haven't you." Lee laughed, quickly pulling out of the carpark. Chloe laughed, nodding slowly.

"I heard what Andy said to you." he told her.

"It's nothing I haven't heard a hundred times before, it was just a bit humiliating that Kirstie heard." she sighed.

"I don't think she'll tell the others though." he reassured her. Chloe shook her head slowly.

"Andy said that you beat him up?" she asked him, slightly nervous about his answer.

"Yeah I did." he said, sighing deeply.

"I really regret doing that, I was just so angry at what he did to you." he explained.

"I got help for my anger when I was in rehab." he added.

"Good, you do seem calmer in general." she said quietly.

"Just please don't beat anyone up because of me." she added. Lee nodded slowly.

"I've just realised I don't know what hotel you are staying at." Lee chuckled, suddenly realising that he was automatically driving them home.

"The one not far from my house?" he asked.

"Yep." she said quietly.

"I can't believe Matt is dating Nathan." she said, trying to fill the silence.

"Me neither, I didn't see that coming." he agreed.

"I think they'll be good for each other though." she said thoughtfully.

"Yeah probably." he agreed, his heart sinking when they pulled up at the hotel and he realised that he was going to have to say goodbye to Chloe once again.

"Thank you for the lift." she said quietly.

"No problem." he replied, his mouth suddenly feeling slightly dry.

"Wait!" he said quickly when Chloe started to open the car door. She paused for a moment, turning to face him.

"Can I come inside with you?" he asked nervously.

"What for?" she asked, her heart pounding against her chest at the thought of being alone with him in a hotel room.

"Just for a cup of tea or something." he told her.

"I just want to spend as much time with you as possible before you go home." he added tentatively. Chloe hesitated for a moment before nodding slowly.

Chapter Four

Chloe smiled at Lee as she silently handed him a mug of tea. He smiled his thanks at her and quickly perched on the bed, watching her closely as she removed her heels and climbed onto the desk opposite him, quickly crossing her legs. Chloe avoided his gaze as she sat silently swirling her tea bag around her mug.

"You look stunning tonight Chlo." Lee whispered, not quite able to tear his eyes away from gazing at her in wonder. Her cheeks coloured as she sat silently, trying to avoid eye contact.

"I saw you dancing on the pole." he tried again when she didn't respond.

"I can't believe I did that." she said quietly.

"I have to admit, I was a bit shocked, but you looked amazing." he told her.

"The girls convinced me." she admitted, smiling slightly.

"Maybe Amy's wildness is rubbing off on you." he laughed.

"I hope not." she giggled.

"She's terrible, she gets up to all sorts." she laughed, rolling her eyes slightly, taking a deep breath and finally looking Lee in the eye.

"I was the same at her age to be fair." he laughed.

"Like tonight for example, she went to the theatre and met some people there and they've all gone out clubbing." she said, rolling her eyes.

"That's standard crazy young person." he smiled, suddenly remembering all the times that he'd done wild things during his youth.

"I just hope she'll be okay." she said thoughtfully.

"I'm sure she will be, she seems pretty tough." he reassured her. Chloe nodded slowly, her stomach churning as she thought about Amy being out late in London with complete strangers. She couldn't help but feel slightly nervous that something might happen to her.

"I'm so happy that you finally have some family in your life." he said thoughtfully, smiling slightly when he realised how much happier she was now that she had them in her life.

"Me too, it makes all the difference. My aunt was quite upset when she found out about everything I'd been through and she wasn't there to help." she explained.

"I bet she was. I felt the same when I found out you'd been sleeping in the park." he told her.

"That feels like so long ago now." she said quietly, quickly gazing down at her lap.

"I know, so much has changed." he sighed, his heart sinking when he was reminded once again that he'd lost her.

"We had good times though didn't we." he smiled. Chloe nodded, glancing up at Lee and smiling at him as she thought about all the fun they'd had together over the years.

"We definitely did." she smiled at him.

"I'll never forget that time we went to the beach with the boys for your leaving do....and you were so happy." he said thoughtfully.

"And I ran off to mess about on the rocks." she smiled. Lee chuckled, nodding slowly.

"And you opened up about your life." he reminded her.

"Oh yes, the boys wanted to get me to drink seawater." she smiled fondly, as she thought of all the good times that she'd had with Lee and the boys.

"And you poured water on Steven's fire." he laughed.

"That's right I did." she giggled.

"I'd forgotten about that." she added.

"Maybe we could go to the beach tomorrow, for old time sake?" he suggested nervously, desperately hoping that she would agree so that he could spend as much time with her as possible, before she was taken from him again.

"That's probably not such a good idea." she said quietly, trying to resist the urge to spend more time with him. She wasn't entirely sure that she trusted herself around him, particularly when they were alone. Despite the fact that she knew in her heart how much she still loved him, she knew she had to remain firm and not succumb to his charms.

"I meant as friends, I would really like to still have you in my life as a friend." he said quietly, snapping her out of her thoughts.

"Maybe, I'll have to see what Amy is doing." she said quietly, glancing up at him when she heard him sigh in disappointment.

"You will say goodbye before you go won't you?" he asked her. Chloe nodded slowly, feeling a pang of guilt when she remembered how she'd left him without even saying goodbye.

"I guess I should go soon." he said quietly, glancing at his watch and gasping when he realised how late it was. It didn't seem possible that the two of them had been in the hotel room, talking for the past couple of hours. Lee reluctantly stood up and walked over to the desk, carefully placing his mug down and trying to avoid thinking about how close his body was to touching Chloe. He glanced down at her for a moment, his breath catching in his throat when he saw her gazing up at him silently. Before Lee realised what he was doing, he slowly reached out and gently tucked her hair behind her ear, his fingers brushing against her cheek as he did so. The hairs on the back of Chloe's neck stood on end as his fingertips softly grazed her cheek. In the space of a few short weeks, she'd forgotten how it felt when he touched her, how her skin tingled under his touch. She took deep breaths, trying to steady herself when his hand lingered in place, his fingertips softly stroking her neck. Lee stared down at her, unable to tear his eyes away from her lips, desperately trying to fight the intense urge to kiss her. He glanced down at his hand, as he felt Chloe reach out to take it and gently place their hands on her lap, smiling slightly as she softly played with his fingers. Chloe trembled under his touch, watching closely as his fingers slowly traced a line up her abdomen to her sternum, finally coming to a stop when he reached the laces on her dress. Chloe sighed deeply, quickly leaning forward and resting her forehead against Lee's shoulder.

"This is wrong, I shouldn't be feeling like this." she whispered to herself.

"It's okay Chlo." he whispered, gently stroking her hair. Before Chloe could talk herself out of it, she sat back and quickly climbed off the desk, and moved a safe distance from him.

"I'm sorry." Lee said quickly, feeling slightly frustrated with himself that he'd almost allowed his desire for her to get the better of him.

"It's okay." Chloe said quietly, trying to ignore the anger she was feeling with herself for still having such strong feelings for him.

"I should go." he said awkwardly.

"You don't have to go." she replied quietly, her heart plummeting at the thought of him leaving. Spending the last couple hours with him had reminded her just how much she had missed being in his presence, how safe and comforting it felt.

"We could watch some tv or something?" she suggested, avoiding his gaze as she sat on the bed, curling her legs under her, conscious of the fact that she was still wearing a short dress. Lee smiled at her as he sat beside her and picked up the remote.

"What do you want to watch?" he asked her as he flicked through the channels.

"Ooh we used to watch this all the time with the boys didn't we!" she exclaimed.

"Yep and you always teased me that I was like one of the characters." he laughed.

"A less creepy version." she said, joining in with his laughter.

"And you do like the ladies." she added.

"I used to be really bad didn't I." he chuckled. Chloe nodded, giggling to herself when she remembered the amount of awkward encounters she'd had with half naked women when she was working with the Eclipse boys.

"I think you're a bit like Harriet." he said, a smile playing on the corner of his lips.

"Really, why?" she frowned.

"Because you are really sweet, but secretly you are a little firecracker." he grinned, smiling at Chloe when she burst out laughing.

"Only sometimes." she laughed. Butterflies swirled in her stomach when she finally locked eyes with Lee, sighing quietly when she felt herself slowly becoming lost in them. Chloe quickly looked away from him and turned her attention to the television, trying to focus her mind on something other than the fact that Lee was lying beside her on the bed. A few moments of silence passed, before Chloe frowned to herself and turned to face Lee. She smiled to herself when she noticed that he had fallen asleep. She quickly switched off the television and carefully climbed off the bed, trying not to wake him. Chloe sighed to herself as she walked into the bathroom and locked the door. She slowly untied the laces and slipped out of her dress, before quickly climbing into the shower, her mind wandering to Lee once again. She'd known from the beginning how difficult it would be to see him again, so she'd planned to avoid him during her visit, but now that she had reached out to him, she couldn't resist the urge to be in his presence. She stared at her reflection in the mirror and silently cursed herself for not being stronger. She knew that they couldn't ever get back together, she couldn't go through the media storm again. It had nearly destroyed her the first time and she knew that she wasn't strong enough to go through it again. It had taken her a few weeks to finally start to feel like herself again, and despite the fact that she was still nursing a broken heart, she no longer felt completely worthless and miserable. Her head knew all of this.....but her heart was yearning to be with Lee, to be able to kiss him and to fall asleep in his arms. To feel cherished and loved again, like he'd always made her feel.

Chloe climbed out of the shower and quickly wrapped a towel around her naked frame, cursing to herself when she realised that she'd forgotten to bring her pyjamas into the bathroom with her. She slowly opened the bathroom door and peered around it, before hesitantly stepping into the bedroom. Chloe jumped when she saw Amy in the corner, quickly rummaging in her suitcase.

"Why is Lee asleep on my bed?" Amy asked, as soon as she laid eyes on Chloe.
"Because he fell asleep watching TV and your bed is the one in front of the TV." Chloe replied. Amy raised her eyebrow sceptically as she glanced between Lee, who was still sleeping soundly on the bed, and Chloe, who was standing in front of her, wearing only a towel after having showered. Chloe glanced at Lee, her cheeks colouring when she suddenly realised what Amy was thinking.
"It's not what it looks like!" Chloe said quickly.
"People always say that." Amy giggled.
"It's not though, I swear nothing happened." Chloe told her firmly.
"Um hum." Amy grinned sceptically.

"Oh whatever." Chloe sighed, quickly picking up her pyjamas and walking into the bathroom.
Chloe could feel Amy watching her closely when she finally emerged from the bathroom.
"I'll need to sleep in your bed." Amy told her. Chloe nodded in agreement, sighing when she realised that her bed was the single sofa bed. Chloe glanced at the double bed, sighing quietly to herself when she realised that Lee was still fast asleep. Chloe quickly picked up the spare blanket and began to make a makeshift bed on the floor.
"Are you sleeping on the floor?" Amy frowned.
"Well yeah." Chloe said quietly.
"Sleep in the double." Amy said quickly.
"Don't be ridiculous." Chloe said shortly.
"You've slept in a bed with him before though." Amy pointed out.
"That's not the point, I have a boyfriend and it's really not appropriate to sleep beside another man when you have a boyfriend." Chloe said quietly.

"Well do you want the bed then and I'll take the floor?" Amy offered.

"No, it's fine, I've slept on worse." Chloe said, as she picked up the spare pillow from the double bed and laid down on the floor, quickly pulling the blanket over herself. Amy climbed into bed and quickly switched off the light. Chloe sighed to herself as she stared at the beads of faint light on the ceiling.

"Chloe?" Amy whispered a few moments later, checking to see if Chloe was still awake.

"What?" Chloe answered.

"Are you sure nothing happened?" Amy asked.

"Positive, we were just talking about old times." Chloe told her firmly.

"I thought you weren't planning to see him again." Amy frowned.

"I wasn't, he turned up at the reunion and ended up giving me a lift home." Chloe explained.

"Oooh." Amy giggled.

"No not like that, I left early because Andy was there and obviously Ben gave me a ride to the reunion and he wasn't ready to leave yet." Chloe told her.

"Ugh, Andy is such a dick." Amy said shortly.

"I know." Chloe sighed, her cheeks colouring when she remembered what Andy had said about her.

"Anyway, how come you're not wasted, you normally are when you've been clubbing?" Chloe asked.

"We went to a bar instead and I only had a couple of drinks." Amy told her. Chloe nodded slowly, the two of them falling silent.

"What are you going to do?" Amy piped up, after a few moments of silence.

"About what?" Chloe asked.

"Lee." Amy whispered.

"What about him?" Chloe sighed, wishing that Amy would spit out whatever it was that she was trying to ask.

"Well you've clearly missed him a lot more than you realised and it's kind of obvious that he still loves you." Amy said quietly.

"You don't have to whisper, he'll be out for the count." Chloe said quietly.

"Don't change the subject." Amy said quickly, instantly realising what Chloe was trying to do.

"I don't know what you want me to say." Chloe said shortly, trying to ignore the fact that Lee was sleeping just a few feet away from her and desperately trying to resist the temptation to climb into the bed and curl up in his arms.

"Do you still love him?" Amy asked, clearly not wanting to drop the subject.

"Of course I do, it's only been a few weeks." Chloe said quietly, choosing not to admit that she'd only realised a few hours ago just how much she still loved and missed him.

"I'm going to try and get some sleep now." Chloe said quickly, before Amy could ask her any further questions.

Chapter Five

Chloe slowly sat up and rested her back against the wall, gently massaging her sore muscles.

"How was the floor?" Amy asked as soon as she realised that Chloe was awake.

"Not too bad." Chloe said sleepily, yawning as she rubbed the sleep out of her eyes.

"Did you have a think about what I said last night?" Amy asked.

"No I didn't, I slept." Chloe lied quickly, choosing not to mention the hours that she'd spent tossing and turning, unable to decide what she should do for the best. She glanced at the bed, smiling slightly when she saw that Lee was still fast asleep. Her heart plummeted when she suddenly remembered that her and Amy were going home tomorrow and today was her last opportunity to spend some time with Lee before she left. She swallowed the lump that was rising in her throat at the thought of saying goodbye to him. Chloe jumped when her phone beeped, notifying her that she had a text. She sighed when she glanced at the display and saw that it was from Martin.

"Oh for god sake." Chloe muttered under her breath when she read the message.

"What is it?" Amy frowned.

"Martin wants me to stay over at his house next weekend." Chloe sighed.

"Oooh." Amy giggled, turning over to face Chloe and wiggling her eyebrows at her.

"He's obsessed with getting me to stay over." Chloe said, rolling her eyes, before quickly putting down her phone.

"He's obviously really into you." Amy said, smiling slightly. Chloe nodded and fell silent. Amy watched her closely, feeling slightly sorry for her when she noticed how much inner turmoil Chloe was in. She clearly had no idea what to do for the best.

"Who's better in bed, between Martin and Lee?" Amy giggled, trying to break the uncomfortable silence.

"Amy!" Chloe exclaimed.

"It's just an innocent question." Amy laughed. Chloe rolled her eyes, glancing at Lee and wincing slightly when she locked eyes with him.

"How long have you been awake?" Chloe squirmed.

"Long enough." he said, smiling slightly at her coloured cheeks.

"We're still waiting for an answer though." he chuckled.

"You'll be waiting a while." Chloe said, smiling slightly as her cheeks coloured even further.

"I reckon that means it's me." Lee chuckled, sitting up in bed and locking eyes with Amy. Amy nodded and burst out laughing.

"How come you are sleeping on the floor?" he asked Chloe, when he turned his attention back to her and finally noticed.

"Well, where else was I supposed to sleep?" Chloe frowned.

"You could have had half of the double bed." he told her.

"I did tell her that you wouldn't mind." Amy piped up, wiggling her eyebrows at Lee.

"That's not the point, it's inappropriate." Chloe pointed out. Lee nodded slowly, a small smile playing on the corner of his lips when he realised that Chloe hadn't stated that she didn't want to sleep beside him, but instead said that it was inappropriate.

The three of them fell silent when Chloe's phone beeped yet again. She sighed, not even wanting to pick up her phone. She couldn't help but feel slightly annoyed that Martin had spent most of the past three weeks, trying to get her into bed with him, being in Lee's presence had reminded her once again how it felt to be valued for more than just her body.

"It's Martin again." Amy said, as she leaned over and picked up Chloe's phone.

"He's sent some pictures." she added thoughtfully.

"I wouldn't open them if I were you." Chloe said quickly.

"Ewww!" Amy exclaimed, screwing her face up in disgust and quickly flinging Chloe's phone onto the floor.

"I did warn you." Chloe said, smiling slightly when she noticed Amy's expression.

"Is it a dick pick?" Lee laughed, quickly climbing out of bed. Chloe quickly crawled along the floor and grabbed her phone.

"Yeah, there are some things you can't unsee." Amy said quickly.

"Let me see." Lee teased Chloe, holding his hand out for the phone.

"No." Chloe laughed. Lee laughed, quickly reaching out to take her phone. Chloe giggled and curled up on top of her phone before Lee could get to it.

"Give it here, I want to see if you've downgraded." Lee laughed. Chloe squealed as he began to tickle her, smiling in satisfaction when she moved away from her phone and he was able to swipe it from her grasp.

"You've definitely downgraded." he told her, as soon as he looked at her phone. Lee's breath caught in his throat as he returned to Chloe's home screen and noticed the picture of the two of them curled up in each other's arms. He couldn't help but remember the night he'd taken that picture, on the night that Chloe had given her virginity to him.

"What's wrong?" Chloe asked, when she noticed him staring at her phone silently, an expression that she couldn't quite interpret, etched on his handsome features.

"Nothing." he said quietly, not quite able to tear his eyes away from staring at the picture. He sighed quietly and reluctantly handed Chloe her phone. Chloe glanced down at the phone in his hand.

"Can you delete the picture please, I really don't want that on my phone?" Chloe asked. Lee nodded slowly, and quickly did as she asked, realising instantly what image she was speaking about.

"I really don't understand why some guys feel the need to do things like that." Chloe said quietly.

"Think yourself lucky you actually get guys send them to you." Amy laughed.

"Maybe he's hoping that you'll reciprocate." Amy laughed. Chloe rolled her eyes and shook her head slowly, glancing up at Lee as he stood up and walked over to the desk, busying himself making a cup of tea, as he tried to tune out what they were saying. He couldn't bring himself to think about Chloe with another man.

"Are you going to stay at his next weekend?" Amy asked.

"I don't know." Chloe said quietly, sighing quietly to herself.

"He's not putting pressure on you is he Chlo?" Lee asked, as he handed her a mug of tea. Chloe shrugged silently, avoiding his intense gaze. Lee sighed deeply, frowning to himself as he watched her closely.

"So, are we going to the beach then?" Lee asked, changing the subject in an attempt to lighten the atmosphere.

"The beach?" Amy frowned.

"Yeah, I suggested it to Chloe last night." Lee told her.

"I am supposed to be meeting up with some friends." Amy lied, smiling slightly to herself when she realised that Chloe and Lee had the opportunity to spend some time alone together. Despite the fact that Amy barely knew Lee, she could clearly see how much he adored Chloe and how relaxed and comfortable Chloe was when he was around. She couldn't help but hope that if they spent some time alone, Chloe would realise how much she still loved and needed Lee.

"Do you want to go Chlo?" Lee offered nervously. Chloe hesitated for a moment, feeling slightly guilty that she was considering spending time with her ex-boyfriend when she had a new boyfriend, but knowing in the back of her mind that she couldn't resist the opportunity to spend some more time with Lee before she returned to Nottingham. Chloe took a deep breath and nodded slowly, finally giving into the temptation. Lee smiled slightly and released the breath he didn't realise he was holding when Chloe nodded.

"I'll need to pop home and change, since I slept in these clothes." he said, glancing down at himself.

"I can come back for you in a bit if you want?" he asked Chloe. Chloe nodded slowly, staring after him as he left the hotel room. Despite the fact that she knew he would be coming back, she couldn't help but miss him already.

"Earth to Chloe!" Amy exclaimed.

"What?" Chloe asked, snapping out of her thoughts.

"I said, what are you going to wear?" Amy giggled.

"I have no idea, something casual." Chloe said, frowning in confusion.

"It's not a date." she quickly added.

"Sure it's not." Amy smiled.

"It's not, now stop it!" Chloe said firmly.

"I have a boyfriend remember and I'm not exactly the kind of person to cheat on someone." Chloe pointed out.

"I know that, but your boyfriend is a twat, maybe it's time you went back to the old one." Amy said.

"It's really cute how Lee calls you Chlo." Amy tried.

"Also he's more handsome than Martin." Amy added.

"He's better than him in every way." Chloe said thoughtfully, almost like she was talking to herself. Amy smiled and raised her eyebrow.

"Don't start." Chloe said quietly, before standing up and walking into the bathroom.

Lee sighed quietly to himself as he sat on the sand and watched Chloe paddling her feet in the ocean. He stared at her, completely mesmerized by how beautiful she looked, her trainers in her hand as she slowly walked along the shore, the water coming to just above her ankles. He couldn't help but remember the last time the two of them were at the beach, on the day that the media storm had started. Lee knew in his heart, that if it wasn't for the media, him and Chloe would still be together. He reluctantly tore his eyes away from staring at Chloe and gazed down at the sand, slowly playing with the grains, wishing not for the first time, that Chloe was still in his life. He'd had the best night sleep that he'd had in weeks last night, feeling comforted just knowing that she was in the room. He knew that she was the one who made him whole, and he had no idea what he was going to do when she returned to Nottingham tomorrow. Lee's head snapped up when Chloe appeared and silently sat beside him.

"Are you okay, you look a bit sad?" Chloe asked worriedly.

"Yeah, I was just deep in thought." he told her, turning to face her and smiling when he noticed her gazing up at him.

"About what?" she asked gently.

"The fact that you are going home tomorrow and how much I'm going to miss you." he admitted, sighing quietly. Chloe sighed and shuffled closer to him, gently resting the side of her head on his shoulder and gazing out at the ocean thoughtfully.

"I'm really sorry that I broke your heart." she told him, feeling another pang of guilt.

"You didn't, the media and the fans did." he told her quickly.

"It was all their fault Chlo, not yours." he added.

"They really broke us didn't they." she said thoughtfully. Lee nodded slowly, sighing in frustration.

"You seem happier now though." he added.

"That's just because I have some family in my life." she told him.

"And a new man." he said, an edge of bitterness in his voice.

"Does he take care of you?" he added. Chloe shook her head slowly.

"No, he's not like you." she said thoughtfully. Lee glanced at her as she said those words, his eyes flickering to her lips when she raised her head and stared at him. Chloe reluctantly looked away from him, trying not to become lost in his gaze.

"He likes to buy me things all the time, and take me to the building site to show off in front of the other builders." she admitted. Lee remained silent, not entirely sure how to respond. Despite the fact that he was simmering that Chloe wasn't being treated right, the last thing he wanted to do was to interfere in her new relationship.

"I've officially become a trophy girlfriend." she added bitterly.

"Just don't do anything you don't want to do and make sure you don't just settle for someone." he told her, trying to keep his voice level.

"You deserve so much." he added quietly. Lee glanced down at Chloe as she rested her head on his shoulder once again and fell silent. He smiled to himself when he realised that she'd fallen asleep. He carefully rested his head against hers, sighing in contentment.

Chloe's eyes snapped open as she quickly lifted her head and gazed around, frowning when she realised that she was at the beach and Lee was sitting beside her, silently staring at his phone. It didn't feel real that she was sitting on the beach with Lee, it felt like she was still dreaming. She glanced at Lee's phone, smiling slightly when she noticed that Lee was staring fondly at the pictures of Chloe feeding the lemurs at the zoo. He glanced at her when he felt her watching him closely.

"We should probably go." Lee said reluctantly, when he glanced at the ocean and saw that the tide was slowly coming in. Chloe nodded and slowly stood up, brushing the sand off her trousers, trying to fight the tears that were filling her eyes when she realised that she was going to have to say goodbye to him. Lee watched Chloe closely as she pulled on her trainers and slowly began to walk back to Lee's car. As soon as she reached the car, Chloe paused, her hand in place on the door handle, not quite able to bring herself to get into Lee's car.

"What's wrong?" Lee asked, watching her closely.

"Nothing, I just need a minute." she said quietly. Chloe's legs shook as she slowly walked over to the bonnet and perched on it, taking deep breaths, desperately trying to fight the way that she was feeling.

"What's going on Chlo?" Lee asked, quickly walking over to her. Chloe glanced up at him as he stood between her legs and placed his hands on her thighs, a look of concern on his handsome features. Chloe hesitated for a moment, before quickly throwing her arms around his neck and holding him tightly, finally giving into the feelings she'd been desperately fighting for the past three days.

"I can't leave you." she sobbed, not even bothering to fight her tears any longer. Lee wrapped his arms around her waist and picked her up, holding her tightly against himself, quickly placing his hands on her hips to support her weight.

"If you don't want to leave me....then don't." he whispered in her ear.

"I want you back Chlo." he told her, finally deciding to seize the moment and tell her how he felt.

"But....what about the media?" she asked quietly, her heart pounding in fear as she thought about the potential of history repeating itself.

"We can come up with a plan for them." he told her softly. Chloe nodded slowly, still slightly afraid of the repercussions, but she knew in her heart that she couldn't live without Lee any longer and the two of them would have to find a way to deal with the potential consequences.

"I love you so much." she whispered softly. Lee smiled slightly as he gently placed her down on the ground. Chloe smiled up at him, unable to tear her eyes away from his as he placed his hand on her neck and softly stroked her cheek with his thumb. Her eyes flickered to his lips when he slowly leaned towards her. She reluctantly turned her head away, feeling slightly guilty when she noticed Lee's confused expression.

"I have to do the right thing. I'll speak to Martin tomorrow when I'm in Nottingham." she told him. He smiled at her, his heart swelling with pride when he was reminded once again what a good person she was.

"It's only a couple of days, by the time I get back to London." she added.

"It's totally fine Chloe, I'm just glad to have you back." he admitted. Chloe smiled. She giggled and wrapped her legs around Lee's waist, when he picked her up again and held her tightly against himself.

"I love you Chloe Evans." he said softly, desperately trying to resist the urge to kiss her.

"I love you too." she smiled.

Chapter Six

Kirstie took a deep breath, sighing quietly to herself when she noticed Chloe sitting silently at Ben's kitchen table, her hands gently wrapped around her coffee mug. Kirstie's heart was pounding against her chest when she sat beside Chloe. Chloe had always meant a lot to Kirstie, she was almost like a sister to her and she couldn't help but feel slightly nervous as to how Chloe was going to handle the news that she was about to find out.

"So what was with the really cryptic text?" Chloe asked as soon as Kirstie sat down. As soon as Chloe had read the text from Kirstie, telling her to come over as there was something that she needed to know before she returned home to Nottingham, Chloe's brain had been working overtime, trying to figure out what was so important.

"Do you have some exciting news?" Chloe tried, when Kirstie remained silent.

"Not exactly." Kirstie said quietly, feeling slightly guilty that she wasn't able to tell Chloe what was going on. Part of her longed to be able to warn her friend, but she knew that it wasn't her information to share, it had to come directly from the source. Kirstie's head snapped up as she heard the doorbell ring.

"I'll be back in a minute." she told Chloe quietly, as she quickly hurried to answer the door. Chloe sat in silence for a few moments, frowning to herself when Kirstie returned, closely followed by Lee. Lee smiled softly at Chloe as he sat opposite her at the table, the two of them watching Kirstie closely as she returned to her original position beside Chloe.

"Right, what's going on?" Lee asked quickly.

"We have to wait for one more person first." Kirstie told them.

"Is it Ben?" Chloe asked.

"It's all very mysterious, gathering us together like this." Lee said.

"Maybe they have a happy announcement." Chloe smiled excitedly.

"Hmm....what have you and Ben been up to I wonder?" Lee chuckled.

"No, it's nothing like that." Kirstie said quickly, her cheeks colouring slightly.

"It's not something bad is it?" Chloe asked nervously, her eyes flickering to Lee for a moment as she felt him watching her closely.

"I can't say, I'm sorry." Kirstie said quietly. Chloe's heart pounded against her chest when she noticed Kirstie's expression. Her face was a mixture of sadness and guilt and in that moment Chloe suddenly realised that the news wasn't something good. Chloe locked eyes with Lee, trying to gauge whether he had come to the same conclusion as her or not. She sighed to herself when she noticed him staring blankly at her, equally as confused as she was. The two of them jumped as the doorbell sounded again. Kirstie took a deep breath, desperately trying to steady her nerves and slowly stood up.

"I've got a really bad feeling." Chloe whispered to Lee as soon as Kirstie left the room.

"About what?" he whispered back. Chloe shrugged silently, her eyes flickering to the doorway. She gasped as she locked eyes with Michelle. Lee turned in his chair, quickly following Chloe's eyeline.

"What's she doing here?!" Lee exclaimed, his eyes wandering to Chloe as Michelle silently took her seat beside him.

"Just give her a chance to speak." Kirstie said quietly as she sat down. Michelle sat in silence, staring at the table, not even able to bring herself to look at any of them. Lee could feel himself becoming more and more nervous about being in Michelle's presence. He couldn't help but remember the last few times that Michelle had been in their lives and how upset and hurt Chloe had been by her behaviour.

"I think we should go." Lee muttered, quickly standing up.

"Chlo?" he asked her, quickly holding his hand out to her, trying to get Chloe away from Michelle before she inevitably managed to hurt Chloe again.

"I know it's difficult, but you need to listen to what she has to say." Kirstie said quickly. Lee remained silent, shaking his head slowly in frustration.

"Please, it's important." Kirstie tried again. Lee sighed deeply, his eyes fixed on Chloe as she reached out and took his hand, squeezing it gently to reassure him. He reluctantly sat down, quickly realising that Chloe wanted to hear what Michelle had to say. Despite the fact that Lee wanted to get as far away as possible from Michelle, he couldn't bring himself to leave Chloe alone with her.

"What's so bloody important then?" Lee said bitterly. Michelle glanced up at Kirstie who nodded at her reassuringly, trying to suppress her own anger when she thought about what Michelle had done to Chloe and Lee.

"I believe I owe you both an apology." Michelle said quietly, finally glancing up and locking eyes with Chloe.

"We've been through this before though when you apologised and then hurt us again." Chloe said quickly.

"You clearly don't like me, so maybe we should just leave it at that and move on with our lives." Chloe added, not entirely sure why they were here. She'd known for a while now that Michelle clearly had something against her, but she'd never been able to figure out what it was.

"Although why we're on the subject, why do you hate me?" Chloe asked.

"I think I've always been a good friend to you." Chloe added.

"Because I was in a bad place and you always seem to have everything." Michelle said quietly.

"What's that supposed to mean?" Chloe frowned.

"You're so beautiful and popular and guys love you wherever you go and do you know how much that hurts when you are the one that has nothing." Michelle explained.

"And then you got a rich, successful boyfriend, who adored you and would do anything for you and that's what I've always wanted." she continued.

"So you were jealous?" Lee rounded on her.

"Yeah I guess I was." Michelle admitted quietly.

"I've been saying that all along.....it's not exactly news." Lee said, rolling his eyes impatiently.

"I know but I became so jealous of what the two of you had that I did something despicable." Michelle said, pausing for a moment as she took a deep breath, trying to steady her nerves. She couldn't help but feel slightly nervous about how Lee was going to react, particularly when she knew how protective of Chloe he was.

"What did you do?" Chloe asked nervously, her heart pounding against her chest. Chloe glanced down at her lap as she felt Kirstie take her hand and squeeze it gently.

"What's going on?" Chloe asked again, starting to panic slightly as she quickly glanced between Kirstie and Michelle. Michelle opened her mouth to speak, quickly closing it again when she couldn't quite get the words to come out.

"For god sake, will you just spit it out!" Lee snapped.

"It was me that exposed the two of you to the media." Michelle blurted, before she could stop herself.

"What?" Chloe whispered, not quite able to believe what she was hearing.

"I told them that the two of you were dating and the date and time that you would be at the airport." Michelle said quietly, returning to staring at the table.

"And I gave them your name, because I knew they would be able to dig up the article about you being stabbed, and then they would find out about you being homeless." Michelle continued.

"But....why would you do that?" Chloe asked quietly.

"Because I told you, I was jealous and I couldn't stand seeing how happy the two of you were together." Michelle admitted.

"We weren't happy though, we were already going through a really difficult time." Chloe muttered, her eyes filling with tears. She slowly took a sip of her coffee, trying to process what she'd just heard. Chloe carefully put down her coffee mug, staring at her hands as they shook uncontrollably.

"I am so sorry, I didn't mean for it to get so out of hand, it all kind of blew up, before I could stop it." Michelle said.

"Do you have any idea what you did to us?" Lee whispered, through gritted teeth, as he tried to hold back his temper.

"I'm sorry." Michelle said, her eyes filling with tears as she finally glanced up at Chloe, her heart breaking a little when she saw the hurt that was written all over Chloe's face.

"Chloe wanted to take her own life because of you." Lee told her, his tone full of menace when he thought about how much hurt she'd caused Chloe.

"I didn't know that." Michelle said sadly.

"Nor did I." Kirstie admitted, glancing at Chloe who had fallen silent, not entirely sure what to say or how to feel.

"Well she did and she was afraid to even leave the house." Lee said quietly.

"You put her through hell!" he exclaimed angrily, causing Michelle to jump.

"I lost her because of you, and ended up in rehab." he added.

"I don't know what else to say other than how sorry I am, I swear I never meant for any of those things to happen." Michelle said quietly.

Lee glanced at Chloe, his heart breaking as she buried her head in her hands and began to cry, no longer able to hold back the tears she'd been fighting.

"This is fucking ridiculous!" Lee said angrily, glaring at Michelle as he stood up and walked over to Chloe, quickly squatting down in front of her and wrapping his arms around her, holding her tightly.

"You really are evil do you know that." Lee said, glaring at Michelle across the table. Chloe slowly wrapped her arms around Lee's neck, her heart breaking a little when she remembered everything that they had been through as a result of the media. It had been bad enough going through two weeks of hell, but it hurt more now that she knew it had been done to them deliberately.

"All of this because you are jealous of her!" Lee said angrily, shaking his head at Michelle when she deliberately avoided his gaze.

"She can't help being beautiful you know." he added, sighing quietly as he softly stroked Chloe's hair.

"I'm sorry." Michelle repeated, not entirely sure what to do or say to repair the damage that she had done. Lee glanced at Chloe as she slowly sat back from him, quickly wiping away her tears. Kirstie sighed sadly when she saw Chloe's tear stained cheeks.

"How did you find out about this?" Chloe asked Kirstie, not even able to bring herself to look at or even acknowledge Michelle.

"She confessed it to me and Kathleen at the reunion when she was really drunk, and we gave her an ultimatum that if she ever wants to be friends with any of us ever again she has to tell you both what she did." Kirstie explained.

"Well I'm done with her for good." Chloe said shortly, quickly standing up, glancing at Lee as he stood up and hovered beside her protectively.

"Wait, please!" Michelle exclaimed.

"I have a train to catch!" Chloe snapped, before quickly walking away. Lee glanced at Michelle as she stood up and made a move to follow Chloe.

"You stay away from both of us.....for good." Lee warned her. Michelle's feet froze to the spot when she heard Lee's words. She nodded slowly, her eyes filling with tears. Lee hurried after Chloe, sighing sadly to himself when he noticed her sitting quietly on the bonnet of his car.

"We need to get you to the train station don't we?" he asked her.

"Well, I had a thought about that." she said quietly. Lee raised his eyebrow and waited for her to continue.

"Rather than us being apart for a couple of days, how about you come with me?" she suggested, not quite able to face the idea of being parted from him.

"Yeah sounds good, I'm not taking the train though." he said, smiling slightly.

"We can take my car." he added. Chloe nodded slowly, her eyes filling with tears when she noticed Michelle hovering on Ben's doorstep, speaking to Kirstie about something.

"Do you think we could maybe stay in Nottingham for a few days?" she asked.

"So that you have longer with your family?" he asked. Chloe nodded slowly.

"Yeah of course we can, I don't have to be back for anything, since I have a year off, thanks to a certain someone." he said bitterly.

"And we can have some time away from our friends, since it's clear you can't trust anyone." she muttered bitterly, before quickly climbing into Lee's car and slamming the door behind herself.

Chapter Seven

Amy glanced up at the hotel doorway as the door opened and Chloe walked in. Amy smiled at her and quickly continued her packing, becoming slightly nervous that they were going to miss their train home.

"Have you already packed?" Amy frowned when Chloe picked up her suitcase.

"I got up early this morning and did it." Chloe told her.

"Okay, well I'm almost done." Amy said.

"So what was your friend's news, is she getting married?" Amy said excitedly. Chloe shook her head slowly and quickly filled Amy in on what had happened with Michelle.

"Oh my god, what a bitch!" Amy exclaimed when Chloe had finished explaining.

"I just can't process how someone could hate me enough to do that." Chloe said, sighing sadly.

"I wouldn't give her another thought." Amy said angrily. Chloe nodded, sighing sadly as her eyes slowly filled with tears.

"Lee is furious with her." Chloe said quietly.

"I bet he is, I don't blame him." Amy said shortly, smiling in satisfaction as she quickly zipped up her suitcase and lifted it off the bed. The two of them remained silent as they slowly walked down the staircase and made their way into the carpark. Chloe smiled when she noticed Lee casually leaning against his car, waiting for her.

"That was quick." Chloe smiled as soon as she reached him.

"It doesn't take me long to pack a bag." he told her.

"Does that mean you threw the stuff in?" Chloe laughed as she quickly placed her suitcase into the back of Lee's car.

"Kind of." he chuckled.

"What are you doing here?!" Amy piped up when she finally caught up with Chloe.

"I'm coming to Nottingham." Lee beamed at her.

"Why?" Amy frowned. Lee glanced at Chloe awkwardly, not entirely sure what she wanted him to say.

"Lee and I have decided to get back together." Chloe announced, smiling slightly when she glanced at Lee. Chloe jumped as Amy let out a shriek of excitement and pulled her into a hug.

"I'm so happy!" Amy squealed, quickly letting go of Chloe and hugging Lee.

"So, are you collecting your stuff and then moving back down?" Amy asked when she eventually calmed down slightly.

"Yes eventually, but I thought we could stay a few days first." Chloe told her.

"Your Mum won't mind will she?" Chloe added nervously.

"Nah, I doubt it, she was expecting you back anyway wasn't she." Amy pointed out.

"I'll call her on the way up and speak to her." Amy added. Chloe nodded slowly.

"Shall we set off then?" Lee asked them.

"Are you going to be alright getting the train on your own?" Chloe asked Amy, feeling slightly guilty that she was abandoning her.

"Yes, I suppose I'll go on the cramped train while you get to ride in the fancy sports car." Amy sighed.

"I can swap with you if you want?" Chloe offered, glancing at Lee who opened his mouth to argue, but quickly closed it again.

"It's fine, I'm teasing you." Amy giggled.

"I'll take you out for a spin in my car one day." Lee told her.

"Ooh yay!" Amy squealed.

"You'll probably be there before us anyway, since the train is quicker isn't it." Chloe told her.

"Good, I can prepare Mum." Amy said, raising her eyebrow at Chloe, before glancing at Lee who was frowning in confusion. Chloe nodded slowly and climbed into Lee's car, glancing at him when he climbed into the driver's seat and quickly pulled away.

"I got your favourite for the journey." Lee smiled, quickly pulling a bag of sweets out of his pocket and handing them to Chloe.

"Thanks." she giggled.

"I need to be good though, I've been binging so much junk food recently." she admitted, smiling slightly when she thought of the evenings that she'd spent on the sofa with Amy, trying to drown her sorrows in food.

"That's because you didn't have me around to cook for you." he laughed. Chloe nodded in agreement, smiling slightly. She jumped and glanced down at her phone when it rang, silently shaking her head and sighing deeply.

"That's the third time Michelle has tried to call me since we left Kirstie's." she sighed.

"Do you want me to answer it and tell her to fuck off?" he offered.

"No, I'll just block her number." she said, quickly blocking the number as soon as her phone stopped ringing.

"It still doesn't feel real that she was behind everything." she said thoughtfully.

"It's disgusting, I don't think she realises just how bad she made you feel." he said angrily.

"Especially when we'd just lost our baby a few weeks beforehand." he added.

"To be fair she didn't know about that." she pointed out.

"I know, but that's not the point, it probably wouldn't have stopped her anyway!" he exclaimed. Chloe nodded slowly, wishing that she could disagree with him, but suspecting in her heart that he was correct.

"Even though she probably didn't mean for it to get as out of hand as it did, she still set the wheels in motion to deliberately make us unhappy and potentially split us up." he ranted.

"And yet she's supposed to be my friend." she said quietly.

"Yeah I know." he sighed, glancing at Chloe when he sensed a change in her body language. As soon as he glanced at her, and noticed the tears in her eyes, he quickly reached over and squeezed her hand gently.

"I'm really looking forward to seeing your family and the town that you are from." he said quickly, trying to change the subject, before Chloe became even more upset than she already was.

"Hopefully you'll like my aunt, she can be a bit intense." she admitted, glancing at Lee nervously, her heart pounding against her chest when she suddenly realised that her aunt Gwen, might not approve of him.

"How intense?" he frowned, suddenly feeling slightly nervous.

"She's just very old fashioned, so you'll need to be on your best behaviour." she told him, smiling slightly when she noticed his horrified expression.

"So no swearing then." he laughed.

"No, definitely no swearing." she chuckled.

"Hopefully she'll like me." he said thoughtfully.

"I'm sure she will, I'm pretty sure Amy loves you already." she smiled.

"Speaking of Amy, do you remember when we came to your house the other day and I told you she's got a new boyfriend?" she asked. Lee thought for a moment, before slowly shaking his head.

"I don't remember much of that day to be honest, I was just so happy to see you." he admitted.

"Well, whatever you do, don't tell my aunt about Amy's boyfriend, he's kind of a secret." she said quickly.

"Why is he a secret, is he dodgy?" he frowned.

"No, but my aunt is very over protective of Amy and she finds it a bit overbearing, which is why she is secretly wild." she giggled.

"Oh shit." he said, bursting out laughing when Chloe glared at him for swearing.

"So is she your aunt on your father's side?" he asked.

"Yes." she replied, opening the bag of sweets and silently handing one to Lee.

"It's just my aunt, her and my uncle split up years ago." she added.

"And they just had Amy?" he asked.

"No, they had Kyle as well, he's the oldest, but he's away at University, training to be a doctor." she explained.

"It was kind of nice when I was growing up, because obviously I am an only child, so the two of them were like my siblings." she continued.

"So if you were close with them, how come you lost touch?" he frowned.

"When we moved to London I was so distracted with everything, and when I lost my parents, I stupidly stayed in London with Andy and then around the time they moved house and Andy left me, I then ended up in the park and lost my phone so when I got a new phone, I didn't even have their numbers." she explained.

"And my aunt doesn't allow them to go on social media." she added.

"Oh wait....what do your family know about your life?!" Lee exclaimed, when a thought suddenly popped into his head. He knew how private Chloe was about her personal life and suddenly felt nervous about potentially letting on something that they didn't already know.

"My aunt just knows what she read in the articles, although thankfully she didn't believe any of Andy's crap." she said quietly.

"As for Amy...I kind of told her everything, which I shouldn't have, but I was in such a bad place when I left you, that it just kind of all came out." she continued.

"You don't have to explain yourself Chlo, I'm just making sure I don't put my foot in it." he told her. Chloe nodded slowly, smiling to herself as she stared at him silently.

"What?" he asked, glancing at her when he felt her watching him closely.

"I just really missed you." she told him softly.

"I really want to kiss you right now." he admitted, smiling slightly to himself.

"Speaking of which, I need to message Martin and ask him to meet with me tomorrow." she said quietly, feeling a slight pang of guilt. Despite the fact that she knew she was doing what was right, she couldn't help but feel guilty that she had to hurt someone else in the process. Chloe glanced at Lee when he quickly switched on the music, beaming like a child when Eclipse's album started to play. She rolled her eyes at him when he began to belt out his section of Broken.

"Aren't you meant to be resting your voice?" she asked him sternly.

"Yeah kind of." he chuckled.

"It's not too bad with certain songs, but I can't do the bigger songs." he added.

"Your voice sounds fine to be fair." she told him.

"It's not too bad, it just doesn't feel a hundred percent." he admitted. The two of them jumped as Chloe's phone began to ring.

"Is that Michelle again?" Lee sighed impatiently.

"No, I blocked her.....it's Martin." she said nervously. Lee glanced at her and quickly switched off the music. Chloe took a deep breath and reluctantly answered the phone.

"Hello." she said nervously, not entirely sure how the conversation was going to go.

"What was with your cryptic text?" Martin asked as soon as she answered the phone.

"It wasn't cryptic, I just asked if we can meet up when I'm back, so that we can talk." Chloe said quietly.

"Is it about you coming over to stay at the weekend?" he asked.

"No." she said shortly. Chloe fell silent, her stomach churning as she thought about what to do. She couldn't quite bring herself to break up with him over the phone, she knew that she owed him a face to face explanation.

"Are you breaking up with me?" he asked quickly when she fell silent. Chloe glanced at Lee, trying to silently ask him what she should do. Lee shrugged at her silently.

"Yes I am, I was hoping to do it when I saw you though." Chloe said sadly, her stomach churning with guilt.

"Are you serious?!" Martin exclaimed.

"I'm afraid so, I realised that I am still in love with my ex, I'm really sorry." she said nervously, her heart pounding against her chest when Martin fell silent for a moment.

"So you've basically wasted my time for the past four weeks!" he snapped.

"Three weeks." she said sarcastically.

"Yeah well maybe you would like to give me all the gifts back then, and the money that I spent on dates!" he said angrily.

"Excuse me, I always paid my own way on the dates and as for the gifts, you can have them back, they were making me uncomfortable anyway!" Chloe snapped, her temper finally flaring.

"I didn't plan for this to happen." she added.

"It's probably for the best anyway, since I slept with someone while you were away." he told her smugly.

"What?" she said, fighting to keep her voice level.

"I was out in a bar and it just kind of happened." he told her.

"Cheating on someone doesn't just happen!" she exclaimed, feeling her temper rising even further as she was reminded of how it felt all those years ago when Andy informed her that he'd been cheating on her.

"Also, I've spent the past few days in close proximity to my ex and haven't done anything, because I would never cheat on anyone!" she cried.

"Yeah well, it's been three fucking weeks, I needed some action!" he exclaimed.

"Just hang up on him Chlo." Lee piped up, when he could no longer stand listening to Martin tear Chloe's character apart. Chloe nodded and quickly hung up the phone, before flinging it onto the dashboard.

"Are you alright?" Lee asked her worriedly.

"Did you hear what he said?" she said quickly.

"Yeah most of it." he answered.

"He seems like a dick." he added.

"Oh my god, I've just thought of something." she said thoughtfully.

"That there's no going back and now you are stuck with me?" he laughed.

"No." she said, smiling slightly.

"If I hadn't broken up with him, he wouldn't have told me that he'd cheated would he, and he would have been expecting to sleep with me at the weekend." she said, screwing her nose up in disgust.

"Yeah probably." he said quietly, swallowing the lump that was rising in his throat.

"I'm assuming, given his comments, that you didn't actually sleep with him?" he asked nervously, slightly afraid of her answer.

"No I didn't." she told him, smiling slightly when she saw Lee release the breath that he was holding.

"Good." he smiled.

"Why is that good?" she smiled.

"I don't know, it just kind of feels like a special thing between us that you've only been with me." he told her.

"It probably shouldn't be a big deal but it kind of is." he added.

"I know, I feel the same, that's why I don't think I could ever sleep with anyone else." she said quietly, her cheeks colouring slightly.

"I haven't been with anyone else since you left either." he said.

"Really?!" she exclaimed.

"Why are you always so surprised?" he chuckled.

"I did tell you that I don't want anyone else." he reminded her.

"I know, but I was gone though." she pointed out. Lee shrugged, glancing at her for a moment before quickly pulling over onto the hard shoulder. Chloe watched as he quickly unclipped his seatbelt and leaned towards her. Her heart pounded against her chest as he kissed her deeply, finally able to give into some of the longing that he'd been feeling for her for the past few days. Her skin tingled under his touch as his hand remained in place on her neck and he softly stroked her cheek with his thumb. She sighed and rested her forehead against his, smiling up at him as he gazed down at her lovingly.

"I've missed you so much." he whispered. Chloe's heart pounded against her chest as she remained silent, unable to tear her eyes away from him. She took deep breaths, trying to control the intense desire that she was feeling for him. Even though they'd only been apart for a few weeks, it had felt like a lifetime. She kissed his lips softly, wishing with all her heart that the two of them hadn't been parted for the last few weeks, but knowing in her heart that it was her fault. Chloe eventually pulled away from him and sighed sadly, feeling another pang of guilt for what she'd done to Lee.

"I hope you know that I'm sorry for everything that I did." she said quietly.

"I at least should have told you to your face that I was leaving......you deserved so much better than a note." she added thoughtfully, feeling slightly sick when she suddenly realised that she had wanted to explain to Martin in person and yet when it was Lee she had left him a note.

"It's okay, I understand why you had to do what you did, you needed to get away." he said sadly, his heart breaking a little when he remembered how miserable Chloe was back then. Lee felt a small flicker of fear when he realised that if Chloe hadn't got away from everything, she could have been tempted to end things and then the two of them would have been parted forever.

"I'm just glad that I've got you back." he said quietly.

Chapter Eight

Lee took a deep breath, glancing at Chloe's aunt's house nervously as they pulled up outside. His stomach was swirling with butterflies as he thought about how much Chloe's family meant to her and how important it would be to her to gain their approval of him. He knew that he had to be on his best behaviour in order to make a good impression.

"Don't look so stressed, you'll be fine." Chloe chuckled, watching Lee closely as he nervously picked at the material on his jeans.

"I just want them to like me." he admitted.

"It's really not a big deal, I'm not close to my aunt anyway, I'm closer to Amy and she already likes you." she smiled at him before quickly climbing out of the car.

"I know, but my Mum adores you, so I'm under pressure." he said, smiling slightly as he lifted their suitcases out of the car and handed Chloe her suitcase when he remembered that she liked her own independence.

"She probably doesn't anymore." she said sighing sadly.

"She does Chlo, anyone who knows you understands." he told her. Chloe nodded slowly, glancing at Lee as they walked towards the house and she sensed his body language stiffen. She smiled at him and gently reached out to take his hand, squeezing it gently in an attempt to reassure him. Chloe took a deep breath, suddenly feeling slightly nervous when she remembered how strict and intense her aunt could be. Despite the fact that her opinion on Lee wouldn't change, regardless of her aunt's opinion, she couldn't help but feel slightly nervous about how her aunt was going to treat him. Chloe slowly pulled her keys out of her pocket and silently unlocked the door, trying to ignore the tension that she was feeling. Lee followed Chloe closely as she wandered around the house, frowning to herself when she realised that her aunt was nowhere to be seen. She wandered into the bedroom she'd been sharing with Amy and smiled at Amy when she noticed her laying on her bed reading a book.

"Hey guys." Amy smiled at them.

"Hey, how was the train?" Lee grinned at her as he perched on Chloe's bed.

"Don't be smug." Amy smiled.

"Where's Auntie Gwen?" Chloe asked her.

"She was a bit frantic when she found out she was getting an extra guest, so she rushed out to the supermarket." Amy told them, rolling her eyes. Chloe nodded slowly, glancing around the room, and sighing to herself when she laid eyes on the mountain of gifts from Martin on her counter. She could feel her blood slowly simmering as she thought about his words to her on the phone and how he'd had the audacity to have a go at her, when he had cheated on her anyway.

"What are you doing?!" Amy exclaimed as she watched Chloe quickly gathering up the gifts and stuffing them into a carrier bag.

"Gathering all of Martin's gifts so that I can take them back to him." Chloe replied shortly.

"Ooh, she's raging." Amy told Lee. He nodded slowly, smiling slightly at Chloe when she locked eyes with him. As soon as she'd gathered up all the gifts, she rummaged in her suitcase and quickly pulled out her makeup bag.

"Why are you staring at me?" Chloe asked Amy as she locked eyes with her in the mirror.

"I've just never seen you so mad before." Amy said.

"I'm not that mad, I'm just determined to prove a point." Chloe told her, as she quickly applied her makeup.

"Are you going to wear something hot?" Amy laughed. Chloe nodded slowly, a small smile playing on the corner of her lips.

"Is this such a good idea, why don't you just stay away from him?" Lee asked, his heart pounding against his chest at the thought of Chloe going to see Martin and him potentially tearing her down again.

"I need to take the gifts back anyway." Chloe pointed out, before quickly picking up her clothes and walking into the bathroom. Lee's breath caught in his throat when she emerged dressed in leather trousers and a tight tank top, the material clinging tightly to her skin.

"You do realise you can post the gifts back to him." Lee sighed, his stomach churning at the thought of Chloe going to a building site, being surrounded by men, when she looked as stunning as she did. He couldn't help but worry that one of them would take advantage of her.

"No, I'm going to take them to the building site and embarrass him in front of his friends." Chloe insisted as she pulled on her leather jacket and pumps.

"If you're worried then you can come with me." Chloe said quickly, smiling slightly when Lee nodded quickly and visibly relaxed.

"Ooh yeah, you have to take your hot boyfriend and the sports car." Amy giggled, clapping her hands excitedly.

"Okay I think I'm ready." Chloe announced, her cheeks colouring slightly when she noticed Lee and Amy staring at her silently.

"What?" Chloe asked, when she couldn't stand the silence any longer.

"You look stunning Chlo." Lee eventually said, desperately trying to hide how attracted he was to her.

"There's one thing missing though." he said softly, quickly rummaging in his pocket and standing up. As soon as he reached her, he gently placed his hands on her hips and turned her so that her back was facing him. Chloe watched in the mirror as he reached around her neck and gently fastened her necklace, his hands lingering in place on her neck. Her eyes filled with tears as she stared down at the necklace Lee had given her all those months ago. He watched her closely as she softly stroked the necklace with her finger, suddenly realising how much she'd missed having it around her neck.

"I'm so glad you kept it." Chloe whispered, locking eyes with Lee in the mirror.

"Of course I kept it." he told her, carefully wrapping his arms around her waist and pulling her close. Chloe trembled slightly when she felt his body pressed against hers, her skin tingling when he placed a soft kiss on her neck. She sighed in contentment, suddenly realising how much she had missed being in Lee's arms. The way that he managed to make her feel so loved and cherished without even having to say a word.

"You guys had better go if you want to try and catch him before he finishes work." Amy piped up, glancing at her watch. Chloe nodded slowly and reluctantly removed herself from Lee's arms, glancing up at him when she felt him watching her closely. Lee quickly picked up his car keys and followed Chloe to his car.
"Are you sure this is such a good idea?" Lee asked, when he pulled out of the driveway.

"Why, what's wrong?" she asked him, frowning to herself as she quickly programmed the sat-nav for the building site.

"I just don't want him to say anything that might upset you." he sighed.

"It's fine, it's not like I care about him." she said quickly. Lee nodded slowly, still not entirely convinced that she was taking the best course of action, particularly when he knew how sensitive she was to things.

"I had a thought about the media and I think I've come up with a plan." he told her. Chloe raised her eyebrow and waited for him to continue.

"I think we should do an article where we tell our side of the story." he said.

"And get everything out in the open...so that the fans know the truth, and then they'll learn to love you like I do." he explained.

"We don't have to expose everything though do we?" she asked nervously.

"No of course not, but we can put the record straight about everything that Andy said about you." he pointed out.

"Have a think about it....I just think it might be a way of making the fans love you and then you won't have to worry about the hate and we can just relax." he said quickly. Chloe nodded slowly, swallowing the lump that rose in her throat when she thought about potentially exposing her life for everyone to read about. She was snapped out of her thoughts when Lee slowly pulled into the building site.

Lee watched Chloe proudly as she quickly picked up the bag of gifts and climbed out of the car, before she could talk herself out of it. Chloe walked towards the front of the car and perched on the bonnet, glancing behind herself at Lee when he sat behind her. He couldn't help but smile to himself when he noticed a group of men watching her, unable to stop themselves from staring at her flawless figure. Chloe narrowed her eyes when Martin did a double take at her as the group walked towards her.

"I believe you wanted these back." Chloe said bitterly, quickly handing the bag to Martin as soon as they reached her.

"Great, I can give them to the next girl that catches my eye." Martin sneered at her as he quickly took the bag that Chloe was holding out to him.

"I hope you realise that just because you are beautiful, that doesn't mean that you can string men along." he added, his breath catching in his throat as his eyes wandered over her figure.

"Says the person who cheated on me as soon as I went away." Chloe snapped.

"Well since you spent most of the time with your ex, I doubt you stayed faithful anyway." Martin pointed out.

"I didn't do anything, because I wouldn't do that to someone." she said quietly, trying to keep her voice level.

"Even though it's been killing me." Lee chuckled. Chloe glanced behind herself, smiling slightly when she locked eyes with Lee. Martin followed Chloe's eyeline, finally able to tear his eyes away from Chloe and focus on Lee.

"You're the ex then?" Martin sneered.

"Yep, although I do have a name." Lee said condescendingly.

"Lee, nice to meet you." he added, a small smile playing on the corner of his lips as he stood up and offered Martin his hand for him to shake. Martin reluctantly shook his hand, watching closely as Lee stepped beside Chloe and placed his hand on her back protectively.

"I actually think that I owe you thanks." Lee said, trying to turn the tables on Martin when he could no longer stand seeing him sneering at Chloe.

"For what?" Martin frowned.

"For being so horrible that she didn't fall out of love with me." Lee chuckled. Martin glared at Chloe, a brief flicker of embarrassment passing over his face when his friends started to laugh from behind him.

"You're very welcome, you'll get bored of waiting around anyway, since she doesn't give up the goods." Martin said smugly.

"Well that side of things have never been an issue with me." Lee said smugly, smiling slightly when he realised that Martin was squirming.

"I just wasn't that into you." Chloe told him. Martin shrugged, trying to hide how gutted he was that things between himself and Chloe hadn't worked out.

"She's the hottest girlfriend you've ever had and you cocked it up." one of Martin's friends teased him.

"Literally." another one of them laughed.

"Maybe it was the picture you sent that put her off." he added.

"Speaking of which, did nobody ever tell you, it's rude not to reciprocate when someone sends you a nude image?" Martin sneered, quickly recovering himself and becoming defensive.

"That was never going to happen." Chloe said shortly.

"That explains why you never showed us the image we were promised." one of the friends laughed.

"Yeah, well I didn't get one did I." Martin said shortly. Chloe swallowed the lump that was rising in her throat, as she tried to process his words. She couldn't help but feel repulsed at the idea that had she sent him a picture of herself, he would have shared it with his friends.

"Wait, so you would have shown them the picture of me?" Chloe checked quietly. Martin nodded slowly.

"That's what men do honey." he said condescendingly.

"That's disgusting." Chloe said quietly.

"It's also a breach of trust, if a woman hasn't consented to that." she added, her blood boiling when they burst out laughing at her.

"If you all want to see her out of her clothes so badly then I suggest you buy Eclipse's new album." Lee said shortly, suddenly feeling a deep anger rising in the pit of his stomach. Chloe glanced at Lee, a small giggle escaping her lips when she saw the smug expression on his face. Before Martin could respond, Chloe turned on her heel and walked away, quickly climbing into Lee's car. Lee glanced at her as he climbed into the car beside her.

"Are you okay?" he asked nervously, afraid that Martin might have upset her with his words.

"I'm fine, his opinion doesn't matter to me." she said quietly. Lee smiled at her, his heart swelling with pride at how much her confidence was growing. He reached towards her and slowly stroked her cheek with his fingertips. Chloe glanced down at his lips as he slowly moved towards her.

"Don't, they are watching." she said, slowly turning her head away, her cheeks colouring when she glanced out of the window and saw the group staring at her.

"Who cares?" he laughed. Chloe glanced at Lee as he slowly trailed his fingertips along her jawline and down onto her neck. She shivered involuntarily, her skin tingling under his touch. He smiled slightly, clearly realising the effect that he was having on her.

"We need to get back to my auntie's." Chloe whispered, desperately trying to ignore the temptation that she was feeling. Lee nodded slowly, a small smile playing on the corner of his lips.

Chapter Nine

Chloe quickly took Lee's hand and squeezed it gently, trying to provide him with some reassurance. She couldn't help but glance up at him and smile as the two of them walked into the house. Her heart swelled with pride when she realised how important it was to Lee that her family approve of him. Chloe's stomach churned as the two of them walked into the living room. They hovered nervously as Gwen watched Lee closely, her eyes narrowing, almost like she was trying to assess him.

"Auntie, this is Lee." Chloe said quietly, trying to break the uncomfortable silence.

"I'm Gwen, nice to meet you." Gwen said, holding her hand out for Lee to shake. Lee reluctantly let go of Chloe's hand and quickly shook hands with Gwen, trying to ignore the nervous butterflies that were swirling in his stomach.

"I had no idea you were planning to get back together with him." Gwen said shortly, turning to face Chloe.

"I didn't plan too." Chloe said nervously, glancing at Lee who gave her a small reassuring smile.

"I did think it was a little strange, since you have a new boyfriend." Gwen said shortly.

"He was a rebound though." Chloe pointed out, sighing deeply to herself as she sat on the sofa and Lee sat beside her.

"I really wish you wouldn't go out dressed like that Chloe." Gwen sighed, when she finally noticed the outfit that Chloe was wearing.

"Auntie, I'm twenty five, and it's not a revealing outfit anyway." Chloe sighed, rolling her eyes impatiently.

"I know, but it doesn't leave much to the imagination does it." Gwen pointed out. Chloe sighed deeply to herself, trying to ignore the frustration that she was feeling. Despite the fact that she knew her aunt was very religious and strict in the way that she brought up Amy and Kyle, she'd been hoping that the same rules wouldn't apply to her.

"I think she looks stunning whatever she wears." Lee said, trying to find a way to encourage Gwen to warm to him.

Gwen raised her eyebrow at him and watched him closely. Even though she'd heard a lot about Lee from Chloe, she wasn't entirely sure what she thought of him. It was clear that he was very handsome and talented and Gwen couldn't help but feel uneasy that he might be taking advantage of Chloe's sweet and vulnerable nature.

"So what do you do for a living?" Lee asked Gwen awkwardly.

"I'm a carer for the elderly." she replied quietly, her eyes fixed on him intensely, almost like she was examining a specimen under a microscope.

"Wow, that must be very rewarding." Lee smiled. Gwen nodded silently.

"I'd better go and sort out dinner." Gwen said, quickly standing up.

"I can make something if you want, I'm quite a good cook." Lee offered hopefully.

"It's already in the oven, I just have to serve it." Gwen snapped, as she quickly walked away.

"Well that was frosty." Chloe said quietly as soon as Gwen left the room. She glanced at Lee, her heart sinking when she noticed him sigh sadly.

"Don't worry about it." she said, quickly turning to face him.

"She really doesn't like me does she." he muttered, his heart sinking in disappointment.

"She's just really old fashioned and strict, and she doesn't like men since her and my uncle split up." she explained. Lee nodded slowly, glancing down at Chloe as she snuggled against him, carefully resting her head on his shoulder.

"Don't stress, it doesn't matter what she thinks of you anyway." she told him. Lee sighed as she placed a soft kiss on his neck.

"It kinda does Chlo." he muttered. Chloe sighed sadly when she suddenly realised how disappointed he was by her Aunt's reaction to him.

"She'll warm to you." she told him. Lee nodded slowly, quickly wrapping his arm around her waist. She glanced up at him for a moment, before slowly placing a series of soft kisses on his neck, smiling slightly when she heard him sigh in pleasure. Lee trembled under her touch as she carefully placed her hand under his shirt, slowly making her way upwards.

"Stop it Chlo, you'll get me into trouble." he whispered hoarsely.

"Dinner is ready!" Gwen called from the kitchen. Lee sighed in disappointment when Chloe moved away from him and slowly stood up, waiting for a moment for him to stand up, before the two of them walked through to the kitchen.

"It smells amazing in here!" Lee exclaimed.

"Can I help with anything?" he offered.

"Everything is under control." Gwen said shortly. Lee sighed in frustration and quickly took a seat opposite Amy at the dining table. Amy smiled sympathetically at him as he sat in silence, watching Chloe pull some glasses out of the cupboard and place them on the table.

"Thank you hunnie." Gwen smiled at Chloe as she picked up two of the plates of food and placed them on the table. As soon as Chloe sat beside Lee, she placed her hand on his knee, trying to reassure him.

"So, Lee, tell me about yourself?" Gwen asked.

"There's not really much to tell." Lee said nervously, not entirely sure what to say.

"I heard that you like the ladies." Gwen said accusingly.

"I used too, but that was before I fell in love with Chloe." he told her. Gwen scoffed sceptically, glaring at him across the table.

"Lee got Chloe a new necklace Mum." Amy piped up, trying to steer the conversation slightly. Gwen's gaze flickered to Chloe's neck, her eyes widening when she noticed the necklace.

"It's not new, he gave it to me months ago, he just gave it back to me today." Chloe explained.

"It looks very expensive." Gwen said quietly. Lee nodded slowly, not entirely sure what to say. He couldn't help but feel like whatever he said or did, Gwen was determined to think badly of him.

"Chlo doesn't like it when I buy her things, so I wanted to buy one gift that showed her how much I love her." he admitted quietly. Gwen nodded slowly, smiling slightly when she noticed Chloe and Lee glance at each other. Even in just a fleeting glance between the two of them, it was clear how much they loved each other.

"Oh Chloe, I forgot to ask, can you do my makeup for Prom on Saturday?" Amy asked excitedly.

"Yes of course." Chloe said, smiling slightly when Amy let out a squeal of excitement.

"Make sure you behave yourself, no getting drunk or getting with boys." Gwen told Amy sternly. Lee smiled slightly when Amy rolled her eyes at him.

"What's the number one rule?" Gwen added, raising her eyebrow at Amy.

"Yes I know Mum." Amy sighed, her cheeks colouring in embarrassment.

"No, tell me what is it?" Gwen insisted.

"No sex before marriage." Amy said shortly.

"Exactly." Gwen said, smiling in satisfaction.

"Which is why you will be sleeping on the sofa." she added, turning to Lee.

"I don't want any funny business, until there is a ring on her finger." she continued, pointing at Chloe.

"Auntie, I'm twenty five." Chloe sighed.

"That's not the point, your father would be turning in his grave if I didn't remind you of the family values." Gwen stated firmly.

"My Dad wasn't religious." Chloe argued.

"Don't argue with me Chloe, both of you know the number one rule!" Gwen snapped. Chloe could feel the anger rising in the pit of her stomach, as she opened her mouth to point out that she wasn't her mother and had no right to tell her what to do, but she quickly closed it again, deciding not to rise to the bait.

"You see young man, the Evans girls have very firm beliefs." Gwen said, turning her attention back to Lee, who was squirming slightly in his chair. Lee nodded slowly, glancing awkwardly at Chloe who remained silent, slowly pushing her food around her plate with her fork. The four of them remained silent for the rest of the meal, the tension in the air so thick that as soon as they had finished eating, Lee gathered the plates and took them into the kitchen to wash up.

"Can you try and make the effort with him please?" Chloe asked Gwen as soon as Lee left the room.

"He's a good guy Mum and he really adores Chloe." Amy agreed.

"I just want to make sure that he doesn't take advantage of you." Gwen said quietly.

"He won't Auntie, I promise. He takes care of me, when I was recovering from being stabbed he barely left my side for two weeks and that was before we even got together." Chloe explained. The three of them fell silent as Lee walked back into the room and hovered awkwardly.

"The washing up is done, is there anything else I can do to help?" he asked nervously.

"I don't think so." Gwen said quietly.

"You could come and watch a film with me." Amy beamed.

"Uh oh." Chloe laughed, quickly realising where Amy was going with the conversation.

"What film?" Lee frowned, glancing nervously at Chloe when he heard her comment.

"My favourite film." she added.

"You just like singing along to the songs." Chloe laughed.

"I know......ooh!" Amy exclaimed, causing everyone to jump.

"And you have a really good singing voice!" she added excitedly. Before Lee could react, Amy stood up and took Lee's hand, quickly dragging him towards the living room. Lee quickly shot Chloe a panicked expression, she shrugged at him, smiling slightly as she watched him being dragged away. Chloe could feel Gwen watching her closely, almost like she was trying to figure something out.

"You really love him don't you?" Gwen eventually asked. Chloe nodded slowly.

"He loves me too Auntie, he takes care of me and he would do anything to protect me." Chloe told her, smiling slightly to herself when she was reminded once again how lucky she was to have found someone like Lee. Gwen remained silent for a few moments, deep in thought about what Chloe had just said.

"I think Amy is working tomorrow, but I'm not working until the evening so maybe the three of us can go out somewhere?" Gwen suggested, trying to make the effort with Lee as Chloe had requested.

"That would be great." Chloe said, smiling slightly.

"We could take him to the waterfall or something." Gwen suggested. Chloe nodded, glancing towards the living room and giggling when she heard Amy singing at the top of her lungs.

"I'd better go and save him." Chloe laughed as she quickly stood up.

Chloe sighed to herself as she laid in bed and glanced at the clock. She'd been awake for what felt like hours, unable to settle and fall asleep. She tossed and turned, slowly becoming more and more frustrated as she listened to Amy sleeping quietly in her bed. Her mind wandered to Lee, who was sleeping on the sofa downstairs. She couldn't help but feel that if she was able to curl up in Lee's arms, she would feel more relaxed. Before Chloe could talk herself out of it, she slowly climbed out of bed, trying not to wake Amy. She quickly padded downstairs, glancing around nervously in case her aunt spotted her.

"What are you doing here?" Lee asked, when he noticed Chloe slowly walking over to him.

"I need a hug." she said quietly.

"Why, what's wrong?" he asked worriedly, quickly sitting up and watching her closely as she carefully sat on his lap.

"Nothing, I just want to be with you." she admitted, her cheeks colouring slightly.

"Aww, Chlo." he chuckled, smiling at her as he laid back down and she laid on top of him, quickly snuggling against him.

"I can't believe my auntie is making you sleep on the sofa." she said sadly, sighing in contentment when she felt Lee wrap his arms around her and hold her tightly against him.

"I didn't think it through, we should have got a hotel." she added.

"It's fine." he said quietly.

"It's not though, we've been apart for weeks. I just want to be with you." she admitted, snuggling her head against his collarbone.

"I know, but it's just a few days." he told her, smiling slightly when Chloe lifted her head and raised her eyebrow sceptically.

"And I want to make a good impression." he added, gently stroking her cheek with his hand. Chloe turned her head and placed a soft kiss on his hand.

"You do realise that my auntie is wrong about my parents, they weren't religious at all, she just likes to think that everyone is like her." she said, smiling slightly.

"I did figure that." he smiled.

"And as for the sex before marriage rule, that was never a thing with my parents, Mum just used to say to make sure you pick someone worthy to be your first." she explained, raising her eyebrow at him. He raised his eyebrow at her, a small smile playing on the corner of his lips.

"She does seem very intense with all the rules and stuff." he sighed.

"I know, it's Amy I feel sorry for." she said, resting her head on his chest and closing her eyes. Lee turned his head and rested it against hers, sighing quietly as he softly stroked her hair, cherishing the feeling of finally being able to hold her in his arms.

Chapter Ten

Chloe's eyes snapped open as she felt someone shaking her gently. She slowly sat up and frowned as she locked eyes with Amy.

"What's wrong?" Chloe asked, quickly rubbing the sleep out of her eyes.

"You must have fallen asleep down here, you need to get up before Mum finds out." Amy hissed. Chloe sighed quietly and slowly climbed out of Lee's arms, trying not to wake him.

"Sorry I didn't mean to wake you." she told Lee softly when she noticed him sitting up slowly.

"It's okay." he said sleepily. Chloe smiled as she felt him wrap his arms around her waist and gently pull her onto his lap, holding her gently as he carefully rested his chin on her shoulder. Chloe shivered slightly as she felt his hair brush against her neck.

"Anyway, I have to go to work, just make sure she doesn't catch you." Amy warned, clearing her throat awkwardly when she noticed the way that Chloe and Lee were gazing at each other longingly. She smiled slightly and quickly left the room, when the two of them didn't even acknowledge her because they were too focused on each other. Chloe and Lee jumped and quickly moved apart when Gwen walked into the room, frowning for a moment when she noticed that they were both still wearing their pyjamas.

"Come on you too, we need to get going." she told them firmly.

"Going where?" Lee frowned, glancing at Chloe.

"We're taking you to see the waterfall." Gwen said firmly.

"What, now?!" Chloe exclaimed, slightly confused as to why they were going out to the waterfall first thing in the morning.

"Yeah, I have to work tonight, so I'll need to get some sleep later this afternoon, so we need to go out now." Gwen said shortly. Chloe nodded slowly and quickly stood up, stretching out her sore muscles as she did so. Despite the fact that she'd slept really well, being curled up in Lee's arms, the two of them laying on the couch together hadn't been particularly comfortable. Gwen glanced between the two of them, frowning slightly.

"Did you sleep down here Chloe?" Gwen asked.

"No, I just came down to see him when I woke up." Chloe lied, feeling a slight pang of guilt for lying but knowing in her heart that if she told the truth her Aunt would be furious and the last thing that Chloe wanted was for her to have a go at Lee when she already knew how gutted he was that her Aunt didn't seem to like him.

"You'd better not have." Gwen said, narrowing her eyes at them suspiciously.

Lee avoided her gaze, feeling slightly uncomfortable with the conversation.

"Right, get dressed, we're going out." Gwen told them firmly.

"Thank you so much for letting us stay with you." Lee said quietly, still trying to make the effort with Gwen, as the three of them walked to the waterfall.

"You're welcome." Gwen replied quietly, glancing at Chloe when she noticed Lee take Chloe's hand, gently intwining their fingers.

"So what are your plans when the two of you get home?" Gwen asked them.

"We don't really have any do we....I need to find a job." Chloe said thoughtfully.

"Since I have a year off, we could always both take a year out and do a lot of holidays and fun stuff?" Lee suggested.

"And then when the tour preparations start again, you could come back and work for us." he continued.

"That would be awesome, we could make a list of all the things that we want to do." Chloe said excitedly.

"As long as you let me pay my own way." she quickly added. Lee nodded slowly, smiling slightly.

"Do you have somewhere to live in London?" Gwen asked, glancing at Chloe. Chloe remained silent, suddenly realising that her and Lee hadn't actually spoken about their living arrangements yet. Lee watched her closely, desperately hoping that she would return to living with him, but trying not to put pressure on her.

"I don't know, I haven't really thought about it." Chloe admitted eventually, glancing at Lee. He smiled warmly at her when the two of them locked eyes.

"I just want to make sure that you don't end up on a park bench again." Gwen piped up, a note of sadness present in her voice.

"No, that will never be happening again." Lee said quickly.

"You're welcome to move back in with me, if you want too?" he offered tentatively. Chloe nodded quickly, smiling up at him.

Lee gasped as they rounded the corner and stood in front of the waterfall. He stared in wonder at the water as it slowly flowed into the pool below.

"How far down do you think it is?" Chloe asked Lee as she stood on the rocks and peered down at the water.

"A couple of meters maybe." he answered, glancing at Chloe for a moment, his heart pounding against his chest when he saw the twinkle in her eyes. She smiled at Lee before turning her attention back to the water. She stared at the still water longingly, trying to figure out if it was deep enough for her to jump into.

"Chloe don't." Lee warned her, when he realised what she was considering. She turned to face him, a cheeky smile playing on the corner of her lips as she quickly removed her jacket and shoes.

"Don't you dare!" Gwen said sharply when she realised what Chloe was about to do. Chloe rolled her eyes and turned her back on the two of them, before quickly jumping off the rocks, a sense of freedom flowing through her as she fell through the air. She gasped and quickly brushed her hair out of her face when she landed in the cold water. Chloe smiled to herself as she treaded water and glanced up onto the ledge and noticed Gwen glaring at her angrily. Lee couldn't help but smile at her when she laughed happily and began to swim around in the water. He watched her closely as she dived under the water and swam towards the waterfall.

"Chloe, you could have hurt yourself!" Gwen shouted as soon as Chloe resurfaced. Chloe shrugged silently, glancing at Lee who quickly looked away from her, trying to resist the urge to burst out laughing at Chloe's incredulous expression.

"Aren't you coming in?" Chloe called to Lee, raising her eyebrow at him. Lee chuckled at her infectious excitement and quickly removed his jacket.

"Don't encourage her!" Gwen told him firmly.

"There's nothing wrong with having a little bit of fun." he said sighing quietly as he removed his shoes and socks.

"That depends if you drown in the process." Gwen pointed out.

"I won't let anything happen to her." he reassured her. Gwen rolled her eyes at Lee as he jumped into the water to join Chloe, taking care not to jump too close to her, in case he injured her. Chloe beamed at him and quickly swam away, towards the waterfall.

"CHLOE?!" Gwen called. Chloe ignored her and continued swimming, giggling loudly when she noticed that Lee was swimming after her.

"CHLOE EVANS!" Gwen tried again. Chloe stopped swimming and rolled her eyes at Lee, before quickly glancing up at Gwen.

"What?!" Chloe called.

"I have to go back to the car for my phone!" Gwen called.

"Okay!" Chloe called back.

"Good, don't hurry back." Lee muttered under his breath. Chloe burst out laughing.

"She's so intense." he added, smiling slightly at Chloe as she laughed.

"I know, she means well though.....I think." she chuckled.

"I'm sure she's over compensating because she feels bad that you had to sleep rough for a year, so she now thinks that she has to act like your parent." Lee said quietly.

"Probably." Chloe agreed. She stared past Lee, her eyes fixed closely on Gwen as she watched her walking away. As soon as she was out of sight, Chloe quickly swam over to Lee and wrapped her arms around his neck, kissing him deeply.

"I take it she's gone then." he chuckled when they eventually pulled apart. Chloe nodded slowly, smiling when she felt Lee place his hands on her hips and pull her close. She placed her hands on the back of his neck and softly stroked his hair, placing soft kisses on his neck. Her skin tingled when he placed his hands under her shirt and slowly stroked her spine with his fingertips. Chloe sighed in contentment, quickly wrapping her legs around his hips.

"Chlo." Lee whispered longingly, his hands grasping the material of her shirt and curling it into a fist as he desperately tried to fight the deep longing that he was feeling for her.

"What?" she mumbled, in between kissing his neck.

"I need you so bad.....this is like torture." he admitted hoarsely.

"Aww, are you struggling baby?" she whispered, as she methodically kissed a trail along his jawline.

"Um hum." he mumbled. Chloe giggled and kissed his lips softly.

"I don't think I'm the only one though." he said, taking deep breaths, to try and steady his heart that was pounding against his chest.

"I don't know what you're talking about." she smiled.

"Oh I see, so you're going to pretend that you're not struggling just as much as I am." he laughed.

"I'm an Evans girl remember, we don't do that kind of thing." she giggled.

"Oh really?" he said, raising his eyebrow sceptically. Chloe nodded quickly, her cheeks colouring slightly. Lee couldn't help but smile at how adorable she was. He kissed her softly, quickly deepening the kiss, desperately wishing that he was able to give into the intense desire that he was feeling for her.

"Chloe!" Gwen's voice called from the rocks. Chloe sighed quietly as the two of them quickly pulled apart and she reluctantly unwrapped her legs from Lee's hips.

"Oh for god sake." Lee whispered in her ear, as he rested his cheek against hers.

"We need to get back!" Gwen called them.

"We should probably go." Chloe sighed.

"I can't get out right now." Lee said, glancing down at his groin. Chloe followed his eyeline and burst out laughing when she saw what he was looking at.

"It's not funny." he grinned.

"Sorry, it's kind of my fault." she giggled.

"Damn right it is." he smiled. Chloe glanced up at Gwen and back to Lee.

"You wait there for a bit and try and cool off." she chuckled, before quickly making her way over to the edge of the water and climbing out.

"Oh for fuck sake." Lee mumbled when he glanced at Chloe and noticed that her top was so wet, that her bra was visible underneath. Chloe followed Lee's eyeline, a small smile playing on the corner of her lips when she noticed what he was looking at. Lee reluctantly tore his eyes away from staring at her and slowly disappeared under the surface of the water, trying to cool himself down. Chloe laughed and slowly climbed back up onto the ridge, squirming slightly when she felt Gwen staring at her intensely.

"For goodness sake Chloe, cover yourself up!" Gwen said firmly as soon as she laid eyes on Chloe.

"I have a bra on, it's no different than a bikini." Chloe sighed.

"It's very different." Gwen said shortly, quickly picking up Chloe's jacket and handing it to her firmly. Gwen gasped as her eyes wandered to Chloe's abdomen and she noticed her scar.

"Is that from when you were stabbed in the park?" Gwen asked quietly. Chloe nodded slowly.

"Can I see?" Gwen asked. Chloe took a deep breath and slowly lifted the corner of her top, her cheeks colouring as she glanced down at her scar. Gwen's eyes were fixed on Chloe's scar as she slowly traced her finger along it.

"I can't even imagine what you must have gone through." Gwen said sadly.

"It's fine, it's in the past now." Chloe said, glancing at Lee as he walked over to them.

"I'm sorry that you had to go through so much on your own, I wish that I'd been there for you." Gwen said, her voice catching in her throat.

"I wasn't alone." Chloe said, smiling at Lee as he stood beside her.

"You didn't go back to the park afterwards did you?" Gwen asked nervously.

"No, I went to live with Lee." Chloe answered.

"There was no way I was going to let you spend a single night on that bench, after I found out." Lee said quietly, his stomach churning like it always did, when he thought about the woman that he loved sleeping rough.

"I'll always remember what you said to me when I was in hospital and you thought that I was sleeping." Chloe smiled at him.

"What did I say?" Lee frowned.

"That you wished I was yours, then you could have protected me." Chloe said quietly. Lee nodded slowly.

"I would literally have taken the knife for you." he told her, gazing down at her softly.

"I know you would have." Chloe whispered, slowly wrapping her arms around his waist and squeezing him gently. Lee smiled at her, quickly moving out of her grasp as he saw some hikers walking towards them. He quickly took her jacket from Gwen and placed it on her, slowly zipping it up.

Chloe glanced at Gwen when she heard her sniff, frowning to herself when she noticed that Gwen's eyes had filled with tears. Before Chloe could react, Gwen walked over to Lee and quickly pulled him into a tight hug. Lee locked eyes with Chloe over the top of Gwen's head, and raised his eyebrow questioningly at her. Chloe shrugged in confusion.

"Thank you for taking care of her." Gwen whispered in Lee's ear.

"It's a privilege." he said quietly.

Chapter Eleven

Lee fidgeted carefully, trying to find a comfortable position as he sat on Chloe's bed, glancing down at Chloe as she stirred in her sleep. He was reminded once again of how beautiful she was as she slept soundly, her back resting against his chest. She mumbled something in her sleep and snuggled her head against his collarbone. Lee softly stroked her hair, still not quite able to comprehend how someone as beautiful and kind hearted as her had fallen in love with someone like him. He knew that he would never be able to fully express how madly in love with her he was, but he knew in his heart that Chloe knew how strong his feelings for her were.

"Chloe!" Amy called as she came bounding into the bedroom. Lee sighed sadly as Chloe jumped, her eyes quickly snapping open.

"Sorry I didn't mean to fall asleep on you." she mumbled sleepily, turning her head to face him.

"I don't have any complaints." he smiled at her, watching closely as she rested the back of her head against his shoulder and relaxed against him, sighing quietly to herself as she rubbed the sleep out of her eyes.

"I'm sorry, I didn't mean to wake you." Amy piped up as she sat on her bed opposite them.

"It's okay, I didn't intend to fall asleep anyway." Chloe said quietly, feeling a deep sense of relaxation when she felt Lee's soft heartbeat against her back. She smiled to herself when he wrapped his arms around her and pulled her close, gently resting his chin on her shoulder, the two of them longing to be close to each other, after spending what felt like a lifetime apart.

"You're turning into an old lady that needs afternoon naps." Amy teased. Chloe nodded slowly, her skin tingling as she rested her cheek against Lee's. Chloe glanced at Amy as she fell silent and stared at her lap awkwardly.

"Did you want me for something?" Chloe asked her, suddenly remembering that Amy had been calling her.

"Yeah kinda." Amy said, glancing nervously at Lee.

"Do you want me to give the two of you some time alone to talk?" Lee offered, when he noticed Amy's body language.

"No, it's okay, just don't tell anyone." Amy said. Lee nodded slowly, glancing at Chloe when he felt her body language stiffen nervously.

"Alex has invited me over tonight." Amy announced quietly.

"Who's Alex?" Lee frowned.

"My boyfriend." Amy answered, glancing at the doorway, nervous that her mother would overhear their conversation.

"And since Mum is working tonight, I'm going to sneak over there." she added.

"Is that such a good idea, if she finds out you'll be grounded forever?" Chloe pointed out.

"She won't find out, she doesn't finish work until the morning and I'll just make sure that I'm back here before her." Amy insisted.

"Just don't tell her." she added.

"We're not going to tell her." Chloe told her, smiling slightly when she noticed the excited twinkle in Amy's eyes.

"You're eighteen, you have your own life." Lee agreed.

"Try telling that to my Mum." Amy sighed.

"She wants me to wait until I'm married before I do anything, but that's not what I want." Amy sighed sadly, wishing in her heart that her mum wasn't so strict with her.

"You have to decide for yourself when you are ready, as long as you make sure that you are certain." Chloe told her.

"I am ready, I need to pop my cherry at some point." Amy said quickly, glancing at Lee when he burst out laughing at her words.

"My virginity has never been a big deal to me, like it has you." Amy added, glancing at Chloe.

"Everyone is different anyway." Chloe said quietly, feeling slightly nervous that Amy would live to regret her actions at a later date.

"You guys need to give me tips." Amy smiled, bursting out laughing when Chloe squirmed against Lee's chest, her cheeks colouring deeply.

"Tips about what?" Lee chuckled as he gently brushed Chloe's hair to one side of her neck, smiling slightly when she shivered involuntarily.

"I dunno, like....." Amy started but trailed off when she became too embarrassed to finish her sentence.

"What?" Lee laughed, glancing at Chloe when she remained silent, clearly not comfortable talking about the subject.

"Well, how do I know what to do....I don't want to be really bad at it?" she asked nervously.

"You just let the guy lead, problem solved." Lee said quickly.

"But I haven't told him that I've never been with anyone before, and I don't want too." Amy pointed out.

"Why not?" Chloe frowned.

"I dunno, I just feel like guys think it's a bit weird." Amy sighed.

"That depends on the guy." Chloe pointed out.

"And you definitely need to tell him Amy." Lee said sternly.

"Why, what difference does it make?" Amy argued.

"Because he'll need to be gentle with you and take things slowly, and if he doesn't know then he might not be." Lee pointed out, glancing down at Chloe when he remembered how worried he had been about hurting her.

"I would have felt really guilty if I hadn't known." Lee whispered.

"And hurt that the woman didn't feel like she could trust me enough to tell me." he added.

"It's okay, Amy knows that you were my first." Chloe said quickly, trying to reassure him when she felt him squirming nervously. Amy nodded in agreement, smiling at the two of them when they glanced at each other and Amy was reminded once again of how in love the two of them were.

"Does it hurt Chloe?" Amy asked her nervously.

"Yes." Chloe admitted, glancing at Lee when she heard him sigh sadly.

"Only a little though." she quickly added, when she realised that he was feeling guilty at the thought that he'd hurt her.

"I was really careful." Lee said quietly.

"I know you were." Chloe smiled at him, quickly placing a soft kiss on his lips.

"So you definitely need to tell him, otherwise it will hurt a lot more." Chloe said, turning her attention back to Amy. Amy nodded slowly, swallowing the lump that was rising in her throat.

The three of them fell silent as Gwen peered around the doorway dressed in her uniform.

"Right, I have to go to work, dinner is in the fridge, you just need to heat it up." Gwen explained.

"Make sure you behave yourselves." she added, before quickly walking away.

"Right, I need to get ready!" Amy squealed as soon as she heard the front door close. Chloe smiled as she watched Amy quickly gathering her keys and phone.

"Do you need me to give you a lift over?" Lee offered, when he suddenly realised that it was dark outside.

"No, it's okay thanks. Alex is picking me up." Amy told him. Amy stared at her reflection in the mirror and smiled slightly when she realised how confident she felt. She squealed in excitement as she heard a car horn beeping from outside.

"That'll be Alex!" she said excitedly.

"Be careful Amy, you don't really know this guy." Chloe said worriedly. Amy nodded slowly.

"And make sure you tell him!" Lee called after her as she walked away. Lee burst out laughing as Amy stuck her middle finger up at him and walked out of the room.

"I really hope she doesn't regret anything." Chloe said quietly.

"I don't think she will, she seems pretty certain." he replied. Lee fell silent for a moment, smiling slightly to himself when he realised for the first time that they had the house to themselves. He glanced down at Chloe as she slowly turned on his lap, smiling slightly when she faced him. She slowly wrapped her arms around his neck and kissed him deeply, her hands slowly trailing down his neck. Lee broke the kiss and quickly pulled her top over her head. Before Chloe had a chance to react he placed his hands on her hips and pushed her roughly onto the bed. She watched as he quickly climbed on top of her.

"Calm down." Chloe giggled.

"It's been weeks Chlo." he whispered hoarsely in her ear.

"I know." she said quietly, gasping in pleasure as he kissed a trail down her neck and onto her sternum. Chloe grasped Lee's shirt in her grip and quickly pulled it over his head. Lee groaned in pleasure as she slowly stroked a trail down his chest. Lee slowly pulled down Chloe's trousers as he placed a series of soft kisses on her abdomen, maintaining eye contact with her the entire time. Chloe pulled her legs towards herself, carefully extracting them from her trousers. She gasped in pleasure and reached down to stroke Lee's hair when he quickly kissed a trail up the inside of her thigh. Lee smiled to himself when Chloe squirmed underneath him, letting out a small whimper when his hand briefly caressed her sensitive area.

"I can't wait any longer." Lee whispered, his breath catching in his throat.

"Me neither." Chloe admitted, arching her back upwards and quickly unclasping her bra.

"You're so beautiful Chlo." he whispered, gazing at her in wonder for a moment.

"I love you." she whispered.

"Do you feel better now?" Chloe asked Lee softly, as she curled up in his arms.

"Yep." he beamed, taking deep breaths to try and get his breath back. She lifted her head and smiled at him, her skin tingling as he wrapped his arm around her waist and slowly traced small circles on her back. Chloe's eyes filled with tears as she snuggled against him. She blinked slowly, cursing herself as one of her tears fell from her eye and landed on his bare chest.

"Are you okay?" Lee asked her quickly. Chloe remained silent and nodded slowly, not entirely sure why she was feeling so emotional.

"Are you crying?" he asked worriedly, quickly turning to face her, his brow furrowing in concern when he noticed the tears in her eyes.

"Did I hurt you?" he asked nervously, his stomach churning with guilt when he realised that he might have accidently hurt her.

"I know I wasn't as gentle with you as I normally am, but I just missed you so much." he continued, before Chloe had a chance to answer.

"I'm sorry, I didn't mean to hurt you." he said sadly, turning on his side and pulling Chloe into his arms, when he noticed the steady stream of tears that were rolling down her face.

"You didn't hurt me, I'm fine." she mumbled against his chest, quickly wrapping her arms around his neck and holding him tightly.

"I'm just emotional because I missed you and I'm so glad that we are back together." she explained.

"Me too." he whispered, softly stroking her hair.

"I love you so much." she whispered, holding him tightly and wishing that she never had to let go.

Chapter Twelve

Chloe slowly pulled down the sleeves of Lee's hoodie and smiled to herself when he pulled on his pyjamas and laid on his side behind her, gently wrapping his arms around her waist and pulling her against him so that he could hold her tightly. She sighed in contentment and closed her eyes, suddenly feeling her eyelids becoming heavy.

"I love you." Lee whispered in her ear as he snuggled his face against hers. He gazed at her fondly, cherishing the feel of holding her tightly in his arms. Lee knew that for as long as he lived, he would never stop loving and adoring Chloe. She meant the world to him and he knew that he was nothing without her.

Chloe jumped, her eyes bolting open as she heard the front door slam, sighing to herself as she reluctantly removed herself from Lee's arms. Lee watched her sadly. Despite the fact that it had been months since she was stabbed, he couldn't help but notice that she was still quite jumpy.

"Come here Chlo." he said, reaching out to take her hand as she sat up and shuffled down the end of the bed. Chloe glanced at his hand, resisting the urge to take it.

"Chlo, come back to bed." Lee tried again.

"I can't......what if it's my auntie.....she might have come home early to check on us." Chloe pointed out, glancing down at herself and beginning to panic slightly when she remembered that she was only wearing her knickers and Lee's hoodie. Her heart pounded against her chest as she heard footsteps quickly climbing the stairs and she realised that she wouldn't have time to change.

"Are you that embarrassed by me?" he teased her, smiling slightly.

"No, I just don't want her to hate you." she muttered, her heart in her mouth as the bedroom door opened. Chloe released the breath she was holding when Amy walked into the room, her face full of anger. She briefly glanced between Chloe and Lee, before quickly walking into the bathroom and slamming the door.

"She's back early isn't she?" Lee frowned when he glanced at the clock and saw how early it still was. Chloe nodded slowly, unable to shake the feeling that something was wrong. She glanced at Lee as he slowly stood up.

"I need a cup of tea, do you want one?" he offered.

"Yes please." she replied, giggling as Lee bent down to her and kissed her lips tenderly. Chloe trembled as he placed his hands on her bare legs, his hands slowly making their way upwards.

"Stop it, Amy is back." she reminded him, smiling at the cheeky twinkle in his eyes.

"You're too beautiful to resist." he smiled, slowly straightening up. Chloe quickly looked away from him, her cheeks colouring as she felt him watching her closely.

"Maybe you should make Amy one too." she said, glancing nervously at the bathroom door. Lee nodded slowly and quickly left the room. As soon as Lee left the room, Amy quickly emerged from the bathroom and threw herself onto her bed, her face red with anger.

"What's wrong Amy?" Chloe asked quickly.

"You and Lee give the worst advice ever." Amy said bitterly.

"Why, what happened?" Chloe asked worriedly, her heart pounding against her chest. Chloe quickly stood up and perched beside Amy on the bed, frowning to herself as Amy shuffled along the bed and rested her head against Chloe's shoulder and wrapped her arms around her waist. Chloe sighed and carefully placed her arm around Amy's shoulders, sensing that she needed a few moments, before she was ready to talk about whatever had happened. Chloe sighed sadly when she heard Amy sniff quietly. Chloe glanced up as Lee walked back into the room and slowly walked over to them, silently handing Amy her cup of tea and placing Chloe's on the bedside table beside her. He glanced at Chloe and raised his eyebrow questioningly when he noticed that Amy was crying. Chloe shrugged at him, still not entirely sure what was going on.

"Did he hurt you Amy?" Chloe asked softly.

"Kinda." Amy said sadly, sniffing quietly as she quickly wiped away her tears.

"Do I need to go and kick his arse?" Lee asked, as he sat on Chloe's bed. Amy shook her head slowly, smiling slightly at his words.

"You need to tell us what happened, we're getting worried?" Chloe asked quietly.

"He broke up with me." Amy said sadly.

"What, why?!" Lee exclaimed, feeling slightly angry at the thought of someone hurting Amy's feelings. Even though he barely knew her, the two of them had bonded over the past week and he had grown quite fond of her.

"Because I did what you told me too and I told him that I'd never been with anyone before." Amy said. Chloe and Lee frowned at each other in confusion.

"And he said that he just wanted something casual and wasn't prepared to be my first, because apparently I would become clingy afterwards." she continued.

"Which is complete bullshit by the way, it's not like I am in love with him, I just really liked him." she ranted.

"Is that even a thing?" Lee frowned.

"I don't know, it was different for us because I was already in love with you." Chloe said thoughtfully.

"Apparently it's a thing." Amy said angrily.

"I shouldn't have said anything to him." she quickly added.

"Yes you should have. If he's going to react like that then he doesn't deserve you." Lee told her.

"There's plenty more fish in the sea, you'll find a good guy one day." Chloe added.

"That's easy for you to say, you have the perfect man." Amy sighed, finally lifting her head from Chloe's shoulder and glancing at Lee.

"Trust me, I'm far from perfect." Lee said quietly.

"I want what the two of you have though." Amy admitted sadly.

"You'll find someone one day, there's no rush though, you're only young." Chloe told her. Amy sighed sadly and nodded slowly, silently taking a sip of her tea.

"Oh no, Alex was meant to be taking me to prom tomorrow night!" Amy exclaimed when she suddenly remembered.

"Can't you ask someone else to go with you?" Chloe suggested.

"It's pretty late notice." Amy said, sighing sadly. Chloe sighed quietly when she noticed the disappointment written over Amy's face. She knew that Amy had been excited about her prom for the past few weeks.

"I'll just save the dress and wear it to your wedding." Amy teased, smiling at the two of them, trying to lighten the atmosphere and hide how disappointed she was. Chloe turned to face Lee, raising her eyebrow at him. Lee frowned at her, glancing at Amy when he finally realised what Chloe was trying to communicate.

"Isn't it going to be a bit weird, a thirty one year old guy going with an eighteen year old?" Lee frowned at Chloe, glancing at Amy for a moment when he saw her looking between him and Chloe hopefully.

"No, it's only as a friend, to make sure she's safe." Chloe pointed out.

"Okay fine." Lee said, not entirely sure if he was comfortable with the situation, but quickly realising how important it was to Amy and Chloe.

"Really?!" Amy exclaimed, quickly placing her cup of tea on the bedside table.

"Yeah, I'll take you....but I'm not going to pretend to be your date, it'll be as friends only." he told her, smiling slightly when she nodded excitedly. Before Lee could react Amy quickly stood up and rushed over to him, quickly throwing herself into his arms. Lee wobbled for a moment, quickly recovering himself and smiling at Chloe as the two of them locked eyes.

"Thank you so much!" Amy squealed in his ear.

"It's fine." Lee smiled.

"Oh my god, I get to go in your car too!" Amy yelled. Lee nodded slowly, bursting out laughing when Amy finally let go of him and danced around the room happily. Chloe laughed, shaking her head as she slowly stood up. Lee smiled at her as she mouthed thank you at him.

"I think she's forgotten about Alex already." Chloe laughed as Amy hurried out of the room. Lee nodded slowly.

"Are you sure you don't mind me going to prom with her?" he asked her.

"No, I think it's a great idea, she adores you." she smiled at him, watching him closely as he stood up. Chloe quickly walked over to him and wrapped her arms around his neck. Lee rested his hands on her thighs and carefully picked her up, gently wrapping her legs around his hips. Chloe's heart pounded against her chest as he kissed her tenderly, quickly deepening the kiss. She giggled as he pressed her body against the wall and kissed her passionately.

"What's gotten into you lately?" Chloe asked breathlessly.

"I just missed you so much." he whispered. Chloe gasped as he began to kiss her neck, smiling slightly as she shivered when he found her sensitive spot.

"My aunt will kill you if you leave a mark." Chloe reminded him as she slowly tipped her head back, her skin tingling under his touch when he placed his hands under her hoodie, holding her waist tightly.

"You can cover it with makeup." he mumbled against her neck.

"I've never seen you like this before." she giggled, smiling to herself when she pushed her hips against him and he let out a small groan of pleasure.

"I want you all the time." he admitted. Chloe's heart fluttered against his chest as he said those words. She slowly tipped her head forward and rested her forehead against his, staring into his eyes as she slowly rotated her hips against him. Lee groaned and placed his hands on the wall behind her, pressing his forehead against Chloe's and kissing her lips softly as he stared at her lovingly. Chloe took deep breaths, trying to control her longing for him as he squirmed against her, gripping her waist tightly as she continued to rotate her hips against him. Lee pressed his head against the wall behind her, his body pressed tightly against Chloe's as he groaned in pleasure.

"I love you." she whispered in his ear. He let out a final deep groan as he released, collapsing against her slightly, breathing deeply as he fought to get his breath back. He slowly lifted his head, staring down at Chloe as she smiled up at him. He placed his hands on her face, slowly stroking her jawline with his thumbs, before gently placing a soft kiss on her lips.

"What are you doing?" Chloe frowned as he carried her over to the bed and carefully placed her down, before quickly laying down beside her.

"I have to return the favour." he smiled at her, gently placing his hand under her hoodie and stroking small circles on her abdomen. She stared up at him as he placed his arm behind her head and slowly stroked her hair. Chloe leaned towards him and kissed his lips softly, gasping against his lips when she felt him place his hand inside her underwear.

"What if Amy comes back?" she asked, beginning to panic slightly.

"It's okay, we'll hear her footsteps coming up the stairs." he reassured her. Chloe nodded, squirming as his soft fingers traced small circles.

"I want you so badly." she whimpered, pressing her body against his and snuggling into him as he continued to massage her.

"I know, but we can't, just in case." he told her. Chloe nodded slowly, her whole body trembling against him as she released. Lee smiled slightly as she bit her lip to prevent herself from crying out. She wrapped her arms around his neck and kissed him deeply, sighing deeply when they eventually pulled apart. She quickly pulled away from him and sat up, pulling down her hoodie when she heard Amy's footsteps climbing the stairs.

"I need to shower again now." Lee chuckled as he slowly sat up.

"Sorry that was my fault." she giggled.

"You can't help being stunning." he smiled, quickly pecking her lips before standing up and walking into the bathroom and closing the door. Chloe glanced up at Amy as she walked into the bedroom.

"Where's Lee?" Amy frowned.

"He's gone for a shower." Chloe told her, laying down on her side and pulling the covers over herself.

"Ooh." Amy said, wiggling her eyebrows at Chloe as she quickly changed into her pyjamas. Chloe rolled her eyes, sighing to herself as Amy watched her closely.

"I need details.....especially since I don't have a sex life." Amy giggled, curling up in bed and laying down on her side so that she was facing Chloe.

"Nor do I, I'm an Evans girl remember." Chloe laughed, fighting to keep her eyes open. Amy burst out laughing.

"I don't really understand why she calls us that, especially when I'm not even an Evans." Amy said, when she eventually recovered herself.

"Because you have Evan's blood in your veins." Chloe said, imitating Gwen's voice.

"That was amazing, you sound just like her!" Amy said, bursting out laughing.

"I can't believe I just did that!" Chloe said, joining in with Amy's infectious laughter.

Lee frowned when he emerged from the bathroom and noticed Amy and Chloe in fits of laughter about something.

"What did I miss?" he smiled. Chloe opened her mouth to tell him, before quickly bursting into laughter again.

"What are you laughing at?" Lee chuckled, glancing between the two of them.

"How bad you are in bed!" Amy laughed. Lee frowned in confusion, glancing at Chloe when she instantly stopped laughing.

"Amy!" Chloe exclaimed.

"Chloe was complaining and then we got the giggles." Amy continued.

"Will you shut up and go to bed!" Chloe said firmly.

"Yes Mum." Amy pouted.

"It's a good thing you are going back to London, before you turn into my Mum." Amy giggled. Chloe shook her head slowly and rolled her eyes. Lee slowly walked over to Chloe and squatted down in front of her.

"I'd better go back to my sofa." he said sadly. Chloe nodded slowly, sighing quietly to herself. Lee sighed and placed a soft kiss on her lips.

"You can stay up here if you want?" Amy suggested.

"I'm not going to tell." she added.

"What time does your Mum normally get home from work?" Lee asked Amy.

"She's normally back just after nine am." Amy told him.

"So as long as you get up before then, it should be fine." she added. Lee raised his eyebrow questioningly at Chloe, smiling slightly when he noticed that she was struggling to keep her eyes open. Chloe nodded slowly. Lee smiled and quickly climbed into bed beside her, watching her closely as she turned to face him and quickly curled up in his arms.

"Just don't have sex right under my nose please." Amy laughed. Lee chuckled, watching Chloe closely when he realised that she'd fallen asleep as soon as she was in his arms. He placed a kiss on her forehead and slowly closed his eyes.

Chapter Thirteen

Chloe sighed sadly as she stood in the kitchen watching Lee chopping fruit. She couldn't help but feel sad that they were leaving Nottingham after breakfast. Despite the fact that Chloe was thrilled to be back with Lee and she knew that she couldn't live without him, she couldn't help but feel upset about the idea of being parted from her family once again. Her confidence had soared since she'd been staying with them and she had finally found somewhere safe and quiet that she felt at home. Butterflies swirled in Chloe's stomach as she thought about the idea of returning to London and potentially being faced with yet another media storm. Gwen smiled at Chloe and Lee as she walked into the room and began to make pancakes. Lee glanced at Chloe, his brow furrowing in concern when he heard her sigh sadly and lean against the kitchen counter.

"Are you okay Chlo?" Lee asked worriedly. Chloe remained silent and nodded slowly, trying to hide how upset she was at the thought of saying goodbye to her family.

"You're very quiet." he prompted her, when she didn't respond.

"I'm fine." Chloe said, smiling falsely.

"She's devastated about leaving us." Amy teased as she walked into the room and stood beside Chloe. Chloe wrapped her arms around Amy's shoulders and pulled her close.

"I'm really going to miss you." Chloe admitted.

"I don't blame you." Amy said sadly, her stomach plummeting at the thought of Chloe leaving. The last few weeks had reminded Amy of how much Chloe meant to her and how much she enjoyed having her around.

"I'm so glad we got back in touch." Amy admitted.

"Me too, at least some good came out of the media." Chloe sighed, glancing at Lee when she felt him watching her closely. His stomach swirled with guilt, when he was reminded once again of how much Chloe went through as a result of his lifestyle. He couldn't help but feel slightly nervous that history was going to repeat itself.

"Did you arrange to do that article yet?" Chloe asked Lee, when she noticed the guilty expression on his face.

"Not yet, I was waiting to speak to you about it again." he told her.

"I think we should just do it and see what happens." Chloe said nervously. Lee nodded slowly.

"Are you guys doing a shoot or something?" Amy asked excitedly.

"Yeah and an article for a magazine, so that we can take control of it this time and tell our side of things." Lee explained.

"We need to show how much of a good person she is, and how much she means to me." he added.

"I want to make sure the fans love Chloe as much as I do." he continued, smiling back at Gwen when she flashed him a small smile.

"Just make sure you get to keep your clothes on this time." Gwen said firmly, feeling slightly sick when she remembered Amy showing her Eclipse's album cover. Chloe nodded slowly, her cheeks colouring.

"Shit!" Lee exclaimed when he accidentally sliced his finger with the knife. He quickly flung the knife onto the counter, silently cursing himself for getting distracted when he remembered how mesmerizing Chloe had looked on the day of the album photoshoot. Chloe slowly walked over to him and held his wrist, inspecting his finger as she watched a trail of blood slowly trickling down his finger. She quickly picked up some kitchen towel and placed it over the wound, gently applying pressure. Lee gazed down at her as she stood in front of him and shyly glanced up at him, her cheeks colouring under his intense gaze. He winced slightly as she applied more pressure to the wound, trying to stop the bleeding. She hesitated for a moment, before placing a soft kiss on the palm of his hand. Lee stared at her longingly, desperately trying to resist the urge to pull her into his arms and kiss her.

"It looks sore." Chloe said softly when she slowly removed the kitchen towel and stared at the wound.

"It's not too bad." he said quietly, placing his other hand on her bare arm and slowly stroking down it, smiling to himself when he felt the goose bumps rising on Chloe's arm.

"I'll get you a plaster." Gwen piped up, snapping Lee out of his thoughts. He reluctantly tore his eyes away from Chloe and smiled his thanks at Gwen when she handed him a plaster.

"I apologise for swearing." Lee said quietly when he suddenly remembered what he'd said.

"I think I can make an exception in these circumstances." Gwen said smiling slightly. Lee glanced at Chloe when she gently took the plaster from his grip and carefully applied it to his finger. As soon as she'd applied the plaster, she placed another soft kiss on his hand, smiling when Lee gently stroked her cheek with his fingertips.

"I love you." she whispered as she stared into his eyes.

"I love you too." he told her, quickly placing a soft kiss on her forehead.

"You guys are so adorable." Amy piped up, snapping Chloe and Lee out of their thoughts.

"They are actually aren't they." Gwen agreed, smiling as she watched the two of them. Amy nodded, her stomach rumbling as Gwen placed the pancakes onto a plate and carried them over to the dining table.

"I think I'll leave cutting the rest of the fruit." Lee chuckled as he glanced down at his finger.

"We should have enough anyway." Gwen said, smiling at him as she picked up the bowl of fruit and placed it on the table. The four of them walked over to the dining table and quickly sat down. Chloe smiled at Lee as he sat beside her and placed his hand on her lap. She reached down and placed her hand on top of his, gently playing with his fingers.

"I'm going to miss having you here Chloe, it's been really nice." Gwen said quietly.

"I'll miss you guys too, thank you so much for letting me stay, I can never thank you enough for helping me through everything." Chloe replied, her eyes filling with tears.

"It's no problem, it's what family is for." Gwen smiled.

"I believe I owe you thanks as well." Lee piped up.

"You've welcomed me into your home and I really appreciate it." he added.

"You're welcome, it's actually been really nice to meet you." Gwen smiled.

"And I really appreciate you taking Amy to her prom last night to make sure that she was safe." she added.

"I made sure she behaved herself too." Lee teased Amy, smiling at her when she rolled her eyes at him.

"I would like to come up and visit more, now that we are back in touch." Chloe said quietly.

"You'll always be welcome up here." Gwen smiled at her.

"If you want too, you can both come and stay with us at some point too." Lee offered.

"We won't both fit in your tiny house." Amy laughed. Gwen frowned for a moment, glancing between Amy and Lee when he joined in with her laughter.

"His house is beautiful Mum, it's like a mansion." Amy told her.

"It's not a mansion." he argued, smiling slightly when Amy raised her eyebrow sceptically.

"It has a swimming pool, a hot tub and a gym!" Amy insisted.

"Fair point." Lee agreed, bursting out laughing when Amy nodded smugly.

"Maybe we should come and stay then." Gwen smiled.

"You're welcome anytime." Lee told her, glancing at Chloe and smiling at her reassuringly. He knew from her body language how upset she was at the thought of having to leave her family.

"Just make sure that you take care of her for us." Gwen said quietly, her eyes filling with tears when she locked eyes with Chloe.

"Of course I will." Lee smiled, slowly curling his fingers over Chloe's and gently stroking her fingernails.

"She means the world to me, I'll always protect her." he added, gazing fondly at Chloe as the two of them locked eyes.

"I know." Gwen smiled at them.

"Do you want a cup of tea?" Gwen offered when they had finally finished breakfast.

"We should probably head off, the boys are coming over this afternoon, so we need to get back." Lee answered, when Chloe remained silent.

"The Eclipse boys?" Chloe asked.

"Yeah, they've been coming over once a week to check on me, they are going to get such a shock when they see you." Lee said, chuckling quietly.

"You haven't told them yet?" Amy asked.

"We haven't told anyone apart from you guys." Lee replied.

"Argh, I'm so jealous that you get to spend the afternoon with the Eclipse boys." Amy said, trying to cheer Chloe up when she sensed how she was feeling.

"It'll be good to see them, I haven't seen them in a while." Chloe said quietly, smiling falsely as she tried to put on a brave face and hide how upset she actually was.

"Hopefully Steven and Adrian aren't mad with me." she added thoughtfully.

"Why would they be mad at you?" Lee frowned.

"Because you dropped out of the tour because of me." Chloe reminded him, sighing quietly to herself.

"Nobody blames you for what happened Chlo." he told her gently. Chloe nodded slowly, not entirely sure if she believed him or not.

"Can I borrow you for a few minutes before we go?" Chloe asked, quickly turning to face Amy. Amy frowned in confusion as Chloe quickly stood up and nodded her head in the direction of the stairs. Lee watched as Amy and Chloe left the room together. He couldn't help but feel concerned that something was going on that Chloe wasn't telling him. She'd been very quiet for the past couple of days, he'd assumed it was a result of the fact that they were due to return to London soon, but he couldn't ignore the feeling that something was wrong. His brain was spinning with the possibilities of what Chloe could possibly need to talk to Amy in private about. Had something happened that she hadn't told him about? And if so what could possibly be wrong that she couldn't talk to him about? Lee could hear Gwen talking to him, but he couldn't process her words, his brain was working overtime, as his eyes wandered up the stairs, unable to stop worrying about Chloe.

"I'm sorry, I need to go and check on her." Lee said quietly, quickly standing up and making his way upstairs. His heart was pounding against his chest as he quickly climbed the stairs. He walked into the bedroom, frowning to himself when he heard voices coming from the bathroom.

"Chlo!" Lee called, quickly knocking on the bathroom door.

"Yes?" she called back.

"Can I come in?" he asked.

"No!" Chloe said sharply.

"We won't be long." Amy agreed, a slight grimace present in her voice.

"Chlo, what's going on?" Lee asked.

"Are you okay?" he added, before she had a chance to respond.

"I'm fine, I just need a few minutes." Chloe told him. Lee sighed and rested his head against the door, flashbacks swirling around his head when he remembered the last time that Chloe had locked him out of a bathroom... on the day that they'd lost their baby. He could hear Chloe and Amy whispering to each other but he couldn't focus on their words, only the memory of Chloe sitting on the bathroom floor, at the studio, covered in blood. He quickly lifted his head and stepped back from the door when Chloe and Amy emerged a few moments later.

"What's wrong?" Chloe asked him quickly, when she noticed that his eyes were full of tears. Lee remained silent, quickly wrapping his arms around her and holding her tightly against himself.

"Can you give us a minute?" Chloe whispered to Amy, when she locked eyes with her over Lee's shoulder. Amy nodded and quickly left the room.

"Lee, what's wrong?" Chloe whispered when he snuggled his head into her shoulder and sniffed quietly.

"Bad memories." he whispered back, pulling her tightly against him.

"I'll never forget the last time you wouldn't let me into the bathroom." he added sadly. Chloe fell silent for a moment, deep in thought as she tried to remember the time that he was speaking about. She sighed deeply when she finally joined the dots in her head. Her stomach swirled with guilt at the thought that she'd opened up Lee's wound, that she knew would never truly heal.

"I'm sorry." she said quietly, wrapping her arms around his neck and softly stroking his hair to try and comfort him.

"I just needed to speak to Amy." she added.

"It's okay, it's just the association of last time." he said quietly, wishing once again, with all his heart, that he could have done something to prevent the loss of their baby.

"I know." she whispered sadly.

Chapter Fourteen

Chloe sighed sadly and wiped away her tears as she gazed out of the car window and watched the landscape rushing by. As they travelled further away from Nottingham and closer to London, Chloe could feel her heart slowly plummeting. She glanced at Lee as she felt him reach over and gently take her hand, squeezing it in reassurance.

"We can go and see them regularly Chlo." he told her, his heart breaking a little when he noticed the steady stream of tears rolling down her cheeks.

"I know, it was just really difficult saying goodbye." she said sadly.

"I understand, and it's worse because you've only just got them back." he said, sighing sadly.

"You seem to have a lot more confidence since you've been with them." he prompted her.

"It helps when you have a family doesn't it." she said quietly.

"Yeah, I can't imagine what it must have been like for you all those years without a family." he agreed. Chloe nodded slowly.

"And the counselling has been really helping too." she said thoughtfully.

"You should make sure that you continue it, if it's been helping." he smiled at her.

"Well apparently you can do it via video call, which means that I won't have to find a new counsellor." she explained.

"London holds a lot of bad memories." she sighed as they drove into the city.

"What?" he frowned in confusion, tearing his eyes away from the road and glancing at her for a moment.

"There have been good things too, but a lot of bad stuff has happened in London." she sighed.

"I got stabbed there, lost both my parents and lost our baby." she continued. Lee nodded slowly, swallowing the lump that was rising in his throat when she mentioned their baby.

"And I'm really scared that the media thing is going to start back up again." she added.

"That's why we need to do the OK magazine article." he said quietly, his stomach churning nervously. Chloe nodded slowly.

"Can we stay in the house for a few days, just us two, until we've done the article?" she asked, her stomach churning at the thought of the media potentially finding out about them before they'd had a chance to release the article.

"If that's what you want." he said.

"It's a good idea, we could do with some time just the two of us, without any pressure." he added thoughtfully.

"After the Eclipse boys go home of course." she said, smiling slightly when she remembered that they were coming over to see Lee. He nodded, a small smile playing on the corner of his lips when he realised how pleased they were going to be when they found out that Chloe was back in their lives.

"I suppose at some point, we'll need to tell all of our friends about us." Chloe said thoughtfully.

"Maybe we could do it after we've done the interview and the shoot, then that way we can tell them just before the article comes out so that they can hear it from us, but there's no time for Michelle to stir up, when it inevitably gets back to her." he explained.

"Sounds like a plan." she agreed.

"I can get everyone over and we can tell them all at once." he suggested.

"I think they'll be very surprised, since they all think I'm in Nottingham." she said, smiling slightly. Lee nodded slowly, chuckling quietly to himself.

"It looks like the boys are already here." Lee said as they pulled into the driveway and he noticed Steven's car. Chloe nodded slowly, swallowing the nervous lump that was rising in her throat as she slowly climbed out of Lee's car. Lee opened the boot and quickly pulled out their suitcases, before quickly handing Chloe hers.

"Don't look so nervous, I promise they are not mad at you." Lee told her as they walked up the driveway.

"I would understand if they are, I think I'd be mad, after all the work they put into the tour." she said sadly, feeling another pang of guilt that her actions had such a detrimental effect on the man that she loved and as a result her three best friends. The Eclipse boys had been good to her over the years and she couldn't help but feel like she had let them down. Despite the fact that it wasn't deliberate, that didn't stop the intense guilt that she was feeling. As soon as they walked into house, Lee glanced at Chloe when he heard Steven, Adrian and Nathan's voices coming from the living room. Chloe watched him closely, smiling slightly when he placed his finger on her lips, before winking at her and walking into living room. Chloe hovered nervously in the hallway, listening closely for the right moment to make her entrance.

"Lee!" Steven exclaimed as soon as he walked into the room.

"Hey." Lee said quietly, trying to hide how happy he was so that the boys didn't become suspicious that Chloe was back in his life.

"Where have you been?!" Nathan exclaimed, quickly standing up and pulling him into a hug.

"I did text you to tell you that I was going away for a few days, and as you can see I've only just got home." Lee said, rolling his eyes.

"We thought you'd gone on a bender again or something." Adrian piped up.

"Nope." Lee said quietly, glancing at Nathan who was watching him closely, a suspicious expression on his face.

"The twinkle is back in your eyes." Nathan pointed out.

"Have you finally decided to listen to us and try and meet someone else?" Steven chuckled.

"Nope, there's nobody else for me." Lee said quickly, a small smile playing on the corner of his lips when he realised that Chloe would be able to hear his every word from her place in the hallway. Steven laughed and made a vomiting noise. Lee shook his head slowly.

Chloe took a deep breath to steady her nerves and slowly walked into the living room, her cheeks colouring as they turned to stare at her.

"Chlo Bo!" Nathan exclaimed, quickly rushing over and pulling her into a tight bear hug. Chloe giggled as Nathan picked her up and squeezed her tightly against himself.

"I can't breathe!" Chloe said breathlessly.

"Sorry." Nathan said, quickly letting go of her and smiling at her flushed cheeks. Chloe glanced at Adrian and Steven nervously for a moment, releasing the breath she didn't realise she was holding when Adrian pulled her into a hug.

"Group hug!" Steven laughed, quickly hugging Chloe from behind. Chloe burst out laughing when she felt Lee and Nathan join in, the four of them squashing her slightly in the middle.

"Now I really can't breathe." she said nervously. Steven and Adrian burst out laughing and quickly let go of her, the four of them watching her closely as she took deep breaths, trying to recover herself.

"I'm so glad you're back, we were worried about you." Adrian told her.

"I'm okay." Chloe said, giving him a small smile.

"I am so sorry about everything that happened, it was all my fault." Chloe said sadly.

"You guys put so much work into the tour and it got postponed because of me." she continued, her eyes filling with tears.

"We totally get it." Nathan reassured her.

"You're our little sister Chloe, your mental health and Lee's is so much more important to us than a bloody arena tour." Adrian told her.

"Besides we're going next year instead." Nathan added.

"Maybe by next year, if the album does well, we won't have to live on a bus, we might get hotels." Steven laughed, trying to lighten the atmosphere when he noticed how upset Chloe was. The four of them burst out laughing, Chloe smiled shyly, still feeling guilty for what had happened but feeling a deep sense of relief that they didn't hold it against her.

"So, are you officially back together?" Adrian asked.

"Yep, I think I wore her down." Lee chuckled, gently wrapping his arm around Chloe's shoulders.

"But what about the media, won't it just get bad again?" Nathan asked, glancing at Chloe nervously, when he remembered how broken she'd been when she was living under the media storm.

"Well, I have a plan." Lee told them, quickly explaining his idea for OK magazine.

"That's a good idea." Steven said.

"Maybe if we show a united front as well, once you make the announcement, we can all back you up on Twitter saying how happy Chloe makes you and how much we all love her and stuff?" Adrian suggested. Lee nodded slowly, smiling at them.

"I kind of wish we'd done all of this in the first place, then the media wouldn't have taken you from me." Lee said sadly, glancing at Chloe.

"It might not work yet, they might still hate me anyway." Chloe said quietly.

"You can't leave him again anyway, otherwise we'll have to go back to babysitting!" Adrian laughed.

"Babysitting?" Chloe frowned.

"Yeah, we took turns didn't we." Adrian teased Lee, smiling when he noticed that he was squirming slightly.

"I was in rehab most of the time." Lee said shortly.

"Only after I kicked your arse into it." Nathan reminded him.

"For the first week, we took turns staying over with him." Steven told Chloe.

"In case he went to beat Andy up again?" Chloe asked, slightly afraid of their answer. Despite the fact that she felt slightly sorry for Lee when she felt him squirming, she knew that he would never open up to her about the weeks that she'd been gone, because he wouldn't want her to feel guilty, but Chloe knew that she needed to know, in the same way that Lee had wanted to know about how she'd coped.

"Yeah partly, we just kept an eye on him." Adrian told her.

"I wasn't that bad." Lee muttered quietly.

"Really, so you didn't keep drinking yourself to sleep then." Steven teased him. Lee opened his mouth to respond but quickly closed it when Nathan interrupted him.

"And you kept calling out for Chloe in your sleep." Nathan said quickly.

"I don't know what you're talking about." Lee mumbled.

"We should have recorded it boys." Steven laughed.

"Stop making me out to be some kind of sissy!" Lee exclaimed.

"You said it not us." Adrian laughed.

"So, is there a particular reason you came over, I assume it wasn't just to embarrass me in front of my girlfriend?" Lee asked quickly.

"We came to check on you." Nathan told him.

"All three of you didn't need to come over for that." Lee pointed out.

"We also came to work on the new song with you." Adrian told him.

"Matt is getting antsy, he wants it written and submitted by the end of the week." Steven explained.

"Great." Lee sighed, glancing at Chloe and sighing in disappointment when he realised that he wouldn't get some time alone with her after all.

"It's okay, I need to unpack anyway." Chloe piped up, trying to hide her disappointment.

"We won't keep him long Chlo Bo, I'm sure the two of you have a lot of catching up to do." Nathan smiled, wiggling his eyebrows at Chloe.

"We've spent the past few days together anyway." Chloe said, trying to appease her guilt by not showing them how disappointed she was that they needed Lee for a while.

"Yeah in Nottingham with your family, it wasn't exactly quality time together." Lee pointed out, smiling slightly when her cheeks coloured.

"They fell in love with you though." Chloe pointed out. Chloe took deep breaths, before turning on her heel and quickly running upstairs.

"Chlo, you forgot the suitcases." Lee called after her, chuckling to himself.

"I'll come back for them in a minute!" she called back. Chloe ran into the bathroom, swinging the door closed behind herself, only just making it in time to vomit down the toilet. She coughed, fighting to get her breath back, quickly taking the hair band off her wrist and tying her hair out of the way. Warm tears rolled down Chloe's cheeks as she continued to vomit. She rested her elbow against the toilet seat and closed her eyes, breathing deeply, in the hope that the intense nausea she was feeling would subside. Ever since the night that Lee was at Amy's Prom and Chloe had spent most of the evening vomiting, she hadn't been able to escape the intense feeling of dread in her stomach. She breathed a sigh of relief when the nausea finally passed, before slowly standing up and rinsing her mouth with mouthwash. She quickly flushed the toilet, and pulled out her hair band, trying to hide the evidence from Lee. Chloe stared at her reflection in the mirror, her heart pounding against her chest as she slowly brushed her hair, not entirely sure what to do or how to even process the situation. She jumped and frowned to herself when she heard the front door close loudly. She slipped off her pumps and slowly padded downstairs, smiling slightly when she noticed Lee sitting on the sofa, his guitar on his lap. She watched him closely as he sat in silence, absent mindedly playing a soft tune on the guitar, a notebook beside him on the sofa. Chloe glanced around the room, frowning to herself when she realised that Adrian, Steven and Nathan were nowhere to be seen. She slowly walked up behind Lee and gently wrapped her arms around his neck, sighing softly to herself as she rested her face against his.

"Where are the boys?" she asked.

"They left." he said quietly, softly singing some lyrics to himself and quickly picking up the notebook to write them down before he forgot them. Chloe nodded slowly and placed a soft kiss on his cheek. She kissed his neck softly and placed her arms under the collar of his shirt, slowly trailing her hands down his chest, smiling slightly when she felt him trembling under her touch.

"I need to get this done Chlo." he said hoarsely, trying to focus his mind on the song and not what Chloe was doing to him. She ignored him and slowly trailed her hands upwards, smiling against his neck when she grazed his nipples and he gasped quietly.

"Chlo stop it." he whispered, reluctantly taking hold of her arms and pulling them out from under his shirt.

"Why?" she whispered, causing Lee's hair to stand on end, when he felt her warm breath against his neck.

"Because if I get this done, we can have the next couple of days, just the two of us, with no interruptions." he told her. Chloe sighed quietly and slowly walked around the sofa, laying down opposite him. She watched him closely as he played the guitar, slowly mumbling song lyrics under his breath. Chloe smiled to herself when she noticed how handsome he looked, she couldn't remember a time when she'd ever been as attracted to him as she was feeling right at this moment. She glanced down at the guitar, wishing that she was sitting on his lap and he was holding her instead of the guitar. Lee glanced up at her for a moment when he felt her watching him closely. Chloe bit her lip, unable to tear her eyes away from him. He picked up his notebook and quickly scribbled down some lyrics. Chloe sighed in frustration, smiling slightly to herself when she had an idea.

"What?" Lee asked when he glanced at her again and noticed the cheeky twinkle in her eyes that he knew all too well.

"Nothing." she said sweetly. Lee raised his eyebrow sceptically, a small smile playing on the corner of his lips when Chloe slowly removed her jeans and laid down on the sofa, stretching out her slim tanned legs. Lee chuckled quietly, quickly realising what she was trying to do when she sat forward slightly and rested her elbow on her knee, slowly running her hand through her hair as she maintained eye contact with him. He reluctantly tore his eyes away from staring at the soft skin on her legs that he longed to stroke and stared at his notebook, trying to focus his mind on the song and not the beautiful woman sitting opposite him. His eyes flickered to Chloe as she fidgeted slightly and he caught a glimpse of her white lace knickers. Chloe smiled to herself when she noticed him watching her closely, a look of deep longing etched on his handsome features.

"I'm so hot." Chloe lied quietly, slowly unfastening the buttons on her blouse and removing it.

"I've been telling you that for months." he told her, misunderstanding what she meant.

His eyes widened when he noticed that she was wearing the corset from the photoshoot. Chloe placed her hands on her abdomen and slowly stroked circles on it, watching Lee out of the corner of her eye, as he continued to watch her closely.

"When did you put that on?" he asked her, his breath catching in his throat.

"Before we left Nottingham." she told him.

"Wait, is that what you and Amy were doing in the bathroom?" he asked, suddenly joining the dots in his head.

"Yes, it ties up at the back, so I can only wear it when someone does it up for me." she said quietly. Lee nodded slowly, unable to tear his eyes away from her. Even though he'd seen her body on numerous occasions, she still managed to take his breath away.

Chloe looked away from him, a small smile playing on the corner of her lips as she bent her left leg, placing her hand on her ankle and slowly stroking her way up her leg, a small gasp escaping her lips when she reached the inside of her thigh. Lee took deep breaths, trying to resist her as she placed her finger on the small gap between the corset and her knickers and traced small circles on it. Before Lee could stop himself he quickly pushed the guitar off his lap and flung the notebook onto the sofa, no longer able to fight the intense desire that he was feeling for her. He shuffled over to her so that he was kneeling over her and quickly removed his shirt.

"You have a song to write remember." Chloe said innocently, gazing up at him through her eyelashes.

"Don't play innocent, you knew what you were doing." Lee chuckled, placing his hand on her leg, frowning to himself when she sat up and stared at him. She slowly moved her head towards his, stopping when their lips were mere centimetres apart.

"Go back to your song." she whispered, giggling when she realised the effect she was having on him and how desperately he wanted her. Lee buried his head into her shoulder and placed a series of soft kisses on her neck, desperately trying to resist the urge to take her right now.

"You can stop that." she told him firmly. Lee lifted his head, frowning to himself as he watched her closely. She smiled cheekily at his wounded expression, enjoying the fact that she was teasing him.

"Please let me touch you Chlo." he pleaded when he realised that he'd never struggled to resist anyone as much as he was struggling right now.

"I don't need you." she told him firmly.

"I can sort myself out." she added, smiling cheekily as she slowly placed her hand inside her underwear. Chloe closed her eyes and let out a small whimper as she began to stroke herself. Chloe opened her eyes slowly as she felt Lee trailing his hands over her corset. His hands eventually lingered in place on her hips, as he took deep breaths, trying to resist the urge to pull her onto him. He couldn't stand the idea of Chloe slowly pleasuring herself underneath him, especially when she wouldn't allow him to kiss her or touch her.

"Please Chlo." he whispered, when she let out a small moan of pleasure.

"It's fine, you go back to writing your song." she told him, unable to stop herself from smiling in satisfaction at him.

"In fact, I'll go upstairs, so that I don't distract you." she added, slowly moving from underneath him, making sure that she 'accidentally' brushed her leg against his groin as she did so.

"Whoops." she giggled as she quickly stood up.

"Where are you going?" he asked, his breath catching in his throat as she walked towards the staircase.

"I told you, I can sort myself out." she said quickly, placing her hand on the banister and turning to face him, bursting out laughing when she saw the incredulous expression on his face.

"But that's meant to be my job!" he called after her as she turned her back on him and began to slowly climb the stairs. Chloe stopped when she was halfway up the stairs and turned to face him, raising her eyebrow at him. He hesitated for a moment before quickly climbing off the sofa and running after her. Chloe squealed and quickly ran upstairs, giggling to herself as she heard him gaining on her. She ran into the bedroom, stopping as she felt Lee's hands on her hips. He turned her to face him and quickly pushed her onto the dressing table. Chloe gasped in shock, placing her hand behind herself to steady her balance, not even caring when she knocked over her makeup. Lee kissed her passionately, forcing Chloe's head back, his hands roaming over her body as he finally gave into the desire. He quickly kissed the corner of her lips and along her jawline, quickly making his way down her neck, sucking at her skin, trying to make a mark and prove a point to her. Chloe smirked at him as she placed her hand on his chest and slowly straightened her arm, gently pushing him away from her. Before Lee could react, she placed her hand in her underwear again and cried out, knowing how much Lee liked it when he made her cry out and how much he would hate it if she did it to herself.

"Stop it." he said firmly, taking her wrist and pulling her hand out of her underwear. Chloe glared at him defiantly as she watched him fumbling with his belt buckle.

"Don't ever do that to me again." he whispered, choosing not to admit that he'd never been as turned on his life as he was at that moment.

"Don't try and reject me then." she smiled.

"No, I won't be making that mistake again." he mumbled as he quickly removed his trousers and boxers. Chloe shuffled to the end of the dressing table and wrapped her legs around his waist, giggling as he placed his hands on her thighs and quickly carried her over to the bed. He flung her onto the bed, the desperation finally getting the better of him. Before Chloe could react he placed his hands on her knickers and quickly pulled them off, flinging them across the room. As soon as he'd discarded her underwear he climbed on top of her and quickly pushed into her, letting out a deep groan of pleasure. Chloe stared up at him, becoming lost in his deep Eclipse eyes as he quickly made love to her.

"I take it the corset is staying on then." Chloe giggled.

"Yeah because you look so hot in it." he admitted breathlessly. Lee watched her closely as she slowly trailed her hand down towards her sensitive area.

"Will you stop doing that?!" he told her firmly, taking her hand in his own and slowly wrapping it around the bed post. Chloe chuckled, her legs trembling as he quickly increased the pace. Chloe whimpered when Lee trailed his hand downwards and began to stroke her sensitive area. She arched her back, quickly tightening her walls around him.

"Jesus Chlo." he whispered. Chloe smiled slightly, calling out his name when she finally released. Lee groaned deeply as he released just after her, collapsing on top of her.

"Be careful." Chloe whispered worriedly.

"What?" Lee frowned.

"I'm smaller than you remember." she said quietly, quickly squirming out from underneath him and glancing at her abdomen nervously.

"I'm always careful with you." he told her breathlessly. Chloe slowly sat up and wrapped her arms around his neck, kissing him softly. The two of them jumped as the doorbell rang. Lee reluctantly climbed off the bed and picked up his trousers, glancing down at his phone and sighing when he saw who was at the door.

"It's my Mum." he told Chloe as he quickly pulled on his boxers and trousers. Chloe nodded slowly, watching as he pulled a shirt out of the drawer and quickly pulled it on.

"At least I get to make another apology." Chloe sighed. Lee smiled slightly before leaning down and placing a soft kiss on her lips.

"Don't take the corset off, I want to do it later." he told her, before hurrying to answer the door.

Chapter Fifteen

Lee smiled at Chloe as she hurried around the kitchen, setting out plates and cutlery. He quickly pulled some wine glasses out of the cupboard and placed them on the counter. Chloe had been keeping busy all day, frantically cleaning the house before their guests arrived. Despite the fact that Chloe knew Lee had a housekeeper, she'd been a ball of nervous energy and had needed to keep busy.

"Where's the alcohol?!" Chloe exclaimed in panic when she opened the cupboard and saw that it was completely empty.

"Nathan cleared out the supply before I came home from rehab, so that I wouldn't be tempted." Lee told her, smiling at how adorable she looked when she turned to face him, a look of panic on her face.

"It's okay though, I've told everyone to bring some alcohol with them." he told her.

"You're not going to be drinking any alcohol are you?" she asked, suddenly feeling slightly nervous that if he had even a small amount of alcohol, he might relapse.

"No I'm not, don't worry." he reassured her when he saw the concern on her pretty features.

"I'll stay sober, so that you're not the only one." she said quietly, quickly looking away from him and slowly picking her fingernails.

"Don't be daft, you can drink if you want too." he told her.

"You could even get drunk if you want, and I can keep an eye on you." he added, smiling slightly when he realised that he still hadn't seen Chloe when she was drunk.

"I want to see your wild side." he prompted when she didn't respond.

"You really don't." she said, smiling slightly.

"Although you were a bit wild the day we came back from Nottingham." he laughed.

"I don't know what came over me." she giggled. Lee burst out laughing when he glanced at her and noticed her coloured cheeks.

"So, who's coming again?" she asked, changing the subject to hide her embarrassment. Lee burst out laughing and wiggled his eyebrows at her cheekily.

"Not like that!" she exclaimed, smiling at Lee as he continued to laugh at her.

"Okay so Ben and Kirstie, Louise and Peter." Lee told her, when he eventually stopped laughing. Chloe nodded and counted the glasses, quickly adding another to the counter when she realised they were one short.

"I wonder if any of them will want to stay over." she said thoughtfully.

"Everyone is staying over." he told her.

"What?!" Chloe spluttered.

"You could have told me, I haven't made the beds or anything!" she exclaimed.

"Will you stop stressing." he chuckled, placing his hands on her hips and pulling her into his arms. Chloe sighed quietly as he held her tightly.

"Why are you so nervous?" he asked.

"I don't know really." she admitted.

"Oh, I have to light the fire!" she exclaimed, quickly removing herself from Lee's arms when she remembered. He smiled at her as he watched her opening drawers in the kitchen and rummaging in them.

"Where is the damn lighter kept now?" she muttered angrily.

"Over here." he told her, turning his back on her and opening a drawer. Chloe gasped as she opened a drawer and noticed a thick black notebook with her name written on the front. As soon as she looked at the handwriting, she knew that it was Lee's. She softly stroked the notebook with her fingers, trying to decide whether she should open the notebook or close the drawer and pretend that she'd never laid eyes on it. Before she could stop herself she picked up the notebook and placed it on the kitchen counter, staring at it silently. Chloe jumped as she felt Lee's warm breath on her neck as he peered over her shoulder.

"Is this yours?" she asked quietly, pretty certain that she already knew the answer.

"Yeah." he said quietly, his cheeks colouring in embarrassment as he watched Chloe staring silently at the notebook.

"Why does it have my name on it?" she asked quietly, desperately trying to resist the urge to open the notebook. Despite the fact that she wanted to know what was inside it, she knew that she had to do the right thing and respect his privacy.

"Because it's a kind of memory book thing that I made when I was in rehab." he told her. Chloe glanced at him as he wrapped his arms around her waist and gently rested his chin on her shoulder, sighing quietly to himself as he stared at the notebook and was reminded of how miserable he was when he was parted from Chloe.

"Can I look at it?" she asked.

"If you want." he replied reluctantly, not entirely sure how he felt about Chloe reading the book. Chloe's hands shook as she slowly opened the notebook and carefully leafed through the pages. Her heart pounded against her chest as she gazed at the photos from their time together. She couldn't help but smile at the selection of selfies, suddenly realising for the first time how happy and in love the two of them looked. Her stomach churned as she turned the page and stared at the pictures of their baby. Memories swirled around her head when she remembered how emotional the two them had been at the scan, when they had finally been able to lay eyes on their baby.

"You kept these." she said sadly as she softly stroked the images with her finger.

"Of course I kept them." he said quietly, biting his lip in an attempt to fight the intense emotions that he was feeling. He knew in his heart that even though he'd been devastated by the loss of their baby, that loss was now exacerbated by the fact that he had lost Chloe shortly afterwards. He couldn't help but wonder whether, if the two of them hadn't lost their baby a few weeks earlier, Chloe might have coped better with the media storm and they wouldn't have been parted as a result.

"What's this?" Chloe asked as she picked up an envelope that was safely tucked inside the notebook.

"I forgot about that." he mumbled. Chloe glanced at him as she felt him squirming against her. Before Chloe could open the letter, Lee quickly reached around her and took it from her grasp, staring down at it thoughtfully. Chloe watched him closely as he slowly stepped back, leaning against the kitchen counter, unable to tear his eyes away from staring at the letter.

"It's not a suicide note or anything is it?" she asked nervously, her brain a swirling mist of memories from the day that she'd first read her father's letter.

"No of course not." he said quickly.

"I just had so much guilt and sadness that I needed to find a way to let it out." he added, an edge of sadness present in his voice.

"Guilt for what, it wasn't your fault that I left?" she frowned.

"I was still carrying the guilt for the way that I treated you after we lost our baby." he told her quietly, his eyes brimming with tears when he was reminded once again of how terrible the past few weeks had been.

"That wasn't your fault, you were hurting." she said quietly. Lee glanced down at his hand as Chloe took it in her own and squeezed it gently.

"And I knew it was my fault that the fans and media turned on you." he added thoughtfully.

"If you hadn't been with me.....if I'd resisted you better then you wouldn't have had to go through everything they put you through." he continued sadly.

"Yes, but if we hadn't got together I would still be miserable, you've made me so happy." she told him.

"And you helped me get my life back on track, so that I wasn't living on a bench anymore. That's a debt I'll never be able to repay." she added, standing in front of him and gently resting her head against his chest, sighing in contentment as she heard his heart beating softly.

"So stop blaming yourself." she whispered. Chloe closed her eyes as she felt Lee wrap his arms around her and hold her tightly, gently resting his head on her shoulder and sighing deeply. He glanced at the note that was still in his hand, trying to decide if he could bring himself to allow Chloe to read it. Despite the embarrassment he felt, he knew that he needed to be completely open about how bad he'd felt when they were parted. She had given her heart, body and soul to him and he knew that he needed to be completely open with her. Chloe glanced up at Lee when he reluctantly stepped back from her and slowly handed her the note.

"I never intended for anyone to read it." he sighed, watching closely as Chloe took the note from him and gazed down at it.

"It's okay if you don't want to share it." she told him.

"I think I need too." he said, his cheeks colouring slightly. Chloe nodded slowly, her hands shaking slightly as she slowly opened the envelope.

"Is it a song?" she frowned when she noticed the writing at the top of the page read: How Do I? by Lee Knight. Lee nodded slowly, not quite able to bring himself to look her in the eye as she read the song lyrics.
"Oh my god." Chloe whispered, her stomach churning with guilt when she suddenly realised just how much he'd been struggling without her. Her heart broke for him, she couldn't stand the thought of him hurting, struggling to get through each day.

"The words are so heartfelt." she added quietly, a small sob escaping her lips. Lee sighed sadly, wrapping his arms around her waist and pulling her back into his arms.

"That's because I missed you so much." he whispered in her ear. Chloe nodded, bursting into tears when she couldn't hold them back anymore.

"I'm so sorry, I never wanted to break your heart." she said, sobbing against his chest.

"You need to stop blaming yourself Chlo." he said softly.

"Is it true what the boys said, that you were calling out for me in your sleep?" she asked tentatively.

"I don't remember much of that time to be honest, I was permanently drunk." he admitted.

"All I know for sure is that I really missed you and kept dreaming about you, so it's probably true." he added thoughtfully. Chloe sighed sadly as she quickly wrapped her arms around his waist, squeezing him tightly, feeling sick to her stomach at the thought of him being so unhappy and calling out for her in his sleep.

"I love you." she whispered against his chest.

"I promise that I'll never leave you again." she added.

"Don't say that Chlo." he said quickly.

"Why not?" she frowned.

"Because I don't want you to feel trapped, you should always feel like you can leave me if you want too, and not be trapped by a promise." he explained, gazing down at her as she lifted her head to stare up at him. The two of them jumped as the doorbell rang. Chloe watched Lee as he opened the kitchen cupboard and pulled out another wine glass.

"Do we have another guest coming that you haven't told me about?" she asked, frowning in confusion. Lee nodded slowly, a small smile playing on the corner of his lips.

"It's a surprise though." he told her. Chloe jumped as the doorbell rang once again.

"You'd better go and answer the door." Lee told her.

Chapter Sixteen

Chloe let out a small squeal of excitement when she opened the front door and laid eyes on Danny. He laughed when she quickly flung herself into his arms and held him tightly.

"It's been too long." she whispered in his ear, her eyes filling with tears when she realised that once again she'd forgotten to keep in contact with Danny.

"I know, I've missed you." he told her, smiling at her when she eventually let go of him.

"What are you doing here?" Chloe asked as she gestured for him to come in.

"Lee invited me over, apparently he wants to talk to me about something." he replied, quickly following Chloe into the kitchen.

"Indeed I do." Lee smiled at the two of them when they walked into the kitchen.

"Is it something to do with the song I wrote?" Danny asked quickly, still slightly confused as to why Lee had called him out of the Eclipse and invited him over.

"What happened with the song in the end?" Chloe piped up, before Lee had a chance to respond.

"Matt managed to sort out your idea of paying me in advance for the song." Danny told her.

"It's on the album." Lee agreed.

"Did you get a fair price?" Chloe asked.

"Yeah I got a really good payment....so I have a little rented place now." Danny smiled.

"Oh my god." Chloe whispered, quickly pulling him into another hug and squeezing him tightly. Her eyes filled with tears of happiness at the thought that Danny was no longer sleeping rough.

"I'll never be able to thank the two of you enough for everything that you did for me." Danny said, his voice breaking slightly as he glanced between Chloe and Lee.

"We didn't do that much." Chloe said shyly, her cheeks colouring slightly.

"Anyway, what did you want to ask me?" Danny asked Lee, when he couldn't stand not knowing any longer.

"I need a favour." Lee said.

"You probably heard about everything that happened to Chloe with the media?" he added. Danny nodded slowly.

"I was actually approached by a journalist." Danny said quietly.

"Really?" Chloe frowned.

"Yeah, it must have been when they found out about you being homeless, a journalist came to the park and was asking for a statement from anyone that knew you." Danny explained.

"Obviously I refused." he added. Chloe nodded slowly, her eyes filling with tears as she was reminded once again of everything that the media and the fans had put her through.

"Thank you." she whispered softly, smiling at Danny when she realised how much of a true friend he was to her. Despite the fact that he was the one friend of hers that desperately needed money, he still hadn't been able to bring himself to betray her trust.

"Anyway I have a plan for the media and fans. I want to make them love Chloe, so I was wondering if you would be prepared to do an article to say about how kind she is and how she helped you to get off the streets?" Lee asked.

"And maybe you could mention that she used to bring you food parcels and stuff." he quickly added. Chloe turned to face Lee, smiling at him when the two of them locked eyes.

"It's the least I can do." Danny said quickly, smiling at Chloe when he noticed her staring at Lee lovingly.

"Thanks, I really appreciate it." Lee said, reluctantly tearing his eyes away from Chloe.

"It's no problem, I owe you guys a lot." Danny pointed out.

"You don't owe us anything." Chloe said quietly. Danny smiled at her.

"Do you have people coming over?" Danny asked awkwardly, when he suddenly noticed the plates and glasses piled on the counter.

"Yeah, but you can stay if you want?" Lee offered.

"No, it's fine, I have to get back anyway, I only popped over to see what you wanted to speak to me about." Danny replied.

"I promise I'll be a better friend and keep in touch more." Chloe told him.

"Don't worry about it, you've had a lot on your plate." Danny reassured her. Chloe smiled as he quickly pulled her into a hug.

"Take care of her." Danny said, turning to face Lee when he eventually let go of Chloe. Lee nodded slowly, smiling to himself when he glanced at Chloe, his heart swelling with pride as he thought about how grateful he was to have her back in his life. As soon as Danny left, Chloe walked over to Lee and gently placed herself in his arms, snuggling her head against his chest.

"You alright Chlo?" he asked worriedly, when he sensed that she was upset about something.

"Yes I'm fine." she mumbled against his chest, trying to ignore the intense fear that was slowly building with each day that passed. Lee wrapped his arms around her shoulders and squeezed her tightly, wishing not for the first time that he could hold her for every moment of the rest of his life.

"Don't squeeze me." she said nervously wincing slightly and quickly squirming out of his grasp.

"Sorry, did I hurt you?" he asked nervously.

"I'm fine, stop worrying." she said quickly, glancing down at herself and trying to resist the urge to rub her sore chest. Chloe jumped, her heart pounding against her chest nervously as the doorbell rang.

"I'll get it." Lee told her, smiling at her when he noticed how nervous she looked. Chloe nodded slowly, hovering nervously in the kitchen as she watched Lee leave the room. She swallowed the nervous lump that was rising in her throat when she heard voices travelling down the hallway. Her eyes flickered to the doorway as Kirstie, Louise, Ben and Peter walked into the room, Lee following closely behind.

"Chloe!" Kirstie squealed as soon as she laid eyes on her.

"Hey." Chloe replied shyly, her cheeks colouring in embarrassment as everyone turned to stare at her.

"I thought you went back to Nottingham!" Louise exclaimed excitedly.

"I did go to pack so that I could come back." Chloe replied, smiling slightly when she noticed how pleased they were to see her.

"I'm so glad you're back." Kirstie admitted, quickly pulling Chloe into a hug.

"Me too." Louise piped up, hugging Chloe as soon as Kirstie let go of her.

"We were wondering why you randomly invited everyone over." Peter smiled at Lee.

"Especially since we haven't seen you for weeks, because you've been too busy feeling sorry for yourself." Ben chuckled. Lee smiled slightly, rolling his eyes.

"Are you planning to stay for good?" Louise asked Chloe.

"I hope so." Chloe said quietly, glancing at Lee who smiled at her reassuringly.

"It depends if the media start on her again." Lee sighed, his stomach churning at the thought of losing Chloe once again.

"What are you going to do about that?" Kirstie asked, glancing at Chloe nervously, her heart sinking when she suddenly remembered just how unhappy Chloe had been.

"We have an article coming out tomorrow." Lee told them.

"Ooh exciting!" Louise exclaimed excitedly.

"They came to the house to interview us and take some pictures." Chloe said quietly.

"Have you done it as a tell all kind of article?" Ben asked.

"Yeah and I made sure that I mentioned how much I love and need Chloe and how if I lose her again, I'll be leaving the band." Lee said.

"You got a bit carried away didn't you." Chloe smiled at him.

"I'm just determined to not let everything get bad for you again." Lee told her gently.

"So, what's new with everyone else?" Chloe asked, trying to get the focus off herself.

"We don't really have any news do we?" Kirstie asked, sighing quietly to herself as she glanced at Ben, her heart breaking a little when she was reminded once again of how desperately her and Ben wanted a baby, but were still unsuccessful. Ben shook his head slowly as his eyes locked with Kirstie, the two of them instantly realising how the other one was feeling. Chloe frowned to herself when she noticed Kirstie sighing sadly. She had known Kirstie for a long time and she couldn't help but feel like something was going on with Kirstie and Ben.

"We have some news." Louise said excitedly, pausing for a moment for dramatic effect.

"Peter is now one of my backing dancers, which means that he can come with me when I start doing all my shows." Louise explained. Peter smiled at her, before gently placing a soft kiss on her lips.

"Aww that's amazing." Chloe smiled. Kirstie smiled at Peter and Louise as she glanced between the two of them and noticed how happy the two of them seemed. Ben beamed at the group as he placed the bags of alcohol that he'd brought, onto the kitchen counter. Lee beamed as he rummaged through the bag and pulled out the bottles.

"I can make everyone a cocktail." Lee beamed.

"Ooh, that sounds exciting!" Louise exclaimed.

"I'm quite good at making cocktails." Lee told them, rummaging in the cupboard and pulling out a cocktail shaker.

"Awesome, we brought snacks as well." Peter told them.

"Something to absorb the alcohol." Louise agreed.

"You guys can make yourselves at home in the living room if you want?" Lee offered.

"We'll set out the food." Louise stated, quickly taking Peter's hand and walking into the living room.

"Do you need us to help with anything?" Kirstie asked Lee, feeling slightly guilty as she watched him mixing cocktails.

"Nope, everything is under control." he smiled at her.

"I can help anyway." Chloe told her. Kirstie nodded and quickly followed Ben into the living room.

"Go and have fun Chlo, you don't have to keep an eye on me, I'm not going to drink." Lee reassured her.

"I know." Chloe said quietly, her stomach churning nervously as she watched Lee making cocktails. She quickly picked up one of the glasses and poured herself some orange juice.

"Don't you want one of my famous cocktails?" Lee grinned, raising his eyebrow at her.

"No, I'll stay sober with you." she told him quietly, squirming slightly as she felt him watching her closely.

"You don't have too, honestly." he told her, frowning in confusion.

"It's fine." she insisted, quickly placing a soft kiss on his lips, before wandering into the living room to join the others.

Chapter Seventeen

Chloe sighed quietly as she placed the pancake mix into the pan, smiling in satisfaction as she quickly added some blueberries. She glanced up at the doorway, smiling at Kirstie as she walked into the room.

"Something smells yummy." Kirstie said, quickly sniffing the air.

"I'm making pancakes." Chloe told her.

"That's a bit random." Kirstie giggled, rubbing the sleep out of her eyes and yawning loudly.

"I just really fancy them." Chloe said quietly.

"Do you want some?" Chloe offered.

"I'm okay thank you, I can't face the thought of food." Kirstie replied, feeling slightly nauseous as she watched the pancakes slowly cooking in the pan.

"Well that's your own fault, you shouldn't have drunk so much." Chloe pointed out, smiling slightly when she glanced at Kirstie and saw her pale complexion.

"I know, I got totally carried away." Kirstie laughed.

"You don't seem too hungover this morning." Kirstie added.

"No, just a little bit." Chloe lied, her cheeks colouring slightly.

"I didn't go as mad as you." she quickly added, her stomach churning with guilt that she was having to lie to her friends. She quickly placed her pancakes onto a plate and sat at the kitchen island.

"I blame Lee....he put a lot of alcohol in those cocktails." Kirstie smiled.

"What are you blaming me for?" Lee asked as he walked into the room.

"Mixing very strong drinks." Kirstie laughed.

"Well the way I remember it, is that you kept asking for more drinks." Lee chuckled.

"You're hungry this morning." Lee laughed when he glanced at Chloe and noticed her eating a mound of pancakes. Chloe nodded slowly, closing her eyes and sighing in pleasure. Lee smiled at her as he quickly reached onto her plate and pulled off one of the pancakes, his eyes glinting cheekily at her.

"Hey, get your mitts off!" Chloe exclaimed, a small smile playing on the corner of her lips. Lee beamed at her as he slowly ate the pancake that he'd stolen. As soon as he finished, he leaned down and quickly placed a soft kiss on her lips. Chloe jumped as she heard Lee's phone ring in his pocket. He quickly pulled it out, glancing down at the screen and sighing when he saw that it was his Mum.

"I should probably get that." Lee said, quickly walking into the living room.

"You guys seem like you are back on track." Kirstie smiled at Chloe, as soon as Lee left the room.

"I think we are, the article comes out today, so hopefully things don't go crazy again." Chloe said quietly, her stomach churning nervously.

"I don't think they will, I think Lee has come up with a good plan." Kirstie smiled, trying to reassure her. Chloe nodded slowly, quickly placing down her fork as she felt a sudden wave of nausea wash over her. She took deep breaths, trying to stop herself from vomiting. Chloe quickly stood up, beginning to panic slightly when she realised that she wasn't going to make it to the bathroom upstairs. She quickly climbed off the stool, throwing herself to the ground and vomiting into the kitchen bin.

"Oh my god, are you okay?!" Kirstie exclaimed when Chloe eventually stopped vomiting. Chloe nodded slowly, wrapping her arms around her abdomen as she vomited once again. Kirstie watched Chloe sadly as she coughed, taking deep breaths to try and get her breath back.

"I thought you said that you weren't hungover." Kirstie chuckled when Chloe finally stopped vomiting and sat back from the bin.

"I think I need to use the bathroom." Chloe mumbled, quickly standing up, staggering slightly as she fought to regain her balance. Chloe quickly clapped her hand over her mouth and ran upstairs, hurrying to make it to the bathroom in time.

"Are you alright?" Ben called after her as she ran past him. Chloe remained silent, afraid to speak in case she accidently vomited, before she reached the bathroom. Ben frowned in confusion and walked into the kitchen, smiling to himself as he walked up behind Kirstie and wrapped his arms around her waist, pulling her close.

"Morning babe." Ben whispered in her ear.

"Hey." Kirstie smiled, sighing in contentment as he held her tightly.

"You smell like a brewery." she giggled, wrinkling up her nose.

"Sorry." he chuckled, squeezing her tightly.

"Ooh, whose are the pancakes?" he asked excitedly when he eventually noticed them on the counter.

"Chloe's." she told him.

"She won't mind if I eat them." he grinned, his eyes twinkling cheekily as he quickly released Kirstie and picked up the plate. She rolled her eyes as she watched him happily tucking into Chloe's pancakes.

"How come Chloe made you pancakes, and wouldn't let me have any of hers?" Lee chuckled as he walked back into the kitchen.

"Technically I stole hers." Ben admitted, beaming like a child when he noticed Lee's incredulous expression.

"So you waited until she was out of the room and swooped in." Lee laughed.

"Yep, like a seagull." Ben chuckled. Lee shook his head and rolled his eyes.

"Where did she go anyway?" Lee asked.

"She was vomiting, so I expect she went to the bathroom." Kirstie told him.

"You definitely put too much alcohol in those drinks." she added.

"You've probably pickled her insides or something." Ben agreed.

"They weren't that strong, you lot are a bunch of light weights." Lee chuckled.

"Is that why we are all really hungover?" Louise giggled as she walked into the room, closely followed by Peter.

"Except you because you didn't drink." Louise laughed when she saw Lee shaking his head at them.

"Smelling those pancakes is making me feel sick." Peter admitted, resting his head against the kitchen island as soon as he sat down.

"I might have to fight Chloe for the bathroom." Peter groaned, as he placed his fingers on his temples and gently massaged his sore head.

"There's so many bathrooms in this house, I think you'll be fine." Ben chuckled.

Lee's eyes wandered upstairs, when he realised that Chloe still hadn't returned from the bathroom.

"I should probably go and check on Chloe." Lee said thoughtfully.

"Yeah, since you've given her a really bad hangover." Kirstie said, smiling slightly when she noticed Lee frowning. Lee nodded slowly, before quickly walking away, his heart pounding as he climbed the stairs. Kirstie's words were constantly swirling around his head as he suddenly remembered that he hadn't made a cocktail for Chloe, she'd insisted on staying sober with him. Lee sighed sadly as he reached the bathroom and leant against the door frame, his heart sinking as he watched Chloe vomiting into the toilet. She coughed quietly, gently resting her elbow on the toilet seat and placing her head in her hands, too exhausted to even lift her head.

"Are you okay Chlo?" Lee asked nervously, feeling slightly guilty when she jumped. Chloe nodded slowly, taking deep breaths to try and get her breath back.

"Oh no." she whispered, as she felt yet another wave of nausea wash over her.

"You should go downstairs and be a good host." she said breathlessly, when she eventually stopped vomiting.

"They don't need me, they are too busy complaining about the amount of alcohol in the drinks." he told her, smiling slightly.

"You did get a bit carried away." she said quietly, her stomach churning nervously. She glanced down at her abdomen, gently placing her hand on it and biting her lip, desperately trying to fight the tears that were filling her eyes.

"You didn't drink though did you." he said quietly. He sighed sadly as Chloe vomited again.

"What's wrong Chloe?" he asked her nervously, his heart breaking a little when she lifted her head slightly and he noticed how pale she was.

"I just don't feel well." she mumbled sadly, quickly tucking her legs underneath her and staring at her lap.

"You were like this before weren't you..." he said thoughtfully, his voice trailing off when he suddenly remembered the last time that Chloe had been vomiting continually.

"I know." she whispered, her hands shaking as she slowly closed the toilet seat and rested her head on it.

"Are you......" he started but trailed off when he couldn't quite bring himself to ask the question that he was dying to know the answer too.

"Probably." she said quietly.

"Probably what?" he frowned, his heart pounding against his chest nervously.

"Nothing." she whispered, not quite able to say the word.

"You've been tired a lot too haven't you." he said thoughtfully, almost like he was thinking aloud.

"And you didn't drink last night." he added, slowly joining the dots in his head.

"Oh my god Chloe....are you pregnant?!" he said quickly.

"I don't know.....probably." she said quietly, quickly wiping away the tears that were steadily flowing down her cheeks.

"What do you mean probably?!" he exclaimed.

"I don't know." she whispered.

"All I know is that I feel the same as I did last time." she added nervously, her stomach churning with fear.

"Shit." he muttered under his breath. Lee swallowed the lump that was rising in his throat, his eyes fixed on Chloe who was crying quietly to herself, her head still resting on the toilet seat. Suddenly all of Chloe's behaviour over the past few days finally made sense to him, the fact that she was sleeping a lot, eating more than usual and constantly telling him to be careful with her. His stomach churned with fear when he suddenly remembered how he hadn't been as gentle with her as usual since she'd come back into his life, because he'd missed her so much.

"How long have you had suspicions?" he asked her.

"Since you took Amy to prom and I spent the whole evening vomiting." she admitted.

"That's over a week ago!" he exclaimed.

"Why the hell didn't you tell me?!" he added, before Chloe had the chance to respond.

"Because I've been trying to pretend that it isn't happening." she said.

"We need to find out." he sighed, feeling slightly sorry for her when he realised how upset she was.

"I can't." she whispered.

"Why not?" he frowned. Chloe glanced up at him as he crossed the room and sat beside her, gently placing his hand on the small of her back. She shrugged, not quite able to bring herself to tell him how afraid she actually was. She'd had a lot of time to think over the past week and she couldn't help but feel afraid that if she was pregnant and the worst was to happen, Lee would return to hating her.....just like last time. Chloe closed her eyes, trying to control the intense fear that she was feeling. She flinched slightly as she felt Lee gently brush her hair out of her face. She slowly opened her eyes when she felt him place a soft kiss on her cheek. Lee sighed sadly when Chloe finally glanced at him, his heart breaking when he noticed how upset she was. Despite the fact that he knew how much Chloe was struggling, he couldn't stop thinking about what was happening. He couldn't stand the idea of not knowing if she was pregnant or not.

"Shall I go out and get a test?" he asked her, gently stroking away her tears with his fingertips. Chloe remained silent, not entirely sure what to say or how she felt. Her eyelids fluttered closed, the exhaustion finally setting in.

"I need to know if I'm going to be a Dad." he prompted her. Chloe quickly clapped her hand over her mouth, a small sob escaping her lips as she nodded slowly. Lee sighed sadly and carefully placed his head on top of hers, in a desperate attempt to provide her with some comfort.

"It'll be okay Chlo." he whispered, trying to convince himself as much as her.

"That's what we thought last time." she muttered sadly.

Chapter Eighteen

Chloe sighed quietly and slowly moved her head off the toilet seat, sitting quietly for a moment when she felt the room spinning. She quickly brushed her hair out of her face when she felt Lee watching her closely.

"We need to get back to our guests, we're being rude." she said quietly.

"I have to go to the chemist." he said firmly, quickly standing up. Before Chloe could respond he quickly left the room. Chloe sighed to herself as she heard the sound of his footsteps running down the stairs. She slowly stood up, quickly wiping away her tears as she walked downstairs, desperately hoping that the others wouldn't notice. Chloe took a deep breath and slowly walked into the kitchen, her cheeks colouring as Louise, Peter, Kirstie and Ben turned to stare at her.

"God, you look rough Chloe!" Louise exclaimed as soon as she laid eyes on her.

"Thanks." Chloe said, smiling slightly.

"Where did Lee go, he grabbed his jacket and left?" Kirstie asked.

"He had to pop into work." Chloe said quietly, feeling slightly guilty that she was lying to her friends once again.

"I have a confession to make." Ben piped up, a cheeky grin playing on the corner of his lips. Chloe raised her eyebrow and waited for him to continue.

"I kind of ate your pancakes." Ben chuckled.

"What do you mean kind of, you did eat them!" Kirstie giggled, laughing when she saw the guilty expression on his handsome features.

"It's fine, I'm not hungry anymore anyway. " Chloe said quietly, leaning against the kitchen counter as she struggled to keep her eyes open.

"You look like you need some rest Chloe." Kirstie said worriedly, watching her closely. Chloe nodded slowly.

"We should go." Kirstie told Ben, quickly taking his hand.

"You don't have to go." Chloe told them sadly, feeling slightly guilty that they felt like they had to leave.

"It's fine, we could probably all do with some rest anyway." Louise pointed out. Chloe nodded slowly and watched as the four of them gathered their belongings and quickly left the house. As soon as Chloe was alone, she walked into the living room and laid down on the sofa, quickly pulling the throw over herself and snuggling into it. The more time that passed the more nervous she became about the thought of doing a pregnancy test. She knew in her heart that neither Lee or herself were strong enough to go through what they'd been through just a few short months ago. Chloe jumped and snapped out of her thoughts when she heard the front door open and quickly close again.

"Chlo?!" she heard Lee's voice calling from the hallway.

"I'm in here!" she called back, glancing up at him as he quickly walked into the living room and sat on the floor beside her.

"That was quick." she said quietly, her eyes darting to the pharmacy bag that was in his hand. Lee nodded slowly, his brow furrowing in concern when he noticed how exhausted she looked.

"Are you okay Chlo?" he asked nervously. She nodded slowly, her eyelids fluttering as she fought to keep them open.

"Don't be stressed about it, it'll be okay." he told her.

"I'm just so scared." she whispered. He smiled sympathetically at her, wishing that he could do something to make her feel better. He slowly placed the bag onto the coffee table, glancing at Chloe as he felt her watching him closely.

"You can do the test whenever you are ready and I'll be there with you." he told her softly. Chloe nodded slowly, sighing quietly as warm tears rolled down her cheeks.

"Just don't end up hating me again okay." she whispered, her skin tingling when Lee reached out and gently wiped away her tears. He gently placed his forehead against hers, sighing deeply when he heard her words. He knew in his heart that he was to blame for her feeling the way that she did. It was a direct result of the despicable way that he'd treated her last time.

"I could never hate you Chloe." he whispered, gently placing a soft kiss on her lips. He watched her as she carefully fidgeted, finally giving into the exhaustion and closing her eyes. Lee smiled slightly when he realised that she'd fallen asleep instantly.

"I love you so much Chlo." he whispered, placing a soft kiss on her lips.

Chloe's eyelids fluttered open as she felt someone softly stroking her hair. She smiled slightly as she locked eyes with Lee and noticed that he was watching her closely.

"Were you watching me sleep?" she asked him.

"Kind of." he smiled.

"Why?" she giggled.

"I dunno, I was just deep in thought." he admitted.

"Plus you're so beautiful, it's difficult not to stare at you." he told her, watching her closely as she slowly sat up.

"Smooth." she smiled, her cheeks colouring slightly.

"Do you feel better now you've slept?" he asked her. She nodded slowly, her stomach plummeting when she glanced at the pharmacy bag and was reminded of their situation once again.

"Maybe we should get it over with." she muttered thoughtfully, her eyes fixed on the bag. Lee followed her eyeline, his stomach churning nervously when he realised what she was looking at. Before Chloe could talk herself out of it, she quickly stood up, staggering slightly when she suddenly felt lightheaded. She glanced down at Lee as she felt him quickly reach out and take her hips, quickly steadying her. He slowly stood up, his hands still in place on Chloe's hips, making sure that she didn't lose her balance again. As soon as Lee stood up, Chloe quickly wrapped her arms around his neck and held him tightly, sighing sadly when she felt him wrap his arms around her and squeeze her gently.

"If you're not ready, we don't have to do it now." he whispered in her ear.

"It's fine." she sighed. Chloe reluctantly removed herself from Lee's arms and quickly picked up the bag, hurrying upstairs, before she started to panic and talk herself out of doing the test. She glanced behind herself at Lee as she walked into the bathroom and pulled out the pregnancy test, frowning to herself when she suddenly noticed that there were two in the bag.

"Why did you get two?" she frowned.

"I wanted to be extra certain either way." he told her. Chloe nodded slowly.

"Can you turn your back, just while I pee on the stick?" she asked him.

"Two sticks." he reminded her, quickly handing her the second pregnancy test.

"Either way, you don't need to watch me do that part." she insisted. Lee smiled slightly and quickly turned his back on her. As he stood silently, staring at the wall, he couldn't help but feel a range of emotions. It almost felt surreal that this was happening to the two of them again, particularly when they'd spent most of the past few weeks apart.

"Okay done." Chloe announced a few moments later. Lee slowly turned around, watching her closely as she quickly washed her hands and sat on the floor, resting her back against the bathtub. Chloe quickly pulled her legs towards herself, trying to protect herself from the inner turmoil that she was feeling. She glanced at Lee for a moment as he silently sat beside her. Chloe silently handed him one of the pregnancy tests, her eyes fixed on the one that was still in her hand.

"How long do we have to wait?" he asked nervously.

"A few more minutes." she replied, glancing at her watch. The two of them sat in silence, neither of them entirely sure what to say to the other. Chloe intermittently glanced at her watch, the time seeming to stretch for an eternity.

"Okay, the time is up." she said eventually, staring at her watch, not quite able to bring herself to look at the pregnancy test in her hand.

"What does yours say?" she asked tentatively, when Lee remained silent.

"It says you're pregnant." he muttered. Chloe took a deep breath and quickly glanced down at the test in her hand.

"So does mine." she whispered.

"It says nine to ten weeks." she said thoughtfully. Lee nodded slowly, quickly pulling his phone out of his pocket and counting back the weeks on the calendar.

"I don't understand how this happened, I made sure I took the pill every day. I was extra careful after what happened last time." she said quietly.

"Well, ten weeks ago we were in Norway." he told her.

"I was definitely careful about taking the pill." she repeated, feeling slightly nervous that he was going to blame her again.

"I know you were." he said quietly.

"Wait....do you think that...." he started but trailed off, his thoughts a complete swirling fog.

"What?" she asked nervously.

"Well....you were sick quite a lot when we were there weren't you. With the food and the travelling and stuff." he explained.

"Maybe you threw up the pill or something." he continued.

"That's not a thing though is it?" she frowned.

"I don't know." he admitted, glancing at Chloe as she wrapped her arms around his neck, carefully leaning against him. He gently wrapped his arm around her shoulders, sighing sadly when he noticed that she was trembling.

"We can ask when we go for a scan." he told her. Chloe nodded slowly, quickly snuggling her head against his collarbone.

"I'm never having sex again." she said quietly, glancing at Lee when he burst out laughing.

"I don't know why you're laughing, I'm being serious." she said firmly.

"You must have really good swimmers." she said quietly, quickly standing up and walking into the bedroom.

Lee frowned in confusion when he heard Chloe walking downstairs. His eyes wandered to the pregnancy tests on the floor, his stomach swirling with excitement at the thought of becoming a father. From the moment that he'd come to terms with Chloe being pregnant the first time around, he knew that he couldn't wait to be a father. As soon as his thoughts wandered to their first baby, he suddenly felt a pang of fear that this baby could also be cruelly stolen from them. Lee snapped out of his thoughts when he heard Chloe's footsteps returning.

Chloe quickly pulled on her pyjamas and climbed into bed, trying not to think about the intense fear that was swirling around her head. She knew that Lee was excited about the prospect of becoming a father, she'd seen it in his eyes from the moment he'd looked at the positive pregnancy test. She angrily wiped away the tears that were slowly rolling down her cheeks, when she realised the pressure that she was now under to make sure that she didn't lose their baby.....again. Her eyes flickered upwards as Lee walked into the bedroom and quickly climbed into bed beside her. Lee quickly wrapped his arms around Chloe's waist, frowning to himself when she squirmed away from him.

"What's wrong Chlo?" he asked nervously.

"What do you think is wrong!" she snapped.

"I just need some time to process it." she quickly added, feeling slightly guilty when she realised that she'd snapped at him. Lee nodded slowly, his heart sinking slightly when he heard Chloe crying softly to herself.

"What are we going to do?" she said eventually.

"We're going to have a baby." he said quietly.

"I'm so scared that history is going to repeat itself." she muttered.

"If it does then we'll just have to deal with it." he said quietly, his heart sinking at the thought of losing another baby.

"But, we almost lost each other last time, and I've only just got you back." she pointed out.

"I won't let that happen again." he said quietly, trying to reassure her. He sighed sadly, his heart breaking as he heard her sobbing quietly to herself.

"Come here Chlo." he whispered, gently placing his hand on her back.

"Chlo." he tried again when she didn't respond.

"I'm fine, I just need to get some sleep." she said sadly. Lee gently placed a soft kiss on her shoulder, his eyes filling with tears as he listened to Chloe crying to herself. He desperately wished that she would allow him to pull her into his arms, so that he could comfort her, but he knew that she needed some time to process her thoughts. Lee quickly wiped the tears from his eyes, feeling slightly nervous that Chloe might turn over and notice. He sighed to himself as he turned onto his back and stared at the ceiling, trying to stop his thoughts from wandering to everything that had happened last time.

Chapter Nineteen

Chloe slowly opened her eyes, gently rubbing the sleep out them as she slowly sat up. She sighed deeply as she felt another wave of nausea slowly washing over her. She quickly stood up and hurried into the bathroom. She cursed under her breath as she rummaged in the medication drawer, frantically trying to find her anti-sickness medication before she started vomiting.

"What are you looking for?" Lee asked from behind her. Chloe jumped, a small squeak of fear escaping her lips.

"Don't sneak up on me!" she exclaimed.

"I wasn't, I just came in to shower." he replied quietly, frowning slightly when he heard her harsh tone.

"Where are the damn anti-sickness tablets?!" Chloe said angrily, rummaging through the boxes of medication. Lee watched as she angrily flung a box of tablets into the drawer and slammed it shut, finally giving up on the search.

"I don't know where you left them." he said sadly, feeling slightly helpless as he watched her quickly sit in front of the toilet and vomit into it.

"It's too bloody late now anyway." she coughed, when she finally stopped vomiting.

Chloe flinched slightly as she felt Lee gently gather her hair in his hand, holding it out of the way.

"Do you have a hair band?" he asked her. Chloe shook her head slowly, clutching her abdomen as she vomited again.

"Don't cry Chlo." he said sadly when he noticed the tears slowly rolling down Chloe's cheeks.

"I'm fine, just have your shower." she said quickly, slowly standing up and flushing the toilet. Lee opened his mouth to respond, but quickly closed it again. He watched her closely, frowning in confusion as she quickly brushed her teeth and walked out of the bathroom. Despite the fact that he knew that she was stressed about their situation, he couldn't understand why she was suddenly being so distant with him. He couldn't think of anything that he had done to upset her. Lee sighed to himself as he climbed into the shower, gently pressing his head against the wall as the hot water trickled down his back. He knew in his heart that he had to find a way to get Chloe to open up to him, rather than pushing him away and shutting him out of her feelings, but he had no idea how to do that. He couldn't help but wish that she was as excited about the prospect of becoming a parent as he was. Even though he knew that she was struggling to come to terms with it, he couldn't help but feel disappointed at her reaction. As soon as Lee climbed out of the shower, he quickly wrapped a towel around his waist and walked into the bedroom, frowning to himself when he noticed that Chloe was snuggled up in bed.

"Are you alright Chlo?" he asked softly, squatting down in front of her.

"I'm fine." she said quickly.

"Please don't start fussing me all the time again." she quickly added. Lee nodded slowly and quickly stood up, his heart sinking slightly as he watched her closely.

"I'm just worried about you." he said sadly.

"Well, I'm fine. I just need a day in bed." she said shortly. Chloe sighed, closing her eyes tightly as she felt Lee watching her closely. Despite the fact that she felt guilty for being so short with him, she knew that she needed some time to process her feelings without him constantly fussing her. She needed some time to control the butterflies that were swirling around her stomach as she thought about the panic that she was struggling to suppress. As much as she tried to push her fear to the back of her mind she couldn't help keep replaying the events of last time over and over again. It felt like history was going to repeat itself, like her life was on a constant loop. She knew deep down that if she lost their baby again, then Lee would undoubtedly blame her, in the same way that he did before. Chloe frowned to herself as she heard Lee sigh deeply and felt him climb back into bed beside her.

"You don't have to stay up here with me." she said quietly.

"It's fine, I want to be by your side." he replied softly. Chloe sighed to herself, slowly turning onto her back and staring at the ceiling thoughtfully. She glanced at Lee as she felt him watching her closely. Her cheeks coloured and she quickly looked away from his intense gaze as soon as they locked eyes.

"Why do you keep staring at me?" she asked, glancing at him as he turned on his side and quickly shuffled closer to her.

"Because sometimes I can't believe that you are mine." he said quietly, his cheeks colouring slightly when Chloe glanced at him.

"I feel lucky enough that you have fallen in love with me, but now I get to have a baby with you." he continued thoughtfully. Chloe sighed deeply as she slowly turned on her side and shuffled closer to Lee, quickly snuggling her body against him.

"If things go to plan this time." she said sadly, her skin tingling when she felt him place his hand under her pyjama top and stroke soft circles on her abdomen.

"I don't even want to think about that." he whispered. Chloe nodded slowly before gently wrapping her arms around his neck. Lee's heart plummeted when he felt her warm tears against his collarbone.

"Please don't cry Chlo." he whispered sadly.

"I'm just so afraid." she whispered against his chest.

"I know." he sighed. Chloe glanced down at Lee's hand, staring at it as he continued tracing small circles on her abdomen. She locked eyes with him as he reached his other hand towards her, gently stroking her cheek with his fingertips.

"Can you make me a promise?" Chloe asked softly.

"What is it?" Lee asked nervously. His heart pounded against his chest as Chloe sniffed quietly and slowly wiped away her tears.

"I don't want things to go the same way that they did last time." she said quietly.

"Me neither." he said quickly, his stomach churning when he was reminded how close he came to losing her.

"If my body lets you down again, don't hate me." she continued, her voice breaking slightly.

"Don't say stuff like that about yourself, you didn't let me down." he told her sadly, his heart breaking when he noticed the pained expression on her face.

"My body did though." she whispered.

"Oh my god....what if I'm like my Mum." she added breathlessly, her heart pounding against her chest, as she felt herself beginning to panic.

"She had three miscarriages!" she exclaimed, taking deep breaths. Lee watched her closely as she slowly sat up and quickly placed her hand on her abdomen. His heart plummeted as he watched her chest rising and falling rapidly. In that moment he knew that she was starting to panic.

"I don't know what's going to happen, but I promise you that you are not going to lose me, I'll always be by your side." he reassured her, quickly sitting up beside her and wrapping his arms around her waist. Lee carefully pulled her onto his lap and placed his chin on her shoulder, holding her tightly against himself in an attempt to calm her down. Chloe closed her eyes tightly, taking deep breaths in through her nose and out through her mouth.

"You need to get your blood pressure down Chlo." Lee whispered in her ear, his stomach churning when he remembered reading in a pregnancy book, all those months ago, that high blood pressure could be harmful to an unborn baby. Chloe nodded slowly, her skin tingling as she felt Lee place a soft kiss on her neck. He breathed a sigh of relief when Chloe sighed deeply and he felt her finally relax against him. Chloe fell silent, her thoughts swirling, she slowly opened her eyes and turned her head to face Lee, smiling slightly when she noticed that he was still resting his chin on her shoulder. She placed a soft kiss on his cheek and gently rested her forehead against his cheek.

"I'm sorry, I didn't intend for this to happen again." she whispered sadly.

"I know you didn't." he said softly.

"Besides you don't need to be sorry, I'm excited to be a Dad." he added.

"Really?" she whispered, not quite able to bring herself to hope that the two of them were going to have a baby together. Lee nodded quickly, smiling at how adorable Chloe looked as she stared at him.

"I think we should wait to tell anyone until you are twelve weeks though, just in case." he told her.

"What about your Mum?" she asked.

"No, I think we shouldn't tell anyone yet." he said quickly. Chloe nodded in agreement.

"Oh no." Chloe whispered, when a thought suddenly popped into her head.

"What is it?" Lee asked nervously, watching her closely as she removed herself from his arms and slowly turned to face him.

"My aunt is going to be furious." she said quietly.

"I'm officially living in sin." she added, smiling slightly.

"Just say that it was immaculate conception, like the Virgin Mary." Lee chuckled. Chloe stared at him for a moment before bursting out laughing at his cheeky expression. As soon as Chloe stopped laughing she quickly wrapped her arms around his neck and kissed him deeply. Her skin tingled under his touch as Lee gently placed his hands under her shirt and rested them in place on her hips. Chloe giggled as he gently pushed her onto the bed, twisting his body so that he was laying down beside her. Lee's eyes flickered to Chloe when she gripped the bottom of his shirt, smiling at him as she slowly unbuttoned it. Lee sighed quietly as she placed her hands against his bare chest, enjoying the feel of his warm skin beneath her fingers. Lee stared at her as she gazed up at him through her long eyelashes. He smiled slightly to himself when he was reminded once again of how beautiful she was. He reached towards her and placed his fingertips on her forehead, slowly stroking down her face. Chloe sighed deeply and closed her eyes, trembling under his touch when he reached her neck. She gasped when she felt Lee's other hand slowly stroking his way up her leg. He grasped the bottom of her pyjama top in his hands and slowly lifted it up, revealing her abdomen. Chloe glanced at him, smiling slightly to herself when she noticed that his eyes were fixed on her abdomen. Her heart swelled with pride as she watched him staring at her abdomen lovingly, as he placed a series of soft kisses. He glanced up at her as she reached down and slowly stroked his hair, sighing in contentment as he carefully rested the side of his head against her abdomen.

"I love you so much." she whispered. Lee glanced up at her, smiling at her as she gazed down at him.

"I love you too." he whispered.

"Please be careful." she said nervously when he returned to stroking her abdomen and staring at it fondly.

"I would never do anything to hurt the baby." he said quietly, frowning slightly at her words.

"I know, I meant, you need to be careful not to fall in love with the baby yet." she told him.

"I don't want your heart to break again." she continued, her heart sinking slightly when she was reminded once again of how devastated Lee had been when she lost their baby. He nodded slowly, sighing quietly to himself.

"I wonder why you aren't showing this time, you had a small bump at ten weeks last time didn't you." he said thoughtfully.

"I think every pregnancy is different though, sometimes you show more than others." she reassured him.

"Yeah I guess so." he said quietly. Lee carefully placed his hands on her waist and pulled her close, kissing her lips softly. Chloe wrapped her arms around his neck, sighing in contentment when they finally pulled apart. She gasped as his hands slowly trailed their way upwards, his thumbs brushing against her breasts. She pulled Lee close, kissing his neck softly, her heart aching for him. She stopped kissing him for a moment, smiling slightly as she removed her pyjama top and he stared at her, a look of deep longing etched on his handsome features. He stared at her for a moment, before quickly kissing her neck, smiling to himself when he felt her trembling under his touch. Chloe's heart pounded against her chest as she gently wrapped her legs around his waist.

"I don't know if we can Chlo." he whispered against her neck.

"Why not?" she whispered, a note of pleading in her voice.

"We might hurt the baby." he said nervously in between kissing her neck.

"But we've been having a lot of sex lately anyway." she pointed out.

"That was before we knew though." he pointed out.

"We can't not have sex for the next six months!" she protested.

"Besides in all the pregnancy books that I read before, it says that it's safe." she added. Lee thought for a moment, smiling slightly as he glanced at her and noticed her incredulous expression.

"I thought you never wanted to have sex again." he pointed out, chuckling slightly. Chloe glared at him defiantly, trying to resist the urge to burst out laughing at his smug smile.

"I can't exactly get more pregnant though can I." she pointed out, raising her eyebrow at him. Lee smiled at her, not quite able to tear his eyes away from the beautiful woman beneath him. He glanced at her abdomen nervously, not entirely sure what to do. Every time that he gazed into her eyes, he felt a deep sense of longing for her.

"Please don't be like this, it'll be fine." she pleaded. Lee sighed quietly, trying to push the baby from his mind. He quickly returned to kissing her neck, slowly making his way along her jawline and down onto her collarbone, smiling against her when he noticed her body trembling in anticipation.

"Maybe we should wait until you are twelve weeks." he said nervously, in between kissing her neck, trying to resist the temptation that he was feeling.

"But you won't want me when I'm fat." she said sadly, her heart plummeting when she suddenly realised that she would no longer be attractive to him when she didn't have what he described as the 'perfect body'. She knew that he could have the pick of any woman that he wanted and she couldn't help but feel like he would be tempted to stray away.

"Chloe, you don't really think that do you?" he asked, instantly stopping kissing her neck as soon as he heard her words.

"Kind of." she admitted quietly, her cheeks colouring as he stared at her intensely. Lee frowned at her, his heart breaking a little that she could possibly think that he would ever want anyone else.

"I won't have the perfect body that you always tell me I have anymore." she said sadly.

"And you're so handsome, you could easily find someone else." she said quietly, reaching up and gently stroking his hair.

"Says the person who everyone wants." he said eventually, his throat feeling slightly dry.

"Besides you won't be fat, you'll be pregnant. It's different." he added, sighing quietly to himself when she looked away from him, her cheeks colouring.

"My body will never be the same though, and you won't want me." she said sadly, her eyes filling with tears at the thought of the man that she loved no longer being attracted to her.

"Please don't say stuff like that about yourself." he told her quietly.

"I will always want you Chlo." he added softly.

"Always." he continued when he noticed her raising her eyebrow sceptically. Chloe nodded slowly, not entirely sure if she believed him. Lee sighed sadly, his chest feeling tight at the thought that she clearly didn't believe him.

"You know how much I love you, surely you don't think I'm that shallow?" he asked her, feeling slightly hurt that she was doubting him.

"I don't know. You know how insecure I am, I can't help it." she said quietly.

"I'm sorry." she added quietly, quickly wiping the tears from her eyes. Lee gently stroked her face with his fingertips, before placing a tender kiss on her lips.

"You don't have to worry, I will always want you." he told her when they eventually pulled apart.

"Even when you are old and wrinkly." he chuckled. Chloe burst out laughing.

"That's different though, because you'll be old and wrinkly too." she giggled.

"Although I'm older than you so in theory I'll be wrinkly first." he laughed, smiling at her adorable laugh.

"That's true." she chuckled. Before Lee could respond Chloe wrapped her arms around his neck and pulled him close, enjoying the feel of his body pressed against hers. Lee kissed her softly, gasping against her lips when he felt her place her hand inside his boxer shorts. He rested his head on her shoulder, gently placing a series of soft kisses on her neck. Chloe shivered involuntarily when she stroked him and a deep groan escaped his lips. She breathed deeply, trying to control the deep desire that she was feeling for him. She gently rested her head against his, smiling slightly when she felt him breathing deeply against her neck.

"I need you to make love to me." she whispered in his ear. Lee slowly lifted his head, a small smile playing on the corner of his lips when he noticed the desperation on Chloe's face.

"We can be careful." she pleaded.

"You keep saying that I have a high sex drive, but I think you secretly have one too." he chuckled. Chloe raised her eyebrow, giggling when she stroked Lee again and he groaned.

"Only with you....because I love you so much." she told him. Lee smiled at her words, his heart swelling with pride.

"You're so amazing." he whispered in her ear.

Chapter Twenty

"Will you stop dicking around?!" Lee exclaimed when Nathan wiped his paint brush on Lee's cheek. Nathan burst out laughing at Lee's incredulous expression.

"You're meant to be helping." Lee added, smiling slightly when Nathan pouted at him.

"I am helping." Nathan protested.

"We still have two more walls to do and we need to get it done before Chloe gets back." Lee said, starting to panic slightly as he gazed around the room and noticed how much painting still needed to be done.

"Why, what difference does it make?" Nathan sighed, chuckling when he noticed Lee frantically painting the wall.

"I want to surprise her." Lee told him.

"Where is she anyway?" Nathan asked.

"She's gone shopping." Lee told him.

"Oh shit." he added when he heard the front door close.

"Lee!" Chloe's voice called from downstairs.

"We're upstairs Chlo!" Lee called back, his stomach plummeting in disappointment when he realised that Chloe was home much earlier than he'd hoped.

"That's the surprise out of the window." Nathan chuckled when they heard Chloe's footsteps slowly climbing the stairs. Lee glanced up and smiled at her as she leant against the doorway, carefully placing her shopping bags on the floor.

"What are you doing?" she frowned, glancing between the two of them. She frowned in confusion when she noticed them holding paint brushes.

"We are painting." Nathan said, beaming proudly.

"Yes but why?" Chloe frowned. Her heart fluttered against her chest as her eyes wandered to the corner of the room and she noticed a small wooden crib.

"Wait, are you making a nursery?" she whispered, her voice breaking slightly when she glanced at Lee and saw him nodding slowly.

"We're attempting too." Lee smiled at her.

"That's really sweet." Chloe smiled, quickly crossing the room to stand beside Lee. He smiled down at her as she wrapped her arms around his waist, her eyes filling with tears as she stared at the crib. Chloe glanced up at Lee, smiling at him as he stared at her. She kissed him softly, giggling to herself as she stroked the paint mark on his cheek.

"Did you miss the wall?" she giggled.

"No, that was Nath." Lee chuckled.

"You probably shouldn't be in here with the fumes." Lee pointed out when he suddenly realised. Chloe nodded slowly, quickly taking his hand and leaving the room, pulling him along with her.

"I have to finish the painting!" Lee protested, bursting out laughing and glancing back at Nathan when he heard him fling the paintbrush into the tray and follow them. Chloe led Lee into the living room, eventually letting go of his hand to remove her jacket.

"Aww Chlo Bo, your little bump is so cute." Nathan beamed as he threw himself onto the sofa. Lee smiled proudly at Chloe as the two of them sat on the sofa. Lee gently wrapped his arm around Chloe's shoulders and kissed her cheek gently.

"How far gone are you now?" Nathan asked.

"She's sixteen and a half weeks." Lee said quickly, before Chloe had a chance to respond. Chloe nodded slowly.

"I notice you painted the nursery blue." Chloe giggled, glancing between the two of them.

"It had to be didn't it." Lee beamed.

"But we went for a baby blue, so that it's unisex." Nathan chuckled. Chloe burst out laughing, smiling at their adorable expressions.

"Are you going to find out what you are having?" Nathan asked.

"Yes, we'll find out at the twenty week scan." Chloe replied.

"We have to tell the fans at some point too." Lee reminded her. Chloe nodded slowly, her stomach churning in anticipation. Despite the fact that most of the fans had grown fond of her, since the article was released, Chloe couldn't help but feel slightly nervous about how they would take the news that she was having a baby with Lee.

"Why don't you tell them at the Apollo gig in a few weeks?" Nathan suggested.

"Yeah we could do actually." Lee said thoughtfully.

"Then that way, you could join us for the meet and greet afterwards, then the fans can meet you." Lee continued, turning to Chloe.

"Is that such a good idea?" Chloe asked nervously.

"I'm sure it'll be fine, they love you now remember." Nathan said quickly.

"Besides I'll be right by your side." Lee reassured her, smiling slightly at her adorable expression.

"Plus it's better to tell them before it gets leaked." Nathan pointed out.

"I guess so." Chloe said quietly, trying to control the butterflies in her stomach.

"Speaking of the baby.....we have something to talk to you about." Lee said, reluctantly tearing his eyes away from Chloe and turning his attention to Nathan.

"You have finally decided to go with the name that I picked?!" Nathan exclaimed hopefully.

"No!" Lee said quickly, chuckling to himself.

"What name?" Chloe frowned, glancing between the two of them, smiling slightly when she noticed Nathan's cheeky expression.

"I think you should call your baby Private." Nathan beamed proudly.

"What?!" Chloe exclaimed.

"That's a ridiculous name!" she giggled.

"Yeah but Private Knight." Lee whispered in her ear.

"We are not naming our baby that!" Chloe exclaimed, bursting out laughing when she noticed Nathan's incredulous expression.

"That's what I said." Lee agreed, rolling his eyes.

"Anyway, we have already asked Kirstie to be the baby's godmother so we were wondering if you would like to be godfather?" Lee asked Nathan. Nathan instantly stopped laughing, the smile slowly fading from his face as he stared at them, his mouth suddenly feeling very dry.

"I would love too." Nathan whispered, his voice breaking slightly as his eyes misted with tears. Chloe smiled as Nathan quickly stood up and crossed the room, perching on the sofa beside her and gently pulling her into a hug. Her heart fluttered with pride when she heard him sniff quietly in her ear. Chloe jumped and glanced at the laptop on the coffee table as it began to chime. Her heart sunk when she read the display and saw that Gwen was calling her.

"Oh no, I forgot that I was meant to be calling my auntie today." Chloe said quietly, her stomach churning nervously.

"You need to tell her about the baby at some point." Lee pointed out, softly stroking Chloe's hair when he realised how nervous she was becoming. Chloe nodded slowly, swallowing the lump that was rising in her throat. She glanced at Lee and sighed deeply to herself.

"You'd better make yourself scarce, otherwise she'll probably have a go at you." Chloe told him sadly, wishing that he could be by her side when she told her aunt the news, but knowing in her heart that Gwen would likely be furious with Lee. Nathan and Lee quickly stood up and moved down the sofa, making sure that they were out of sight of the laptop. Chloe nodded slowly and reluctantly answered the call.

"Hi Auntie." Chloe said nervously, her stomach churning with butterflies.

"Hello, Chloe, how are you?" Gwen asked.

"I'm fine, how are you?" Chloe asked.

"I'm well thank you." Gwen replied. Chloe nodded slowly, opening her mouth to speak, but quickly closing it again, when she couldn't quite bring herself to say the words.

"You asked to speak to me about something?" Gwen prompted.

"Yes.....I....erm..." Chloe started but trailed off, her eyes darting over the laptop to Lee who nodded at her reassuringly.

"What is it?" Gwen asked.

"Lee hasn't left you has he?!" Gwen quickly added, before Chloe had a chance to respond. Chloe shook her head slowly.

"We're going to have a baby together." Chloe said quietly.

"What?" Gwen asked, frowning in confusion.

"I'm pregnant." Chloe said quietly, her eyes quickly darting away from the screen as her cheeks coloured nervously. Time seemed to stretch for an eternity as Gwen remained silent, staring at Chloe, not quite able to comprehend what she was telling her. Chloe eventually glanced back at the laptop, her heart breaking a little when she saw the disappointment written all over Gwen's face.

"Auntie?" Chloe said quietly.

"I don't know what you want me say Chloe." Gwen said sternly, slowly shaking her head.

"Are you angry with me?" Chloe asked nervously.

"No, just very disappointed." Gwen told her. Chloe nodded slowly, swallowing the lump that was rising in her throat.

"You knew the values that you've been raised with and I thought you were better than that and that you were a good influence for Amy." Gwen continued.

"I was raised differently though!" Chloe protested, her heart pounding against her chest when Gwen glared at her.

"You can't use that as an excuse, you know as well as I do that your father would be turning in his grave." Gwen said matter of factly.

"Dad wasn't religious." Chloe muttered under her breath, trying to hold back the tears that were filling her eyes.

"Where's Lee anyway, I think I need to have a word with him?" Gwen said angrily, completely disregarding what Chloe had just said.

"He's out." Chloe lied quickly.

"Well tell him to call me!" Gwen snapped.

"Auntie?!" Chloe called when she noticed Gwen searching the keyboard for the hang up button.

"There's nothing else to say Chloe." Gwen said sternly, quickly ending the call. Chloe stared at the laptop numbly as she slowly brought her legs up against her, trying to protect herself from the hurt that she was feeling. She ran her hand through her hair, sighing in frustration as she slowly rested her back against the sofa.

"I guess I'm back to not having a family again." Chloe whispered to herself, quickly wiping away the tears that were steadily rolling down her cheeks. She glanced down at her abdomen, gently resting her hand on it, and sighing sadly to herself. Chloe glanced up at Lee as he quickly crossed the room and sat beside her.

"Come here Chlo." Lee whispered, gently wrapping his arm around her shoulders and pulling her close. Chloe buried her head in his shoulder and allowed the tears that she'd been fighting to flow freely.

"You don't really think that your Dad would be disappointed in you do you?" Lee whispered, softly stroking her hair.

"No, he wasn't religious anyway." she said quietly.

"I just can't lose my family, I've only just got them back." she added sadly.

"Do you want me to talk to her?" Lee offered, his heart breaking a little when he noticed how upset she was.

"No, she'll be nasty to you." she said quickly.

"So?" Lee countered. Chloe shook her head quickly, not quite able to face the idea of her aunt being cruel to the man that she loved with all her heart.

"Your aunt seems like a pain in the neck." Nathan pointed out. Chloe nodded, closing her eyes when Lee placed a soft kiss on her forehead. Her skin tingled when she felt his warm breath against her face as he sighed deeply, gently resting his face against hers.

"She'll probably come around." Lee told her.

"And you still have Amy, she was happy when you told her wasn't she." he continued. Chloe nodded slowly, lifting her head and smiling at Lee when she noticed him staring at her lovingly.

"I think I need a bath." Chloe said sadly, her skin tingling as Lee gently wiped away her tears with his thumb. Lee nodded slowly, sighing sadly when she slowly stood up and walked away.

Chloe climbed out of the bath and quickly pulled on her pyjamas, trying to push Gwen's words out of her mind. Despite the fact that she'd known that Gwen would be disappointed in her, that didn't stop the hurt that she was feeling. She couldn't help but hope that Lee was right and that eventually Gwen would come around to the idea. The last thing that Chloe wanted to do was to lose her family once again. Her eyes flickered to the mirror as she stared at her bump. Chloe stared down at her abdomen as she placed her hand on it, still not quite able to believe that she was carrying a baby inside her. She sighed sadly to herself as she turned sideways and realised how noticeable her bump was. Despite the fact that she was still able to hide it under baggy clothes, she couldn't help but feel a pang of concern that Lee would become less and less attracted to her, the more weeks that passed. She knew in her heart that she wasn't strong enough to lose him. Chloe sighed and slowly walked out of the bathroom, her stomach swirling in excitement as she walked past the nursery room. Despite the insecurities that she was feeling, she couldn't help but feel excited about the idea of having Lee's baby. She picked up her shopping bags and quickly made her way downstairs, frowning to herself when she heard Nathan singing in the living room. Chloe smiled, her heart swelling with pride as she stood in the living room doorway, glancing between the two of them when Lee joined in with the chorus. The two of them fell silent when they noticed Chloe hovering awkwardly in the doorway.

"Don't stop on my account." Chloe smiled at them.

"It's fine, we were just rehearsing." Lee told her, his eyes flickering to her bump. His heart swelled with pride when he noticed how perfect it looked.

"Matt has managed to arrange this Apollo gig and now he is stressing that our lead singer won't be able to sing." Nathan chuckled.

"My voice is fine now." Lee said, rolling his eyes.

"Yeah but we need to check if you can do the big vocal in Breathe Easy, otherwise we need to drop it from the set." Nathan pointed out. Chloe smiled, chills running down her spine, as Lee began to sing the verse, slowly building for the high part. She gasped, her hand darting to her abdomen when she felt a strange fluttering sensation. Lee instantly stopped singing, when he noticed Chloe staring at her abdomen nervously.

"What's wrong Chlo?" Lee asked nervously, beginning to panic slightly. Nathan turned to follow Lee's eyeline, the two of them frowning to themselves as Chloe stared at her abdomen silently.

"Chloe!" Lee exclaimed worriedly.

"Do it again." Chloe said quickly.

"Do what?" Lee frowned.

"Sing." Chloe said quickly.

"Why, what's going on?" Lee asked her.

"Please just do it!" Chloe exclaimed. Lee frowned to himself, quickly doing as she asked.

"Oh my god!" she exclaimed when she felt the fluttering sensation once again.

"Will you please tell me what's going on?!" Lee exclaimed, breathing deeply to try and suppress the panic that he was feeling.

"I think the baby just moved." she muttered, her eyes filling with tears as she slowly glanced up, a small sob escaping her lips when she locked eyes with Lee.

"Really?" Lee whispered, his voice breaking slightly.

"I think so." she nodded.

"Private must like it when you sing." Nathan smiled.

"Stop calling our baby that!" Lee said sternly, glancing at Nathan when he burst out laughing.

"There's a little baby living inside me." she whispered, the realisation finally dawning on her. Lee nodded slowly, quickly crossing the room to stand in front of her, the two of them unable to tear their eyes away from her abdomen.

"It's so amazing." Chloe sobbed, her skin tingling when Lee placed his hand on top of hers. Chloe leaned forward, gently resting her head against Lee's shoulder.

"I love you so much little baby." Chloe whispered, her heart pounding against her chest.

"You mean Private." Nathan piped up. Nathan burst out laughing when Lee reached over and clipped him around the back of the head.

Chapter Twenty One

"You totally ruined the moment then." Lee told Nathan sternly when he noticed Chloe giggling quietly.

"Actually I enhanced it." Nathan beamed. Lee shook his head and rolled his eyes, glancing down at Chloe when she reluctantly removed herself from his arms.

"You should sit down, you look tired." Lee said worriedly. Chloe nodded and slowly sat on the sofa beside Nathan.

"I'll make you a cup of tea." Lee told her, trying to exit the room, before the tears of happiness that he was fighting spilled out of his eyes. Chloe smiled at Nathan as he smiled at her and gently wrapped his arm around her shoulders.

"How are you doing Chlo Bo?" Nathan asked her.

"I'm fine." she told him, gently resting her head against his shoulder, fighting to keep her eyes open.

"The sickness isn't so bad now, which has been nice." she told him.

"Did Lee show you the pictures of the baby?" she added, quickly tucking her legs underneath her.

"Yep and the video." he smiled at her.

"Of my little god child." he added proudly, glancing at Chloe's bump. Chloe nodded slowly, smiling slightly to herself.

"Are you feeling okay about becoming a mother?" he asked her.

"I think so. I mean it is scary, but I think I can do it, and I'll have Lee, so it'll be okay." she replied quietly.

"Although I am a bit worried about the giving birth part." she admitted, swallowing the lump that was rising in her throat when she thought about the pain that she would have to endure.

"It'll be worth it though." Nathan pointed out, snapping her out of her thoughts. Chloe nodded slowly, gently closing her eyes, no longer able to fight the exhaustion that she was feeling. Nathan glanced at Chloe, smiling slightly when he realised that she'd fallen asleep. His eyes flickered up as Lee returned, carrying a cup of tea and quickly setting it down on the coffee table.

"You're too late, she's already fallen asleep." Nathan chuckled. Lee nodded slowly as he slowly sat on Chloe's other side. He watched her closely, smiling slightly at how adorable she looked as she slept peacefully. Lee placed his hand on her leg, longing to be close to her.

"I hope you realise how lucky you are." Nathan said quietly.

"I definitely do." Lee said quietly, staring at Chloe fondly.

"Even after all this time, I still don't feel like I deserve her." Lee admitted.

"And yet she's the one who thinks she doesn't deserve me." he continued, shaking his head slowly.

"I still can't believe that you are going to be a Dad." Nathan said quietly, glancing at Chloe as she fidgeted in her sleep. She opened her eyes for a moment, before gently resting her head on Nathan's lap and quickly falling back asleep.

"Me neither, I never pictured myself having a family, until I started dating Chloe." Lee said, smiling slightly.

"It's going to be a good looking baby with your guys gene pool." Nathan smiled, glancing between the two of them.

"It's ridiculous how beautiful she is." Lee said fondly, still not able to tear his eyes away from Chloe.

"And yet she doesn't believe it." he added, sighing sadly.

"She's a lot more confident than she was though." Nathan pointed out.

"Yeah kind of." Lee said quietly, sighing quietly to himself.

"What?" Nathan frowned.

"She was getting a lot more confident, until we found out she was pregnant." Lee said, slowly tracing small circles on Chloe's leg.

"And now she keeps asking me all the time if I still want her." he continued. Nathan raised his eyebrow, frowning in confusion.

"Because she thinks that I won't want her anymore now that her body is changing." Lee explained.

"Aww bless her, that's a shame." Nathan said sadly.

"It kind of hurts me a little bit that she doubts my love for her all the time." Lee admitted, his heart plummeting when he was reminded once again that Chloe's confidence in her body was slowly fading.

"I don't think she doubts your love for her, she probably just thinks that you won't be attracted to her anymore." Nathan pointed out.

"Which is completely untrue!" Lee exclaimed, cursing himself when Chloe fidgeted in her sleep.

"I'm really not that shallow." he added quietly.

"I know, you know that she always doubts herself though." Nathan sighed. Lee's eyes flickered to Chloe as he heard her mumble his name in her sleep.

"Maybe I need to find a way to prove to her that I love her for who she is and not her body." Lee said thoughtfully.

"You could plan a romantic evening for her?" Nathan suggested.

"I don't think that's going to cut it." Lee said quietly.

"I was thinking more along the lines of proposing to her." he added.

"That's a big step." Nathan pointed out.

"Not really, I've known for a while that I want to make her my wife one day." Lee told him. Nathan smiled at his words, not quite able to believe how much Lee had changed since being with Chloe. Even though Nathan had known for years that Lee had a secret soft side that he liked to hide from everyone, he'd never imagined that Lee would fall so hard for Chloe. Chloe's eyelids flickered open for a moment, her ears pricking up when she heard Lee talking about her.

"I don't really know what else to do to help her, I don't think she believes me when I tell her that she is beautiful and that I think her bump is adorable." Lee said, snapping Nathan out of his thoughts.

"And I love her even more now that she is carrying my baby." he added.

"The pregnancy does really suit her, she is definitely glowing." Nathan agreed.

"I know." Lee smiled. Chloe slowly sat up, gently rubbing the sleep out of her eyes, her cheeks colouring when she noticed Nathan and Lee watching her closely.

"What?" Chloe asked, glancing between the two of them.

"Nothing." Nathan said, quickly looking away from her.

"Were the two of you talking about me?" she asked.

"Nope." Lee said quickly, his heart pounding nervously at the thought she might have heard him speaking to Nathan about his plans.

"What's in the shopping bag?" Lee asked quickly, trying to distract her when he felt himself squirming under her intense gaze.

"Oh, well, I did something bad." she admitted nervously.

"You brought a sex toy." Nathan beamed, bursting out laughing when Chloe's cheeks coloured deeply.

"No of course not!" she said quickly.

"I was out buying clothes and I saw these." she added, gently rummaging in the bag and pulling out a selection of baby grows and blankets.

"I know we said we were going to wait and go shopping for baby things together but I saw them and just couldn't resist." she explained. Lee smiled as he gazed at the items.

"You're not mad are you?" she checked, feeling slightly guilty that she had gone back on their deal.

"No of course not." Lee smiled at her.

"Besides I brought a crib." he added. Lee's heart swelled with pride when Chloe picked up one of the baby grows and gently laid it on her abdomen, smiling down at it, her eyes twinkling happily.

"That's so cute." Nathan said happily. Chloe nodded slowly, glancing up at Lee as he slowly leant towards her and placed a soft kiss on her lips.

"Anyway, I'd better leave you lovebirds to it." Nathan piped up, quickly standing up.

"You don't have to go." Chloe said quickly.

"I have a date with Matt anyway." Nathan beamed. Chloe nodded slowly, smiling as Nathan leaned over and gently pulled her into a hug.

"Take care Chlo Bo, make sure he looks after you." Nathan told her. Chloe glanced at Lee when he quickly stood up and picked up her mug of tea.

"I'm going to make you a fresh one." Lee told her, when he noticed Chloe raise her eyebrow at him questioningly.

"Oh and make sure you take care of my god child." Nathan told Chloe as he reached the doorway and quickly turned back to face her.

"Little...." Nathan started, pausing for dramatic effect.

"Don't you dare." Lee warned him, a small smile playing on the corner of his lips.

"I didn't do anything!" Nathan said, holding his hands up in surrender. Chloe smiled at Nathan as he left the room, Lee following closely behind.

"Take care of Private!" Nathan called from the hallway. Chloe frowned when she heard a commotion from the hallway.

"Ow, you bastard!" Nathan exclaimed.

"Serves you right!" Lee exclaimed.

"Maybe you'll think twice before calling my baby that again." Lee laughed.

"What you mean Private." Nathan laughed. Chloe's head snapped to the hallway as she heard the sounds of them fighting. She frowned to herself as she heard Nathan let out a groan of pain.

"You're such a dick." Lee laughed.

"Speaking of which, I won't be able to have sex tonight now!" Nathan groaned.

"I did warn you." Lee laughed.

"We'll have to revoke your god parent status if you keep on!" Chloe called out.

"Yeah exactly." Lee agreed. Chloe smiled to herself as she heard Nathan and Lee burst out laughing.

"Now sod off home." Lee told him when they'd eventually stopped laughing.

"Lee!" Chloe called when she heard the front door open and close.

"What's up?" he asked, peering his head around the doorway.

"What did you do to him?" she asked, smiling slightly when she noticed his flushed cheeks.

"I gave him a wedgie." he laughed.

"Nice." she giggled.

"You don't have to make me a cup of tea, I don't really fancy one anyway." she told him. Lee nodded slowly, before quickly crossing the room and laying down on the sofa behind her.

"Come here then." he said softly. Chloe smiled slightly as she carefully curled up in front of him, sighing in contentment as he wrapped his arms around her and gently pulled her against him. She glanced at him when he gently brushed her hair to one side and rested his chin on her shoulder. She glanced down at his hands that were gently resting in place against her abdomen. He placed a soft kiss on her neck, smiling slightly when she placed her hands on top of his, snuggling against him.

"I can't believe you felt the baby move." he whispered in her ear.

"Clearly the baby likes it when you sing." she smiled.

"What did it feel like?" he asked her.

"I don't know really.....it's difficult to explain, kind of like a fluttering feeling, almost like butterflies but more intense." she explained.

"Speaking of singing, we'd better hope the baby doesn't have a pair of lungs like you, it'll be the loudest baby ever." she giggled.

"My voice isn't that high pitched." he laughed.

"Ermm, excuse me, what about the end of Fly By!" Chloe giggled.

"Yeah, I'll give you that one." he chuckled, squeezing Chloe gently against himself.

"Speaking of the baby, did Kirstie agree to be godmother?" he asked her. Chloe nodded slowly, her thoughts swirling when she remembered how distracted and emotional Kirstie had seemed earlier.

"I'm a bit worried about her." she told him thoughtfully.

"Why?" he frowned.

"I don't know, she just seemed a bit quiet and emotional." she pointed out.

"Maybe she was emotional because she's happy that you asked her to be god mother?" he suggested.

"I don't think so, she seemed emotional before that, when we were looking at baby clothes and stuff." she told him.

"I did ask her, but she said that everything is fine, but I just have a bad feeling." she added thoughtfully.

"She might just be feeling sad because Ben is away in Norway recording with the A1 boys." he reminded her.

"Maybe." she said thoughtfully, still not quite able to shake the feeling that something was going on with Kirstie. She couldn't help but feel a little hurt that if there was an issue, Kirstie didn't feel able to confide in her.

"I'm sure she's fine." he reassured her, gently placing a soft kiss on her cheek.

"I hope so." she said quietly. She sighed quietly to herself when she felt Lee gently kissing her neck.

"I heard you and Nathan talking about me." she told him.

"Which part?!" he said quickly, instantly stopping kissing her neck, his heart pounding nervously against his chest.

"That you think I'm beautiful and love me even more now that I'm carrying your baby." she told him, smiling slightly.

"That's not a secret though, I've been telling you that for weeks." he said quietly, breathing a sigh of relief.

"I just wish you believed me." he added sadly.

"I do believe you. I know how much you love me." she said quietly, slowly turning over so that she was facing him.

"I love both of you." he whispered, gently placing his hand on her bump. Chloe smiled slightly, before kissing him deeply.

"So don't listen to your insecurities okay." he told her when they eventually pulled apart.

"You don't need to, because you are so beautiful." he added, staring at her as he gently stroked her hair.

"You don't get it do you?" she sighed.

"Nope, not really." he admitted.

"Just because you love someone, that doesn't mean that you find them attractive anymore." she pointed out.

"And I don't feel attractive anymore, I'm never going to have a good body again." she added, turning over on the sofa so that her back was facing him, in the hope that he wouldn't notice the tears that were slowly filling her eyes.

"Chloe." he sighed deeply as he gently rested his head on her shoulder, his heart breaking a little when he snuggled his face against hers and felt her warm tears against his cheek.

"Of course I'm attracted to you, you're so beautiful." he whispered in her ear as he softly stroked her hair. Chloe sniffed sadly when she felt Lee wrap his arms around her waist and pull her close.

"You wouldn't tell me even if you weren't." she sighed.

"Chlo, please stop." he whispered sadly, no longer able to bear hearing her tearing herself down.

"I'll be fine, I'm just tired." she said quietly, trying to drop the subject when she realised that she was hurting Lee. He sighed sadly to himself when Chloe closed her eyes and fell asleep instantly. He couldn't help but wish that Chloe believed him when he told her how amazing she was.

Chapter Twenty Two

Chloe sighed as she glanced at the bedroom clock, not entirely sure what had woken her when she realised that it was only midnight. She slowly lifted her head, gently placing a soft kiss on Lee's lips, smiling slightly to herself when she noticed him sleeping soundly. She glanced down at her stomach, giggling quietly to herself when she heard it growling loudly. She carefully climbed out of bed, trying not to wake Lee. She slowly padded downstairs, quickly flicking on the kitchen light and rummaging in the cupboards, smiling in satisfaction when she found a bunch of bananas. Chloe slowly peeled them before placing them on the counter and carefully chopping them with a knife. She quickly picked up a slice and placed it into her mouth, smiling in satisfaction when she was finally able to satisfy her cravings. She continued slicing the banana, jumping when she heard the doorbell ring. She gasped, glancing down at her finger as she nicked the end of it with the knife. She placed her finger in her mouth, quickly sucking the small amount of blood off her finger, peering around the doorway, her eyes fixed nervously on the front door. Chloe jumped as the doorbell chimed once again. Her heart pounded against her chest as she tip toed along the hallway, not entirely sure what to do. Her stomach churned nervously as she glanced at the clock in the hallway, not entirely sure who would be visiting so late. She cursed under her breath when she realised that she'd left her mobile phone upstairs and so couldn't even log onto the app and check the security camera at the front door. Chloe stood beside the door, her feet frozen to the spot, a small squeak of fear escaping her lips when the letterbox opened.

"Please let me in Chloe!" a panicked voice called through the letter box. Chloe sighed deeply when she instantly recognised the voice. Chloe quickly placed the door on the chain and slowly opened it, carefully peering around the gap.

"What do you want Michelle?!" Chloe said shortly, her temper slowly growing as soon as she laid eyes on the person that had tried to ruin her life. Michelle stared at Chloe for a moment, a small sob escaping her lips when she finally laid eyes on a familiar face. Chloe gasped to herself when she noticed the swellings on Michelle's cheekbones and the small trail of blood that was flowing down her cheek from her split lip. Chloe closed the door, quickly removing the chain, before opening it once again.

"What happened?" Chloe asked as she watched Michelle stagger into the house.

"It's a long story." Michelle whispered, falling to her knees in relief as soon as she was safely inside the house. Despite the fact that she knew how much Chloe and Lee hated her, she couldn't help but feel safer with them than she would be alone. Michelle placed her head in her hands, trying to process what had happened, not quite able to comprehend everything. Chloe watched in horror as Michelle placed her head in her hands and began to sob loudly.

"You need to tell me what happened?" Chloe asked gently, quickly kneeling down in front of her.

"I can't!" Michelle exclaimed. Chloe gasped when Michelle began to sob hysterically.

"I know you hate me, but please don't kick me out!" Michelle exclaimed. Chloe nodded slowly, the deep anger and resentment that she felt for Michelle slowly disappearing when she realised how distraught she was over whatever had happened. She couldn't help but feel a deep surge of sympathy for her. In all the years that Chloe had known Michelle, she'd never seen her in such a state. Her eyes were wide, her whole body trembling with fear. Chloe thought for a moment, not entirely sure what to do to help the devastated woman that was sobbing and crying hysterically on the floor. Michelle eventually fell sideways, no longer having the strength to hold herself up, collapsing onto the floor and curling into a ball, desperately wishing that she could wake up from this nightmare.

"LEE!" Chloe called loudly, desperately hoping that Lee would hear her.

"No please don't!" Michelle cried, beginning to panic slightly when she thought about being face to face with Lee again.

"He hates me." she added nervously, not entirely sure how Lee was going to react to seeing her. Chloe shrugged, breathing a sigh of relief when she heard Lee's footsteps. Michelle quickly stood up, leaning against the wall for support.

"I should go." Michelle said quickly.

"You don't have to go." Chloe said quietly.

"What's wrong?!" Chloe heard Lee calling to her. She glanced up the stairs, sighing quietly to herself when she noticed Lee staring silently at Michelle, his jaw hardening as soon as he laid eyes on her.

"What the hell are you doing here?!" Lee asked, a note of menace present in his voice.

"I didn't know where else to go." Michelle admitted, knowing in her heart that she should leave the house, but not quite able to bring herself to be alone.

"Well you've come to the wrong place, we've no interest in you." Lee told her as he slowly walked downstairs, glaring at Michelle the entire time.

"I think something has happened." Chloe told Lee, quickly taking his hand and squeezing it gently, trying to calm him down. Lee shook his head slowly, not entirely sure why Michelle had decided to darken their door with her problems, particularly after everything that she had done to them.

"What is it then?" Lee sighed, glancing down at Chloe when he noticed her watching Michelle closely, a look of deep sympathy etched on her pretty features.

"Oh my god, Mark didn't hurt you did he?!" Chloe exclaimed when Michelle fell silent. Michelle shook her head slowly, not entirely sure how to tell them what had happened to her. She knew in her heart that as soon as she said the words aloud, everything would suddenly feel more real.

"I got raped." Michelle muttered.

"What?" Chloe whispered, her heart sinking into the pit of her stomach.

"I got raped!" Michelle exclaimed, slowly sliding her back down the wall, quickly bringing her legs up against her body and wrapping her arms around them, rocking her body slightly as she sobbed.

"Oh shit." Lee muttered under his breath. Chloe glanced at him for a moment, before turning her attention back to Michelle, who was softly sobbing her heart out on the floor.

"You need to call the police." Chloe told Lee as she reluctantly let go of his hand and crossed the room, quickly kneeling down in front of Michelle and hugging her tightly. Michelle hesitated for a moment before quickly wrapping her arms around Chloe. Chloe's eyes filled with tears as she listened to Michelle's sobs of anguish. Despite the way that she felt about Michelle, she wouldn't wish what had happened to her on anyone.

"The police will be here soon, they said you need to keep your clothes." Lee announced quietly as he walked back into the room. Michelle nodded slowly, smiling at Chloe when she eventually sat back, her eyes fixed on Michelle sadly.

"I don't have anything to change into anyway." Michelle said quietly.

"I could lend you some clothes?" Chloe offered, wishing in her heart that she was able to do more to help.

"I doubt they would fit me." Michelle said, smiling slightly when she remembered how slim Chloe was.

"Chlo, can you come here for a minute please?" Lee asked from behind her. Chloe nodded and slowly stood up, frowning when she turned to face Lee and saw that he was holding his hand out to her. She quickly took his hand, gasping in shock as he pulled her towards himself and handed her the hoodie that he was holding.

"Can you put this on please?" he whispered in her ear.

"What for, I'm not cold?" Chloe frowned.

"Please just do it." he insisted. Chloe frowned for a moment, before quickly doing as he asked. As soon as Chloe had placed the hoodie over her head, Lee quickly grasped the bottom of it and gently pulled it down over her bump.

"I don't want to find a picture of your bump in the paper in the morning." Lee whispered in her ear, glancing over her head and narrowing his eyes at Michelle suspiciously.

"I didn't realise that you are pregnant Chloe." Michelle said, finally noting her bump as she watched them closely. Chloe nodded slowly, her eyes darting to Lee when she heard him sigh quietly.

"This had better not be a set up to gain more information on us." Lee warned Michelle, his temper rising at the thought of her doing anything to hurt Chloe or their baby.

"I don't think she's sick enough to have made something like this up." Chloe mumbled. Lee raised his eyebrow sceptically, not entirely sure if he could bring himself to believe that she just happened to end up at their door.

"I didn't know where else to go, and despite the fact that you hate me, I knew that you would protect me!" Michelle snapped.

"What?" Lee frowned, not entirely sure what she was talking about.

"Because you'll always protect Chloe, so if I'm with her then maybe you'll protect me too." Michelle explained.

"And you hate the person that did this to me far more than you hate me!" she continued, a small sob escaping her lips. Lee frowned, glancing at Chloe who shrugged at him, not entirely sure what Michelle was trying to tell them. Before Chloe and Lee could respond, Michelle quickly dropped her trousers, turning her thigh to face them. Chloe gasped when she saw the deep scratches, clearly made by fingernails when Michelle was held down.

"Do you believe me now?!" Michelle exclaimed, her eyes fixed on Lee. Lee nodded slowly, his complexion slowly turning pale.

"Oh and just so that you hear it from me rather than the police....it was Shayne." Michelle announced.

"What?" Chloe whispered, her legs suddenly feeling weak as she tried to process Michelle's words. Michelle nodded slowly as she quickly pulled her trousers back up, feeling slightly guilty when she noticed the guilty expression on Chloe's face.

"Oh my god." Chloe whispered, her stomach churning with guilt when she realised that all of this was her fault. She was the one who had brought Shayne into everyone's lives. If it hadn't been for her, Michelle and Shayne would never even have met. Chloe glanced at Lee when she felt him watching her closely, an expression on his face that she couldn't quite interpret.

"I knew he was going to rape you that day in the bathroom." Lee said quietly, swallowing the lump that was rising in his throat, when he realised how close Chloe had come to having her life changed forever. He shook his head slowly, trying to clear the images that were swirling around his head.

The three of them jumped as the doorbell rang. Chloe numbly walked over to the door and slowly opened it, gesturing to the police to come into the house.

"We've had a report of a rape." one of the police officers said.

"Yes, it wasn't me, it was Michelle." Chloe said quietly, pointing to Michelle.

"Is there a room that we can use?" the police officer asked.

"The living room." Lee said quietly, quickly gesturing to the living room. Chloe sighed sadly as she watched Michelle walk into the living room, closely followed by the police women. As soon as the door was closed behind them, Lee quickly wrapped his arms around Chloe's waist and pulled her close, burying his head in her shoulder.

"It's okay, I'm okay." she whispered in his ear, as she gently stroked his hair, in an attempt to calm him down. Lee breathed deeply, quickly grasping the material of Chloe's hoodie and curling it into his fists, desperately trying to hold her as tightly as possible.

"He's such an animal." he whispered.

"I know." she whispered, sniffing slightly as she tried to control the tears that were filling her eyes.

"I think we should let her stay for a couple of days, until Mark is back from Norway." she added nervously, not entirely sure how Lee was going to react, but knowing that she needed to reach out and help Michelle in her moment of need, particularly when Chloe knew that she was partly responsible.

"Yeah I know." Lee whispered in her ear, holding Chloe even tighter as he fought to control the flashbacks that were swirling around his head. He couldn't stop thinking about what would have happened to Chloe if he hadn't been there to intervene.

"Be careful of the baby." she reminded him nervously. Lee nodded slowly, releasing his grip slightly, but not quite able to bring himself to release her completely.

Chapter Twenty Three

"You can probably let go of me now." Chloe smiled, when after what felt like an age, Lee was still holding her tightly, not quite able to bring himself to let her go. He wanted to hold her tightly in his arms, to know that she was safe, while he fought to control the intense fear that he was experiencing. Even though he knew he was being irrational, he couldn't stop thinking about what could have happened to Chloe on the night of the record label party. He sighed deeply, thanking his lucky starts that he'd been at the party that night, and was able to protect Chloe from being violated. He couldn't help but feel sick to his stomach at the thought of anyone doing anything to harm her, particularly when she was so precious to him. Lee reluctantly let go of Chloe when the living room door opened and the police women walked out, smiling at Chloe and Lee as they walked past. As soon as they left the house, Chloe glanced into the living room, sighing quietly when she heard Michelle let out a small sob.

"Maybe you should go and get some rest?" Lee suggested to Chloe. She glanced up at him as he hovered beside her protectively.

"We can't leave her." she pointed out, feeling slightly guilty at the thought of going to bed and leaving Michelle alone.

"I can deal with her, you need to get some sleep." he insisted. Chloe glanced down at her abdomen as Lee reached out and stroked it softly with his fingertips.

"You're growing a little person." he added, smiling slightly at Chloe when she smiled up at him. The two of them fell silent as Michelle walked into the hallway, glancing between the two of them awkwardly.

"I should probably leave you both in peace, I'm really sorry for just turning up out of the blue." Michelle said sadly, quickly wiping away the tears that were steadily rolling down her cheeks. Chloe glanced at Lee, raising her eyebrow at him. Lee sighed deeply, knowing in his heart that he couldn't turn Michelle away in her time of need. Despite the fact that he wanted nothing more than to keep Michelle as far away from the two of them as possible, he knew that he had to do the right thing.

"You can stay for a couple of days if you want?" Lee offered hesitantly, his voice catching slightly in his throat, as he struggled to get the words out.

"Are you sure I wouldn't be imposing?" Michelle asked nervously, not quite daring to hope that she wouldn't have to return home and be alone.

"You shouldn't be on your own." Chloe pointed out, clearly realising how Michelle was feeling.

"You could stay with us until Mark gets back." Chloe added.

"As long as you are sure?" Michelle asked tentatively, glancing between the two of them nervously. Lee nodded slowly, his eyes darting to Chloe when she stepped forward and quickly pulled Michelle into a hug, trying to provide at least a small amount of comfort.

"There's a bed in the spare room." Lee told Michelle, before quickly taking Chloe's hand and leading her upstairs.

"We'll be just down the hall!" Chloe called out to her as Lee led her away.

"Shouldn't we stay with her?" Chloe asked him quickly.

"She'll be okay, you need to get some rest." he told her, watching her closely as she slowly climbed into bed. He quickly climbed into bed beside her, smiling at her as she laid on her side and stared up at him, her cheeks colouring when she noticed him watching her closely. Chloe closed her eyes, sighing quietly as her thoughts wandered to Michelle and what she had been through. She suddenly felt a wave of nausea wash over her as her brain swirled with images of Michelle being assaulted by Shayne. Chloe jumped, her eyes snapping open when she felt Lee softly stroking her hair.

"You should try and get some sleep too." she told him, smiling slightly when his fingertips lingered on her cheek.

"I can't stop thinking about what could have happened that night." he admitted, swallowing the lump that was rising in his throat at the thought of anyone doing anything to harm Chloe. Chloe sighed deeply, her heart breaking a little at the deep sadness that was written on Lee's face. She placed a soft kiss on his palm, smiling slightly when he gently stroked her cheek with his fingertips.

"You don't need to worry I'm fine." she reassured him, her skin tingling under his touch as he continued to stroke her cheek.

"I'm just so glad that I was there to stop him." he muttered.

"Me too." she said quietly, suddenly feeling slightly afraid at the thought of what could have happened to her if Lee hadn't protected her that night. He sighed quietly as he gently rested his head against Chloe's, suddenly feeling a deep sense of contentment when he inhaled her familiar scent.

"I'm glad he didn't take my virginity before I was able to give it to you." she said thoughtfully. Lee slowly lifted his head, his eyes fixed on Chloe as she stared up at him.

"That's a horrible thought." he whispered, trying not to become angry at the thought of someone robbing Chloe of her choices.

"You hated me back then though." he pointed out, trying to distract himself from the images that were swirling around his head.

"I didn't hate you, I thought you hated me." she said, smiling slightly. Chloe smiled to herself when she thought back to all those months ago and how much things had changed.

"I would never have thought back then that one day we would be having a baby together." she said thoughtfully, smiling slightly as she stared at her bump, carefully placing her hand on it. Lee smiled as he watched her staring fondly at her abdomen. Chloe glanced up at him, her cheeks colouring when she noticed that he was watching her closely.

"Me neither, so much has changed." he agreed thoughtfully.

"I guess it's a good thing we decided to stop pretending to hate each other." she giggled. Lee nodded in agreement, smiling slightly.

"I'm so glad that I have you, you make me so happy." he told her gently. Chloe smiled as she leant forward and placed a soft lingering kiss on his lips. Lee shuddered as she placed her hand underneath his pyjama top and gently traced small circles on his chest. He placed his hand on her hip and pulled her close. Chloe giggled as he ran his hand down her thigh, carefully wrapping her leg around his hips. A small gasp escaped her lips when Lee buried his head in her shoulder and placed a series of soft kisses on her neck.

"I am so in love with you." she whispered in his ear, sighing deeply as she snuggled against his collarbone. Lee smiled as he continued to kiss her neck, methodically making his way upwards and along her jawline. Chloe continued tracing small circles on his chest, smiling cheekily to herself as she slowly made her way downwards. Lee shivered under her touch when she softly stroked her hand along his trouser line.

Chloe glanced down at Lee's hands as he placed them on her hips and slowly lifted her pyjama top. She glanced down at her exposed bump and sighed quietly to herself.

"What's wrong?" he asked, instantly stopping kissing her neck when he noticed the change in her body language. He slowly lifted his head from her neck and gazed at her longingly as he waited for her to respond.

"Nothing, I'm fine." she muttered, not quite able to bring herself to tell him about her insecurities since she knew that he wouldn't understand. He watched her closely as she quickly removed her shirt from his grasp and pulled it back down, quickly covering herself up, her cheeks colouring slightly as he stared at her. She sighed quietly to herself as she felt his eyes burning a hole in her head.

"Why do you keep staring at me?" she asked, avoiding eye contact with him.

"Because you're so beautiful." he breathed, not quite able to tear his eyes away from her.

"Where's all the confidence that you built up gone?" he added when she didn't respond.

"I don't know." she admitted. He sighed sadly as she squirmed against him, her cheeks colouring in embarrassment as she stared down at her bump. Even though he knew that Chloe had always been plagued by insecurities, he couldn't understand why all of the confidence that she'd built up had slowly ebbed away.

"Is this because you are pregnant?" he asked her. Chloe nodded slowly, her eyes filling with tears.

"I just feel so fat." she admitted quietly. Lee frowned in confusion, his eyes wandering to her bump.

"You only have a small bump anyway." he pointed out.

"I know, but I'm going to get bigger....and what if....." she started, trailing off when she couldn't bring herself to finish the sentence.

"What if what?" he asked quickly. Chloe sighed deeply.

"What if you don't want me anymore." she said quietly. Lee stared at her as she laid on her side, silently picking her fingernails, not quite able to bring herself to look at him. He shook his head slowly, not quite able to comprehend how someone as naturally beautiful as her, managed to doubt herself all the time. Even though her body had changed, the pregnancy suited her and in Lee's eyes she was even more attractive to him than normal, now that she was carrying his baby.

"Does this look like someone who isn't attracted to you?!" he exclaimed in disbelief, quickly throwing the duvet off himself and gesturing to his groin.

"I guess not." she said, smiling slightly when she followed his eyeline.

"There you go then." he said, smiling smugly at her. Her eyes flickered upwards as he slowly moved his face towards her, stopping when his lips were mere centimetres away from hers.

"So no more talking negatively about yourself Miss Evans." he beamed at her. Chloe burst out laughing at his cheeky expression.

"You're killing me." he chuckled, quickly wrapping his arms around her waist and pulling her against him, sighing in contentment when he felt her body pressed against his. Chloe's skin tingled when Lee buried his head into her shoulder and placed a series of soft kisses on her neck. She sighed happily and placed her hand on the back of his neck, gently stroking his hair, smiling slightly when she heard Lee sigh in contentment. She rested her head against his shoulder, softly closing her eyes, as the exhaustion finally set in.

The two of them jumped and instantly pulled apart as they heard an ear splitting scream coming from down the hallway. Chloe turned to face Lee, her eyes wide with panic when she suddenly remembered that Michelle was sleeping in one of the spare rooms.

"It's okay, she probably just had a bad dream." Lee reassured Chloe as she quickly sat up in bed.

"I should go and check on her." she said thoughtfully, her heart breaking a little at the thought of everything that Michelle had been through. Chloe knew better than anyone what it was like to be plagued with nightmares and afraid to fall asleep. Lee watched her closely as she quickly climbed out of bed.

"Maybe I should sleep in her bed with her, so that she's not alone." she pointed out.

"Chloe...." Lee argued, trailing off when Chloe turned to face him and raised her eyebrow.

"What's wrong?" she asked, frowning in confusion when she noticed his concerned expression.

"Is it such a good idea for you to be alone with her all night?" he asked worriedly, not quite able to bring himself to fully trust Michelle after everything that she had done to them.

"I don't want too, but I feel bad for her, I know what it's like to have nightmares and the only time I felt safe was when you were with me." she explained, sighing quietly to herself at the thought of not being able to spend the night curled up in his arms. The two of them locked eyes, clearly feeling the same way.

"Why don't we ask her if she wants her mattress in here with us?" he suggested, trying to find a compromise that would ease Chloe's guilt. Chloe nodded slowly, smiling at him as he quickly climbed out of bed.

"You go back to bed, I'll sort it." he told her quickly. Chloe nodded slowly, yawning to herself as she quickly climbed back into bed. As soon as Lee left the room she closed her eyes, sighing quietly to herself as she waited for him to return. Her eyes snapped open, her gaze wandering to her bump when she felt the familiar fluttering sensation. She smiled to herself, softly stroking her abdomen with her fingertips.

"You're definitely getting more active little baby." she said softly, smiling to herself as she felt another wave of love wash over her. Despite the fact that she was slightly apprehensive about becoming a mother, she felt an overwhelming sense of love for her unborn baby. Chloe glanced at the doorway as she heard footsteps approaching. She glanced down at her bump, quickly climbing out of bed and pulling on Lee's hoodie. She sighed in contentment as she sat on the bed, quickly pulling down the sleeves on the hoodie, feeling a deep sense of relaxation, like she always did when she was wearing Lee's hoodie. Chloe snuggled down under the covers, glancing up as Lee walked into the room, carrying a mattress, closely followed by Michelle.

"Thank you." Michelle said quietly when Lee quickly placed the mattress on the floor. Michelle quickly sat on her bed and began to arrange the blankets, suddenly feeling slightly self-conscious that she was sleeping in the same room as Chloe and Lee, particularly when she knew how they felt about her.

"Are you sure this is okay Chloe?" Michelle asked awkwardly, when the two of them locked eyes.

"Yes it's fine." Chloe said quietly, smiling reassuringly as she turned on her side to face Michelle. Chloe glanced behind herself as she felt Lee climb into bed beside her and gently wrap his arms around her waist, resting his chin on her shoulder. She glanced down at his hands as they rested in place on her bump, his fingers stroking it softly. A small gasp escaped her lips when she felt the baby move again.

"Are you okay?" he asked worriedly, glancing at Chloe's hands as she placed them on top of his and quickly linked their fingers.

"I'm fine, it just feels really strange when the baby moves." she said quietly, her voice breaking slightly with emotion. She still couldn't quite comprehend how it was possible to love something so much, even though she hadn't met their baby yet. Chloe turned to face Lee, smiling at him when she noticed his eyes filling with tears.

"You need to get some sleep." he told her, smiling down at her as she rested her head against his collarbone and snuggled against him. Chloe sighed in contentment and closed her eyes when she felt Lee softly stroking her hair.

"Night guys." Michelle called as she quickly switched off the bedroom lamp.

Chapter Twenty Four

"Morning beautiful." Lee smiled at Chloe as she padded into the kitchen. He couldn't help but smile at her when he noticed that she was still wearing her pyjamas. His eyes darted to her bump, smiling slightly to himself when he saw how adorable she looked. Chloe followed his eyeline, her cheeks colouring when she realised what he was staring at.

"I think I need to get some bigger pyjamas." she said quietly, her cheeks colouring when she suddenly realised how much her pyjama top clung to her bump.

"You could always just sleep in my hoodie when your pyjamas don't fit you anymore?" he suggested.

"Speaking of your hoodie, I'll go and put it on now." she said quietly.

"You don't have to hide Chlo." he said softly, his heart sinking a little when he realised how self-conscious she was becoming.

"I guess I know that." she muttered.

"Being pregnant isn't something to be embarrassed about." he told her.

"I'm not embarrassed about being pregnant, I just don't like the way that I look." she replied, slowly folding her arms across her chest as she leant her back against the kitchen counter.

"You know what I'm like though, I'm always scared that I'm going to lose you." she added, sighing quietly to herself as she carefully perched on the counter. Lee sighed deeply, his heart breaking a little as he stared at her sad expression. He quickly crossed the room, his breath catching in his throat as he stared down at her longingly. He placed his hands on her thighs, and gently wrapped them around his waist, smiling slightly when she finally gazed up at him.

"You know how much I love you, do you really think that I'm going to go anywhere?" he said softly.

"And you know how much I want to be a father." he added when she didn't respond.

"I would never stop you from seeing the baby if we broke up anyway." she told him, her heart breaking a little at the thought of losing him.

"Chlo...stop." he whispered.

"I wouldn't though, I know how much you love the baby already." she said, smiling proudly at him.

"A lot." he said quietly.

"I know." she smiled.

"But that doesn't even come close to how much I love you.....I lived without you before and I hated every minute of it." he explained.

"I know, me too." she said quietly, as she gently wrapped her arms around his neck.

"I know that I'm being silly, but I can't help it." she added.

"I just know how much you liked my body and how it won't ever be the same again." she continued, sighing sadly to herself. She couldn't help but feel a twinge of sadness when she remembered that she'd only just started to feel confident in her own skin and now all the confidence that she'd built up had slowly faded. Lee sighed sadly to himself as he softly stroked Chloe's hair, wishing in his heart that he knew what to say to make her believe him.

"I still love your body Chlo." he whispered in her ear. Her skin tingled under his touch when she felt him place his hands underneath her shirt and slowly stroke the base of her spine. Chloe stared up at him, her legs feeling weak as she slowly became lost in his deep blue eyes. She couldn't help but notice how handsome he was when he was wearing his pyjamas and his hair was messy.

Her eyes darted to his lips as he smiled at her and placed a tender kiss on her lips, chuckling to himself when he felt her trembling under his touch.

"I didn't think it was possible to love someone as much as I love you." she admitted, gently resting her forehead against his.

"Me neither." he agreed. Chloe smiled, before quickly kissing him softly. She jumped and pulled away from him as Michelle walked into the room. Lee sighed quietly and turned to face Michelle, who was glancing between the two of them awkwardly.

"Sorry, did I interrupt something?" Michelle asked nervously as she hovered in the doorway.

"No not at all." Chloe replied, quickly climbing off the kitchen counter.

"I was just telling Chloe how much I love her." Lee said, making a point to remind Michelle that no matter what she did, she wouldn't be able to come between them. Michelle smiled at him, trying to make the effort, even though she realised that she would never be able to make up for what she did to them.

"What do you want for breakfast Chlo?" Lee asked her.

"I can make something in a bit." Chloe told him.

"It's fine, you go and chill in the living room, I'll bring something in for you." he told her. Chloe nodded slowly, quickly placing a soft kiss on his lips before walking into the living room. Lee remained silent as he rummaged in the fridge and quickly pulled out a selection of fruit.

"You can help yourself to anything from the fridge." Lee told Michelle when he felt her watching him chopping the fruit.

"Thank you." Michelle said awkwardly, her stomach churning with tension. Despite the fact that Lee was making the effort to be kind to her, Michelle could clearly sense that he was still furious with her underneath the facade that he was putting on. Michelle silently poured some cereal into a bowl, her hands shaking with tension. She smiled to herself when she walked over to the fridge and noticed an ultrasound image of a baby held in place by a magnet.

"Is that your baby?" she smiled, as she quickly pulled the milk out of the fridge.

"Yep." he replied shortly, when he realised what she was looking at.

"Wow, the two of you must be so excited!" she exclaimed. Lee nodded slowly, not entirely sure if she was being genuine or not.

"How far gone is Chloe?" she asked.

"Almost seventeen weeks." he said shortly.

"Aww, congratulations." she smiled.

"I don't really want to talk about our baby with you." he said dismissively, his stomach churning with anger when he remembered everything that Chloe went through at the hands of the press, all as a result of Michelle's petty jealousy. He knew that he would never be able to forgive her for hurting the person that meant the world to him, he knew that he was nothing without Chloe and thanks to Michelle's actions, he'd almost lost her for good.

Before Michelle had a chance to respond, Lee picked up the bowl of fruit and walked into the living room, smiling when he noticed Chloe sitting cross legged on the sofa.

"Thank you." Chloe smiled when Lee handed her the bowl of fruit and sat beside her. His eyes darted upwards when he saw Michelle walk into the room and perch nervously on the sofa opposite them.

"Are you warm enough, or do you want me to light the fire?" Lee offered, turning his attention back to Chloe.

"I'm okay at the moment." Chloe smiled at him, her heart pounding against her chest when she was reminded once again of how sweet and caring he was towards her.

"How are you doing Michelle?" Chloe asked, reluctantly tearing her eyes away from Lee.

"I'm fine." Michelle said, smiling falsely, trying to put on a brave face to hide how upset she really was about everything that had happened.

"Did you manage to get some sleep?" Chloe asked, not entirely convinced that Michelle was doing okay. She couldn't help but feel sorry for her when she saw the swelling on her lip and the dark circles under her eyes from a lack of sleep.

"I got some." Michelle said quietly.

"Thanks for letting me sleep in your room last night." she added awkwardly.

"You're welcome, I know what it's like to have bad nightmares after a traumatic experience." Chloe said, smiling reassuringly at her. She glanced at Lee for a moment as he wrapped his arm around her shoulders, gently stroking the bare skin on her arm.

"I noticed the picture of your baby on the fridge." Michelle said quickly, trying to change the subject, before she was no longer able to fight the tears that she was hiding. Chloe nodded slowly, glancing at Lee when she felt his body language stiffen.

"I'm so happy for both of you." Michelle smiled.

"Thank you." Chloe smiled.

"Are you going to find out what you are having?" Michelle asked excitedly. Chloe opened her mouth to respond, quickly closing it again when Lee beat her too it.

"That's enough!" Lee warned. He glanced at Chloe as she quickly turned to face him, slightly shocked by his outburst.

"The baby topic of off the table." he told Michelle sternly.

"I didn't mean to offend you, I am genuinely happy for you." Michelle tried nervously, glancing between him and Chloe, slightly confused as to what she had done wrong.

"No you're not, you just want information." Lee said suspiciously, not quite able to bring himself to believe that her questions were innocent.

"And I'm telling you now.....if you ever.....ever do what you did to Chloe again, I will hire the best lawyers money can buy and I will sue you for breach of privacy." Lee warned, his tone slightly menacing.

"And I will make up random shit about you and plaster it all over the papers." he added.

"Lee stop." Chloe said quietly, quickly placing her hand on his thigh, trying to calm him down.

"I don't want her hurting you again, I don't think she realises how bad things were for us." he said quickly.

"Why don't you go and make me a cup of tea?" Chloe said quickly, trying to distract Lee before things escalated. She knew how protective he was of her and their baby and she couldn't help but feel slightly nervous that he would lose his temper at the thought of Michelle doing anything to hurt either of them. Lee nodded slowly, sighing deeply to himself as he tried to hold his tongue. Despite the fact that he sympathised with Michelle's situation and wouldn't wish what had happened to her on anyone, that didn't mean that he trusted her and he knew in his heart that he would never forgive her. Chloe watched him closely as he sat on the sofa, finally falling silent. He placed his hand on her cheek and kissed her softly. Chloe sighed in disappointment when he eventually moved away from her and walked into the kitchen.

"Sorry about that." Chloe said as soon as Lee left the room. Even though she knew that Lee hadn't really done anything wrong, she knew how cutting his words could be sometimes.

"It's okay, he doesn't trust me. I don't blame him." Michelle sighed, feeling another wave of guilt when she thought about what she'd done to them.

"He's just protective." Chloe said quietly, not quite able to bring herself to tell her that she didn't trust her either.

"You're so lucky." Michelle said thoughtfully.

"I know." Chloe agreed, still not quite able to understand how someone like Lee had fallen in love with her.

"He would literally do anything for you." Michelle said quietly. Chloe nodded slowly.

"Whereas Mark doesn't seem to give a shit about me!" she added angrily.

"What are you talking about?" Chloe frowned, glancing up as Lee walked into the room and silently handed her a cup of tea. She smiled when he curled up on the sofa beside her, gently resting his head on her lap and staring up at her. Chloe placed her bowl of fruit on the arm rest of the sofa and softly stroked his hair, smiling to herself when Lee sighed deeply, finally feeling relaxed. Lee snuggled his head against her bump and closed his eyes.

"Well obviously I told him what happened and he asked if I wanted him to come back from Norway early and I said that I was fine because he didn't seem like he cared anyway." Michelle explained, sighing sadly to herself when she watched the way that Lee and Chloe were with each other.

"I really wish I had someone that treats me the way Lee takes care of you." Michelle sighed sadly. Lee raised his eyebrow at Chloe, smiling slightly as Chloe bit her lip, trying to stop herself from bursting out laughing at his cheeky expression.

"Maybe he didn't come home because you said that you were doing okay?" Chloe pointed out, not entirely sure what to say to make Michelle feel better.

"That's not the point though, I want a guy that cares about me enough to cut a trip short when I've been assaulted!" Michelle said angrily.

"I mean Lee came home early from Germany, just because he missed you." she added.

"If Chloe was assaulted, nothing she said or did would stop me from getting the next available flight." Lee said quickly, slowly turning over so that he was facing Michelle, his head still in place on Chloe's lap.

"I know, and that's partly why I was so jealous of the two of you, because I want what you have." Michelle told them. The three of them jumped as Michelle's phone rang. She sighed quietly to herself and pulled it out of her pocket, her heart sinking a little when she realised that Mark was calling her. She angrily flung her phone onto the coffee table, glancing up at Chloe as she saw her eyes flicker to the display.

"Aren't you going to answer him?" Chloe asked.

"What for, he doesn't care anyway." Michelle muttered angrily.

"Just answer him, it's a bit harsh otherwise." Chloe tried.

"You'll make him worry." she added. Michelle sighed and quickly picked up her phone before walking out of the room.

Chapter Twenty Five

Lee sighed in relief as soon as Michelle left the room. He glanced up at Chloe smiling slightly when she continued softly stroking his hair.

"I'm finding it really difficult being around her." he admitted.

"I know, but we have to do the right thing." she said quietly, not entirely sure how comfortable she was at the thought of having Michelle around, but knowing in her heart that she needed to be there for her in her time of need.

"I get it, but at the same time, she is not our problem." he pointed out, sighing deeply. Chloe nodded slowly, sighing quietly to herself when she realised that Lee would never forgive Michelle for what she had done to them, even though she couldn't blame him, she couldn't help but feel uneasy with the tense atmosphere in the house. Chloe's heart fluttered as Lee turned over to face her and planted a soft kiss on her bump, smiling at her when their eyes locked. She watched him closely as he reached out and gently took her wrist in his grasp, placing a tender kiss on her hand as he stroked small circles on her wrist.

"I still can't quite believe that Shayne did that to her." she said thoughtfully, her stomach churning with guilt once again.

"I feel partly responsible." she added.

"Why?" he frowned.

"Because I brought Shayne into her life, she wouldn't have even met him if it wasn't for me." she said quietly, sighing deeply to herself.

"Not really, she saw him at the masquerade ball didn't she, so they potentially would have met anyway." he reminded her.

"I guess so." she muttered.

"I can't even imagine what she must be going through." she said thoughtfully.

"I think she's putting on a brave face." she continued.

"Yeah probably." he said quietly, feeling slightly sorry for Michelle at what she had been through. Lee frowned at Chloe when he noticed her watching him closely, raising her eyebrow at him.

"What?" he asked, frowning in confusion.

"You need to be kind to her, I know you don't like her, but she's been through a terrible ordeal." she explained. Lee sighed quietly, not entirely sure how to respond. Despite the fact that he knew Chloe was right, he wasn't sure how to suppress the deep anger that he felt towards Michelle.

"Imagine if it was me." she prompted.

"I don't even want to think about that." he replied quickly, swallowing the dry lump that was rising in his throat.

"I didn't mean it like that, I meant that you would want someone to take care of me wouldn't you?" she pointed out.

"No, I would take care of you myself." he said shortly. Chloe raised her eyebrow at him, sighing in frustration.

"I know what you're saying, I get it." he said quietly.

"Mark is a bit of a dick isn't he." he added thoughtfully. Chloe nodded slowly, feeling really sorry for Michelle as she thought about how she would feel if Lee didn't seem to care about her. The two of them fell silent as Michelle walked into the room. They watched as she perched on the sofa, quickly wiping away the tears that were steadily rolling down her cheeks.

"Is Mark coming home?" Chloe asked hopefully. Michelle sniffed and shook her head sadly.

"Don't be daft, he doesn't give a damn." she added, angrily flinging her phone onto the coffee table.

"Why don't you ask him to come back to support you?" Chloe suggested.

"I shouldn't have to ask though should I, he should want to be here for me." Michelle argued, biting her lip to prevent herself from bursting into tears. Chloe nodded slowly, not entirely sure what to say to make Michelle feel better. She glanced at Lee as he slowly sat up and crossed his legs on the sofa. She smiled at him as he gently placed his hands on her hips and pulled her onto his lap. Chloe sighed in contentment when Lee brushed her hair to one side and rested his chin on her shoulder.

"I hope you know how lucky you are." Michelle said quietly as she stared at the two of them dreamily. Chloe nodded slowly, glancing at Lee when she felt him kissing her neck softly.

"I am so sorry that I ever tried to come between both of you." Michelle said, her stomach churning with guilt when she suddenly realised how happy and in love the two of them were. Lee sighed as he placed his chin on Chloe's shoulder, peering at Michelle suspiciously.

"I really am sorry, I'll never do anything like that again." Michelle tried, her cheeks colouring as she locked eyes with Lee.

"I can't ever forgive you for what you did to us." Lee admitted, feeling slightly guilty when he noticed Michelle's face drop. Even though he didn't want to hurt her, particularly after everything that she'd been through, he knew that he had to be completely honest with her.

"Maybe if I explain why I did what I did?" Michelle tried, desperately wishing that she could turn the clock back.

"You don't have to explain." Chloe said quickly, not entirely sure that it was such a good idea for Michelle to be talking about everything that had happened, when she was still coming to terms with what Shayne had done to her.

"We know why you did it anyway, because you are jealous." Lee said quietly. His eyes flickered to Chloe as she fidgeted on his lap, wincing slightly and placing her hand against her abdomen.

"Are you alright Chlo?" Lee asked quickly, his brow furrowing in concern.

"It's just cramps." she muttered, gently massaging her abdomen. He smiled sympathetically at her and softly stroked her hair, trying to distract her from the pain that she was feeling.

"I take it you don't want me to explain then?" Michelle said quietly, staring to feel slightly frustrated with the fact that they didn't seem willing to give her a chance.

"If you want to explain then you can, it's your choice." Chloe told her, resting the back of her head against Lee.

"I basically let my insecurities get the better of me, I've always been insecure about people not wanting me and Mark always has a way of making me feel like he is ashamed to be seen with me." Michelle explained.

"I think that's just the way that Mark is, he's not ready to commit." Lee pointed out, his eyes still fixed on Chloe as she silently massaged her bump, wincing slightly.

"I know, but it was horrible when I saw how Lee was so into you and how he would do anything for you, and it's not fair, because I wanted that too." Michelle explained, her cheeks colouring slightly when Lee glanced at her and shook his head slowly, still not quite able to comprehend how her insecurities had turned her so bitter. Chloe was plagued with insecurities too, but he knew that she would never punish anybody else in order to help herself feel better.

"And I started to resent you because you are so beautiful and it drove me crazy that wherever we went guys were so into you all of the time." Michelle continued, sighing quietly to herself when she glanced at Chloe and began to wish that she looked like her yet again.

"I don't think that's true." Chloe argued.

"It is though, guys are besotted with you." Michelle insisted.

"Even if that is true, you didn't have to try and destroy me." Chloe said quietly.

"And you knew how much I need him." Chloe added, glancing at Lee who was still resting his chin on her shoulder. Chloe gently took Lee's hand and placed it on her lap, softly playing with his fingers.

"I didn't Chloe, I swear. I wasn't thinking clearly. I never meant for everything to get so out of hand." Michelle said sadly.

"I wish I could take back what I did." she added. Chloe nodded slowly, not quite able to bring herself to look Michelle in the eye.

"There will never be any going back, I almost lost her because of you." Lee told her firmly, glancing at Chloe when she squeezed his hand reassuringly.

"I'm getting all the stick for all of this, but I wasn't the only one!" Michelle snapped bitterly, her temper finally starting to fray.

"What's that supposed to mean?" Lee asked quickly, his eyes darting towards her.

"Nothing just forget it." Michelle said shortly.

"No, I want to know what you meant." Lee insisted.

"It was Shayne's idea....he realised how much I hated you, and suggested that we work together to bring you down." Michelle explained quickly, glancing at Lee nervously, not entirely sure how he was going to react.

"Are you shitting me?!" Lee exclaimed, his stomach churning angrily at the mention of Shayne. Michelle shook her head slowly.

"You set the whole thing up together?" Chloe asked quietly, not quite able to process what Michelle had just said.

"Yes.....I'm so sorry." Michelle said hesitantly, her heart breaking a little when she noticed that Chloe's eyes had filled with tears.

"If it makes you feel any better he came to see me the other day to ask me to gather more information on you both and I said no." she added.

"What did you tell him?!" Lee asked, an edge of anger present in his voice.

"Nothing!" Michelle exclaimed.

"I meant it when I apologised to you both at Kirstie's, I won't do anything to hurt either of you again." she continued.

"And when I told him that he didn't take it very well." she explained.

"Wait, is that why he attacked you?!" Chloe cried, finally joining the dots in her head. Michelle nodded slowly.

"And he was high on drugs I think." Michelle sighed. Chloe's heart plummeted, her stomach churning with guilt when she suddenly realised that Michelle had been assaulted because she'd refused to do anything else to hurt them. Her heart broke further when she saw tears rolling down Michelle's cheeks. Lee glanced at Chloe as she slowly climbed off his lap and knelt on the floor in front of Michelle, gently wrapping her arms around Michelle and pulling her into a hug. Michelle clung to Chloe tightly as she began to sob, finally letting out all the emotions that she'd been keeping in check. Chloe held her tightly, trying to provide her with some comfort, but not entirely sure what to say or do to help her feel better.

"I'm so sorry." Chloe whispered, sniffing quietly as she tried to fight the tears that were filling her eyes.

"I'm fine." Michelle whispered, slowly releasing Chloe and sitting back.

"I just need some fresh air....I need to go and get some clothes anyway." she added, trying to put on a brave face and fight how she was feeling. She sighed quietly to herself, suddenly feeling slightly afraid at the thought of returning to her house alone, when the last time that she was there she'd been assaulted by Shayne. Chloe turned to face Lee, raising her eyebrow at him, when she realised how Michelle was feeling. Lee frowned at her for a moment before sighing deeply when he realised what she was suggesting.

"I can take you if you want?" he offered reluctantly. Michelle nodded slowly.

"We'll go in a bit." Lee told her. Chloe smiled at him, her heart surging with pride.

"Are you sure you're okay?" Chloe asked Michelle, turning her attention back to her.

"I'm fine, I just need some air, can I go and sit in the pool room for a bit?" Michelle asked Lee. He nodded slowly, watching her closely as she quickly left the room.

"This is so awful." Chloe said quietly, resting her elbow on the sofa and running her hand through her hair in frustration.

"I have no idea how to help her." she added thoughtfully.

"Why are you getting upset?" he asked her softly, when he noticed that her eyes were filling with tears.

"Because it's a horrendous situation, he basically raped her because she refused to hurt us again." she said quietly.

"That's so messed up." she added quickly.

"He's a vile human being." he agreed. Chloe nodded slowly as she quickly stood up.

"Maybe you should go and get Michelle's clothes on your own, she's probably not ready to go back to where it happened yet?" she suggested. Lee nodded slowly, feeling slightly nervous about the idea of leaving Chloe alone with Michelle.

"I think she's proven that she's not going to stab us in the back again." she said, when she noticed Lee's expression.

"I should probably get dressed." he said.

"Me too." she agreed.

"You don't have to, you could have a pyjama day." he smiled at her, following her as she climbed the stairs. Chloe smiled slightly as she walked into the bedroom, her heart sinking when she noticed Michelle's mattress in the corner. Every time that she was reminded of what had happened to Michelle, her stomach churned with guilt. Chloe perched on the end of the bed, glancing at Lee when he sat beside her. As soon as he was beside her, Chloe wrapped her arms around his waist and snuggled against him, smiling to herself when he placed his arm around her shoulders. She closed her eyes, sighing in contentment.

"How are your cramps?" he asked her, placing his other hand on her bump.

"They are okay now." she muttered, her skin tingling under his touch as he stroked the bare skin on her arm, his other hand tracing small circles on her abdomen.

"I love you." she whispered, slowly opening her eyes and glancing up at him. Lee smiled at her and rested his forehead against hers, staring down at her lovingly. She placed a soft kiss on his lips, before closing her eyes and snuggling her face against his, feeling comforted by the feel of his warm breath on her face.

"You can sleep if you want too, I can go to Michelle's later on." he told her, when he realised that she was fighting the urge to fall asleep in his arms. Chloe nodded slowly, relaxing into his arms and finally falling asleep.

Chapter Twenty Six

Chloe frowned as her eyelids slowly fluttered open. She glanced up at Lee, her cheeks colouring when she noticed him gazing down at her.

"Sorry." she said quietly.

"Sorry for what?" he asked, frowning at her.

"I didn't mean to fall asleep on you." she said, smiling slightly.

"It's fine Chlo." he said quietly, placing a soft kiss on her forehead. Chloe smiled as he wrapped his arms around her shoulders and rocked her playfully. She giggled as Lee quickly pulled her onto his lap. He laughed as he wobbled and fell backwards on the bed, glancing up at Chloe as she fell forward on top of him. She gasped, quickly placing her knees on the bed, either side of him, trying to steady her balance. She sat up slightly, her cheeks colouring as Lee lay on the bed, staring up at her.

"Sorry, I didn't crush you did I?" she asked quietly.

"Of course not, you're really light." he chuckled, placing his hands on her hips.

"Why do you keep apologising all the time?" he added. Chloe shrugged, glancing down at his hands that were still in place on her hips. Lee sat up slightly, watching Chloe closely as he rested his elbows on the bed. She leant forward slightly, slowly wrapping her arms around his neck and sighing deeply. He slowly placed his hands under the material of her pyjama top and gently stroked her spine, gazing down at her longingly as she snuggled against him. Chloe glanced up at him, her cheeks colouring slightly when they locked eyes. Lee smiled at her, before kissing her deeply.

"I have to shower and get dressed." she said quickly as soon as they pulled apart. Lee watched her as she quickly climbed off him and stood up, rummaging in the cupboard for her clothes. He frowned to himself when she avoided his gaze and walked into the bathroom.

Chloe sighed to herself as she stood in the shower and allowed the warm water to flow down her back. She placed her hand against the wall of the shower and hung her head angrily. The tears that were flowing down her cheeks, quickly being washed away by the water. She couldn't help but feel a deep sense of frustration with herself, she'd thought the days were gone, where she was plagued by insecurities, but the thought of the man that she loved seeing her naked body, filled her with a deep sense of dread.

She knew that Lee could have any woman that he wanted and it made her feel sick to her stomach, the thought of him being repulsed by her fat body.

Chloe jumped and whirled around, her heart pounding against her chest when Lee opened the door to the shower cubicle and climbed in beside her. She glanced down at herself, her cheeks colouring deeply when she suddenly felt exposed and vulnerable. She squirmed into the corner of the cubicle, wishing that she had some way of covering her naked frame. She glanced down at Lee's hands as he placed them on her ribs and gently pulled her towards himself. Chloe squirmed away from his grasp, avoiding his gaze as she slunk into the corner.

"Don't you want me anymore Chlo?" he asked sadly, slightly confused as to what was going on with her.

"Of course I do." she said quietly, glancing up at him and smiling slightly when she saw the water from the shower, slowly dripping off his hair.

"You look really hot when you're wet." she added, not quite able to tear her eyes away from him.

"So do you." he smiled, trying to resist the urge to stare at her body.

"I remember when I first started working with you and the boys and you were filming the video for I Can, and I remember thinking how handsome you looked when you were singing under the rain machine." she explained, completely disregarding what he'd said to her.

"Well that was naughty, you were still dating Andy back then." he chuckled. Chloe nodded slowly, giggling quietly to herself. Lee stared down at Chloe as he moved closer to her. He gazed down at her longingly, his body mere inches from hers. She glanced up at him for a moment, her cheeks colouring as she quickly returned to gazing at the ground.

"You need to stop being so self-conscious Chlo." he told her as he gently placed his hands on her cheeks and slowly tilted her face so that she was looking at him. She nodded slowly, swallowing the lump that was rising in her throat.

"Don't look at me then." she said quietly, gently placing her hand on his bare chest and smiling slightly when she felt his heart pounding under her touch. She glanced up at him when he sighed deeply. Her stomach churned with guilt when she realised that he didn't understand the way that she was feeling.

"You don't get it do you?" she said sadly.

"No, because you are so beautiful." he told her.

"And just because you have a small bump, doesn't mean that you aren't beautiful anymore." he added, before slowly burying his head in her shoulder and placing a series of soft kisses on her neck, no longer able to fight the desire that he was feeling for her. Chloe sighed quietly, not quite able to bring herself to argue with him. She knew that no matter what she said, he wouldn't understand how it felt to be embarrassed to undress in front of the person that she loved. She slowly wrapped her arms around his neck, her skin tingling as he kissed his way along her jawline, hesitating for a moment when he reached her lips. Her eyes flickered to his when he gazed at her for a brief moment, before kissing her lips softly. He placed his hands on her waist as he quickly deepened the kiss. She smiled at him, slightly breathless when Lee eventually pulled away from her and slowly kissed his way down her neck and onto her sternum. She placed her hand on the back of his neck, gripping his hair tightly in her grasp.

"At least I know that I still turn you on." she smiled slightly when she glanced down at him.

"For now anyway." she added quietly.

"I don't think that's ever going to be an issue." he whispered, gently resting his forehead against her chest. Chloe smiled slightly as she jumped towards him, wrapping her legs around his hips.

"No not yet." he said firmly, quickly placing his hands on her hips.

"I knew you didn't want me." she said quietly, her cheeks colouring as she slowly unwrapped her legs from his hips. She slowly shook her head as she backed away from him, gasping slightly when her back hit against the wall.

"I want to help you love your body." he told her.

"Good luck with that." she sighed. Lee raised his eyebrow at her as he turned to the shelf and quickly picked up a bottle of shower gel and squeezed some into his hand, smiling cheekily at Chloe as she watched him closely. Her skin tingled under his touch when he placed his hands on her shoulders and methodically trailed them down her arms, stopping for a moment when he reached her hips, before slowly making his way upwards.

"You do realise that I can wash myself." she smiled, gasping when he reached her breasts and began to gently massage them. Lee remained silent, quickly placing his hands on her hips and slowly turning her away from him. She glanced down at his hands when he gently pulled her body against his, sighing to herself when she felt his soft heartbeat against her back. He placed his hands on her lower back and slowly began to massage her sore muscles with his thumbs. She glanced at him when he rested his chin on her shoulder, smiling to herself as she rested her cheek against his. She glanced down at his hands as he placed them on her bump, slowly tracing small circles with his fingertips. Chloe trembled against him when he returned to kissing her neck, smiling to himself when he slowly ran his hand up the inside of Chloe's thigh and she squirmed against him. Lee's hand stopped just before he reached her sensitive area and slowly trailed his way back down.

"Stop teasing me." Chloe pleaded, her voice catching slightly when his hand slowly made its way upwards once again.

"As you wish." he whispered in her ear, smiling to himself when Chloe shivered involuntarily. Before Chloe could react, he placed his hands on her waist and turned her to face him. She giggled as he carefully picked her up and wrapped her legs around his hips. Chloe smiled as he carefully placed her back against the wall of the shower. She wrapped her arms around his neck and buried her head in his shoulder, snuggling against him, still not quite able to believe that it was possible to love someone as much as she loved him.

Lee smiled at Chloe as she quickly pulled on his hoodie over the top of her clothes and tied her hair up in a messy bun. She slowly rubbed her eyes, fighting to keep them open as she suddenly felt exhausted. She carefully placed one foot in front of the other as she slowly walked downstairs, glancing behind herself at Lee as he followed closely behind her.

"Woah!" Lee exclaimed, quickly reaching out and grasping Chloe's arm to steady her as she staggered on the stairs.

"Are you okay?" he asked quickly, his hand still in place on her arm. Chloe nodded slowly, glancing at him as she felt him watching her closely.

"Are you sure?" he asked, feeling slightly nervous that if he let go of her arm, she would stagger again and fall down the stairs.

"I'm just really tired." she told him. He watched her closely as she leant against him, fighting to keep her eyes open. She smiled when she felt Lee place his arm under her legs and carefully pick her up, staring down at her when she wrapped her arms around his neck.

"I think I can walk you know." she said quietly as Lee carefully carried her downstairs.

"I don't want you falling over." he told her.

"You're worried about the baby." she said quietly, closing her eyes slowly as she desperately tried to fight the intense fatigue that she was feeling.

"I don't want anything to happen to either of you." he said softly as he walked into the living room and carefully placed her onto the sofa.

"I love you both so much." he whispered as he squatted down in front of her, smiling slightly when she curled up on the sofa. Chloe smiled at him as he softly stroked her hair. She slowly stroked his cheek with her fingertips, her skin tingling when he placed a soft kiss on her wrist. Their eyes flickered to the doorway as Michelle walked into the room, glancing between the two of them awkwardly.

"Are we going then?" Michelle asked Lee, swallowing the nervous lump that was rising in her throat at the thought of returning home. Despite the fact that she knew how much Lee hated Shayne, she couldn't help but wonder if he cared enough to protect her from him, if he did happen to turn up at Michelle's house.

"It's okay, I'll go." Lee told her.

"Are you sure?" Michelle frowned. Lee nodded slowly, his eyes still fixed on Chloe.

"Do you want a blanket?" Lee asked, when he noticed Chloe pulling down the sleeves on his hoodie.

"I'm okay, your hoodie is cosy." she smiled, slowly leaning forward and resting her cheek against his, sighing in contentment as she inhaled his familiar scent.

"I love you so much." she whispered in his ear.

"I love you too." he whispered back. Chloe smiled slightly, her heart fluttering against her chest, like it always did when he told her that he loved her.

"My heart will belong to you for the rest of my life." she said quietly, her voice breaking slightly. His breath caught in his throat as he stared at the love of his life, still not quite able to believe how amazing she was. When he'd finally realised that he was in love with her, he hadn't realised just how much his love for her would grow over time. To the point where he knew that he couldn't function without her. He sighed sadly to himself when he noticed that Chloe's eyes were slowly filling with tears.

"These pregnancy hormones are really putting you through the ringer aren't they." he said sadly. She nodded slowly, staring at him as he softly wiped away her tears with his thumb.

"Do you want me to stay?" he offered, still not entirely comfortable about leaving Chloe alone with Michelle.

"No, it's okay." Chloe said quietly. Lee nodded slowly, his eyes wandering to her bump as he gently stroked it with his fingertips.

"Don't worry, we'll be fine." Chloe told him, following his eyeline and smiling proudly at him.

"What?" he chuckled, when he noticed her watching him closely.

"I'm so glad you're my baby's Daddy." Chloe said softly, smiling at him. He stared at her silently, suddenly feeling overcome with emotion at her words. He bit his lip, desperately trying to fight his tears, the last thing he wanted to do was to let down his guard in front of Michelle.

"I'll keep an eye on her for you." Michelle piped up from behind them. Lee nodded slowly, appreciating that she was trying to be kind, but not feeling any reassurance.

"Nathan is coming over later, to help me finish painting the nursery." Lee told them, reluctantly standing up, his heart breaking a little when Chloe stared up at him.

"Once we've finished the painting, we can go out somewhere nice for a treat, just the two of us." Lee told Chloe, smiling at her when she nodded slowly.

"Nath can stay with you until we get back, so that you don't have to be alone." Lee said, turning his attention to Michelle. Michelle nodded and silently handed him her front door key.

"Do you know where I live?" Michelle asked.

"You live with Mark don't you?" he asked.

"Nope." Michelle said shortly.

"I could text you my address." she added.

"Oh wait, I don't have your number!" she quickly added, staring at him and raising her eyebrow expectantly.

"No you don't." Lee said shortly, having no intention of giving her his number, in case she tried to find a way to come between him and Chloe again. Michelle rolled her eyes slightly, before picking up the notebook and pen from the table. She quickly wrote down her address and tore the page out of the notebook.

"Be careful, I've arranged for the paparazzi to be waiting outside the house for you." Michelle said sarcastically as she handed Lee the sheet of paper, her temper finally fraying that him and Chloe continued to doubt her motives.

"That's not funny." Lee snapped. Michelle rolled her eyes and shrugged at him.

"Be careful, I can easily kick you out." he warned her.

"I'll see you later Chlo." he added, quickly walking away before he could talk himself out of it. Chloe sighed quietly when she heard the front door close.

"I don't get how he wants me to keep an eye on you but yet I can't phone him if anything happens anyway!" Michelle exclaimed, angrily throwing herself down on the sofa.

"You don't need to keep an eye on me anyway, I'm fine....I'm just tired." Chloe argued.

"He won't be long anyway." Chloe added.

"He'll probably rush back because he doesn't trust me with you." Michelle said bitterly.

"Can you blame him though?" Chloe frowned.

"How many times do I have to apologise?!" Michelle exclaimed.

"Just because you've apologised, doesn't mean that we will suddenly trust you again." Chloe pointed out.

"He's always been really protective of you though hasn't he." Michelle said quickly.

"What's that supposed to mean?!" Chloe rounded on her, slowly sitting up on the sofa. Michelle opened her mouth to speak, quickly closing it again when Chloe cut her off.

"He's just a very loving and protective person and he would do anything for me." Chloe said quickly.

"And the baby." she added.

"I know, I can see that. He's very attentive with you." Michelle said quietly, sighing to herself when she felt another twinge of jealousy. Whenever she saw how Lee treated Chloe and how sweet and tender he was with her, she couldn't help but wish that she had someone like him in her life to cherish her.

"That's because he cares.....a lot." Chloe said, smiling fondly when she realised once again how lucky she was to have Lee in her life. Chloe placed her hand on her abdomen, smiling slightly as she stroked small circles on her bump with her fingernails.

"I wonder if Nathan and Lee are going to rehearse while he's here." Chloe said thoughtfully.

"Do they have a gig coming up or something?" Michelle asked.

"Yes, in a few weeks." Chloe told her.

"The baby likes it when Lee sings." she added, staring at her abdomen fondly.

"Really?" Michelle frowned.

"Yes, it always moves." Chloe smiled.

"God, I hate saying it, I can't wait until we can find out what we are having." she added, quickly laying back down on the sofa.

"What are you hoping for?" Michelle asked.

"I don't mind really, Lee really wants a girl though so it would be nice to be able to give him a girl." Chloe told her, gasping quietly when she felt the baby move again.

"You're like your Dad, you don't sit still." Chloe giggled, speaking softly to her bump.

"Can I feel?" Michelle asked, slowly reaching towards Chloe.

"No!" Chloe said sharply, squirming away from Michelle before she could touch her.

"It's too early for you to be able to feel the movement anyway." Chloe told her.

"I wasn't going to do anything to hurt you or the baby." Michelle said quietly, feeling slightly hurt that Chloe was so suspicious of her.

"I don't let anyone touch my bump, except Lee." Chloe said quietly.

"Why?" Michelle frowned.

"I'm just very protective." Chloe sighed, her cheeks colouring slightly as Michelle stared at her. Chloe yawned quietly and slowly closed her eyes, no longer having the energy to stay awake.

Chapter Twenty Seven

Michelle jumped and carefully placed her book that she was reading on the coffee table, when she heard the doorbell ring. She glanced at Chloe, smiling slightly to herself when she noticed that she was sleeping soundly on the sofa. She sighed and slowly stood up as the doorbell sounded once again. Michelle walked along the hall and slowly opened the front door, gasping as she laid eyes on Shayne.

"What are you doing here?!" she exclaimed, frowning at him as he staggered and leant against the doorway. She rolled her eyes slightly when she gazed at his pupils and noticed how dilated they were.

"I think the more appropriate question, is what are you doing here?" he sneered at her.

"I thought you hated them." he added, smiling smugly at her, as he tried to focus on her face that was slowly swirling.

"You shouldn't be here." she said firmly, quickly moving to close the door, gasping as Shayne reached out to place his hand on the door, preventing her from closing it. Michelle groaned as she fought to close the door, her stomach churning in fear when she realised that he was too strong for her. She watched in horror as he forced the door open and quickly walked into the house.

"What do you even want, you're breaking your bail conditions?" she asked nervously, quickly stepping back from him and swallowing the nervous lump that was rising in her throat.

"Yeah I heard that you reported me, even though you gave consent." he muttered, shaking his head slowly.

"I did not give consent." she snapped, her temper starting to rise that he was trying to suggest that she'd made up the charges.

"You would say that wouldn't you, the truth is you just feel guilty that you cheated on your boyfriend, and it's easier to blame me rather than face up to what you did." he sneered at her. Michelle shook her head slowly and stared at him, not entirely sure how to respond. Despite the fact that she felt a deep sense of anger at Shayne's words, she couldn't help but feel slightly nervous of what he was capable of. She had witnessed first hand, how quickly his temper could turn and from her experience as a nurse she could clearly see that he was high on drugs.

"Maybe you should leave." she tried, fighting to keep her voice level.

"Not until you drop the charges!" he said angrily, quickly stepping towards her. Shayne smirked as a small squeak of fear escaped her lips. He laughed when she quickly stepped back, gasping as her back made contact with the wall.

"I'm not going to drop them, you know what you did." she told him, surprising herself by how brave she suddenly felt.

"Just drop the damn charges!" he yelled, his temper finally snapping.

"What's going on?" Michelle heard a small voice say from the living room doorway. Michelle's heart plummeted into the pit of her stomach as she saw Chloe slowly walking into the hall. Michelle glanced between Chloe and Shayne, suddenly feeling rigid with fear at the thought of Shayne doing something to hurt Chloe, particularly when she was pregnant.

Chloe gasped as she slowly walked into the hallway and noticed Shayne glaring at Michelle menacingly. She froze in place, her legs suddenly feeling very heavy.

"Oh look, it's Lee's little stylist." Shayne said, smirking at Chloe as he patronised her.

"Why are you here?" Chloe asked quietly, her gaze fixed on the floor as she tried not to do anything to antagonize Shayne. She glanced up at him as he stood in front of her, staring down at her silently. Chloe slowly backed away from him, not entirely sure what he was going to do, but knowing in her heart that she needed to protect her baby. She gasped in shock as Shayne reached towards her and grabbed her hoodie, quickly pulling her towards himself. Michelle hurried over to stand behind Shayne and grabbed his elbow, desperately fighting with him to try and pull him away from Chloe. Shayne pushed her away with his elbow, smiling to himself when Michelle staggered backwards, hitting her head against the radiator and collapsing in a heap on the floor. Chloe stared at Michelle, her heart pounding against her chest when Michelle remained completely motionless. She released the breath she didn't realise that she was holding when she saw Michelle taking steady breaths. Her eyes flickered to Shayne when he placed his hands on her hips and pushed her against the wall roughly. Chloe froze in fear, desperately racking her brain to try and think of something to escape the situation. She squirmed slightly, trying to remove herself from his grip, sighing in frustration as he pressed his body against hers, completely pinning her against the wall.

"Please don't hurt me, I haven't done anything to you." she said nervously.

"You're the one that got away." he said softly, completely disregarding what she had said. Her stomach churned in disgust as he began to softly stroke her hair. She swallowed the bile that was rising in her throat as he leaned towards her and placed a soft kiss on her neck. She squirmed slightly, trying to free herself from his grasp, sighing in frustration when she realised that she was completely pinned against him.

"Stop." she pleaded, moving her head away from him. Shayne laughed condescendingly and placed his hand on her throat, holding her head tightly in place as he returned to kissing and sucking her neck. Chloe's eyes filled with tears when she suddenly realised that he was trying to leave a mark on her neck to prove a point to Lee.

"You're so beautiful." he whispered in between kissing her neck. Chloe let out a small whimper of fear when she felt his hand slowly trailing up the inside of her thigh. Before she could talk herself out of it, she placed her hands on his chest and shoved him as hard as she could. Shayne staggered for a moment as she caught him unawares. Chloe seized her opportunity and squeezed past him, quickly running towards the front door, knowing in her heart that her only hope was to get herself out of the house and away from Shayne as fast as possible. A small shriek of fear escaped her lips as Shayne reached out and grasped her hood, roughly pulling her backwards and flinging her onto the floor. Chloe gasped, fighting to get her breath back as she slowly sat up, placing her hands on the floor behind her to steady herself.

"You need to behave yourself.....otherwise things are going to get ugly." he sneered, gazing down at her like she was an ant under his boot. Chloe watched him, as his eyes darted all over the room frantically. She knew that he had taken something and she couldn't help but feel slightly afraid of what he might be capable of. She gasped to herself as she saw him slowly raise his foot, she instinctively curled into a ball and turned her back to face him, desperately trying to do something to protect her unborn baby. She cried out in pain as he repeatedly kicked her back, another shot of pain ricocheting through her body, every time that his foot made contact. Chloe remained silent, her body burning as she fought to get her breath back when he eventually stopped kicking her. She glanced up at him when he squatted down in front of her and grasped her hoodie in his hand, quickly pulling her to her feet and flinging her onto the stairs. She yelped in pain when her already sore back made contact with the stairs, wincing when her forehead cracked against the banister. The room swirled as she suddenly felt light-headed. She pressed her hand against her forehead, gasping when she noticed the trace of blood on her hand. She stared up at him numbly, feeling too weak and in too much pain to react to anything. Her heart pounded against her chest when Shayne slowly climbed the stairs and positioned himself on top of her.

"Please don't do this, I'll do anything!" she pleaded, her voice coming out in loud sobs, when she realised what he was about to do to her. Shayne ignored her, smirking to herself as he quickly spread her legs. She squirmed underneath him, trying to fight to get away, sobbing loudly when she realised that he was too strong for her. He placed his legs on top of hers, pinning her legs underneath his.

"Don't touch me!" she exclaimed when he fumbled with the button on her jeans. Chloe began to sob loudly, trying to squirm away from him as he slowly unzipped her jeans.

"Lee will kill you if you touch me." she sobbed, desperately trying to squirm away from him.

"Are you threatening me, you little bitch!" he exclaimed angrily. Before Chloe could respond, he took her hair in his fist and angrily hit her head against the banister, smiling in satisfaction when she cried out in pain, her head slumping onto the stair. She remained still, no longer able to focus on anything that was happening, the room was swirling so much.

"I want to see this amazing body that everyone always talks about." he said hoarsely.

"LEE!" she screamed desperately, knowing in her heart that he was too far away to hear her. She closed her eyes tightly, her heart pounding against her chest when she felt Shayne slowly pulling her hoodie over her head. She took deep breaths, trying to steady her breathing, desperately trying to convince herself that it was Lee's body that was pressed against hers.

"Wait, are you pregnant?" he asked, his voice dripping with disgust. Chloe slowly opened her eyes, remaining silent as she watched him staring numbly at her abdomen.

"That's gross." he added, slowly climbing off of her and sitting below her on the stairs, his eyes fixed on her. Chloe slowly sat up, gently wrapping her hand around the banister to steady herself as she sat trembling silently, afraid to move or say anything in case she antagonized Shayne. A steady stream of tears rolled down her cheeks as she stared at her bump, feeling herself starting to panic that Shayne now knew that she was carrying Lee's baby. She knew that Shayne loathed Lee and wanted revenge on him, and she couldn't help but feel a pang of fear that the easiest way for Shayne to hurt Lee would be to do something to the baby. Chloe's eyes flickered to Michelle who was slowly sitting up, resting her back against the radiator as she slowly regained full consciousness. Shayne jumped, turning to face the doorway when he heard a car pull into the drive loudly. He turned to face Chloe, a look of panic in his eyes. Before Chloe could react Shayne reached out to grasp her wrist and quickly stood up, pulling her with him. She staggered slightly, gasping as he pulled her back against his chest, quickly wrapping his arm around her throat.

"If you say anything or try anything, I will kick that baby out of you." he whispered menacingly in her ear.

Chapter Twenty Eight

Lee quickly climbed out of his car and ran as fast as he could down the driveway, his heart pounding against his chest at the thought of Shayne doing anything to harm Chloe. As soon as he'd received the notification on his phone that Shayne was at the door, he'd rushed to his car and dashed home as fast as he could. His heart had been in his mouth as he'd sped home, able to hear the commotion and Chloe screaming for him, but unable to do anything about it. Lee rushed into the house, skidding to a stop when he noticed Shayne standing in the doorway, his arm wrapped around Chloe's neck as he held her tightly against himself. His heart sunk into the pit of his stomach when he locked eyes with Chloe and noticed the trail of blood trickling down the side of her face. A deep sense of anger slowly built in his stomach, his eyes fixed on the swelling on her cheek. As soon as Chloe locked eyes with Lee, she burst into tears, no longer able to hide how afraid she was. Even though she felt a small sense of relief that Lee was home, she knew in her heart that Shayne would do whatever he could to hurt Lee, and that she was likely to bear the brunt of his temper.

"It's okay, don't cry princess." Shayne said condescendingly, smirking at Lee as he softly kissed away Chloe's tears. Chloe jerked her head away from him, trying to supress the nausea that she felt whenever he touched her.

"Take your hands off her!" Lee warned, a note of aggression present in his voice as he watched Shayne placing soft kisses on Chloe's cheeks.

"Stop squirming or I'll have to hurt you again." Shayne said quickly, his eyes darting to Chloe as she tried to squirm away from him.

"You wouldn't dare!" Lee said menacingly, quickly stepping towards Shayne. Shayne jumped and stepped backwards, pulling Chloe with him, quickly tightening his grip on her throat. Chloe gasped, fighting to get her breath back. Shayne smirked at Lee when Chloe stood silently, taking deep breaths. Lee quickly assessed the situation, desperately trying to resist the urge to rip Chloe from Shayne's arms. He knew in his heart that if he tried anything, Shayne would lash out and hurt Chloe, and the last thing he wanted was for anything to happen to her.

"You're too late anyway." Shayne said, smirking at Lee.

"I already got what I wanted." he added, maintaining eye contact with Lee as he trailed his hand down the side of Chloe's body, his hand gently resting in place on her hip. Shayne glanced down at his hand as he slowly placed his hands inside Chloe's jeans. She whimpered as she felt him slowly stroking her underwear with his fingers. Lee's brain swirled with a mist of thoughts, when he followed Shayne's eyeline and noticed for the first time that Chloe's hoodie had been discarded on the floor. His heart plummeted further when he noticed that Chloe's jeans were unfastened. His breath caught in his throat when he remembered the moment that he'd heard Chloe pleading with Shayne and desperately calling out for Lee to help her. Given that he knew what Shayne was capable of, he knew in his heart that he was too late to prevent Chloe from being sexually assaulted by Shayne. He bit the inside of his lip, trying to fight the wave of emotions that he was feeling when he suddenly realised that his nightmare had come true and that he had let Chloe down at the moment when she'd needed him.

"You are so dead." Lee muttered, as he clenched and unclenched his fists, trying to resist the urge to launch himself at Shayne. Shayne chuckled, smirking at Lee.

"Shayne stop.....she hasn't done anything to you!" Michelle exclaimed from her position on the floor.

"I know, but she is his Achilles heel." Shayne argued, smiling at Lee when he noticed how much he was struggling to control his temper.

"And she's beautiful." he added, placing a soft kiss on Chloe's shoulder.

"Chlo." Lee whispered, desperately wishing that he could do something to protect her. Chloe locked eyes with Lee, trying to become lost in his deep Eclipse eyes and convince herself that it was Lee's lips that were placing a series of kisses on her shoulder.

"Why do you care, you've ruined her anyway." Shayne said, smiling at Lee as he rested his chin on Chloe's shoulder.

"Everyone always used to talk about her amazing body, and you've ruined it by putting a baby inside her." Shayne continued, when he realised that Lee wasn't going to respond to the bait.

"Or maybe that's why you did it, since you've always been possessive of her. You wanted to make sure that you limited her options." he continued. A twisted smirk appeared on Shayne's face as he slowly placed his hands underneath Chloe's pyjama top and rested them on her abdomen.

"Take your hands off my baby!" Chloe hissed, before she could stop herself. She squirmed, trying to get away from him, gasping loudly when his grip on her neck tightened. She glanced at Lee, realising that she needed to do something to protect her and the baby. Before Shayne could react, Chloe leaned forward slightly and quickly moved her head backwards, smiling in satisfaction when her head made contact with Shayne's face and she heard his nose crack. Shayne cried out in pain and instinctively clutched his nose. Chloe seized her opportunity and squirmed out of his grasp. She ran upstairs, knowing that she had to get herself and her baby as far away from Shayne as possible. Before she could reach the top of the stairs, her legs buckled from under her and she collapsed in a heap halfway up the stairs.

Lee glanced at Chloe as she made her way upstairs, as soon as she was safely out of range of Shayne, Lee seized his opportunity and darted across the room towards Shayne. Before Lee could reach him, Shayne bolted out of the house. Lee ran after him, stopping in the doorway when he noticed Michelle blocking his exit.

"Get the hell out of my way!" Lee shouted.

"Just leave it." Michelle pleaded with him.

"I'm going to kill him for what he's done!" Lee exclaimed, his temper finally snapping.

"I know and I know that he deserves it, but you can't end up in jail." Michelle argued.

"Especially when you are going to be a father." she added. Lee glared at her, taking deep breaths as he tried to control his temper. Despite the temptation that he was feeling to chase after Shayne and make him pay for hurting the woman that he loved, he knew that Michelle was right. Lee took a deep breath, finally calming down slightly. He glanced up at Chloe, his heart breaking a little when he saw that she was curled up in a ball, her head gently resting on one of the stairs. He quickly climbed the stairs and sat beside her, frowning to himself when she didn't even glance up at him. He watched her closely as she remained still and silent, staring into space.

"Are you okay?" he asked nervously, softly reaching out and stroking her hair with his hand. He frowned at her as she remained silent, not even acknowledging his touch.

"Chlo?" he tried, leaning over and placing a soft kiss on her cheek, trying to resist the urge to panic when she still didn't respond. His heart broke a little when she blinked slowly and a steady stream of tears rolled down her cheeks. His eyes filled with tears as he watched her heart slowly breaking, he still couldn't quite process the thought that Chloe had been sexually assaulted and he hadn't been able to do anything to protect her. He knew in his heart that he would never forgive himself for allowing Shayne to harm her.

"Chloe, please talk to me." he pleaded sadly, quickly wiping away the tears that were filling his eyes. Lee gently leaned over and placed a series of soft kisses on her cheeks, desperately trying to find a way to provide her with some comfort.

"I'm okay." she whispered softly, closing her eyes tightly, her brain still swirling with a mist of thoughts. She couldn't help but feel a pang of fear when she realised what she had been through, and how easily things could have been so much worse. She'd always been proud of the fact that she'd only given herself to Lee, and she felt sick to her stomach at the thought that if it hadn't been for Shayne being repulsed by her pregnant body, then she would have been robbed of that forever.

Lee's eyes wandered to Chloe's jeans when he suddenly noticed that they were still unfastened. He slowly reached out to fasten them, trying to preserve her dignity when he glanced at Michelle and noticed her watching them closely.

"Don't touch me." Chloe gasped, squirming away from him as her eyes quickly snapped open.

"Chloe, I would never take advantage of you." he said quickly, holding his hands up in front of her. Chloe nodded slowly, breathing a sigh of relief when she realised that it was Lee that was sitting beside her.

"I know, I'm sorry." she whispered, shuffling towards him and gently resting the side of her head against his leg.

"I'm the one who is sorry, this is all my fault." he whispered sadly, biting his lip in an attempt to control the emotions that he was feeling. Chloe flinched slightly, glancing up at him for a moment when he gently stroked her hair, not entirely sure what to say or do to comfort her.

"I wish I'd been able to protect you." he muttered thoughtfully. Lee's eyes snapped to Michelle when she handed him a damp cloth. He'd been so focused on Chloe that he hadn't even noticed her leaving the room, let alone returning. He silently took the cloth from her, glancing down at Chloe as she slowly sat up and held out her hand for it.

"I'll do it Chlo." he said softly. Chloe glanced up at him, sighing to herself when she noticed that his eyes were filling with tears. She remained silent, watching him closely as he gently wiped away the blood from her face. His hand eventually came to a stop as he carefully pressed the cloth against the swelling on her cheekbone. He locked eyes with her, his stomach churning with guilt when he noticed her gazing at him sadly.

"I never should have left you alone." he said quietly, desperately wishing that he could turn the clock back and not leave Chloe alone and unprotected. She nodded slowly and carefully stood up, leaning on the banister for support when she felt the room spinning.

"Where are you going?" he asked nervously, watching her closely.

"To wash." she replied numbly, feeling the sudden urge to clean away the smell of Shayne's aftershave that was still lingering on her skin. Lee nodded slowly, his eyes fixed on Chloe as she walked away. As soon as Chloe was out of sight, he placed his head in his hands, digging his fingernails into his scalp in frustration.

"What did he do to her?" Lee asked quietly, glancing up at Michelle.

"I don't know." Michelle replied sadly.

"Did he rape her?" he asked quickly, his stomach churning at the thought of it.

"I honestly don't know, I tried to pull him away from her and he pushed me. I hit my head on the radiator and blacked out." Michelle explained, her eyes fixed on Lee as she perched on the step below him.

"I'm sorry." she whispered, her heart breaking a little when she realised how upset Lee was about the situation. Even though she knew that he was trying to hide how he was feeling, the pain and anger was written all over his face. Lee glanced down at his knee when he felt Michelle place her hand on it.

"Do you want me to go and check on Chloe?" she offered, wishing that she could do something to help.

"No, you stay away from her." Lee said shortly, a note of warning in his voice.

"Since this is all your fault, I don't want you anywhere near her!" he added menacingly.

"Wait, what did I do?!" Michelle exclaimed in disbelief.

"You led him to her." he said shortly, fighting to keep his voice level.

"And you let him in the door." he added, his temper flaring.

"And thanks to you, the little bastard got away!" he exclaimed. Michelle opened her mouth to respond, but quickly closed it again, not entirely sure how to respond. The two of them jumped, their eyes flickering to the doorway as Nathan walked into the house.

"Oh god, what's happened?" Nathan asked quickly, as soon as he noticed Lee's expression.

"It's a long story." Lee whispered, quickly pulling his phone out of his pocket and logging onto the security system app. He knew that due to the fact that Shayne had gone on the run, that he needed to hand the recordings to the police, to ensure that Shayne got sent down for a long time and was out of their lives for good.

"I need the contact details for the detective dealing with your case." Lee told Michelle shortly.

"I'll go and get it." she said, quickly leaving the room, feeling relieved that she was able to do at least something to help. Before Lee could stop himself, he switched on the recording, his heart breaking when he listened to Chloe pleading with Shayne. It felt like someone was punching him in the chest. As soon as he heard her screaming for him, he curled into a ball on the stairs, not even caring when he slid down several steps. Nathan watched in horror as Lee sobbed silently to himself, a look of deep anger and anguish etched on his face.

"Lee, tell me what's going on?" Nathan asked nervously.

"Ask Michelle." Lee muttered.

"And keep her away from me while you're at it." he added angrily.

Chapter Twenty Nine

Chloe sighed in relief as she climbed into the bath and relaxed into the water. She picked up the sponge from the counter and scrubbed her skin, desperately trying to remove the lingering sensation of Shayne's touch. She gasped in pain when she rested her back against the bathtub, forgetting for a moment that she was injured. Her eyes misted with tears as she started down at her abdomen, a sudden wave of fear washing over her. She sat in silence, desperately racking her brain to try and remember if Shayne had done anything that might have caused harm to her baby. The events were on a constant loop in her mind, she remembered how she had desperately curled into a ball as Shayne kicked her, in an attempt to protect the baby. She blinked slowly, sighing to herself and resting her elbow against the side of the bathtub, her heart pounding against her chest at the idea of losing the baby. Her heart had broken when she lost their first baby, and she knew that she wasn't strong enough to go through the process again, particularly when she was further along this time and regularly felt the baby move inside of her. The deep and intense love that she felt for her baby was like nothing that she had ever felt before and she knew in her heart that Lee felt the same way. Chloe took a deep breath, trying to supress the panic that she was feeling, and splashed some water on her face, quickly scrubbing her neck with the sponge. She suddenly felt a deep surge of anger at what Shayne had done to her, particularly when she'd never done anything to hurt him, but yet he seemed hell bent on destroying her life. She placed her hands on either side of the bath frame and gingerly lifted herself up, wincing at the pain in her back. Tears continued to fall from her eyes as she carefully pulled on her clothes, a small squeak of pain escaping her lips when she twisted. She sighed deeply to herself as she carefully sat on the bathroom floor and crossed her legs, staring in silence at her hands that were resting in her lap. She watched as her tears slowly rolled off her chin and dripped onto her lap, her heart breaking a little every time her eyes wandered to her bump.

"I love you so much little baby." she whispered, carefully placing her hand on her bump and softly stroking it with her fingernails.

"Why do you keep staring at me?!" Lee snapped when he could no longer stand Nathan staring at him.

"Because I've never seen you so upset and angry, and I'm worried about you." Nathan told him, as he sat beside Lee on the sofa.

"Well what do you expect?!" Lee exclaimed, angrily flinging his phone onto the coffee table when he'd finally sent the email to the police. Nathan sighed deeply, staring at Lee as he tried to rack his brain for what he could possibly say to help him feel better.

"This is not your fault." Nathan told him, his stomach churning a little when he thought about what Chloe had been through. He felt sick to his stomach at the thought of anyone doing anything to hurt Chloe's kind soul. Given how upset and angry Nathan was feeling, he couldn't possibly imagine what Lee must be feeling, given how important Chloe was to him.

"Of course it's my fault." Lee said shortly, snapping Nathan out of his thoughts.

"But you can't blame yourself, you can't be with her twenty four seven." Nathan pointed out.

"I know that, but how come whenever she needs me I'm never there, I didn't stop her from being stabbed and now I let her get assaulted!" Lee said angrily.

"You weren't even together when she was stabbed." Nathan pointed out.

"And like I said, you can't always be with her, just in case something happens." he added. Lee nodded slowly, sighing deeply when he realised that Nathan was right. Despite the fact that he knew Nathan was correct, it didn't ease the intense guilt that he was feeling for letting Chloe down in her time of need. He couldn't help but feel slightly resentful of Michelle, as he knew in his heart that if he hadn't left the house to fetch her clothes for her, he would have been able to protect Chloe from Shayne.

"Do you want me to stay over for a few days?" Nathan offered, sensing that Lee needed his support. Lee nodded slowly, his eyes fixed on his hands that were resting in place on his lap. No matter how hard he tried, he couldn't seem to stop his hands from shaking.

"It'll be extra protection for Chloe if he does turn up again." Lee said thoughtfully.

"I doubt he will." Nathan said quietly.

"Why did you have to stop me from going after him?!" Lee exclaimed, his gaze wandering to Michelle who was sitting on the sofa opposite him.

"This could all have been over.....she could have been safe!" he added, his temper finally snapping. Michelle stared at him in numb shock, not entirely sure how to respond.

"I just didn't want you to do something that you would regret." Michelle said quietly, her stomach churning when she noticed the hatred in Lee's expression as he stared at her.

"More likely you didn't want me to hurt him because this is another one of your twisted games." Lee said shortly. Lee gasped when he suddenly realised what he needed to do. The only way that Chloe was going to be safe was if Lee eliminated the issue and he knew that he needed to make Shayne pay for what he did to her.

"You know him better than I do....where would he go?" Lee rounded on Michelle.

"I have no idea." Michelle said quietly.

"I don't know him that well anyway." she quickly added.

"The police will find him anyway." Nathan said quickly, trying to diffuse the tension as he glanced nervously between Michelle and Lee.

"Not if I find him first." Lee said firmly, frowning to himself as he racked his brain, desperately trying to think about where he should start looking for Shayne.

"You can't go after him, Chloe needs you." Nathan argued. Lee's eyes snapped up as Chloe walked into the room and hovered nervously in the doorway, her cheeks colouring when the three of them turned to stare at her.

"Please don't go after him." Chloe said softly, her heart breaking a little when she locked eyes with Lee and noticed how upset he was.

"Just let the police deal with it." she added. Lee nodded slowly, his temper calming down slightly as soon as Chloe had entered the room. He shot her a small smile as she crossed the room and stood in front of him, gazing sadly at him when she reached out to take his hand, squeezing it reassuringly. His eyes remained fixed on her as he quickly crossed his legs and held her wrist tightly, slowly pulling her towards him. She allowed him to pull her towards himself, glancing down at him when he wrapped his arms around her waist tightly and rested his head against her abdomen. She placed her arms around his head and held him tightly, softly stroking his hair when she heard him sigh sadly to himself. Her heart broke for him when she heard him sniff sadly.

"Don't get upset, we're okay." she whispered, biting her lip to fight her emotions so that she didn't upset him further. She knew in her heart that if he realised that she was injured then he would feel even more guilty than he already did and the last thing she wanted was for him to go after Shayne. Lee raised his head slowly and stared up at her. Chloe turned her back on him and slowly sat on his lap, grimacing in pain when he quickly wrapped his arms around her waist and pulled her close. She took deep breaths, trying to control the stabbing pain in her back as Lee held her tightly against himself. He gently brushed her hair to one side and rested his chin on her shoulder, feeling a deep desire to hold her as tightly as possible so that he knew she was safe. Chloe glanced down at his hands as he rested them on her bump, she smiled slightly and placed her hands on top of his, quickly linking their fingers. She fidgeted, trying to loosen his grip on her slightly so that she wasn't in so much pain.

"I would never hurt you Chlo." he told her softly when he noticed that her body was trembling against him.

"I know you wouldn't." she said softly. She flinched slightly when she felt Lee place a series of soft kisses on her neck.

"Please don't do that." she said quietly, squirming away from him when she was reminded of the moment when Shayne had kissed her neck.

"Sorry." he said quietly. He watched her closely as she turned her head to face him and gave him a small reassuring smile. She placed a soft kiss on his lips, before gently resting her forehead against his. He softly stroked her cheek with his fingertips, frowning to himself when he noticed a red mark on her neck, that was hidden slightly by her hair. He slowly moved her hair aside, his breath catching in his throat as he stared at the mark.

"What's this?" he muttered, as he stroked the mark with his fingertips.

"Maybe it was you this morning." Chloe said quickly, her stomach churning with guilt as she lied to him. Despite the guilt that she was feeling, she knew that if she told Lee what had happened that he would be enraged and would likely go looking for Shayne and she couldn't face the thought of Lee getting hurt or ending up in jail.

"No, it definitely wasn't me." he said quietly, fighting to keep his voice level as he felt his temper slowly rising. He felt a deep sense of anger in the pit of his stomach that Shayne had left a mark on the woman that he'd loved, almost like he'd 'branded' her just to hurt Lee.

"It's not a big deal." Chloe said quickly, trying to diffuse the situation when she noticed Lee's nostrils flaring in anger. Lee sighed deeply and quickly curled up on the sofa, carefully pulling Chloe with him. She sighed in contentment as she curled up against him, her body finally relaxing when she felt him curled up behind her, his body resting tightly against hers. Despite the pain in her back, she couldn't bring herself to move away from him.

"You need to tell me what he did to you Chlo?" he whispered in her ear.

"Nothing, I'm fine." Chloe lied quickly, her eyes filling with tears as flashbacks swirled around her head once again. Her eyes filled with tears when she remembered how close she had come to being raped, and never belonging to just Lee again.

"Don't lie to me Chloe, I heard the recording." he snapped.

"What recording?" she frowned, turning her head to face him.

"The security system, I saw Shayne at the door and then I could hear him talking as I drove home." he told her.

"I heard you scream for me." he prompted, glancing down at her as she turned her body to face him, gently placing her hand on his chest as she snuggled her body against his.

"He didn't rape me, he just made out to you that he did, to wind you up." she told him, choosing not to mention everything that had happened and how close she had come to being raped by him.

"But you weren't wearing my hoodie and your jeans were undone." Lee frowned.

"Well, he didn't rape me." she said quietly.

"I didn't ask you what he didn't do, I asked what he did do." he snapped impatiently, feeling slightly frustrated that she wasn't opening up to him. Despite the intense relief that he'd felt when he realised that she hadn't been raped, he still knew that something had happened and he desperately needed to know what it was.

"I'm fine." Chloe whispered, not quite able to bring herself to talk about what had happened.

"Chloe please tell me." Lee pleaded.

"Can we just drop it please?" she said quietly, slowly wiping away the tears that were rolling down her cheeks.

"Lee!" Nathan said quickly when Lee opened his mouth to continue interrogating Chloe.

"Just leave it today, you can talk about it tomorrow." Nathan quickly added when he realised how upset Chloe was getting. Lee sighed quietly and reluctantly nodded, trying to stop his brain spinning with all the possibilities. He watched Chloe closely as she placed her hand on her bump, her eyes misting with tears when she remembered that the reason Shayne hadn't raped her was due to the fact that she was pregnant. She couldn't help but wonder if he was telling the truth when he'd said that he was repulsed by her body or whether somewhere deep inside him, there was a small glimmer of goodness that couldn't bring himself to harm a baby. All she knew for certain was that she had the baby to thank for her life not being changed forever. Chloe clapped her hand over her mouth when a small sob escaped her lips.

"I think we should get the baby checked over." Chloe said quietly.

"Did he do something to hurt the baby?!" Lee exclaimed, beginning to panic slightly.

"It's my baby too, I have a right to know!" he added, before Chloe had a chance to respond.

"No he didn't, the only time he touched the baby was when you were there, just before I head butted him." Chloe told him.

"But he threw me to the ground a couple of times, so just for peace of mind, I want to get the baby checked over." she continued. Lee nodded slowly, his stomach churning nervously at the thought of losing their baby. He glanced down at Chloe when she snuggled against his chest and sobbed quietly. He rested his head against hers, the tears that he'd been fighting slowly rolling down his cheeks. Chloe glanced up at him as he held her tightly, sniffing quietly to himself as he held her. She jumped slightly when Lee suddenly pushed her away and sat up.

"I'll ring the midwife." he told her, quickly leaving the room before he broke down. The last thing he wanted was to be vulnerable in front of Michelle. Nathan glanced at Chloe as she slowly sat up. She smiled at him as he wrapped his arm around her shoulders and pulled her close. He remained silent, not entirely sure what to say to comfort her.

"I can't lose the baby Nathan." she said quietly, a small sob escaping her lips. Before Nathan could respond, she quickly stood up and ran upstairs, suddenly needing some time alone.

Nathan locked eyes with Michelle and sighed quietly to himself. The two of them remained silent, neither of them entirely sure what to say or how to process the situation. Their eyes flickered to the doorway when Lee walked back into the room, his eyes widening nervously when he noticed that Chloe was no longer in the room.

"I think she went upstairs." Nathan told him. Lee nodded and slowly turned to leave the room, pausing for a moment when Nathan called out to him:

"Don't start grilling her again, she needs to process everything." Lee nodded slowly and ran upstairs, sighing to himself when he noticed Chloe curled up on top of the bed. She glanced up at him when he curled up beside her, gently reaching out to stroke away her tears with his thumb.

"The midwife is coming over first thing tomorrow." he told her gently. Chloe nodded slowly.

"And the police are coming over later to talk to you." he said quietly.

"Why?" she frowned, her heart sinking at the thought of having to talk about what happened.

"Because we need to make sure he goes down for a long time, so that he can't hurt you anymore." he told her, his voice dripping with disdain. She nodded slowly and closed her eyes, no longer having the strength to argue with him.

"Chlo.....I-" he started.

"I don't want to talk about it, I just want to sleep." she interrupted him. She opened her eyes and glanced at him when she felt him watching her closely.

"I was only going to say that I love you." he told her, watching closely as she softly stroked her bump. She nodded slowly and closed her eyes.

Chapter Thirty

Chloe's eyes snapped open, grimacing when she felt the intense pain in her back. She squirmed out of Lee's arms, desperately trying to free herself from his grip so that she wasn't in so much pain. She sighed to herself as she placed her hands behind herself and slowly sat up, breathing deeply as she waited for the pain to pass. She glanced at the clock sighing to herself when she noticed that it was only five am. Her eyes flickered to Lee when he fidgeted slightly in his sleep, clearly unsettled by the fact that she was no longer in his arms. Despite the fact that she longed to curl up in Lee's arms, she knew that he would hold her tightly in his arms, as a desire to make her feel safe, and she could no longer tolerate the pain. She sighed to herself as she reluctantly climbed out of bed and slowly made her way downstairs, carefully curling up on the sofa as soon as she reached the living room. She picked up one of the cushions and hugged it tightly, digging her fingernails into it as an attempt to fight the pain that she was feeling.

Chloe jumped, glancing up as she saw Nathan walking into the room, carrying a smoothie in his hand.

"What are you doing up?" she asked him as he sat beside her on the sofa.

"I always get up early, I've just been working out in the gym." he told her, quickly picking up the throw and placing it over when he noticed that she was trembling.

"I'm not cold, I just can't stop trembling lately." she said quietly, her cheeks colouring in embarrassment as he watched her closely.

"You've been through a lot that's why." he sighed, not quite able to bring himself to ask Chloe what had happened.

"What are you doing down here anyway?" he asked her.

"I just needed a bit of space." she said quietly.

"He's not been questioning you again has he?" he sighed. Chloe shook her head slowly, sighing quietly to herself. She knew that she would have to tell Lee what had happened eventually, but she was hoping that Shayne would be caught first, so that there was no chance of Lee lashing out and going after Shayne. Chloe let out a yelp of pain as she fidgeted slightly, glancing at Nathan when she felt him watching her closely, his brow furrowing in concern.

"Are you okay?" he asked worriedly. Chloe nodded slowly, her eyes filling with tears.

"I need to tell you something." she said quietly, her heart pounding against her chest at the thought of telling him what had happened to her. She couldn't help but feel nervous that he would tell Lee, but she knew that she needed some help from someone and he seemed like the best person.

"Oh no." he said quietly.

"What?" she frowned.

"Please tell me you didn't lie about not being raped?" he asked quickly, his stomach churning nervously.

"No of course not." she said quietly, smiling slightly when Nathan breathed a sigh of relief.

"If I tell you then you can't tell anyone.......especially Lee." she added.

"Okay." he said tentatively.

"I mean it, he can't know yet." she said firmly.

"Promise?" she asked.

"But...." he started, trailing off when Chloe interrupted him.

"Please Nathan, I need to talk to someone." she pleaded. Nathan sighed deeply, his stomach churning at the thought of keeping something a secret from his best friend, particularly when it involved Chloe. He felt his resolve slowly wavering when Chloe stared up at him, a sad expression on her pretty features. Despite the fact that he wasn't entirely comfortable with the situation, he knew that he couldn't turn her down in her time of need.

"Okay fine.....I promise." he said hesitantly. Chloe nodded slowly.

"When Shayne was here, I tried to fight him off, he got angry and threw me to the floor. He went to kick me so I turned my back on him to protect the baby. And my back has been really sore ever since, so I was wondering if you could check it for me." she explained. Nathan nodded slowly, swallowing the lump that was rising in his throat. He watched her closely as she slowly sat up, wincing in pain when she grasped the bottom of her pyjama top and slowly lifted the back up. Nathan gasped in shock, his stomach churning as he gazed at her back and the sheer amount of dark bruises that were present.

"Jeez Chlo Bo." he muttered, unable to tear his eyes away from the bruises. His heart plummeted further when he lifted her shirt up to her shoulders and noticed the boot-shaped bruise that was present between her shoulder blades.

"Is it bad?" she asked nervously.

"Yeah, you must be in so much pain." he said quietly. Chloe nodded slowly, quickly pulling her top back down, in case Michelle or Lee walked into the room.

"We should probably get you checked out, you might have broken ribs or something." he told her.

"But then we'll have to tell Lee!" she exclaimed, starting to panic slightly.

"And he'll be furious, and want to go after Shayne." she added.

"It should be fine, we can say that I'm taking you out for a walk or something and we'll got to A and E." he told her, smiling at her reassuringly.

"Or the other option is that we ask Michelle to check you over, since she's a nurse?" he suggested.

"I don't think that's a good idea, she'll probably tell Lee, to try and come between us again." she said thoughtfully, still not entirely sure that she trusted Michelle fully. Nathan nodded in agreement.

"Go and get dressed then, I'll take you now." he told her firmly.

"Just make sure you tell Lee that you are going out, so that he doesn't panic when he wakes up and you're gone." he added. Chloe nodded slowly, her stomach churning at the thought of having to lie to Lee, but she knew in her heart that it was her only option. Not only did she not want him to go searching for Shayne, she also didn't want him to have to carry any more guilt than he already was. She quickly stood up, her heart sinking further as she slowly climbed the stairs. She wandered into the bedroom, quickly picking up a set of clothes and walking into the bathroom. As soon as she was dressed she quickly emerged from the bathroom and perched on the bed, gasping in pain as she leaned over to pull on her trainers.

"What are you doing up so early?" Lee's voice said from behind her. Chloe jumped when she heard his voice, keeping her back to him so that she wouldn't have to look him in the eye as she lied to him.

"I'm going for a walk." she said shortly.

"Yeah very funny." he chuckled.

"Come back to bed Chlo, you need to rest." he added, as he turned on his side, resting his head against his hand and frowning to himself as he watched her slowly pulling on her trainers.

"I already told you, I'm going for a walk." she stated, slowly standing up and pulling on her jacket.

"No you're not." he told her firmly, his stomach churning at the thought of her leaving the house alone when Shayne was still on the loose.

"Excuse me?" she asked, raising her eyebrow as she turned to face him.

"It's not safe, you need to stay inside until Shayne is caught, just in case." he pointed out, swallowing the lump that was rising in his throat at the thought that Shayne could be anywhere at any time, he could even be watching the house, waiting for Chloe to leave, and they would have no idea until it was too late.

"I can't live in fear for the rest of my life, I need some fresh air." she argued.

"It's not the rest of your life, just until Shayne is caught." he insisted. Chloe glared at him defiantly, knowing that he was right, but realising that Nathan was correct and she needed to get checked over. Lee sighed deeply as she stared at him, an angry expression on her pretty features. He knew in his heart that he was smothering her, but at the same time, he couldn't bear for her to be out of his sight so soon after everything that had happened.

"At least let me come with you." he said, finally deciding to compromise with her. He couldn't help but feel happier at the idea that he would at least be by her side to protect her.

"It's fine, Nathan is coming with me." she told him, quickly zipping up her jacket and glancing down at herself to check that her bump was hidden. Given that they hadn't announced to the fans about the baby yet, the last thing she wanted was for her bump to be noticed when she was out in public.

"No Chloe, I'll go with you." he insisted. Despite the fact that he trusted Nathan, he wanted to make sure that he was with Chloe, so that he could protect her himself if necessary.

"I'm not discussing it anymore, I'm going out." she told him firmly.

"Why can't I go with you?" he frowned, his heart breaking a little at the thought that she didn't want him with her.

"Because I don't want you too, I'm going with Nathan." she sighed, feeling a pang of guilt when she saw the look of hurt flicker across his face for a brief moment before he quickly recovered himself.

"Well tough, you're carrying my baby, so I either go with you or you don't go at all!" he snapped defensively. She glared at him for a moment, shaking her head in disbelief.

"You're such a dick sometimes!" she snapped, her eyes filling with tears when he mentioned their baby and she was reminded once again that they weren't yet certain that everything was okay. She stared at the ground numbly, not entirely sure what to do for the best, knowing in her heart that she needed to get herself checked over, but not entirely sure how she was going to accomplish that without Lee finding out about her injuries, since he wouldn't let her leave the house without him. Lee sighed sadly to himself and slowly climbed out of bed, his heart breaking a little when he realised that he'd managed to upset her. The last thing he wanted to do was upset her, particularly when she was still upset after whatever had happened with Shayne, but he couldn't bring himself to be parted from her. As soon as he stood in front of her, he reached out and softly stroked her cheek with his fingertips, sighing quietly to himself when she turned her face away from him.

"I'm sorry, I didn't mean to upset you." he said softly. Chloe remained silent, her eyes fixed on the floor.

"I just want to protect you." he added sadly, his heart sinking when he noticed the steady stream of tears that were flowing down her cheeks.

"Nathan is quite capable of protecting me." she pointed out. Lee sighed to himself when he heard her words. He knew in his heart that Nathan was able to protect her, but he wanted to make sure that he didn't let her down again.

"It's non-negotiable Chlo." he told her firmly. She glanced down at her hips when Lee placed his hands on them and pulled her towards himself, trying to pull her into his arms. He sighed quietly when she squirmed out of his grasp and quickly backed away from him.

"Don't be like this Chlo." he sighed.

"Just leave me alone." she said shortly, glaring at him angrily as she stormed out of the room, slamming the bedroom door behind herself. She ran downstairs, glancing at Nathan when she noticed him hovering in the hallway, clearly waiting for her.

"Are we going then?" Nathan asked as he fell into step beside her.

"Yes and quickly." she told him as she hurried out of the house, trying to get away before Lee decided to follow her.

"Have you spoken to Lee?" he asked.

"Yes and he said I can't go, but I'm going anyway." she said firmly as she quickly walked out of the house.

Chapter Thirty One

Chloe smiled at Nathan as he fell into step beside her and quickly looped his arm through hers, making sure that he kept her close, so that he knew that she was safe. He couldn't help but feel an intense burden when he suddenly realised that he was responsible for protecting the love of Lee's life and their baby. Chloe glanced at Nathan as he stared down at his phone and quickly typed something on it.

"What are you doing?" Chloe frowned.

"I'm just texting Lee to tell him that you are with me and you're safe, so that he doesn't panic." he told her.

"I did tell him that I was going out." she said quietly, sighing deeply when she remembered how unreasonable Lee was being about the whole situation.

"Although I don't think he realised that I was sneaking out despite being told that I wasn't allowed too." she added thoughtfully, feeling slightly guilty that she'd made him worry.

"Like a child." she continued, an edge of bitterness present in her voice.

"He's just really worried about you Chlo Bo." he said quietly, taking her hand as they finally arrived at the hospital.

"Why don't you go and sit down, I'll check you in?" Nathan suggested. Chloe nodded slowly and perched awkwardly on one of the chairs, her cheeks colouring slightly when the other people at reception stared at her. She frowned to herself, slightly confused as to why they were staring at her. She gasped quietly when she remembered that she had a large swelling present on her cheek. She squirmed slightly in her seat, suddenly feeling very self-conscious. She sighed in relief when Nathan returned and quickly sat next to her. He wrapped his arm around her shoulders, his stomach churning with guilt when she gasped in pain.

"Sorry, I forgot." he said gently.

"It's okay." she said quietly, resting the side of her head against his shoulder. She jumped and slowly pulled her phone out of her pocket, her stomach churning when she noticed that Lee was calling her.

"Oh my god, this is really stressing me out." she said nervously, as she quickly turned off the sound on her phone and stared at the display as Lee continued trying to get hold of her.

"I don't know what to do.....if I don't answer he's going to worry and if I do answer he's going to want to know where I am and I can't exactly tell him can I?!" she exclaimed, starting to panic slightly.

"I'll message him again and tell him to give you space." he sighed, quickly sending Lee a text.

"He's just so intense sometimes, I can't bear it." she said quietly.

"He just wants to make sure that nothing happens to you." he pointed out.

"I know and I could understand it if I was going out alone, but I'm with you." she said quietly.

"I know." he sighed, gently taking Chloe's hand and squeezing it reassuringly.

"I think he's riddled with guilt that he wasn't there to protect you when you needed him." he told her.

"Imagine how you would feel if you were him, and plus he knows that Shayne hurt you to get to him so he blames himself." he continued.

"It's not his fault though." she muttered, her eyes filling with tears.

"He's carrying all that guilt and the anger at Shayne for hurting you." he explained.

"And he's worried about the baby, just like you are." he added.

"That's another reason that he can't know about this, he's feeling guilty enough already." she said thoughtfully, her heart breaking a little as she thought about how Lee must be feeling.

"I get it, but I still don't like it when he tells me I can't do things." she sighed.

"That's because you're a strong independent woman." he chuckled, trying to find a way to cheer her up when he noticed that she was starting to get upset. Chloe nodded slowly, the trace of a small smile playing on the corner of her lips. The two of them fell silent, glancing up when they heard Chloe's name being called.

"Do you want me to come with you?" he offered, watching Chloe closely as she carefully stood up. She nodded slowly, feeling comforted as she followed the doctor, Nathan walking closely behind her.

"Right Miss Evans if you can take a seat please." the doctor told them. Chloe gingerly sat down, quickly reaching out to take Nathan's hand as he sat beside her.

"I'm Doctor Jones, what can I do for you today?" she asked, smiling warmly at them.

"I was the victim of an assault and was kicked repeatedly on my back and I have been in a lot of pain ever since." Chloe explained.

"Okay, let's have a look at you then." Doctor Jones said kindly.

"If you remove your jacket and shirt and I can have a good look at your back." she added. Chloe glanced at Nathan nervously, her cheeks colouring slightly at the thought of undressing in front of them, particularly when she was so self-conscious of her body. Before she could talk herself out of it, she slowly removed her jacket, her cheeks colouring as she lifted her shirt, her eyes wandering to her bump and the still very visible scar on her abdomen. She smiled at Nathan as he reached over and gently squeezed her hand, trying to provide her with some reassurance.

"I didn't realise that you are pregnant!" the doctor exclaimed.

"Yes, almost seventeen weeks." Chloe said quietly.

"Have you had the baby checked over?" the doctor asked.

"We have a midwife coming over later." Chloe told her.

Chloe slowly turned her back on the doctor, starting at a mark on the wall as she tried to forget that she was half naked in front of the doctor and Nathan. Chloe gasped in pain as the Doctor carefully examined her back, gently pressing her hand against each of her ribs in turn. She cried out when she couldn't stand the intense pain any longer.

"You definitely have several broken ribs." the doctor told her, glancing at Nathan and frowning at him for a moment.

"I'm not having an X-ray!" Chloe said quickly, suddenly fearing for the safety of the baby.

"You won't need one, we don't perform an X-ray for broken ribs, we just leave them to heal." the doctor told her, watching Chloe closely as she quickly pulled her clothes back on.

"They should heal in a few weeks, just make sure that you take it easy and if you need to take pain relief you can take paracetamol." she continued.

"That won't harm the baby will it?" Chloe asked nervously.

"No it should be fine, just make sure that you avoid Ibuprofen." the doctor explained. Chloe nodded slowly, knowing in her heart that she wasn't prepared to take any medication, in case she somehow harmed the baby.

"I'll make do without anything." she said quietly, almost like she was talking to herself. Doctor Jones nodded slowly, quickly turning her attention to Nathan.

"Can I have a moment alone with Miss Evans please?" she asked. Nathan glanced at Chloe, who nodded slowly.

"I'll be at reception." Nathan told her as he slowly stood up and left the room.

"Is there anything else you would like to talk about?" the doctor asked as she watched Chloe awkwardly pulling on her jacket.

"No, I don't think so." Chloe replied quietly.

"Is that your partner that is in with you?" the doctor asked.

"No, he's just a friend." Chloe said quietly, her brow furrowing in confusion.

"Just remember if there's anything you need to talk about we are here for you." the doctor told her, gently placing a hand on Chloe's knee.

"It's not like that." Chloe said quickly, finally joining the dots in her head.

"My boyfriend would never hurt me, it was an assault by someone else, it has been reported to the police." she added. The doctor nodded slowly, smiling sympathetically at Chloe as she slowly stood up.

"Make sure that you get plenty of rest and take things easy." the doctor stated. Chloe nodded slowly.

"Thank you." Chloe said as she walked out of the room. She sighed to herself as she slowly walked over to Nathan. As soon as she reached him, she took his hand, suddenly feeling vulnerable and seeking some comfort.

"Come on, we should get you home." he said, as he led Chloe out of the hospital.

"I don't want to go home yet." she said quietly as they walked, her heart sinking at the thought of returning home to face Lee. She couldn't help but feel slightly nervous that he would be angry that she had snuck out without him and she knew that she would face a barrage of questions.

"Why not?" he asked, snapping her out of her thoughts.

"I just need some breathing space." she admitted.

"Can we go to the cemetery?" she asked, feeling a sudden desire to spend some time with her parents.

"If you want too." he smiled at her.

Lee sighed to himself as he stared at his phone, with every hour that passed he became more and more nervous that something had happened to Chloe. Even though he knew in his heart that Nathan would do whatever it took to protect her, he couldn't help but wish that he was able to take care of her himself, especially since he knew that her and the baby were his responsibility. He glanced up at Sheila as she walked into the room and handed him a cup of tea as she sat beside him on the sofa.

"You didn't have to come over Mum." he said quietly.

"I want to support you both." she told him gently, smiling at him when he wrapped his arm around her shoulders. She sighed to herself when she realised that his hands were shaking.

"She'll be okay, Nathan will take care of her." she told him.

"I guess I know that." he sighed.

"Are you doing okay sweetheart?" she asked as he gently rested his head on her shoulder and sighed sadly, still not quite able to suppress the intense fear that he was feeling. He nodded slowly, his mouth suddenly feeling dry when he remembered how helpless he'd felt as he'd watched Shayne holding Chloe.

"I'll be fine." he said, smiling falsely.

"I'm just really worried about Chloe." he added.

"What did he actually do to her?" she asked.

"I don't know." he admitted, his heart sinking when he was reminded that Chloe still wouldn't open up to him.

"I have asked her loads of times and she won't tell me. She wouldn't even let me in with her when she spoke to the police." he continued.

"She probably just needs some time to get her head around whatever happened." she said, softly stroking his hair and sighing to herself when she heard him sniff sadly.

"I need to know what happened Mum." he said sadly.

"I know sweetheart, your brain is spinning with possibilities isn't it." she muttered. Lee nodded slowly, his eyes filling with tears at the thought of Shayne harming Chloe.

"The worst part is that it's all my fault. He hurt her to get to me." he whispered, wiping away the tears that were filling his eyes.

"It's not your fault, everyone knows how much Chloe means to you and that you wouldn't do anything to hurt her." she told him. He nodded slowly, still feeling sick to his stomach with guilt.

"What time is the midwife coming over?" she asked, trying to distract him.

"In about an hour." he said quietly.

"I hope Chloe is back in time, she's been gone for hours." he added nervously.

"I'll try calling her again." he continued, quickly picking up his phone.

"Just leave her, she probably needs some time." she told him, gently taking his phone out of his grip and placing it in her pocket. Lee nodded slowly, sighing to himself as he closed his eyes, trying to fight the images that were swirling around his head.

Whenever he closed his eyes he could see Chloe's face, her eyes pleading with him to help her as Shayne held her tightly against himself.

"You really need a haircut." Sheila chuckled to herself, trying to distract him from worrying about Chloe.

"I like it a bit longer." he smiled, slowly opening his eyes. Lee's eyes flickered to the hallway as he heard the front door open and close. He released the breath he didn't realise he was holding when Chloe walked into the room. He quickly stood up and crossed the room so that he was standing in front of her, his eyes darting all over her body, checking for signs of injury.

"Thank god you're okay." he muttered, unable to tear his eyes away from her as he watched her staring at the floor.

"I did tell you that I would take care of her." Nathan piped up. Lee nodded slowly, his eyes still fixed on Chloe. He took a step closer to her, frowning to himself when she quickly backed away from him, gasping when her back hit against the wall behind her.

"Please don't do that to me again." Lee muttered, his stomach churning as he thought about the possibility of Shayne finding out that she had left the house. Chloe nodded slowly, feeling a pang of guilt for making him worry.

"I'm sorry." she whispered, glancing up at him as he stepped closer to her and gently placed his hands on either side of her neck, softly stroking along her jawline with his thumbs.

"Do you have any idea how worried I was?" he said quietly. She nodded slowly, not entirely sure what to say to him.

"I love you so much." he breathed, gently wrapping his arms around her waist and pressing his body against hers, suddenly feeling an overwhelming desire to hold her close and never let her go. Chloe's heart pounded against her chest as Lee placed his head against the wall behind her, his body pressed tightly against hers. His heart broke a little when he suddenly realised that her whole body was trembling nervously against him.

"I'm really sorry, I know you just want to protect me." she whispered, her stomach churning with guilt as she thought about the fact that she wasn't able to be honest with him.

"You don't have to apologise Chlo." he said quietly. She wrapped her arms around his neck tightly and closed her eyes. She gasped her eyes snapping open when the feel of Lee's body pressing against hers suddenly reminded her of when Shayne's body was against her, when he pinned her down on the stairs. He slowly raised his head, frowning in confusion when he noticed the fear on her face.

"What's wrong?" he asked worriedly.

"I'm fine." she whispered, trying to control the panic that she was feeling.

"It's okay Chlo." he told her, holding her tightly in an attempt to make her feel safe.

"Please don't pin me." she whispered, a small squeak of fear escaping her lips. Lee quickly let go of her, almost like he'd received an electric shock. His heart sunk into the pit of his stomach as he stood in silence, trying to process her words.

"I wasn't Chlo." he said sadly, his heart breaking when he realised that she was afraid of him.

"I would never do anything to hurt you." he added, when she remained silent, taking deep breaths to try and steady her nerves.

"I know." she whispered, her cheeks colouring in embarrassment as she glanced up at him and saw that he was staring at her, a look of deep sadness on his handsome features.

"I'm sorry." she said quietly, quickly reaching out to take his hand and squeezing it reassuringly.

"You don't have to keep apologising Chlo, you haven't done anything wrong." he said softly,

"I think I need to get some rest." she said quietly, suddenly feeling the desire to leave the room when she felt everyone's eyes watching her.

"Do you want me to come with you?" he offered sadly, watching her as she slowly climbed the stairs.

"No, I'll be okay." she said quietly.

Chapter Thirty Two

Lee sighed sadly to himself as he watched Chloe climbing the stairs. As soon as she disappeared out of sight, he found himself longing to follow her, to always be by her side, making sure that she was safe. Despite the fact that he still had no idea exactly what had happened to her, he could clearly see that she was attempting to hide how much she was struggling from him. He slowly walked over to the sofa and perched on the end of it, gently resting his elbows on his knees, his brain spinning with possibilities.

"Was she okay when you were out?" Lee asked Nathan, trying to distract himself from the images that were swirling around his head.

"Yeah she wasn't too bad. We spent a lot of time in the cemetery." Nathan replied. Lee nodded slowly, his heart breaking a little when he realised that she often visited the cemetery at times when she felt alone and like she had nobody else to turn too.

"She probably just needed to tell her parents what had happened." Sheila piped up, glancing at Lee when she heard him sigh sadly to himself. Lee nodded, glancing down at his leg as it began to bounce up and down.

"Did you manage to find out exactly what happened?" Lee asked Nathan, not entirely sure that he was ready to hear about whatever Chloe had been through, but knowing in his heart that he couldn't bear the unknown.

"No, I stood out of earshot, so that she could have some privacy, but close enough that I could check that she was safe." Nathan explained.

"I just wish that she would tell me what happened." Lee admitted quietly, gently massaging his temples as he heard the sound of Chloe screaming for him as he was driving home echoing around his brain.

"I'm sure she will do, she just needs some time." Sheila reassured him, gently placing her hand on his knee.

Chloe sighed, her eyes filling with tears as she lay on the bed, unable to stop fidgeting as she tried to find a comfortable position. No matter what she did, the pain in her chest was unbearable. She slowly picked up a pillow and held it tightly against herself, snuggling into it. She couldn't help but wish that she could curl up in Lee's arms, so that she felt safe, but every time that she tried she was reminded of Shayne.

She jumped and slowly sat up as the bedroom door opened. She quickly wiped the tears from her eyes, her heart sinking when she noticed Lee gazing at her sadly.

"The midwife is here." he told her, swallowing the nervous lump that was rising in his throat. She nodded slowly and stared at her hands that were gently resting in place on her lap. Lee pulled the chair out from the dressing table and placed it beside the bed, watching Chloe closely as he sat down beside her.

"It'll be alright Chlo." he said softly, as he placed his hands on top of hers and squeezed them gently.

"Will it, what if it's not?" she whispered, her eyes filling with tears once again.

"Then I'll kill him." he muttered under his breath, suddenly feeling a deep sense of anger in the pit of his stomach. Chloe opened her mouth to respond, her stomach churning nervously at his words, but quickly closed it again when the midwife walked into the room.

"Hello Chloe, how are you doing today?" she asked.

"I'm alright." Chloe replied quietly, glancing nervously at Lee as she fidgeted on the bed, unable to get comfortable because of the intense pain in her back.

"So since we've not met before, my name is Sarah and I'm a private midwife." she told them.

"I was told that you were the victim of an assault?" she asked. Chloe nodded slowly, her eyes fixed on her lap as she felt Lee's eyes burning a hole into her head.

"Okay, so I'll check your baby over for you to make sure that everything is as it should be." Sarah said, as she rummaged in her bag and pulled out a portable ultrasound machine.

"Okay if you can just lay back and lift your shirt up for me." Sarah said, glancing between Chloe and Lee when they remained silent. Chloe nodded slowly and did as she asked, a small gasp escaping her lips as she rested her back against the bed frame. The two of them remained silent as Sarah quickly applied some gel to Chloe's abdomen.

"So, you're seventeen weeks aren't you?" Sarah checked, glancing at Chloe as she slowly moved the probe around, searching for the baby.

"Yes." Chloe said quietly, her heart pounding against her chest with every moment that passed.

"I haven't felt the baby move since I was attacked either." she added, glancing at Lee when he quickly turned to face her.

"What?" he whispered, his stomach churning nervously as he tried to process Chloe's words.

"That's okay, it's probably just a coincidence." Sarah said, smiling reassuringly at Chloe. Lee swallowed the lump that was rising in his throat, his eyes fixed on Chloe as he suddenly felt paralysed with fear that something had happened to their baby. Chloe glanced at him for a moment, her heart breaking a little when she noticed that his eyes had filled with tears. She knew in her heart that neither of them were strong enough to lose their baby. Lee smiled at her as she reached across and gently stroked his hair, trying to provide him with some comfort. He turned his head slightly and placed a soft kiss on her wrist.

"There we go." Sarah said happily when she finally located the baby. Chloe and Lee turned to face the ultrasound machine, their eyes misting with tears as they gazed fondly at their baby.

"Is everything okay?" Chloe asked nervously.

"Yes everything is fine, you can see the heartbeat there." Sarah said, pointing to the screen. Chloe nodded slowly, quickly releasing the breath that she didn't realise she was holding. Her eyes were fixed on the screen as she watched her baby's heartbeat fluttering quickly on the screen. Lee sniffed quietly, trying to fight the wave of relief that he was feeling and resist the urge to burst into tears. Chloe didn't react as he placed a soft kiss on her cheek and gently rested the side of his head against her shoulder, his eyes fixed on the screen.

"So thankfully everything is okay." Sarah smiled at them when she eventually removed the probe and carefully wiped the gel from Chloe's abdomen. Chloe nodded slowly, quickly wiping away the tears of relief that were steadily rolling down her cheeks and pulling down her shirt.

"Thank you so much for coming over." Lee smiled at Sarah as he watched her slowly packing away her equipment.

"You are very welcome, I'm pleased that I was able to put your minds at rest." she replied, smiling between the two of them when she noticed how relieved they both looked. The two of them remained silent as they watched Sarah quickly leaving the room. Lee quickly perched on the bed beside Chloe, staring down at her as she silently gazed up at him. Her eyes flickered to his lips as he laid down on his side beside her. He hesitated for a moment before placing a soft kiss on her lips. Her heart pounded against her chest nervously as she kissed him back. She sighed sadly to herself when they eventually pulled apart and Lee stared down at her. His stomach churned when he glanced down at her neck and he stared at the very noticeable mark that Shayne had left on her. He sighed sadly to himself as he stroked it softly with his fingertips.

"Are you going to tell me what he did to you Chlo?" he asked nervously, his desperation to know exactly what she had been through getting the better of him.

"I'm so glad the baby is okay." she mumbled, trying to change the subject.

"I know, me too." he sighed. Chloe's stomach churned when she felt him place his hand on her side and slowly trail it downwards. Her breath caught in her throat, when his hand eventually came to a stop and rested in place on her bump. She instinctively squirmed away from his touch, her stomach churning with guilt when she heard him sigh deeply.

"Chlo." he whispered sadly, not entirely sure what to say to make her feel better. She glanced down at his hand when he softly trailed the tips of his fingers on her bump, not quite able to fight the need that he had to touch their baby.

"Don't!" she said sharply, quickly moving away from him. Her heart broke for him when she glanced at him and noticed that his eyes had filled with tears. She knew that she was breaking his heart and couldn't help but feel an intense guilt that she was denying him the baby, particularly when he was relieved that the baby was okay. Chloe ran her hand through her hair in frustration, desperately wishing that she was able to fight the intense flashbacks that swirled around her brain whenever Lee unknowingly did anything that reminded her of Shayne's touch. She knew that she couldn't keep pushing him away, particularly when she was craving his comfort, but she had no idea how to allow him to comfort her without the intense fear from taking over.

Lee couldn't help but stare at her as she gazed at him silently. Even though he knew that she was still suffering because of what she had been through, it still felt like someone was stabbing in the heart whenever she moved away from him. He wanted nothing more than to be able to hold her and their baby close, to be able to feel Chloe's soft heartbeat against his chest as he held her. He desperately wanted to help her feel safe, but had no idea how to do so when she was constantly moving away from his touch.

"You're not afraid of me are you?" he asked, sighing sadly as he watched Chloe slowly sit up and shuffle down the end of the bed.

"No of course not." she said, glancing up at him.

"You keep moving away from me all the time." he said, trying to prompt her. Chloe remained silent, not entirely sure what to say, without telling him the truth that whenever he touched her, she was reminded of Shayne's touch.

"You blame me don't you." he said, sighing deeply.

"No, I don't." she muttered, the guilt that she was feeling suddenly intensifying.

"It doesn't matter if you do....I blame myself." he admitted, his heart plummeting when Chloe stared at him silently. Every time that he looked at her, his eyes were drawn to the mark on her neck and the swelling on her cheek.

"I don't blame you, I swear." she said firmly. Lee nodded slowly, swallowing the lump that was rising in his throat. He still felt sick to his stomach that she'd been hurt because of him. His thoughts wandered back to when she was stabbed and he promised her that he would never allow anyone to harm her again. He knew in his heart that he'd let her down....even though she would never admit it to him. Chloe sighed deeply as she carefully stood up and left the room, trying to escape the uncomfortable silence.

Chapter Thirty Three

Chloe glanced up as Michelle walked into the kitchen, smiling at her as soon as they locked eyes. Michelle watched Chloe closely as she slowly poured herself a glass of water and quickly downed it, avoiding Michelle's gaze as she felt her staring at her.

"Are you okay Chloe, you look upset?" Michelle asked softly. Chloe nodded slowly, smiling falsely at her. She couldn't bring herself to open up to Michelle, after everything that she had done, Chloe knew that she would never trust her again.

"I'm sorry I've not really been checking on you." Chloe whispered, suddenly feeling a wave of guilt when she realised that she had completely forgotten about Michelle and everything that she had been through.

"It's fine, you've had a lot going on." Michelle smiled at her.

"Mark is back from Norway later anyway, so he's coming to pick me up." she added.

"Good....make sure he takes care of you." Chloe told her. Michelle nodded slowly, raising her eyebrow sceptically. She couldn't help but wish, once again, that Mark was the kind of person who actually seemed to care about her.

"He's been calling quite a lot, so he must care." Chloe pointed out, when she noticed Michelle's sceptical expression.

"Maybe." Michelle shrugged.

"I actually want to thank you for letting me stay here, I don't know what I'd have done without you the past few days." Michelle said, biting her lip to prevent herself from bursting into tears when she was reminded of everything that she had been through.

"It's okay, you don't have to thank me. It's what anyone would have done in the circumstances." Chloe told her.

"No, it's not, particularly after everything that I did to you. I really appreciate it." Michelle insisted, quickly pulling Chloe into a hug.

"And I'm so sorry for leading Shayne to you, I will never forgive myself." she continued.

"It's not your fault." Chloe whispered, her eyes filling with tears.

"You've been through so much already and now this." Michelle whispered in her ear.

"And you're pregnant." she added, her heart breaking at the thought of anything happening to Chloe's baby. Michelle knew that she would never forgive herself if Chloe lost her baby as a result of trying to help her.

"The baby is fine." Chloe told her, choosing not to mention her own injuries. Michelle watched her closely as she carefully extracted herself from Michelle's grip.

"Thank god, I'm so pleased." Michelle said quietly, breathing a deep sigh of relief.

"Me too." Chloe smiled, gently placing her hand on her bump and softly stroking it with her fingernails. Michelle smiled at her, following closely behind as Chloe walked into the living room. Chloe froze, her cheeks colouring as she walked into the living room and Nathan, Lee and Sheila instantly stopped talking and turned to face her.

"Were you talking about me?" she asked as she carefully sat between Lee and Nathan.

"Lee was just telling us the good news, that everything is okay with the baby." Sheila piped up, smiling at Chloe. Chloe nodded slowly glancing at each of them in turn, still not quite able to shake the feeling that they'd been talking about her. She raised her eyebrow at Nathan, sighing quietly to herself when his cheeks coloured and he quickly looked away from her, avoiding her gaze.

"You were talking about me weren't you?!" Chloe insisted, her temper starting to fray.

"We're just worried about you Chlo." Lee told her, watching her closely as she tucked her legs onto the sofa. Chloe shook her head slowly, glancing down at his hand as he rested it in place on her knees.

"Well I'm fine." she said shortly, feeling slightly frustrated that everyone was constantly fussing her.

"The baby is fine, so I'm fine." she added shortly, her cheeks colouring as everyone stared at her. She squirmed in her seat, trying to make herself as inconspicuous as possible. She gasped in pain as she twisted and felt a searing pain in her back.

"Are you okay?" Lee asked quickly, his brow furrowing in concern.

"Yes I already told you." she replied.

"But you gasped, did the baby move again?" Lee asked her. Chloe shook her head, sighing in frustration. Even though she knew that everyone cared about her, and she appreciated their concern, she couldn't help but feel like a specimen under a microscope as everyone stared at her. She slowly pulled the hood of her jumper over her head as the room fell silent, everyone's eyes still fixed on her.

"Let's see what's on TV." Michelle piped up when she couldn't stand the awkward silence any longer. Chloe shot Michelle a small smile when she quickly picked up the remote and switched on the television.

"Ooh, this is a good film." she announced as she quickly selected the channel.

"I've never seen it before." Chloe replied, glancing at Lee who was still watching her closely. She sighed to herself and turned to face the television, her stomach churning nervously as she felt him watching her closely. Even though she knew that his intense concern was coming out of a place of love, she couldn't help but wish that she could hide from the world. To be able to process everything that had happened without constantly having to hide how afraid and sore she was. Having to constantly lie to the man that she loved was finally starting to take its toll on her, and even though she knew that she was doing the right thing, to protect Lee from the inevitable anger that he would feel, she couldn't help but feel sick with guilt that she wasn't being open and honest with him.

She stared at the television, trying to engross herself in the film as a distraction from the anxiety and intense inner turmoil that she was feeling. As she glanced at the glass of wine in Michelle's hand, she couldn't help but wish that she could drown her own sorrows in alcohol. She'd have given anything to be able to escape the way that she was feeling, at least for a few moments.

"Oh my god, no matter how many times I watch it, I always cry when Ellie dies." Michelle muttered, a small sob escaping her lips as she stared, transfixed at the screen.

Lee glanced at Chloe, his heart plummeting when he noticed that her eyes had filled with tears. He couldn't help but feel slightly frustrated with Michelle, that she had insensitively switched on a film that he knew would remind Chloe how it felt when she lost her mother. He sighed sadly to himself when he noticed her slowly wiping away her tears. Chloe jumped when Lee wrapped his arms around her waist and tried to pull her onto his lap. She cried out in pain and quickly squirmed away from his grip. Lee instantly let go of her, sighing quietly to himself.

"I forgot I'm not allowed to touch you anymore." he snapped defensively when he gazed around the room and noticed everyone staring at them.

"I just don't want to sit on your lap." she said quietly, her cheeks colouring

"Whatever." he muttered, the frustration finally getting the better of him. He had no idea how he was supposed to help her when she constantly squirmed away from him. Despite the fact that he knew it was a result of whatever Shayne had done to her, it still hurt him deeply every time that she moved away from him, almost like she was afraid of him or disgusted by him. Even though she had denied the fact that she blamed him, he couldn't help but feel like she was secretly disappointed in him for not protecting her.

Chloe glanced at Nathan when he reached over and gently squeezed her hand in an attempt to reassure her. She smiled at him, a small part of her wishing Lee understood her in the same way that Nathan did. That he realised how scared and trapped she felt whenever he tried to hold her in his arms. Even though she knew in her heart that Lee would never do anything to hurt her, the fear that she'd felt when Shayne held her down would still come flooding back. Before Chloe could stop herself she gently rested the side of her head against Nathan's shoulder and linked her arm through his, snuggling against him in a desperate attempt to feel safe. Nathan glanced at Lee nervously, not entirely sure what to do. He could clearly see the hurt in Lee's eyes that Chloe was turning to Nathan for support rather than him, but at the same time, he couldn't bring himself to move away from her when she clearly needed some comfort. Chloe slowly raised her head, glancing between the two of them awkwardly, when she sensed the tense atmosphere. Her stomach churned with guilt when she saw the hurt written on Lee's face.

"I'm going to bed." Chloe said quietly, before quickly standing up and leaving the room.

Chloe wiped away the tears that were steadily flowing down her cheeks as she slowly climbed the stairs. She sighed deeply when she heard footsteps climbing the stairs behind her.

"You don't need to go to bed just because I am." she said shortly, not even turning around.

"I'm not, I was hoping to talk to you." she heard Sheila's voice say from behind her. Chloe froze in place and slowly turned to face her.

"I thought you were Lee." Chloe said quietly.

"Yeah I guessed that." Sheila laughed. Chloe smiled slightly, staring at the floor as the two of them fell silent.

"Do you need someone to talk too Chloe?" Sheila offered.

"No, I'm fine." Chloe said quietly.

"And I really don't need a lecture from anyone about how I should open up to Lee about what happened." she added.

"He's just trying to help you Chloe, he wants to help you feel safe." Sheila pointed out.

"I know that, but I still can't tell him. He's your son, you know what he's like." Chloe said quickly.

"What do you mean?" Sheila frowned.

"If I tell him what happened, he'll probably go looking for Shayne and I don't want that to happen." Chloe explained.

"Especially when he's going to be a father." she continued, sighing quietly as her eyes wandered to her abdomen. Sheila nodded slowly.

"Don't forget you can always talk to me if you need too!" Sheila called after Chloe as she walked away from her. Chloe nodded and walked into the bedroom, sighing in relief when she closed the door behind herself and realised that she was finally free from the intense gazes of everyone.

Chapter Thirty Four

Chloe's eyes snapped open, her eyes widening in panic when she realised that the bedroom lamp was switched on. She quickly pulled the duvet over her head and curled up in a ball under the covers, trying to find a way to feel safe. She felt an intense stabbing pain in her chest as she sobbed quietly to herself, unable to stop the flashbacks from swirling around her head. No matter how much time passed, she couldn't seem to stop thinking about what Shayne had done to her and how it felt when he touched her, against her will. Vomit rose in her throat when she closed her eyes and saw the twisted smirk on Shayne's face as he spread her legs and pinned her down. Her stomach turned at the thought of what he was going to do to her, her heart breaking a little that the special bond between her and Lee, that meant the world to her, would have been broken. She knew in her heart that she would never sleep with another man, it meant too much to her that she'd only ever been with Lee. Chloe jumped as she heard Lee's voice from behind her:

"Did you have a nightmare Chlo?" he asked softly.

"No, I'm fine." she lied, clapping her hand over her mouth when a small sob escaped her lips.

"I heard you, you were calling out." he pointed out, his heart breaking as he stared at her. Even though she had her back to him, he knew that she was crying to herself. He longed to reach out and pull her into his arms, but he knew that his Mum was right, he needed to give her some space and allow her to come to him when she felt ready to do so. She slowly opened her eyes, glancing down at her hands that were shaking uncontrollably.

"I'm just so afraid." she whispered, no longer able to hide from him how she was feeling.

"You don't have to be afraid Chlo, I won't leave your side until he is caught." he told her. Chloe nodded and slowly turned to face him, gently pushing the duvet down so that she was no longer buried underneath it. She jumped slightly when she noticed that he was laying on his side, facing her, watching her closely, a look of concern on his handsome features.

He gasped quietly to himself when he noticed her tear stained face and how wide her eyes were with fear. She quickly pulled the sleeves on his hoodie down over her hands, desperately trying to find a way to comfort herself and hide from the world. Chloe shuffled over to him, glancing up at him nervously as she hesitated for a moment. Her heart pounded against her chest as she felt the warmth radiating from his body. His breath caught in his throat as she carefully rested her body against his. He glanced down at her and raised his arms to wrap them around her, before quickly lowering them when he suddenly remembered that she couldn't bear to be held. He stared down at her, unable to tear his eyes away from her as her body trembled against him.

"You're okay Chlo." he whispered in her ear, desperately trying to resist the urge to touch her. She flinched slightly as he gently placed his hand on the side of her face and softly stroked her hair, trying to comfort her without causing her fear to increase.

"He almost took me!" she exclaimed, sobbing uncontrollably against him.

"What are you talking about?" he frowned, swallowing the bile that was rising in his throat as he tried to process her words.

"I would never have just been yours again." she continued, almost like she hadn't heard what he'd said.

"You don't belong to me anyway Chlo." he told her, his eyes filling with tears when he realised what she was suggesting. His brain began to swirl with thoughts as he desperately tried to resist the urge to ask her what she had been through. He couldn't help but feel whatever Shayne had done to Chloe it was something bad. It suddenly made sense to him why she was so afraid, and why she couldn't bear to be held. Chloe quickly wiped away the tears that were rolling down her cheeks, wrapping her arms around her chest to try and control the intense pain that she was in.

"I don't know how to feel safe." she sobbed against his chest.

"It's okay, I'll keep you safe Chlo." he told her, continuing to softly stroke her hair.

"Every time I close my eyes, I can feel him touching me." she whispered, no longer having the energy to sob. He sighed deeply as she rested her head against his collarbone and snuggled her body against his. Lee placed a soft kiss on her forehead and continued stroking her hair, wishing in his heart that he knew what to say or do to make her feel better.

"I'll never let him touch you again." he whispered, his stomach churning with guilt once again, that he wasn't able to protect her when she needed him. Chloe nodded slowly, her stomach churning at the thought of Shayne returning to the house. Up until that moment she hadn't really processed that he knew exactly where she was. She gasped as a thought suddenly popped into her head:

"He must have been watching the house." she whispered nervously.

"I know." he agreed.

"Why do you think I don't want to leave your side?" he added. Lee sighed sadly to himself as Chloe sniffed quietly, her body still trembling against him. As soon as Lee had seen Shayne at the house, he'd quickly realised that it wasn't a coincidence that he'd happened to turn up when Lee wasn't home. He'd clearly been watching the house for some time, patiently waiting for the moment when Michelle and Chloe were alone and defenceless.

"What if he comes back for me?" she said breathlessly as she fought to suppress the panic that she was feeling.

"I don't think he would dare." he told her firmly, his eyes filling with tears when Chloe stared at her hands, desperately trying to stop herself from trembling uncontrollably.

"What can I do to make you feel safe?" he asked her, when he couldn't stand feeling helpless any longer.

"I don't know." she said softly. He sighed deeply to himself and gently rested his face against hers, slowly placing a soft kiss on her cheek. His heart pounded against his chest, his temper building slightly when his eyes wandered to the mark on Chloe's neck.

"I'm so sorry Chlo, I never should have left you on your own." he whispered, closing his eyes for a moment and sighing to himself when the tears that he'd been fighting fell from his eyes and dropped onto Chloe's cheek. Chloe sighed deeply, finally relaxing against him. Lee smiled slightly when he felt Chloe finally relaxing.

"I love you so much." she whispered, sighing sadly to herself when she felt Lee's tears on her cheek.

"I love you too." he whispered back, still wishing that he could turn the clock back and protect her from everything that had happened to her. The two of them remained silent as Chloe slowly closed her eyes, sighing in contentment to herself when she felt Lee's face still resting against hers. She snuggled closer to him, suddenly feeling an intense need to be close to him.

"Is the baby okay Chlo?" he asked her, when he suddenly remembered that she'd been calling out for the baby in her sleep.

"Yes, why?" she frowned in confusion.

"You were calling out in your sleep and you said something about the baby." he told her, watching her closely as she slowly lifted her head and stared at him.

"What did I say?" she asked him.

"Most of it was incoherent, but you mentioned the baby." he replied, instinctively moving his hand towards her bump, quickly moving his hand away before he touched her, when he remembered how she had reacted last time. Chloe watched him closely as he sighed sadly to himself, his eyes fixed on her bump. She sighed quietly, suddenly feeling a wave of guilt wash over her when she realised how upset he was about the whole situation.

"The baby is fine, it was just a dream." she quickly reassured him. Lee smiled at her as she gently took his hand in hers and carefully placed it on her abdomen.

"I'm sorry I kept the baby from you." she said softly.

"You didn't Chlo." he whispered, his eyes misting with tears as he stared at their hands gently resting in place on her bump, unable to tear his eyes away.

"It reminded me of when Shayne touched our baby." she said quietly, her eyes filling with tears once again.

"It's okay, you don't have to explain yourself." he said quietly. Chloe nodded slowly, quickly resting her head against his chest once again, sighing in contentment as he stroked her hair, his other hand softly stroking her bump.

"Get some sleep Chlo....I won't let anything happen to you." he reassured her softly. Chloe nodded slowly and gently closed her eyes.

Chapter Thirty Five

Lee frowned to himself as he slowly opened his eyes and squinted in the bright sunlight that was shining through the window. He glanced down at Chloe, smiling to himself when he noticed that she was still curled up against him. She was curled into a tight ball, her head resting gently on his chest. He stared at her longingly, smiling to himself when he was reminded once again of how beautiful she was. His brow furrowed in concern when she fidgeted in her sleep, her movements gradually becoming frantic.

"It's okay Chlo." he whispered softly, gently brushing the swelling on her cheek with his thumb. Even though he knew that she was fast asleep and couldn't hear him, he liked to think that he was able to comfort her in some small way. His heart broke a little when he saw the look of fear on her face. Even though he was tempted to wake her, he knew that he couldn't, the only thing that he could do was to wait and hope she wouldn't be too upset and afraid when she woke. He jumped slightly, watching her closely as she quickly turned onto her side, her back facing him. He glanced down at her hips, frowning to himself when he noticed that her top had risen up slightly. He quickly took the material between his hands, slowly pulling her top back down, fearful that she would be cold. Lee froze, his eyes widening when he laid eyes on the dark bruises on her lower back. His stomach churned as he stared at them, unable to tear his eyes away from them. His thoughts swirled uncontrollably when he quickly realised that they had been caused by Shayne. Before he could stop himself he rested the side of his head against Chloe's hips, snuggling himself into her. His eyes filled with tears when he thought about what Chloe may or may not have been through as a result of Shayne. He placed his hand on Chloe's legs, gently stroking small circles with his fingertips, closing his eyes, trying to distract himself from the images that were swirling around his head.

"I can't believe I didn't protect you, especially when I promised you last time." he whispered sadly, gently taking the material of her pyjama trousers in his hand and curling it into his fist, desperately trying to control the inner turmoil that he was in. He'd never felt so guilty, angry and upset all at the same time. He sighed to himself, softly closing his eyes as he snuggled himself closer to her, needing to be as close to her as possible.

"I'm sorry Chlo." he whispered, no longer able to fight the tears that were slowly rolling down his cheeks. He opened his eyes and slowly shook his head, desperately trying to clear the images of the bruises on Chloe's back. He couldn't help but wonder what else she had kept from him and what other injuries she had. He suddenly felt sick to his stomach that she didn't feel able to tell him exactly what she had been through. He jumped slightly as Chloe fidgeted and slowly sat up, a frown present on her pretty features when she noticed him curled up beside her, his head still in place on her hips. Chloe gazed down at him, her heart sinking a little when she noticed the tears that were rolling down his cheeks. She sighed to herself and softly stroked his hair, not entirely sure what he was upset about. He remained still, not even reacting as she stroked his hair, his brain still reeling with what he'd seen.

"Are you okay?" she asked softly, sighing to herself when he didn't respond. She leant forward to rest her body against his, to try and provide him with some comfort. A small whimper of pain escaped her lips as she started to sit forward and felt a tearing pain rip through her back. She quickly laid back down on the bed, taking deep breaths as she waited for the pain to subside. Her stomach plummeted when she glanced at Lee and noticed that he still hadn't moved and that tears were still steadily rolling down his cheeks.

"Come here." she said sadly. Lee slowly lifted his head and gazed at her sadly. Despite the fact that he longed to curl up with her, to be able to rest his head against her chest and listen to her soft heartbeat, he knew that it would cause her fear to increase and that was the last thing that he wanted. She'd already been through enough and she was more important to him than himself.

"Lee." she whispered, when he remained silent, unable to tear his eyes away from her.

"No, Chlo." he mumbled, his voice catching in his throat.

"I don't want you to be afraid." he added.

"I'm okay." she told him, knowing in her heart that when he held her she would likely be reminded of Shayne's touch, but at that moment she knew that he needed her to comfort him, and she couldn't deny him. She watched him closely as he slowly shuffled closer, hesitating for a moment before gently placing his head on her chest. Chloe sighed quietly as she wrapped her arm around his neck and softly stroked his hair, gently snuggling her face against his. He shivered under her touch as she stroked the hair on the back of his neck. Chloe flinched for a moment when she felt him place his hand on her abdomen.

"I would never do anything to hurt either of you." he whispered in her ear, his heart sinking when he felt her flinch.

"I know." she whispered.

"You both mean the world to me." he told her, sniffing quietly. Chloe smiled to herself, her heart swelling with pride when she was reminded once again how lucky she was to have him in her life.

"What's wrong, did you have a nightmare or something?" she asked, still slightly confused as to why he was so upset.

"No not exactly." he said, sighing deeply. His eyes flickered to Chloe as she placed a soft kiss on his forehead.

"I think we need to have a chat Chlo." he said quietly as he slowly stroked small circles on her bump.

"Why, what's wrong?" she asked, her stomach churning nervously.

"You need to tell me what happened." he said quietly. Chloe sighed deeply and fell silent, her stomach churning as her thoughts wandered to Shayne. Lee slowly lifted his head, his gaze fixed on her as he waited for her to respond. She remained silent, quickly looking away from his intense gaze, her cheeks colouring.

"Please baby, I need to know." he said quietly, trying to prompt her.

"No you don't." she said shortly. She winced as she quickly moved away from him and carefully sat up, shuffling over to the edge of the bed and placing her legs over the side of the bed.

"Chlo." Lee said quietly from behind her. Her eyes misted with tears when she heard the deep sadness in his voice. She couldn't help but feel sick with guilt at what she was doing to him, she knew that not knowing what had happened to her was slowly tearing him apart and that his brain was likely spinning with the possibilities. But she knew in her heart that he would be blinded by rage and would want to make Shayne pay for hurting her. She jumped slightly, snapping out of her thoughts when she felt Lee place a soft kiss on her shoulder.

"I'll tell you when he's arrested." she said thoughtfully, almost like she was talking to herself.

"Why, what difference does it make?" he frowned.

"Because you'll kill him." she whispered, her stomach churning nervously. She slowly turned to face him, tucking her legs onto the bed and resting her hands on her lap. She glanced up at him as she felt him watching her closely. Her heart broke when he quickly wiped away the last of his tears.

"I can't not know any longer Chlo." he said softly, his stomach churning with guilt that he was putting pressure on her, but he knew in his heart that he couldn't stand the unknown any longer, especially now that he had seen her bruises. She sighed sadly and reached towards him, softly stroking his cheek with her fingertips.

"I can't tell you yet." she whispered, her eyes filling with tears.

"But I've seen your bruises." he said quietly, swallowing the lump that was rising in his throat. Chloe gasped and quickly moved her hand away from him, almost like she had received an electric shock.

"How did you....." she started, trailing off, her brain swirling as she tried to figure out how he could possibly have seen the bruises on her back.

"Wait....did you lift my top up while I was asleep?!" she asked quickly as she shuffled away from him.

"No of course not." he frowned, feeling slightly hurt that she even considered that he would do something like that to her.

"Your top rose up when you turned over, I actually pulled it back down so that you didn't get cold." he explained, watching her closely as she avoided his gaze. Chloe nodded and remained silent, sighing quietly to herself at the tension in the room. She couldn't help but think back to the time before Shayne had attacked her, when she would only feel relaxed when she was in Lee's presence. Ever since that fateful night she hadn't been able to relax around him, partly due to the fact that his touch reminded her of Shayne but largely because she knew that she was hiding the truth from him. Despite the fact that she only wanted to protect him from his own temper, that didn't stop the intense guilt that she was feeling. Her eyes flickered to Lee when he moved closer to her, stopping when he was sitting in front of her.

"How far up did my top go?" she asked nervously, suddenly feeling slightly fearful that he had seen the boot print shaped bruise that Nathan had described.

"Only a little." he said quietly, frowning slightly at her words.

"Why?" he quickly added, when he suddenly realised that she seemed to be suggesting that she had other injuries.

"I just wondered." she said quietly, quickly looking away from his intense gaze.

"Chlo?" he insisted, sighing in frustration.

"Promise me something." she muttered, finally looking him in the eye. He nodded slowly, raising his eyebrow as he waited for her to continue.

"I'll tell you everything, if you promise not to do something stupid, like go looking for him." she stated firmly.

"I promise." he said quickly, his desperation to know what had happened to her causing him to not give much thought to what she was asking of him. She narrowed her eyes at him suspiciously.

"I won't do anything stupid Chlo." he reassured her. She nodded slowly, opening her mouth to speak and quickly closing it again when she suddenly realised that she had no idea how to start telling him everything that had happened.

"Start at the beginning Chlo." he prompted. Her eyes filled with tears as she slowly shook her head, trying to clear the images that were swirling around her mind. She swallowed the lump that that was rising in her throat when she remembered how it had felt when Shayne touched her.

"He had me pinned against the wall and was kissing my neck, and I knew that he was trying to prove a point to you. And I felt his hand stroking up my leg, so I shoved him as hard as I could." she explained quietly, her cheeks colouring as she stared at her hands that were gently resting in place on her lap, unable to look him in the eye.

"And I must have caught him unawares, because I managed to squeeze past him and I ran." she continued, glancing up at Lee for a moment. He remained silent, hanging on her every word, as he waited for her to tell him everything that had happened.

"But he grabbed my hood and pulled me back. He threw me to the ground and I knew that he was going to kick me, so I turned my back on him." she said quietly.

"To protect the baby." he muttered. She nodded slowly, her eyes filling with tears as she stared down at her bump. Lee quickly reached over to squeeze her hand, frowning to himself when she quickly pulled away from his touch. A steady stream of tears rolled down her cheeks as she placed her hand on her bump and stroked soft circles with her fingernails.

"He wanted to make sure that I behaved so he repeatedly kicked my back, hence the bruises." she muttered.

"Then he flung me onto the stairs and climbed on top of me." she said, a small sob escaping her lips as she tried to get everything out before she broke down and couldn't speak about it any longer.

"He unfastened my jeans and removed my hoodie." she whispered, a small sob escaping her lips when she remembered how it felt when Shayne had spread her legs and pinned her under him, his body pressed tightly against her. She fell silent, not quite able to bring herself to say anymore.

"Was that when you screamed for me?" he asked her, trying to fight the intense anger that he was feeling at the thought of anyone doing anything to harm Chloe.

"Kind of, I threatened him first, that you would kill him if he touched me. That's when he hit my head against the banister." she told him.

"I'll never forget the way that you screamed." he said quietly, slowly closing his eyes for a moment and sighing deeply.

"Well thankfully he stopped when he noticed that I am pregnant." she said quietly.

"So I have the baby to thank for that." she added thoughtfully.

"I don't understand....why would he care about the baby?" he frowned.

"He was high on something wasn't he, who knows what was going through his mind." she said quietly, not quite able to bring herself to tell him that Shayne had been disgusted by her no longer 'perfect' body. She couldn't help but feel sick to her stomach when she thought about his words that day. Even though she didn't want him to be attracted to her anyway and felt a deep sense of relief that he wasn't, that didn't stop the small sense of hurt that someone had finally confirmed the way that she'd been feeling about her body for the past few weeks.

"And you know the rest because you were there." she whispered, slowly wiping away the steady stream of tears that were rolling down her cheeks. He nodded slowly, watching her closely as she sat in silence, crying softly to herself. He couldn't help but wish that he hadn't promised Chloe that he wouldn't go looking for Shayne, he'd have given anything to be able to make him pay for hurting the woman he loved. Chloe glanced at him, her stomach churning nervously as she carefully moved closer to him. She gently placed herself on his lap and rested the side of her head against his shoulder, snuggling against his collarbone. She squirmed nervously as she felt Lee gently place his arm around her hips.

"Please don't hold me." she whispered.

"I won't." he whispered back, his heart breaking a little when he felt her trembling against him. He jumped slightly when she began to sob hysterically against him, finally releasing the emotions that she'd been keeping in check for a while.

"I keep feeling him spreading my legs and pinning me down!" she exclaimed, quickly wrapping her arms around Lee's neck and clinging to him tightly. He froze, not entirely sure what to say or do to comfort her. He desperately wanted to hold her tightly against him, but he knew in his heart that her fear would intensify. Lee turned his face to hers and gently planted a soft kiss on her forehead, his eyes filling with tears as she continued to sob.

"I can still feel his erection against my leg!" she sobbed, her voice breaking slightly. Lee swallowed the vomit that was rising in his throat at her words.

"It's okay Chlo." he whispered, trying to suppress the intense nausea that he was feeling.

"Don't let him have me." she said quietly, when she didn't have the energy to sob any longer.

"I won't leave your side until he's caught." he reassured her.

"Even though I promised that I wouldn't go after him, if he turns up here, he's fair game." he added, a note of menace present in his voice. Chloe nodded slowly and softly closed her eyes.

Chapter Thirty Six

Lee sighed quietly to himself as he stared at Chloe, who was still curled up against him, clinging to him tightly. His heart broke for her when he noticed the steady stream of tears that were rolling down her cheeks. He carefully placed his arm around her shoulders and softly stroked her neck with his fingertips, not entirely sure how to comfort her when she couldn't stand to be held.

"You're okay Chlo." he whispered in her ear, gently stroking the hair on the back of her neck. She nodded slowly, knowing in her head that he was right, but not quite able to bring herself to believe it in her heart, or to stop herself from trembling. She placed her arms across her chest and stared down at her hands, sighing in frustration when she noticed that they were shaking uncontrollably. Lee followed her gaze, sighing sadly when he noticed what she was looking at. He placed his hand over hers and placed a soft kiss on her hands, not quite able to tear his eyes away from her. He couldn't help but feel another surge of anger when he thought about what Shayne had done to Chloe and how her life had almost been changed forever. He desperately wanted to make him pay for hurting the person that meant the world to him. Lee sighed deeply to himself when he remembered the promise that he'd made to Chloe that he wouldn't go after Shayne....he wished that he could take it back. He'd have given anything to be able to hunt him down and teach him a lesson, to show him what happens if you mess with Chloe. His mind wandered to when he'd hunted down Andy because he'd dared to hurt Chloe, and what Andy had done to her was nothing compared to what Shayne had done. A small part of him couldn't help but feel like he was letting her down for not making Shayne pay for hurting her.

"Are you sure you don't want me to go after him?" he offered, taking deep breaths to try and control his temper when she lifted her head and gazed up at him, a look of deep sadness etched on her face.

"No!" she exclaimed quickly, beginning to panic slightly that he would go back on his promise and go after Shayne.

"You made a promise." she reminded him, her heart pounding against her chest that her worst fear was coming true.

"I know." he whispered. Chloe sighed sadly to herself and wrapped her arms around his neck, gently placing a series of soft kisses on his neck as an attempt to distract him from the deep anger that she knew he was feeling. He stared at her longingly, his skin tingling under her touch. She glanced up at him, her eyes flickering to his lips as he slowly moved his face towards hers. She flinched slightly when his lips made contact with hers, her heart pounding against her chest as he placed a tender kiss on her lips.

He watched her closely as she gently rested her forehead against his and closed her eyes.

"Please don't go after him." she whispered, a note of pleading in her voice.

"I won't, I made you a promise." he said reluctantly.

"I just don't want you to get hurt." she said quietly, her stomach churning as her thoughts returned to everything that she had been through. Her eyes filled with tears when a thought suddenly popped into her head. She knew that she'd been pushing Lee away for the past few days as a result of the intense fear that she was feeling, and she couldn't help but feel concerned that she was going to lose him as a result of what Shayne had done to her. Before she could stop herself, she placed her head in her hands and sobbed quietly, the thought of losing the most important person in her life, being too much for her to bear.

"Oh Chlo." Lee whispered, his heart breaking as he watched her breaking down. He had never felt so powerless. When he'd taken care of her after she'd been stabbed, he'd at least been able to hold her and he knew what to say to reassure her, but now he felt completely powerless. He stared at Chloe as she quickly climbed off his lap and rushed into the bathroom, suddenly feeling the urge to vomit. She threw herself to the ground, only just making it in time to vomit into the toilet. She cried out in pain and clutched her chest, the force of vomiting, tearing through her already sore ribcage.

Lee sighed sadly to himself and threw himself backwards onto the bed, staring at the ceiling as he listened to Chloe vomiting in the bathroom. Despite the fact that he felt a deep sense of relief that he now knew about everything that had happened to her, he couldn't stop the images from swirling around his brain. The thought of Shayne spreading Chloe's legs and pinning her under his body made him feel sick to his stomach. He ran his hands through his hair and took deep breaths, trying to control his temper so that he didn't break his promise to her. He turned his head when he noticed Chloe walking back into the living room. She avoided his gaze and quickly rummaged in the drawers, pulling out some clothes. The two of them jumped, their eyes flickering to the bedroom door when they heard a knock.

"What?" Lee asked shortly, slowly sitting up and perching on the end of the bed. He sighed when the bedroom door opened and Sheila walked in.

"Bloody hell Mum, I asked what you wanted, I didn't say that you could just walk in!" he exclaimed, glancing at Chloe when she glanced down at herself in her pyjamas, her cheeks colouring.

"I just came to ask if you need anything from the shops?" Sheila said, glaring at Lee sternly.

"No, I don't think so." Lee sighed.

"Oh my god Chloe, look at you!" Sheila exclaimed when she turned to gaze at Chloe.

"What is it?!" Chloe asked quickly, a note of panic in her voice as she quickly looked down at herself.

"I haven't seen your bump before." Sheila said dreamily, unable to tear her eyes away from Chloe's abdomen. Chloe's eyes followed Sheila's, her cheeks colouring when she realised what she was staring at.

"My little grandchild." Sheila said softly, her eyes misting with tears when she glanced at Lee. He shot her a small smile, his heart surging with pride when he glanced at Chloe. Chloe gasped and instinctively took a step backwards when Sheila reached out to touch her bump.

"Please don't do that." Chloe said firmly, finally looking Sheila in the eye.

"Why, what's the big deal?" Sheila frowned.

"Drop it Mum." Lee said firmly, glancing at Chloe when she walked into the bathroom and quickly closed the door.

"Why is she keeping the baby from everyone?" Sheila snapped as soon as Chloe left the room.

"She's not Mum, stop it!" Lee replied firmly, quickly jumping to Chloe's defence.

"She's just really overprotective because of what happened last time." he explained.

"I get that, but that doesn't give her the right to be possessive. It's your baby too." she pointed out.

"It's not like that Mum, she hasn't been keeping me from the baby." he said quietly, starting to get slightly frustrated that his Mum didn't seem to understand how Chloe was feeling.

"Besides I think it shows that she's going to be an amazing Mum. She loves the baby so much already." he added thoughtfully, smiling slightly to himself as he thought about the idea of the two of them becoming parents in a few months. Sheila nodded slowly, still not entirely comfortable with what she percieved as Chloe being possessive of the baby, but she decided not to press the matter.

"I still can't quite belive that I'm going to be a grandmother." she smiled at him, trying to ligten the mood.

"I can't believe I'm going to be a Dad." he smiled back.

"No, I have to admit, I never thought you'd find someone to settle down with." she laughed.

"Me neither." he admitted.

"The funny thing is, I couldn't imagine you and Chloe not being together now." she told him.

The two of them fell silent as the bathroom door opened and Chloe walked into the bedroom, her eyes fixed on the floor.

"Anyway, I have to go to the shops, do you want me to pop over later?" Sheila offered. Lee glanced at Chloe for a moment, frowning to himself when he noticed her sigh sadly.

"No, I think we should be okay." Lee told Sheila, realising instantly that Chloe wanted some peace and quiet.

"Okay, see you guys then." Sheila said quietly, before quickly leaving the room. Chloe breathed a sigh of relief and walked over to Lee, stopping when she was standing in front of him. He stared up at her, smiling slightly as she softly stroked his hair.

"I haven't been keeping the baby from you." she sighed in frustration.

"I know, she doesn't know what she's talking about." he mumbled, trying to fight the intense desire that he was feeling for her as she stood in front of him. She smiled at him as he leant forward and placed a soft kiss on her abdomen. Chloe sighed in contentment and wrapped her arms his head, holding him tightly against herself.

"I love you." she whispered, squirming slightly when Lee gently wrapped his arms around her hips. She took deep breaths, trying to steady her nerves. Lee's head snapped up when he heard Chloe sniff quietly to herself.

"I'm sorry." he whispered, quickly releasing her from his grip.

"I just really want to hold you." he added, watching her sadly as she stared at him, her eyes filling with tears.

"I know, I'm sorry." she mumbled, quickly wiping the tears from her eyes. She hesitated for a moment before slowly reaching out and taking his hands on her own. He watched her closely as she placed his hands on her back and gave him a small reassuring nod. Lee smiled at her and gently pulled her against him, sighing in contentment as he rested his head against her chest and inhaled her familiar scent.

"I've missed this." he whispered, not quite able to bring himself to let her go. She nodded slowly, breathing deeply as she tried not to let her mind wander to Shayne. He placed a soft kiss on her neck when he felt her body finally relax against him. Lee jumped and raised his head when he felt Chloe quickly remove herself from his arms.

"I'm going to be sick again." she told him, before quickly hurrying into the bathroom.

Chapter Thirty Seven

Chloe sighed quietly and rested her head against the toilet seat when she finally stopped vomiting. She wrapped her arms around her chest, trying to control the searing pain in her ribs, the force of vomiting ripping through her chest. She whimpered quietly when she coughed, trying to clear her throat. Chloe quickly tucked her legs underneath her frame, sniffing quietly to herself as she grit her teeth, waiting for the pain to pass.

"Are you okay?" Lee asked her as he walked into the bathroom and leant casually against the door frame. She nodded slowly, continuing to take deep breaths.

"Maybe we should get you checked out." he said thoughtfully, almost like he was talking to himself.

"Why?" she frowned.

"Because of everything you've been through, and we got the baby checked didn't we." he said quietly, his stomach churning nervously at the thought of something being wrong with Chloe.

"This isn't him." she said, her voice dripping with disdain.

"It's probably the baby." she quickly added, placing her elbow on the toilet seat and resting her head against her hand. Lee nodded slowly and quickly crossed the room, sitting beside her on the floor. He placed his hand on her back, slowly rubbing her back, in an attempt to comfort her. She cried out in pain and quickly shuffled away from him. He stared at her in shock, not entirely sure what he'd done.

"Did I hurt you?" he whispered sadly, his heart breaking when he noticed the look of pain on her features.

"A little." she admitted.

"It's okay though, they'll just take a few weeks to heal." she added, slowly sitting up and carefully resting her back against the bathtub.

"What will?" he frowned in confusion.

"I have broken ribs." she said quietly.

"What?" he whispered. She nodded slowly, her stomach churning with guilt when she suddenly realised that she'd forgotten to tell him.

"We definitely need to get you checked out if you think you have broken ribs." he said quietly, swallowing the lump that was rising in his throat.

"I went to the hospital the other day and they told me." she explained.

"Nathan took me." she added when he remained silent.

"On the day you said you were going for a walk?" he checked, feeling slightly sick at the thought that he'd argued with her about her leaving the house. She nodded slowly.

"I should have been there with you." he whispered, his stomach churning with guilt that he hadn't been by her side at the hospital. Even though it was a small comfort to him that Nathan had been with her, he still couldn't help but feel like he'd let her down once again.

"It wasn't your fault though, I was trying to protect you from the anger I knew you would feel." she explained, snapping him out of his thoughts.

"Besides you wouldn't have liked being there, the doctor thought Nathan was responsible." she added, smiling slightly.

"There's nothing else you haven't told me is there?" he asked quickly, completely disregarding her words.

"No, I don't think so." she said quietly. He stared at her, his thoughts swirling about her injuries.

"Chlo, can you get undressed please?" he said quickly, no longer able to fight his desperation to check her over. She frowned at him and placed her hand on the edge of the bathtub, using it for support as she carefully stood up.

"I'm being serious." he prompted, staring up at her from his place on the floor.

"Why?" she asked him, watching closely as he stood up.

"I want to check you over." he said quietly, gazing down at her as he stood in front of her.

"The doctor already did it." she sighed, her cheeks colouring at the thought of undressing in front of him.

"I know, but for my own piece of mind, I need to check that you are okay." he told her. She shook her head, and stepped backwards.

"But I'm gross." she whispered under her breath, Shayne's words still swirling around her head.

"What?" he asked.

"Nothing." she said quickly.

"Did you just say that you are gross?" he frowned.

"I am though." she muttered.

"Says who?" he asked quickly, his heart breaking a little when he noticed that her eyes had filled with tears. She shrugged silently, quickly looking away from him, not quite able to bring herself to tell him what Shayne had said about her. She glanced up at him and sighed deeply when she suddenly realised how important it was to him that he was able to check her over for injuries. Despite the fact that she felt sick to her stomach at being completely vulnerable in front of him, she knew that she needed to reassure him. She wasn't the only one that was hurting as a result of Shayne's actions, and she couldn't bring herself to deny him of the small comfort that he was seeking.

"I'll run you a bath." he prompted her. Chloe nodded, watching him closely as he switched on the taps and slowly poured some bubble bath into the bath. She stared down at the buttons on her top, jumping slightly when Lee appeared in front of her. She quickly looked away from him and returned to staring at the buttons. Her hands shook as she slowly unfastened the top button. She cursed herself under her breath when her hands were shaking so much that she was struggling to undo the buttons.

"Do you want me to do it?" he offered, his hands hovering below hers. His skin tingled when her fingers brushed against his.

"No, it's fine." she said shortly. She sighed deeply, quickly deciding to remove her leggings, in the hope that her hands would stop shaking and she would be able to unfasten the buttons on her shirt. Chloe avoided Lee's intense gaze as she slowly unfastened the buttons, her stomach churning nervously as she stared down at herself. Even though her shirt was open at the front, she left it on, not quite able to bring herself to reveal her back to him.

Lee's eyes widened as he stared at her, his mouth suddenly feeling slightly dry at how beautiful she looked. His eyes flickered to the dark blue lace underwear set that she was wearing. He smiled slightly when he noticed how her bra perfectly cupped her breasts.

"Did you buy a new set?" he asked hoarsely, trying to control the deep desire that he was feeling for her. She nodded slowly, her eyes fixed on the floor, her cheeks colouring deeply when she felt him staring at her.

"My boobs are getting bigger, so I had to buy some new underwear." she said quietly.

"Yeah I noticed." he mumbled, not quite able to tear his eyes away from her body.

"You look so hot Chlo." he added, gently placing his hands under the material of her shirt and resting them in place on her hips. She glanced up at him for a moment, before quickly looking away when she noticed him staring at her, a look of deep longing on his face.

"I don't though." she whispered under her breath. Lee sighed sadly to himself and slowly turned her around so that her back was facing him.

"Look how beautiful you are." he said softly, as he gazed at her in the mirror. Chloe smiled slightly when the two of them locked eyes in the mirror. She maintained eye contact with him, determined not to look at her body. She sighed quietly when he wrapped his arms around her waist and held her tightly against himself, gently resting his chin on her shoulder.

"You're ready to go." she said quietly, when she felt his body pressed against hers. He nodded slowly, quickly burying his head on her shoulder and kissing her neck softly.

"Because you're stunning." he whispered in between kissing her neck. Chloe sighed quietly and carefully removed herself from his arms, her cheeks colouring as she turned to face him.

"I thought you wanted to check me over for injuries." she reminded him.

"I do, I just got distracted." he said, smiling slightly and quickly shaking his head to try and focus his mind on something else, other than how desperately he wanted her.

"In fact, just forget it!" she snapped, quickly leaning over and pulling her leggings back on. Lee frowned at her words, watching her closely as she slowly buttoned her shirt back up.

"If you wanted me to undress because you wanted sex you could have just said, rather than trying to manipulate me." she said angrily, her temper finally snapping. She couldn't help but feel humiliated that she'd undressed for him, despite the fact that she didn't want too, and he had no intention of checking her over anyway.

"Manipulate you?" Lee frowned, not entirely sure what she was talking about.

"You made out you wanted to check me over, which I told you the doctor had already done it. And I went along with it to put your mind at rest, but you just want sex!" she exclaimed angrily.

"It's not like that Chlo." he said sadly, sighing to himself when he reached out to touch her cheek and she quickly squirmed away from him.

"Don't." she warned him, an edge of anger present in her voice when she finally locked eyes with him.

"This is ridiculous...I've never manipulated you and I've never used you for sex either." he said shortly.

"Just because someone tried to take advantage of you, doesn't mean that I would ever do that!" he added angrily, suddenly feeling a deep sense of hurt that she felt he was capable of something like that.

"I don't want to talk about it anymore." she said shortly, her stomach turning as she thought about Shayne once again. Before Lee could respond she quickly leaned over and switched off the bath taps when she suddenly noticed how full the bath tub was.

"Where are you going?" he frowned as she squeezed past him and walked out of the bathroom.

"I need some time out." she said dismissively, sighing to herself as she walked away from him and he followed her.

"It's not safe for you to go out though." he reminded her.

"I know that." she snapped. Lee sighed in frustration when she walked into the spare room, quickly slamming the door closed behind herself. He shook his head slowly, still not quite able to comprehend that she thought so little of him. Ever since they'd been together, he'd given her everything and she meant the world to him. Even though he knew that she was being over sensitive as a result of what she'd been through, that didn't stop the hurt that he was feeling. He pressed his forehead against the bedroom door, wishing that he could stay by Chloe's side, but knowing in his heart that she needed some time alone with her thoughts. His heart broke a little when he glanced at the bottom of the door and saw her shadow and heard her sobbing quietly to herself.

"Chlo." he whispered softly, trying to resist the urge to open the bedroom door so that he could comfort her.

"I need some time alone." she replied. Chloe breathed a sigh of relief when she heard Lee's footsteps finally walking downstairs. She slowly stood up and walked over to the bed, quickly curling up on top of it. She wrapped her arms around the pillow and snuggled into it, not even bothering to fight the tears that were steadily rolling down her cheeks. She sighed angrily to herself when her thoughts wandered to Shayne. She pressed her fingers against her temples wishing that she could drill the memories of that fateful night out of her head. She'd have given anything to go back to the way things were before that night. To be able to stop constantly thinking about the way it felt when he'd touched her and pinned her body underneath his.

Despite the fact that she had everything she wanted she couldn't help but feel trapped in her own home. Having to almost constantly conceal from Lee just how bad she was feeling was finally starting to take it's toll on her. She couldn't help but feel like he didn't understand her or the way that she was feeling, and he expected her not to recoil from his touch, because of the reminder of Shayne. She felt a pang of guilt when she realised that whenever she instinctively moved away from him, she was hurting him, but she couldn't figure out how to stop the memories of that fateful encounter from swirling around her head.

A small part of her longed to be back in the park on her bench, away from everyone, to finally be alone with her thoughts. Even though she'd been struggling, everything had seemed so much simpler when she was alone and she didn't have to pretend.

She smiled to herself, her eyes wandering to her abdomen when she felt the familiar fluttering sensation.

"I take it you don't like the idea of living in the park then." she smiled, gently placing her hand on her bump and stroking soft circles with her fingertips.

"I wasn't seriously considering it anyway, although I could just imagine your Dad's face if I told him I was going back there." she smiled, gasping quietly when she felt her baby move once again.

She sighed to herself when she heard her stomach grumble. Despite the fact that she didn't want to leave the spare room and go downstairs, especially when she knew that she would face a barrage of questions, she knew that she needed to eat something. She carefully opened the bedroom door and peered around it, before hurrying downstairs before she could be noticed. As soon as she reached the kitchen she rummaged in the fridge and pulled out the leftover pasta bake that Lee had made the day before. She impatiently tapped her fingernail against the kitchen counter as she stared at the microwave, waiting for the food to be ready. She let out a small squeak of fear when Nathan walked into the kitchen.

"Sorry I didn't mean to make you jump." he said, smiling sympathetically at her. Chloe shrugged, remaining silent as she continued to stare at the microwave, her cheeks colouring slightly when she felt Nathan watching her closely. As soon as the food was ready, Chloe quickly pulled it out of the microwave and rummaged in the drawer for a fork.

"Do you want to talk Chlo Bo?" he offered.

"Nope, I'm sick of talking about it." she said shortly.

"Have you and Lee had an argument?" he prompted her.

"Where is Lee anyway?" she asked, completely disregarding his question.

"In the gym, taking his anger at Shayne out on his body." he sighed, his heart sinking when he thought about what Chloe and Lee had been through.

"When you see him, tell him that I'm sleeping in the spare room tonight." she said dismissively. Nathan opened his mouth to respond, but quickly closed it again when Chloe cut him off.

"And that I want to be left alone." she added, before quickly walking away.

Chapter Thirty Eight

Chloe sighed to herself when she glanced at the clock and saw that it was almost midnight. She'd laid awake for hours, tossing and turning as she desperately tried to fall asleep. Every creak that the house made, and every noise from outside caused her stomach to churn with fear. Even though she knew that she was being unreasonable and Shayne wouldn't be able to get into the house unnoticed, she couldn't seem to escape the fear that she would open her eyes and he would be staring down at her. She ran her hand through her hair in frustration and quickly switched on the bedroom lamp. She carefully sat up, wincing at the pain in her chest. Her thoughts wandered to Lee who was sleeping in the bedroom next to her. Despite the fact that she was struggling to be around him at the moment, she knew in her heart that he was the only person that could make her feel safe. Her stomach churned with guilt when she thought about what she'd said to him. She knew that he would never manipulate her or take advantage of her, but as a result of what she'd been through she'd doubted his motives.

Before she could talk herself out of it, she quickly climbed out of bed and made her way to their bedroom. She hesitated for a moment, her hand resting in place on the doorknob when she suddenly felt slightly nervous that Lee might be angry with her after the way that she'd treated him. She slowly opened the door, sighing quietly to herself as she walked over to the bed and noticed Lee curled up on his side. She carefully lifted the duvet and climbed into her side of the bed, her gaze fixed on him. As soon as she was beside him, she could feel herself slowly starting to relax. She was back where she was meant to be, beside the man that she loved and that would do anything to keep her safe. Chloe laid on her side, facing him, not quite able to tear her eyes away from him as he slept soundly. She reached towards him and gently stroked his face with her fingertips.

"I'm sorry." she whispered sadly, her stomach churning with guilt that she kept pushing him away when he only wanted to take care of her and comfort her. She smiled slightly when his eyes slowly flickered open and he gazed at her for a moment, his expression softening when he realised who she was.

"Are you okay Chlo?" he asked nervously. She nodded slowly, swallowing the lump that was rising in her throat.

"I'm really sorry for earlier." she muttered.

"It's fine, I understand that you are hurting." he reassured her, suddenly feeling a deep sense of contentment now that she was by his side. He hadn't been able to stop thinking and worrying about her the whole day that they'd been apart.

"That's not an excuse for me to accuse you of that though." she said quietly, glancing at him when she felt him watching her closely.

"I know that you didn't mean it, you're just sensitive at the moment and I get it." he told her softly. Chloe nodded slowly, her gaze wandering to his chest, suddenly wishing that she could curl up against him. Lee stared down at her as she shuffled closer to him and tentatively placed herself against him. He couldn't tear his eyes away from her as she carefully snuggled against him, sighing to herself when she rested her head against his chest, the sound of his soft heartbeat echoing in her ear. He sighed sadly when he felt her body trembling against him. She flinched instinctively when he rested his head against hers and placed a soft kiss on her forehead.

"I won't hurt you." he whispered sadly, wishing not for the first time, that he could wrap his arms around her and hold her close.

"I know you wouldn't." she said quietly, her eyes filling with tears when she thought about how much she continued to accidentally hurt the man that she loved. He stared at her sadly, wishing that he could do something to take away the mental and physical pain that she was feeling.

"Try and get some sleep Chlo." he whispered sadly, sighing quietly as he softly stroked her hair. She nodded slowly, sighing in contentment when he rested his face against hers. Chloe closed her eyes, her heart pounding against her chest when Lee placed his hand on her hips and snuggled against her, cherishing the feel of her by his side. He couldn't help but wish that he was able to hold her tightly in his arms, but he knew that she was still too afraid.

Chloe awoke with a start, quickly bolting up in bed and switching on the bedside lamp. She placed her hands behind herself and breathed deeply, trying to steady her nerves. Her nightmare was still swirling around her head, the images of what had happened on a constant loop in her mind. A small sob escaped her lips as a steady stream of tears rolled down her cheeks. She glanced at Lee, sighing to herself when she realised that he was sleeping soundly, blissfully unaware that she needed his comfort. Chloe curled into a ball on the bed and sobbed hysterically, quickly clapping her hand over her mouth to try and stifle the sound so that she didn't wake Lee. She quickly climbed out of bed and began to pace the bedroom, not quite able to calm down the panic that she was feeling. Even though she knew that it was only a nightmare, she couldn't quite erase the thoughts. She took deep breaths, trying to control her heartbeat that she could feel pounding against her chest, not quite able to bring herself to stop pacing. Chloe angrily wiped away the tears that were still flowing down her cheeks, her heart breaking a little when her gaze wandered to her bump. She quickly glanced at the bedroom clock, sighing to herself when she noticed that it was only three am. She perched on the end of the bed, glancing down at her shaking hands, desperately trying to steady her nerves. Her stomach churned when her eyes wandered back to her abdomen. She swallowed the lump that was rising in her throat, desperately trying to fight the intense nausea that she was feeling as she thought about her nightmare.

She sighed sadly as she stood up and wandered into the bathroom and ran herself a bath, desperately trying to find a way to calm her nerves. Chloe pushed the door ajar and removed her pyjamas, before carefully climbing into the bath. She sighed to herself as she tentatively laid down, gently resting her head against the bath frame and covering her body with the bubbles. Her heart pounded against her chest as she closed her eyes and her thoughts wandered back to her nightmare. She placed her hand on her bump, not even trying to hold back the tears that were rolling down her cheeks. She turned onto her side and curled into a ball, trying to find a way to relax. Even though she knew that her nightmare wasn't real, it had touched a raw nerve and she couldn't stop thinking about it. She jumped when she heard a gentle tap at the bathroom door. Lee stared at her as he crossed the room and sat on the floor beside her, his heart breaking for her when he noticed the tears that were rolling down her cheeks. Chloe quickly glanced down at herself, sighing in relief when she realised that her naked frame was completely hidden by the bubbles.

"What's going on Chlo?" he asked softly, carefully reaching out and stroking away her tears with his thumb.

"I had a bad nightmare." she said quietly.

"About Shayne again?" he asked sadly. She nodded slowly, sniffing sadly to herself.

"Tell me." he prompted her, his stomach churning nervously.

"I dreamt that the baby was his." she whispered, not quite having the energy to sob any longer.

"It was just a bad dream Chlo." he whispered, his stomach churning with anger at the very mention of it.

"I know, but it was horrible." she muttered, quickly wrapping her arms around his neck and pulling him close. He sighed sadly, gently stroking her hair, his heart breaking when he heard her sniffing quietly to herself.

"It's your baby." she whispered over and over, trying to remind herself of reality, in the hope that she could erase the nightmare from her head.

"I know, it's okay." he whispered softly.

"And I'm yours too." she said quietly, eventually unwrapping her arms from around his neck and sitting back.

"I don't like it when you say that." he sighed, gently taking her hand in his and placing a soft kiss on it.

"If he'd raped me, I wouldn't be your little Chlo anymore." she said thoughtfully, completely disregarding what he'd said.

"I don't own you Chloe." he told her firmly, watching her closely as she slowly wiped away the tears that were rolling down her cheeks.

"I know, I didn't mean it like that." she muttered.

"I just like the fact that I've only been with you." she added.

"It means a lot to me." she continued, sighing quietly when she locked eyes with him.

"It means a lot to me too." he smiled at her.

"I know how lucky I am." he added. Chloe smiled slightly, before gently placing a soft kiss on his lips. She fidgeted slightly, trying to find a comfortable position when her ribs began to throb painfully. She placed her hands on the sides of the bath frame and carefully sat forward, trying to relieve the pressure on her back. Lee gasped in shock as he laid eyes on her back, finally realising the full extent of her bruises. His heart plummeted when he noticed the boot print between her shoulders. Chloe glanced behind herself when she felt Lee gently brush his fingers against her back.

"He really is an animal." he whispered sadly, taking deep breaths to try and control the anger that was rising in his stomach as he stared transfixed on her back. Chloe slowly turned to face him, her stomach churning with guilt when she noticed that his eyes had filled with tears.

"Don't get upset, I'm okay." she whispered.

"You're not though, he broke your bones." he mumbled, swallowing the bile that was rising in his throat.

"I really want to kill him." he added, a note of menace present in his voice.

"No don't!" Chloe exclaimed, beginning to panic slightly when she noticed how angry he was becoming. He sighed deeply, glancing at Chloe for a moment when she placed a soft kiss on his cheek.

"I need you.....and so does the baby." she said quietly.

"Yeah I know, the only reason I haven't gone after the little bastard is because I made you a promise." he said, sighing angrily. Chloe nodded slowly and placed her hand on his cheek, softly stroking his hair with her fingertips. She glanced over his shoulder, sighing to herself when she realised that the towels were hanging up on the other side of the room.

"Could you pass me a towel so that I can get out please?" she asked tentatively, her cheeks colouring at the thought of standing naked in front of him. Lee nodded slowly, his heart sinking as he picked up a towel and gently handed it to her. Even though he knew that she was struggling because of what Shayne had done to her, he couldn't help but wish that she hadn't lost all the body confidence that she'd built up over the past few months. He knew in his heart that Shayne wasn't the only reason for the way that she was feeling, she'd been struggling with her body confidence ever since she'd started to develop a bump. His heart plummeted at the thought of her confidence slowly getting worse over the next few months. He wanted nothing more than for her to love her body and be confident in her own skin.

"Can you turn your back please?" she asked nervously, snapping him out of his thoughts. He nodded slowly and quickly turned his back on her, sighing sadly to himself.

As soon as Lee turned his back on her, Chloe slowly climbed out of the bathtub, quickly wrapping the towel around her naked frame, relaxing a little now that she was no longer completely vulnerable in front of him. She glanced up at Lee for a moment, checking that he still had his back to her, before quickly drying herself and pulling on her pyjamas.

"You can turn around now." she said quietly as she stood behind him and placed her hand on his back, smiling slightly at how broad and muscular he was. Her eyes flickered to his when he turned to face her and stared down at her longingly. Her skin tingled under his touch when he stroked her bare arm with his fingertips, his eyes flickering to her lips for a moment. She smiled slightly when she noticed that he was struggling to stay awake.

"I'm sorry I woke you." she said quickly.

"You should go back to bed." she added when he didn't respond.

"Aren't you coming too?" he frowned when he realised what she was suggesting. She shook her head slowly, her heart pounding against her chest at the thought of going back to sleep and being confronted by nightmares once again.

"I can't go back to sleep." she whispered sadly.

"It felt so real....so vivid. And if I go back to sleep, I'll be reminded how it felt to have his baby inside of me." she explained, her eyes filling with tears.

"So, you get some sleep, I'll go and watch some TV or something." she added, smiling falsely at him.

"But....Chlo..." he started, his voice trailing off when he realised that he had no idea what to say to comfort her.

"Can I hold you?" he asked impulsively, his eyes filling with tears as he stared at the woman that he loved and realised how much inner turmoil and sadness she was feeling. She glanced up at him, her stomach churning nervously at the thought of him holding her. Even though her stomach was churning with fear, she couldn't bring herself to deny him when he was upset. She nodded slowly, swallowing the nervous lump that was rising in her throat.

"Just be gentle with me, I'm in a lot of pain." she muttered.

"I know." he said quietly. He glanced at Chloe for a moment before carefully wrapping his arms around her and gently holding her close.

Chapter Thirty Nine

Lee smiled down at Chloe when he eventually let go of her, his heart pounding against his chest as she gazed up at him, a small twinkle present in her eyes. She frowned as he quickly walked out of the bathroom and returned a few moments later with a selection of blankets.

"What are you doing?" she asked, smiling at the cheeky expression on his face. He smiled at her, before quickly reaching out to take her hand and leading her downstairs.

"We can chill on the sofa and have a movie marathon." he announced as soon as they entered the living room. Chloe smiled at his infectious excitement, watching closely as he laid out the blankets on the sofa. She carefully perched on the sofa, sighing to herself when she curled into a ball and pulled the blanket over her frame. Lee hesitated for a moment, a small smile playing on the corner of his lips when Chloe shuffled forward on the sofa, staring up at him as she waited for him to curl up behind her. As soon as he laid down behind her, Chloe shuffled backwards, gently resting her body against his and sighing in contentment. Lee sighed happily as he rested his chin on her shoulder and snuggled his face against hers. He moved his arms towards her, longing to hold her against himself, but quickly stopped himself when he remembered that she was struggling at the moment. Chloe glanced down at Lee's hand as it hovered beside her bump, making small movements as he clearly tried to fight his desire to touch the baby. She turned her head slightly, giving him a small smile when he raised his eyebrow questioningly.

"Is it okay if I....." he started, trailing off as his eyes flickered to her abdomen. Chloe smiled at how adorable he was and gently took his hand in hers, carefully placing it against her bump. Her skin tingled as his hand rested in place, his fingers gently playing with hers.

"You don't have to ask my permission, it's your baby too." she said softly, resting the back of her head against his collarbone and gently closing her eyes. Lee stared at her, not quite able to tear his eyes away from the person who meant the world to him. The intense love that he felt for her on a daily basis, never failing to take his breath away.

"I love you so much Chlo." he whispered in her ear, smiling slightly when she shivered involuntarily.

"I love you too." she whispered back, quickly leaning over to the coffee table and picking up the remote control.

"We should have a marathon, just like old times." she giggled when she switched on the television and scrolled through Lee's saved movies.

"Oh yeah, I remember when we used to make the boys watch movies with us." he laughed, smiling fondly when he remembered all the fun he'd had with Chloe over the years.

"Remember we watched that film so many times we ended up learning all the words to the soundtrack didn't we." he chuckled.

"Oh yes, I forgot about that." she agreed, bursting out laughing, a small whimper of pain escaping her lips when she felt a searing pain in her chest as she laughed. She turned onto her back, gasping slightly as she fought to control the pain. Her eyes flickered to Lee as he gazed down at her sadly, watching her closely as he softly stroked her hair, to try and distract her from the pain that she was feeling.

"Although your singing was a lot better than mine." she smiled, trying to reassure him that she was alright. He raised his eyebrow, a small trace of a smile playing on the corner of his lips. She fidgeted slightly, trying to find a comfortable position. Chloe gazed up at Lee and gently stroked his cheek with her fingertips as he laid on his side beside her, staring down at her, a look of concern on his handsome features.

"Don't look so worried, I'm alright." she reassured him, her heart breaking a little when she saw the look of deep sadness on his face.

"Are you taking anything for the pain?" he asked worriedly. Chloe shook her head slowly, sighing quietly to herself when he frowned at her.

"I am worried that it might harm the baby." she pointed out.

"And I would rather tolerate the pain than do anything to hurt our baby." she added, her eyes wandering to her bump. She watched Lee as he carefully lifted the bottom of her shirt and stared in wonder at her abdomen. His eyes were fixed on it as he leant forward and placed a soft kiss on her abdomen, his heart yearning for the day that he could finally hold their baby. Chloe sighed in contentment when Lee rested his head against the side of her abdomen, his eyes fixed on her bump as he traced small circles on it. He smiled to himself when he felt Chloe reach down and softly stroke his hair. It suddenly dawned on him how much he had missed being this close to her.

"Are you cold?" he asked gently, when he noticed for the first time that Chloe was trembling. She shook her head slowly, watching him sadly as he lifted his head and gently pulled her pyjama top back down.

"Is it because I'm touching you?" he muttered, moving away from her slightly, his stomach churning with guilt that he'd caused her fear to resurface.

"No, it's okay." she whispered, watching him closely as he laid down behind her, his gaze fixed on her. She turned to face him and gently placed a soft kiss on his lips, before snuggling her head against his chest.

"I'm just afraid all the time, but it's not your fault." she mumbled against his chest.

"You don't need to be afraid." he said, sighing deeply. Chloe nodded slowly, her eyes filling with tears as she placed her hand on his chest, quickly grasping the material of his pyjama shirt in her hand and curling it into her fist.

"I think you need to get some sleep Chlo." he said quietly, when he noticed that she was struggling to keep her eyes open. She flinched slightly when he placed his hand behind her head and softly stroked her hair.

"I can't." she said firmly, her eyes snapping open in fear.

"But you know that I won't let anything happen to you." he pointed out.

"I know, but you can't protect me from the nightmares." she sighed sadly.

"I can be by your side when you wake up though." he said quietly, his heart breaking a little at the look of fear on her face. Chloe shook her head slowly, still not quite able to allow herself to fall asleep.

"I'll be okay, we need to do our movie marathon anyway." she replied quickly, taking deep breaths to try and steady her nerves. She quickly turned her away from him and carefully rested her back against his chest. Lee sighed sadly as he gazed down at her and quickly switched on the movie. It was clear that she was exhausted and was in desperate need of sleep, but he couldn't help but feel a deep sense of sadness that she was too afraid to fall asleep. He felt a small glimmer of hope as she gazed up at the television. He couldn't help but hope that she would relax into the movie and eventually fall asleep.

Lee sighed in contentment as he stared down at Chloe sleeping soundly in his arms. He stroked her hair softly, unable to tear his eyes away from her. He glanced up at

Nathan as he walked into the room. Nathan frowned in confusion when he realised that it was lunchtime and Chloe was still fast asleep.

"She finally fell asleep." Lee told him, speaking in hushed tones so that he didn't wake her.

"Has she not been sleeping very well?" Nathan asked, glancing at Chloe for a moment.

"No, she's been having really bad nightmares, she was awake most of the night." Lee sighed, gently placing a soft kiss on Chloe's shoulder.

"The pain in her ribs probably won't be helping her sleep either." Nathan pointed out. Lee nodded slowly, sighing sadly to himself.

"I never thanked you for taking her to the hospital." Lee said quietly.

"It's not a big deal, she's like my little sister, I wanted to do something to help her." Nathan replied, his stomach churning when he remembered the bruises on Chloe's back.

"Even though I did tell her that you wouldn't be happy about it." he added, smiling slightly.

"I'm not angry with her. I know why she kept it from me." Lee said softly, continuing to stroke Chloe's hair.

"Because of your temper." Nathan pointed out.

"Yeah I know, I just want to protect her though." Lee sighed sadly.

"She knows that, but she wants to protect you too." Nathan said. Lee nodded, his eyes flickering to Chloe once again. The two of them jumped as Chloe's phone began to ring. Chloe bolted awake and quickly sat up, crying out in pain when she twisted her ribs.

"It's just your phone Chlo." Lee said, glancing at the coffee table where her phone was ringing loudly. Nathan quickly leaned over to pick up her phone and handed it to her. Chloe smiled her thanks, frowning to herself when she saw that it was an unknown caller.

"I don't know who it is." Chloe whispered, her stomach churning nervously. Even though she knew in her head that Shayne didn't have her phone number, she couldn't stop the small swirl of fear that it might be him calling her. She locked eyes with Lee, realising instantly that he'd had the same thought.

"Do you want me to answer it?" Lee offered, holding his hand out for the phone and swallowing the nervous lump that was rising in his throat. Chloe shook her head slowly, her hands shaking as she answered the phone....

Chapter Forty

Chloe sat in silence as she quickly hung up the phone. She'd sat in silence for most of the phone call, her mouth too dry to be able to respond to anything that was being said to her. She placed her elbows on her knees and gently rested her chin on her hands, not entirely sure how to process what she'd just been told.

"It wasn't Shayne was it?" Lee asked quickly, his stomach churning nervously. Chloe shook her head slowly. He watched her closely as she opened her mouth to speak but quickly closed it again.

"They've finally got him." she mumbled thoughtfully, almost like she was talking to herself.

"What?" Lee whispered, not quite able to bring himself to hope that Shayne had finally been caught. Chloe glanced at him and nodded slowly, sighing to herself as she sat in silence, gently picking her fingernails.

"But...how....when?!" Lee exclaimed, his mind racing with questions.

"I don't know, I didn't ask." Chloe replied quietly. She sat in numb shock, not entirely able to process that she no longer needed to be afraid of Shayne hurting her. She'd been afraid every waking moment over the past few days, and couldn't quite comprehend that she had nothing to be afraid of anymore. There was no longer a possibility of her waking up or turning a corner and being face to face with the person from her nightmares.

"Are you okay Chlo?" Lee asked nervously. She nodded slowly, staring at her hands that were in place on her lap, sighing deeply to herself as she suddenly felt an intense wave of relief wash over her.

Chloe jumped, glancing at Nathan in confusion when Lee stood up and quickly hurried out of the room. She couldn't help but panic slightly that he was going to the police station. She released the breath she didn't realise she was holding when she heard him running upstairs.

"Where's he going?" she frowned.

"God knows." Nathan replied.

"Maybe he really needs to use the toilet." he added, chuckling slightly. Chloe burst out laughing.

"Don't make me laugh." she told him, quickly clutching her ribs.

"Sorry." he said, smiling reassuringly at her. Her eyes flickered to the doorway when Lee reappeared, fully dressed, carrying two backpacks in his hand. Chloe raised her eyebrow questioningly, smiling slightly when she noticed the cheeky twinkle in his eye.

"What are you up to?" she smiled.

"We're going out. You need to get dressed." he told her.

"Where are we going?" she frowned.

"I'm not telling you, so don't keep asking." he beamed at her, quickly miming zipping his lips closed. Chloe rolled her eyes playfully and tentatively stood up. Even though she hated surprises, she couldn't help but feel excited about the idea of finally being able to leave the house. She couldn't remember the last time that her and Lee had gone out and done something together....just the two of them.

"Oh Chlo!" he called after her as she climbed the stairs. She stopped and slowly turned to face him, raising her eyebrow questioningly.

"Make sure you wear something that covers your bump, just in case we get spotted." he reminded her. Chloe nodded slowly and quickly climbed the stairs.

"You do realise that you're going to have to tell the fans about the baby eventually." Nathan pointed out.

"Oh really....I hadn't thought of that. I just figured that nobody will notice and if we get seen out with the baby I'll say it's yours." Lee teased him, rolling his eyes.

"I was just saying." Nathan laughed, holding his hands up in surrender.

"I'll tell the fans at the Apollo gig." Lee told him, smiling at the thought of him and Chloe no longer having to hide their excitement.

"That's a bit risky isn't it?" Nathan frowned.

"No not really, if they're going to kick off about it then they will anyway. I don't give a shit." Lee stated, walking into the kitchen and sighing to himself when Nathan followed him.

"Aren't you worried that they are going to turn on Chloe again?" Nathan asked, watching Lee closely as he rummaged in the fridge and stuffed a selection of food into the backpacks.

"Yeah a bit, but I think most of the fans love her now anyway." Lee sighed.

"Besides they know that if they make me choose between her and the band, it'll always be Chloe." he added, smiling to himself when he thought about her.

"Charming." Nathan chuckled.

"Her and the baby have to be my priority." Lee shrugged, his eyes flickering to the doorway when Chloe walked into the room. He sighed to himself when he noticed that she'd applied makeup to cover the mark on her face and neck. His heart pounded against his chest as he stared at her, not quite able to tear his eyes away from the beautiful woman in front of him.

"And yet you thought you weren't going to be a good Dad." she smiled at him, her heart fluttering at his words.

"C'mon then, we're going." he smiled at her, quickly reaching out to take her hand.

Chloe glanced at Lee, her eyes lighting up in excitement when they pulled up at the beach. He smiled at her, his heart bursting with pride when he realised that it was the first time he'd seen her smile properly since Shayne had attacked her. She quickly climbed out of the car and picked up her backpack, wincing slightly as she pulled it onto her back.

"No, give me that!" he exclaimed sternly, holding out his hand for the backpack.

"It only has towels in it, it's really light." she argued, trying to ignore the pain in her back.

"I don't care, you have broken ribs, you shouldn't be carrying a backpack." he insisted, quickly placing his hand underneath the backpack to support it's weight while he waited for Chloe to remove it. She sighed in defeat and carefully removed the backpack, smiling at him when he beamed at her like a child.

"I've never been to this beach before." she stated, glancing at her hand as Lee gently took it in his own as they walked down the track.

"Me neither, it looks nice though." he smiled, gazing out at the ocean in the distance. Lee climbed over the rocks and jumped onto the sand, turning back to face Chloe and offering her his hand to help her over the rocks. Chloe smiled at him as she took his hand and allowed him to help her, her heart swelling with pride when she realised instantly that he was concerned about her falling and hurting their baby. As soon as they reached a secluded area, Lee rummaged in the backpack and quickly placed the towels on the sand. He sat down and carefully began to arrange the food. Chloe smiled at him as she sat beside him, her eyelids suddenly feeling heavy as she gazed out at the ocean. Before Chloe could talk herself out of it, she shuffled over to him and placed her head on his shoulder, quickly wrapping her arms around his waist, her eyes still fixed on the ocean. He smiled down at her and carefully wrapped his arm around her shoulders, before placing a soft kiss on her forehead. She sighed deeply to herself as she stared at the deep blue water that was crashing against the rocks, glancing down at her hands and smiling slightly when she noticed that for the first time in a few days, they were no longer shaking.

"How are you feeling about Shayne being caught?" he asked tentatively, slightly afraid that he would say something to upset her.

"Relieved, I guess." she said quietly, still not quite able to believe that her ordeal was over. Despite the fact that she still had the memories of that fateful night swirling around her head, she at least knew that Shayne could no longer harm her and she no longer had to deal with the fear that Lee's temper would eventually snap and he would be unable to stop himself from hunting down the man that had dared to hurt Chloe.

"I'm also glad that you can't go looking for him now." she added, glancing up at him. He nodded slowly, smiling slightly at her words. He couldn't help but feel a surge of pride as he watched her closely and noticed how relaxed she was now that she was out of the house and at the beach.

"I think we needed to get out of the house." he said quietly, his eyes flickering to her lips as she stared up at him. Chloe nodded in agreement, sighing in contentment as Lee laid down on the towels and laid on his side, gazing up at her. She hesitated for a moment before laying down beside him and placing herself in his arms. He turned on his back, smiling at her as she snuggled against him.

"I keep thinking about poor Michelle." she admitted thoughtfully.

"Why, do you think she was involved?!" he said quickly, a slight edge of menace present in his tone.

"No, I just know how bad I've been feeling and he didn't even rape me. It must be so much worse for her." she explained, her eyes filling with tears when she was reminded once again of everything that she had been through.

"And she doesn't even have anyone to take care of her like I do." she added thoughtfully, glancing up at him and placing a soft kiss on his neck.

"Hopefully Mark will look after her." he said quietly, sighing when he realised that Chloe was right. She raised her eyebrow sceptically and sighed to herself, her stomach churning with guilt.

"Maybe I should reach out to her?" she said thoughtfully.

"That's probably not such a good idea." he said quickly, his heart pounding against his chest nervously as he thought about Michelle doing something to hurt Chloe again. She'd been through enough in her life and he knew that it was his responsibility to protect her and their baby.

"You look really beautiful Chlo." he whispered, gazing down at her longingly.

Chloe sighed and placed her hand under his shirt, slowly making her way up to his chest. Lee took deep breaths, his heart pounding against his chest as she stroked soft circles with her fingertips.

"Chlo." he whispered hoarsely, feeling weak under her touch. Chloe gazed up at him through her eyelashes, feigning a look of innocence.

"Chlo stop." he said, quickly taking her hand in his and removing it from underneath his shirt.

"Why?" she said, smiling cheekily at him.

"Because I won't be able to hide how much I want you." he whispered, sitting up slightly and gazing down the beach at the group of people. She smiled to herself and carefully sat up, wincing slightly at the pain in her back.

"Changing the subject slightly, but can we go to the cemetery on the way home?" she asked, swallowing the lump that was rising in her throat when she suddenly remembered that it was her Mum's birthday tomorrow. Lee nodded slowly, glancing down at Chloe as she curled up on the towel and gently rested her head on his lap, falling asleep instantly.

Chapter Forty One

Chloe sighed quietly to herself, gazing around at the landscape as Lee parked at the cemetery. Her heart sunk, like it always did when she was reminded once again of her situation. Even though she never forgot that her parents had left her, her heart still broke a little when she remembered all the happy times that the three of them had spent together. She smiled at Lee when he reached over and took her hand, squeezing it in reassurance.

"Do you want me to come with you or would you rather I wait in the car?" he offered nervously.

"No, it's okay, you can come with me." she smiled, quickly letting go of his hand and tentatively climbing out of the car, wincing in pain when she twisted awkwardly.

Lee followed her closely, quickly falling into step beside her and gently wrapping his arm around her waist. As soon as Chloe reached her parent's grave, she dropped to her knees, her stomach churning when she read their names on the headstone.

"I really miss you both." she mumbled under her breath, glancing at Lee as he sat beside her.

"Oh I forgot to tell you that we got the baby checked and everything is okay." she mumbled, her eyes filling with tears when she was reminded that her parent's wouldn't get the opportunity to meet her baby. She knew in her heart that they would have been thrilled by the idea of becoming grandparents. Lee sighed quietly when he glanced at Chloe and saw that her eyes had filled with tears. He understood instantly how she was feeling and couldn't help but wish that there was something that he could do to bring her parents back.

"I could really do with having you around right now Mum." she admitted quietly. She slowly wiped away the tears that were rolling down her cheeks, unable to tear her eyes away from the headstone, even when she felt Lee gently rest the side of his head against her shoulder.

"You could show me how to be a good Mum." she continued, sighing sadly to herself.

"I don't think you need to worry about that." Lee said softly.

"You're going to be a great Mum." he added, gently wrapping his arm around her waist and pulling her close. Chloe placed her hand on his chest and snuggled against him, trying to fight the tears that were filling her eyes. Chloe nodded slowly, her stomach churning nervously at the thought of being responsible for someone that she loved so much and that would be completely reliant on the two of them. She glanced back to the headstone, a small swirl of anger stirring inside of her when she thought about how she'd lost both of her parents within the same year. Despite the fact that she understood that her father was struggling to cope without her mother, that didn't make his actions any easier for her to bear. Even after all these years she couldn't help but feel slightly angry with her father for abandoning her in her time of need, particularly when he'd promised that he would always be there for her. Her stomach churned when she glanced at Lee and a thought suddenly popped into her head. She knew that Lee couldn't function without her, he'd said it on numerous occasions and it had been proven accurate when she'd left him behind and he'd ended up in rehab. Her heart plummeted with fear at the thought of something happening to her, and Lee potentially following in her father's footsteps. She knew first-hand how it felt to be completely alone in the world and the last thing she wanted was for history to repeat itself and their baby to have to go through the same thing as her. Chloe glanced up at Lee, sighing quietly to herself as he gazed down at her, a confused expression on his handsome features.

"Promise me you won't do what my father did?" she asked quickly, before she could stop herself.

"What do you mean?" he frowned, glancing at the grave for a moment, before his gaze turned back to her.

"If something happens to me..." she started trailing off when Lee interrupted her.

"Chlo don't." he said quickly, not even wanting to think about a life without her.

"No I mean it, if something happens to me.....you can't abandon our child." she said quietly, her heart sinking when she heard her father's words swirling around her head. How he'd promised her that when they lost her mother they would get through each day together and that he would always be there for her.

"I really don't want to talk about this Chlo." he whispered, his eyes wandering to her abdomen as his stomach churned in fear at the thought of anything happening to the person who meant the world to him.

"You need to promise me though.....I know what it feels like to lose both parents close together...and I don't want that for our child." she said quickly, beginning to panic slightly.

"And I'll make you the same promise in return." she prompted.

"What?" he frowned, struggling to think straight because his brain was working overtime.

"That if anything happens to you, I won't do anything to myself, for the sake of our child." she said quietly, her eyes filling with tears at the thought of living in a world without him. He sighed sadly as he stared at her, his heart breaking a little when he noticed that her eyes had filled with tears.

"Okay I promise." he whispered reluctantly. Chloe nodded slowly, quickly wrapping her arms around his neck and holding him close.

"I love you so much." she whispered in his ear.

"I love you too Chlo." he whispered back.

"Just make sure that you don't leave me." he whispered, wrapping his arms around her and holding her carefully, desperately trying to resist the urge to hold her as tight as possible and never let go.

"What do you fancy for dinner?" Lee asked Chloe as soon as they arrived home.

"Hmm, I'm not sure really." she admitted, frowning to herself as she removed her shoes and noticed that Nathan's were no longer in the hallway.

"I messaged him and said that he can head home, since we don't need to guard you anymore." he told her, realising instantly what she was frowning at. Chloe nodded slowly.

"Why don't I make a pizza or something?" he suggested.

"Sounds good." she smiled.

"I'm just going to go and put my pyjamas on." she told him, feeling a sudden desire to wear something more comfortable. He nodded slowly, smiling warmly at her as he watched her climbing the stairs.

Chloe wandered into the bedroom and quickly picked up a makeup wipe, sitting in silence as she removed her makeup. As soon as she was finished she quickly removed her clothes, sighing quietly to herself when she glanced at her reflection in the mirror. She swallowed slowly, suddenly feeling a wave of nausea wash over her. She clapped her hand over her mouth and rushed into the bathroom, quickly kneeling on the floor and vomiting into the toilet.

"You really need to stop doing this to me little baby." she mumbled, clutching her sore chest as she took deep breaths, trying to get her breath back.

"Especially when I'm sore." she said quietly, slowly sitting back as she felt the nausea slowly passing. She gingerly stood up, quickly grasping the sink when she felt the room swirling slightly. As soon as she recovered her balance she quickly brushed her teeth and walked into the bedroom, a small squeak of fear escaping her lips when she noticed Lee perched on the end of their bed. His eyes quickly glanced up from his phone when he heard Chloe squeak.

"Shit." he muttered, his breath catching in his throat as he stared at her, standing before him in her underwear. He stared at her silently, unable to tear his eyes away from her figure. He shook his head slowly as he stared at the woman he loved, standing before him in her underwear, still not quite able to comprehend that she had no idea how mesmerising she was. Chloe's eyes darted to the floor, not quite able to look him in the eye, her cheeks colouring deeply as she felt him staring at her. Her eyes flickered to him when he reached behind himself and picked up a pillow, quickly placing it over his lap.

"Surely you can't be good to go already, I didn't even touch you?" she frowned, not entirely sure what had gotten into him lately.

"I know....but you're so beautiful." he breathed, his breath catching in his throat. Chloe watched him closely as he closed his eyes and took deep breaths, desperately trying to control how attracted he was to her. He knew that she was still recovering from everything that she had been through as a result of Shayne and the last thing he wanted to do was to push her before she was ready. Before Chloe could talk herself out of it, she took a deep breath and crossed the room, stopping when she was stood directly in front of him. Lee slowly opened his eyes, jumping slightly when he noticed that she was standing mere centimetres from him. He glanced up at her, forcing himself to maintain eye contact with her. She impulsively wrapped her arms around his head and held him tightly against her abdomen, suddenly feeling an overwhelming need to be close to him. He placed his hands on her hips, sighing in contentment as he rested his head against her, his skin tingling under her touch when she softly stroked his hair. Chloe shivered involuntarily when she felt his hair brush against her abdomen. She stared down at him as he lifted his head and planted a series of soft kisses on her stomach. Lee glanced down at Chloe's hands as she took hold of the pillow on his lap and quickly discarded it onto the floor. Her hands shook as she knelt on the bed and carefully positioned herself on his lap, her heart pounding against her chest as she wrapped her arms around his neck. Lee placed his arms around her hips, holding her close. He sighed deeply, as she placed a soft kiss on his cheek, methodically making her way along his jawline and down onto his neck.

"I want you so bad Chlo." he said hoarsely, softly stroking the base of her spine with his fingertips.

"Since I'm yours you can have me whenever you want." she whispered against his neck, smiling in satisfaction when he shivered under her touch.

"I know, but you're sore Chlo." he whispered sadly, his stomach churning at the thought of hurting her. Given that she couldn't laugh or move without being in pain, he couldn't bear the idea of inflicting any more pain on her than she was already feeling.

"I'll be okay." she mumbled, glancing down at her hands as she placed them on the bottom of his shirt and slowly lifted it over his head, quickly discarding it on the floor. Chloe placed her hands against his bare chest, cherishing the feel of his bare skin against hers.

"You're so warm." she whispered thoughtfully, almost as if she was talking to herself.

"That's because you make me hot." he muttered, placing a kiss on her shoulder and slowly kissing his way down her bra strap. Chloe sighed quietly and gently rested her forehead against his bare chest, suddenly realising how much she had missed his comfort. She gasped as he kissed his way along the lace trim on her bra, sighing deeply when he reached her sternum. Chloe glanced at him, softly stroking his hair when he rested his forehead against her chest. She trembled when she felt his warm breath against her chest. She smiled slightly when he glanced up at her, a look of deep longing etched on his handsome features. In that moment she suddenly realised how much he was struggling to resist her. Even though she'd been having intense doubts about her new body shape, and concerns that he would no longer be attracted to her, it suddenly dawned on her that he still wanted her.

"It's okay, you don't have to fight it." she whispered in his ear, gently wrapping her arms around his head and holding him close.

"I don't want to hurt you." he mumbled against her chest.

"I'll be fine." she reassured him, gently placing her hands on the side of his face and slowly lifting his head. She gently placed a tender kiss on his lips. Lee hesitated for a moment before quickly kissing her back, not quite able to bring himself to resist her advances. When they eventually pulled apart, Chloe sighed deeply and rested her forehead against his cheek.

"Let me see your back first." he said quietly, still desperately trying to resist the beautiful woman that was sitting in front of him. Chloe nodded slowly and quickly climbed off the bed, her cheeks colouring slightly as she stood in front of him, his eyes gazing in wonder at her body. Before Lee could stop himself he placed a soft kiss on her bump and quickly placed his hands on her hips, looping his thumbs through her underwear. He sighed deeply and quickly removed his thumbs, before he was unable to stop himself from removing her underwear.

"Stop fighting it.....I want you." she whispered.

"I need to check that you are okay first." he said softly, knowing that he was being unreasonable but he knew in his heart that he needed the reassurance. She sighed in defeat and perched on his lap, slowly turning her back on him. He sighed sadly, his heart breaking when Chloe turned her back on him and he laid eyes on her bruises. Even though he'd seen the marks on her back before, it still caused his stomach to churn with a mixture of sadness and anger whenever he was reminded of what she'd been through. He carefully brushed her hair to one side and softly stroked the marks with his fingers, sighing deeply to himself. Chloe twisted around to glance at him, a small yelp of pain escaping her lips when she twisted wrong.

"Oh Chlo." he said quietly, his heart breaking as he watched her. She sat in silence, taking deep breaths as she tried to supress the intense pain in her chest. Lee watched her sadly, desperately wishing that he could do something to take her pain away. He carefully wrapped his arms around her waist and held her close against himself, trying to find a way to help her. Her eyes filled with tears as she carefully rested her back against his chest, her breathing short and shallow.

"Take deep breaths Chlo." he whispered in her ear, placing a soft kiss on her neck.

"It hurts more when I take deep breaths." she admitted, sighing quietly. She closed her eyes and rested the back of her head against Lee's chest, flinching slightly when she felt him wrap his arm around her shoulder and gently wipe away the tears that were spilling out of her eyes. Chloe sighed in relief as the warmth of his chest against her back soothed the intense pain.

"Your warmth is helping." she told him quickly, trying to reassure him when she sensed how much he was struggling with seeing her in pain.

"Is it a stabbing pain?" he asked her, gently stroking her hair.

"Kind of, and it feels like there is pressure in my chest." she said quietly, wincing slightly as she fidgeted.

"You know what will probably help." he said quietly.

"What?" she asked, frowning when she felt Lee reaching behind her and quickly unclasp her bra. He kept the two parts of the clasp in his hands, making sure that her breasts were still covered. Despite the fact that he wanted to provide her with some relief from the pain, the last thing he wanted was for her to feel like he was taking advantage of the situation.

"Actually that does feel a bit better." she said, sighing in relief.

"See." he smiled, gently placing a soft kiss on her head.

"Maybe you shouldn't wear a bra for the next few weeks while you heal?" he suggested.

"Don't be ridiculous." she said quickly, her cheeks colouring as she thought about being in public without wearing a bra.

"You do realise you don't have to hold onto it though." she added.

"I wasn't sure if you wanted me to take it off or not." he said quietly.

"Not really, but it's okay." she said quietly.

"I know how self-conscious you've been lately." he muttered. Chloe nodded slowly, swallowing the lump that was rising in her throat.

"Even though you have nothing to be self-conscious about, you're so beautiful." he whispered in her ear.

"It's partly because I was scared that you wouldn't want me anymore." she said quietly.

"But it seems like you do." she quickly added.

"Of course I do." he said softly. She nodded, quickly reaching behind herself and removing the clasps from his grip. She slowly removed her bra, watching as it tumbled to the floor. Chloe slowly turned to face him, her cheeks colouring slightly when his eyes flickered to her bare chest.

"I'm loving your bigger boobs." he smiled at her. She glanced up at him, a small smile playing on the corner of her lips. Her heart pounded against her chest when he kissed her lips softly for a moment before quickly deepening the kiss. She wrapped her arms around his neck, her bare skin tingling under his touch when he placed his hands on her hips. Chloe gasped when he buried his head in her neck and placed a series of soft kisses, smiling against her neck when he found her sensitive spot. She shuddered when he blew his warm breath against her neck. She slowly wrapped her arm around his head, softly running her hand through his hair. A small whimper escaped Chloe's lips when Lee slowly kissed along her collarbone and down onto her breast. She placed her hands against his chest, slowly trailing them downwards. Lee watched her closely, his whole body trembling with anticipation. Chloe's hands shook as she fumbled with his belt. He carefully pushed her onto the bed so that he could remove his trousers and boxers. Her cheeks coloured as she stared at her hands that were in place on her lap, realising that she needed to pluck up the courage to remove her panties. Even though she could clearly see how desperately Lee wanted her, she couldn't help but think that she would never like her body again, particularly after Shayne had confirmed her fears. He placed his hands on her hips and pulled her towards him.

"What are you doing?" she asked when he pulled her onto his lap.

"You need to take charge Chlo." he mumbled, burying his head in her chest and softly kissing her breasts.

"But...." she started, trailing off when his tongue flicked against her nipple.

"Then you can make sure you only do movements that don't hurt your ribs." he pointed out, mumbling against her chest. Chloe nodded slowly, realising that he was right but her heart sinking at the thought of it.

"What's wrong?" Lee asked her when he noticed the change in her body language. She remained silent, not entirely sure how to admit her feelings to him.

"I just don't want to take charge." she admitted, her cheeks colouring as he stared at her.

"Why not, you've done it before?" he asked, frowning in confusion.

"Because I don't." she said firmly, not quite able to bring herself to tell him that she didn't want to have to look down at her body.

"But you need too." he insisted, sighing quietly to himself.

"It's so much better when you make love to me though." she mumbled to herself, her cheeks colouring when she glanced at Lee and saw a small smile playing on the corner of his lips. Lee shook his head slowly, his heart breaking a little when he noticed the disappointment on Chloe's face. As she sat staring up at him with her deep blue eyes, he could feel his resolve slowly wavering. He quickly tore his eyes away from her, still not quite able to face the idea of causing her pain. She sighed deeply as she stared at his back, her heart sinking when she realised that he was determined to resist her. Her eyes misted with tears as she quickly reached down the end of the bed and picked up Lee's shirt, quickly pulling it over her frame. Lee's head snapped up as she shuffled to the side of the bed and carefully stood up. She glanced down at herself, smiling slightly when she noticed how large Lee's shirt was on her.

"Where are you going?" Lee frowned as he watched her stand up.

"I think the moment has gone." she said quickly, avoiding eye contact with him.

"But...Chlo..." he started, trailing off when he suddenly realised that he had no idea what he was going to say.

"You keep saying that you can't resist me, but clearly you can." she snapped, quickly walking past him, her feet freezing in place when he reached out and grasped her wrist in his grip. Her skin tingled when he placed his hands under the shirt and rested them on her hips, gently pulling her towards himself. Chloe gasped, when he softly trailed his fingertips along the inside of her thighs. A small whimper escaped her lips when his fingertips 'accidentally' brushed against her sensitive area. Lee glanced up at her, before gently placing a series of soft kisses on her thighs, smiling in satisfaction when she placed her hand on his head and curled his hair into her fist.

"Lee." she whimpered, a note of pleading in her voice.

"What?" he smiled, feigning ignorance. She trembled when he rested his head against her abdomen, his warm breath against her underwear.

"Just take me please." she begged, placing her knees onto the bed and straddling him.

"Take you where?" he grinned, enjoying the fact that he was teasing her. He grasped the bottom of her shirt in his hands and slowly lifted it over her head, making sure that his fingers brushed their way up her frame. Before Lee could react, Chloe quickly removed her panties and pushed herself onto him, smiling to herself when Lee groaned deeply. She wrapped her arms around his neck, pressing her body tightly against his, her chin resting in place on his shoulder. Lee buried his head in her shoulder, quickly kissing her neck, his hands resting in place on her hips. Before he could talk himself out of it, he gripped her hips and slowly turned her, gently placing her on the bed. Chloe gazed up at him through her long eyelashes, glancing down at his hands as he placed them on her thighs. Lee quickly removed his hands, glancing at Chloe nervously when he suddenly remembered how upset she'd been at the memory of Shayne spreading her legs.

"What's wrong?" she asked, placing her elbows behind her and tentatively sitting up.

"Nothing." he said quietly, swallowing the lump that was rising in his throat. Chloe frowned for a moment, a small gasp escaping her lips when she suddenly joined the dots in her head.

"It's okay." she reassured him, slowly spreading her legs and watching him closely as he positioned himself on top of her. A small whimper escaped her lips when he slowly pushed himself into her, his eyes gazing into hers. He kissed her lips tenderly as he carefully made love to her, trying to resist the urge to give into the deep passion that he was feeling for her. The last thing he wanted to do was to harm her or their baby. He smiled at her as he gazed down at her, realising once again how beautiful she was and how lucky he was to have her in his life.

"What?" Chloe frowned, when she noticed him staring at her.

"You're just so beautiful." he breathed, completely mesmerized by her as he watched her slowly coming undone underneath him. He reached down and slowly began to stroke her sensitive area, smiling to himself when she cried out in pleasure, gripping the bed frame tightly in her fists.

"I love you." she whined, smiling to herself when she tightened her walls around him and he groaned quietly. She wrapped her arms around his neck, holding him tightly against herself as he quickly increased the pace.

"I love you more." he whispered, groaning deeply when he finally released. As soon as she felt Lee release, she released herself, her whole body trembling against him. Lee smiled at her as he lounged on the bed beside her, placing his hand on her abdomen and slowly stroking small circles on her bump.

"It's been far too long since you made love to me." she whispered as she quickly snuggled her body against him, gently resting her head on his chest.

"It's only been a week." he chuckled, glancing down at his hand when Chloe linked her hand through his, the two of them stroking her bump affectionately.

"That is a long time for us." she giggled, shivering slightly when as he softly stroked her hair.

"True." he laughed, smiling at her when she gazed up at him, a cheeky twinkle in her eyes. She eventually tore her gaze away his, her cheeks colouring when she glanced down at herself and suddenly remembered that she was naked. Lee jumped slightly when she sat up with a start and picked up Lee's shirt, quickly pulling it over her naked frame.

"You have to stop hiding from me Chlo." he said softly as he slowly sat up, his gaze fixed on her. She jumped slightly as he wrapped his arms around her waist and carefully pulled her onto his lap. Her skin tingled under his touch when he brushed her hair to one side of her neck and kissed her neck softly.

"I'm not hiding." she whispered, glancing down at his hands as he placed them under her shirt, gently resting them in place against her bump.

"You are though." he insisted, sighing quietly to himself as he held her against his chest. Chloe turned her head to face him when he placed his chin on her shoulder. He smiled at her as she gently placed a soft kiss on his cheek.

"You have no reason too. You're so beautiful." he whispered in her ear, smiling slightly when she shivered involuntarily. She glanced down at herself when Lee slowly trailed one hand downwards and the other upwards, his fingers slowly trailing over her breasts. She trembled against him as his hand slowly trailed up the inside of her thigh, eventually coming to a stop when he reached her sensitive area.

"Why does sex with you feel so good?" she mumbled, gasping when he began to stroke her sensitive area, his other hand gently caressing her breasts.

"Luckily for me, you have nobody else to compare me too." he chuckled. She giggled quietly, the hairs on the back of her neck standing on end when he began to kiss her neck.

"Are you ready to go again already?" she frowned, glancing at him, smiling slightly when he nodded slowly.

"Because you are so damn hot." he mumbled against her neck, smiling to himself when she squirmed against him.

"I love you with all my heart." she whispered.

Chapter Forty Two

Chloe slowly opened her eyes, squinting in bright sunlight. She frowned to herself as she slowly focused on her surroundings and gazed around the room, suddenly realising that she was curled up on the couch in the Eclipse boy's dressing room. She slowly sat up, her stomach churning nervously at the thought of the impending announcement. Even though she knew that they needed to tell the fans at some point, she couldn't help but feel slightly nervous about how they were going to take the news. Her eyes snapped up as Matt walked into the room, carrying a large box under his arm.

"What have you got in there?" she asked him, slowly rubbing the sleep out of her eyes.

"The boys outfits for the meet and greet later." he told her.

"So you're styling them now." she giggled, smiling slightly at the frustrated expression on his face.

"Well, I don't have you anymore do I." he teased her, bursting out laughing when she smiled at him.

"I just don't want to be around the fans anymore after what they did." she explained.

"Today is the exception." she added when she noticed the confusion on his face. Chloe sighed quietly to herself and gently placed her hand on her bump, once again wishing that Lee wasn't in the public eye. She'd have loved to be able to live her life under the radar, rather than everything her and Lee did being constantly scrutinised. Her eyes wandered to Matt when he sat opposite her on the sofa and carefully opened the box that he'd been carrying.

"Are you going to show me the outfits then?" she frowned, watching him closely.

"I just have hoodies for the boys to wear." he told her, quickly pulling a hoodie out of the box and handing it to her. Chloe smiled slightly when she turned it over and noticed the dates of the tour printed on the back.

"I like how it has their surnames printed on the back." she said, smiling when she noticed that she had Steven's hoodie in her hand.

"Yeah I thought that was a nice touch." he chuckled. Chloe frowned to herself when Matt glanced at her, a cheeky smile playing on the corner of his lips. She watched as he rummaged in the box and silently handed her a bag.

"What's this?" she frowned.

"A present for you." he beamed. Chloe smiled and carefully opened the bag, gasping quietly when she pulled out a tiny matching hoodie. She carefully placed it on her lap, unable to tear her eyes away from it.

"It's so cute." she whispered, carefully stroking the sleeve with her thumb.

"It's for the little one." he announced, his eyes flickering to her bump for a moment.

"The baby needs to fit in with the boys." he added, chuckling to himself. Chloe nodded slowly, her eyes filling with tears as she stared down at the miniature hoodie in her lap. Until that moment she'd been able to push it to the back of her mind that Lee would be going on tour next year. She knew in her heart that she wouldn't be able to accompany him, it didn't seem fair to her to travel around the country with a baby. She blinked slowly, her heart breaking at the thought of being parted from Lee for two months, when the two of them had barely been apart since they'd started dating.

"Oh no, I didn't mean to upset you." Matt said quickly, when he noticed the tears streaming down Chloe's cheeks.

"It's okay, it's not your fault." she whispered, angrily wiping away her tears.

"I've just realised that I won't be able to go on the tour." she added quietly, her stomach churning at the thought of it.

"Of course you will." he argued, frowning slightly at her words.

"No I can't." she sighed. It felt like her heart was being ripped out of her chest and stomped on, the thought of being away from Lee's side for what felt like a lifetime. Her mind wandered to a few months ago when she'd left Lee and returned to Nottingham, how miserable she'd been when she was no longer in his presence. Six weeks had felt like a lifetime and she knew that two months away from him would be unbearable.

"But I just assumed that you and the baby would be accompanying Lee." Matt frowned, snapping her out of her thoughts.

"And I know you don't work with the boys anymore, but you know that you are welcome to come with us." he added.

"I know, but it's not fair on the baby." she pointed out, sighing deeply to herself.

"The baby will only be four months old, we can't be on the road all the time, surrounded by fans, trying to live off a tour bus. And the baby will keep the boys up at night and they won't be well rested to perform." she explained, glancing at him when he sighed and nodded in agreement, quickly realising that she was correct.

"Have you spoken to Lee about it?" he asked.

"No, I have been trying not to think about it." she admitted, staring down at the hoodie on her lap.

"I think you need to tell him....he won't be happy about it." he told her. Chloe nodded slowly, her stomach churning at the thought of telling Lee. She knew that he wouldn't be happy about the idea of leaving her behind. Her heart plummeted when she suddenly realised that he wouldn't want to go on the tour without her. He would rather let down the boys and the fans and once again it would be her fault.

"I'll tell him another time, I can't tell him just before he goes on stage." she said thoughtfully, glancing at Matt when she heard him sigh deeply.

"Don't worry, I won't let him pull out of the tour again." she added, her stomach churning with guilt when she remembered how Lee had pulled out of the tour the first time around.

"Yeah good luck with that." he sighed, unable to shake the feeling that Lee would refuse to leave Chloe's side, particularly when they had a young baby. Chloe jumped and quickly wiped away her tears when the door to the dressing room opened and Adrian, Steven, Lee and Nathan walked into the room. She quickly looked away from them, desperately hoping that Lee wouldn't notice the tears that had filled her eyes.

"Lee was just telling us about the announcement." Steven said quickly.

"What announcement?" Matt frowned.

"I'm going to tell the fans about Chloe being pregnant." Lee told him.

"On stage or at the meet and greet?" Matt checked, glancing at Chloe when he noticed her squirming nervously.

"On the stage when I speak to the crowd." Lee said quietly, glancing at Chloe and frowning slightly when he noticed the tears that had filled her eyes. She sighed to herself and quickly wandered over to the makeup chair and began to apply her makeup, trying to give herself at least a shred of confidence before she had to face the fans. She glanced at Lee in the mirror when he stood behind her and gently placed his hands on her shoulders. Her skin tingled as he leant over and gently rested his chin on her shoulder, his warm breath on her neck.

"Don't get upset, I won't let them come between us again." he whispered in her ear. She nodded slowly, her stomach churning with a mixture of nerves and dread at the thought of being away from him for two months.

"I won't Chlo, if things get bad again, I'll leave the band and we can go and raise our baby off the grid." he whispered.

"You would do that?" she asked, slowly putting down the makeup brush and locking eyes with him in the mirror.

"Yeah of course I would." he reassured her.

"I won't lose you again." he added, brushing her hair to one side and placing a soft kiss on her neck.

"The two of you are my priority." he mumbled against her neck, keeping his voice low so that he wasn't overheard.

"I know." she mouthed at him in the mirror, glancing up when she noticed Nathan rummaging in the hoodies.

"What are these for?" he rounded on Matt.

"The four of you need to wear them during the meet and greet." Matt told them, sighing when Steven rolled his eyes at him.

"What for?" Steven sighed.

"To advertise the tour obviously." Matt said impatiently. Chloe sighed to herself and continued applying her makeup, trying to distract herself from the intense desire that she was feeling for Lee as he continued to place soft kisses on her neck. She shivered under his touch as he softly stroked her hair, his hand slowly trailing down her shoulder and onto her arm. Her skin tingled under his touch as he slowly traced small circles on her arm with his fingertips.

"Stop it." she whispered, glancing nervously at the boys in the mirror when she shivered involuntarily.

"They aren't watching anyway." he whispered against her neck, smiling in satisfaction when she trembled against him. He locked eyes with her in the mirror, smiling cheekily at her as he traced his fingertips along her collarbone, slowly making his way towards her chest, his fingers eventually resting against the heart on the end of her necklace.

"You even had one made for private." Nathan piped up from across the room, beaming to himself when he picked up the small hoodie. Lee sighed deeply and quickly turned to face Nathan, glaring at him across the room, his heart swelling with pride when his eyes flickered to the hoodie.

"It's so cute." Adrian laughed.

"Are you trying to turn my baby into a billboard now?" Lee grinned at Matt.

"No, I just figured the baby is a part of our little family and I didn't want it to be left out." Matt answered, glancing nervously at Chloe.

"I think this is your one." Steven announced, quickly throwing Lee's hoodie at him, bursting out laughing when he swiftly caught it.

"It won't be mine for very long anyway." Lee beamed.

"Please don't start....just wear the damn thing!" Matt snapped. Lee frowned at him, slightly confused as to why Matt was suddenly being so waspish.

"I meant because Chloe will probably adopt it." Lee said, glancing at Chloe and smiling at her when he saw the trace of a small smile playing on the corner of her lips.

"I already have the one from your last tour." she smiled, carefully standing up.

"Yeah but this one is nicer." Lee laughed. The six of them fell silent as the door to the dressing room opened and Bobby walked into the room, closely followed by Jonny. Chloe glanced at Lee, squirming slightly when she felt Jonny watching her closely. Bobby smiled at her as he quickly crossed the room and pulled her into a hug.

"I haven't seen you for ages Chloe." Bobby told her.

"I know, I'm sorry. Things have been a bit intense." she replied, her stomach churning with guilt when she suddenly realised that she hadn't been there for Bobby during his time of need.

"Yeah I heard about Shayne attacking you." Bobby said, smiling sympathetically at her when he eventually released her from his grip. Chloe glanced at Lee when she felt him place his hand on the small of her back, suddenly feeling slightly nervous that speaking about Shayne would cause her to be upset.

"I have the envelope for you." Lee said, quickly rummaging in his pocket and handing the envelope to Bobby.

"This is a lot of responsibility." Bobby said quietly, as he tentatively took the envelope.

"Are you bribing our stage staff now?" Adrian laughed.

"No of course not." Lee laughed. Bobby smiled at Chloe and Lee, before quickly leaving the room to make the preparations.

"It's the gender of our baby." Chloe quickly told them when the four of them raised their eyebrows questioningly.

"Are you twenty weeks already?!" Nathan exclaimed, his eyes darting to her abdomen. Chloe smiled slightly and nodded slowly.

"But you don't look any bigger than when I last saw you." Nathan frowned, glancing at Lee nervously.

"The midwife said that I'm not showing very much but it's nothing to worry about, I'm just measuring small." she reassured him, smiling to herself when she noticed how concerned he looked. She couldn't help but feel a surge of pride at how much Nathan cared about the baby already.

"We had the gender scan a couple of days ago, and we figured we would do the reveal at the end of the show." Lee explained.

"In the confetti cannons, blue for a boy, pink for a girl." he added.

"That's actually really cute." Matt smiled.

"Wouldn't you rather do it yourselves somewhere private?" Nathan frowned, glancing at Chloe.

"In an ideal world yes, but we need to make the fans feel involved so that hopefully they don't hate on us again." Lee answered, glancing at Chloe when she nodded slowly.

"And we'll keep the name a secret until the baby is born." Chloe agreed, her heart sinking a little about her life being so public, but she knew in her heart that they were making the right decision. She knew what she was getting into when she chose to date Lee and she would never ask him to leave the band on her account.

"Wait, so we don't get to know the name?" Adrian laughed, pretending to pout at the two of them.

"Not even the godfather?" Nathan prompted, wriggling his eyebrows cheekily. Chloe shook her head slowly, smiling at Nathan's cheeky expression.

"We haven't spoken about names yet anyway have we?" Lee said, turning to face Chloe.

"Just the middle names." she smiled at him.

"We can tell them the middle names can't we?" Lee asked her.

"Basically if it's a girl it'll be Paul and Emilia for a girl." Chloe announced.

"My parents' names." she quickly added, glancing up at Lee when he placed a soft kiss on her head.

"That's actually really sweet." Nathan smiled. Lee nodded, glancing at Jonny for a moment, his stomach churning when he realised that he was sitting across the room, his eyes fixed on Chloe. She glanced at Lee when she noticed his body language stiffen, quickly following his eyeline. As soon as she locked eyes with Jonny, he raised his eyebrow at her.

"I need to use the bathroom." Chloe announced, squirming under Jonny's intense gaze. Lee nodded slowly, watching her closely as she left the room, quickly closing the door behind her. Lee glanced at Nathan when he walked over to him and quickly slipped a small box into his pocket.

"It finally arrived then." Lee muttered.

"Yep, I collected it this morning." Nathan told him.

"Thanks." Lee smiled at him. His eyes flickered to Jonny when he stood up and walked across the room.

"Where are you going?!" Lee demanded. Jonny froze in place and slowly turned to face him.

"Don't even think about following her!" Lee warned him.

"I'm really not that invested in your girlfriend." Jonny replied, smirking at Lee.

"I think we both know that's not true." Lee argued.

"Although I heard that you can make her feel things that I can't." he added, chuckling slightly when the smirk slowly disappeared from Jonny's face. Jonny opened his mouth to respond, but quickly closed it when Chloe walked into the room, glancing around nervously when she picked up on the tense atmosphere. As soon as she was in the room, she quickly walked over to Lee and stood beside him, wrapping her arms around his waist and resting her head against his chest.

"You weren't sick were you?" he asked her, placing his arm around her shoulders and softly stroking her hair. She shook her head slowly, fighting to keep her eyes open.

"Why don't you have a nap during the show, Matt can come and get you just before I make the announcement?" Lee suggested.

"I'll be okay." she said quietly.

"You look really tired though." he said quietly, sighing when he noticed that she was struggling to keep her eyes open.

"I'm always tried though." she stated, glancing up at him and giving him a small smile.

"Besides I like watching you on stage." she added. Lee smiled at her, before gently placing a soft kiss on her lips.

"You boys should really get going, you need to do your sound check." Matt announced.

"Oh, I almost forgot!" Lee exclaimed, beginning to panic when he noticed the boys getting ready to leave the room. His eyes flickered to Jonny, who was still hovering in the room.

"This is just for the people I trust, so you can get out." Lee told him firmly. Jonny shrugged and quickly left the room.

"That was a bit harsh." Chloe muttered.

"He's a dickhead." Lee replied.

"What is it then?" Nathan prompted.

"I'm just telling you guys that the official story is that Chloe and I planned to have a baby. I don't want anyone to know that it just happened." Lee told them firmly, glancing at Chloe when she took his hand and squeezed it gently.

"Why, what difference does it make?" Steven frowned.

"I don't want Chloe getting stick for so called trapping me, even though she didn't, that's what people will think." Lee explained. He glanced at the five of them in turn, breathing a sigh of relief when they nodded in agreement.

"Right, we really have to go." Matt said as he ushered them out of the dressing room.

Chapter Forty Three

Chloe smiled at Lee, her heart surging with pride as she sat in the theatre, watching the boys doing their sound check. She couldn't help but notice how relaxed and happy he looked when he was performing with the boys. She fidgeted in her seat, wincing slightly and rubbing her bump, trying to ease the cramps that she was feeling. She rested her elbow against the armrest, placing her head against her hand and closing her eyes, finally giving into the intense fatigue that she'd been fighting all day.

Lee glanced down at Chloe, smiling to himself when he noticed that she'd fallen asleep. He couldn't tear his eyes away from her as she slept soundly, her hand gently resting in place on her abdomen. His heart surged with pride when he was reminded once again, how beautiful she was. He snapped out of his thoughts when Nathan elbowed him in the ribs, alerting him to the fact that he'd missed his cue to start singing. Matt sighed and quickly switched off the music, glaring at Lee, a look of frustration on his face.

"Start again from the top." Matt said firmly. Lee nodded slowly, his eyes wandering to Bobby when he noticed him sitting in front of the stage, slowly pulling the envelope out of his pocket. Before he could stop himself Lee quickly placed the microphone back onto the stand and hurried to the edge of the stage, quickly jumping down in front of Bobby. Bobby jumped when Lee quickly swiped the envelope out of his grasp.

"Sorry, I need to find out with Chloe first." Lee said. Bobby nodded slowly, smiling slightly. Matt sighed deeply as he watched Lee place the envelope into his pocket and climb back onto the stage.

Chloe awoke with a start, glancing around the theatre and frowning to herself when she noticed that the stage was empty. She turned to her side, jumping slightly when she noticed that Lee was sitting beside her, gently tracing small circles on her arm. He smiled at her, maintaining eye contact as he placed a soft kiss on her shoulder.

"Were you watching me sleep?" she smiled.

"No, I was waiting for you to wake up." he chuckled, watching her closely as she lifted the arm rest between them and shuffled closer to him, snuggling into his arms.

"I don't know what I'm going to do without you." she mumbled to herself, her skin tingling under his touch when he placed his hand on her lap and slowly traced small circles on her leg.

"I'm not going anywhere Chlo." he whispered softly. She nodded slowly, her stomach churning at the thought of being parted from him.

"I have a surprise for you." he told her, smiling cheekily as he rummaged in his pocket and pulled out the envelope, gently placing it on her lap. Chloe glanced down at it, slightly confused as to what was going on.

"I thought you wanted Bobby to do the reveal." she frowned, realising instantly what was in the envelope.

"We can still do that, but maybe we should find out before everyone else." he pointed out, his stomach churning nervously.

"And I kind of want to be by your side when we find out." he added thoughtfully, not entirely comfortable with the idea of being parted from Chloe when the two of them found out the gender of their baby.

"And I know that you won't want to be on the stage." he continued. Chloe shook her head slowly, carefully picking up the envelope.

"Maybe you should open it." she suggested.

"We'll do it together." he told her, gently taking hold of her hand and placing it on one end of the envelope, his hand resting in place on the other end. She smiled at him as they quickly opened the envelope and pulled out the slip of paper.

"It's a girl." she whispered. Lee nodded slowly, his heart souring against his chest at the thought of having a baby girl.

"Oh my god." she whispered, her heart pounding against her chest as she stared down at her bump. She glanced at Lee when she heard him sniff quietly, his eyes still fixed on the piece of paper.

"Are you okay?" she asked softly. He nodded slowly, quickly wrapping his arms around her waist and pulling her onto his lap. She wrapped her arms around his neck, sighing in contentment as he held her tightly, burying his head in her shoulder.

"I'm just so happy." he whispered, trying to hold back the emotions that he was feeling.

"We're going to have a baby girl." he whispered, his eyes filling with tears of happiness.

"I know." she said quietly, gently stroking the hair on the back of his neck. She gasped, quickly wrapping her legs around his waist when he suddenly stood up and spun around, no longer able to hide his excitement. He'd been thrilled since he'd first discovered that he was having a baby with Chloe, but he'd been hoping that they would have a baby girl together.

"We're going to have a baby girl!" he exclaimed excitedly.

"Ssh." she giggled, bursting out laughing when he carefully set her down on the back of one of the chairs.

"She's going to be a mini you." he said, his face brimming with pride.

"She'll definitely be a daddy's princess." she giggled.

"And she's not allowed to date......ever." he laughed.

"Right steady on, that's a long way off." she said, bursting out laughing when she noticed the cheeky twinkle in his eyes. She watched him as he knelt in front of her and gently rested his forehead against her abdomen, gently placing a series of soft kisses on her abdomen.

"I can't wait to hold our baby Chlo." he admitted, shivering slightly when Chloe softly stroked his hair.

"I know, me neither." she whispered. Lee placed his hands on either side of the chair and slowly stood up, leaning over to kiss Chloe's lips. She wrapped her arms around his neck, her heart pounding against her chest when he quickly deepened the kiss.

"I love you so much." she whispered, gently resting her head against his chest, when they eventually pulled apart.

"I love you too." he whispered back, placing a soft kiss on her neck.

"I love both of my girls so much." he added, gently resting his hand on her bump. Chloe smiled against his chest, her heart swelling with pride as she thought how much of an amazing father he was going to be and how lucky their child was to have him in their lives.

"LEE!" Matt's voice bellowed from the corridor, causing Chloe to jump.

"You'd better go." she giggled, smiling at Lee when he sighed quietly and slowly straightened up. He rolled his eyes and quickly placed a soft kiss on her lips.

"I'll let Bobby know to use pink confetti." she told him, smiling at how happy he looked.

"Okay guys, we only have one more song to go I'm afraid!" Steven announced, chuckling to himself when the crowd let out a chorus of groans.

"But before we do that, Lee has something that he would like to say." Nathan said, smiling at Lee.

"Yes indeed I do." Lee smiled back, his gaze wandering to Chloe who was standing at the side of the stage, her frame hidden by the curtain. She smiled at him, giving him a small nod of encouragement.

"So first of all, as you all know I have a girlfriend. And I am the luckiest man in the world because she is the kindest, purest, most beautiful woman that I've ever met." Lee said, his heart swelling with pride as he glanced at Chloe and saw her cheeks colouring.

"He's talking about me guys." Nathan said, pretending to be embarrassed.

"Shut up you dick." Lee laughed, elbowing him in the ribs playfully. The two of them burst out laughing, joining in with the crowd.

"Anyway so since Chloe is the love of my life, we have decided that the time is right to take a big step." Lee continued tentatively, his heart pounding nervously at the thought of making the announcement to the fans. Despite the fact that he knew that he was doing the right thing and that they would have to tell the fans eventually, he couldn't help but feel a wave of fear that they would turn on Chloe and troll her once again. He took a deep breath, desperately trying to calm his nerves.

"So Chloe and I are going to have a baby in August." he blurted, before he could talk himself out of it. His stomach churned nervously as the theatre fell silent, a ripple of shock passing around the room. A few moments of silence passed before the theatre finally erupted into a chorus of cheers and clapping. Nathan smiled at Lee, quickly wrapping his arm around his shoulders, still not quite able to believe that his best friend had finally fallen in love with someone and would soon become a father.

"And I get to be godfather of course." Nathan piped up, winking at Lee.

"Wait....what about us?" Steven teased.

"No, I'm the best friend." Nathan countered.

"Which is why I get to name the baby." he added, beaming at Lee when he glared at him.

"Don't start this shit again." Lee warned, a small smile playing on the corner of his lips when he listened the crowd laughing at their banter.

"Anyway as I was about to say, we are going to perform one more song." Lee said quickly, before Nathan could tell the crowd the annoying nickname that he'd made up for the baby.

"And at the end of the song we are going to reveal the gender of our baby. So the confetti will be blue if it's a boy and pink for a girl." he continued, glancing at Chloe and winking at her when she smiled at him.

"But before that....here is Chloe's favourite song.....this is Broken." Lee announced, his heart pounding against his chest like it always did when he sung the song that he wrote about his feelings for Chloe. He couldn't help but think back to the time when he thought he was going to lose her from his life forever. He'd never even dared to hope that she would reciprocate his feelings for her, let alone that she would fall desperately in love with him and be carrying his baby. As long as he lived, he knew that he would never stop thanking his lucky stars that she was prepared to share her life with him.

Chloe smiled to herself, her heart pounding against her chest when she heard Lee's amazing vocals singing his part of the song that he'd written about her. Whenever she heard their song, it always made her feel weak at the knees. She knew how lucky she was to have someone like Lee in her life. Someone who loved and cherished her and would do anything to protect her, even to his own detriment. She jumped slightly when the song finished and the confetti cannons exploded, releasing pink confetti into the air, causing the crowd to erupt with excitement. Lee glanced at Chloe for a moment before he was enveloped in a group hug by Adrian, Steven and Nathan.

"C'mon Chlo Bo!" Nathan called out to her, as soon as he let go of Lee. Adrian smiled at her, gesturing for her to join them on the stage.

"I think she needs some encouragement guys." Steven said, when he noticed Chloe slowly shaking her head at them. He raised his arms and waved his hands up and down, signalling to the crowd to give her some encouragement. Chloe stomach churned with fear as she stood backstage, listening to the crowd chanting her name, her feet frozen in place, not quite able to bring herself to walk out onto the stage and be stared at by thousands of people. She locked eyes, slowly shaking her head at him.

"She's too shy to be on the stage." Lee quickly told them, jumping to Chloe's defence.

"She will be with us at the meet and greet, so those of you that have tickets, you'll be able to meet her then." Lee announced to the crowd before quickly walking off the stage, hurrying over to Chloe. As soon as he reached her, he quickly pulled her into a hug, squeezing her gently, his heart pounding against his chest as he thought about their daughter that they would finally get to meet in a few short months.

"I need to grab you guys for a chat about the new single." Matt announced, as soon as Adrian, Steven and Nathan joined them backstage. Lee sighed quietly and reluctantly let go of Chloe, glancing back at her for a moment as he followed Matt.

Chapter Forty Four

Lee's eyes wandered to Chloe as he walked into the dressing room, closely followed by Adrian, Steven and Nathan. He smiled at her when he noticed that she was curled up on the sofa, sound asleep.

"She's stolen your hoodie already." Nathan laughed. Lee nodded slowly as he sat on the floor in front of the sofa, suddenly feeling content now that he was beside her.

"She can keep it if she wants." Lee said softly, gazing fondly at her.

"I can't believe that you are having a girl." Adrian grinned.

"I know, I can't believe it either." Lee replied.

"I love them both so much." he added, reaching out and softly stroking Chloe's hair. He stared at Chloe as he watched her chest slowly rising and falling, not quite able to bring himself to tear his eyes away from her. Ever since he'd found out that Chloe was pregnant, it was almost like he'd fallen even deeper in love with her than before. Especially now that she was showing, he found himself longing for her almost constantly.

"Right, we need to go!" Matt announced as he walked into the room purposefully.

"Ssh." Lee said quickly, slightly afraid that he was going to wake Chloe.

"Chloe is asleep." Nathan told him quietly.

"Well she needs to come with us anyway, so we'll need to wake her." Matt pointed out, rolling his eyes in frustration.

"No." Lee said firmly.

"She's been having bad fatigue as part of the pregnancy, so she needs to rest." he added, glancing up at Matt when he heard him sigh deeply.

"She's carrying precious cargo." he continued, gently resting his hand against her bump and placing a soft kiss on her lips.

"Well she can sleep later can't she, once the meet and greet is over!" Matt snapped, his temper finally starting to rise as he glared at Lee.

"What's your problem?" Lee rounded on him.

"Your attitude is my problem." Matt said shortly.

"And what's that supposed to mean?" Lee insisted, frowning at Matt's words.

"You pulled out of the tour last time and let a lot of people down and we have managed to reschedule everything around you and you're not even that invested!" Matt exclaimed angrily. Lee opened his mouth to respond, quickly closing it when Matt continued to rant.

"And I know that Chloe means a lot to you, but you have other commitments too, you can't expect the rest of us to keep picking up the slack for you because you've disappeared somewhere or you've forgotten to start singing!" Matt ranted.

"He couldn't help the fact that he was in rehab." Steven piped up, not entirely sure what had gotten into Matt. Even though he knew that Lee wasn't as invested in the band as the rest of them, he understood that it was because he was fully committed to Chloe and their baby.

"I know that, but I shouldn't have to keep prompting you to do things all the time." Matt sighed.

"So you either wake Chloe up or she can stay there while the four of you do the meet and greet." he continued.

"You don't need to be such a dick." Lee snapped, glancing at Chloe as she stirred slowly.

"I hope you realise that if you pull out of this tour, the record label will probably drop you." Matt pointed out, his temper still simmering when he noticed Lee watching Chloe closely. Even though he knew that he was being unfair to Lee, he couldn't help feeling a deep sense of frustration that he'd managed to convince the record label to give the band another chance and now his gut was screaming at him that Lee would pull out of the tour once again, as soon as he discovered that Chloe would be remaining behind.

"What the hell has gotten into him?" Adrian muttered as they watched Matt leave the room, slamming the door behind himself.

"God knows." Steven shrugged, staring intently at his phone, the conversation clearly boring him. Lee jumped slightly as Chloe sat up behind him and wrapped her arms around his neck, gently resting her chin on his shoulder.

"Did I get you into trouble?" she whispered sleepily.

"Don't worry about it." he replied, placing his hands on her arms and planting a soft kiss on her forearm. Chloe's eyes flickered upwards, her heart sinking as she locked eyes with Nathan. She knew from his expression that she had managed to cause a problem between them.

"Sorry, I don't mean to cause problems." Chloe said quietly, glancing around nervously at them.

"Matt's just in a mood it's fine." Nathan said quickly.

"Besides you can't help falling asleep." he added, smiling at Chloe when the two of them locked eyes.

"I think maybe you need to give her a night off, she looks shattered." Steven chuckled, winking at Lee. Lee glanced at Chloe, smiling slightly when he noticed her cheeks colouring.

"It's the pregnancy." Lee said quickly, a small smile playing on the corner of his lips when Steven raised his eyebrow sceptically.

"I'm sure that's what it is." Steven laughed, before quickly leaving the room.

"I'm going to go and talk to Matt, see if I can calm him down." Nathan announced, as he followed Steven. Adrian smiled to himself when he saw Lee slowly turn his head to face Chloe, gently placing a soft kiss on her lips. Lee didn't even break eye contact with her when Adrian quickly excused himself, sensing that they needed a moment alone.

"It was so nice to see you on stage again doing what you love to do." she muttered, softly stroking his hairline with her fingertips, her heart swelling with pride when she remembered how happy and content he'd seemed when he was on stage performing with the boys.

"And you looked really hot." she smiled, planting a series of soft kisses on his neck, quickly resting her chin on his shoulder. Lee smiled slightly, struggling to focus on her words when she placed her hands underneath his shirt, slowly stroking her way down his chest.

"I wanted you so bad." she whispered in his ear, smiling slightly when he shivered under her touch.

"What do you mean 'wanted'?" he smiled.

"I meant want." she said quickly, giggling quietly.

"You're getting as bad as me." he chuckled, smiling at her when she continued kissing his neck.

"I blame the hormones." she whispered against his neck, a small smile playing on her lips.

"Oh so it's the baby's fault is it." he grinned, trembling under her touch when her hands slowly trailed their way upwards.

"Um hum." she mumbled, desperately trying to fight the deep desire that she was feeling for him.

"We need to wait until later." he grinned, quickly moving away from her touch before he accidentally revealed how attracted he was to her.

"We should go before Matt has another meltdown." he prompted her, standing up and holding out his hand to her. Chloe nodded, sighing quietly to herself as she took his hand and slowly stood up.

"I love how you've adopted my hoodie already." he smiled, watching closely as she quickly removed it and handed it to him.

"I couldn't resist. I was cold when I came through here." she told him, a small smile playing on the corner of her lips.

"I just need it for tonight and then you can have it." he muttered, wrapping his arm around her shoulders and placing a soft kiss on her forehead.

"Do you have a jacket or something to wear if you are cold?" he asked. She nodded slowly as she walked over to the coat rail and removed her leather jacket, quickly pulling it on.

"I should probably leave it unzipped though shouldn't I." she sighed, glancing down at her bump, her stomach churning nervously at the thought of everyone staring at her.

"Yeah probably. If they are able to see your bump, they'll feel more involved." he said quietly, sighing sadly to himself when he noticed Chloe nodding reluctantly. He couldn't help but feel a pang of guilt that he was putting her into a situation that she didn't feel comfortable with.

"I just want to protect you both from the hate." he muttered softly, almost like he was talking to himself.

"I know, it's okay." she reassured him, trying to ignore the butterflies that were swirling in her stomach.

"I don't want anyone touching our baby though." she added.

"No that's fine, they won't." he reassured her, his eyes flickering to her bump.

"You're the only person that's allowed to touch her while she's inside me." she muttered, taking his hand and gently placing it on her abdomen. Her skin tingled under his touch, like it always did when he touched her. Chloe rested her forehead against his shoulder, the two of them staring down at her bump, neither of them able to comprehend that they were having a baby girl together.

They jumped as the door to the dressing room was flung open, the force of it causing the door to hit against the wall.

"Are you actually going to grace us with your presence at some point this evening?!" Matt exclaimed as soon as he laid eyes on Lee. Lee opened his mouth to respond, quickly closing it again when he glanced at Chloe and noticed her squirming. Despite the fact that his temper was flaring, the last thing he wanted was to cause drama and upset Chloe, when he knew that she was already worried about the meet and greet.

"We were just about to come through." Chloe said quietly, frowning to herself at Matt's waspish tone.

"Well if you're not too busy, we're ready for you." Matt snapped, opening the dressing room door and standing with his back against it, gesturing for Lee to leave the room. Lee gently took Chloe's hand and squeezed it, trying to provide her with some reassurance. Matt glared at Lee as he walked past, Chloe following closely behind.

She remained close to Lee as the two of them walked into a room and quickly joined Nathan, Adrian and Steven at the table. Chloe shot Lee a small smile when she noticed him winking at her, before quickly pulling on his hoodie. She tentatively sat beside Nathan, perching on the edge of the chair, her stomach churning with nerves.

"You look like you want the ground to swallow you up." Nathan chuckled, quickly taking her hand and squeezing it gently.

"This kind of thing isn't really my scene." Chloe mumbled, squirming nervously as she noticed the fans lining up across the room. She glanced at Lee as he sat beside her and arranged the album promo shots in front of himself.

"Oh, and don't you dare mention that you call our baby 'private'." Lee warned, leaning across Chloe to whisper to Nathan.

"I wasn't going too." Nathan laughed.

"Good, I don't want to wake up in the morning to find that bloody hashtag trending on twitter." Lee said, a small trace of a smile playing on the corner of his lips. Chloe glanced down at the photographs in front of her and quickly pushed them towards Lee, her heart plummeting as she stared at the photoshoot from all those months ago. She couldn't help but feel a twinge of sadness as she gazed at herself in the corset. Despite the fact that she knew in her heart that Lee was still attracted to her new body, she couldn't help but wish that she could return to all those months ago, when she'd finally gained some body confidence. To be able to hold her head high and finally feel comfortable in her own skin once again. Her eyes misted with tears as she stared, transfixed at the photographs. Her eyes flickered to her bump when she felt the familiar fluttering sensation as her baby moved inside of her. She sighed sadly, suddenly feeling an intense wave of guilt wash over her, knowing in her heart that she adored her baby already and didn't wish that she wasn't pregnant, just so that she could have her 'perfect' body back.

"Oh my god Lee, I can't believe I'm finally getting to meet you!" an excited fan squealed as she quickly leaned over the table and pulled Lee into a hug.

"I've wanted to meet you for so long!" she added, hugging him tightly.

"It's nice to meet you too." Lee chuckled.

"Thank you." he replied.

"Have you heard our new single yet?" he asked her, smiling when she eventually let go of him. She nodded slowly

"You wrote that song didn't you." she smiled. Lee nodded, quickly handing her back the album.

"Quite a lot of the songs are written by you aren't they." she beamed at her, staring at him longingly.

"Broken is definitely my favourite one that I've written though." Lee said, glancing at Chloe and smiling at her. The fan nodded, shooting him one last smile before she moved onto Nathan.

"Hello." Lee smiled as another fan approached them and handed him her album.

"Can you write it for Donna please?" she asked him.

"Yeah of course." he smiled. Chloe glanced up, her cheeks colouring when she noticed Donna watching her closely. As soon as they locked eyes, Donna shot Chloe a small smile. Chloe smiled back.

"I didn't actually realise until earlier that you are the model with Lee on the album." Donna smiled at her. Chloe nodded slowly, her stomach churning nervously.

"She looked even more stunning than usual that day." Lee smiled, gently placing his hand on the small of Chloe's back. Chloe smiled her thanks when Donna quickly nodded in agreement, before moving along the table.

"Hi, my name is Paige." a fan said when she approached Lee. He smiled at her and quickly pulled her into a hug, when he noticed that her whole body was trembling nervously.

"Congratulations on the baby, I'm so excited for the two of you." she smiled, glancing between Chloe and Lee.

"Thank you, she's doing well." Chloe said, quickly standing up beside Lee, so that Paige was able to see her bump.

"Oh my god, you have such a cute bump!" Paige exclaimed, her eyes fixed on Chloe's abdomen.

"Do you have any names in mind yet?" Paige asked.

"We've not really spoken about names yet have we." Chloe said, glancing at Lee.

"No, we were waiting until we knew what we were having." Lee agreed.

"We can give her a name this weekend." Chloe smiled, gazing down at her bump affectionately and carefully resting her hand against it. Paige smiled warmly at them before quickly walking away.

"Oh my god!" a fan squealed as she ran over to them, throwing herself into Lee's arms. He staggered slightly, bursting out laughing when he eventually recovered his balance.

"Nice to meet you too." he chuckled.

"And you must be Chloe!" she squealed, quickly turning to face Chloe as soon as she released Lee from her grasp. Chloe nodded shyly, smiling slightly as the fan pulled her into a hug. Chloe glanced at Lee, raising her eyebrow in confusion, smiling at him when he shrugged.

"It's so good to meet you both." the fan said excitedly, bouncing up and down on the spot as she let go of Chloe.

"It's nice to meet you too." Chloe smiled.

"Can I have a picture with you?" the fan asked Lee, quickly pulling out her mobile phone.

"Of course." Lee smiled at her, standing beside her as she took a selfie with the two of them.

"Would you like me to take a picture of the two of you together?" Chloe offered, holding her hand out for the phone.

"That would be amazing, thank you!" the fan squealed, quickly handing Chloe her phone and beaming as she took the picture.

"Thank you so much." she added, her face red with happiness as she gazed at the picture of herself with Lee. Chloe nodded slowly, glancing at Lee as he took her hand.

"That was the last one." Matt announced.

"So does that mean I can go or are you going to get your panties in a twist again?" Lee asked sarcastically.

"No you can go." Matt said shortly.

Chapter Forty Five

Chloe sighed quietly to herself as she rested her elbow against the car door and leant her head against it, desperately trying not to fall asleep until they were home. She glanced at Lee for a moment, smiling to herself when she noticed how happy he seemed. He'd barely been able to stop smiling since the moment he'd first found out that they were having a baby girl. Her heart swelled against her chest, her stomach churning with excitement at the thought of the two of them becoming parents. Despite the intense fear that Lee had felt at the beginning she knew in her heart that he was going to be an amazing father to their child. He was such a thoughtful and loving person and she knew that he would do anything to protect both her and their baby. As she sat deep in thought, she couldn't help but realise how lucky she was to have someone like him in her life, particularly when she knew that he could have any woman that he wanted, a point which had been proved today when she was reminded how the fans were with him. So many women would have given anything to have a baby with Lee Knight, and she couldn't help but feel lucky that she was the one who got the privilege.

"I think the fan event went quite well in the end." Lee stated, snapping her out of her thoughts.

"Yes it could have been worse." she said, smiling at him as he glanced at her, before quickly turning his attention back to the road.

"Is that code for you didn't enjoy it?" he chuckled.

"It's just not my thing is it, I'm not a people person like you are." she smiled.

"Although it was nice to see how much the fans adore you." she added, smiling to herself.

"I think they are fond of you too." he told her, smiling slightly as he thought about how much the fans were slowly growing to love Chloe like he did.

"Where are we going?" she asked, frowning when she suddenly noticed that he'd taken the turning for the motorway, rather than the one for his house.

"It's a surprise." he said, grinning to himself. Chloe smiled, quickly racking her brain as she tried to figure out what was going on and where he was taking her.

"We're not going to Nottingham are we?" she asked nervously, her heart plummeting at the thought of it.

"No." he said quietly.

"Because there wouldn't be much point." she told him.

"Is your Aunt still not speaking to you?" he asked.

"Nope." she said sadly, biting her lip as she fought the tears that were filling her eyes. Her mind wandered to all those weeks ago when she'd told her Auntie that her and Lee were having a baby. Even though she knew that she would be disappointed in her, as a result of her beliefs, Chloe hadn't expected her Auntie to cut her off completely.

"At least Amy is excited about the baby." he said, sighing quietly to himself when he sensed how upset Chloe was about the whole situation.

"Maybe we could invite her to stay with us soon." he added, trying to lighten the atmosphere.

"That would be good." she said quietly, closing her eyes when she could no longer fight the exhaustion that she was feeling.

Chloe's eyes snapped open as she glanced around, trying to figure out where she was. She sighed in contentment when she realised that she was in Lee's arms. He smiled down at her as he carefully carried her towards the hotel.

"Sorry, I didn't mean to wake you." he said, softly placing a kiss on her forehead.

"It's fine, but I can walk though." she smiled, giggling at his cheeky expression as he carefully placed her on the ground. He quickly walked back to the car, returning a few moments later with their bags.

"Are we spending the weekend here?" she frowned.

"Yep, I thought we could do with a weekend away." he said, smiling when he noticed her excited expression.

"Yes, but where are we?" she laughed, quickly reaching over and taking her bag from his grasp.

"We're at a hotel." he teased her, laughing as he took her hand and the two of them walked towards the hotel.

"I can see that." she laughed.

"We're in Portsmouth." he told her.

"Just a little trip somewhere that's not too far away." he added, holding the hotel door open for her and following her into reception.

"Also I checked in online." he added, quickly removing the key card from his pocket and handing it to her. Chloe nodded, glancing around as she searched for their room. As soon as she found it she walked into the room and placed her bag onto the bed.

"It's so sweet of you to organise a trip away." she said, smiling at him as she slowly turned to face him.

"I know." he smiled at her, a cheeky twinkle in his eye.

"How did you know what to pack?" she giggled as she turned her back on him and rummaged through her bag.

"Because I know you really well remember." he smiled, gently wrapping his arms around her waist and pulling her close, sighing in contentment when he rested his chest against her back. Chloe placed her hands on his arms, smiling as he playfully rocked her from side to side. She nodded slowly, her eyes brimming with tears as she removed the items, suddenly realising that he'd packed all of her favourite items.

"You're so amazing." she whispered.

"How did I get so lucky." she added, her voice breaking with emotion. She smiled slightly when he held her tighter and placed a soft kiss on her neck.

"The same way that I did." he whispered softly, smiling slightly as she trembled against him when she felt his warm breath against her neck. He glanced down at her when she yawned and relaxed against him.

"Are you tired Chlo?" he asked, an edge of worry present in his voice. She nodded slowly.

"Maybe you should have a lie down." he suggested. Chloe nodded once again, reluctantly removing herself from his arms. He watched closely as she placed her cosmetic bag onto the bedside table and quickly removed her jacket and shoes. She carefully laid down on the bed, removed a makeup wipe and quickly removed her makeup before she fell asleep once again. She smiled at Lee as he curled up on the bed beside her, carefully placing his head on her lap. He turned to face her, smiling up at her as the two of them locked eyes. She smiled to herself when she noticed the cheeky glint in his eye. Her heart pounded against her chest when he grasped the bottom of her shirt in his hand and slowly began to unfasten the buttons, carefully revealing her abdomen. She sighed in contentment as he snuggled his head against her abdomen, gently placing a series of soft kisses on her bump.

"I can't wait to meet our daughter." he whispered, his heart pounding against his chest as he thought about their baby and how desperately he wanted to meet her. Chloe nodded slowly, her eyes misting with tears as she watched Lee staring fondly at her bump. He sighed happily and slowly traced small circles with his fingers, the intense love that he felt for their baby clearly showing on his face. His eyes flickered to her when she rummaged in her cosmetic bag and quickly pulled out the Bio Oil. He frowned to himself, raising his head as she slowly sat up.

"What's that for?" he asked, glancing at the bottle in her hand.

"It's to help with stretch marks and stuff." she told him, slowly unscrewing the lid.

"But you don't have any stretch marks." he frowned, his gaze flickering to her bump for a moment.

"I know, but it might help to prevent them." she said sadly.

"It's also helping with my scar." she added, sighing sadly to herself. Lee sighed deeply, his heart breaking a little at the deep sadness that was written on her face. Even though he knew that she had always been a self-conscious person, he couldn't help but wish that there was something that he could say or do to help her realise how beautiful she was. Chloe glanced at him as he held out his hand and raised his eyebrow at her.

"What?" she frowned.

"I'll do it." he said, a small smile playing on his lips.

"I'm quite capable." she argued.

"I know, but I want too." he insisted. She nodded slowly, smiling slightly as she handed him the bottle.

"Do you remember the last time that we were at a hotel together?" she asked.

"Yes I do." he said quietly, his brain swirling with memories.

"Maybe you should sleep on the floor again, just for old times' sake." he added, bursting out laughing when he noticed her shocked expression. She glared at him for a moment before quickly joining in with his laughter. Goosebumps rose on her arms as she felt Lee gently rubbing the oil into her abdomen. He glanced up at her, smiling slightly to himself when she trembled under his touch. Lee stared at her abdomen as he slowly stroked his way along her scar. He couldn't help but smile to himself when he remembered how he'd taken care of her after she was stabbed. If felt like a lifetime ago, so much had changed. His breath caught in his throat as he remembered the day that they had told each other how they felt and he'd finally been able to call her his girlfriend. Chloe carefully sat up, resting her shoulders against the headboard, watching Lee closely as he slowly unfastened the remaining buttons on her shirt, maintaining eye contact with her. She smiled slightly as he parted the material and stared longingly at her torso.

"I really like it when you wear the white set." he whispered, his eyes fixed on her white lace bra.

"Why?" she giggled, her heart pounding against her chest when she realised that he couldn't tear his eyes away from her.

"It suits you." he whispered hoarsely, as he placed his hands on her shoulders and slowly moved her shirt down her arms.

"Also it reminds me how pure you are." he mumbled against her chest as he rested his forehead against her sternum, kissing her softly. Chloe glanced down at him as he slowly lifted his head, gazing up at her longingly. He placed his hands on her hips and slowly removed her leggings, his fingers methodically trailing down her bare skin as he did so.

"You're so beautiful." he breathed in wonder as he sat back and stared at her, his heart pounding against his chest. Chloe stared at him, squirming slightly under his intense gaze.

"You always do this." she mumbled, her cheeks colouring in embarrassment as he continued to stare at her.

"Do what?" he frowned.

"Undress me and then stare at me." she said quietly, sighing to herself when she noticed that he was still fully dressed.

"Only because I can't believe my luck." he said. She nodded slowly, her heart plummeting as she glanced behind him and gazed at her reflection in the mirror. Before Lee could react, Chloe quickly picked up her shirt and pulled it on, cursing to herself as she attempted to fasten the buttons, her hands shaking nervously.

"Don't hide from me Chlo." he whispered, his heart breaking a little when he realised what she was doing. She glanced down at her hands as he carefully took them in his own, to prevent her from fastening the buttons. She sighed quietly to herself, her eyes fixed over his shoulder at her reflection in the mirror. Her gaze didn't falter when Lee gently unfastened the buttons and slowly parted the material of her shirt.

"Your body is so beautiful." he whispered, placing his hands on her waist and softly stroking her bra with his thumbs. Before Chloe could respond, he buried his head into her shoulder, placing a series of soft kisses on her neck. She gasped in pleasure, her eyes flickering to his hands for a moment as her skin tingled under his touch. He slowly trailed his hands upwards, quickly grasping the material of her shirt in his hands and slowly moving his hands down her arms. Her eyes remained fixed on her reflection as Lee quickly removed his hoodie. He frowned to himself when he was finally able to tear his eyes away from Chloe's mesmerising figure and follow her eyeline. His heart plummeted when he realised that she was staring sadly at her own reflection.

"What's wrong Chlo?" he whispered, gently placing a soft kiss on her cheek. Chloe remained silent, sighing quietly to herself as she rested her cheek against Lee's, her skin tingling when she felt his warm breath against her cheek.

"Tell me Chlo." he mumbled, placing a series of soft kisses on her cheek. She gently wrapped her arm around his head, holding him close as he kissed his way along her jawline, smiling to himself when she trembled under his touch. She gasped quietly, placing her hand in his hair and curling it into her fist when Lee found the sensitive spot on her neck. A small whimper escaped her lips as she felt him gently trailing his fingertips along the inside of her thigh. She sighed in disappointment when Lee slowly raised his head, staring down at her, a look of deep longing etched on his handsome features.

"You need to start loving your beautiful body Chlo." he said softly, when he noticed her squirming under his gaze.

"I just feel gross." she whispered, watching him closely as he removed his shirt, his eyes fixed on her. Her eyes flickered to the mirror once again, before quickly looking away, desperately trying to convince herself that she still had her 'perfect' body. She stared down at her bump, affectionately resting her hand on her baby and smiling to herself as she thought about her baby girl.

"Nobody thinks that." Lee piped up, snapping her out of her thoughts. Her gaze remained fixed on her hand, her heart bursting with pride when Lee followed her gaze, gently placing his hand beside hers and softly stroking her fingernails.

"They kind of do." she mumbled thoughtfully, almost like she was speaking to herself.

"Who does?" he frowned, his head quickly snapping up when he heard her words.

"Just forget it." she said quickly, her cheeks colouring when she realised that she'd spoken aloud. She sighed sadly to herself, Shayne's words swirling around her head. Despite the fact that it was a few weeks ago, she couldn't help but feel slightly ashamed that her body was no longer desirable.

"Did someone tell you something negative about yourself?" he asked, quickly picking up on the tension in her body language. Chloe sighed quietly, not quite able to bring herself to tell him what Shayne had said to her, particularly when she knew how angry he would be about it. She placed her hands on his chest, and kissed his lips tenderly.

"Stop trying to distract me Chlo." he whispered when they eventually broke apart. She ignored him and placed a soft kiss on his cheek, slowly making her way along his jawline. He groaned quietly, his skin tingling under her touch as she slowly trailed her hands down his chest. She giggled as Lee placed his hands on her hips and quickly pulled her onto his lap, kissing her lips passionately.

"I love you." she whispered breathlessly.

Chapter Forty Six

Chloe sighed happily and smiled to herself as she slowly opened her eyes. She quickly pulled down the sleeves of Lee's hoodie and wrapped her arms around the pillow, hugging it tightly against herself. She stretched slowly, her heart pounding against her chest when she felt the familiar fluttering sensation in her abdomen. Despite the fact that she'd been able to feel her baby moving inside her for some time, she still couldn't quite believe that she was carrying a tiny baby. She turned over in bed, hoping to tell Lee that their baby was moving once again, frowning to herself when she suddenly realised that Lee was no longer beside her. She carefully sat up and picked up her phone from the nightstand, gasping when she realised that it was almost noon. Chloe quickly climbed out of bed and ran a hairbrush through her hair, smiling slightly when she glanced at herself in the mirror, wearing Lee's new hoodie. She quickly walked into the bathroom, smiling to herself when Lee glanced up at her from the bath tub. Her breath caught in her throat as she gazed in wonder at him, the small droplets of water dripping off his hair. Lee couldn't help but stare at Chloe as she casually leant against the doorframe, her eyes fixed on him. He smiled slightly as she stood in his hoodie, her beauty still radiating from her despite the baggy material. His gaze wandered to the edge of the material that stopped in the middle of her thighs.

"Why did you let me lie in for so long?" she asked, suddenly feeling slightly guilty that she had wasted so much of their time by sleeping.

"Because you looked so peaceful." he smiled at her, his heart pounding against his chest when he remembered how Chloe had fallen asleep almost as soon as he'd made love to her.

"And I know the pregnancy has been making you really tired so I want to make sure that you are getting enough rest." he added. Chloe nodded slowly, her eyes flickering to the bath water as she watched the steam rising out of the bath, suddenly feeling an intense urge to climb into the bath with him. As soon as the two of them locked eyes, Lee raised his eyebrow at her, realising instantly what she was thinking. Before she could talk herself out of it she slowly removed Lee's hoodie, smiling slightly when she locked eyes with him and noticed his eyes wandering over her body. She glanced down at her underwear, suddenly deciding that she felt more comfortable leaving it on. Chloe carefully climbed into the bath, sighing in contentment as she sat between Lee's legs and gently laid her back against his chest. Her skin tingled as he wrapped his arms around her waist and held her tightly, cherishing the feel of her body against his. He smiled down at Chloe, placing a soft kiss on her cheek as she snuggled her head against his collarbone.

"Why are you still wearing your underwear?" he asked softly, gazing down at her and frowning to himself. Chloe shrugged, closing her eyes softly as she relaxed against him, smiling slightly when she felt his soft heartbeat against her back.

"What were you saying last night about feeling gross?" he asked, gently placing a series of soft kisses on her neck.

"It's nothing." she whispered, turning her head and resting her cheek against his, her skin tingling as he continued placing soft kisses on her neck.

"Chlo." he mumbled against her neck.

"It's just one person's opinion anyway." she said quietly, trying to convince herself almost as much as him.

"I've never had much body confidence anyway, so it just confirmed what I was already thinking." she continued, glancing down at Lee's hands as he placed them on her bump, gently stroking the baby with his fingertips.

"You are not gross Chlo and you never have been." he told her firmly, his heart breaking a little at her lack of confidence.

"I know that you don't think that." she said quietly, smiling slightly when she remembered how desperately he wanted her. Lee nodded slowly, his gaze wandering to his hands when Chloe linked their hands, the two of them affectionately stroking her bump.

"Tell me who said that about you Chlo." he prompted, carefully wrapping his arm around her shoulders and softly stroking her hair. She opened her mouth to respond, quickly closing it again when she suddenly realised how angry he would become as soon as he found out that it was Shayne. Ever since that fateful night a few weeks ago, Shayne had become Lee's Achilles heel, the one person who made his temper flare from nowhere.

"It doesn't matter really does it." she whispered, her cheeks colouring when she felt him watching her closely.

"Of course it does." he insisted, his brain swirling as he tried to figure out who had said something so nasty to Chloe.

"It was Shayne." she blurted, when she suddenly realised that he was going to continue asking her until she told him who had made the comment about her.

"That's why he didn't rape me I guess, because he said that I am gross." she explained, her eyes filling with tears as she stared down at her bump. Lee's hands froze in place, his stomach churning with anger that someone like Shayne could say something so despicable to Chloe, especially something that wasn't true.

"Don't get angry." she said quickly, turning her head to face him when she felt his body language stiffen, his heart pounding against her back.

"How dare he say something like that to you!" he snapped, his nostrils flaring angrily.

"You've been struggling with your confidence all this time because you believed that he was telling the truth." he ranted angrily.

"I wasn't feeling great about my body before he said what he did." she pointed out to him, quickly wiping away her tears and hoping that he wouldn't notice.

"Yeah but he made it worse!" he exclaimed angrily, his stomach churning with guilt when he caused Chloe to jump in shock.

"He's such a nasty bastard." he whispered, softly stroking her hair, in an attempt to reassure her and calm himself down.

"Please tell me that you don't believe him." he added, glancing down at her as she snuggled her head against his collarbone, gently placing a soft kiss on his neck. She remained silent, slowly kissing her way up his neck and along his jawline. She shivered as she turned on her side and felt Lee place his hand on the small of her back, gently stroking the base of her spine.

"I really wish that you would love your body as much as I do." he whispered, staring into her deep blue eyes as she slowly lifted her head and gazed up at him through her long eyelashes.

"You've seen the effect that you have on me." he smiled at her, trying to supress his anger at the fact that thanks to Shayne she'd spent the past few weeks believing that she was undesirable.

"I know." she mumbled, a small smile playing on the corner of her lips. She placed her hand on his cheek, and held his head tightly against hers, smiling against his neck when she continued planting kisses and he shivered under her touch. A small whimper escaped her lips when he placed his hand between her legs and softly stroked the inside of her thigh.

"Do you really not think I'm gross?" Chloe mumbled as she slowly sat up, glancing down at his hand that was resting in place against her underwear.

"Of course not." he said quietly, sighing deeply as he sat up and carefully pulled her into his arms.

"I know you don't believe me, but you're the most beautiful person I've ever met." he whispered in her ear.

"And you know how easy it is for you to turn me on." he continued, slowly releasing her from his grasp and staring down at her longingly. She gently rested her forehead against his, her heart pounding against her chest as she gazed at him, still not quite able to believe that she had someone like him in her life.

"I'm so lucky to have you." she muttered, gently placing a soft kiss on his lips.

"It's a mutual thing Chlo." he whispered back, placing his hands on her waist and softly stroking her bra with his thumbs. Chloe nodded slowly, quickly standing up and climbing out of the bath as she made a snap decision.

"Where are you going?" he asked, watching her closely as she stood in front of him, her cheeks colouring as he watched her closely. She remained silent, a small smile playing on the corner of her lips when she noticed the droplets of water dripping from his hair. She bit her lip, trying to fight the deep desire that she was feeling for him.

"See, how can you not love that breath taking body." he muttered, resting his chin on the bathtub, unable to tear his eyes away from her. She smiled slightly, her legs feeling slightly weak when she locked eyes with him and noticed how desperately he wanted her. Lee swallowed the lump that was rising in his throat as he watched Chloe slowly reach around her back and unfasten her bra, her hands shaking nervously. His eyes flickered to her bra as it tumbled to the floor. His eyes widened when she placed her thumbs through her panties and slowly removed them, carefully stepping out of them. He smiled as he locked eyes with her, still not quite able to believe how beautiful she was. Despite the fact that he'd seen her body on numerous occasions, she still managed to take his breath away. He slowly stood up and climbed out of the bathtub, his eyes fixed on her as she stood in front of him, watching him silently, her cheeks colouring slightly as his eyes wandered over her body. She glanced up at Lee, locking eyes with him as he stood in front of her, his body mere inches from hers. Her legs trembled with anticipation as she felt the warmth radiating from his body. She rested her forehead against his chest, her heart pounding against her chest, when he softly stroked her hair, the hairs on the back of her neck standing on end.

"I love you so much." she whispered, placing a soft kiss on his bare chest, smiling to herself when she was reminded once again how much she adored him. Her skin tingled under his touch when he placed his hands on her hips, slowly trailing his way upwards, his fingers stroking her spine as he did so. His hands eventually came to a stop, gently resting them on her waist. She glanced down at his hands as he slowly turned her away from him and gently pulled her back against his chest.

"Look how beautiful you are." he whispered in her ear, gently placing his hands on her bump. Chloe glanced up, her cheeks colouring as she locked eyes with him in the mirror. She sighed in contentment and placed her hands on top of his, gently linking their fingers. A small gasp escaped her lips when Lee buried his head into her shoulder and placed a series of soft kisses on her neck. She rested the side of her head against him, closing her eyes, shivering involuntarily as he stroked small circles on her bump. He slowly raised his head, gazing at her in the mirror, a small smile playing on the corner of his lips when the two of them locked eyes and he saw the deep lust that she was feeling for him. Chloe locked eyes with him, a cheeky twinkle in her eyes as she pushed her hips against him and slowly rotated them, smiling in satisfaction when Lee groaned deeply, resting his chin on her shoulder. Her heart pounded against her chest when she rotated her hips again and Lee curled his hands into fists, squeezing her hands tightly, needing to grip onto something as he felt a deep sense of pleasure flowing through his veins. She tilted her hips backwards and rotated her hips painstakingly slowly, enjoying the fact that she was teasing him.

"It turns me on so much when you do that." she whispered, locking eyes with him in the mirror when another deep groan escaped his lips.

"Stop it Chlo." he mumbled, gripping onto her hips to prevent her from moving again, when he suddenly realised that he could no longer resist her.

"Why?" she whispered, glancing down at his hands as he pushed her away slightly and slowly turned her so that she was facing him.

"Because I need to be inside you." he admitted, his breath catching in his throat as he gazed longingly at the beautiful woman standing in front of him. Before Chloe could respond he picked her up and roughly placed her on the counter, his hands gripping onto her hips tightly. He quickly pushed into her, no longer able to fight the desperation that he was feeling for her.

"Be careful of the baby." she whispered, pressing her body against his, her hands gripping tightly to the counter.

"I know." he mumbled.

Chapter Forty Seven

Lee smiled at Chloe as the two of them walked through the shopping centre and she quickly took his hand, squeezing it gently, her stomach churning nervously as almost everyone that they passed stared at them.

"I think a lot of people recognise you here." she said quietly, glancing at him for a moment.

"Most of them are staring at you." he told her, smiling to himself when he noticed another passer-by that was unable to tear his eyes away from Chloe.

"I doubt it." she muttered, her cheeks colouring when she felt him watching her closely.

"You're so cute." he grinned, wrapping his arm around her waist and pulling her against him.

"I told you that the pregnancy really suits you." he told her, smiling at her when she giggled. He couldn't help but feel a surge of pride as he stared at her in her fitted jeans and tank top, smiling slightly to himself that she finally felt able to show off her bump. He knew in his heart that she felt better about her body now that she had finally opened up to him about what Shayne had said to her and he'd been able to reassure her that he still found her desirable. He couldn't help but wonder if part of her new found confidence was as a result of them finally revealing their news to the fans, and the overwhelming love and support that they'd received. The two of them could finally relax and no longer had to hide their baby from the world.

"Why are you staring at me?" Chloe asked, snapping him out of his thoughts.

"I like it when you are more confident." he admitted, smiling proudly at her. His mind wandered to the countless times over the past few weeks that she'd refused to fully undress in front of him, his heart swelling with pride as he remembered how different she'd been earlier. How she had been able to bring herself to stand in front of him and undress as he'd gazed at her in wonder, completely mesmerized by her beauty.

"I think some of it is hormones." she said thoughtfully, frowning slightly to herself when she suddenly realised that she currently didn't feel the need to hide from the world.

"Sometimes I feel more vulnerable than others. You're lucky you don't have to deal with hormones like women do." she continued, a small smile playing on the corner of her lips.

As soon as they entered the store, Chloe let go of Lee's hand and strode over to the baby section.

"Slow down a bit." he laughed as he hurried after her, smiling at her evident excitement.

"This is so cute!" she exclaimed, holding up an animal print baby grow against her bump.

"To be fair, I think she will look cute in whatever she's wearing." he smiled, his gaze fixed on the baby grow.

"She's going to be so beautiful." he added, his eyes misting with tears when he glanced at Chloe. She nodded slowly, gently placing her hand on her bump.

"Especially if she inherits her grandmother's looks." she said thoughtfully, her eyes filling with tears as she thought of her mother.

"She probably will since you look like your Mum." he told her.

"I love our baby girl so much already." she whispered, her eyes fixed on her bump as she carefully stroked soft circles on it.

"I know, me too." he muttered, gazing down at Chloe as he stood at her side, their bodies mere inches from each other. Chloe glanced up at him, smiling as the two of them locked eyes and he placed a soft kiss on her forehead.

"I love you both so much." he whispered in her ear.

"I love you too." she mumbled, gazing up at him longingly. He glanced down at her hand as she placed it under his shirt and stroked soft circles on his chest, longing to be close to him. She rested her head against his chest, closing her eyes and sighing deeply to herself, her heart pounding against her chest, the deep love that she felt for him on a daily basis, still managing to take her breath away. Chloe trembled against him when he placed his hand on her bump, gently stroking soft circles with his fingertips.

"Stop it Chlo." he whispered hoarsely, smiling to himself when he felt Chloe slowly trail her hands down his chest, her fingers methodically trailing circles as she did so.

She glanced up at him, raising her eyebrow, a cheeky glint in her eyes, when she realised the effect that she was having on him. He quickly took her hand in his own and removed it from underneath his shirt, reluctantly tearing his eyes away from hers in an attempt to fight the deep desire that he was feeling for her. Chloe smiled cheekily as she snuggled her head against his collarbone and placed a series of soft kisses on his neck.

"What has gotten into you today?" he smiled, glancing down at his groin nervously and breathing a sigh of relief when he realised that he hadn't yet revealed the way that he was feeling about her.

"I think it's hormones." she giggled, glancing up at him as he quickly stepped back from her so that he was safely out of range of her touch.

"You've reached the randy stage." he smiled, bursting out laughing when her cheeks coloured deeply.

"Maybe a little." she mumbled, a small smile playing on the corner of her lips.

"Well I'm not going to complain." he grinned, carefully reaching out to take her hand and gently twirling her around. His heart swelled with pride as she burst out laughing, her face lighting up with happiness.

"Anyway, stop distracting me." he grinned, placing a quick kiss on her lips, before walking away to scan the shelves for baby clothes. Chloe smiled at him, rolling her eyes slightly as he grinned cheekily at her from across the aisle. She jumped as a shop assistant appeared behind her.

"Can I help you with anything?" Karen the shop assistant offered.

"We're just stocking up on a few things." Chloe smiled, slowly turning to face Karen, following her eyeline when her eyes flickered to Chloe's bump. Karen's eyes lit up, a dreamy expression on her face as she stared at Chloe's abdomen.

"Is this your first baby?" Karen asked. Chloe glanced at Lee across the store, her stomach churning when she thought about their first baby that they'd lost. She knew in her heart that no matter how much time passed, the pain would never fully subside. She nodded slowly, not quite able to bring herself to talk about the traumatic experience of losing a child.

"You're so lucky." Karen smiled, her eyes still gazing in wonder at Chloe's bump.

"I know." Chloe whispered, placing her hand at the base of her bump and cradling it. Chloe's eyes snapped up as Lee crossed the store, quickly walking towards her.

"Hey Chlo, look what I found!" he exclaimed excitedly, holding up a baby grow in front of her, his gaze flickering to Karen for a brief moment, before he turned his attention back to Chloe. She burst out laughing as she stared at the baby grow and read the words 'Made in Portsmouth'. Lee grinned at her, his eyes twinkling cheekily.

"That's not going to work though, since your baby was made in Norway." she giggled, her cheeks colouring when she glanced at Karen.

"I know, but it's funny." he agreed.

"We should get one made that says Norway on it." he continued, bursting out laughing when he saw the incredulous expression on Chloe's face.

"Erm....no." Chloe said quickly, a small smile playing on the corner of her lips.

"Spoil sport." he chuckled.

"On that note I think we have everything." she grinned, glancing into the basket that was on her arm.

"Yeah we can get the bulkier things when the new car arrives next week." he agreed. Chloe frowned as he reached over and carefully un hooked the basket from her arm and began to walk towards the till.

"Wait, you can't buy everything!" she exclaimed, quickly following him.

"I want to treat my little princess." he argued, his gaze flickering to her bump. Chloe sighed to herself as she watched him walking away, her stomach churning with guilt like it always did when he wouldn't allow her to buy things.

She remained silent as she slowly walked back to Lee's car, sighing deeply to herself as she climbed inside and gazed out of the window.

"Are you feeling bad about me buying the clothes Chlo?" Lee asked when he pulled out of the carpark, frowning to himself when he suddenly realised that Chloe hadn't said a word since they'd left the store.

"A little." she sighed.

"I don't like it when you buy things, it makes me feel like everyone thinks that I'm with you for your money." she continued, her stomach churning at the thought of everyone judging her.

"I know, but nobody is going to know are they." he pointed out.

"And besides, I've told you before that there's no point in me having money if I can't spend it on the people that I love. I want to be able to treat my girls." he added, glancing at her for a moment when she placed her hand on top of his, that was resting casually on the gear stick. He smiled at her, softly stroking her fingernails.

"I really should get a job." she said thoughtfully, staring down at his hand as she gently pulled it towards her and placed it on her lap.

"That's probably not such a good idea Chlo." he said quickly, his heart sinking at the thought of her having to work. He knew that she'd been struggling with fatigue as a result of the pregnancy and he couldn't help but feel afraid that something would happen to her or their baby if she pushed herself too hard.

"I guess employers won't want to employ someone that is pregnant." she said thoughtfully, her eyes wandering to her bump.

"I didn't mean that, I meant that you've been exhausted a lot and I don't want you overdoing it." he told her, squeezing her hand gently.

"It's good that if you don't feel up to doing anything you don't have too." he added.

"I guess so, and I don't want anything to happen to our baby girl." she said quietly, realising that she was being over cautious, but not quite able to stop the fear that was swirling around her head.

"I quite like getting to spend every day with you." he admitted, smiling slightly as he thought about how much he was cherishing the time that the two of them had together before the baby arrived. She smiled, quickly pulling his hand towards her face and placing a soft kiss on it. He glanced at her for a moment as she fidgeted, wincing slightly as she tried to find a comfortable position.

"Are you okay?" he asked quickly, his heart pounding against his chest nervously.

"It's just cramps." she said, smiling falsely as she tried to reassure him. She winced as she gently massaged her sore abdomen.

"And she likes to fidget." she added, gasping slightly as she felt her baby moving inside of her. She glanced down at her hand, frowning slightly when she suddenly realised that she'd felt her baby's movement against her hand as well as inside of her. Chloe glanced at Lee, a small smile playing on the corner of her lips at the thought that if they timed it right, Lee would finally be able to feel his baby moving.

"She takes after her Dad already." he laughed, snapping Chloe out of her thoughts. She nodded slowly, deciding not to mention the realisation that she'd just come to, in case she got his hopes up unnecessarily. He frowned at their hands when she placed his hand on her bump and held it in place, almost like she was waiting for something. She waited with baited breath, desperately hoping that the baby would move and Lee would be able to feel it. He glanced at her as she sighed deeply, her stomach plummeting with disappointment.

"I thought we were going back to the hotel." she frowned, glancing at Lee in confusion when she noticed that he'd pulled up at the beach.

"We are, but I thought we could make a little stop off first." he smiled at her. Chloe's eyes lit up in excitement as she quickly climbed out of the car, glancing at Lee as be appeared beside her. As soon as they reached the beach, she removed her trainers and socks and slowly waded into the water, glancing down at her feet and sighing in contentment as the water pooled around her ankles. Lee couldn't help but gaze in wonder at her as she swirled her feet around in the water, her eyes sparking with happiness. She slowly walked along the shoreline, carrying her trainers in her hand. His heart pounded against his chest as he was reminded once again of how naturally beautiful she was. As soon as he walked over to her he took her hand and walked beside her along the beach, glancing at her for a moment as she gazed up at him.

"I'm so in love with you." she whispered, pausing for a moment as she turned to face him.

"I love you too Chlo." he whispered, gently brushing his fingertips against her cheek.

"And our baby girl." he added, gently resting his other hand on her bump. Chloe nodded slowly, smiling to herself as she followed his eyeline, the two of them gazing down at her bump.

"We need to give her a name." he mumbled, his eyes brimming with tears at the thought of finally being able to hold their baby girl in a few short months.

"Maybe we should give her a Norwegian name." she giggled, smiling when she remembered the baby grow that Lee had wanted to get made.

"That's a really good idea." he laughed.

"I was joking." she said quickly, bursting out laughing when she noticed the cheeky glint in his eyes.

"I know, but it's cute." he said, smiling at her as they continued walking along the shore line.

"Something traditional like Sigrid?" he suggested, bursting out laughing when he glanced at Chloe and saw her screwing her nose up in disgust.

"What about Lillian?" he tried.

"After the whale?" she asked quietly, her stomach churning when she was reminded of how miserable she was when she'd lost their baby and felt like she was slowly losing Lee too. She'd never felt so alone. Chloe shook her head slowly, her gaze turning to Lee when he pulled his phone out of his pocket and typed a search into the internet. She jumped as Lee gasped quietly and stopped suddenly, his eyes fixed on his phone.

"What's wrong?" she asked him quickly, her heart pounding against her chest nervously.

"I have the perfect name." he said quietly, his voice breaking with emotion. She raised her eyebrow and waited for him to continue.

"Freyja." he stated, glancing up at Chloe for a moment and staring deeply into her eyes.

"The Norse goddess of love." he added thoughtfully.

"Freyja Emilia." she whispered thoughtfully, placing her forehead against his chest, her eyes fixed on her bump.

"I think it's cute." he mumbled, resting his chin on the top of Chloe's head.

"It's perfect." she whispered, her eyes filling with tears as she finally raised her head and gazed into Lee's eyes, her heart brimming with pride when she noticed the tears that were filling his eyes. He nodded slowly, before gently placing a soft kiss on her lips.

Chapter Forty Eight

Lee glanced up from his phone, his eyes wandering to Chloe as she fidgeted in her sleep. He couldn't help but smile at her as she slept soundly, a look of deep relaxation on her pretty features. He slowly pulled the blanket over her naked frame, determined to preserve her dignity at the same time as making sure that she wasn't cold. Lee turned on his side to face her, not quite able to tear his eyes away from the woman who had stolen his heart. Before he could stop himself, he placed a soft kiss on her lips, gently resting his forehead against hers as he watched her chest slowly rising and falling, his heart bursting with pride. He sighed in contentment as he softly stroked her hair, his fingertips trailing on her cheek.

"I didn't realise it was possible to love someone as much as I love you." he whispered thoughtfully. His eyes flickered to the watch on his wrist, his stomach churning nervously when he realised the time. He quickly stood up and wandered into the bathroom.

Chloe's eyelids flickered open, frowning to herself when she realised that the light was still on in the hotel room. She slowly sat up in bed, glancing down at herself when she suddenly realised that she was still naked. As she leant over the bed, she quickly picked up Lee's shirt, smiling slightly to herself when she remembered how he'd quickly discarded it on the floor in his desperation for her. She sighed in contentment when she pulled the shirt over her naked frame, a small smile playing on the corner of her lips as she inhaled his familiar scent. She quickly pulled a hairbrush through her hair and tucked her legs under her frame, glancing around the room when she suddenly realised that Lee was no longer beside her. Her eyes flickered upwards as Lee walked into the room, a towel wrapped around his waist. Chloe's heart pounded against her chest as she watched the small droplets of water dripping from his hair.

"Good morning." he said sarcastically, a small smile playing on the corner of his lips when the two of them locked eyes.

"I can't believe I fell asleep again." she grinned, rubbing the sleep out of her eyes.

"Literally as soon as you closed your eyes." he chuckled, glancing at her as she shuffled over to the edge of the bed, her eyes twinkling as she gazed at him. He couldn't help but smile at her when he realised how much her confidence was slowly improving. There was a time when she would never have fallen asleep naked, because she'd made sure to cover herself up, but now she clearly felt comfortable enough in her own skin to do so, at least when she was around him. He glanced down at her hand as she gripped the towel around his waist and quickly pulled him closer.

"What are you doing?" he laughed, gazing down at her as she stared up at him through her long eyelashes. She remained silent, her eyes fixed on his as she placed a series of soft kisses on his chest. He gasped quietly, the hairs on the back of his neck standing on end.

"Stop it Chlo, I've just showered." he mumbled reluctantly, desperately trying to resist her advances. She smiled cheekily when he rested his hand on her head, softly stroking her hair.

"I'm sure you can shower again." she mumbled against his chest, smiling in satisfaction when she felt him trembling under her touch. He closed his eyes, taking deep breaths as he tried to fight the deep desire for her.

"We have to go out though." he said hoarsely, fighting to keep his voice level.

"Do we?" she frowned, her head snapping up. He sighed in disappointment when she finally stopped kissing him, gazing up at him as she waited for him to respond.

"I made a dinner reservation for us." he explained, leaning forward and placing a soft kiss on her forehead.

"And we're probably going to be late for it." he added, his stomach churning nervously when he thought about his plans for the evening. Chloe nodded slowly her heart sinking in disappointment as she gazed at his bare chest, trying to ignore how desperately she wanted him.

"But I want you." she whispered, placing her hands on his hips and methodically trailing her fingers down his V-line. He took her hand in his own and gripped it tightly, suddenly feeling the need to grasp something when she kissed his stomach, glancing up at him for a moment, her eyes twinkling cheekily.

"Surely you can't want me again already?" he mumbled, trying to distract himself from what she was doing to him. He smiled to himself when she nodded slowly, biting the corner of her lip as she gazed up at him. Lee burst out laughing when he saw the incredulous expression on Chloe's face, shaking his head slowly.

"It's only been about an hour." he chuckled, bursting out laughing again when she shrugged.

"I don't know what's come over me." she admitted, joining in with his laughter.

"Me neither, you are definitely worse than me." he grinned, resting his forehead against hers and sighing in contentment as he inhaled her familiar scent. Her heart pounded against her chest when he placed a soft lingering kiss on her lips.

"We really have to get ready to go out Chlo." he muttered, softly stroking her cheekbone with his fingertips. She sighed deeply to herself, a small part of her wishing that they could spend the evening alone in the hotel room.

"Surely you're not going to try and resist me." she said, smiling smugly at him as she placed her hands behind herself on the bed and leaned backwards, staring up at him and raising her eyebrow.

"We have to get ready to go out." he repeated, trying not to stare at her but not quite able to tear his eyes away. She glanced down at herself, smiling slightly when an idea suddenly popped into her head. She carefully sat up, a small smile playing on the corner of her lips when she noticed that his eyes were fixed on her and that despite the fact that he kept telling her that they needed to get ready to go out, he was still standing in front of her.

"I guess I should get changed then." she said innocently, trying to resist the urge to burst out laughing when he bit his lip and nodded reluctantly. Lee smiled to himself when he noticed the cheeky glint in Chloe's eyes. His breath catching in his throat when she stared down at herself and slowly began to undo the buttons on her shirt, glancing up at him with every button that she unfastened. He swallowed the lump that was rising in his throat, his heart pounding so fast that it felt like it was going to burst out of his chest.

"Chlo." he mumbled, taking a step closer to her when she finally removed the shirt. He stood in front of her, his body mere inches from hers, gazing down at her as he took deep breaths. He gently placed his hands on her neck and softly stroked her jawline with his thumbs, sighing deeply to himself as he stared at the beautiful woman that he still couldn't quite believe was in love with him.

"What?" she mumbled, gazing up at him innocently.

"You just take my breath away sometimes." he breathed, slowly leaning down and placing a soft lingering kiss on her lips.

"Please don't try to resist me." she whispered, her heart pounding against her chest as she stared at the towel that was still wrapped around his waist, gently placing her hands on it, desperately trying to resist the urge to remove it. He watched her closely as she slowly raised her head, gazing up at him, a look of pleading in her eyes.

"I don't know why I even try anyway." he muttered, quickly removing the towel from his waist and climbing onto the bed, placing his knees on either side of her. Chloe laid back on the bed, her heart bursting against her chest when he carefully climbed on top of her, taking care not to crush her small frame.

"I love you so much." she whispered, her eyes twinkling happily as she wrapped her arms around his neck.

"I have a present for you." Lee told Chloe as he emerged from the bathroom and rummaged in his bag. She frowned at him as she dried herself off and quickly pulled on her underwear, smiling slightly when he glanced at her, his eyes lighting up when he noticed that she was wearing his favourite white lace set.

"Well technically my Mum picked it, but I pointed her in the right direction." he admitted, chuckling to himself, when he reluctantly tore his eyes away from staring at her perfect body.

"You didn't have to buy me anything." she muttered, her stomach swirling with guilt when he handed her a gift bag. He raised his eyebrow at her, watching her closely as he waited for her to open her present. She gasped as she opened the bag and pulled out a fitted black dress. She held it up against herself, her cheeks colouring slightly when she realised how fitted it was.

"Don't worry, it's a maternity dress." he said, quickly noticing her expression. She glanced down at her bump, sighing slightly as she thought about everyone staring at her.

"It might not fit me." she muttered, still staring at the dress in her hands. She jumped slightly as Lee appeared in front of her.

"I think you'll be fine. You are measuring small for twenty one weeks." he told her, gently tracing his fingers on her bump.

"I guess so." she said quietly, stepping back from Lee so that she could step into the dress. She blushed as she glanced up at Lee, quickly gathering her hair and turning her back on him, her skin tingling as he silently zipped up the dress, his fingers brushing against her spine as he did so. He rested his chin on her shoulder gazing at her reflection in the mirror, smiling slightly to himself when he saw how mesmerising she looked.

"I love you." he whispered, smiling to himself when Chloe shivered as she felt his warm breath on her neck.

"I love you too." she said softly, her eyes fixed on Lee in the mirror as she sat down and began to apply her makeup. She couldn't help but notice how handsome he looked in his skinny jeans, shirt and waistcoat. He reluctantly turned away from her and pulled on his leather jacket, placing his hand into his pocket to check that he had everything he needed for the evening. His stomach churned nervously, his eyes briefly flickering to Chloe as he thought about what he was planning to do.

"You look so beautiful Chlo." he told her, watching closely as she ran a hairbrush through her hair, the waves gently rippling down her shoulders. She slowly stood up, placing her feet into her pumps and gazing up at him shyly.

"Thank you for the dress." she mumbled, trying to supress the guilt she was feeling that he'd brought her something once again. She couldn't help but wish that she was in a financial position to be able to spoil him in the same way that he could her. She gazed up at him, her skin tingling under his touch when he stroked her bare forearm with his fingers.

"You look really handsome in a waistcoat." she told him, smiling to herself when she remembered all those years ago when she'd first started working with the Eclipse boys and Lee had been wearing a waistcoat during the video-shoot.

"I really want to take it off you." she mumbled, placing her hands against his chest, her fingers lingering against the buttons.

"Well you can't." he grinned, gently trailing his fingers up her forearm and along her collarbone, eventually coming to rest on her neck. He smiled in satisfaction when she shuddered under his touch.

"Stop teasing me then." she muttered, smiling slightly when she noticed the cheeky glint in his eyes.

"I'm not." he smiled, stroking small circles on her neck. He burst out laughing when she raised her eyebrow at him sceptically.

"Seriously though, we really have to go." he told her, glancing down at her as she sighed deeply and rested her forehead against his chest. He placed his hand on the back of her head, softly stroking her hair with his fingertips. Lee glanced at his watch, his stomach churning nervously. A small sigh of disappointment escaped his lips when she raised her head, gazing up at him silently. She jumped, gasping slightly as her phone began to ring. Her eyes scanned the room frantically, trying to remember where she had left the phone. Lee smiled when he realised that Chloe's ringtone was his version of 'Broken' that he'd recorded for her. Chloe gasped, quickly placing her hand on her bump when she felt Freyja moving around inside of her. Butterflies swarmed in her stomach when she realised that she was able to feel the movement under her hand. She glanced up at Lee as he picked up her phone from the counter and handed her mobile to her.

"It's Kirstie." he prompted, frowning at her when she glanced at the phone in his outstretched hand but didn't take it. His eyes flickered to the phone when it eventually rang out.

"Unzip me a second." Chloe said, quickly turning her back on him and gathering her hair to one side.

"No Chlo, we have to go out." he sighed, trying to resist the temptation to do as she asked.

"Please just do it!" she exclaimed, her hand still resting in place on her bump as she waited for Freyja to move once again. He frowned at her waspish tone, before quickly doing what she asked. He glanced down at her as she took his hand in hers and carefully placed it inside her dress. She sighed in contentment and turned her back on him, her gaze wandering to her bump when she felt him stroking soft circles with his fingertips.

"What am I waiting for?" he asked, resting his chin on Chloe's shoulder and glancing down at her when she gently placed her hand on top of his. She remained silent, waiting with baited breath for Freyja to move, desperately hoping that Lee would finally be able to feel their baby moving inside of her. She sighed deeply to herself, her heart sinking in disappointment after what felt like an eternity of waiting. Her skin tingled when Lee slowly traced small circles on her bump, carefully pressing his body against hers. Chloe's heart pounded in her chest as she rested her back against Lee's chest, sighing in contentment to herself when she felt his soft heartbeat against her back.

"Oh my god." he whispered, a small gasp escaping his lips when he finally felt Freyja moving under his touch. His eyes misted with tears as he suddenly felt overcome with emotion that he'd finally felt his baby moving. Since the first moment that Chloe had felt Freyja move inside of her, he'd been longing for the moment that he would be able to feel the movement too. Chloe glanced behind herself, shooting Lee a small smile when she noticed that his eyes had filled with tears.

"It's so amazing." he whispered, his voice breaking with emotion.

"I know, I still can't quite believe it." she agreed, turning her head to plant a soft kiss on his cheek. He nodded slowly, pressing his hand against her bump when Freyja moved once again. Chloe placed her hand on top of his, gently linking their fingers as the two of them tried to fight the powerful emotions that they were feeling.

Chapter Forty Nine

Chloe glanced up, her eyes wandering to the bar when she heard a woman laughing loudly. She rolled her eyes when she suddenly realised that the woman in question was flirting with Lee. Her stomach churned when she noticed the skin tight, short dress that the woman was wearing. Chloe rolled her eyes when the woman laughed once again, flicking her hair as she placed her hand on Lee's arm. She sighed to herself, her insecurities swirling around her head as she stared transfixed on the beautiful woman. Despite the fact that Chloe knew in her heart, how much Lee adored her, she couldn't help but worry that she would one day lose him to someone more beautiful than her. She carefully placed her hand on her bump, gazing down at her baby affectionately, trying to distract herself from what was happening. Chloe slowly kicked off her shoes and tucked her legs onto the sofa, fidgeting slowly as she tried to find a comfortable position She winced, softly massaging her abdomen in an ill-conceived attempt to relieve the cramps in her abdomen.

"Is everything okay?" Lee asked nervously, as soon as he returned to the table and sat beside her. Chloe nodded slowly, her gaze remaining fixed on her lap. She glanced over to the bar as she felt someone watching her closely, her heart plummeting when she realised the woman that had been flirting with Lee was still watching her closely. She sighed and quickly tore her eyes away, glancing down at Lee's hand as he rested it on her lap, softly stroking small circles on her bare legs.

"What's going on Chlo?" he asked, not quite able to shake the feeling that something was bothering her.

"Nothing." she mumbled, glancing up at him for a moment, before sighing deeply and quickly averting her eyes. Her gaze flickered to the woman at the bar, who was still staring, her gaze transfixed on Lee as she took a swig of her drink. Lee frowned to himself when he noticed Chloe's eyes darken. He followed her gaze, his stomach plummeting when he instantly realised what she was looking at.

"Just ignore her." he sighed, his heart breaking a little when he saw the look of deep sadness on her face. She nodded slowly, smiling slightly when he placed a soft kiss on her cheek, sighing in contentment when he rested his face against hers, inhaling her familiar scent.

"People always flirt with you anyway." she whispered sadly as she rested her head on his shoulder and snuggled against his collarbone, her cheeks colouring when she glanced up at him and saw that he was gazing at her longingly. He watched her closely as she winced in pain and gently massaged her bump, trying to do something to ease the pain that she was feeling.

"Is Freyja moving again?" he asked, gently placing his hand on top of hers.

"No, it's just cramps." she mumbled. Lee nodded slowly, sighing quietly when he saw Chloe's eyes flicker to the bar once again. She relaxed against him, wrapping her arms around his waist and snuggling into his arms. He wrapped his arm around her waist, his other hand still stroking her bare legs as he desperately tried to find a way to reassure her that he only had eyes for her.

"Do you miss being single and hooking up with a different woman most nights?" she mumbled against his neck, glancing up at him when he sighed deeply at her words.

"No not at all." he said quickly, gazing down at her, still not quite able to comprehend the fact that she constantly doubted herself and his feelings for her.

"Even though they were beautiful models." she muttered, glancing over at the woman at the bar once again, her heart sinking when Chloe noticed that she was still watching them closely.

"So are you though." he whispered, gently placing a soft kiss on her forehead.

"You don't understand because you've never had a hook up, but it's totally different when you love someone." he added, shooting her a small smile when she lifted her head to stare at him.

"I just feel like you have so many beautiful women to compare me too." she muttered, her heart pounding against her chest as she stared into his deep Eclipse eyes.

"There's no comparison though Chlo, I promise you." he whispered, trying to reassure her.

"Whenever I see your beautiful body, I can't believe my luck. I love you so much that all the hook ups mean nothing to me. And you know it means the world to me that you chose me to give yourself too." he continued. She smiled at him, her heart pounding against her chest at his words. He smiled back at her, before placing a soft lingering kiss on her lips.

"You do know how much I love you don't you?" he asked nervously.

"Of course I do." she smiled at him, slowly raising her head.

"And I get insecure sometimes because I know how amazing you are and everyone always wants to take you from me." she continued.

"It happens with you too though." he pointed out, smiling slightly to himself when he remembered how almost every man that laid eyes on Chloe was mesmerised by her. He couldn't help but feel a surge of pride that he was the one that she loved with all her heart.

"I guess so." she mumbled, her eyes wandering to her bump. Even though she appreciated that he was trying to make her feel better, she knew in her heart that nobody wanted her now that she was pregnant. Lee on the other hand, still had numerous adoring fans that would do anything to take him from her.

"I also feel bad that....." she started, trailing off when she felt her cheeks colouring deeply.

"What?" he prompted her, frowning when he noticed how embarrassed she was.

"That you don't get to do all of your fun stuff that you liked doing before we got together." she muttered, her cheeks colouring even further. He frowned at her, not entirely sure what she was talking about or why she constantly underestimated the way that he felt about her. He sighed deeply when the realisation finally dawned on him.

"Are you speaking about the threesomes?" he asked, glancing down at her hands as she rested them on her lap. She nodded slowly, not quite able to bring herself to look him in the eye.

"I would understand if you wanted to do them again." she mumbled.

"Are you suggesting that I should cheat on you?" he asked quickly, frowning in confusion.

"No of course not!" she exclaimed, glancing around the room nervously when she suddenly realised that she raised her voice.

"I just meant that if you really wanted one, we could." she mumbled nervously, her cheeks colouring once again. He gazed at her for a moment, not quite able to process her words.

"Is this your way of saying that you want to try having one?" he grinned, teasing her when he eventually recovered himself.

"Am I not enough for you Chlo?" he laughed, smiling at her when he noticed her squirming in her seat. Chloe smiled at the cheeky glint in his eyes, before wrapping her arms around his neck, softly stroking the hair on the back of his neck.

"Of course you are." she smiled, quickly placing a soft kiss on his lips. The two of them sprung apart when the waitress arrived at the table and handed them their food, smiling warmly as she glanced between the two of them.

"You secretly want to try a threesome don't you?" he beamed, grinning at her cheekily as soon as the waitress was safely out of earshot.

"No, I really don't!" she exclaimed, bursting out laughing when he raised his eyebrow sceptically.

"But I am prepared to do it if you really want too." she added quickly, her cheeks colouring deeply as her eyes wandered to her lap, her stomach swirling nervously at the thought of undressing in front of someone that wasn't Lee. Her brain swirled with a mist of thoughts, a lump rising in her throat as she thought about someone else touching her. She knew that she wouldn't be able to bear someone else's touch, particularly when it meant the world to her that she'd only ever been with Lee.

"I couldn't think of anything worse." he said quickly, snapping her out of her thoughts. Chloe frowned to herself as she finally locked eyes with him, raising her eyebrow and waiting for him to continue.

"I wouldn't be able to watch somebody else touching you, or kissing you.....or worse making love to you." he explained, swallowing the vomit that was rising in his throat at the very thought of it.

"The things we do together are a special bond between us.....and I don't want to share you." he added, smiling to himself when he noticed her glazed expression.

"What?" he asked, a small smile playing on the corner of his lips as she continued to stare at him.

"I just love you so much." she whispered, her eyes misting with tears as she stared transfixed on him, thanking her lucky stars once again. She knew how lucky she was to have someone like Lee in her life. How much he cared about her and cherished her and she knew that he would do anything for her.

"I love you too." he whispered back, gently wrapping his arms around her waist and carefully pulling her onto his lap. Chloe sighed in contentment, her heart pounding against her chest as she wrapped her arms around his neck and clung to him tightly.

"So no more talk of getting other people involved okay." he mumbled in her ear, his stomach still churning at the thought of her suggestion. She remained silent, nodding slowly, trying to hide how relieved she was that he had rejected her suggestion.

"You're more than enough for me Chlo......you always have been." he whispered softly.

Chapter Fifty

Lee glanced at Chloe as they walked along the seafront, smiling to himself when he noticed how beautiful she looked in the faint moonlight that was shining across the ocean. She smiled, glancing down at her hand as he took it and squeezed it gently.

"Where are we going?" she frowned, glancing at Lee when they reached the car and continued walking, his hand still gently gripping hers.

"We're taking a little detour." he said quietly, a small smile playing on the corner of his lips. She nodded slowly, racking her brain as to where they could be going. She couldn't help but notice how mysterious and secretive he had been lately. Chloe stopped, her feet frozen to the spot as she gazed up at Spinnaker Tower. She stared at the tower, completely mesmerized by how breath-taking it was, fully lit up under the night sky.

"Wow!" she breathed, her breath catching in her throat as she gazed in wonder.

"Welcome to Spinnaker Tower." he said quietly, smiling at her when he noticed her eyes lighting up.

"Do we get to go inside it?" she asked hopefully, her stomach churning with excitement. Lee nodded slowly, his heart pounding against his chest as he led her towards the tower. His heart sunk when they entered the tower and he realised that the elevator was out of order.

"Maybe we should come back another day?" he suggested, his eyes flickering to Chloe's bump.

"Why?" she frowned.

"Because there are a lot of stairs." he pointed out, gazing up at the stairs.

"And you probably won't manage all of them." he added, slowly becoming concerned that as a result of her pregnancy the stairs would be too much for her.

"Do you want to bet?" she asked, glaring at him defiantly. He smiled slightly, his heart swelling with pride when he saw the determination on her pretty features.

"Chlo?!" he called after her, watching helplessly as she let go of his hand and began to slowly climb the stairs. He fell into step beside her, remaining close so that he could keep an eye on her. Chloe sighed to herself when she felt Lee intermittently glancing at her. Despite the fact she loved how much he cared about her and wanted to protect her, she couldn't help but feel slightly frustrated when he tried to smother her. Chloe took deep breaths, continuing to climb the steps, trying to hide from Lee how exhausted she was suddenly feeling. He watched her closely as she reached out and grasped the handrail when she suddenly felt lightheaded. She halted, glancing around nervously as she tried to get her breath back and stop her head from swirling. Lee watched closely as she carefully sat down on one of the steps, her hand sliding down the handrail.

"This is ridiculous Chlo, you shouldn't be overdoing it." he sighed, trying not to become frustrated with her that in her stubbornness she wasn't listening to him.

"I'll be okay." she replied quietly, glancing up at him for a moment, quickly looking away when she noticed him watching her closely. Lee nodded slowly, his gaze fixed on her as she placed her hand on her bump and massaged it softly, trying to supress the cramps that she was feeling. Her gaze flickered to Lee for a brief moment as he sat beside her, watching her closely.

"I think we should go back to the car." he suggested, his stomach churning nervously at the thought of anything happening to Chloe or Freyja.

"I'll be fine, we can just take it slow and steady." she told him, her eyes fixed on her bump.

"Speaking of the baby, we need to figure out the birthing plan when we get home." she added, trying to keep him talking so that he wouldn't continue arguing with her.

"I think all of that should be your decision, since you're the one that will be giving birth." he pointed out, swallowing the lump that was rising in his throat at the thought of Chloe being in pain. Even though he knew that it was a necessary part of childbirth, he still couldn't quite stomach the idea.

"Do you mind if I have the baby in your house, rather than going to hospital?" she asked tentatively, not entirely sure how he would feel about it. She knew how much he worried about something happening to her and the baby and she couldn't help but feel like he would prefer her to be in a hospital, in case something went wrong. Lee fell silent, thinking for a moment. He sighed deeply when he saw the hopeful expression on her face.

"If you would feel better about it, I could go to the hospital instead." she said quietly, shooting him a small smile when she saw the worried expression on his handsome features.

"I just couldn't bear it if anything happened to either of you." he mumbled, taking deep breaths to try and suppress the intense fear that he was feeling. It had nearly destroyed him losing their first baby and Chloe a few weeks later and he knew that he wasn't strong enough to lose her again. Chloe smiled sympathetically and shuffled closer to him, gently resting the side of her head against his shoulder. He gazed down at her for a moment before placing a soft kiss on her head.

"We'll be okay." she whispered, trying to reassure him.

"I hope so, I can't lose either of you." he whispered back, his eyes filling with tears as he rested his head against hers.

"How about as a compromise we have a private midwife that we can call to come to the house when you go into labour?" he suggested, relaxing a little at the thought that they wouldn't be alone.

"That way if something doesn't go to plan, we have someone that can help." he continued. Chloe glanced up and nodded slowly, her heart surging with pride when she was reminded how much her and the baby meant to him. She knew in her heart that he would do anything for the two of them. He watched her closely as she tentatively stood up, grasping the handrail for support, fearful that she would fall over and harm their baby. She glanced at Lee for a moment, smiling at him when he placed his hand under her elbow to provide her with some support.

"Are you sure you're okay to do this Chlo?" he asked, an edge of worry present in his voice. Chloe nodded slowly and carefully began to climb the stairs, glancing down at her bump when she felt Freyja moving inside of her.

"Do you want to be with me at the birth?" she asked him, trying to distract herself from the exhaustion that she was feeling.

"Yes of course I do." he replied quickly, frowning in confusion at her words.

"I just wasn't sure if you would want to be there or not, I know that you hate seeing me in pain." she pointed out, her stomach churning with guilt when she noticed the flicker of hurt on his face.

"I do want you there, but I don't want you to be uncomfortable with it." she continued.

"I don't like the idea of you being in a lot of pain, but I still want to be there for you." he reassured her, gently taking her hand and holding it tightly, swallowing the lump that was rising in his throat at the thought of the woman he loved being in excruciating pain. Despite the fact that he longed for the day that the two of them could finally hold their baby, he couldn't help but feel partly responsible for the task that Chloe now faced. Chloe smiled at him and wrapped her arm through his, leaning against him slightly as she continued climbing the stairs. He gasped and quickly steadied her when she wobbled slightly on a step.

"You do want me there don't you Chlo?" he asked tentatively.

"Yes of course I do." she smiled, glancing up at him for a moment when she felt him watching her closely.

"The pain won't be so bad if I have you by my side." she added, smiling to herself when he stopped dead in his tracks and turned to face her, quickly planting a tender kiss on her lips.

"You know that I'll always be by your side." he whispered in her ear.

"I know." she mumbled, gently wrapping her arm around his neck and softly stroking his hair.

"The two of you are my whole world." he continued, gazing down at her bump as he stroked soft circles with his fingertips.

"You're my whole world too." she mumbled, gently resting her forehead against his shoulder.

"I love you so much Chlo." he whispered, his voice breaking a little as he thought about his plans. Chloe smiled slightly, a small shiver travelling down her spine when he softly stroked her hair.

"I need to conquer these steps." she giggled, quickly lifting her head and moving away from him, before she was no longer able to fight her desire for him. Lee nodded slowly, sighing in disappointment. He placed his hands on her waist, keeping her steady as she continued climbing the steps. His eyes remained fixed on her, making sure that she didn't stumble or lose her balance.

Chloe breathed a deep sigh of relief when she took the last step as the two of them finally reached the top floor of the tower. She glanced at Lee as he stood beside her, collapsing against him slightly in relief.

"Maybe you should sit down for a minute Chlo." he said worriedly, glancing down at her as she leant against him.

"I'll be okay." she reassured him, smiling to herself when she felt him place a soft kiss on her forehead. She took his hand and led him over to the window, gasping as she gazed down at the landscape. She stared in wonder at the illuminated harbour, smiling to herself as she gazed at the ocean, perfectly highlighted by the moonlight.

"It's so amazing up here." she muttered, her voice breaking a little as she stared at the mesmerising landscape, suddenly feeling small and insignificant in the landscape.

"Kirstie told me that the tower is beautiful at night." he agreed, glancing at Chloe and smiling to himself when he noticed the look of wonder on her pretty features. He took a deep breath, trying to steady his nerves as he reluctantly tore his eyes away from Chloe and rummaged in his pocket, concentrating on his hands as he fought to stop them from shaking.

"I got you a present." he said softly, glancing down at the small parcel in his hand as he handed it to her. Chloe smiled up at him, carefully taking the parcel from his grasp.

"Well technically it's for Freyja." he added, chuckling nervously to himself. Chloe's heart swelled with pride as she unwrapped the parcel and laid eyes on a pink baby grow with the words 'Baby Knight' written across it. She burst out laughing when she glanced up at him and noticed the cheeky twinkle in his eyes. Her heart pounded against her chest when she was reminded once again how fortunate she was to be carrying his child. She knew that a lot of women would love to be in her position and she never for a single moment took that for granted.

"Ermm, excuse me, what if I want to give her my surname." she teased him, a small smile playing on the corner of her lips as she tried to keep a straight face. Lee opened his mouth to respond, quickly closing it again when he noticed the cheeky glint in her eyes.

"You can if you really want too." he smiled.

"But....." he continued, pausing for dramatic effect as he rummaged in his pocket. Chloe glanced down at his hands, her heart pounding against her chest when he placed his hand on her hip and slowly turned her away from him. She sighed in contentment as he rested his chest against her back and placed his chin on her shoulder, gently wrapping his arms around her waist. Chloe gazed out of the window, mesmerized by both the landscape and the feeling of Lee's soft heartbeat against her back. He sighed deeply as he planted a series of soft kisses on her neck, cherishing the feel of holding her in his arms. She glanced down at her bump when she felt Lee loosen his grip slightly and gently rest something in place against it, frowning to herself when she realised that it was another baby grow.

"The first one is to go with this one." he whispered in her ear, smiling slightly when she shivered involuntarily. She frowned to herself as she tried to read the words in the reflection of the window.

"What does it say?" she frowned, trying to read it upside down. A small gasp escaped her lips as she read the words: 'Mummy, will you marry Daddy?'

Chapter Fifty One

"What?" Chloe whispered thoughtfully, almost as if she was talking to herself.

"Marry me." he mumbled, wrapping his arms around her waist and holding her tightly, rocking her slightly.

"Really?" she whispered, slowly turning around to face him. Lee nodded slowly, swallowing the lump that was rising in his throat as she wrapped her arms around his neck.

"You really want me to be your wife?" she checked, still not quite able to comprehend what was happening.

"Of course I do." he mumbled, his voice breaking slightly as he stared at the woman that he wanted to spend the rest of his life with. Chloe bit her lip, trying to fight the tears that were filling her eyes, her emotions a mixture of excitement, happiness and shock. She kissed Lee's lips tenderly, still not quite able to comprehend that someone as special as him had fallen for someone like her. She knew that as long as she lived, she would never fully deserve him.

"You need to give me an answer Chlo." he chuckled, staring down at her when they eventually pulled apart.

"Of course, I'll marry you." she whispered, her voice breaking slightly, as she fought to get the words out. Lee breathed a deep sigh of relief, his heart pounding against his chest, his eyes filling with tears of happiness. Chloe smiled when he wrapped his arms around her waist and pulled her against him, holding her tightly. He buried his head in her shoulder, breathing deeply as he inhaled her familiar scent.

"You make me so happy." Chloe sobbed against his chest, not quite able to express how madly in love with him she was. She knew in her heart that as long as she lived he was the only man that she would ever want. He smiled at her words, eventually releasing her from his grasp and gazing down at her lovingly. Her heart melted as she locked eyes with him, her legs feeling weak at the way he was staring at her. Eventually he tore his eyes away and rummaged in his pocket, smiling to himself when he pulled out a ring box. Chloe gasped as he presented her with a silver ring, with a deep blue sapphire in the middle, flanked by two diamonds.

"It matches your necklace." he smiled as he carefully removed the ring from the box and gently took her hand in his grasp, his eyes filling with tears as he gently slid the ring onto her finger. Chloe nodded slowly, gently wiping away her tears, her eyes fixed on the ring on her finger.

"I can't wait to be your wife." she whispered, trying to fight the tears that were filling her eyes.

"You're officially stuck with me now." he grinned. Chloe giggled, quickly wrapping her arms around his neck and holding him against her.

"The ring is so beautiful." she breathed, holding up her hand and gazing at it.

"You're so beautiful." he muttered.

"Smooth." she giggled.

"You'll have to get used to it." he laughed, wrapping his arms around her and holding her tightly against his frame.

"Mrs Knight." he whispered in her ear, his heart swelling with pride at the thought that he would one day be able to call her his wife.

"Excuse me, I might want to keep my maiden name." she teased. Lee slowly removed her from his arms, staring down at her, trying to decide if she was teasing him or not.

"You don't want to be Mrs Knight?" he asked, his stomach sinking slightly at the thought of her not wanting to share his surname. Chloe shrugged, not entirely sure how she felt about it. Due to the fact that she was still flying high from Lee's proposal, she couldn't process anything, let alone make a decision about her surname.

"Where is everyone anyway?" she asked, changing the subject, frowning when she glanced around the tower and suddenly noticed that they were completely alone.

"I hired the whole tower, because I know how self-conscious you are." he told her, smiling proudly to himself. Chloe smiled at him, glancing down at her hand when she felt him take it in his own and quickly plant a soft kiss on her ring, as he gazed up at her, a cheeky twinkle in his eyes.

"You're so amazing." she whispered, gently stroking his cheek with her fingertips. Her skin tingled under his touch when he placed his hands on her hips and softly stroked small circles on her spine. She stared up at him, still not quite able to believe that she could now call him her fiancée. Chloe shivered involuntarily as his hands slowly trailed up the side of her dress, eventually coming to a stop on her waist. She sighed deeply, quickly resting her forehead against his chest.

"I think we need to get back to the hotel room." she muttered, goosebumps rising on her arms when she felt him stroking her hair. She slowly lifted her head to stare at him when he didn't respond. Lee gazed at her for a moment, bursting out laughing when he noticed the pleading in her eyes.

"C'mon then." he chuckled, quickly taking her hand and leading her back down the stairs.

Chloe grinned at Lee as she quickly took his hand and led him into the hotel room, pushing the door closed behind them with her foot.

"Steady on." he laughed, smiling down at her when she pushed him against the wall and quickly unfastened the buttons on his waistcoat. She gazed up at him through her eyelashes, before placing a soft kiss on his lips. He closed his eyes, resting the back of his head against the wall as Chloe placed a kiss on the corner of his lips, methodically kissing along his jawline and down onto his neck. He placed his hands on her waist, a small shiver travelling down his spine when he felt Chloe place her hands underneath his shirt. Lee opened his eyes, frowning down at Chloe when she eventually moved away from him. He watched her closely as she gathered her hair to one side and slowly turned her back on him, taking deep breaths as she locked eyes with him in the mirror.

"Unzip me then." she whispered. Lee placed his hands on her zip, sighing deeply to himself when he realised that he needed to resist her advances.

"I can't Chlo." he mumbled reluctantly. She frowned for a moment, raising her eyebrow at him as she waited for him to continue.

"We have to go." he told her, sighing in disappointment as he stared at her longingly.

"Why?" she muttered, slowly turning to face him.

"I have a surprise planned." he said quietly, slowly reaching out to stroke her cheek with his fingertips, sighing quietly as she gently rested her forehead against his .

"What surprise?" she asked quickly, slowly turning to face him.

"If I tell you then it won't be a surprise will it." he chuckled, sighing to himself as he stared down at the beautiful woman in front of him, who was still gazing up at him longingly. Her gaze remained fixed on his when he placed his fingers on her cheek, stroking soft circles with his fingertips. Chloe sighed in pleasure and closed her eyes, placing a soft kiss on his palm.

"Can't we just stay here for a little bit?" she asked, a note of desperation present in her voice.

"Don't tempt me." he mumbled, desperately trying to resist her advances.

"You keep doing this to me." she giggled, smiling to herself when she remembered how he'd tried to resist her earlier when they needed to get to the restaurant.

"Besides you gave into me last time." she pointed out, a cheeky twinkle in her eyes as she gazed up at him, biting her lip as she placed her hands underneath his shirt and slowly trailed them downwards.

"We need to get packed Chlo, we can't be late." he muttered, shivering under her touch. She frowned at his words, not entirely sure what he was talking about. Her stomach churned nervously when she suddenly realised that he might have planned some form of party to celebrate their engagement.

"You haven't planned something big have you?" she asked tentatively. He shook his head slowly, a small smile playing on the corner of his lips.

"What's going on then?" she asked, unable to stand the idea of not knowing any longer. He shook his head slowly and mimed zipping his lips closed, determined not to tell her anything that might give something away.

"Well you still need to unzip me." she said stubbornly, a small smirk playing on the corner of her lips as she turned her back on him, her eyes fixed on him in the mirror.

"No I don't." he said, reluctantly tearing his eyes away from the zip in a desperate attempt to resist her request. He smiled when he locked eyes with her in the mirror and noticed her raising her eyebrow at him.

"I want to wear something more comfortable." she pointed out, maintaining eye contact with him in her determination to convince him to do as she asked. He nodded slowly, his resolve wavering when he noticed the hopeful expression on her pretty features. Lee's hands shook in anticipation as he slowly unzipped her dress, his fingers trailing down her spine as he did so. He closed his eyes, taking deep breaths as his fingers remained in place on the base of her spine. Chloe shuddered when she felt his warm breath on her neck, his fingers still stroking her skin. Lee eventually opened his eyes, his gaze fixed on Chloe as she carefully stepped out of the dress and slowly turned to face him, a small smile playing on the corner of her lips when she noticed the look of deep longing that was etched on his handsome features. He sighed deeply, unable to tear his eyes away from her as she stood before him in her underwear.

"You're so beautiful Chlo." he muttered, his heart pounding against his chest as he stared, completely mesmerized by her beauty. Her cheeks coloured as she quickly looked away from him, staring at the ground for a moment before glancing back up at him when she heard him sigh deeply. She smiled at him when the two of them locked eyes, gazing at him innocently. He sighed deeply, running his hand through his hair in frustration when she eventually tore her eyes away from his, turning her back on him and slowly bending over to pick up her dress.

"I know what you are trying to do." he chuckled, watching her closely as she slowly straightened up, her eyes fixed on his in the mirror. He placed his hand on her back, softly trailing his fingertips down her spine, smiling to himself when she shuddered under his touch. Chloe sighed in disappointment when he eventually stopped touching her.

"Are you alright Chlo?" he asked, frowning to himself when he noticed that her eyes had misted with tears. She nodded slowly, biting her lip to try and fight the overwhelming emotions that she was feeling. Despite the fact that she knew she was overreacting and she could see how much Lee was struggling to resist her, she couldn't help but feel a pang of hurt that he was rejecting her.

"Don't worry Chlo, I do want you." he muttered quickly, instantly realising how she was feeling. Chloe nodded slowly, not entirely sure how to respond.

"Badly...." he continued, his stomach churning with guilt when he realised that he'd accidentally upset her. Before he could say anything else, Chloe quickly pulled on her skinny jeans and a top, glancing at him for a moment as she pulled on his new hoodie, her eyes flickering to the ring on her finger as it sparkled in the light. He sighed deeply and quickly walked over to her, carefully pulling her into his arms and holding her tightly.

"I just don't want us to be late for your surprise." he whispered in her ear.

"I know." she sighed sadly.

"I love you." she added, gently wrapping her arms around his neck and relaxing into his arms.

Chapter Fifty Two

Chloe glanced at Lee as the two of them sat in his car as it sped down the motorway. She stared down at their hands when she felt him reach across and take her hand in his, squeezing it gently.

"You're very quiet Chlo." he prompted, glancing at her for a brief moment, before turning his attention back to the road.

"I'm just tired." she muttered.

"And I still can't believe it." she continued, staring down at the ring on her finger, her heart swelling with pride that she was able to call herself Lee's fiancé.

"I'm so happy you said yes." he smiled, glancing at her when she giggled quietly.

"As if I would ever say no." she beamed. Lee smiled to himself when he noticed Chloe gazing in wonder at the ring on her finger, her eyes fixed on it as she slowly twirled it around her finger.

"Do you like the ring?" he asked tentatively.

"I love it, it's so beautiful." she mumbled, her voice breaking a little that he'd brought her something that she knew would have been very expensive.

"It must have cost a lot of money." she continued, her stomach swirling with guilt. Lee nodded slowly.

"I wanted to get you something really precious, to show you how much you mean to me." he told her.

"I already know how much I mean to you." she smiled at him, her eyes darting to her abdomen when she suddenly felt Freyja moving inside of her once again.

"How much we both mean to you." she added, slowly pulling Lee's hand towards her and carefully resting it in place on her bump. He gasped in shock as he felt their baby move under his touch, his eyes brimming with tears.

"It's so incredible." he whispered.

"She's definitely an active baby." she giggled, her eyes flickering to Lee's hand when she felt him tracing soft circles on her bump. Chloe nodded slowly, softly closing her eyes and sighing in contentment, Lee's touch finally relaxing her.

"We're almost there, you need to close your eyes!" he exclaimed suddenly, causing Chloe to jump.

"What?" she frowned in confusion.

"I don't want you to realise where we are going until we get there, so you need to close your eyes." he explained. Chloe nodded slowly and quickly did as he asked, her stomach swirling with nerves for what he could possibly have planned.

"Are they closed?" he asked.

"Yes." she replied.

"Are you sure?" he chuckled.

"I know how much you hate surprises." he continued.

"I promise my eyes are closed." she giggled, squeezing his hand playfully.

"Okay good." he said quietly, before quickly taking the exit off the motorway and driving through the town, glancing at Chloe when he finally pulled into the carpark. He hurried around to the passenger side of the car and opened the door, placing his hands under Chloe's elbows and helping her to stand. He stood behind her, carefully helping her to walk, since she still had her eyes closed. Her skin tingled under his touch when he rested his hands on her hips and carefully guided her in front of him, taking care to keep her safe from harm. She frowned to herself when Lee gently stopped her, his hands finally leaving her hips.

"Okay, you can open them now." he told her. Chloe frowned to herself when she realised that his voice sounded further away than before. She slowly opened her eyes, squinting in the bright light, gazing around the room as she tried to take in her surroundings. Her heart pounded against her chest, her eyes flickering to the bar when she suddenly realised that she was in a pub.

"Do you remember the last time that we were here?" she heard Lee's voice from behind her. Chloe slowly turned to face Lee, smiling at him when she realised that he was standing on a small stage above her, staring down at her happily.

"Oh my god, this is the pub where we first met." she whispered, her eyes misting with tears. Lee nodded slowly, staring down at Chloe, his hands trembling with emotion as he watched her eyes filling with tears.

"I was standing right here." he mumbled, pointing down at the stage beneath his feet.

"And you walked through that door......and I couldn't take my eyes off you." he continued, pointing to the door behind her. Chloe nodded slowly, biting her lip to try and fight the tears that were threatening to spill out of her eyes. Her mind wandered to that fateful day all those years ago when she'd taken her Mum to the pub in an attempt to cheer her up. She knew in her heart that if it hadn't of been for that day, she would never have met Lee, and he would never have become the love of her life. Chloe glanced down at her bump, blinking slowly as the tears that she'd been fighting to hold back finally spilled from her eyes. She sighed deeply and closed her eyes, the images of her mother swirling around her head. How the two of them had sat at a table, Chloe's mother Emilia happily singing along to the music. A small smile played on the corner of Chloe's lips when she remembered how Emilia had tried to encourage Chloe to speak to Lee. She sighed deeply as her eyes wandered to the bar, and remembered how whenever she glanced up, she had locked eyes with Lee as he stared at her, completely mesmerised by this woman, despite the fact that he'd not even uttered a word to her.

"Go on Chloe, just go and talk to him!" Emilia insisted, placing her hand on Chloe's elbow and pushing her towards the bar.

"There's no point Mum, I start at university soon." Chloe argued, rolling her eyes at the excitement on her Mother's face.

"Seize the moment Chloe and go and talk to him." Emilia insisted, staring at Chloe sternly.

"Besides I want a drink anyway, you can go and get it for me." she continued, a small smile playing on the corner of her lips. Chloe sighed deeply, smiling slightly when she noticed the cheeky twinkle in her Mum's eyes.

"I know what you are trying to do Mum and it won't work." Chloe giggled, bursting out laughing when her Mum gently shoved her towards the bar.

"Besides a guy like him can have anyone he wants so he won't be interested in someone like me anyway." she continued, still slightly confused as to why her Mum was so determined to get her to talk to Lee.

"Just go." Emilia chuckled, placing her hand on Chloe's back and gently shoving Chloe towards the bar.

Chloe sighed deeply to herself as she slowly walked towards the bar, her eyes deliberately avoiding Lee. She knew that her Mum was trying to boost her confidence, and was always telling her how beautiful she was, but she was under no illusions. Someone like Lee would never be interested in her in the real world, that wasn't how life worked, and even if he was, she had too much going on to be ready for a relationship at this moment in time.

"Can I have a glass of water and some white wine please?" Chloe asked the barman. He nodded slowly and began to prepare her drinks. She glanced at Lee, her cheeks colouring when she locked eyes with him as he sat on the stool beside her. Her eyes flickered upwards when Nathan walked over and began to speak to Lee. She turned her attention away from them and smiled at the barman as he handed her the drinks.

"Thank you." she said quietly, quickly taking a large swig of wine. She gently massaged her sore temples, sighing quietly to herself as her head began to pound, the intense noise of the pub finally starting to affect her. Chloe placed her finger on the rim of her wine glass and slowly traced circles on it, her eyes filling with tears as she thought about her mother's diagnosis. No matter how many weeks had passed, she still couldn't quite process that her mother wasn't going to recover, and that she would eventually have to say goodbye to one of the most important people in her life. She bit her lip, trying to control the tears that were filling her eyes, jumping as she felt someone push against her back. She staggered slightly, quickly grasping the bar to steady herself.

"Oh my god, I'm really sorry." she heard a voice say from behind her.

"It's fine." she said quietly, slowly turning around and glancing at Lee.

"It was an accident, I wasn't paying attention to my surroundings." he insisted.

"It's fine honestly, don't worry about it." she told him, quickly looking away from his intense gaze. She could feel him watching her closely as she downed the rest of her glass of wine and gestured to the barman for a refill.

"Is the show really that bad?" he chuckled, smiling at her as she took another deep gulp of wine.

"No, the performance was great." she told him, glancing at Nathan when he shot her a small smile.

"So, are you here with your boyfriend?" Lee asked, glancing around the bar for a moment.

"Nope, I came with my Mum." she answered.

"I got her the tickets as a treat." she added, choosing not to mention that her and her father had hoped that the event would help to cheer her mother up and give her something to aim for.

"She's a big fan then?" he asked, trying to get her to open up to him. Chloe nodded slowly, before quickly taking another sip of her drink. Lee paused for a moment, watching her body language closely. He couldn't quite bring himself to tear his eyes away from the most beautiful woman that he'd ever seen. He frowned to himself when she sighed deeply, slowly stroking circles on the bar. Even though he barely knew her, he could sense that she was distracted and had a deep sense of sadness behind her eyes.

"I'm Lee by the way." he piped up, trying to get her to speak to him in his desperation to get to know her better.

"I know." she replied, a small smile playing on the corner of her lips.

"Chloe." she added, finally turning to face him. Lee took a sharp intake of breath when the woman that he'd been mesmerized by, since the moment she'd walked through the door, finally turned to face him, gazing up at him with her deep blue eyes.

"Can I buy you a drink?" he offered, his eyes fixed on her.

"No, I'm okay thank you. I have to be careful not to drink too much." she said, smiling to herself when she thought about her wild tendencies that she had when she was under the influence of alcohol. Chloe glanced at her Mum, giving her a small wave when she noticed her watching closely.

"Do you have wild tendencies?" he laughed.

"I'd probably end up dancing on a table or something." she giggled, glancing at Lee when she noticed him watching her closely. Lee took a sip of his drink, his eyes still fixed on Chloe, his heart pounding against his chest when he realised that she was, if possible, even more beautiful when she laughed. He couldn't stop his eyes from wandering over her flawless hourglass figure that was perfectly highlighted by her white fitted dress. Despite the fact that he spent most of his life surrounded by beautiful women, he'd never been this captivated by someone before. He couldn't quite put his finger on what it was, all he knew was that he wanted her desperately, and felt a strong desire to get to know her for the person that she was. Lee raised his eyebrow, resisting the urge to tell her how entranced her was by her presence. He shook his head slowly, trying to clear his head and organise his muddled thoughts.

"So, what do you do for a living?" he asked her, trying to engage her in conversation once again.

"I don't have a job at the moment, I start at University in September." she told him, sighing deeply to herself at the thought of being parted from her parents at such a difficult time, but she knew in her heart that they wouldn't allow her to drop out of the course.

"What are you studying?" he asked.

"Make-up, so that I can be a stylist." she explained. Lee nodded slowly, frowning to himself when he noticed the change in her body language. He smiled sympathetically at her when he suddenly realised that she had become distracted and lost in thought once again.

"You can be a stylist to the stars." he grinned, teasing her to try and lighten the atmosphere. She nodded slowly, smiling at him as he teased her playfully, his blue eyes twinkling cheekily.

"So, are you enjoying the band being back together?" she asked, trying to shift the focus off herself.

"Yeah, it's been good. We are starting off with some little gigs and hopefully we can work our way up to the big arenas again soon." he told her.

"You'll have to come and see us when we go on tour." he continued.

"Sounds like a plan." she smiled, quickly turning away from him as the two of them fell silent. Chloe jumped, her skin tingling when she felt someone carefully stroke their fingers down her forearm.

"Can I help you?" she asked sarcastically, instantly turning to face the person, sighing to herself as she locked eyes with a young man.

"I saw you across the pub and just had to come and speak to you." he muttered, gazing down at her longingly.

"I'm Jack." he added, reaching out to take Chloe's hand and planting a soft kiss on it, maintaining eye contact with her the entire time.

"Chloe." she replied quietly.

"You are the most beautiful woman that I have ever seen." Jack muttered, his eyes fixed on Chloe. She smiled her thanks, glancing down at his hand as he placed it between her shoulder blades, slowly trailing his fingers down her spine. Lee's stomach churned as he watched Jack gazing longingly at her. Even though he could understand why he was spellbound by her, that didn't stop the jealousy that he was feeling.

"So, do you know when you are going on tour?" Chloe asked, turning her attention to Lee as she turned her back on Jack, trying to ignore his advances.

"Not yet....we need to...." Lee started, trailing off when Jack spoke once again.

"Are you going to get your coat Chloe?" Jack interrupted, smirking at Lee smugly over the top of Chloe's head.

"What for?" Chloe frowned, glancing at Jack for a moment.

"So that I can take you somewhere nice for dinner." he grinned, wiggling his eyebrows at her. Lee sighed angrily as he took a swig of his drink, the hairs on the back of his neck standing up as he watched Jack flirting with Chloe. The way that he was staring at her like she was a piece of meat, and the cocky, over the top attitude that he had causing his blood to boil. Especially when he deliberately interrupted him and then had the audacity to smirk about it. He tore his gaze away from Chloe and Jack, trying to focus on something else, before he accidentally revealed how angry Jack was making him.

"I don't want to go out for dinner." Chloe said shortly, her temper slowly starting to rise.

"Aww, princess, don't get snippy." Jack retorted, quickly reaching out to stroke Chloe's cheek with his fingertips. Chloe quickly pulled her head away, glaring at him angrily.

"I'll get my jacket and then I'm taking you out for dinner." Jack grinned smugly, glancing at Chloe for a moment before walking away. Chloe sighed deeply, her temper simmering as she watched him walking across the bar, turning back to her briefly and winking at her. She glanced at Lee as he shot her a small sympathetic smile, as he gently wrapped his arm around her shoulders.

"Is he annoying you babe?" he asked gently. Chloe nodded slowly.

"I think I'm just going to call it a night and head home." she told him.

"Preferably before he comes back over here." she added, glancing up when she noticed Jack steadily walking back towards them.

"C'mon, I'll walk you back to your Mum." he said kindly, placing his hand on her waist protectively.

Chloe jumped, snapping out of her thoughts when she heard music from behind her. She whirled around, gasping as she gazed at the stage and noticed that Steven, Adrian and Nathan had appeared beside Lee. Her heart pounded against her chest when Adrian sang the opening lines to 'Broken'. Chloe gazed at Lee, her eyes brimming with tears as he watched her closely. A small gasp escaped her lips as Lee began to sing his verse, his soft yet powerful voice causing her to feel weak at the knees. Chloe gently wiped away her tears, her eyes flickering to her abdomen when she felt Freyja moving inside of her. Her heart swelled with pride at the thought that her baby girl clearly loved hearing Lee sing. Lee stared at Chloe, unable to tear his eyes away from her when the song finally came to an end. His heart soared when a small sob of happiness escaped her lips. She watched him closely as he quickly jumped down from the stage and gently pulled her into his arms, holding her tightly. Chloe snuggled her face against his collarbone, sighing in contentment when he placed his chin on her head.

"I love you so much." she whispered, her voice breaking with emotion as she tried to fight the intense range of emotions that she was feeling. A mixture of elation that she was going to marry the love of her life and sadness at the memories of her mother. She couldn't help but wish once again, that her parents hadn't been stolen from her. She'd have given anything to have them with her on her wedding day and for them to meet her baby. Lee quickly released Chloe from his grasp, smiling when Nathan, Steven and Adrian took in turns hugging her, the three of them thrilled by the exciting news.

"I can't believe that you are getting married." Steven beamed, clapping Lee on the back.

"Me neither, I never thought you would settle down." Adrian agreed, bursting out laughing when Lee glared at him.

"Well I have." Lee smirked, gently wrapping his arm around Chloe's shoulders.

"And I've settled down before you guys." he continued, glancing down at Chloe as she stared up at him, her eyes twinkling happily.

"I can't believe how lucky I am." he sighed, leaning forward to whisper in Chloe's ear.

"We need to celebrate guys!" Nathan exclaimed, causing Chloe to jump. Chloe nodded slowly, smiling slightly to herself when she gazed around the pub and noticed for the first time they were completely alone except for the barman.

"Did you hire the whole pub?" she frowned, turning to face Lee. He nodded slowly before placing the softest of kisses on her forehead.

"I'll get the first round in." Steven stated, quickly walking towards the bar.

"Don't forget Chloe can't drink!" Lee called after him.

"I'm not going to forget that am I!" he called back. Lee nodded slowly, before turning his attention back to Chloe. She glanced down at her abdomen when she felt Lee place his hand inside the pocket of his hoodie that she was still wearing, and softly stroke her bump with his fingertips.

"The three of us are going to be a proper family." he mumbled, resting his forehead against hers.

"I know, I can't wait." she muttered.

Chapter Fifty Three

"Oh my god, I can't believe it!" Louise squealed, causing Chloe to jump. Chloe giggled when Louise flung herself towards her and quickly pulled Chloe into a hug.

"I actually can't believe it!" Louise squealed when she finally released Chloe from her grasp.

"Me neither, why didn't you say anything?!" Kirstie cried, clapping her hands together in excitement.

"He only asked me at the weekend, and I wanted to wait and tell you in person." Chloe pointed out, smiling at their infectious excitement.

"I need to see the ring!" Louise said excitedly, her heart sinking when she glanced at Chloe's left hand and noticed that her baggy jumper was covering where the ring would be.

"Ssh, it's not common knowledge yet." Chloe said quickly, glancing around nervously when a group of people turned to stare at them.

"You shouldn't have told me in a shopping centre then, you know how excited I get." Louise giggled, lowering the tone of her voice. Chloe nodded slowly, her stomach churning nervously at the thought of the fans finding out before Lee had the chance to make the announcement.

"Although we did wonder why Lee invited everyone over for the evening." Kirstie smiled, glancing down at Chloe's hand as she slowly rolled up her jumper sleeve. Louise gasped in shock as she stared at the beautiful ring on Chloe's finger. She stared, mesmerized by the diamonds and sapphire that sat in the centre, shining in the light from the store.

"Wow, it's beautiful." Kirstie breathed, glancing at Chloe and smiling when she noticed how happy Chloe seemed. Louise nodded in agreement, her eyes misting with tears as she pulled Chloe into another hug.

"I'm so happy for you both." Louise whispered in Chloe's ear.

"Thank you." Chloe muttered.

"We need details about the proposal." Kirstie teased, as she turned to scan the rails, searching for a new pair of jeans.

"He asked me when we were at the top of Spinnaker Tower." she told them, smiling to herself when she'd remembered the moment that Lee had placed the baby grow on her bump and asked her to be his wife. Despite the fact that a couple of days had passed since the proposal, it still didn't seem real to her.

"There was a little message on a baby grow, asking Mummy to marry Daddy." she continued.

"Oh my god that's so sweet!" Louise cried, her eyes glazing over dreamily.

"And then we had a little celebration with the Eclipse boys." Chloe added, her heart swelling with pride when she remembered how excited they had been for her and Lee.

"We need to celebrate tonight." Kirstie piped up, bouncing up and down excitedly at the thought of celebrating.

"Especially since we are staying over at Lee's anyway....plus Ben and Peter will be there to celebrate with us." Louise agreed, raising her eyebrow at Chloe hopefully.

"It's up to Lee, it's his house." Chloe said quietly, her stomach churning nervously at the thought of the group celebrating. She couldn't help but remember the last time when they had drunk so much alcohol and partied most of the night away and due to the fact that she was pregnant she wouldn't even be able to join in with them.

"We can grab some booze while we are out." Louise piped up, completely disregarding Chloe's comment. Chloe sighed and rolled her eyes, quickly turning her back to scan the rails.

"Oh guys, I forgot to say. When I come back from being on tour, Peter and I are going to get a little place together." Louise announced, grinning at the group, her eyes twinkling with excitement.

"Ooh, that's exciting!" Kirstie squealed.

"I remember when I moved in with Ben, it was just amazing!" she continued, sighing happily to herself when she remembered how excited she had been to move in with him.

"I know, I literally can't wait." Louise agreed, smiling at Kirstie's infectious excitement.

"Congratulations, I'm really happy for you." Chloe smiled, quickly pulling Louise into a tight hug.

"Thank you." Louise said, smiling at Chloe when she released her from his grasp.

"I guess I'll need to tell Lee at some point." Louise chuckled.

"I'm sure he'll be fine about it, he's quite fond of Peter and he knows that he treats you right." Chloe pointed out. Louise nodded in agreement, a warm feeling spreading in her heart as she thought about how protective Lee was over her. Due to the fact that she didn't have a sibling in her life, she appreciated the fact that he cared about her, like a sister.

"Getting your own place with the man you love is such a good feeling." Kirstie announced, smiling widely at Louise's excitement.

"Also, I'm just going to put this out there, but sex is so much better when you have your own place." she added, giggling quietly to herself. Chloe's cheeks coloured as she glanced around the store nervously, fearful that they would be overheard.

"Isn't that right Chloe?" Kirstie beamed, turning to Chloe for an ally.

"I guess so." Chloe shrugged in response, choosing not to mention to the group that she only slept with Lee when the two of them lived together.

"Maybe I should get something sexy to wear then?" Louise said thoughtfully, her eyes flickering to the lingerie section of the store.

"Although I bet having sex just after you have got engaged is even better." Louise teased, wiggling her eyebrows at Chloe as she tried to include her in the conversation. Chloe's cheeks coloured deeply as both Kirstie and Louise turned to stare at her.

"I wouldn't know." Chloe mumbled, her eyes fixed on the floor. She squirmed slightly as she felt the two of them staring at her. Louise and Kirstie frowned, the two of them glancing at each other for a moment, before turning their attention back to Chloe.

"Are you seriously suggesting that you haven't had any hot, 'we just got engaged sex'!" Louise exclaimed in disbelief, gesturing inverted commas.

"Why are you guys so interested in my sex life?" Chloe sighed, finally glancing up at them and quickly looking away when she squirmed under their intense gazes.

"Don't avoid the question " Kirstie giggled.

"No we haven't." Chloe snapped.

"Although, I don't really understand what difference it makes anyway." she continued, becoming slightly frustrated that they were so interested in her private life. Despite the fact that she knew they liked to discuss sex lives, she didn't feel comfortable contributing to the conversation. She'd always been a very private person and wanted to keep their personal business between Lee and herself.

"But....." Louise started, trailing off when Chloe sighed in frustration.

"I get really bad fatigue with my pregnancy, so I haven't felt up to it." Chloe said shortly.

"Besides, it's only been a couple of days since we got engaged anyway and Lee understands." she continued defensively. Louise nodded slowly and quickly reached out to take Chloe's hand, leading her over to the lingerie section of the store.

"We need to find you something that you will feel amazing in." Louise beamed, her eyes darting to Chloe's bump for a moment, before she turned her attention to the rails.

"That's quite difficult at the moment, I can't exactly wear a corset can I." Chloe sighed, her eyes flickering to her bump. Even though she knew that she was measuring small for being five and half months pregnant, she couldn't help but wish that she still had her flat stomach that enabled her to pull off the corset, that she knew Lee couldn't resist her in.

"No, but we can find you something that gives you a bit of a confidence boost." Kirstie suggested.

"Who said anything about me needing a confidence boost?" Chloe snapped defensively.

"Nobody." Louise said quickly. Chloe frowned when she noticed the two of them glance at each other nervously, their cheeks colouring in embarrassment. She couldn't escape the feeling that they knew something that they were keeping from her.

"Ooh, what about this one?" Kirstie said excitedly, as she picked up a dark purple lace, panties and bra set.

"I won't look good in that." Chloe mumbled, her cheeks colouring as her eyes wandered to her bump and she thought about how visible it would be in just a bra and panties. Her heart pounded against her chest as she placed her hand on her abdomen, smiling to herself when she felt Freyja moving under her touch.

"This one is perfect." Louise stated, quickly picking up a purple baby-doll set. Chloe gasped as she gazed at the beautiful fitted material on the bust, perfectly highlighted by the lace pattern. The silk material flowed from the waist, stopping at the mid thigh. Louise winked at Chloe when she rummaged on the shelf and pulled out a matching set of panties.

"I don't think I can pull that off either." Chloe sighed, glancing up at Louise for a brief moment.

"Sure you can, it clips together at the front, underneath the bra part and then it gets loose, so it'll hide your bump if you feel self-conscious about it." Louise told her.

"I guess so." Chloe muttered, smiling slightly as she stroked the soft silky material.

"You're so beautiful Chloe, just work it." Kirstie smiled at her.

"You'll drive Lee crazy when you wear it." Louise pointed out, winking at Chloe as she walked over to the checkout, to purchase the set before Chloe could respond.

"Especially since he's even more attracted to you lately." Kirstie smiled.

"What?" Chloe frowned, finally locking eyes with Kirstie for the first time since they'd started the conversation.

"Of course he is." Kirstie nodded, beaming happily at Chloe.

"How do you know that?" Chloe asked, narrowing her eyes suspiciously. Kirstie shrugged, her heart pounding her chest nervously when she suddenly realised what she had said.

"Kirstie?" Chloe prompted.

"Maybe you told me about it." Kirstie said quickly, panicking slightly.

"No, I definitely didn't." Chloe said shortly, her brain spinning as she tried to process her thoughts. She couldn't escape the feeling that Kirstie knew more than she was letting on.

"Did Lee say something?" Chloe asked, her stomach churning at the thought of it. Kirstie opened her mouth to respond, quickly closing it again when Louise reappeared, smiling broadly as she handed Chloe the shopping bag.

"Call it an engagement present." Louise grinned.

"Thank you." Chloe said quietly, still not entirely sure if Lee had been discussing her insecurities with her friends.

"We should probably head back to the boys." Kirstie pointed out, squirming slightly under Chloe's intense gaze.

Lee glanced up from his phone as Chloe walked into the room. He smiled at her as she sat on the sofa beside him, her gaze fixed on him.

"Where are the girls?" Lee asked her.

"In the kitchen, making drinks with Peter and Ben." she replied, sighing quietly to herself as she fidgeted, trying to find a comfortable position that eased her cramps. Lee smiled sympathetically as he watched her.

"Is Freyja giving you hassle again?" he asked watching her closely as she carefully massaged her abdomen, trying in vain to provide herself with some relief.

"Ssh." she said quickly, glancing up at the doorway nervously.

"Her name is meant to be a secret." she added. Lee nodded slowly, breathing a small sigh of relief when he checked the doorway and noticed that it was clear.

"Speaking of secrets, I need to ask you something." she started, sighing to herself at the thought of him potentially discussing their private life with her friends. He raised his eyebrow and waited for her to continue. Chloe opened her mouth to ask the dreaded question, quickly closing it again when Nathan strode into the room, throwing himself onto the sofa beside her. She sighed in frustration, glancing at Lee who gave her a small reassuring smile. Nathan glanced between the two of them, frowning to himself as they fell silent.

"Have I interrupted something?" he asked. Chloe shook her head slowly and sat in silence, picking her fingernails.

"How is my god daughter?" Nathan asked, smiling as he glanced at Chloe's abdomen.

"She's fine." Chloe said quietly. Lee stared at her as she carefully shuffled along the sofa. He crossed his legs, watching closely as she sat on his lap, gently resting her back against his chest.

"You really have adopted my new hoodie haven't you?" Lee chuckled, trying to diffuse the tense atmosphere. He couldn't help but wonder what it was that Chloe was about to ask him, before Nathan walked into the room. She nodded slowly, glancing up at him for a moment, before snuggling her head against his collarbone. Chloe sighed in contentment when Lee wrapped his arms around her, holding her tightly against himself, his fingers gently stroking the material of her leggings.

"Are you falling asleep again?" he whispered, when he suddenly noticed that she was struggling to keep her eyes open. She nodded slowly, carefully rubbing the sleep out of her eyes.

"You've been really tired with the pregnancy haven't you?" Nathan piped up, smiling sympathetically at her. Chloe nodded slowly, sighing in contentment when Lee placed a soft kiss on her forehead and stroked her hair.

"Just close your eyes Chlo." he whispered in her ear.

Chapter Fifty Four

"So, we need wedding gossip!" Louise squealed as she hurried into the room, carrying a bottle of wine and some glasses in her hands. She beamed at Lee as she set them out on the table and poured everyone a glass of wine. Kirstie, Ben and Peter sat beside her on the floor, quickly helping themselves to the wine. Lee sighed deeply, glancing down at Chloe as she stirred in his arms, her eyelids slowly fluttering open. He couldn't help but feel slightly frustrated that Louise had woken Chloe, especially when he knew how much she was struggling with fatigue. Chloe glanced up at Lee, staring at him fondly, before gently placing a soft kiss on his lips. Lee's eyes flickered to Louise when she handed him a glass of wine.

"No, I'd better not." he said quickly, gazing down at Chloe as she watched him closely. He wrapped his arms around her waist, quickly linking their hands to try and keep his hands busy as an attempt to resist the glass of wine that he was being offered.

"You'll probably be okay with one glass." Chloe mumbled softly, giving him a small reassuring smile.

"I don't want to risk it." he muttered, placing their hands against Chloe's bump and softly stroking it with his fingertips. Chloe snuggled her face against his, sighing in contentment when he placed his chin on her shoulder.

"I'll pass thanks Lou." he said quietly, gazing at Louise as she reluctantly placed the glass of wine onto the coffee table.

"Surely you can have one?" Ben frowned.

"Probably, but I don't want to be tempted. I can't go back to how things were before." he pointed out, sighing deeply as he thought about how he'd spent weeks drowning his sorrows in alcohol until eventually he'd ended up in rehab.

"You won't." Chloe said quietly, trying to reassure him.

"I want to make sure I am here for you and our baby girl." he said firmly, gazing around at the group, a stern expression on his handsome features, giving them the silent cue that the subject was closed. Chloe smiled, a warm feeling spreading in her chest as he pulled her close, holding her in his strong but gentle arms.

"Anyway, we need wedding gossip!" Kirstie piped up when she suddenly realised that they had digressed.

"What do you want to know?" Chloe giggled, smiling at their infectious excitement.

"All the little details." Louise grinned.

"We haven't really planned much have we." Lee told them. Chloe shook her head slowly.

"But it's going to be a very low key wedding, just family and close friends." Chloe explained.

"You should get the boys to perform at your ceremony." Ben chuckled.

"That's a really good idea." Lee agreed, glancing at Chloe and smiling when he noticed the twinkle in her eyes.

"We could sing Broken for you." he continued, smiling down at Chloe as she gazed up at him fondly.

"That would be amazing." she whispered, softly stroking his cheek with her fingertips.

"Especially since it's our song." he whispered in her ear, smiling slightly when she shivered involuntarily. Chloe nodded slowly, gently resting her forehead against his, her eyes flickering to his lips for a brief moment. She placed a soft, lingering kiss on his lips, her cheeks colouring when she suddenly realised that the others were still in the room.

"What about bridesmaids?" Louise piped up, winking cheekily at the two of them. Chloe glanced at Lee awkwardly, sighing to herself when he shot her a small reassuring smile.

"Amy has agreed to be my bridesmaid." Chloe said tentatively, her eyes flickering to her hand when Lee squeezed it gently, trying to provide her some reassurance. Louise raised her eyebrow, almost like she was waiting for Chloe to continue.

"It's going to be a small wedding so I only have one bridesmaid." Chloe explained, glancing up at them, her stomach churning nervously when she noticed the disappointment on their faces. Louise nodded slowly, trying in vain to hide her disappointment from Chloe. Even though she understood Chloe's decision, she couldn't help but feel disappointed that her and Kirstie wouldn't be more involved with the process.

"You can both help me with the planning side of things though." Chloe suggested, trying to appease some of the guilt she was feeling at the fact that she'd hurt her friends. Kirstie nodded slowly, smiling at Louise when she clapped her hands excitedly.

"Wait, isn't that my job?" Lee chuckled, removing one of his hands from Chloe's pocket and wrapping his arm around her shoulders, his fingers gently caressing her neck.

"You can't help me choose a dress, you're not allowed to see it." Chloe giggled, her skin tingling under his soft touch.

"OMG, we have to go dress shopping!" Louise squealed, causing everyone to jump.

"Yes, let's go tomorrow!" Kirstie joined in, the two of them raising their eyebrow at Chloe hopefully.

"Just slow down a minute." Chloe said quickly, smiling at their infectious excitement.

"We're not getting married until next Spring." Lee quickly explained.

"What?!" Louise exclaimed.

"But that's ages away." she continued, sighing in disappointment.

"Well the baby isn't due until August anyway." Chloe pointed out, a small smile playing on the corner of her lips when she felt Lee softly stroking circles on her bump with the hand that was still resting in the pocket of his hoodie that she was wearing.

"So?" Ben frowned, quickly taking a large swig of his drink.

"I would like to be able to get my figure back so that I feel good on my wedding day." Chloe explained, her cheeks colouring slightly as the group stared at her.

"Even though you're beautiful anyway." Lee whispered in her ear, before gently planting a soft kiss on her neck.

"I'm carrying excess baggage." she smiled, her eyes darting to her bump.

"You're carrying a baby, not baggage." Kirstie pointed out, rolling her eyes. Chloe frowned for a moment when she noticed the exasperation in Kirstie's tone, but she decided not to dwell on it.

"And then we are going on the tour in January." Lee reminded them. Chloe glanced at Nathan, watching him closely as he squirmed awkwardly. She frowned to herself, her heart sinking when she noticed his body language. It was clear that Matt had discussed with Nathan that Chloe wouldn't be joining them on the tour, because she had to prioritize her baby girl. Nathan opened his mouth to say something, quickly closing it again when Chloe slowly shook her head, subtly giving him the signal that she still hadn't discussed her plans with Lee. Her stomach churned with guilt when she felt him watching her closely, clearly picking up on the change in her body language.

"So we figured that it's better to get married when we are back home from the tour." Lee continued.

"There's a lot to figure out with a wedding though isn't there, so there's no rush." Peter said, shooting Chloe a small smile when he noticed her squirming uncomfortably. Lee nodded in agreement, wrapping his arms around Chloe's waist and holding her close, gently resting his chin on her shoulder. He sighed in contentment as she rested her face against his, her eyes flickering to the engagement ring on her finger.

"Since you want something low key, maybe you could get married on a beach or something?" Kirstie suggested.

"Or a boat." Lee chuckled, glancing down at Chloe when she burst out laughing.

"You like the sea remember." he laughed. Chloe nodded slowly.

"I think a beach is a better idea." Nathan grinned.

"Wherever you decide to do it, you need to make sure there's an aisle for you to walk down." Louise smiled.

"That's the best part, watching the groom's face when he sees the bride arrive and watches her walking down the aisle towards him and he is mesmerized." she continued, a dreamy expression on her face.

"I don't have anyone to give me away though." Chloe said sadly, sighing deeply as her thoughts wandered to her father. Her eyes filled with tears when she remembered that her parents wouldn't be a part of her special day. She couldn't help but feel a deep pang of sadness that they were missing out on so much. Not only would they never get to meet their granddaughter, but they wouldn't be able to share her wedding day.

"Don't get upset." Lee whispered in her ear, when he heard her sniff quietly to herself. She placed her hands on top of his, linking their fingers, smiling to herself when he rocked her slowly, trying to distract her from the sadness that she was feeling.

"Can't you get Nathan to give you away, since you guys are close?" Kirstie suggested. Nathan nodded quickly, his eyes lighting up hopefully.

"Wait a second." Chloe said quickly, sighing slightly when Nathan's face fell. Despite the fact that she would love for Nathan to give her away on her wedding day, she couldn't help but realise that Lee would want him to be his best man. Even though she felt a strong bond with Nathan, he was like a big brother to her, she couldn't deny Lee his best friend.

"It's okay Chlo." Lee reassured her when he sensed her hesitation.

"But, he'll be your best man won't he?" Chloe asked, turning to face Lee. He thought for a moment, glancing over the top of Chloe's head at Nathan. Even though Nathan was Lee's best friend, he couldn't deny Chloe of the only person that he knew she would feel comfortable enough with to give her away, particularly when he knew how upset she was that it couldn't be her father. He knew that for as long as he lived he would always put Chloe's feelings above his own and do what was right by her.

"It's fine, I think Nath should give you away." he told her.

"Besides I can ask Si to be my best man." he continued, smiling warmly at her when he noticed the happy sparkle in her eyes.

"But...." Chloe started, trailing off when Lee interrupted her.

"Honestly, it's fine." Lee interrupted, before Chloe could argue with him. Chloe nodded slowly, quickly wrapping her arms around his neck and hugging him tightly, her eyes filling with tears as she realised once again how lucky she was to have someone like Lee in her life. Someone that would literally do anything he could for her and their baby. Chloe carefully stood up and walked over to Nathan, glancing at him as he stood up and pulled her into his arms, hugging her tightly, his eyes misting with tears.

"I would be honoured to give you away Chlo Bo." Nathan whispered in her ear.

"Thank you." she whispered back, swallowing the lump that was rising in her throat. Chloe slowly turned to face Lee, shooting him a small smile when she noticed him gazing at her. Her heart pounded against her chest as he mouthed I love you to her.

"I think I need a beer." Nathan mumbled, quickly walking into the kitchen, trying to hide the tears of happiness that were filling his eyes.

"Let's go for a swim in the pool!" Louise piped up, quickly standing up and taking Peter's hand, pulling him after her.

"Is that such a good idea?" Ben chuckled, raising his eyebrow at Kirstie when she stood up.

"C'mon, it'll be fun." Kirstie beamed, giggling at Louise's infectious excitement. Chloe ignored them, unable to tear her eyes away from Lee as she slowly walked towards him and sat on his lap, placing her legs on the sofa either side of him. She quickly wrapped her arms around his neck, holding him close as she fought to control the intense range of emotions that she was feeling. Lee wrapped his arms around Chloe's waist, placing a soft kiss on her shoulder. He could hear the others speaking to each other in the background, but he couldn't make out what they were saying, he was too focused on Chloe. He took a deep breath, inhaling her familiar scent. Chloe carefully sat back and slowly fidgeted, trying to find a comfortable position. Lee glanced down at her, watching closely as she massaged her bump, wincing slightly.

"Have you got cramps again?" he whispered, his voice slightly hoarse. She nodded slowly, glancing at the others as they hovered, clearly waiting to see if Chloe and Lee were planning to join them. Chloe started to stand up, glancing down at her hips when Lee quickly gripped them, preventing her from standing. She frowned in confusion, her gaze fixed on him.

"We'll catch you up." Lee told them, sighing quietly when they finally left the room.

"Don't you want to go in the pool?" Chloe asked him. He shook his head slowly, his gaze still fixed on Chloe, a look of deep longing on his face. She nodded slowly, wincing as she fidgeted, desperately trying to find a comfortable position that eased her cramps.

"You really need to stop fidgeting Chlo." Lee whispered in her ear, an edge present in his voice.

"Why, what's wrong?" she frowned, her gaze fixed on him as he stared at her. He sighed deeply, placing his hands on Chloe's back and pulling her close. Chloe shuddered when he rested his forehead against her shoulder, and she felt his warm breath against her neck.

"You've turned me on so bad." he whispered, his heart pounding against his chest as he tried to resist the beautiful woman who was still sitting on his lap.

"But I didn't do anything." she said quietly, watching him as he slowly raised his head, watching her closely, a look of deep longing etched on his handsome features.

"No, but that perfect arse did." he smiled, placing his hands on her hips, his eyes still fixed on her. Chloe glanced down at his groin, a small giggle escaping her lips when she realised what she'd accidentally done. She gazed up at him through her eyelashes, her cheeks colouring under his intense gaze.

"Don't look so innocent." he smiled, bursting out laughing at her expression. She raised her eyebrow at him before slowly rotating her hips, smiling to herself when Lee gasped. Before Lee could react she wrapped her arms around his neck, pressing her cheek against his. She placed a series of soft kisses on his neck as she methodically rotated her hips once again, chuckling to herself when Lee groaned quietly and gripped the material of her hoodie, quickly curling them into fists.

"I need you so bad Chlo." he whispered breathlessly.

"I know, it's okay baby." she whispered in between kissing his neck. He shivered involuntarily when she began to softly stroke the hair on the back of his neck.

"It's been a few days too." he mumbled, trying to keep himself talking to distract himself from the intense desire that he was feeling for her.

"I know, that was my fault, I'm sorry." she whispered. Lee slowly lifted his head to make eye contact with her.

"You don't have anything to apologise for." he reassured her.

"I just meant that it's making it more difficult for me to resist you." he explained, smiling slightly when her cheeks coloured. Chloe nodded slowly, before placing a soft lingering kiss on his lips.

"The girls were teasing me about it earlier." she told him.

"Teasing you about what?" he muttered, placing a soft kiss on her forehead.

"That apparently the sex is really good just after you've gotten engaged." she said, rolling her eyes.

"How would they know." he frowned.

"They've never been engaged." he laughed.

"True." she giggled. She stared at him for a moment, her cheeks colouring deeply when she suddenly remembered that she was wearing the sexy underwear set that Louise had brought for her underneath her hoodie and leggings. She bit her lip, trying to ignore the longing that she was feeling for him and how much her skin tingled under his touch. Even after all this time, she still felt weak at the knees whenever she was in his presence. Her eyes flickered to his hand when he placed it on her neck, gently stroking her jawline with his fingertips.

"I have a surprise for you later." she told him, wiggling her eyebrows at him. He raised his eyebrow at her, waiting for her to continue. She slowly turned around so that she had her back to him, smiling to herself when she felt his body trembling against her.

"You have to stop teasing me." he whispered in her ear, quickly resting his chin on her shoulder. Chloe smiled to herself when she placed her hands on his and linked their fingers, slowly moving his hands from her hips. Lee watched closely as she placed his hands underneath her hoodie, slowly pulling them upwards. He frowned to himself when he felt the silky material underneath his touch. Chloe shivered involuntarily when she placed his hands on her breasts and quickly removed her hands. Her skin tingled under his touch as his soft fingers trailed along the lace trim of the nightgown. She sighed in contentment, resting the back of her head against his shoulder, his fingers methodically making their way inside of the bra.

"Did you buy a new set?" he mumbled. Chloe nodded slowly, trying to ignore the goosebumps that were rising on her arms.

"Although technically Louise got it for me." she whispered. The two of them jumped when they heard a joyful scream coming from the direction of the pool room. Chloe sighed and reluctantly moved away from Lee's touch, slowly standing up.

"We should probably go and be good hosts." she said reluctantly.

"But...." he protested, his heart sinking in disappointment as soon as Chloe had climbed off his lap.

"I'm sure you can wait until later." she beamed, giggling slightly when she noticed his pained expression.

"I don't think I can." he sighed, a small smile playing on the corner of his lips. He stared at Chloe, unable to tear his eyes away from her, his brain swirling. His imagination was running wild at the thought of what Chloe was wearing underneath her clothes. Chloe wiggled her eyebrows at him, realising instantly what he was thinking as he gazed at her. She slowly walked away from him, smiling to herself as she felt his eyes on her.

Chapter Fifty Five

Chloe's cheeks coloured as she walked into the pool room and the four of them turned to face her. She couldn't help but smile at their happy expressions as they stood in the pool together. Chloe sighed to herself as she sat on one of the loungers, gently tucking her legs under her, wincing slightly as she rubbed her sore abdomen.

"Where's Nath?" she asked them when she suddenly realised that he was nowhere to be seen.

"He popped into the kitchen to fetch us some more drinks." Peter told her. Chloe nodded slowly.

"Aren't you coming in to join us Chloe?" Louise smiled at her.

"No, I'm okay thank you." she replied, her cheeks colouring at the thought of undressing in front of them. Despite the fact that her body confidence was growing she still couldn't bring herself to undress in front of them. Lee was the only person that she'd ever been able to feel fully comfortable with, enough to make herself vulnerable with him.

"We won't be looking at you." Kirstie reassured her, quickly realising that she felt self-conscious in front of them.

"We're all in our underwear anyway." Ben laughed. Chloe shot them a small smile, not entirely sure how to explain that she couldn't bring herself to undress in front of them, especially since she was still very self-conscious of the scar on her abdomen.

"Ooh, you could wear the nightgown we got earlier!" Louise exclaimed excitedly, wiggling her eyebrows at Chloe.

"I think I'll pass." Chloe replied, her cheeks colouring deeply.

"It's probably for the best, I doubt Lee would be able to keep his hands off you." Louise giggled, glancing over at Ben and Peter as they play fought in the pool.

"What have I done?" Lee asked as he quickly strode into the room.

"Nothing." Louise said quickly, shooting Chloe a small wink, before swimming over to join Peter and Ben.

"What was all that about?" Lee asked Chloe as he perched beside her on the lounger. Chloe rolled her eyes and shrugged, sighing to herself as she felt another wave of fatigue wash over her.

"What took you so long to come through?" she asked him, carefully rubbing her tired eyes.

"I had to take care of something." he grinned, winking at her when she turned to glance at him. Chloe burst out laughing, her cheeks colouring as soon as she realised what he was talking about. Lee joined in with her infectious laughter, his heart pounding against his chest as he watched the woman that he adored with every fibre of his being. He still couldn't quite believe how privileged he was to get to be the one that was able to call her his fiancée.

"What are you two laughing at?" Kirstie giggled.

"Nothing." Lee said quickly. Chloe gazed up at him as he placed a soft kiss on her forehead.

"You should get in the pool with them." Chloe suggested.

"It'll be fun." she continued. Lee nodded slowly, raising his eyebrow at her as he slowly removed his shirt, his eyes fixed on her. A small smile played on Chloe's lips as she gazed at his broad, toned chest. She placed her hand against his abs, sighing quietly when she felt his warmth.

"Don't, otherwise I'll have to leave the room again." he muttered, his skin tingling under Chloe's touch. Before Chloe could respond, Lee stood up and removed his jeans, and quickly jumped into the pool. As soon as he resurfaced he beamed at Chloe when he realised that he'd managed to splash her.

"You did that on purpose." Chloe giggled, when she noticed the cheeky expression on his handsome features. He wiggled his eyebrows at her, as he ran his hand through his hair, pushing it out of the way. Chloe bit her lip, trying to ignore how handsome he looked.

"He was probably trying to get you to undress." Louise grinned. Chloe smiled, her heart bursting with pride when Lee eventually pulled his gaze away from her and swum over to Louise, grabbing hold of her playfully.

"I suggest you apologise for saying that." he teased her, chuckling playfully.

"I can't apologise for something that is true." Louise argued, a small shriek escaping her lips when spun her around and dunked her under the water.

"You alright Chlo Bo?" Nathan asked when he appeared from behind her. A small yelp of fear escaped Chloe's lips.

"Sorry, I didn't mean to startle you." he said gently, as he walked over to the edge of the pool, carefully placing the drinks down, ready for when the group eventually finished messing around.

"It's fine, I was just deep in thought." she smiled at him, watching as he pulled a lounger over so that it was resting against hers.

"About your upcoming nuptials?" he asked her.

Chloe shook her head slowly. He grinned at her as he laid down on the lounger, placing his hands behind the back of his head and crossing his legs.

"What's going on Chlo Bo, you're very quiet?" he asked, an edge of concern present in his voice.

"I'm just tired, I'm always tired lately." she sighed, carefully laying down on the lounger.

"Maybe you should have a nap then." he suggested. Chloe nodded slowly, turning onto her side and watching him closely, fighting to keep her eyes open.

"Thank you for agreeing to give me away." she mumbled, moving her arms so that they were covering her chest as an attempt to keep warm, the slight dampness of her clothes causing her to feel cold.

"It's fine, I honestly can't wait." he smiled at her.

"You'll be Mrs Knight before you know it." he continued.

"I haven't decided what I'm doing about my surname yet." she admitted, glancing at Nathan when he raised his eyebrow at her and waited for her to continue.

"I just feel like my surname is the final connection I have to my family, especially since I don't have their wedding rings anymore." she said, sighing quietly to herself.

"But it's a difficult one, because I want to be Mrs Knight." she continued thoughtfully.

"Well you've got plenty of time to decide and you have the baby to concentrate on first." he pointed out. Chloe nodded slowly. Nathan frowned to himself as he watched Chloe and suddenly noticed that she was shivering.

"Come here Chlo Bo." he offered, holding out his arm to her. Chloe smiled at him as she shuffled closer, quickly wrapping her arms around his chest and snuggling against him for warmth. Nathan wrapped his arm around Chloe's shoulders and held her close.

"You do realise that I love you right." she mumbled, fighting to keep her eyes open.

"Are you feeling okay?" Nathan chuckled, glancing at her for a moment.

"Yes, I'm fine." she giggled.

"I meant like a big brother." she added.

"I know what you meant, I was joking." he teased her, frowning to himself when he realised that her eyes were filling with tears.

"Are you crying?" he asked her, his brow furrowing in concern.

"It's just hormones." she reassured him, quickly wiping the tears from her eyes. She closed her eyes and fell asleep instantly, feeling comforted by being in Nathan's strong arms. He smiled down at Chloe as he watched her sleeping soundly in his arms, still not quite able to comprehend how much happier she was now that her and Lee were finally together. Even though her confidence was still lacking in certain areas, she was a far cry from the ghost of a person she was back when, unbeknown to them, she'd been living on the streets. His stomach churned with guilt at the thought of her living on a park bench, struggling to get through each day. He thought of her as his little sister and found himself wishing that he'd known about her predicament so that he could have helped her.

"Right, we need to do shot guys!" Louise squealed excitedly, placing her hands on the edge of the pool and pulling herself out of it. She beamed at the others as they climbed out and she handed each of them a drink.

"I'm still not drinking." Lee told her, quickly handing her the drink back. Louise rolled her eyes.

"Nath, how about you, since Lee's being boring?!" Louise called over to him.

"No thanks." he said quietly.

"Chloe has fallen asleep on me, so I'm kind of stuck." he added, glancing down at Chloe for a moment as she fidgeted in her sleep. Lee quickly picked up a towel and wrapped it around his neck, scrubbing his hair as he walked over to the lounger beside Nathan and Chloe and sat on it, watching her closely.

"She's fine." Nathan said, before Lee could ask the inevitable question. Lee smiled slightly and nodded slowly.

"You don't need to worry about her so much all of the time." Nathan pointed out, when he noticed that Lee's gaze was still fixed on Chloe.

"Nothing is going to happen to her." he prompted when Lee still hadn't responded.

"I can't help worrying, the two of them are what I live for." he sighed deeply, watching Chloe's chest slowly rise and fall.

"Besides we know what it's like to lose a baby, and neither of us can go through that again." he muttered, glancing behind himself nervously to check that he wasn't overheard. He sighed in relief when he realised that they were too busy debating their drinks to pay any attention to him. He sighed deeply as his gaze flickered back to Chloe.

"And as for Chloe, you know that I can't function without her." he said softly.

"You won't have too." Nathan reassured him. Lee nodded slowly.

"If this is because of Shayne, he's locked up." Nathan said thoughtfully.

"I know." Lee said quietly, swallowing the lump that was rising in his throat as he thought about just how much Chloe had been through and how many times he'd nearly lost her for good. Nathan and Lee instantly stopped talking when the others bounded over to join them, quickly sitting beside them on the floor.

"Ooh, she's fallen asleep on another man!" Ben cried, teasing Lee, his voice slurring slightly.

"That's got to sting." Ben added, chuckling to himself as he teased Lee.

"Not really, she's always been close to Nathan." Lee said quietly, rolling his eyes at Ben.

"Besides I'm not a jealous person." he added.

"A little overprotective maybe but not possessive." he continued thoughtfully.

"A little overprotective?" Nathan grinned.

"She's been through a lot though hasn't she, and I don't want her to suffer through anything else." Lee explained, his eyes flickering to Chloe as she mumbled in her sleep.

"I have to look after them." he added thoughtfully. Kirstie smiled at him, her heart swelling with pride as she watched Lee closely. The way that he stared at Chloe, with such love and admiration, she knew that he would do anything for her.

"You're going to be a great dad." Louise smiled at him.

"And husband." Kirstie grinned, the two of them bursting out laughing when Lee's cheeks coloured deeply.

"She seems to be doing better since Shayne was caught." Kirstie said thoughtfully, quickly taking another swig of her drink. Lee nodded slowly.

"How is her body confidence now?" Kirstie asked.

"She's getting there." Lee told her, sighing quietly to himself.

"She's never been a very confident person though has she." Louise pointed out.

"It's worse since she fell pregnant though." Lee told them, shooting a small sympathetic smile at Chloe, his heart pounding against his chest when he noticed that she was still fast asleep.

"Why, because of her bump?" Louise asked, frowning slightly.

"A combination of that and what Shayne did to her." he sighed deeply, his stomach churning in anger as he thought about what Chloe had been through at the hands of Shayne.

"Plus she thinks that I'm not as attracted to her anymore, which is completely untrue." he continued.

"I kind of get it though." Louise piped up, squirming slightly when Lee quickly turned to face her.

"You have a lot of girls after you don't you." she quickly explained, squirming under his intense gaze. Lee nodded slowly.

"I think her confidence is improving though." Nathan pointed out.

"She's so much better than she was a few weeks ago." Lee agreed.

"She wouldn't even undress in front of me." he told them. Louise scoffed sceptically, raising her eyebrow at him.

"Aww that's a shame bless her." Kirstie said sympathetically, her heart breaking a little at her best friend's confidence being so low. Lee nodded slowly, sighing to himself.

"I don't believe you, you're a highly sexed guy. I doubt you would have waited weeks." Ben laughed.

"Who said anything about waiting weeks?" Lee frowned.

"You did." Ben frowned.

"She would wear my hoodie during sex, because it's so big on her." Lee said quickly, instantly regretting the words as soon as they were out of his mouth.

"It was horrible." he admitted, his stomach churning slightly when he remembered how much he'd hated seeing her with next to no confidence.

"Sex is never horrible." Ben laughed.

Chloe stirred slowly, carefully sitting up, her eyes focused on Lee as he turned to stare at her, a slightly nervous expression on his handsome features.

"Did you just say that having sex with me was horrible?" she rounded on him, her temper slowly rising as she thought about his words.

"Because if so, maybe you should have told me, rather than everybody else!" she exclaimed, her cheeks colouring as felt the group staring at her. She quickly stood up, wishing that she could disappear and not face their judgemental opinions.

"I didn't mean it like that." Lee said quickly, his stomach churning with guilt when he realised how embarrassed and humiliated she felt.

"You really know how to make someone feel like a piece of shit!" she shouted, no longer able to contain her anger.

"Chloe, he wasn't...." Nathan started, trailing off when she interrupted him.

"Stay out of it!" she said quickly.

"Please Chlo, let me explain." Lee pleaded, quickly standing up in front of her.

"Leave me alone!" she said angrily, making a move to walk past him, her temper rising further when he moved to block her.

"Chlo." he muttered, placing his hands on her waist and trying to pull her close.

"Don't touch me!" she said angrily, placing her hands on his chest and pushing past him.

"Chlo!" Lee called desperately, his heart breaking a little as she walked away from him.

"Oh, and if I'm that bad, maybe you should go and screw a random model like you used too!" she shouted, hesitating in the doorway for a moment before walking away.

Chapter Fifty Six

Chloe ran upstairs, desperately trying to get as far away from everyone as possible. Her stomach churned when she heard Nathan calling out to Lee, telling him not to follow her and allow her some time alone with her thoughts.

As soon as she reached the bedroom, she carefully laid down on the bed, wrapping her arms across her chest and curling into a ball, trying to hide from the world and the intense shame that she was feeling. Her heart had shattered into pieces when she'd awoken to Lee telling the group about how she used to wear his hoodie and that having sex with her was, in his words 'horrible'. She clapped her hand over her mouth as a small sob escaped her lips. She'd always known that she wasn't good enough for him, and he had a lot of women to compare her too, but she never expected that he felt like that. She slowly stood up, staggering slightly as she walked into the bathroom, her stomach churning as she gazed at her reflection. She slowly removed her leggings and hoodie, gazing sadly at herself. Chloe turned sideways, tears rolling down her cheeks as she stared at herself in the nightgown that Louise had brought for her.

"I'm not beautiful at all." she whispered to herself, her heart plummeting when she suddenly realised that Lee had been lying to her all this time. She stared at her reflection in a daze, gradually becoming more and more angry and upset with every moment that passed. Before she knew what she was doing, she picked up Lee's electric toothbrush and threw it at the mirror, trying to destroy her reflection. She watched in satisfaction as a large smash mark appeared in the centre of her reflection, the ripples slowly making their way along the mirror.

Chloe dressed in a daze, slowly making her way downstairs, hesitating for a moment when she heard the sound of voices coming from the pool room. She slipped on her trainers and carefully opened the front door, taking care not to alert the others to her intentions. She knew that they would try to stop her and she needed some time to clear her head. Her stomach churned nervously as she placed her hand on the front door knob, hesitating for a moment before slowly turning it.

Kirstie glanced at Lee, smiling sympathetically at him as his eyes wandered to the doorway once again. She could tell by his body language that he desperately wanted to follow Chloe so that he could explain everything to her. It was clear how much it was killing him to be away from her side, unable to check whether she was okay or not.

"Why don't you go and check on her?" Kirstie suggested, her heart breaking a little for him when she realised how lost he seemed without Chloe by his side.

"Because I'm doing what Nathan said and giving her some space." he sighed, an edge of bitterness present in his voice. He remained silent as he picked up an empty beer bottle and began to pick at the edges of the label, trying to keep his mind occupied.

"She just needs some time to cool off." Louise told him.

"She totally misunderstood what I was trying to say, because she only heard part of it." he said, angrily running his hands through his hair.

"Are you talking about Chlo Bo?" Nathan asked as he walked back over to join the group, quickly handing Ben and Peter a fresh beer. Kirstie nodded slowly.

"She's probably just having a bath and going to bed early." Nathan pointed out.

"Especially since she's been feeling really exhausted lately." he continued.

"I guess so." Lee said quietly, sighing to himself when he realised that they were right. Despite the desperation that he felt to check on Chloe and to explain himself to her, he knew that he needed to give her some time to calm down. He'd accidentally humiliated her in front of her friends and he knew that she would take it harshly.

"Although she has been gone for a while." Peter pointed out, glancing at his watch and frowning when he realised how much time had passed. Lee's eyes widened as he gazed around the group nervously. He quickly stood up, glancing down at his knee as he felt Nathan place his hand on it, subtly telling him to stay where he was.

"If she sees you, she's probably going to get angry again." Nathan pointed out.

"I can't avoid her forever though." Lee said quietly, slowly sitting back down as he felt the group watching him closely.

"Just for a little while." Nathan told him reassuringly.

"You have to keep her blood pressure down." Ben slurred, chuckling quietly to himself.

"I can go and check on her if you want?" Kirstie offered, feeling slightly sorry for Lee when she saw the deep sadness on his handsome features. He nodded slowly, shooting Kirstie a small smile as she stood up and quickly walked out of the room.

"I can't believe what an idiot I am." Lee muttered thoughtfully.

"Really, we've all known it for years." Ben teased him.

"I knew that Chloe doesn't like her private life being discussed, but yet I keep doing it." Lee continued, completely disregarding Ben's comment.

"We only knew about her body confidence issues because you asked us for advice on how to help her." Nathan reminded him.

"Actually, I asked you and Kirstie, not everyone else. It was never meant to be a group topic." he said quickly, an edge of anger present in his voice.

"Don't start getting snippy." Louise told him sternly, quickly downing her glass of wine. Lee rolled his eyes angrily, desperately trying to resist the urge to snap back at her. He knew that he was taking his frustration at himself out on the group and he was determined not to let that happen. The group fell silent, none of them sure what to say to lighten the tense atmosphere. Lee's eyes flickered to the doorway when Kirstie walked back into the room, a confused frown on her face.

"Errm guys, I couldn't find Chloe." she announced, glancing around nervously.

"What?!" Lee spluttered, quickly standing up.

"She's probably locked herself in the bathroom or something." Ben said quickly.

"I checked the bathroom, and I'm worried that something is wrong, because the mirror was smashed." Kirstie explained.

"It looks like she threw something at it." she continued, turning to stare at Lee, her eyes narrowing accusingly at him. Despite the fact that she knew Chloe had completely taken the conversation out of context, she couldn't help but feel slightly frustrated at him that he'd managed to upset her best friend, particularly when she was pregnant. Kirstie knew how precious the baby was to the two of them and how much Chloe had been struggling with fatigue and nausea and she couldn't help but feel like Lee had added to her already full plate, because he hadn't kept his mouth closed.

"Right, I'm going to check on her. If we all search the house, she has to be somewhere." Lee said, standing up and quickly taking charge, his stomach swirling nervously.

"Would she maybe have gone to the gym room or something." Louise suggested as she hurried to check.

"This house is massive, surely you can't be expecting us to search the whole thing!" Ben exclaimed, rolling his eyes, the conversation clearly boring him. Kirstie sighed as she placed her hand under Ben's elbow and quickly pulled him to his feet, glaring at him angrily.

"I'll check upstairs." Lee said, quickly bolting out of the room and running upstairs. His heart pounded against his chest nervously as he walked into their bedroom, frowning to himself as he gazed around the room and saw that Chloe was nowhere to be seen. He sighed deeply as he wandered into the bathroom, his eyes fixed on the mirror. His stomach churned with guilt when he quickly realised that thanks to his words, Chloe had clearly been so repulsed by her own reflection that she'd needed to destroy it.

"Lee!" Kirstie shouted from downstairs, snapping him out of his thoughts. He sighed in relief, quickly following the sound of Kirstie's voice when he realised that she had clearly located Chloe. He frowned to himself when he noticed her standing in the front doorway, her complexion slightly pale.

"What's wrong?" he asked her.

"The front door wasn't closed properly." she replied. He frowned to himself, gazing at the gap between the door and the door frame, his brain spinning with possibilities.

"Maybe you guys left it like that earlier when you came in." he suggested, swallowing the lump that was rising in his throat.

"She wouldn't sneak out would she?" Kirstie asked, raising her eyebrow at him. Lee opened his mouth to respond, quickly closing it again when he had no idea whether Chloe was angry enough to want to leave the house.

"Well?!" Lee rounded on Nathan when he hurried into the room. Nathan shook his head slowly.

"For god sake, this is ridiculous." Lee muttered, his stomach churning nervously.

"I even tried calling her phone...." Nathan started.

"And?" Lee asked quickly, before Nathan could finish his sentence.

"It's in the pool room on the lounger, it must have fallen out of her pocket when she was sleeping." Nathan explained. Lee sighed deeply, running his hands through his hair in frustration. Lee raised his eyebrow hopefully when Louise and Peter walked into the room, both of them shaking their heads solemnly.

"Which part of the house is Ben checking?" Nathan asked, quickly rounding on Kirstie.

"He isn't, he crashed out on the sofa." Kirstie admitted, her cheeks colouring in embarrassment.

"She's sneaked out somewhere." Lee said, shaking his head slowly, his heart pounding against his chest as he felt himself slowly beginning to panic. His eyes flickered to the doorway as he began to pace uncontrollably.

"What the hell was she thinking?!" he exclaimed, quickly placing his hands in his pocket when he realised that they were shaking.

"Going out at this time of night on her own." he added.

"And she's bloody pregnant!" he added, his stomach churning at the thought of anything happening to Chloe or Freyja. Before anyone could respond, Lee swiped his keys off the counter and hurried out of the front door.

"Hold up a minute!" Nathan called, quickly hurrying after him.

"What?!" Lee exclaimed, quickly turning around to face him.

"We should put our heads together to figure out where she would go." Nathan protested.

"And we can organise a search party." he added.

"The girls should stay in the house where it's safe." Lee said quickly.

"What are some places that she is likely to go?" Nathan asked as he watched Lee quickly climbing into his car.

"You can go to Danny's, ask Peter to check the studio." Lee said bluntly, when he realised that Nathan was determined to help him search for Chloe.

"Where are you going?" Nathan asked.

"To the cemetery." he stated, quickly closing the car door and pulling away so fast that the tyres squeaked.

Chapter Fifty Seven

Chloe slowly opened her eyes and rubbed them sleepily, frowning to herself when she suddenly realised that she wasn't in her own bed. She racked her brain as she glanced down at herself, her confusion growing when she suddenly realised that she was curled up on a park bench. She wrapped her arms across her chest, shivering in the cold temperatures. Chloe blew softly into her hands, desperately trying to warm them. She gasped when she felt Freyja moving inside of her, her eyes flickering to her bump when she suddenly felt rigid with fear. Her heart pounded against her chest as she slowly sat up, sighing deeply to herself as she pressed her hand against her forehead, trying to stop her head from spinning. She quickly reached out to grasp the handrail of the bench when she felt herself becoming light headed.

"Chloe." she heard a voice whisper from behind her. She frowned to herself, peering through the darkness to try and discover the source of the sound. She slowly turned back to her original position, a small squeak of fear escaping her lips when she saw a familiar face staring at her through the darkness.

"Andy." she whispered, frowning in confusion, still not entirely sure where she was or how she had got there. She blinked a few times, trying to focus on her surroundings.

"Have you taken something Chloe?" Andy asked her, his brow furrowing in concern.

"I don't know how I got here." she whispered.

"Where am I?" she continued.

"Aden Park." he said, frowning slightly as he placed his hands on her brow and noticed that she was running warm. Chloe gasped in shock, the realisation finally dawning on her as she gazed around and realised that she was back on her bench. Back at the place where everything had begun, all those months ago. She frowned in confusion, not entirely sure why, whenever she felt at her lowest, she always felt an overwhelming desire to return to the bench that she'd once called home.

"I have to get home." Chloe stated, slowly standing up, quickly sitting back down again and grasping the handrail when her head began to spin. She gazed down at her bump, her stomach churning with guilt when she realised that she'd accidentally risked their life of her baby. Freyja was one of the most precious things in her life and she knew that she couldn't live without her. Her eyes misted with tears as she stared at her bump, gently resting her shaking hands on it, sighing to herself when she realised that she wasn't even wearing a jacket.

"Do you want me to call someone for you?" Andy offered. Chloe nodded, bursting into tears when she suddenly remembered that she didn't have her phone on her.

"What's going on Chloe?" he asked, an edge of concern present in his voice.

"I don't know, I feel really weird." she admitted, blinking slowly as she tried to focus on her surroundings.

"Have you been drinking or something?" he asked.

"No, of course not." she said quickly.

"It's the anniversary of your Dad's death tomorrow isn't it." he said quietly, almost like he was talking to himself.

"How do you know that?" she asked, frowning to herself.

"I haven't told anyone that." she continued.

"I was in your life when it happened remember." he said quietly, frowning when she gazed at him, almost like she was staring through him. In all the years that he'd known Chloe, he'd never seen her so vacant, almost like she was having an out of body experience.

"I'm surprised you remembered." she mumbled, slowly wiping the tears from her cheeks. She glanced down at her neck, sighing quietly to herself when she was reminded once again that she was no longer in possession of her parent's wedding rings. Barely a day passed when she didn't think of her parents and how gutted she was that they would never meet her daughter. As she slowly raised her head, she frowned to herself when she suddenly realised that Andy had disappeared. She gazed around the park, trying to figure out where he had gone or whether he was merely a figment of her imagination. Chloe sighed deeply to herself, tears rolling freely down her cheeks as she thought about what to do. Her brain was so foggy that she couldn't think clearly, and every time that she stood up she would feel too dizzy and lightheaded to stand.

"I'm so sorry Freyja." she whispered, laying back down on her bench and wrapping her arms across her bump, trying to keep herself and her baby warm. She closed her eyes, desperately wishing that she was back home in the warm, rather than shivering on a park bench, like she used too.

"Chloe?" she heard a voice whisper through the darkness.

"Go away." she mumbled, not even daring to hope that she wasn't imagining the voice that was calling to her.

"Chloe, open your eyes." the voice tried again. Chloe sighed to herself as she slowly opened her eyes, frowning as she laid eyes on Danny.

"What are you doing here?" she asked softly, trying to focus on his features that were out of focus.

"Looking for you, everyone is really worried about you. Lee has everyone out searching." he explained.

"Why?" she asked, rubbing her sore head as she slowly sat up.

"Nathan said you've been missing for a couple of hours." he told her. Chloe frowned at his words, gasping in shock when she suddenly realised that she had no idea where all that time had gone. All she knew was that she was furious with Lee and had needed to get some fresh air, she didn't even remember the journey to the park.

"He came to my house to see if I'd seen you, so I figured I'd check the park." he continued. Chloe nodded slowly.

"Did you see Andy?" she asked him, her brain still swirling with confusion.

"Who?" he frowned.

"Never mind." she replied, slowly standing up, quickly grasping the handrail of the bench when she began to wobble.

"Are you alright?" he asked, quickly placing his hand on her arm to steady her.

"I feel weird." she admitted. He pulled her body against him, slightly concerned that she would fall and injure herself or the baby.

"You're freezing Chloe." he pointed out, staring down at her sympathetically.

"We need to get you home as soon as possible." he continued, watching closely as she leant against him, struggling to keep her eyes open. She nodded slowly, jumping slightly when he carefully picked her up.

"I think I can walk you know." she mumbled sleepily.

"I don't think you can." he insisted, glancing down at her as she wrapped her arms around his neck and rested her head against his shoulder. He gasped as her cold hands made contact with his skin.

"You're probably hypothermic." he said thoughtfully as he quickly carried Chloe home, hurrying to get her warm as quickly as possible.

"I just hope the baby is okay." she muttered, sniffing quietly to herself.

Chapter Fifty Eight

Chloe glanced up at Danny, smiling at him as he gazed down at her as they waited for someone to answer Lee's front door. Danny shot Kirstie a small smile as she opened the door, breathing a sigh of relief when she noticed Chloe safely in his arms. He quickly stepped into the house and walked into the living room, carefully placing Chloe onto the sofa. As soon as she was on the sofa, Chloe curled into a ball, desperately trying to keep warm. She glanced up at Louise as she perched beside her on the sofa, gazing down at her in concern when she noticed Chloe shaking uncontrollably.

"Where have you been Chloe?" Louise asked, gently pulling the throw over Chloe's frame. She remained silent, pulling her arms over her chest and blowing onto her hands.

"I'll give Lee a call." Kirstie announced, quickly leaving the room.

"You look freezing Chloe." Louise said sympathetically, her heart breaking a little for her best friend as she watched her whole body trembling. Chloe nodded slowly, her teeth chattering. The two of them jumped as the front door quickly opened.

"Any news?!" Nathan called as he stepped over the threshold. Louise opened her mouth to answer, quickly closing it again when Nathan walked into the room, his gaze flickering to Chloe who was still curled up on the sofa.

"Danny brought her back a few minutes ago." Louise told him, smiling at Danny as she glanced at him and saw that he was lighting the fire to try and warm Chloe.

"I'll make you a hot water bottle." Louise stated, quickly standing up and leaving the room. Chloe glanced up at Nathan as he sat beside her on the sofa, his brow furrowing in concern as he watched her closely.

"What happened Chlo Bo?" he whispered softly.

"I don't know." she whispered back, her teeth still chattering.

"Come here." he said quietly, slowly opening his arm to her and watching her closely as she shuffled over to him and curled up in his arms, desperately seeking some warmth. Nathan gasped when he felt Chloe's hands against him and he suddenly realised how cold she was.

"I'm so cold." she whispered, her whole body trembling against him. Nathan sighed deeply, quickly grasping the throw and pulling it over the two of them.

"What were you doing out in the cold?" he asked softly, his heart breaking a little when he noticed her eyes filling with tears.

"I don't know, I don't remember." she admitted, still not entirely sure how she had ended up at the park.

"I don't feel right." she continued, closing her eyes tightly as she tried to stop the room from spinning.

"What are you talking about?" he asked, his brow furrowing in concern.

"You were pretty out of it when I found you." Danny piped up, from his position on the floor. The three of them jumped as the front door opened, banging against the wall loudly. Chloe glanced at Nathan nervously as she heard the front door slam closed. Her stomach churned as Lee walked into the room, his intense gaze fixed on her, his jaw set in anger. Lee placed his hands on the back of the sofa, taking deep breaths to try and control the anger that he was feeling. As soon as Kirstie had called, he'd felt an intense wave of relief that Chloe was safe, but that was soon replaced with anger. He couldn't help but feel a deep sense of frustration, that she'd wandered off in the dark, without telling anyone where she was going, putting both her and their baby at risk of harm.

"Where the hell have you been?!" he hissed, when he could no longer control his temper.

"I just went for a walk to clear my head." Chloe said quietly, not quite able to bring herself to look him in the eye. Despite the fact that she was still angry with him for humiliating her in front of her friends, she knew that her actions were wrong. Even though she'd only intended to go for a short walk along the street, she'd somehow ended up at the park. Her eyes filled with tears as she thought about the baby she was carrying and how she would never forgive herself for accidentally endangering her daughter.

"In the dark!" Lee exclaimed, his temper still flaring.

"Here you go Chloe." Louise smiled as she walked back into the room and handed Chloe a hot water bottle. Chloe smiled her thanks, quickly placing it on her lap. Louise glanced between Chloe and Lee, squirming slightly when she picked up on the awkward atmosphere.

"Are you cold?" Lee asked, a note of sarcasm in his voice. Chloe nodded slowly, still not able to bring herself to make eye contact with him.

"Well that's what you get for going out late at night, without even wearing a jacket!" he said angrily.

"You could have at least taken your phone, or even bloody told someone where you were going!" he continued ranting.

"I'm sorry okay." she mumbled, her stomach churning with guilt as she thought about her actions.

"Where did you even find her?" Lee rounded on Danny.

"After Nathan came to see me and told me what had happened, I went to check the park." Danny answered.

"She was on her bench." he continued.

"You went to Aden fucking park?!" Lee shouted, causing everyone to jump. Chloe opened her mouth to respond, quickly closing it again when Lee cut her off.

"This is a joke, you know how dangerous that place is, you almost died the last time!" he continued.

"I didn't mean too I kind of ended up there." Chloe admitted, beginning to panic slightly when she realised how angry Lee was with her.

"The even worse part is that you put the baby at risk too. You're carrying precious cargo, you have to be more careful!" Lee exclaimed angrily. Chloe nodded slowly, quickly wiping away the tears that were flowing freely down her cheeks.

"I think maybe you should back off." Nathan warned, when he realised how upset Chloe was by the whole situation.

"This has nothing to do with you." Lee snapped, his eyes darkening as he glanced at Nathan.

"Just go upstairs and cool off, before you upset her even more." Nathan told him firmly. Lee stared at Chloe who was silently picking her fingernails nervously, not even looking him in the eye. He shook his head, still not quite able to comprehend that she could be so reckless. Chloe glanced up as she watched Lee walking away from her, quickly striding upstairs. She jumped slightly when she heard the bedroom door slam shut. As soon as Lee left the room, Chloe turned to face Nathan, wrapping her arms around his neck and snuggling against him, seeking warmth as well as comfort.

"I really didn't mean for this to happen." she sobbed against his chest, no longer able to hold back the emotions that she'd been fighting.

"I know Chlo Bo." he whispered, placing a soft kiss on her forehead.

"I don't even remember how I got to the park, it was like an out of body experience. I remember leaving the house and the next thing I knew, I woke up on my bench." she rambled, beginning to panic slightly at the thought that it would happen again.

"It's instinct that's why." Danny piped up. Chloe lifted her head to gaze at him, raising her eyebrow at him as she waited for him to continue.

"Whenever something happens that I am struggling to process or when I need a time out from something, I find myself wanting to return to my bench." he explained.

"We still see it as home." he added thoughtfully.

"Everything was so much simpler when we lived there." she agreed.

"And we had each other's backs didn't we." he grinned, trying to cheer her up. Chloe nodded slowly, quickly wiping away the last of her tears.

"You shouldn't go there in the dark though, you know first-hand how dangerous that place is." Danny told her gently.

"I know." she sighed.

"If you ever need to go there to clear your head, I can take you so that you're not alone." Danny offered.

"In the daytime though." he added, smiling slightly. Chloe nodded, smiling slightly when he grinned at her.

"Thank you for bringing me home." she said quietly, watching him closely as he slowly stood up.

"No problem. I should probably head back though." he told her.

"I'll call you tomorrow." he added, before quickly walking away.

"Maybe we should get you checked out Chloe, you're quite pale." Louise piped up.

"I'm fine." Chloe said, gently massaging her sore temples.

"Have you got a sore head?" she asked. Chloe nodded, sighing deeply to herself.

"Do you want me to get you a paracetamol?" Louise offered.

"No it's okay, I don't want to risk the baby." she replied.

"Even though I already did that." she continued, her eyes misting with tears.

"I think I have a migraine pen thing in my bag." Louise stated, quickly standing up and hurrying upstairs. As soon as Louise left the room, Chloe curled into a ball against Nathan, crying quietly to herself. In all the years that she'd been alive, she couldn't remember a time when she'd ever been so disappointed in her behaviour. She knew how privileged she was to be having a baby, and she couldn't help but feel that she'd reneged on her responsibilities.

"Lee's right." she whispered.

"What?" Nathan asked softly.

"I'm going to be such a shit Mum." she sobbed, curling the material of his shirt into her fist as she fought the anger that she was feeling with herself.

"He didn't say that." he pointed out.

"He didn't need too, it was pretty obvious that he was thinking it." she said, sighing sadly to herself.

"I need to be punished." she mumbled thoughtfully, almost like she was talking to herself. Nathan opened his mouth to respond, quickly closing it when Louise returned, quickly handing Chloe the migraine pen.

"Thanks." Chloe mumbled as she quickly applied it.

"I think I'm going to head to bed, since it's pretty late." Louise told them.

"Will you be alright Chloe?" she added.

"Yes, I'll be fine." she replied, smiling falsely.

"I'll stay with her." Nathan reassured her.

"Did you just say that you need to be punished?" he rounded on Chloe as soon as they were alone.

"No." she said quickly.

"Yes you did." he insisted.

"I'm ugly and apparently sex with me is bad and I'm a shit mother that can't even keep my baby safe when she is inside me, let alone when she is born." she said sadly. Nathan sighed deeply, wrapping his arms around her and holding her tightly against him, not entirely sure what to say to comfort her.

"As soon as the baby is born, I'm going back to my bench." she said thoughtfully.

"For a visit with Danny?" he asked, quickly wiping away her tears with his thumb.

"No, to live." she stated, matter of factly.

"Lee can raise the baby, she'll have a life of luxury and she'll be safe with him. Then I can go back to where I belong." she continued.

"What's brought all of this on?" he asked, frowning in confusion.

"I'm just done Nathan." she whispered, still not able to stop herself from crying softly to herself. He sighed deeply, quickly realising that she didn't know what she was saying.

"Close your eyes Chlo Bo, you need to get some sleep." he said softly.

Chapter Fifty Nine

Chloe jumped, her eyes flickering open as she heard a sound from the hallway. Her stomach plummeted as she gazed into the faint moonlight that was streaming in the window, and locked eyes with Lee.

"Sorry, did I wake you?" he asked quietly, sighing to himself when Chloe nodded slowly. She slowly sat up, gently rubbing the sleep out of her eyes.

"I forgot about the squeaky floor board." he said, a small smile playing on the corner of his lips as he hovered awkwardly.

"What are you doing down here?" she asked, nervously.

"I came to see you." he told her.

"If you've come to make me feel guilty, don't bother, nothing you can say will make me feel any worse than I already do." she stated, her eyes brimming with tears.

"I came to check on you, because you haven't come to bed." he said quietly, watching Chloe closely as she stood up and walked into the kitchen. He sighed deeply to himself as he followed her. Even though he knew that her actions had been wrong, he couldn't help but feel slightly guilty that it was his comments that had caused her to leave the house in the first place. Anyone that knew Chloe, knew that she had always been insecure about the way that she looked and he couldn't help but feel that he'd accidentally opened an old wound for her.

Chloe glanced up at Lee, quickly turning away from him and hanging her head in shame. She tapped her fingernail against the kitchen counter as she waited for the kettle to boil, squirming slightly as she felt Lee's watchful gaze burning a hole in the back of her head.

"Have you warmed up now?" he asked tentatively.

"Yep." she said shortly, quickly wiping away the tears that were rolling down her cheeks. She couldn't even bring herself to look at him, her brain completely scrambled with a mixture of anger, sadness and guilt at what she'd done. Her hands shook as she slowly poured the boiling water into her mug, carefully placing the tea bag inside. She closed her eyes slowly, taking deep breaths as she felt the room beginning to spin again. Lee frowned at her when he noticed her slowly turn, grasping the kitchen counter as she wobbled slightly.

"Chlo?" he frowned, as he took a step towards her. She slowly opened her eyes, frowning when she realised that Lee was only a few feet from her, yet his voice appeared distant, almost like it was calling to her from the darkness.

"I'm fine." she said quickly, the words echoing around her head.

"I think we need to talk Chlo." he said gently, reaching out to stroke her cheek, frowning to himself when she recoiled from his touch.

"Not at this time of night we don't." she said firmly, not really in the mood to talk to him, especially in the early hours of the morning. She ran her hand through her hair, blinking quickly as she tried to focus on her blurred surroundings. She gasped, watching as she dropped the cup, her gaze fixed on it as it fell in slow motion, before clattering onto the stone floor. Chloe fell to her knees, the last of her strength that she was using to hold herself up, finally waning.

"Chloe, what's going on?" he asked worriedly, his stomach churning in fear as he watched her sitting on the floor, gazing in silence at the broken fragments.

"I don't know." she mumbled, almost like she was talking to herself. He stared at her, watching closely as she buried her head in her hands and began to sob uncontrollably.

"I gave you everything." she cried, her breath coming out in loud sobs.

"I'm sorry that I'm not good enough for you." she continued, continuing to sob as she slowly picked up the fragments. He stared at her, not entirely sure how to respond to her words. In all the years that he'd known Chloe, he'd never seen her acting in this way. Her expression was distant and vacant and she seemed to have no idea what she was saying or doing.

"Chloe stop." he whispered, quickly kneeling down beside her, his stomach churning with guilt when he suddenly realised how much he had managed to upset her.

"And I'm not good enough for Freyja either." she mumbled to herself, no longer having the energy to sob. Lee sighed deeply, gently placing his hand on her leg, trying to provide her with some comfort. He jumped as she quickly moved away from his touch.

"Don't touch me." she told him sternly.

"Go back to bed, I'm fine." she whispered, trying to convince herself as much as him. Even though she had no idea what was happening to her or why she was unable to think clearly or focus on her surroundings, all she knew was that she wanted to be as far away from Lee as possible. To face the fear that she was feeling, without him gazing at her. She stared down at the china fragment in her hand and curled it into her fist, suddenly feeling the need to grasp something. She stared numbly at her hand, watching the droplets of blood drip onto the floor.

"Chlo!" Lee cried, when he suddenly noticed that she was bleeding.

"Here, give me that." he said quietly, gently uncurling her fingers and removing the fragment from her grip. She stared at the ground in numb silence, not even reacting when Lee picked up a cloth and gently wiped away the blood, sighing quietly to himself as her hand continued to bleed. He placed the cloth over the wound, carefully applying pressure. His eyes were fixed on her as he placed a soft kiss on her fingers.

"Please can you just leave me alone." she whispered, her voice breaking slightly.

"I'm worried about you." he mumbled, his stomach churning nervously as he watched her.

"I'm fine." she whispered, closing her eyes when she felt the room beginning to spin. Her eyes snapped open as she felt herself slowly becoming warm. She placed her hand on the collar of her hoodie, pulling the material away from her skin, to try and cool down. She took deep breaths as she gradually felt herself becoming hotter and hotter. Lee glanced at her as she quickly pulled her hand away from him and removed her hoodie, desperately trying to find a way to cool down. His breath caught in his throat as he stared at the purple lace baby doll nightgown that she was wearing. It seemed like so long ago that she'd told him she had a surprise for him later on that evening. He stared at her perfect body, not quite able to tear his eyes away, completely mesmerized by her beauty once again.

"I believe this is yours anyway." she said, snapping him out of his thoughts as she flung the hoodie towards him.

"You're so beautiful." he breathed, still not able to tear his eyes away from her.

"Don't you dare." she warned him, her tone slightly menacing.

"I thought having sex with me is horrible." she added, a note of bitterness present in her voice. She shook her head angrily, quickly placing her hand on the kitchen counter and slowly pulling herself to her feet.

She glanced down at herself, her cheeks colouring when she suddenly realised that she was still wearing the nightgown that she'd been planning to surprise him with. As she glanced back up at Lee, sighing deeply to herself when she realised that his eyes were still fixed on her, she felt the room beginning to spin uncontrollably. Her vision blurred, before the room was plunged into darkness.

Chapter Sixty

Lee watched in horror as Chloe stood for a moment, wobbling slightly before she collapsed in a crumpled heap on the floor. His heart pounded against his chest as he suddenly felt rigid with fear, not entirely sure what to do to help her. He gently placed his hand on her cheek, softly stroking her skin with his fingertips.

"Chlo?" he whispered nervously, glancing at her chest for a moment as he watched it rising and falling slowly.

"Chloe, please wake up." he pleaded, time seeming to stretch for an eternity as he gazed at her, his hands shaking in fear. He breathed a deep sigh of relief as her eyelids fluttered open and she frowned in confusion at him. She blinked slowly, trying to focus on her surroundings, a look of realisation dawning on her features when she locked eyes with Lee.

"What happened?" she whispered, raising her head slightly, gently pressing her hand against her forehead when she felt her head pounding painfully.

"I think you passed out." he whispered back, his heart still pounding against his chest as he watched her closely, still not able to escape the fear that he was feeling that something was seriously wrong with her. He knew that he would never be strong enough to lose her. He was snapped out of his thoughts when Chloe slowly sat up, taking care not to lose her balance.

"Slowly Chlo." he said, quickly reaching out to hold her elbows to steady her. She sighed to herself as she rested the side of her head against the kitchen cupboard, closing her eyes as she tried to stop her vision from spinning.

"I think we need to get you checked out Chlo." he muttered, gently stroking her hair, his stomach churning with guilt that he hadn't realised that she wasn't feeling well until this moment.

"I'll be okay." she replied, slowly opening her eyes and gazing down at her lap. Her cheeks coloured as she stared down at herself and suddenly realised that she was still wearing the baby-doll nightgown that Louise had purchased for her.

"I need to go and put some clothes on." she muttered, her hand gripping tightly onto the kitchen counter as she tentatively pulled herself to her feet, taking care not to lose her balance. The last thing that she wanted was to do anything to harm her baby girl, especially when she meant the world to her.

"Maybe you should just put my hoodie back on." he suggested, quickly standing up and reaching out to steady her when she wobbled slightly. Chloe glanced down at his hands that were still in place on her hips, sighing quietly to herself. Even though she was still furious with Lee for his comments, she didn't quite have the energy to argue with him, particularly when she was afraid to be alone as she had no idea what was happening to her.

"I don't want to wear it." she muttered, her stomach churning with anger at the thought of wearing his clothes after what he'd said about her. She couldn't even bring herself to be in his presence, let alone wearing his clothes. Her eyes misted with tears as she gazed down at herself, Lee's eyes burning into her as he stared at her, not quite able to tear his eyes away from her. Despite the fact that he was worried for her wellbeing, he couldn't help but admire how beautiful she looked, her flawless figure perfectly highlighted by her leggings and the silk, lace nightgown that she was wearing.

"You can stop staring at me now." she said shortly, as she angrily pushed herself away from the counter and slowly began to walk towards the stairs, taking her time as she felt the room spinning.

"I can't help it." he admitted, a small smile playing on the corner of his lips. He watched her proudly as she slowly walked towards the stairs, a determined expression on her pretty features. No matter how hard her tried, he couldn't escape the feeling that something was wrong with her.

"Don't go there." she warned him, not even turning to face him. Lee sighed as he crossed the room and stood beside her, watching closely in case she somehow lost her balance or fainted once again.

"I still think we need to get you checked out." he insisted, starting to become slightly frustrated with her.

"I said I'm fine!" she snapped.

"Yeah sure you are." he snapped back, as he quickly reached out to steady her when she wobbled.

"Get off me!" she exclaimed, quickly pulling her wrist out of his grip.

"I'm just trying to help Chlo." he muttered sadly.

"Well, I don't need your help." she said quietly, continuing to climb the stairs, her hand holding tightly onto the banister.

As soon as she reached their bedroom, she rummaged in the drawer and quickly pulled out one of her hoodies, staggering slightly as she pulled it over her head, sighing in relief now that she was covered up. She perched on the end of their bed, staring down at her hands as she tried to focus her vision. She jumped when Lee squatted in front of her and gently placed his hands on hers, staring up at her, his brow furrowed in concern.

"Please let me take you to the hospital Chlo." he pleaded with her, his heart breaking a little when he noticed how pale she was.

"I just need to sleep it off." she insisted, slowly standing up. Lee sighed as she walked away from him and wandered into the bathroom. He ran his hand through his hair in frustration, as he heard her vomiting into the toilet. Before he could stop himself he leant against the bathroom door frame, watching her closely.

"Chlo." he muttered, sighing sadly when she carefully sat back, tucking her legs underneath herself.

"Nathan can take me to the doctors in the morning if I'm no better." she said quietly, before quickly vomiting into the toilet once again.

"You don't need Nathan, I'll take you." he said firmly, trying to suppress the anger that was slowly building in his chest. She remained silent, not quite able to summon the energy to argue with him. Chloe placed her hands on either side of the toilet and slowly pushed herself to her feet, carefully trying not to lose her balance.

"At least if you won't get checked over, you need to come to bed and rest." he suggested, watching her as she squeezed past him and walked into the bedroom.

"Don't worry, I am going to rest." she said shortly, glaring at him from across the room.

"Come to bed then." he prompted.

"I'm going to sleep downstairs." she stated, walking away from him.

"But I want to keep an eye on you." he protested, not quite able to bring himself to leave her side when something was clearly wrong with her. Chloe shrugged, sighing deeply to herself as she walked into the hallway, turning to face Lee when she noticed that he was following her.

"Stop keep smothering me!" she exclaimed, finally reaching the end of her tether with his constant fussing.

"I'm not smothering you, I'm really worried about you!" he snapped.

"And the baby." he quickly added. Chloe scoffed and shook her head slowly, the frustration that she was feeling finally boiling over.

"Please let me take you to the hospital Chlo." he pleaded, desperately trying to convince her to agree.

"I already told you, I'm fine." she said angrily.

"For god sake Chloe!" he exclaimed, his temper finally snapping.

"Do you actually give a shit about our baby?!" he cried angrily. Chloe froze in shock, gripping onto the banister as she tried to process his words.

"How could you even think that?" she mumbled, not entirely sure how to respond. She couldn't understand how he could possibly think something like that about her, particularly given how protective she was of their baby. His words had cut through her, like a shard of glass ripping into her heart. Lee opened his mouth to speak, quickly closing it again when he realised that he had no idea what he was about to say. As soon as he'd noticed the flicker of hurt on her face, he knew that he'd hurt her deeply. He hadn't intended to say those words and he knew in his heart how much Chloe loved and cared for their baby, he was just so frustrated that she wasn't listening to him.

"You're such a dickhead!" she shouted, her hurt quickly turning into anger. Lee quickly reached out to grasp her arm, instinctively trying to pull her towards him when he noticed that her eyes were brimming with tears.

"Let go of me!" she exclaimed angrily, quickly pulling her arm out of his grasp. She staggered slightly, losing her balance in her haste to pull away from Lee's grasp. Chloe stepped backwards, trying to regain her balance. She felt a sickening jolt as her foot fell through the air. A small squeak of fear escaped her lips as she fell backwards, in slow motion, reaching towards the banister, her hand falling into thin air.....

Chapter Sixty One

Lee's stomach turned as he hurried to Chloe as she lay in a crumpled heap on the floor at the foot of the stairs. As soon as he reached her, he flung himself to the ground beside her, his stomach churning nervously as she swallowed and slowly sat up, shuffling over to the base of the stairs. Her gaze remained fixed on the ground as she rested the side of her head against the bottom step, biting her lip to try and control the pain that she was feeling. Lee watched her closely, numb from shock at what he'd just witnessed. He knew that for as long as he lived, that he would never forget the sight of Chloe tumbling down the stairs. His gaze flickered to her left wrist when she took it in her hand, wincing slightly as she held it tightly, trying to keep it still.

"What the hell is going on through here?!" Nathan exclaimed as he hurried into the hallway, his eyes darting between Lee and Chloe as he took in the scene.

"We have to take Chloe to hospital." Lee said firmly, trying to suppress the panic that he was feeling. He quickly stood up, taking charge of the situation to try and control the intense fear that was swirling around his stomach.

"Did she fall down the stairs or something?" Nathan asked, suddenly making the connection between the sounds that he had heard coming from the hallway. Lee nodded slowly, quickly pulling on his jacket and shoes.

"Can you drive us, so that I can keep an eye on her?" Lee asked, swallowing the dry lump that was rising in his throat.

"Yeah sure." Nathan said quietly. Chloe's eyes flickered upwards when Lee appeared in front of her, his face mere inches from hers.

"C'mon Chlo, we have to go." he told her firmly. He quickly reached out to take her hands, pulling her to her feet. She cried out in pain, pulling her wrist out of his grasp. Chloe winced as she landed roughly on the floor.

"Sorry, I didn't mean to hurt you." Lee muttered, his stomach churning with guilt as he watched her gently massaging her sore wrist.

"I think I've broken my wrist." she admitted, gritting her teeth in pain.

"It's instinct to put your hand down when you have a fall." Nathan told her, when he quickly reappeared, holding his car keys.

"I was trying to protect the baby." she whispered. Lee nodded slowly, swallowing the bile that was rising in his throat that as a result of his argument with Chloe, the two of them could lose their baby. Freyja was so precious to the two of them and he knew that neither of them would be able to cope without her in their lives. Lee hesitated for a moment before carefully scooping Chloe up and holding her carefully in his arms. She resisted him for a brief moment, before realising that she was too weak to fight against him. Lee watched her as she wrapped her arms across her chest, carefully resting her injured wrist against her arm, to try and ease the pain she was feeling.

"I'm sorry." she whispered, snuggling against his collarbone, in a vain attempt to provide herself with some comfort.

"You have nothing to apologise for Chlo." he replied, quickly walking towards the front door, shooting Nathan a small smile when he opened the door for him and allowed him to pass.

"None of this is your fault." he added, carefully placing Chloe into the back of Nathan's car. She nodded slowly, glancing up as Nathan climbed into the driving seat and quickly started the car.

"Can't you come and sit with me?" she mumbled, a note of pleading in her voice as she gazed at Nathan.

"I can sit with you Chlo." Lee piped up, trying to ignore the hurt he was feeling that she was turning to Nathan for support instead of him.

"I'll be fine, you can sit in the front with Nathan." she said quietly.

"I need to keep an eye on you." Lee argued.

"I said I'm fine." she snapped.

"Yeah that's what you said earlier." he snapped back.

"Lee, just stop arguing and get in the car." Nathan said firmly, rolling his eyes as Lee as he glared at him.

"This is wasting time, we need to get her to the hospital." Nathan pointed out. Lee nodded slowly and eventually admitted defeat, quickly climbing into the passenger seat.

Chloe's eyelids fluttered open, as she squinted in the brightness of the hospital lights. Nathan smiled as she slowly raised her head from his shoulder and locked eyes with him.

"I think they are ready for you Chlo Bo." he told her, glancing at Lee nervously when he felt him watching the two of them closely, unable to tear his eyes away from the love of his life, who was continually pushing him away and turning to another man for comfort in her time of need. Chloe tentatively stood up, quickly reaching out to hold Nathan's shoulder when she felt herself wobbling.

"Do you want me to come with you Chlo?" Lee called after her as she slowly walked towards the doctor that was waiting for her.

"No, I'll be fine." she called back, not quite able to bring herself to be in Lee's presence after his words. Even though she was desperately trying to forget about what he'd said, she couldn't bring herself to move on from it. He'd opened all of her insecurities and she couldn't help but wonder if he'd ever found her beautiful, or whether his words were merely a means to an end. She'd always known in her heart that he was so much better than her and way out of her league, but now she had the final proof. Despite months of him telling her how beautiful she was and how much making love to her was the best sex he'd ever had, he'd confirmed what she had suspected all along.....that it wasn't, and was in his words 'horrible'.

"Okay, take a seat for me please Chloe?" the doctor asked, snapping her out of her thoughts when they finally reached a small room in the hospital. Chloe perched on the end of the bed, watching the doctor as he closed the door behind himself and took a seat beside the bed.

"So, I'm Dr West." he stated, quickly introducing himself.

"I heard that you had a bad fall." he prompted her. Chloe nodded slowly, swallowing the dry lump that was rising in her throat as she was reminded once again of Freyja. She remained silent, gently placing her hand on her lap and carefully massaging her sore wrist.

"Your wrist looks very swollen." he told her, following her eyeline.

"I put my hand down to break my fall." she explained.

"Okay, I'll need to check you over." he said, watching her closely when she nodded slowly. He carefully reached out to take her wrist, gently palpating it.

"Sorry." he said quietly when she winced in pain.

"I think we're going to need to order an X-ray for your wrist." he told her, removing the stethoscope from his neck and listening to her heart.

"Your vitals seem fine." he said thoughtfully.

"What caused you to fall, have you been feeling lightheaded at all?" he continued.

"Yes, I wasn't feeling well all day. I have been lightheaded and confused. Almost like an out of body experience." she explained.

"I ended up at a park earlier and I still have no idea how I got there." she mumbled, frowning thoughtfully to herself as she racked her brain to try and remember what had happened.

"And has that happened before?" he asked, nodding slowly when Chloe shook her head.

"I have been really struggling with fatigue though." she told him.

"And how long has that been going on for?" he prompted.

"A few weeks, I just assumed it was because of the pregnancy." she said thoughtfully.

"I think we'll do a blood test as well, just to check on everything. I'll get a nurse to organise that and we can get an x-ray sorted as well." he said, smiling warmly at her.

"My baby will be okay, won't she?!" she called after him as he started to leave the room.

"We'll do an ultrasound scan to check, but I'm sure everything will be fine." he said, trying to reassure her.

"It shouldn't be too long." he smiled.

Chapter Sixty Two

Chloe sighed deeply as her eyes flickered to the window of her hospital room and she locked eyes with Lee. He shot her a small smile as he stared at her, a look of concern etched on his handsome features. Her stomach churned with guilt when she noticed the look of deep longing on his face. From just one look, she could clearly see that he was desperate to be by her side, supporting her, but was trying to respect her decision for space. Even though she knew that she was hurting him, she was still struggling to be in his presence. Whenever he was near her, she could hear his words swirling around her head. It felt like she was being repeatedly punched in the stomach, the thought that the man she loved didn't find her desirable and had spent the whole of their relationship leading her to believe that he did. Her eyes misted with tears at the thought of how exposed she now felt and how sick to her stomach at the thought of ever having to undress in front of him again.

It had cut her to the bone when he'd suggested that she didn't care about their baby, particularly after everything that they had been through last time. Her mind wandered to when she'd lost their first baby and how Lee had accused her of not caring or grieving the loss of their child. Warm tears rolled down her cheeks as she heard his words on a constant loop in her mind.

She was snapped out of her thoughts when Lee walked into the room, hovering nervously in the doorway. He sighed deeply when he saw her quickly wiping away the tears that were rolling down her cheeks.

"I need to know that you are both okay Chlo." he muttered.

"The doctor is going to give me an ultrasound when he comes back with the blood results." she said quietly, gazing down at her wrist as she massaged it, not quite able to bring herself to make eye contact with him.

"How's your wrist?" he asked, his heart still breaking that she was being so distant with him. Despite the fact that he understood why she was upset with him, he couldn't help but wish that she would allow him to comfort her. He desperately wanted to hold her in his arms, to feel her soft heartbeat against his chest. To hold the woman that he loved with all his heart. He closed his eyes for a moment, sighing to himself when he thought about how it felt to watch her falling down the stairs, almost in slow motion.

"It's broken." she muttered, snapping him out of his thoughts.

"They are going to put a cast on it." she continued, trying to keep herself talking in an attempt to avoid the awkward atmosphere. Lee nodded slowly, his eyes fixed on Chloe as he perched beside her on the bed, his eyes flickering to her hands that were still in place on her lap. He carefully placed his hand on top of hers, longing to be close to her. Chloe glanced down at her hands when she felt Lee softly stroking her fingernails. Before she could stop herself she squirmed away from his touch, gasping in pain when she quickly moved away from his touch.

"Chlo." he whispered, his heart breaking a little as she moved away from him, her face contorting in pain.

"I don't know what you want from me." she muttered, resting her head against the pillow as the room began to spin once again.

"We really need to talk." he said quietly, trying to resist the urge to touch her. He was longing to reach out and stroke her cheek.

"I think we've said everything that we need to say." she said shortly, closing her eyes for a moment. Lee sighed to himself and reluctantly tore his eyes away from her. Despite the fact that he deeply regretted arguing with Chloe and the words that she'd overheard in the pool room, he couldn't understand why she was so closed off to him that she wouldn't allow him to explain. If only she would listen to him, he knew that he could fix things. But she seemed determined to push him away, even though he was desperate to try and fix things with her.

Chloe's eyes flickered to the doorway, raising her eyebrow expectedly when Doctor West walked into the room.

"Okay, so we have your blood results back and it turns out you are very anaemic. Your levels are very low, so we are going to put you onto fluids and an Iron infusion and then we'll give you some medication to take at home for the next few months." he explained.

"What caused it?" Lee frowned, his gaze flickering between Chloe and the doctor.

"It can sometimes occur in pregnancy, but it will certainly explain why you have been so fatigued the past few weeks." he answered, shooting Chloe a small sympathetic smile. Lee sighed deeply to himself as he stared at Chloe. He shook his head slowly, mentally cursing himself that he didn't notice that she wasn't well sooner. He'd just assumed that her intense fatigue was part of her pregnancy. His stomach churned with guilt when he suddenly realised that if he'd noticed sooner that something wasn't right, he could have prevented the whole situation.

"We'll get everything set up and apply the cast, but we'd like to keep you in for twenty four hours for monitoring." he continued. Chloe opened her mouth to argue, quickly closing it again when she realised that it was her only option. Despite the fact that she couldn't stand the idea of being stuck in hospital, she knew that she had to do what was best for her baby. She swallowed the lump that was rising in her throat as she thought about the fact that it would be the first time since her father's death that she wouldn't be able to visit his grave on the day that he'd passed away. Chloe frowned to herself as her thoughts wandered to her father, images swirling around her head of a conversation with Andy that she'd had in the park.

"Is it possible with anaemia to have hallucinations?" she asked the doctor, still not entirely sure if her conversation with Andy had actually taken place or if it was a figment of her imagination.

"Potentially yes. Some patients have had hallucinations." he answered. Chloe nodded thoughtfully, her thoughts swirling as she tried to figure out whether she had imagined the conversation with Andy.

"It happened when I was at the park, but I can't figure out if it was real or not." she continued thoughtfully.

"You'll probably never know." Doctor West pointed out, carefully picking up her right hand and carefully placing a canula.

"What did you see Chlo?" Lee asked.

"Nothing much." she said quickly.

"It probably wasn't real anyway." she continued watching the doctor closely as he attached fluids to her arm and quickly administered the Iron into the fluid bag.

"You should start to feel better in a couple of hours, once the infusion takes effect." the doctor explained.

"Do you know if the baby is okay?" Lee asked, no longer able to stand not knowing if his baby girl was safe.

"I am just going to go and get the ultrasound scanner to check for you." he replied, shooting Chloe a small smile as he left the room. Chloe's eyes wandered to Lee as he sighed deeply to himself, gently resting his hands on the counter behind himself and leaning against it. His gaze flickered to her bump when Chloe fidgeted slightly and quickly pulled down the blankets and pulled up her hoodie ready for when the doctor returned. Her cheeks coloured slightly when she suddenly realised that she was still wearing the lingerie set, she quickly tucked it under the hoodie.

Lee pushed himself off the counter, no longer able to fight the intense need to keep himself busy. She frowned to herself as she watched him pacing nervously, his brow furrowed in concern. His eyes misted with tears as his thoughts wandered back to a few months ago when he'd walked into the bathroom and found Chloe on the floor, covered in her own blood, cradling their lifeless baby in her hand. He couldn't help but think about all the times that he'd seen Freyja on the ultrasound scan and heard her strong heartbeat, and felt her movement underneath his touch. She seemed so full of life, that he couldn't quite bring himself to comprehend life without her. In the same way that he couldn't imagine his life without Chloe by his side. The two of them turned to stare at the doorway as the doctor returned, the ultrasound scanner in his hand. Chloe slowly pulled her shirt up, her eyes fixed on her bump as the doctor applied some gel and gently rested the probe on her abdomen. Her gaze flickered to Lee for a brief moment when he finally stopped pacing, his eyes locked on the screen. Chloe's eyes misted with tears as the doctor carefully moved the probe around her abdomen, his eyes fixed on the screen as he searched for her baby.

"Okay, there's your baby." he muttered, smiling to himself when he finally located the baby.

"Is everything okay?" Chloe asked quickly, her heart pounding against her chest nervously.

"Yes, everything seems fine, she has a strong heartbeat." he replied. Chloe breathed a sigh of relief and finally relaxed, resting the back of her head against the pillows and gazing up at the ceiling, her eyes filling with tears of relief.

"Thank you." Lee mumbled, biting his lip to try and fight the tears that were filling his eyes. The last thing that he wanted to do was to be vulnerable in front of the doctor.

"You're very welcome." he smiled as he gently wiped the gel from Chloe's abdomen and gently pulled her hoodie back down.

"I'll go and chase up someone to apply your cast." he added, before quickly leaving the room. As soon as the doctor left the room, Chloe slowly pulled the blanket over her frame, holding it tightly against her neck as she shivered.

"I'm so relieved that Freyja is okay." Lee stated, wiping the tears of joy from his eyes as he sat on the chair beside the bed. Chloe nodded in agreement.

"I should have taken better care of you Chlo." he said thoughtfully

"Not really, I can take care of myself." she said shortly.

"You really have to stop pushing me away Chlo." he said quietly, sighing deeply to himself. Chloe rolled her eyes at him, and curled into a ball, quickly turning onto her side so that her back was facing him. She gently massaged her sore wrist, desperately trying to fight the tears that were filling her eyes. Despite the fact that she was still in a lot of pain and felt vulnerable and anxious, she wanted nothing more than to be left alone. The last thing she wanted was to have to face Lee, and be reminded of his words whenever she looked at him.

Lee's heart plummeted as he gazed at Chloe's back and heard her sniff quietly to herself. He knew that she was still angry with him, but he couldn't help but wish that she would allow him to explain, rather than constantly pushing him away. Before he could stop himself he climbed onto the bed carefully curling up behind her. Chloe jumped slightly as she felt Lee snuggling against her, his chest against her back. He placed his chin on her shoulder, gently planting the softest of kisses on her cheek.

"Why are you crying?" he whispered in her ear, softly wiping away her tears with his finger.

"No reason." she lied, not really in the mood to open up to him.

"I just need to sleep." she whispered, softly closing her eyes.

"Yeah you need to rest." he whispered in her ear, gently placing his arm around her waist and resting his hand on top of hers. She flinched and moved her hand away from his touch when he linked their fingers.

"Chlo." he muttered, his heart plummeting when she moved away from him.

"Can you just give me some space?" she asked, a note of pleading in her voice. Even though she knew that he was trying to provide her with some comfort, she couldn't quite bear his touch. Lee opened his mouth to argue, quickly closing it again when he realised that he needed to respect her wishes, particularly when he knew that it was his fault that they were in this situation. He reluctantly walked over to the door, hesitating for a moment.

"I love you Chlo." he told her. His heart sunk even further in his chest when she didn't respond to his words. He took one last longing look at her, before quickly leaving the room.

Chapter Sixty Three

"Why aren't you with Chloe?" Nathan asked Lee as soon as he walked over to him, quickly handing him a coffee.

"She wants some space." Lee said sadly, gazing in at her hospital room window, desperately wishing that he could remain by her side....always.

"Besides, she's having her cast fitted anyway." he continued, reluctantly tearing his eyes away from Chloe and turning to face Nathan when he sat opposite him.

"Are you doing okay?" Nathan asked worriedly, when he saw the sadness written on Lee's face.

"Chloe and the baby are okay, so I'm okay too." he whispered, still not entirely sure how to process how cold Chloe was being with him. She was the one person in the world that he always longed to be by her side, to cherish and protect her. His mind wandered to a few months ago when she was attacked by Shayne and how much his heart had broken when she'd continued to push him away. It had been difficult enough for him when she pushed him away as a result of fear, but this time, she was angry with him and he had no idea how to fix things.

"You don't look okay." Nathan prompted, not entirely sure what to do to help fix the situation that he knew was slowly tearing Lee apart.

"All of this is my fault." he muttered.

"She ended up in the park because of what I said about her, and she fell down the stairs because I tried to pull her close." he continued, sighing sadly to himself and running his hand through his hair in frustration.

"You didn't know that any of that would happen." Nathan countered, feeling slightly sorry for his best friend.

"No, but I should have noticed that she wasn't well. It's my responsibility to take care of her." he argued.

"And now she hates me." he continued, biting the inside of his lip in an attempt to fight the intense emotions that he was feeling.

"She doesn't hate you, she's just hurt and angry." Nathan sighed, wishing that he knew what to say to fix things for Lee and Chloe.

"She's probably still angry about what you said in the pool room." he continued.

"Yeah probably, but she won't let me explain." Lee sighed.

"What you have to remember is that she's always really struggled with her insecurities and she thinks that you said sleeping with her is horrible." Nathan explained.

"Which is complete bullshit!" Lee said quickly, his stomach churning with guilt that he'd accidentally hurt the woman that he loved.

"And it probably doesn't help that you used to criticize her all the time before the two of you got together, it's probably opened an old wound." Nathan told him, sighing sadly to himself.

"Imagine how you would feel if you thought she'd said that about you." he prompted, gazing at Lee as he nodded slowly.

"And you're a lot more confident than her." he continued.

"I'm such an idiot." Lee muttered, finally realising what he'd accidentally done.

"She's had a rough few hours, just give her some time." he added. Lee nodded, turning his attention back to Chloe. He shot her a small smile when they locked eyes through the window.

"Okay sweetie, if you can place your wrist on the pillow." her nurse Paula asked, when she placed a pillow on Chloe's lap. She quickly did as Paula asked, watching closely as she sat beside her and carefully began to manipulate her wrist. Chloe cried out in pain as Paula managed to pull the bone back into the correct position.

"That's the worst part over." Paula told her.

"Didn't you treat me when I was stabbed?" Chloe asked, trying to keep herself distracted from the pain as Paula carefully began to apply the cast to her wrist.

"Yes, I think I did." Paula said thoughtfully.

"I remember worrying that you had nowhere to live." she added. Chloe nodded slowly, her stomach churning as she remembered how it had felt when she lived at the park, to be completely alone and helpless. She sighed as her eyes flickered to the window, her cheeks colouring as she locked eyes with Lee. Chloe quickly turned away from his intense gaze, staring down at her lap.

"I see you still have that handsome boyfriend of yours." Paula beamed, smiling at Lee for a brief moment. Chloe remained silent, trying to push Lee from her mind, since she couldn't seem to bring herself to forget his words that had cut her to the quik.

"Although, I think he's maybe more than a boyfriend now though isn't he?" Paula giggled, wiggling her eyebrows playfully when she finally noticed the sapphire ring on Chloe's finger.

"Yes, he's my fiancée." she said quietly, her eyes wandering to her ring. She reached over and slowly pulled her ring off her finger, gazing down at it thoughtfully as she held it in her hand.

Lee gasped as he stared at Chloe through the window and noticed her slowly removing the engagement ring from her finger. His heart pounded against his chest as he could feel himself beginning to panic slightly that Chloe no longer wanted to be with him. He couldn't quite bear the thought of Chloe no longer being a part of his life. He'd already lost her once and he knew in his heart that he wasn't strong enough to do so again.

"It's alright sweetie, you can still wear the ring, even though you're having a cast." Paula reassured her when she realised what Chloe was doing. She nodded and slowly placed the ring back onto the finger, sighing quietly as she stared at it.

Before she could stop them, warm tears rolled down her cheeks. Despite the fact that she knew Lee and Nathan were just the other side of the window, she had never felt so alone. Like nobody understood her.

"Is everything okay?" Paula asked nervously.

"Yes." Chloe said quietly, gently wiping away her tears.

"It's just been a rough couple of days." she added, sighing quietly to herself.

"What's been going on?" Paula prompted her, sensing that she needed someone to talk too. Chloe hesitated for a moment, not entirely sure if she wanted to open up to her or not.

"Anything you say is confidential hun." Paula told her.

"We've just been arguing a bit and he said a couple of things that really hurt me." she started.

"He was probably just angry, we've all said things that we don't mean when we are angry." Paula pointed out.

"I don't think so, it was something that he never told me, I overheard him telling our friends when I thought he was asleep." she explained, swallowing the bile that was rising in her throat as she thought about Lee's words in the pool room.

"And it really hurt me. I don't know how to get over it." she continued.

"Maybe you need to talk to him about it and explain how you feel." Paula suggested.

"I can't even stand being around him." Chloe admitted, surprising herself at how easy it was for her to admit.

"I've always known that he is out of my league and now he's finally admitted it." she added.

"I literally have nothing, no home, no job and nowhere to go." she continued.

"You feel worthless?" Paula asked tentatively.

"Yes and trapped." she admitted, sighing quietly to herself.

"I'm sure he didn't intend for you to feel trapped, he's probably just trying to provide for you." Paula said.

"And the way that he looks at you, it's pretty obvious how much he adores you." she added.

"I know, but I still feel trapped." Chloe sighed.

"What you have to remember as well, is that things always feel worse when you don't feel well." Paula stated.

"And your hormones will be all over the place, which is probably adding to it." she continued.

"I guess so." Chloe said thoughtfully.

"Also it's the anniversary of my father's death today." she continued.

"Oh no, I'm so sorry sweetie." Paula said, squeezing her hand sympathetically.

"And this will be the first year since he passed away that I haven't been able to visit his grave." she explained, biting her lip to prevent herself from crying.

"Maybe your fiancée will take you to the graveyard when you are discharged from hospital." Paula said quietly.

"I haven't told him." she replied quietly.

"It's none of his business." she added, an edge of bitterness present in her voice.

"You need to be careful not to push everyone away, especially since you are pregnant. You need a lot of emotional support." Paula told her.

"And even though I hardly know you, it's quite clear that you've been through a lot. So you need a support system around you." she continued.

"I don't need anyone. I need to get my independence back." she replied firmly. Chloe eyes wandered to the window when she noticed movement out of the corner of her eye. She sighed to herself when she saw a group of fans that had clearly noticed Lee and Nathan and were chatting excitedly to them.

"Could you close the blind please?" Chloe whispered, fearful that the fans would notice her through the window. Paula nodded, quickly standing up and doing as she asked.

"Thank you." Chloe said quietly, breathing a sigh of relief that she was now out of sight of the fans.

"Do you have someone that you can speak too?" Paula asked worriedly, when she suddenly noticed the deep sadness on Chloe's beautiful features.

"Not really, nobody really understands me." Chloe sighed.

"And how insignificant I feel compared to Lee. It's like my insecurities just get the better of me sometimes." she added thoughtfully.

"That will definitely be heightened by your pregnancy." Paula told her.

"Besides you shouldn't feel insignificant compared to him, you are a very beautiful young woman." she insisted, smiling slightly when Chloe's cheeks coloured deeply. She frowned to herself as she felt an unfamiliar sensation in her lower abdomen. Her hands shook as she carefully moved the blankets, staring down at herself. A small sob escaped her lips when she noticed traces of blood on her sheets.

"Oh my god." she whispered.

"What's wrong?" Paula asked, quickly noticing that Chloe had gone rigid with fear.

"I'm bleeding." she muttered.

"You have to save my baby!" she screamed, the panic quickly beginning to set in.

Chapter Sixty Four

Paula quickly hurried around the side of the bed, following Chloe's eyeline as she quickly assessed the situation. Her complexion slowly turned pale when she noticed the fresh blood stain on the sheets.

"I can't lose her!" Chloe screamed hysterically, causing Paula to jump.

"Firstly, you have to calm down, otherwise you'll increase your blood pressure." Paula told her gently. She carefully took Chloe's hand in her own, gently squeezing it in reassurance to try and calm her down.

"I'll go and get the doctor. I need you to keep calm and still okay." Paula said firmly, staring at Chloe until she looked her in the eyes. Chloe nodded slowly, calming down slightly as Paula smiled warmly at her.

"It's probably nothing to worry about, so don't panic." she told her as she quickly left the room, hurrying to find a doctor. As soon as Paula left the room, Chloe buried her head in her hands and burst into tears, loud sobs of anguish escaping her lips as she fought to control the intense fear that she was feeling. She knew that she had to remain calm, but she couldn't suppress the fear that something was going to happen to her beautiful baby girl.

"You can't leave me Freyja." she sobbed, every moment that she waited for the doctor to return feeling like an eternity.

"I need you too much." she whispered, closing her eyes and taking deep breaths to try and suppress the panic that she was feeling. The last thing she wanted to do was to make things worse for her baby. Her eyes snapped open when the door opened and Paula returned, quickly followed by Doctor West.

"So, you've had some bleeding?" he asked Chloe. She nodded slowly.

"Okay, I'll need to examine you and then we'll give you another ultrasound." he explained.

"Examine me....down there?" Chloe asked, her cheeks colouring at the thought of it.

"Yes, I need to make sure that your cervix is still closed." he told her. Chloe nodded slowly, her eyes fixed on her hands as she placed her hand on the top of her leggings, struggling to remove them one handed.

"Would you like me to help you?" Paula offered kindly. Chloe nodded, not quite able to bring herself to look them in the eye. Her hands shook as Paula carefully removed her leggings. She couldn't help but squirm in embarrassment when she carefully removed Chloe's underwear.

"Right, I need you to bend your knees and spread your legs." Doctor West told her, shooting her a small reassuring smile. Chloe reluctantly did as he asked, her cheeks colouring even further as she sat in front of the two of them, feeling completely exposed. Even though she knew that she had to do what was right for her baby, she couldn't help but wish that she didn't have to do this.

Her cheeks coloured even further as she gazed down at the doctor as he examined her. She closed her eyes and rested the back of her head against the pillow, gazing up at the ceiling lights, trying to take her mind off what was happening.

"I forgot to ask if you want me to fetch your fiancée?" Paula piped up, clearly trying to distract Chloe. She shook her head slowly, her eyes filling with tears as she thought about him.

"His name is Lee isn't it?" she asked.

"Yes." she replied, sighing to herself when she felt the tears that had filled her eyes, slowly flowing down her cheeks.

"He's in that famous band isn't he?" Paula asked, still trying to keep Chloe talking.

"He's in Eclipse. So is Nathan." she answered.

"They are going on tour again next year." she continued, quickly realising what Paula was trying to do, but going along with it, in order to keep her blood pressure down. Chloe knew that she needed to do whatever she could to help her baby. She quickly sat up, clutching her abdomen when she felt a sudden and intense pain. Chloe curled her toes, trying to control the pain that she was feeling. Doctor West frowned at her, watching her closely as her face contorted in pain.

"Was that a contraction?" Paula asked, the colour slowly draining from her face as she turned to face the doctor.

"What?!" Chloe exclaimed, when the pain finally passed. The doctors eyes flickered to the bed when some fluid rushed out from between Chloe's legs.

"That wasn't my waters was it?!" Chloe cried, her heart pounding against her chest.

"Yep, I think it was." the doctor told her, quickly removing his gloves and flinging them into the bin.

"We need to get her some antibiotics and set up a heart monitor on the baby." he stated, quickly turning to face Paula. She nodded and hurried out of the room.

"This can't be happening." Chloe said quickly, her hands beginning to shake.

"I'm only twenty two weeks!" she exclaimed.

"Try not to panic, it's what we call early labour." the doctor told her, perching beside her on the bed and carefully rolling up her hoodie.

"I know what it is, I've read about it, but she's too young to survive being born." she pointed out.

"Take deep breaths for me, everything is going to be okay." he told her, quickly moving the probe around to search for the baby. She cried out in pain as she felt another contraction ripping through her.

"You have to stop it!" she exclaimed breathlessly.

"I can't lose her!" she continued hysterically.

Chloe's eyes snapped to the doorway as Paula quickly returned and handed the monitor to the doctor.

"You can pop the antibiotic injection into her IV line." he told Paula.

"Everything is fine on the scan, we're going to attach this monitor to your abdomen so that we can monitor any changes to your baby's heartbeat." he explained.

"I know it's scary but most premature labours stop on their own. If that's not the case then we will give you some medication to stop it." he continued.

"Just stop it now!" Chloe screamed, the frustration and panic that she was feeling finally starting to get the better of her.

"It's okay hun." Paula reassured her, gently placing her hand on Chloe's shoulder. Chloe quickly reached down and pulled her leggings back on, no longer able to stand feeling completely exposed. Chloe cried out in pain as she felt yet another, more intense contraction.

She jumped slightly, her eyes darting to the door when it opened and Nathan walked into the room, the colour slowly draining from his face as he took in the scene, quickly noticing the looks of concern on everyone's faces.

"I heard you crying out Chlo Bo." he told her, his heart breaking for her when he noticed how panicked and afraid she looked, a steady stream of tears still rolling down her cheeks.

"Nathan!" Chloe sobbed, completely breaking down as soon as she saw a familiar face.

"What's going on?" Nathan asked tentatively.

"She's going into early labour." Paula told him. Nathan's eyes widened as he stared at Chloe, swallowing the dry lump that was rising in his throat.

"I should fetch Lee." he eventually said.

"No, don't!" Chloe exclaimed quickly. She held out her hand towards Nathan, sighing in relief when he took her hand, squeezing it gently.

"He should be here Chloe." Nathan told her, placing his hand behind her head and softly stroking her hair, in an attempt to calm her down.

"All of this is his bloody fault!" she exclaimed, her blood boiling at the thought that she could lose her baby as a result of Lee's actions.

"But if the baby is coming then he should still be here." Nathan pointed out, trying to get through to her in her panicked state. Chloe nodded slowly, no longer having the energy to argue with him. She held onto his hand tightly as he tried to walk away from her.

"Please don't leave me, I'm scared." she whispered, a note of pleading in her voice.

"Would you like me to go and fetch him?" Paula offered, glancing at Chloe for a moment when she nodded slowly.

"He's probably in the canteen, he was going to get Chloe some food." Nathan told her.

"You should send someone, I'll probably need you back here." the doctor piped up. Paula nodded and quickly left the room.

"Can you sit with me?" Chloe asked Nathan. He nodded and carefully sat beside her on the bed, glancing down at her as she shuffled closer, gently resting her head against his chest. She gripped his shirt, curling the material into her fist when she felt another contraction.

"I can't believe that this is happening!" she sobbed against Nathan's chest.

"Right, we need to stop this labour." the doctor rounded on Paula as soon as she returned to the room.

"The contractions are getting more frequent and Mother and baby are getting distressed." he continued, his eyes darting to the monitor.

"I'll fetch the drugs." Paula stated, hurrying back out of the room.

"This will work won't it?" Chloe asked nervously.

"Yes it should do." he replied.

"What if it doesn't?!" she exclaimed, starting to panic once again.

"Let's not think like that." he replied, trying in vain to keep her as calm as possible.

"She won't survive though will she?!" she cried. The doctor opened his mouth to respond, quickly closing it again when the door burst open and Lee hurried into the room, his feet frozen to the spot as his eyes darted between Chloe and the doctor.

"What the hell is going on?!" he asked quickly.

"Didn't they explain?" the doctor asked.

"They said that she's in labour." he answered, his eyes flickered to Chloe as a small whimper of pain escaped her lips and she snuggled closer to Nathan.

"But it's too early isn't it?" he frowned, his mouth suddenly feeling dry.

"Yes, it's far too early, that's why we are going to stop it." he replied, smiling at Paula when she returned and handed him the medication.

"I'm going to need you to sit like you were before." the doctor told Chloe.

"You can't deliver her!" she exclaimed, glancing at Lee as he walked over to her other side.

"We're not going to deliver her, I need to put the medication into your vagina." he explained. Chloe nodded, slowly lifting her head from Nathan's chest. She could feel Lee's eyes watching her closely as she tried to remove her leggings, cursing under her breath when she realised that her hands were shaking too much.

"Don't." she warned Lee when he placed his hand on her hips, trying to help her. He quickly removed his hand, almost like he'd received an electric shock.

"I'll do it sweetie." Paula told her, quickly helping Chloe.

"Would you like me to sign your cast for you?" Nathan joked, trying to distract her from the embarrassment that he knew she was feeling. He smiled to himself when a small giggle escaped Chloe's lips.

"I'm not a groupie you know." she smiled.

"Okay, we're done." the doctor told her. Paula smiled at Chloe and carefully helped her to cover herself.

"It'll be a little while before it takes effect so you'll probably still have contractions for a while, but we'll keep the monitor on the baby." he continued.

"Stay with her and let me know of any changes." he said, turning to Paula as he left the room. Lee's stomach churned when Chloe cried out in pain, digging her fingernails into Nathan's shoulder.

"The medication isn't working!" she exclaimed, her heart pounding against her chest.

"You need to give the medication time to work." Paula reassured her.

"You feel really hot Chlo Bo." Nathan told her.

"It's because she's panicking." Paula sighed.

"We really need to keep her calm, it's not good for the baby." she added.

"Take deep breaths Chloe." Nathan told her. Chloe nodded, slowly curling into a ball and pulling the blanket over herself, holding it tightly.

"What usually calms her when she is stressed?" Paula asked, glancing between the two of them. Her eyes flickering back to Chloe when she winced, curling into a tight ball when she felt another contraction.

"I have to hold her usually." Lee piped up, sighing to himself as he watched Chloe and felt completely powerless.

"But she's angry with me." he added.

"It's worth a try though." Nathan said, quickly standing up and gesturing for Lee to take his place. Lee nodded and slowly walked around the bed. He perched beside Chloe, staring down at her as she took deep breaths, not even glancing up at him.

"Everything is okay Chlo." he whispered, placing his hand on her neck and softly stroking her cheek with his fingertips.

"The baby is going to be fine." he tried, carefully leaning forward and resting his cheek against hers, sighing to himself when she felt her warm tears against his cheek.

"No thanks to you." she muttered under her breath. Lee quickly sat back, staring down at her, his stomach churning at her words.

"How could you lie to me for so long?" she asked, finally making eye contact with him as she glared at him angrily. He sighed to himself and ran his hand through his hair in frustration when he realised that his presence wasn't calming her down, if anything he was making her worse. His eyes darted around the room, stopping when he noticed her phone on the counter. He rummaged in his pocket and pulled out a bluetooth headphone, carefully placing it into Chloe's ear. As soon as he picked up her phone, he quickly searched through it for one of her father's videos, pressing play on the first one that he found. A small sob escaped Chloe's lips when she heard her father's voice. She closed her eyes, finally calming down as she listened to him.

"I'm so sorry Dad." she muttered, feeling slightly guilty that she wasn't at his graveside.

"I love you." she whispered.

Chapter Sixty Five

Chloe sighed to herself as she sat on Lee's sofa, gently tucking her legs under her frame and glancing up at Nathan as he sat beside her. Even though she felt trapped when she was in Lee's house, she had spent the whole of the past two days that she was in hospital, desperate to get home. She placed her hand on her bump, gently massaging it, still thanking her lucky stars that Freyja was safe, and still inside of her, developing in the way that she was meant to be. Chloe glanced up as Lee walked back into the room and tentatively handed her a mug of tea. She smiled her thanks, keeping her gaze focused on her lap as he sat beside her on the sofa. Her eyes flickered to his hand as he placed it on her knee, stroking soft circles on her leg. Her stomach churned slightly under his touch as she tried to resist the urge to move away from him.

"Can I ask a favour?" she asked Nathan. He nodded slowly, raising his eyebrow at her as he waited for her to continue.

"When you go home later, could you give me a lift to the cemetery?" she asked hopefully.

"Yeah of course." he replied.

"I can take you Chlo?" Lee offered, glancing between the two of them.

"It's fine, Nathan said he'll take me." she said shortly, not even able to bring herself to make eye contact with him.

"I need to visit my Dad, since I missed the anniversary of his death." she continued, trying to keep talking to distract from the awkward atmosphere.

"Really?" Nathan frowned.

"I was in hospital wasn't I." she said quietly, shooting Lee and angry look. He frowned at her for a moment, his stomach churning when he suddenly realised what she was suggesting. Even though he knew in his heart that it was his fault that Chloe had fallen down the stairs and the two of them had almost lost their baby as a result, but never for a moment did he think that she would blame him.

"I'm happy to take you." he tried, swallowing the dry lump that was rising in his throat.

"I said no." she snapped, the anger starting to build in her stomach

"But then I could wait for you and give you a lift back." Lee pointed out, desperately trying to get her to allow him back into her life. He couldn't stand how distant and cold she was being with him. Even though she hadn't gone anywhere, he couldn't help but feel like he was slowly losing her.

"I can walk back." she argued, her blood slowly starting to boil that he was being so persistent. Lee opened his mouth to argue, quickly closing it again when Chloe cut him off.

"Stop being so possessive of me." she said angrily.

"I'm not, I just want to protect you, there's a difference." he argued, his stomach churning at the thought of something happening to her, particularly when she was still recovering from her ordeal. Even though he knew that he was being a bit unreasonable, he couldn't help but feel the fear that he'd felt on the night that she disappeared and he was terrified that something had happened to her and their baby.

"You'd better lock me in a tower then and never let me out." she said quietly, snapping him out of his thoughts.

"This isn't helping, maybe the two of you need to talk." Nathan suggested, sighing sadly to himself as he glanced between the two of them and noticed how miserable they both looked.

"What's the point?" Chloe sighed, staring down at her bump as she stroked soft circles on it.

"When are you going to stop pushing me away Chlo?" Lee said quietly, when he couldn't stand it any longer. Chloe shrugged, not entirely sure what to say.

"Why don't the two of you talk, I'll go and make some dinner." Nathan said, quickly standing up and leaving the room, before either of them could argue with him. Chloe sighed to herself, her eyes fixed on her hands as the room suddenly fell silent.

"I'm really sorry for everything Chlo." he said tentatively. She nodded slowly, remaining silent.

"I never should have said that you don't care about the baby, I was just angry and worried about the two of you." he continued, desperately hoping that Chloe would respond to him or at least acknowledge his presence.

"You're so wrong anyway." she said quickly, trying to suppress the deep anger that she felt whenever she was in his presence.

"You saw how panicked I was when she tried to come early." she added.

"I know." he whispered, his stomach churning with guilt when he was reminded how close they had come to losing their baby as a result of his actions.

"I'll never forgive myself for what happened." he said quietly, his eyes brimming with tears. Chloe glanced up at him, finally locking eyes with him as she raised her eyebrow, waiting for him to continue.

"If I hadn't tried to pull you close....." he started, his voice trailing off when it began to break. She glanced down at his hand as it moved from her leg, gently resting it against her bump. Chloe sighed as he gently stroked soft circles with his fingertips. Her heart broke a little for him when she noticed that his eyes had filled with tears.

"It was just instinct to pull you close.....I never meant for any of this to happen." he whispered. Chloe jumped slightly when he placed his hands on her hips and quickly leant forward, resting his forehead against her bump and placing a soft kiss on it.

"I'm so sorry Freyja." he mumbled, the tears that he'd been fighting spilling out of his eyes and flowing down his cheeks. Chloe sighed deeply, the deep anger that she was feeling dissipating slightly when she saw how much his heart was breaking. Before she could stop herself she placed her hand on his head, softly stroking his hair, trying to provide him with some comfort. She gasped, smiling slightly to herself when she felt Freyja fidgeting inside of her. Lee slowly lifted his head, his eyes still fixed on her bump as he quickly wiped away his tears.

"I think she's telling you that she is okay." she smiled.

"That I'm forgiven." he smiled back. Chloe nodded slowly.

"I hope you know that I would never do anything to harm her deliberately. It was an accident." he said quietly, gently placing a soft kiss on Chloe's forehead.

"I know." she muttered sadly, turning her head away from him as he leaned towards her to plant a soft kiss on her lips.

"That's not why I'm angry at you." she continued, her heart sinking once again when she thought about his words. He frowned to himself for a moment, sighing quietly when he remembered his words in the pool room. With everything that had happened, it seemed like a lifetime ago.

"It's not what you think." he told her.

"Let me guess, I didn't hear correctly." she said shortly, rolling her eyes when she realised that he was going to try and pull the wool over her eyes, rather than admit how he truly felt.

"I think you misheard what I was saying." he said quietly, glancing at Chloe when she scoffed sceptically.

"I heard enough, I know that you think sex with me is horrible." she muttered.

"You could have told me how you felt." she continued, her eyes filling with tears at the thought of the man who she had given her heart too, didn't find her attractive. She'd always feared that he would no longer find her desirable when she didn't have her 'perfect' body.

"Is it because of the pregnancy?" she asked sadly.

"Chlo stop." he whispered, his stomach churning with guilt.

"Sex with you has never been horrible." he whispered.

"I've told you before, making love with you is the best sex I've ever had, because it's meaningful." he explained.

"I've given you everything, I even gave you my first time." she muttered, wiping away the tears that were flowing down her cheeks.

"I know, and I know what an honour it is." he said quietly, sighing sadly when he noticed how upset she was.

"It means a lot to me that you've only been with me." he told her, softly stroking away her tears with his thumb.

"So why is it horrible then?" she sniffed.

"It's not, I swear." he said quickly.

"We have amazing sex." he added.

"The only time I didn't enjoy it was when it was your first time, because I hated hurting you. But you knew that because I told you at the time." he explained.

"I mean come on, that time when we pulled an all nighter. That day when you were wearing the corset, making love in the log cabin in Norway." he continued thoughtfully, smiling to himself as the memories swirled in his head. Chloe frowned at him as he picked up a cushion from the sofa and quickly placed it on his lap, smiling slightly when the two of them locked eyes.

"See, it's even turning me on just thinking about it." he admitted.

"It doesn't take much for someone to turn you on though." she sighed, still not entirely sure if she believed him or not.

"Not for you it doesn't." he smiled.

"You know how badly I want you...all of the time." he whispered, placing his hand on her neck and stroking her lips with his thumb. Chloe shook her head slowly, trying to fight the tears that were filling her eyes once again.

"Why did you say what you did then?" she asked, raising her eyebrow sceptically.

"The guys were asking me if your confidence has improved." he started.

"How did they even know about that?" she interrupted him.

"Remember a few weeks ago, when you couldn't undress in front of me at all?" he asked. She nodded slowly and remained silent, waiting for him to continue.

"I asked Kirstie and Nathan for advice. I wanted to know what I could do to help you because I couldn't stand seeing you like that, with no confidence." he explained.

"I had no idea that they would discuss it with the others." he added, sighing sadly when he noticed the steady stream of tears that were rolling down her cheeks.

"I feel so exposed." she whispered, her cheeks colouring in embarrassment.

"I did ask you not to discuss our personal business with anyone." she added, sighing quietly to herself.

"I know, I'm sorry. I just wanted to help." he sighed.

"That's what I said was horrible." he added.

"What?" she frowned.

"I said that it was horrible seeing you with no confidence." he told her.

"So you do think having sex with me is horrible?!" she exclaimed quickly.

"No, just the situation!" he said quickly.

"It's not nice seeing the person that you love, hiding all the time because you were embarrassed." he quickly explained.

"Imagine how you would feel if it was me." he prompted her.

"You knew that I had no confidence, before you decided to date me. So you knew what you were getting into." she snapped defensively.

"I know, and I still take some of the responsibility for your lack of confidence." he sighed, wishing with all his heart that she could see how beautiful she was.

"You've lied to me all this time, I bet you never even thought I was beautiful." she muttered, her brain a swirling mist of thoughts.

"Where did that come from?" he frowned.

"That's completely untrue, you're the most beautiful person I've ever met." he added quickly.

"Yeah right, I can't believe I fell for that line." she snapped, quickly standing up, glancing at Nathan as he walked back into the room. Lee opened his mouth to respond, quickly closing it again when she interrupted him.

"I need some air, can we go to the cemetery now?" Chloe asked Nathan, biting her lip to fight the tears that were filling her eyes.

"If you want too, I can bring you back here afterwards too." he replied. Lee stared at Chloe, not entirely sure what was happening. He'd thought that the conversation between the two of them had been progressing well, but now it seemed like they were suddenly back to square one. He couldn't help but feel slightly hurt that she didn't seem to believe him.

"And I'm sorry if the sex is bad....but you're the one who taught me." she snapped, before turning on her heel and walking away.

Chapter Sixty Six

"Wait up Chlo Bo!" Nathan called when he noticed Chloe quickly climbing out of his car and striding across the cemetery. He quickly locked the car and hurried after her.

"You don't have to come with me." she told him, her heart sinking like it always did when she reached her parent's grave.

"I want to make sure that you are okay." he told her, watching her closely as she dropped to her knees in front of her parent's grave. Her eyes were fixed on the headstone as she sat in silence, picking at the grass.

"I'm fine." she said shortly, quickly shutting down the conversation.

"Hey Dad." she whispered.

"I'm sorry that I haven't been to see you sooner. I hope you aren't too disappointed, but the baby decided to try and come early, and I had to make sure that she was okay." she continued, sighing quietly to herself.

"Your granddaughter that you'll never get to meet." she added, her eyes misting with tears.

"I would give anything to have you both here with me, then maybe I wouldn't feel so overwhelmed and alone." she whispered, gently wiping away the tears that were rolling down her cheeks.

"I tried to reach out to Auntie Gwen the other day, but she's still not speaking to me." she sighed.

"And I know it shouldn't bother me, but I just feel so alone." she added, clapping her hand over her mouth when a small sob escaped her lips.

"You're not alone Chlo Bo, you have so many people that love and care about you." Nathan piped up from behind her, his heart breaking a little when he suddenly realised how much she was secretly suffering. He couldn't help but wonder if the fallout with Lee was the straw that broke the camel's back and that she could no longer take any more pain and suffering in her life.

"Nobody understands me though." she argued.

"Once I have the baby, I need to get my life back on track. Get a job and move back to Nottingham." she muttered.

"What?" Nathan frowned.

"Nothing." she said quickly, squirming slightly when she realised that she'd said that aloud.

"I need to get my own independence, so that I'm not worthless anymore." she said thoughtfully, almost like she was talking to herself.

"You're not worthless." he sighed, quickly kneeling down beside her and watching her closely, a look of concern on his handsome features.

"What's brought all of this on Chlo Bo?" he asked.

"It doesn't seem like it's just your argument with Lee." he prompted, when she didn't respond.

"I've been feeling a bit trapped for a while. I have no job, barely any money and since I'm pregnant I have no prospects. I just feel completely worthless and vulnerable." she explained.

"And I feel alone, like nobody understands me. My body confidence is at an all-time low, even more so after what Lee said." she continued, staring at her hands that were resting in place on her lap.

"Didn't he explain the context of the comment?" he frowned.

"Yes, but I still think there was some truth behind his words, he's probably been lying to me this whole time." she sighed, her heart breaking at the thought of it.

"You know him better than anyone, surely you don't think that he would do that." he pointed out. Chloe shrugged, still not quite able to control the doubts that were swirling around her head.

"I've always known that he can do better than me anyway." she said thoughtfully.

"You need Lee though, he's the love of your life. You can't keep pushing him away." he pointed out.

"I'm just so done with everything." she admitted, gently placing her head on his lap and curling into a ball.

"Maybe you need to speak to someone." he added, slightly concerned for Chloe's wellbeing.

"You can't trust anyone, things always get repeated." she said matter of factly.

"I meant like a therapist or something." he suggested.

"You've been holding onto so much for so long that maybe it's starting to boil over." he added. Chloe remained silent, her eyes still fixed on the gravestone as she rested her head in Nathan's lap. She couldn't help but wish that she could be reunited with her parents, she'd have given anything to see them again.

"Why did you have to kill yourself?" she whispered, sighing sadly to herself as she thought about the possibility that if it hadn't been for his suicide, her father might still be in her life.

"I really need you." she sighed.

"But you couldn't bear life without Mum." she continued.

"He must have really loved her." Nathan piped up.

"They adored each other." she told him, a small smile playing on the corner of her lips.

"Like you and Lee." he said, smiling down at her.

"I really don't want to talk about Lee." she said quickly, desperately trying to put her walls up as a defence to the deep hurt that she was feeling. She couldn't help but feel slightly frustrated in herself that she'd fallen for lies, just like she had when she was dating Andy.

"Are you sure that a lot of this isn't your hormones being all over the place?" he asked. Chloe shrugged, quickly standing up and brushing the dirt off her trousers. As soon as her thoughts had wandered to Andy, she'd been reminded of her conversation with him in the park. She knew in her heart that she needed to know whether it had actually happened or whether it was a figment of her imagination.

"Where are you going?" Nathan asked, quickly following her as she walked back towards the car.

"I'm going to Aden Park." she told him, hoping that if she stepped foot in the park, her brain would be able to piece together the memories of exactly what did or didn't happen.

"Is that such a good idea?" he protested.

"It's broad daylight and you are with me." she pointed out, quickly climbing into Nathan's car. He shook his head slowly, still not entirely sure what had gotten into her or why she was acting so irrationally, but he knew that he needed to humour her so that he didn't cause her any further stress.

"Lee's going to kill me." he sighed as he pulled out of the cemetery.

"Don't tell him then." she replied firmly.

Nathan watched Chloe closely as she slowly walked ahead of him, gazing thoughtfully around the park. He sighed to himself when she perched on the bench that used to be her home, staring silently at the landscape.

"Why exactly are we here?" he asked as he perched beside her on the bench.

"Because I need to find something out." she said quietly, not entirely sure if she wanted to open up to him, when she knew that like everyone else, he wouldn't understand her.

"I've just realised that I had more prospects when I lived here than I do now. At least I had a job." she said thoughtfully.

"You have got to stop thinking that you are worthless. You've gained so much, Lee's house is as much yours as it is his, you're engaged and you have a baby on the way." he sighed.

"I don't want to talk about it anymore, because nobody understands anyway." she said shortly. Chloe's eyes scanned the horizon, frowning to herself when she noticed someone walking towards her. She smiled as the figure got closer and she realised that it was Megan.

"Chloe, what are you doing here?!" Megan exclaimed as soon as she noticed her.

"Just visiting." Chloe replied, smiling when Megan pulled her into a hug.

"Oh my god, you're pregnant!" Megan exclaimed, when she eventually noticed her bump. Chloe nodded slowly, smiling to herself as she thought about her beautiful baby girl.

"Is this the father?" Megan asked, glancing at Nathan for a moment.

"No, definitely not." Chloe giggled, smiling at Nathan when she noticed him squirming awkwardly.

"Anyway, how are things with you?" Chloe asked.

"Please tell me, you don't still live here?" she added.

"Yeah unfortunately." Megan sighed.

"Make sure if you come here to visit that you don't come alone, the crime rate has gone up in the park." she warned them.

"Right, we are definitely leaving." Nathan said firmly, quickly standing up.

"Not yet." Chloe said firmly.

"Did you see me here a couple of nights ago?" she asked, turning her attention back to Megan.

"No, why?" Megan frowned.

"I wasn't feeling well and had a weird out of body experience and I ended up here. I had a conversation with someone, but I don't know if it was real or not." Chloe explained.

"Who did you speak too, I could ask around?" Megan asked.

"It's okay, it was my ex." she sighed.

"Andy?!" Nathan exclaimed.

"We're here for that tosser!" he added.

"Only because I need to know if I imagined it or not." Chloe sighed, rolling her eyes at him. Megan's head snapped to the other side of the park as she heard shouting and the sound of a commotion.

"Oh great." Megan muttered.

"What is it?" Chloe asked, following her eyeline.

"It's all kicking off again." she sighed.

"C'mon." Nathan said firmly, quickly taking Chloe's elbow and pulling her to her feet.

"But..." she protested.

"I'll never forgive myself if I let anything happen to you or the baby." he said quickly. Chloe sighed in defeat and nodded when she realised that he was right.

"It was nice to see you again." she told Megan. Megan nodded, smiling at them as she watched them walking away. Nathan wrapped his arm around Chloe's waist, holding her close to ensure that she was safe.

"Chloe?" she heard a familiar voice say from behind her. Her feet froze to the spot as she slowly turned around, gasping as she stood face to face with Andy.

"Andy." Chloe breathed, glancing at Nathan when she heard him sigh deeply.

"What are you doing back here?" Andy asked.

"I came to see if I did actually speak to you that night or whether it was a hallucination." she told him.

"No, it definitely happened. You were pretty out of it though." he said quietly, glancing nervously at Nathan. He couldn't help but remember the last time that he'd seen Nathan, when Lee had turned up at his house to make him pay for what he'd done to Chloe. His head swirled with flashbacks when he remembered how Nathan had to pull Lee off him as he beat him up.

"He won't hurt you." Chloe told him, when she sensed Andy's trepidation.

"We really need to get out of here Chlo Bo." Nathan tried, glancing across the park nervously when he noticed the violence intensifying.

"Come to a cafe with us or something, I need to speak to you?" Chloe asked him. Andy hesitated for a moment, glancing at Nathan for a moment, before nodding slowly.

Chapter Sixty Seven

Andy wrapped his hands around his coffee as he sat opposite Chloe in the cafe, his eyes flickering to Nathan as he watched him nervously, not entirely sure if Nathan was going to hurt him or not. He knew how protective Lee and Nathan were of Chloe and that they had plenty of reasons to hate him.

"So why are you here to see me, I thought you hated me?" he asked Chloe, when he couldn't stand the awkward silence any longer.

"I kind of do." Chloe admitted, still not quite able to forgive him for everything that he had done to her over the years.

"I really broke your heart didn't I?" he sighed, his stomach churning with guilt as he gazed into the innocent eyes of the woman that he'd almost broken. Even though he knew it was a result of the mental health problems and gambling addiction that he had at the time, he knew that it was no excuse for his behaviour. Chloe nodded slowly, swallowing the dry lump that was rising in her throat.

"I needed you, I didn't have anyone else." she admitted, sighing quietly to herself when she remembered the moment that he'd packed his bags and left her, only for her to discover that he'd left her in debt.

"I know, I'll never be able to make that up to you." he muttered, quickly looking away from her intense gaze.

"I also ended up homeless because of the debt that you left me with." she continued, her stomach churning with anger.

"And you almost destroyed her, by spreading bullshit in the press. Just so that you could make some more money to squander on gambling!" Nathan added angrily.

"I know, I am so sorry for everything. Even though I know that I'll never be able to make it up to you." he sighed deeply.

"No you won't." she replied shortly, glaring at him over the top of her mug.

"If it makes you feel any better, I live in the same park that you used to live in." he said quietly, his cheeks colouring with embarrassment.

"Why would that make me feel better?" Chloe frowned, not quite able to process his words.

"You live in the park?" Nathan checked, not entirely sure if he trusted him or not. Andy nodded slowly, quickly looking away from their intense gazes.

"But surely you made a lot of money from selling your story?" he continued, narrowing his eyes suspiciously at him.

"I lost every penny that I have on gambling." he sighed.

"I got help for it, but it was too late, I'd already lost everything by then." he added. Chloe nodded slowly, feeling slightly sorry for Andy as he gazed in silence at the table, tracing small circles on it with his thumb. Despite the fact that she would never forgive him for what he had done to her over the years, she still sympathised with his plight. She knew better than anyone what it was like to live in the park, to be looking over your shoulder every moment of every day, and the constant fear of starvation. Even though in her head she hated him, her heart still longed to reach out to him, to provide him with the help that she'd desperately craved when she was in the same situation.

"Well that's on you. When Chloe was homeless it was because of you, but this was your fault." Nathan pointed out, an edge of bitterness present in his voice.

"Couldn't you get a job?" Chloe suggested, placing her hand on Nathan's knee to try and calm him down.

"Not so far." he sighed. Chloe sighed deeply, quickly racking her brain to try and figure out how she could help him. Despite the fact that she knew that she didn't owe him anything, her heart was too big to allow him to be left to suffer.

"I have to use the restroom." he stated, snapping her out of her thoughts as he quickly stood up and walked away.

"What are we even doing here Chlo Bo?" Nathan rounded on her as soon as Andy was out of earshot.

"Well originally I wanted to find out if I imagined the conversation I had with him in the park on the night I ended up there, but I think we've cleared that up already." she said thoughtfully.

"Now I think I might be able to find a way to help him." she continued.

"Why would you want to do that?" he frowned, still not entirely sure what had gotten into Chloe or why she was acting so strangely.

"Because I know what it feels like to be in his position." she pointed out.

"Also, it'll give me something to focus on." she added. Nathan opened his mouth to argue with her, quickly closing it again when she continued speaking.

"I think you have enough going on without taking on anyone else's problems." he sighed, wishing that he could get through to Chloe, but knowing in his heart that she was too stubborn to listen to him. When she made up her mind, there was nothing anyone could do to sway her.

"I could come and drop food off for him and Megan every day." she said thoughtfully, her eyes lighting up at the thought of being able to do something productive to help. Something that meant she could give back and give her a sense of purpose, so that she didn't feel so insignificant and worthless.

"Is this because of what you said earlier?" he asked, quickly realising that she was trying to find something to focus on, to distract herself from how miserable she was feeling.

"Which part?" she frowned.

"The feeling worthless part and being done with life." Nathan said quietly, glancing around the cafe nervously, fearful that they might be overheard.

"I just want to keep busy." she said firmly.

"But you need to sort out the root cause, plastering over a wound doesn't help it heal." he pointed out.

"No need to get philosophical." she replied, a small smile playing on the corner of her lips at his words.

"It's true though, you need to fix your own problems first, starting with patching things up with Lee." he tried again, sighing in frustration when she shook her head slowly, refusing to listen to him.

"I don't want to talk about Lee." she said shortly.

"But, I don't understand. If he's explained everything then why are you still angry with him?" he sighed, running his hand through his hair in frustration.

"Because firstly, I'm not sure if I believe him, and secondly I need to distance myself from him a little bit." she said firmly.

"What are you talking about?" he frowned, still not entirely sure what had gotten into her. In all the years that he'd known Chloe, he'd never seen her happier than when she was with Lee and he knew that the two of them made each other whole.

"For self-preservation." she said quietly, giving him the subtle hint that she was done discussing the subject. She couldn't quite bring herself to open up to him about how hurt she was by Lee's words. Nathan had been Lee's best friend for years and she couldn't help but feel concerned that her words could be repeated to Lee. Chloe didn't want him to know how exposed she now felt and how vulnerable her feelings for him made her. The slightest little thing that he did, cut her deeply and she knew that she needed to raise her barriers so that she wasn't so easily hurt by his words and actions. She needed to be stronger.

Nathan sighed at her words, wishing that he knew what to say to her to fix the situation. The two of them fell silent as Andy returned to the table, glancing between the two of them awkwardly, clearly picking up on the tense atmosphere.

"I should probably head back soon." he said quietly, glancing at Nathan for a moment when he nodded quickly.

"If you meet me outside this cafe at two pm every day, I'll bring some food for you and Megan." Chloe said quickly, glancing at Nathan when she saw him shaking his head disapprovingly.

"You don't have to do that." Andy sighed, his stomach churning with guilt once again at everything that he had done to Chloe and now in his darkest time, she was extending a helping hand.

"It's fine, it gives me something to focus on." she insisted.

"Besides I don't think your boyfriend will like it." Andy pointed out, squirming nervously at the thought of Lee's reaction.

"It's none of his business." she said, glancing at Nathan when he scoffed sceptically.

"And besides, we're not going to tell him." she said firmly, narrowing her eyes at Nathan.

"Are you serious?!" Nathan exclaimed.

"You're just going to create more problems when he inevitably finds out." he sighed.

"He doesn't own me Nathan." she said firmly, rolling her eyes.

"Besides, I'll take precautions, I won't go to the park, that's why I said to meet here." she continued.

"You shouldn't meet him alone either, I don't trust him." Nathan said firmly.

"I am sitting right here you know." Andy sighed.

"I know, I wish that you weren't." Nathan replied, narrowing his eyes at Andy, giving him the silent warning that if he messed with Chloe, he would have him to answer too.

"Also if you tell Lee, I will never forgive you." Chloe stated, rounding on Nathan. He nodded slowly, sighing deeply to himself that he was now embroiled in a situation that he knew wasn't going to end well.

"Right, I'll see you tomorrow." she told Andy, before quickly standing up and walking away.

Chapter Sixty Eight

"Hey." Nathan smiled at Lee as he walked into the gym, sitting opposite Lee as he watched him working out. Lee shot him a small smile, before turning his attention back to the weights that he was lifting, in a desperate attempt to keep himself distracted.

"What's going on?" Nathan asked, realising instantly that something was wrong. Lee shook his head slowly, not really in the mood to talk about his life that he couldn't help but fear was slowly unravelling before his eyes.

C'mon Lee, what is it?" Nathan tried again, sighing to himself when Lee remained silent, pretending that he hadn't heard his words.

"Where's Chlo Bo?" he tried, frowning to himself when he suddenly realised that he hadn't seen Chloe on his way through the house.

"Out with Danny." he muttered, sighing deeply to himself. Nathan frowned when Lee carefully set down the weights and picked up a towel, wrapping it around his neck.

"Same place she always is." he said quietly.

"Huh?" Nathan frowned, still not entirely sure that he was following the conversation.

"I've barely seen her the past few days. She spends most of the time in bed." he told him.

"Really?" Nathan asked.

"Other than when Danny arrives at the same time every day and the two of them go out for a walk." he continued, sighing sadly to himself as he thought about how much he missed Chloe. How he desperately wished that he could hold her as she slept or that she would even be in the same room with him for longer than a few minutes.

"Maybe she's still exhausted from being in the hospital." Nathan suggested, his heart breaking a little when he suddenly realised how much his best friend was hurting.

"No, she's avoiding me." he answered, placing his back against the wall and slowly sliding down it.

"Maybe you should talk to her." Nathan sighed.

"I've tried!" Lee exclaimed.

"She won't listen to me, she's distant and cold with me. She barely even acknowledges my existence." he continued thoughtfully.

"I get what I did was wrong, but I have apologised and explained myself. I don't know what else to do." he muttered, placing his head into his hands, digging his fingernails into his scalp in frustration.

"Perhaps it's partly her hormones." Nathan sighed, not entirely sure what to say for the best.

"Maybe she just wants to be left alone." he added.

"But yet she can go out with Danny every afternoon." Lee pointed out, slowly lifting his head to stare at Nathan, who quickly looked away from his intense gaze, squirming slightly.

"I feel like I'm slowly losing her." he whispered.

"And I don't know what to do about it." he continued, rambling slightly.

"I don't think there's anything you can do. You just have to be there for her and hope that whatever it is, she comes back to you eventually. Nathan sighed.

"That's easier said than done though, when she means the world to me." Lee pointed out.

"I still think she should speak to someone." Nathan said thoughtfully. Lee frowned at him for a moment, raising his eyebrow as he waited for him to continue.

"I'm just worried about her." Nathan said quietly, choosing not to mention all of the things that Chloe had said to him on the day that they went to the cemetery. He couldn't help but feel a deep sense of fear that Chloe was slowly unravelling, the effects of her traumatic life finally catching up on her.

"Me too." Lee admitted, sighing sadly to himself.

"Anyway, I need to shower." Lee said, quickly standing up, before Nathan could notice the tears that were filling his eyes.

"You can make yourself comfortable in the living room, I won't be long." Lee said, quickly walking away.

Nathan sighed sadly to himself as he walked into the living room and perched on the sofa, his brain swirling with a mist of thoughts. He couldn't help but wish that he could snap his fingers and everything between Chloe and Lee would be fixed, the two of them would be happy and full of excitement at their engagement and the fact that would soon get to meet their baby. His head snapped up as the front door opened and closed, the sound of Chloe's laughter filling the hallway. She walked into the living room, closely followed by Danny, her feet freezing to the spot when she noticed Nathan perched on the sofa. He frowned in confusion when he gazed at her and noticed that she was wearing tight trousers and a fitted tank top. Nathan couldn't understand why she was wearing something so fitted, when her confidence was at an all-time low.

"What are you doing here?" Chloe asked Nathan as she sat on the sofa, positioning herself in the corner, tucking her legs onto the sofa. She glanced at Danny, shooting him a small smile when he sat beside her.

"I came to check on you and Lee." Nathan replied.

"How are you doing?" he added.

"Fine." she said quietly, glancing at the stairs nervously when she heard movement upstairs.

"Are you still doing food drop offs?" he asked.

"Yes." she said quietly, rolling her eyes when she heard him sigh deeply.

"It's harmless though isn't it." she said shortly.

"And I've been going with her, so that she isn't alone." Danny piped up, smiling warmly at Nathan.

"I just don't trust that ex-boyfriend of yours." Nathan said quickly.

"I know, neither do I." Chloe agreed. She squirmed uncomfortably in her seat when she heard Lee's footsteps, slowly making their way downstairs.

"I knew I should have gone straight upstairs." she muttered under her breath.

Before Lee could walk into the living room, Chloe quickly stood up and hurried into the kitchen.

"Hey Danny, how's it going?" Lee asked as soon as he walked into the room.

"All good." Danny replied, smiling at Lee as he placed his elbows on the back of the sofa and leant on it.

"I think Chloe is in the kitchen if you're looking for her." he told him. Lee shrugged, not quite able to bring himself to go searching for her when he knew that she wouldn't want him around anyway. His eyes flickered to the doorway when she walked back into the room, his eyes widening when he gazed longingly at her figure. He quickly averted his eyes before he was unable to stop himself from staring at her. Chloe's cheeks coloured under Lee's intense gaze. She quickly walked over to the radiator and pulled off her hoodie, before quickly pulling it over her head, suddenly feeling self-conscious now that Lee was in the room. She returned to the corner of the sofa, snuggling against the cushions, smiling back at Danny when he shot her a small smile. Lee gazed at the back of her head, a small smile playing on the corner of her lips when he noticed that her hair was shimmering under the living room lights. Before he could stop himself he placed his hand underneath her hair, gently stroking her neck with his fingertips, cherishing the feel of her soft, warm skin under his touch.

"You look so beautiful Chlo." he whispered, his voice breaking slightly. She remained silent, not entirely sure how to respond to his words. Despite the instinct that she felt to move away from his touch, she couldn't quite bring herself to humiliate him in front of their friends.

"How's your wrist?" he asked, his eyes flickering to her cast as he softly rested his chin on her shoulder, cherishing the feel of being so close to her after what felt like a lifetime apart. He couldn't quite bring himself to think about what he would do if Chloe never came back to him, he knew in his heart that he would never be strong enough to lose her.

"It's sore." she muttered, her eyes filling with tears when she felt Lee's warm breath against her neck. She couldn't understand what was happening to her and why she was feeling this way about him. She'd always felt relaxed and safe in his presence, but now she felt vulnerable, although he didn't quite feel the way about her that he'd led her to believe. Chloe jumped slightly as Nathan quickly stood up and walked into the kitchen, returning a few moments later with a collection of beer bottles.

"Let's play a drinking game." Nathan suggested, beaming proudly at himself as he handed Danny a beer and threw himself down onto the sofa.

"You do realise I can't drink." Chloe reminded him, sighing quietly to herself.

"Nor can I." Lee said, his eyes fixed on Chloe as she fidgeted slightly, gently massaging her sore abdomen.

"Yeah but me and Danny can." Nathan chuckled, taking a swig of his beer.

"We need to play a game." he added, wiggling his eyebrows at Chloe when she groaned, a small smile playing on the corner of her lips when she noticed the excitement on his face.

"Uh oh." Danny laughed.

"Let's do, tell the group something that you've never told anyone before." Nathan piped up, gazing around at the group as everyone fell silent, racking their brains to try and think of something. Lee sighed to himself as he walked around the sofa and sat down, glancing at Chloe as he sat beside her, his heart sinking as he wished that he could pull her into his arms and hold her close. He'd have given anything to wrap his arms around her as she perched on his lap, like she used too, back when she could still stand his touch.

"Right, shall I go first?" Nathan asked, gazing around at the group.

"If you want too." Chloe said softly.

"I think you probably should, since you're the one who wants to play the game." Danny agreed.

"Okay, so my secret revelation is......" he started, pausing for dramatic effect.

"I had a secret, loving relationship with Lee for about a year." he grinned, shooting Lee a wink. Chloe gasped in shock, glancing between Lee and Nathan, her eyes wide in shock.

"No you didn't you lying bastard." Lee said, bursting out laughing at the cheeky twinkle in Nathan's eyes.

"That never happened." he continued.

"I know, but your face was hilarious." Nathan beamed.

"The look of disgust you mean." he replied, glancing at Chloe for a moment, when he felt her watching him closely. Nathan's jaw dropped as he gazed at Lee, placing his hand on his heart, pretending to be offended.

"You're like my brother, it would be like incest." Lee laughed. Nathan smiled at him, slightly pleased with himself that for a moment Lee had finally forgotten about his problems.

"Tell me about it." Nathan agreed, giving Chloe a small wink when she smiled at him.

"I once stole some underwear from a department store." Nathan grinned.

"That's not exactly the shock revelation that I was expecting." Lee chuckled.

"Okay my turn." Danny said quietly, quickly downing the rest of his beer and starting on another bottle.

"Maybe you should slow down a bit." Chloe chuckled, bursting out laughing when he wiggled his eyebrows at her as he finished the second bottle.

"Okay, well your secret is that you're an alcoholic." Nathan laughed, handing him another bottle.

"Not exactly." he replied, not quite able to look any of them in the eye as he sat in silence, picking at the label on the beer bottle.

"Oh c'mon you have to say." Chloe prompted him, frowning to herself as he glanced between her and Lee, squirming slightly.

"It can't be any worse than mine." Nathan grinned.

"Your's wasn't that bad." Chloe giggled.

"It's just a bit awkward." Danny muttered, smiling at Chloe for a moment before quickly looking away.

"You have to tell us." Chloe insisted, raising her eyebrow expectedly.

"Okay fine." Danny said, sighing deeply to himself. He stared at Lee for a moment, before quickly locking eyes with Chloe, a small smile playing on the corner of his lips as she gazed up at him expectantly.

"I don't know how to tell you this...." he started, trailing off when he couldn't quite find the words to say.

"Oh for god sake, spit it out. The suspense is killing me." Nathan chuckled.

"I've never told anyone this, but I'm in love with you." Danny stated, his gaze fixed on Chloe.

"What?!" Chloe squeaked, her stomach churning nervously.

"I mean, look at that bum." he continued, gently slapping Chloe's rear.

"Stop it." she giggled, her eyes wandering to his hand.

"I thought you are gay?" Lee piped up, frowning to himself.

"I am." he replied quickly.

"Sorry, it was the alcohol." Danny laughed, glancing nervously at Lee who remained silent, avoiding his gaze.

"So what's your actual secret?" Nathan asked.

"I honestly don't have one, the only secret I had was that I'm gay but you guys know that now. Other than that, my life is pretty boring." he admitted.

"Although if I had to admit something, I have had a bit of a crush on you for a while." he admitted, his eyes wandering to Nathan.

"Are you teasing us again?" Chloe checked, gasping quietly to herself when Danny shook his head slowly. Nathan opened his mouth to respond, quickly closing it again and swallowing the dry lump that was rising in his throat.

"That's not exactly what I thought you were going to say." he eventually managed.

"I guess I was just a bit of a groupie. It was a few years ago though." Danny said quietly, squirming awkwardly.

"Chlo Bo?" Nathan said quickly, trying to distract from the awkwardness that he was feeling.

"Anything that we say doesn't leave the four of us right?" she checked, glancing around at them nervously, her cheeks colouring when she locked eyes with Lee.

"Of course." Nathan smiled.

"I'll probably have forgotten by tomorrow anyway." Danny grinned, taking another large gulp of beer. Chloe nodded slowly, taking a deep breath as she pressed to tell them her biggest secret, that she'd never planned to tell anyone.

"Just after I lost my Mum, things were really bad and my Dad wasn't coping at all. I felt really alone and was obviously grieving....so I started self-harming." she said quietly, not quite able to look any of them in the eye.

"Didn't anyone realise?" Danny frowned, his stomach churning at the thought of someone as kind and pure as Chloe, feeling the need to harm herself.

"No, I was clever with it." she said quietly.

"What does that mean?" Nathan asked quickly.

"Well obviously when my Mum was really sick she wanted to pass away at home, so the hospice nurse used to come in and visit her. I managed to get hold of some needles." Chloe explained, sighing to herself as she stared at Nathan's blank expression.

"If you put a needle into the vein in your hand or your arm, it bleeds quite a bit and just leaves a bruise. So it's difficult to notice." she continued, surprising herself at how easy it was to admit to them.

"That explains why you don't have any scars." Lee said thoughtfully, his stomach churning as he thought about her words. He couldn't quite process how someone as perfect as her had felt so lost and helpless that she'd needed to punish herself in order to deal with everything. His heart pounded against his chest as he stared down at her as she slowly traced circles on her leg, not quite able to look them in the eye. Her cheeks coloured deeply when she suddenly realised that she'd divulged her biggest secret to them and now she could never take that back. It was something that she'd been planning to take to her grave.

"You never told me that." Lee whispered, his heart breaking a little at the thought of her sitting alone, watching the blood drip from her arm. Chloe shrugged, her gaze still fixed on her lap as Lee shuffled closer to her and carefully wrapped his arm around her shoulders.

"I thought I knew everything about you." he said softly, still not quite able to process her revelation.

"It was years ago anyway." she said quietly, glancing up at him for a moment as he stroked her arm with his fingertips.

"I know, but I can't bear the thought of you hurting yourself." he muttered, placing a soft kiss on her cheek.

"Anyway, Lee, it's your turn." Nathan piped up, trying to deflect from Chloe when he noticed her squirming, her cheeks still coloured. Lee shook his head slowly, his eyes still fixed on Chloe.

"No, I'm not having it, fair is fair." Nathan tried.

"I'm an open book that can't keep his mouth shut anyway, so you know pretty much everything about me." Lee pointed out, sighing to himself as he reluctantly tore his eyes away from staring at Chloe.

"I don't believe that for a second." Nathan smiled.

"I'm still not doing it." Lee snapped.

"There's only one thing that I've never told anyone, and it's personal." he continued.

"That's the whole point of the game." Danny chuckled.

"I don't care. I said no." he insisted, determined not to be persuaded into saying something that he was going to regret. He glanced at Chloe for a moment as she stared up at him, a frown present on her pretty features.

"I should go to bed anyway." she said, desperately trying to resist the urge to ask him what his secret could possibly be, that he didn't feel able to share, particularly after what she had just admitted to the group. Lee sighed to himself as he watched Chloe slowly standing up. As she left the room, he found himself longing to follow her, like an invisible bungee rope that was constantly pulling him to her side.

Chapter Sixty Nine

As soon as Chloe left the room, Lee sighed deeply to himself, placing his head in his hands, still not entirely sure how to process what Chloe had said. In all the years that he'd known her, he'd never had an inkling that she'd ever felt the need to harm herself. He couldn't quite understand why someone as amazing and special as her could possibly feel so worthless that she'd needed to hurt herself in order to feel better.

"Why, were you being weird and not telling us your secret?" Nathan asked, snapping him out of his thoughts.

"Because I don't want too." he replied shortly, lifting his head to gaze at him. Nathan opened his mouth to respond, quickly closing it again when Lee cut him off.

"Just drop it." he said shortly, glaring at Nathan, silently warning him that the subject was off limits.

"I think I need a beer." Lee said shortly, his eyes flickering to the stairs as his thoughts wandered back to Chloe and how desperately he wanted to be by her side.

"Why don't you go and check on her if you are worried?" Danny suggested, following Lee's eyeline.

"Because she doesn't want me around, and I have to be careful." he replied, sighing deeply to himself.

"Careful of what?" Nathan frowned.

"I don't want to stress her out." Lee sighed.

"It's like trying to choose between my heart and my head. My heart is yearning to be with her, but I know in my head that she doesn't want me around." he continued thoughtfully, desperately wishing once again that things were back to the way they had used to be between the two of them. Chloe had been his whole world for so long, that he didn't quite know how to function without her.

"I still can't believe what she said." he muttered thoughtfully.

"During the game?" Nathan asked, sighing sadly to himself when Lee nodded slowly.

"I just don't understand why she wouldn't tell me." he said thoughtfully, closing his eyes for a moment to try and clear the images that were swirling around his head. No matter how hard he tried, he couldn't seem to delete the images of the woman that he loved, sitting alone in a room, silently watching the blood dripping from her arm. Her anxiety slowly easing with every drop that was spilled.

"Well by the sounds of it, she's never told anyone." Nathan said quickly.

"She pretty much knows everything about me." Lee said thoughtfully.

"I actually can't deal with this anymore." he admitted, stroking small circles on his knee, not quite able to make eye contact with either of them as he desperately fought the tears that were filling his eyes.

"Deal with what?" Danny asked him.

"Constantly being pushed away, I feel like I'm not even in her life anymore." he replied, sighing sadly to himself.

"I don't even understand what I'm supposed to have done to deserve it." he continued.

"Like I said the other day, I think she is struggling." Nathan reminded him. Lee nodded slowly, trying to ignore the fear that was churning in his stomach.

"Maybe the things that I said to her, finally pushed her too far." he said thoughtfully, his eyes flickering to the beer on the table as he tried to resist the urge to consume it. Nathan watched Lee closely as he fell silent, staring at the beer bottle. Lee quickly reached over and swiped the bottle from the table, glancing at Nathan when he felt him watching him closely.

"Don't!" Nathan said firmly, quickly swiping the bottle from Lee's hands before he could open it.

"It's just one beer." Lee argued.

"I don't care. This is how it started last time, with you trying to drown your sorrows." Nathan explained.

"And do you really want to go back to that place when you have a child on the way." he continued. Lee sighed deeply, his eyes wandering upstairs once again.

"Maybe you should go and check on her." Nathan suggested, quickly realising how desperately Lee needed to see Chloe. He nodded slowly, quickly standing up.

"Just try not to upset her." Nathan called after him as he walked away.

Lee smiled to himself as he climbed into bed, his eyes fixed on Chloe as she slept on her side, her back facing him. He couldn't tear his eyes from her as he laid beside her, watching her chest slowly rising and falling. His heart yearned to be able to pull her into his arms and hold her close. He'd never for one moment contemplated how miserable and lost he would feel without her, but now that she was continually pushing him away, he longed to be close to her, to pull the woman that he loved into his arms and hold her. Before he could stop himself he turned onto his side and shuffled closer to her, resting his chin on her shoulder. He smiled to himself as he placed his hand on her arm, gently stroking circles on her skin. Chloe fidgeted in her sleep, slowly opening her eyes, frowning to herself as she felt Lee's chest against her back. She glanced down at her arm when she felt Lee's fingers tracing soft circles on it. Chloe glanced behind herself, her cheeks colouring as she locked eyes with Lee. She quickly turned away from him, squirming under his intense gaze.

"Sorry, I didn't mean to wake you." he whispered in her ear.

"It's okay, I'm glad you did." she said quietly, closing her eyes for a moment as she tried to forget about her nightmare.

"Why, what's wrong?" he asked, frowning to himself when he heard her sniff quietly to herself.

"I'm fine, it was just a bad dream." she mumbled, placing her hand on her cast and massaging her sore wrist.

"Tell me." he replied, gently brushing her hair away from her cheek and tucking it behind her ear.

"Ever since I was in hospital, I keep having nightmares about the baby." she muttered, still trying to clear the images from her head.

"What do you mean nightmares?" he asked, his eyes fixed on her as she quickly wiped away the tears from her cheeks, clearly trying to hide them from him.

"That she comes too early, and there's nothing they can do to save her." she whispered, her voice breaking slightly. She sighed sadly to herself, closing her eyes tightly and pressing her fist against her forehead, trying to remove the images of her precious baby coming to harm.

"It's okay, it was just a dream." he reassured her. Chloe nodded slowly, realising that he was correct, but not quite able to stop the images from swirling around her head.

"I know." she whispered, not quite able to bring herself to tell him the enormous responsibility that she felt to keep their baby safe. She knew that she was the only person that could ensure that Freyja was carried to term and couldn't face the possibility of losing her. Chloe jumped, her eyes snapping open when she felt Lee's hand trailing down her side. She glanced down at herself as he gently lifted her hoodie and placed his hand against her bump, sighing in contentment as he felt her warm skin against his hand. Chloe stiffened as he snuggled his chest against her back, his fingers tracing small circles on her bump. He sighed sadly to himself when he sensed the change in her body language.

"Do you want me to stop touching you Chlo?" he asked sadly, his heart plummeting.

"No, it's okay." she replied quietly, trying to resist the urge to move away from his touch.

"I promised that I would never keep the baby from you." she continued, her eyes fixed on his hand.

"I want you too, not just the baby." he admitted, gently placing a soft kiss on her shoulder. Chloe remained silent, blinking slowly as the tears that she'd been fighting finally rolled down her cheeks. She sniffed quietly to herself, torn between pulling away from Lee or curling up in his arms. Lee sighed sadly to himself when he felt Chloe's warm tears against his cheek.

"What's going on Chlo?" he asked gently.

"I'm fine." she said quickly, sniffing quietly to herself.

"I'm getting really worried about you." he prompted her, his stomach churning nervously as he stared at her, still not able to figure out why she was acting so out of character.

"You don't need too, I'm fine." she insisted.

"You're not Chlo." he said quietly, sighing to himself when he realised that she wasn't going to open up to him.

"I've never seen you like this." he continued, desperately trying to find a way to reach her.

"Maybe you don't know me as well as you think." she snapped, her temper finally starting to fray.

"No, I realised that earlier." he said quietly.

"Is this about the self-harming thing?" she said, quickly moving away from his touch and sitting up, resting her back against the pillows.

"Because you can talk. You didn't even tell us your secret!" she added, an edge of anger present in her voice.

"I can tell you right now, if you want?" he offered, sighing deeply as he sat on the end of the bed, watching her closely, not entirely sure what he'd done to anger her.

"I don't want to know, I was just saying." she said dismissively, not even able to bring herself to look at him. Chloe stared at her hands that were resting in place on her lap, frowning in confusion to herself. She couldn't understand why she suddenly felt such anger towards the man that she loved and why she was so desperate to push him away all the time.

"You can't keep pushing me away Chloe." he tried, his heart sinking when she remained silent, not even tearing her eyes away from her lap. He sighed to himself as he slowly made his way up the bed, stopping when he was in front of her. Chloe flinched when he placed his hands on her neck and gazed down at her, his lips mere inches from hers. She remained still when he placed a soft, lingering kiss on her lips.

"You have to let me help you Chlo." he whispered, resting his forehead against hers.

"I don't want you to ever hurt yourself again." he continued.

"Oh for god sake, that was years ago." she snapped, quickly moving away from him and standing up.

"Do you promise that you haven't done it recently?" he asked her, still not able to shake the feeling that she was struggling more than she was letting on.

"I haven't done it for years." she said quickly.

"But it would make sense, especially since you're anaemic." he said nervously, not entirely sure how she was going to respond, but not able to stop himself from asking the question that he was dying to know the answer too.

"That's because I have a deficiency." she said quietly.

"Besides, I would never do anything that might impact the baby." she added, an edge of anger present in her voice. Lee nodded slowly, finally feeling a wave of relief wash over him at her words. He watched her closely as she locked eyes with him, glaring at him across the room.

"We can't go on like this Chlo, we have a baby on the way." he tried, his heart breaking as he watched her closely.

"Well, I don't know what you want me to say." she said shortly. Lee quickly stood up and walked over to her, frowning to himself as she slowly backed away from him. She wobbled slightly as she backed into the desk, placing her hand behind her to steady herself as she sat down.

"Just answer me something." he whispered, staring down at her. Chloe remained silent as she waited for him to continue.

"Do you still love me?" he asked, swallowing the dry lump that was rising in his throat. His heart pounded against his chest, the seconds that it took for her to answer feeling like hours as he waited with baited breath for the answer to the question that he was dreading but needed to know.

"Of course I still love you." she whispered, her stomach churning with guilt at what she was doing to him. Her eyes flickered to him when he stepped closer to her, his body mere inches from hers.

"Stop it." she whispered, placing her hand on his bare chest. He raised his eyebrow at her as he placed his hands on either side of her, gently resting them against the desk.

"I didn't do anything." he mumbled, staring down at her as he placed his fingers on her collarbone, gently trailing them down her necklace chain, eventually coming to a stop when he reached the pendant.

"Come back to me Chlo." he whispered, gently resting his forehead against hers.

"I haven't gone anywhere." she whispered back, trembling slightly as his fingers traced small circles on her chest. He nodded slowly, deciding not to argue with her as he cherished being closer to her than he'd been in what felt like forever.

"I don't want you suffering in silence." he mumbled, placing a soft on her lips.

"You're not alone." he continued, watching her as she sat back, moving away from his touch.

"I should get back to bed." she said quietly, carefully standing up.

"Yeah you need to rest." he sighed, watching her sadly as she climbed into bed and turned her back on him, quickly switching off the lamp.

Chapter Seventy

"What are you guys doing here?" Lee frowned as he opened the front door and stood face to face with Kirstie and Ben.

"Are we not allowed to pop in and visit our favourite couple?" Kirstie grinned, smiling at Lee as he gestured for them to enter the house.

"You'll have to follow me into the kitchen, I'm cooking breakfast." he told them, quickly making his way back into the kitchen. Ben beamed at him as he perched at the breakfast bar, watching Lee as he continued cooking.

"Shall I make tea and coffee?" Kirstie offered.

"Yeah that sounds good." Lee said, smiling at her.

"What are you making anyway?" she asked, peering over the pan.

"Eggs Benedict." he told her, smiling slightly when she raised her eyebrow.

"What?" he frowned, as she wriggled her eyebrows cheekily.

"The last time you made that was when you and Chloe pulled an all-nighter, am I to assume that's the case again?" she giggled, elbowing him in the ribs as she teased him.

"Oooh spill." Ben chuckled, smiling his thanks at Kirstie when she handed him a mug of coffee.

"There's nothing to tell." Lee said quietly, sighing to himself. A small smile played on the corner of his lips as his mind wandered to all those months ago when he returned from Germany. How he'd finally felt whole again as soon as he was in Chloe's presence.

"C'mon don't be boring." Ben chuckled.

"My sex life is off limits, I'm respecting Chloe's wishes." he replied shortly, choosing not to mention the fact that Chloe hadn't been near him for the past couple of weeks.

"Where is Chloe anyway?" Kirstie asked, sitting beside Ben at the kitchen island.

"She's still in bed. I thought I'd make her breakfast." he told them.

"How's she been, I haven't seen her since the night she disappeared?" she asked, her stomach churning nervously when she noticed Lee sigh sadly to himself. Even though she had no idea what was going on, she couldn't help but notice the deep sadness, hidden behind his eyes.

"She's fine." he said quietly, not entirely sure what to say. He knew that Chloe was a private person and he couldn't help but feel that she wouldn't want him discussing her with them, particularly if they didn't already know about the situation.

"I have been trying to call her for the past couple of weeks, but she never picks up." she tried, trying to ignore the concern that she was feeling for her friend.

"Really?" Lee frowned, suddenly realising for the first time that Chloe was even being distant with her best friend. He felt a small wave of relief wash over him that he wasn't the only person that Chloe was pushing away, but that was quickly replaced by concern over her wellbeing. No matter how much he racked his brain, he couldn't seem to figure out why Chloe was suddenly isolating herself. The only thing he could possibly think of was that everything that she'd been through in her life, had finally caught up on her. Combined with the fear of losing the baby and her hormones, she was no longer able to cope with everything. He found himself wishing once again that she would allow him to help her in her time of need.

"Yeah, that's why I came over really, to check on her." Kirstie said sadly, still not entirely sure if she had done something to upset her friend.

"She's fine, she's just been resting a lot." he reassured her, shooting her a small smile when he suddenly noticed how worried she was about Chloe. He couldn't help but share her concerns, his heart sinking as he took a sip of his coffee.

"Well she really wasn't feeling well was she." Ben piped up.

"And then she fell down the bloody stairs." Kirstie sighed.

"And the baby decided to try and come early." Lee said thoughtfully.

"What?!" Kirstie spluttered, coughing on her tea. Lee nodded slowly, his stomach churning as his mind wandered back to when Chloe was in the hospital. He knew in his heart that they were lucky that they hadn't lost their baby.

"The shock of her falling down the stairs, caused her to go into early labour." he muttered, swallowing the dry lump that was rising in his throat.

"That must have been scary." Ben said, shooting him a small sympathetic smile.

"We almost lost the baby." he admitted, sighing sadly to himself.

"Are they both okay now?" Kirstie asked quickly. Lee nodded slowly, smiling slightly when he plated up the food.

"That looks amazing....I'm jealous." she added.

"Yeah where's ours?" Ben agreed.

"Well it's not my fault you turned up unannounced." he said quietly. He jumped slightly as the doorbell rang.

"Who else have you two invited?" he sighed, glancing at their blank expressions. He hurried to answer the door, gasping in shock when he noticed Amy standing on the doorstep.

"Amy?!" he exclaimed.

"Hey dude." she smiled, quickly pulling him into a hug.

"Have you come to stay?" he asked, his eyes wandering to the suitcase beside her.

"If you don't want me here, I can stay in a hotel." she replied.

"Don't be ridiculous." he said, quickly picking up her suitcase and leading the inside.

"Does Chloe know you're here?" he asked.

"Nope. She called me last night and she was in floods of tears." she explained.

"She was?" he frowned, feeling slightly hurt that he had no idea that she was upset last night.

"What was she upset about?" he asked, racking his brain to try and remember if he could possibly have done something to upset her.

"Everything is getting on top of her I think." she replied, sighing sadly to herself.

"So I got in my car and came down. I have a week off work anyway." she continued. Lee nodded slowly, his heart pounding against his chest hopefully. He couldn't help but hope that if Chloe had some family by her side, she would finally start to open up and heal herself of whatever demons she was struggling with.

"She's upstairs if you want to see her." he told her, his eyes flickering to the staircase for a moment, a look of deep longing on his handsome features.

"In fact, you can take her breakfast up if you want." he suggested, quickly walking into the kitchen to collect the plate and handing it to her.

"Do me a favour?" he asked. Amy nodded slowly, raising her eyebrow at him questioningly.

"Remind her that I love her." he said softly. Amy nodded slowly, her heart breaking for him as she quickly climbed the stairs. She frowned to herself as she opened the bedroom door and noticed that Chloe was curled up under the covers, staring in silence at the bedroom wall.

"Amy?" Chloe whispered, quickly sitting up as soon as she laid eyes on her. Amy nodded, quickly placing the plate of food on the counter. Chloe's eyes filled with tears as she quickly climbed out of bed and hurried over to Amy, pulling her into a tight hug.

"I'm so happy you are here." Chloe whispered in her ear.

"I came to check on my sister from another mister." Amy replied, smiling at Chloe when she eventually released her.

"I can't believe I haven't seen you since you and Lee came to Nottingham." Amy said, her eyes misting with tears when she noticed the steady stream of tears that were rolling down Chloe's cheeks.

"I know, it's been far too long." Chloe agreed, smiling at Amy as she sat on the bed.

"Right, sit down and tell me what's been going on." she said sternly, patting the bed beside her. Chloe smiled slightly and quickly did as Amy asked, squirming slightly under her intense gaze.

"I'm fine." Chloe said quietly.

"Nope, I'm not having that. I've known you a long time, I could tell just by talking to you the other night that you're not doing great." Amy insisted.

"Is that food for me?" Chloe asked when she finally noticed the food on the desk.

"Don't try and change the subject." Amy said firmly.

"I didn't drive four hours for you to tell me that everything is fine.....so spill." she insisted.

"Since when did you get so bossy." Chloe giggled, smiling at the stern expression on her face.

"I'm turning into my mother." she told her, joining in with her laughter. Amy stared at Chloe, raising her eyebrow at her as she waited for her to open up.

"I don't really know what's wrong with me." Chloe admitted, sighing in defeat when she realised that Amy wasn't going to leave her alone until she opened up to her.

"I've been feeling really weird." she continued.

"Hormonal kind of weird?" Amy asked.

"Kind of but I just want to be alone all the time. My anxiety has been really bad and I keep panicking about things." she said quietly, surprising herself at how easy it was to open up to Amy.

"What are you panicking about?" Amy prompted her.

"Everything.....something happening to the baby is the main thing." she admitted.

"That's normal though, you know what it's like to lose a baby and you don't want to go through it again. And the early labour will have scared you." Amy explained, reaching over to squeeze Chloe's hand.

"I'm not going to be a good Mum anyway, I have nobody to show me what to do." Chloe said quietly, her thoughts wandering to her parents.

"And Auntie Gwen doesn't want anything to do with me anymore." she added sadly.

"I'm working on that, but you know what she's like." Amy said, rolling her eyes at her mother's behaviour. Chloe nodded slowly.

"I just feel so worthless Amy." Chloe whispered.

"I have no home, no job and hardly any money. How am I supposed to provide for my baby?" she continued.

"I've allowed myself to rely on Lee too much." she added. Amy watched Chloe as she stood up and began to pace the bedroom, her hands shaking, her breathing short and sharp as she started to panic.

"It's just all too much." she admitted, running her hand through her hair in frustration.

"The thing that Lee said to you?" Amy frowned, not entirely sure why after everything that Lee had done for Chloe, she couldn't seem to forgive him for one flippant comment that was taken out of context.

"All of it.....I miss my parents, I'm worthless, Michelle's betrayal, the media, being stabbed and homeless. It's all too much...and that's not to mention losing our first baby." she ranted, becoming slightly hysterical as she continued to pace.

"And being attacked by Shayne." she continued.

"Chloe, I think you need to calm down. It's okay to accept that things have got on top of you." Amy reassured her.

"You've been through so much, it's not weakness that you are struggling." she continued.

"I just need my strength back and my independence. At least when I lived on the bloody bench, I had my independence and a job." Chloe ranted, clearly not hearing Amy's words.

"Yeah but all of your money was going on paying off Andy's debt and you never knew if you would get a meal or not." Amy pointed out.

"Lee has done a lot for you. He protects you and takes care of you and he's been there for you." Amy pointed out.

"You can't keep pushing him away when you need him and he needs you." she continued.

"He doesn't though, he needs the baby, but he'll be fine without me." she whispered.

"Besides he doesn't want me anyway." she muttered, dropping her knees, the last of her strength finally leaving her. She quickly removed her hoodie when she felt herself burning up.

"Oh my god." Amy whispered, her eyes filling with tears as she stared at Chloe's bump, completely transfixed.

"What?" Chloe whispered, glancing down at herself.

"That's the first time I've seen your bump. It suddenly feels real now." Amy whispered, her heart swelling with pride that Chloe was going to have a baby.

"You're measuring small for almost six months though aren't you?" Amy asked, an edge of worry present in her voice.

"That's what everyone says, but the doctor said it's fine, apparently some people only have a small bump." Chloe explained, staring down at her bump as she stroked small circles on it.

"I think I want to move back to Nottingham." Chloe whispered thoughtfully to herself.

"What, where did that come from?" Amy frowned, quickly climbing off the bed and sitting next to her on the floor.

"I just really want to run away." she admitted, taking deep breaths as she felt herself beginning to panic once again.

"Chloe breathe." Amy said sternly, when she realised what was happening.

"You need to stay with Lee, you can't throw away what the two of you have. You both adore each other." she continued, placing her hands on Chloe's cheeks, forcing her to make eye contact with her.

"I need to distance myself from him!" she exclaimed, still continuing to panic.

"No you don't, you can't push him away. You'll regret it." Amy argued.

"Did you know that the last three months of pregnancy can increase your anxiety, maybe that's what this is, it's intensifying your insecurities." she continued.

"I don't know what it is, all I know is that I need to get away and be alone somewhere." she muttered. Before Amy could respond, Chloe buried her head in her hands and began to sob hysterically, finally releasing all of the pent up emotions that she'd been keeping in check for some time.

"I can't keep fighting anymore, I don't have the strength." she sobbed. Amy watched her silently, not entirely sure what to say or do to help her.

"Of course you can, you're the strongest person I know, to have gone through everything that you've been through in your life." Amy told her, sighing sadly to herself when she realised just how much pain Chloe was in.

"And with Lee by your side, you can take on the world." she continued.

"The two of you can raise your baby girl together." she added when Chloe didn't respond.

"No, when I have the baby, I'm going back to the park where I belong!" Chloe sobbed.

"What?" Amy whispered, frowning at her words.

"I'm not letting that happen." she said quickly.

"It's the only home that I have. I don't want to endanger the baby, so I will wait until she's born and then go back." Chloe insisted.

"Don't be ridiculous." Amy said quickly, slowly becoming more and more concerned about Chloe with every moment that passed. She couldn't help but notice that her thoughts seemed random and irrational, almost like she had no idea what she was saying or doing. Like she was stuck in a constant state of panic and didn't know which way to turn for the best.

"Lee wouldn't let that happen either." Amy said quickly, her stomach churning at the thought of Chloe returning to the park where she almost lost her life.

"He doesn't want me anyway." Chloe whispered, falling forwards, her head landing on Amy's shoulder.

"And I don't blame him." she added sadly. Before Amy could say anything, Chloe burst into tears once again, no longer able to maintain the barriers that she'd kept in place for the past couple of weeks.

"Of course he does, he loves you." Amy said quietly, trying to reassure her. Chloe's head snapped up as the bedroom door opened and Lee walked into the room, a cup of tea in his hand. His feet froze to the spot as he saw Chloe on the floor, quickly wiping the tears from her cheeks as she tried to hide them from him. His hands shook, his eyes not leaving Chloe as he carefully placed the cup onto the counter, out of harm's way.

"You alright Chlo?" he asked nervously, watching her closely as she quickly stood up and searched the room, frantically looking for her hoodie. She breathed a sigh of relief when she finally located it and pulled it on, covering herself up.

"What do you want?" she asked, when she noticed him hovering awkwardly.

"Kirstie and Ben are here to see you." he told her. Chloe sighed deeply and walked out of the room.

Chapter Seventy One

Chloe smiled at Amy as she stripped down to her underwear and ran towards the pool, a small squeal of excitement escaping her lips as she jumped into the water.

"Is one glass of wine really all it takes to bring out your wild side." Chloe giggled, as soon as Amy resurfaced.

"I don't need wine, I've always been wild." Amy argued, pouting at her.

"Only when your Mum isn't around." Chloe pointed out, smiling at Amy when she burst out laughing.

"Are you coming in then?" Amy asked, raising her eyebrow hopefully, her stomach sinking in disappointment when Chloe shook her head slowly.

"I thought we established that you are hot and still have a body to die for." Amy grinned.

"No, you decided that." Chloe argued, her cheeks colouring at the thought of stripping down to her underwear.

"Did you have a think about what I said the other day?" Amy asked, quickly climbing out of the pool and reclining on the lounger.

"Which part?" Chloe asked, laying down on the lounger beside Amy's and staring up at the ceiling lights.

"About speaking to your midwife." Amy prompted, sighing to herself when Chloe shook her head slowly.

"I think you should. I'm convinced you have prenatal depression." she continued.

"I don't have any such thing." Chloe replied firmly.

"You have pretty much all of the symptoms." Amy insisted.

"How would you know?" Chloe frowned, slowly becoming frustrated that Amy was constantly nagging her to speak to her midwife.

"Because I looked on the NHS website." Amy told her.

"Speaking of the baby, you do realise you're going to be her unofficial Auntie." Chloe said, trying to change the subject.

"Just like I'm your unofficial sister." Amy smiled.

"Exactly." Chloe smiled.

"Have you named her yet?" Amy asked, her eyes lighting up hopefully when Chloe nodded, a small smile playing on the corner of her lips.

"It's a secret though, we agreed not to tell anyone." Chloe told her, her heart swelling with pride when she remembered the day that she'd walked along the beach with Lee and he'd suggested the name Freyja, after the Norse goddess of love. Amy smiled slightly when she noticed a brief happy twinkle in Chloe's eyes, before it was quickly replaced with sadness once again.

"I was actually going to ask you something." Chloe said tentatively.

"What is it?" Amy frowned.

"What are your long term plans?" Chloe asked.

"Huh?" Amy replied.

"I just wondered if you maybe wanted to get a flat together or something?" Chloe asked, desperately hoping that she would agree.

"But you live here." Amy sighed, her stomach churning that Chloe seemed unable to be content with her life and was determined to lash out.

"Have you not been listening, I want to get my independence back." she sighed.

"I don't think that's the answer to it, I think you are clutching at straws." Amy pointed out.

"And what is the answer to it then?" Chloe said shortly, gradually becoming frustrated that once again nobody seemed to understand her.

"You need to get some help." Amy insisted. Chloe rolled her eyes and shook her head, trying to control the anger that was swirling in her stomach.

"So you keep saying." Chloe snapped.

"Besides, aren't you forgetting about something?" Amy prompted, rolling her eyes when Chloe glanced at her, raising her eyebrow at her questioningly.

"Lee." she sighed.

"I'm not going to keep the baby from him, I would never do that." Chloe pointed out, completely misunderstanding what Amy was trying to say.

"I meant you." Amy tried, still not quite able to figure out if Chloe still wanted to be with Lee or whether she was slowly giving up on their relationship. Amy frowned to herself as she watched the realisation finally dawn on Chloe's face. She knew in her heart that Chloe had no idea what she wanted to do, only that she felt the need to escape from her problems. The two of them jumped as they heard the front door open and close. Chloe glanced at Amy, her eyes widening when she noticed that she was still wearing her underwear.

"Cover yourself up." Chloe said quickly, glancing nervously at the doorway.

"It'll only be Lee getting back won't it?" Amy asked.

"And he only has eyes for you anyway." she added, winking at Chloe.

"He's been at rehearsals with the boys though." Chloe pointed out.

"So?" Amy frowned.

"So, normally when the boys have been rehearsing, they come back here and hang out afterwards." Chloe explained.

"So put some bloody clothes on." she hissed, glancing at the doorway when she heard footsteps approaching. Amy rolled her eyes, quickly doing as Chloe asked.

"It's no different than a bloody bikini." she muttered under her breath. Chloe opened her mouth to respond, quickly closing it when Adrian, Nathan and Steven walked into the room.

"Well hello ladies." Steven beamed, wiggling his eyebrows at them.

"Have you been drinking?" Chloe chuckled.

"Maybe a little on the journey here." Adrian beamed, placing a pack of beer on one of the spare loungers. Chloe glanced at Amy when she noticed that she was stood in silence, her feet frozen to the spot as she gazed in awe at Adrian and Steven.

"This is my cousin Amy." she told them, suddenly remembering that Amy had only met Lee and Nathan on her last visit to London.

"Oh my god, this is so exciting!" Amy squealed, rushing over to them and hugging both of them in turn.

"She's a bit of a fangirl." Nathan chuckled, smiling to himself when he remembered how over excited Amy had been the first time that he'd met her.

"I noticed." Adrian chuckled, as Amy clung onto his neck, not quite able to bring herself to let go of him.

"We've decided to have a pool party." Nathan announced, before quickly removing his shirt and jumping into the pool, smiling at Chloe as he splashed her.

"I've only just got out of the pool." Amy beamed, sighing to herself when her phone started to ring.

"Oh great, it's my Mum." she said quietly, rolling her eyes at Chloe.

"I'd better get this." she sighed.

"We'll save you a beer." Adrian called after her as she walked out of the room. Chloe smiled at Adrian and Steven as they both picked up a beer and joined Nathan in the pool, the three of them messing around together.

"Aren't you coming in Chloe?" Adrian called to her, feeling slightly sorry for her as she sat on the lounger, a look of deep sadness on her pretty features. Chloe slowly stood up and walked over to the edge of the pool, carefully sitting down. She smiled at Nathan as he swum over to her and placed his chin on her knee, the droplets of water dripping off the end of his hair.

"What are you wearing under your hoodie?" he asked her.

"Just a vest top thing." she whispered, hesitating for a moment before slowly removing her leggings, her cheeks colouring slightly when Nathan shot her a small reassuring smile.

"Where's Lee anyway?" she asked him, trying to distract herself from the embarrassment that she was feeling in the hope that it would pass.

"He dropped us off and went to get pizza." he replied.

"We're staying over tonight, because we have rehearsals again tomorrow afternoon and it's just easier." he continued.

Also it means we can get drunk!" Steven called out.

"Right c'mon, stop faffing and come and join us." he added, smiling at her.

"Have you forgotten that I have a cast on that I can't get wet?" she asked, giggling at his infectious excitement.

"You'll be fine, you can go in up to your waist." he pointed out. Chloe nodded slowly, her hands shaking as she slowly removed her hoodie and discarded it onto the floor. She glanced down at her hips when Nathan placed his hands on them and carefully lowered her into the pool. Chloe gasped as she stood in the pool, the water rising to her waist.

"Just relax and have some fun Chlo Bo." he smiled at her.

"I really want to go under." she admitted, finally relaxing now that she was in the water.

"You've always been a mermaid haven't you." he chuckled.

"Give me your hand then." he added, holding out his hand for her cast. He held it safely out of the water as Chloe quickly dunked herself under the water, laughing happily when she resurfaced.

"Chloe, come and join us in the deep end." Steven called to her.

"I can't get my cast wet." she called back. Steven smiled at her as he quickly swam over to her.

"Wrap your arms around my neck." he instructed her when he reached her. Chloe giggled as she did as he asked, smiling happily when he carefully took her over to the deep end of the pool.

"Operation cheer Chloe up is a success." Adrian smiled at her.

"He told you about everything?" Chloe asked nervously, her cheeks colouring.

"He hasn't told us anything, but we're not stupid, we've known you both a long time. We can tell that something is going on." Steven explained. Chloe glanced at Nathan for a moment, sighing to herself when she noticed him squirming slightly.

"It's none of our business anyway, we just want to cheer you up." Steven told her, slowly spinning himself around, smiling at her infectious laughter. Nathan eyes flickered to the doorway when he noticed Lee walking in, carrying boxes of pizza.

"You do realise you have a really nice set Chloe." Steven chuckled.

"Set of what?" she frowned.

"Boobs of course." he grinned. Chloe frowned at his words, quickly following his eyeline, her cheeks colouring deeply when she suddenly realised that her top was completely see through.

"Oh my god, I'm really sorry." she whispered, feeling herself beginning to panic.

"Trust me, you really don't need to apologise." Steven stated, winking at her.

Steven's eyes flickered to Lee when he heard him angrily place the pizza boxes onto one of the loungers, glaring at him angrily across the room.

"I need to get out." Chloe said quietly, desperate to cover herself up. Steven nodded slowly and moved out of the deep end of the pool, placing his hands on her hips and carefully lowering her into the water. As soon as her feet were back on the ground, Chloe hurried over to the ladder, keeping her gaze fixed on the ground, too embarrassed to look any of them in the eye. Once she was out of the pool, she glanced down at herself, sighing sadly when she realised how visible her lace bra now was. She quickly wrapped her arms across her chest as she hurried over to the lounger, breathing a sigh of relief when she pulled it over her head. Chloe glanced at Lee, squirming slightly under his intense gaze. As soon as she locked eyes with him, she could clearly see that he was angry. He quickly looked away from her, glaring at Steven across the room.

"I need to go and check on Amy." Chloe whispered, quickly scurrying out of the room, hurrying to escape the awkward atmosphere.

Chapter Seventy Two

Lee sighed sadly to himself as he watched Chloe quickly walking away from him. His stomach churned with a mixture of sadness and anger. He couldn't understand why, when she had no body confidence at all, she'd somehow managed to strip half naked and climb into the pool. Even though he wanted her to have more confidence in herself and her appearance, he couldn't help but feel a twinge of sadness that she seemed to have more confidence when he wasn't around. He knew that his comment the other night had made the situation worse, but he couldn't help but wish once again that she believed him when he told her that she'd misunderstood his words. That she'd completely taken the comment out of context. He sighed angrily to himself as he thought about all of the times over the past few weeks that she'd pushed him away, both mentally and physically and how his heart broke a little each time.

"Are you going to glare at me for the rest of the evening?" Steven asked, snapping Lee out of his thoughts. Nathan frowned to himself, glancing between Lee and Steven, not entirely sure why Lee seemed so angry.

So c'mon then what's the problem?" he continued, quickly placing his hands on the edge of the pool and pulling himself out.

"I just don't appreciate you making eyes at Chloe as soon as I leave the house." Lee snapped, his temper growing when Steven wrapped a towel around himself and rolled his eyes impatiently.

"Don't be ridiculous, I didn't do anything." Steven replied.

"I heard you." Lee said shortly, still glaring at Steven across the room.

"You were flirting with her." he continued, trying to control the deep anger that was swirling in his stomach. He couldn't help but feel slightly jealous that Steven had been closer to Chloe than Lee had in what felt like a lifetime. He desperately wanted to hold her, or even be in her presence without feeling like she didn't want him around. His heart plummeted at the thought of things never returning to normal between them and the possibility that he was slowly losing her forever.

"I was not flirting with your girlfriend." Steven said firmly.

"Fiancée." Lee replied firmly, narrowing his eyes at Steven.

"Whatever. I still wasn't flirting with her." Steven sighed.

"It was just a joke." he continued.

"What a load of bullshit, you couldn't take your eyes off her!" Lee exclaimed, his temper slowly starting to fray.

"She's a beautiful woman, people check her out wherever she goes." Nathan pointed out, not entirely sure what had gotten into Lee. He couldn't help but wonder if Lee's outburst was a result of the fact that he was paranoid that he was slowly losing Chloe. In all the years that Nathan had known Lee, he'd never known him to be possessive of Chloe and he couldn't help but feel that he was terrified that someone was going to take her from him. Depriving him of his reason for existing.

"Besides he only looked, it's not like he actually did anything." Adrian piped up.

"I am a man, can you really blame me." Steven pointed out, bursting out laughing when he glanced at Adrian and raised his eyebrow at him.

"I don't care, keep your eyes to yourself." Lee said shortly.

"And your inappropriate comments." he continued.

"What's gotten into you?" Adrian frowned, glancing between Lee and Nathan, his frown deepening when he noticed Nathan squirming awkwardly.

"He becomes unreasonable when he's sexually frustrated." Steven said dismissively.

"That's bullshit!" Lee said defensively, choosing not to mention that Steven wasn't a million miles away from the way that he was feeling. The sexual frustration that he was feeling, mixed with the hurt and loneliness and how much he was longing to hold Chloe and love her, causing him to lash out.

"You forget how long I've known you Lee." Steven insisted.

"Not as well as you think." Lee replied.

"Even though it's been three fucking weeks." he added, under his breath, running his hand through his hair in frustration.

"What?" Steven asked.

"Nothing." Lee said quietly, quickly leaving the room, before he said something else that he was going to regret.

Lee hesitated for a moment as he stood outside of the bedroom door, not entirely sure if he wanted to enter the room or not. As much as he still longed to be with Chloe, he couldn't help but feel trepidation at the idea of being in her presence. Despite the fact that he couldn't bring himself to stop trying to get her to allow him back into her life, every time that she rejected him, it felt like his heart was being ripped out of his chest. Nathan's words swirled around his head, when he'd told him to be patient and wait until Chloe came back to him. He bit his lips to fight the tears that were filling his eyes, trying to ignore the desperation that he felt to know when that day would come if at all. Being constantly deprived of the woman that he loved made his chest feel tight, like he couldn't quite breathe in the same way as before. His mind wandered to the boys who were having fun downstairs, the three of them binging on beer and pizza. He couldn't help but wish that he was able to drown his sorrows with alcohol. To finally escape from the tight feeling in his heart and the mixture of hurt and uncertainty that were constantly swirling around his head.

He placed his hand on the doorknob, carefully opening it, his heart fluttering against his chest when he noticed Chloe sitting at the dressing table, staring in silence at her reflection in the mirror. She glanced at him for a brief moment as he entered the room and slowly began to brush her hair, trying to keep her hands busy. Her stomach swirled nervously as Lee walked up behind her, standing behind her, and gazing at her in the mirror.

"Did you have a shower?" he asked, trying to break the uncomfortable atmosphere, as she sat in silence, not even locking eyes with him. Chloe nodded slowly, the hairs on the back of her neck standing on end when she felt his warm breath against her neck.

"I smelt of chlorine." she muttered, swallowing the nervous lump that was rising in her throat.

"You smell amazing." he whispered, taking a deep breath to try and slow his heartbeat that was pounding against his chest.

"And you looked stunning when you were in the pool." he continued, a small smile playing on the corner of his lips as he thought about how mesmerising she'd looked. Her shirt completely see-through to her purple lace bra that perfectly cupped her breasts, her damp hair that had clung to her head.

"Although you always look even more beautiful when you've been in the pool." he prompted her. Chloe locked eyes with him when she felt him place his hand on the back of her neck and stroke soft circles with his fingertips. Her stomach churned nervously as his fingers slowly made their way along her collarbone, methodically stroking down her bra strap. He brushed her hair to one side with his other hand and placed a series of soft kisses on her neck, his other hand eventually coming to a stop when he reached her bra. Chloe glanced down at herself, squirming slightly under his touch as he gently cupped her breast, continuing to stroke small circles.

"I need you so bad Chlo." he admitted, gently pressing his body against hers.

"I know." she mumbled, sighing to herself as she rested the back of her head against his chest. Her stomach churned as he continued to stroke her breast, his chest rising and falling rapidly against her back. Chloe's heart plummeted when she realised how desperately he was longing for her. He eventually removed his hand and slowly trailed them down her side, watching her closely in the mirror. Lee frowned to himself, his heart sinking when he noticed that she was not reacting to his touch. There was a time, a few weeks ago when she shivered and trembled under his touch, but now she seemed disconnected and disinterested. Chloe squirmed against him when he slowly lifted the bottom of her pyjama top, placing his hands against her bare stomach, sighing in contentment as he rested his hands against her bump.

"Did she just move?" he frowned, eventually stopping kissing her neck and resting his chin on her shoulder. Chloe nodded slowly, gazing fondly at her bump. Her eyes flickered to his hands when he grasped the base of her top and slowly lifted it up, gazing at her longingly in the mirror.

"I can't." she said, quickly squirming away from his touch. Her cheeks coloured as he stared at her, not entirely sure what he'd done wrong.

"Why not?" he mumbled, trying to ignore the hurt that he was feeling when she moved away from his touch once again. He couldn't help but feel like she was repulsed by him.

"I just don't want too." she muttered, her gaze fixed on the floor as her cheeks coloured deeply. She couldn't understand what had gotten into her lately. Her brain was constantly swirling with doubts and anxiety, like a blender that she couldn't seem to press the stop button on. There was a time when she would melt under Lee's touch and want nothing more than to be in his presence, but now she wanted to be alone.

"I can't keep doing this Chlo." he muttered, snapping her out of her thoughts.

"Don't then." she muttered, quickly walking over to the bed and perching on the end of it, her gaze still fixed on her lap.

"I haven't asked you too." she added, her stomach starting to swirl with anger.

"Maybe I'm not ready to give up on you yet." he said quietly, trying to prompt a response from her, or even for her to look at him. His heart broke a little as she stared at her lap, his stomach churning at the thought of her slowly slipping through his fingers, nothing that he said or did seeming to have any effect.

"Chlo." he whispered, desperately trying to reach her. He couldn't help but feel hurt that she was able to partly undress in front of the other Eclipse boys. Almost like she seemed happier and more relaxed when he wasn't in the room.

"Just leave me alone!" she exclaimed, no longer able to stand being in his presence. The very sound of his voice, causing her temper to flare from nowhere.

"I don't understand what I've meant to have done, for you to keep treating me like this!" he cried, his desperation slowly turning into frustration.

"You're just angry because you want sex and you're not getting any!" she snapped, finally locking eyes with him and raising her eyebrow at him, almost like she was daring him to deny what she knew to be true.

"Is that what you really think?" he muttered, swallowing the dry lump that was rising in his throat. Her words had cut through him like glass at the thought that she truly felt that way. Chloe shrugged, returning to gazing at her lap, not entirely sure what to think or how to feel.

"I fell in love with you for your heart, not for what's between your legs!" he said angrily, the deep hurt that he felt turning into anger.

"Whatever." she replied shortly. Lee shook his head slowly, trying to resist the urge to shout at her, to scream at her how much hurt she was causing him by continually pushing him away, especially when he'd done nothing wrong. He hesitated for a moment before quickly picking up his jacket and pulling it on.

"Where are you going?" she frowned.

"I'm done with this." he said shortly.

"I'm staying at my Mum's tonight." he added, quickly leaving the room, before she had a chance to respond.

Chapter Seventy Three

Chloe glanced at Amy, shooting her a small smile as she threw herself onto the sofa beside her. Amy watched Chloe closely as she placed her hand on her bump and gently massaged it.

"Is she moving again?" Amy asked, her eyes glazing over as she stared, transfixed at Chloe's bump, still not quite able to believe that Chloe was going to be a mother.

"She fidgets quite a lot lately." Chloe said, smiling proudly at her bump.

"Is it sore when she moves?" Amy asked, completely mesmerized.

"A little, but I quite like it, because it means that she is okay." Chloe replied.

"Are you scared of becoming a mother?" Amy asked.

"Since she wasn't exactly planned was she?" Amy prompted, before Chloe had a chance to respond.

"No she wasn't." Chloe said quietly, sighing deeply to herself. She couldn't quite bring herself to admit how afraid she was at the thought of giving birth to her baby and becoming a mother.

"I just hope that I can do a good job for her." Chloe whispered, her eyes brimming with tears.

"I think you'll be a great Mum." Amy smiled at her, reaching over to squeeze her hand in reassurance.

"Your Mum was incredible, so you've had a good role model." she continued.

"I know." Chloe whispered, swallowing the lump that was rising in her throat at the thought of her mother.

"And Lee will be a good Dad." Amy prompted. Chloe nodded slowly, her body language stiffening at the mention of Lee's name.

"What's wrong?" Amy asked, instantly noticing the change in Chloe's body language.

"Nothing." Chloe said quietly.

"Oh c'mon Chloe." Amy insisted.

"We had a big argument last night." Chloe sighed.

"About what?" Amy asked.

"I've just been feeling different lately and I don't know why." Chloe admitted, rolling her eyes at Amy when she raised her eyebrow questioningly.

"Normally when he touches me, it's electric, I can't even explain it, but it's not like that anymore. I don't feel anything." Chloe said quietly, her stomach churning as she finally admitted her feelings to someone.

"And he wanted sex last night...." Chloe started, trailing off when her cheeks coloured, surprising herself that she was able to talk about this subject with someone.

"And you didn't enjoy it?" Amy prompted, her heart breaking a little when she noticed the deep sadness on Chloe's pretty features.

"I didn't sleep with him." Chloe told her, glancing up at Amy when she fell silent.

"Surely this can't just be because of that comment he made?" Amy muttered, frowning when she remembered the time that she'd spent with Chloe and Lee in Nottingham and how clear it was that they couldn't take their hands off each other. The constant longing looks between them that showed how desperately they longed to be in each other's presence.

"I don't know, I feel weird." Chloe whispered, quickly wiping away the tears that were spilling out of her eyes.

"I keep thinking that maybe I'm falling out of love with him." she continued, sighing sadly to herself.

"I don't think that's the case." Amy sighed.

"I know you don't want to hear this, but lack of interest in sex is also a symptom of prenatal depression." she added tentatively, not entirely sure how Chloe was going to react.

"I don't have depression." Chloe said firmly. Amy opened her mouth to respond, quickly closing it again when Chloe cut her off.

"How was your night with the boys?" Chloe asked, desperately trying to change the subject as she wiped away the last of her tears.

"Fine." Amy said, the trace of a small smile playing on her lips.

"What?" Chloe frowned, realising instantly that she was hiding something.

"Nothing." Amy grinned, her cheeks flushing.

"Amy, I grew up with you, you can't lie to me." Chloe insisted, smiling slightly when she noticed Amy squirming in her seat.

"Okay well....basically.... I have joined your club." Amy said, smiling to herself. She couldn't help but feel slightly pleased that she'd managed to cheer Chloe up a little.

"I'm pretty sure I don't have a club." Chloe frowned, still not entirely sure what she was talking about.

"You kind of do, you gave your first time to one of Blue." Amy piped out, wiggling her eyebrows cheekily. Chloe frowned for a moment, trying to process her thoughts and figure out what Amy was trying to tell her.

"Are you trying to tell me that you slept with one of them?" Chloe frowned, her stomach churning at the thought of it.

"I spent the night with Steven." Amy said proudly.

"What?!" Chloe exclaimed.

"Are you kidding me?!" she continued, still not quite able to process Amy's words.

"It's really not a big deal." Amy giggled.

"Actually it kind of is." Chloe insisted.

"What were you thinking?!" she added, trying to suppress the anger that was swirling in her stomach.

"It was just a one night thing." Amy said, rolling her eyes.

"You gave away your first time as a one night stand?" Chloe said incredulously.

"So what?" Amy snapped defensively, not entirely sure why Chloe was so bothered by her life choices.

"My virginity doesn't mean the same to me as yours did to you." Amy sighed.

"What's your Mum going to say?" Chloe said quickly.

"Obviously I'm not going to tell her." Amy pointed out.

"But you seem to have turned into her. It's my life and my body and it was my decision!" she continued, her temper finally snapping.

"What's going on?" Nathan asked as he walked into the room, closely followed by Steven.

"Chloe is trying to act like my Mother, that's what's going on!" Amy shouted, finally reaching the end of her tether.

"Maybe you would like to explain what is going on." Chloe said angrily, quickly rounding on Steven. He glanced between Chloe and Amy, squirming slightly as he finally made the connection in his head.

"You should be ashamed of yourself." Chloe said, her voice dripping with disdain.

"Oh for god sake, it was consensual, don't make out that it wasn't!" Amy exclaimed, her cheeks colouring slightly as she felt Nathan's eyes burning a hole into her head.

"You deliberately took advantage of her!" Chloe continued, not quite able to get her temper under control.

"He did not take advantage of me!" Amy exclaimed, before Steven had a chance to respond.

"But he's old enough to be your father, it's disgusting!" Chloe shouted.

"Wait a minute, I think everyone needs to calm down." Nathan said quickly.

"She can make her own decisions Chloe, neither of us have done anything wrong. And it's not really any of your business." Steven pointed out.

"She's like my little sister and you took advantage of her." Chloe said bitterly.

"It was her first time, but to you, she's just another notch on the bed post!" she continued angrily.

"What is it with everyone having a go at me lately." Steven muttered under his breath.

"How is it any different to what you did?!" Amy rounded on Chloe.

"Excuse me?" Chloe asked, raising her eyebrow questioningly.

"You gave your virginity to Lee....so how is it any different." Amy said shortly.

"There's a big difference, firstly there's only six years between me and Lee, but Steven is old enough to be your father!" Chloe said angrily.

"And secondly, I waited until I fell in love with someone." she added, squirming slightly when she locked eyes with Steven, suddenly realising that Amy had exposed her secret to him.

"I'm not like you though, I didn't want to wait!" Amy exclaimed, running her hand through her hair in frustration.

"And you have no right to judge my choices." she added.

"Well whatever, don't come crying to me when you realise that you regret it!" Chloe said angrily, quickly standing up. Her stomach churned when she heard the front door opening and closing. Lee frowned as he walked into the living room and noticed Amy, Chloe, Nathan and Steven, standing in silence, glaring at each other, the air thick with tension.

"What's going on?" he asked, flinging his keys onto the coffee table.

"I always seem to be in the dog house." Steven said, taking one last look at Amy before quickly walking out of the room.

"Chloe?" Lee tried, frowning when he noticed the look of anger on her face.

"Nothing, just forget about it." Chloe said quickly, taking deep breaths to try and control her temper.

"Figures." he muttered under his breath.

"What?" Chloe rounded on him.

"Well why bother talking to me. It's not like I'm your fiancée or anything." Lee said shortly.

"Do you want me to go and get the baby's dummies for you?!" Chloe said angrily, still not quite able to control the deep anger that she was feeling.

"What are you talking about?" he sighed, not really in the mood to keep hitting his head against a brick wall.

"So that you can spit it out, just like you spat your dummy out last night!" she snapped.

"Oh whatever." Lee scoffed, slowly shaking his head.

"You're actually a nightmare lately." he added, no longer able to suppress the hurt and frustration that he was feeling. Chloe nodded slowly, biting the inside of her lip to prevent herself from bursting into tears at his words.

"Lee, just leave it." Nathan piped up, his heart breaking a little as he gazed at Chloe. He still couldn't escape the feeling in his gut that something wasn't right with Chloe. She was acting completely out of character and he couldn't understand why Lee couldn't seem to see it, particularly when he knew her better than anyone.

"I have to go and meet Danny anyway." Chloe said quietly.

"So, you'll get a break from me!" she added angrily, glaring at Lee as she walked past him. As soon as she was in the hallway, she perched on the stairs, carefully pulling on her trainers. Her eyes misted with the tears that she was desperately trying to hold back.

"I really don't want to be here anymore." she whispered to herself, digging her fingernails into her scalp as she tried to find a way of releasing the deep sadness and hopelessness that she felt.

"I think it's a good idea to go and get some fresh air." Nathan said, causing Chloe to jump when she suddenly realised that he'd appeared in the hallway.

"I didn't mean the house, I meant I don't want to live anymore." she muttered, suddenly feeling a deep sense of calm, now that she had finally admitted it to herself.

"Don't say that Chlo Bo." he sighed, his heart breaking for her. He remained silent, not entirely sure what to say to help her feel better. His eyes flickered to her as she quickly stood up.

"Do you want me to come with you?" he offered. Chloe shook her head slowly.

"Promise me that you won't do anything stupid." he tried, suddenly feeling afraid at the idea of her being out of his sight and potentially doing something to harm herself.....or worse.

"Don't be ridiculous, I would never do anything to hurt the baby." she replied, matter of factly.

Chapter Seventy Four

Chloe jumped as she walked towards the front door and it opened before she reached it. She frowned to herself as she stood face to face with a dark haired woman that she didn't recognise. Her eyes flickered to the ground when she noticed that the woman was dragging a suitcase across the threshold.

"Who are you?" Chloe asked quickly, slightly confused as to what was going on.

"I'm Steph." she smiled.

"And you must be Chloe?" Steph asked, raising her eyebrow questioningly. Chloe nodded slowly, swallowing the dry lump that was rising in her throat.

"Are you okay, you look a bit upset?" she added, smiling widely at Chloe.

"I'm fine." Chloe said firmly, shooting a small smile at Nathan when she felt him place his hand on the small of her back, trying to provide her with some reassurance.

"Didn't Lee explain about me?" Steph asked, glancing awkwardly between Chloe and Nathan. Chloe shook her head slowly, her stomach churning nervously.

"I was going too, but I got side-tracked." Lee said quickly as he walked into the hallway.

"Steph is a very old friend." Lee explained.

"I'm not that old." Steph giggled.

"We lost touch but she managed to track me down." Lee smiled.

"It was meant to be a surprise. I went to his Mum's to find out where he lived to surprise him, but this one decided to turn up before I had the chance to surprise him." she grinned.

"Well I didn't know did I." Lee chuckled.

"You always did ruin surprises." Steph chuckled, rolling her eyes playfully.

"Are you staying over or something?" Chloe piped up, her stomach churning nervously.

"I said she can stay for a while." Lee said firmly, his tone making it clear that the subject wasn't up for debate.

"I'm really pleased to meet you Chloe, I've heard a lot about you." Steph smiled at her, trying to diffuse the awkward atmosphere.

"Really like what?" Chloe frowned.

"Maybe you've heard what a nightmare I am." she added, her stomach churning with anger once again.

"Here, let me take that." Lee said quietly, quickly reaching out to take Steph's suitcase, determined not to react to Chloe's words. Steph smiled her thanks at him as he quickly took her suitcase upstairs.

"Let's go and have a cup of tea. You can tell me all about the baby." Steph suggested, trying to make the effort to be friends with Chloe.

"I'm sure Lee has already told you anyway." Chloe said quietly, her heart sinking at the thought of Lee spending the evening with Steph when she'd spent the evening alone, crying herself to sleep. She couldn't understand why in all the years that she'd known him, he'd never once mentioned this woman to her.

"Besides I have to be somewhere." she added, quickly walking out of the house.

Chloe's heart plummeted into the pit of her stomach as she closed the front door behind herself and heard the sound of Lee's laughter coming from the living room. She sighed deeply to herself, resting the back of her head against the front door, staring at the ceiling, trying to ignore the panic that she was feeling in the pit of her stomach. As soon as she was in the house, her feelings of anxiety and helplessness were heightened, almost like she had no idea what to do or who to turn too. She reluctantly placed one foot in front of the other, sighing sadly to herself when she heard the sounds of joyous laughter travelling from the living room. Chloe hovered awkwardly, watching closely as Lee and Steph had a dance off on the game console. A small squeal of joy escaped Steph's lips as the tempo increased and the two of them began to dance faster.

"You have such an unfair advantage!" Steph giggled.

"Well you shouldn't have challenged me then!" Lee pointed out, bursting out laughing when Steph collapsed in a heap on the floor.

"No, I think I've learnt my lesson." she agreed.

"At least you've managed to get Mr Grumpy to finally crack a smile." Steven piped up from the sofa.

"It's all part of my charm." Steph beamed, winking at Lee. Steven nodded slowly, his eyes flickering to Amy as she fidgeted on the sofa, reluctantly tearing his eyes away from her when she glanced at him.

"So, are we getting on the drink then?" Steph asked.

"Yeah, if Nathan ever gets back with the booze." Adrian said, glancing at his watch and frowning when he suddenly realised how long Nathan had been gone.

"He's taking his sweet time isn't he." Steph said, glancing at the doorway, shooting Chloe a small smile when she locked eyes with Chloe. Lee followed her eyeline, suddenly feeling slightly guilty when he realised that he hadn't even heard Chloe enter the room. She slowly walked into the room, her gaze fixed on the floor as she felt everyone watching her closely. As soon as she reached the sofa, she tucked her legs underneath her frame, quickly picking up a cushion and hugging it tightly, trying to gain at least a small amount of comfort.

"How far gone are you now Chloe?" Steph asked, trying to fill the uncomfortable silence.

"Almost seven months." Chloe replied quietly.

"Wow, you must be so excited!" Steph smiled. Chloe nodded slowly, remaining silent as she picked her fingernails, not quite able to escape the feeling that none of them wanted her around. Her mind wandered to when she'd been standing in the hall and the sounds of laughter that she'd heard, and now the room was silent and tense.

"Ah, the cavalry is here!" Steph exclaimed, clapping her hands excitedly when Nathan walked into the room, carrying a crate of beer.

"I take it we are okay to stay over again?" Steven checked.

"Yeah, there's plenty of spare rooms." Lee replied. Nathan quickly placed the beer on the table and sat next to Chloe.

"Are you alright Chlo Bo?" he whispered in her ear, frowning to himself when Chloe nodded reluctantly. He glanced down at her hands, his heart plummeting when he realised that she was shaking. Nathan couldn't escape the deep feeling of dread that he felt whenever he looked at Chloe and the concern that he felt when he realised how much she was struggling, almost like she was clinging onto her sanity by the skin of her teeth.

"Here you go dude!" Steph exclaimed, quickly picking up a beer and throwing it at Lee. He smiled at her as he swiftly caught it.

"He's not supposed to be drinking." Chloe said quickly, before she could stop herself.

"I can have one." Lee said firmly.

"I feel kind of bad that you can't drink with us Chloe." Steph said, shooting Chloe a small smile.

"It's okay." Chloe said quietly, swallowing the lump that was rising in her throat.

"That's why I could never have a baby, I wouldn't be able to not drink for nine months. That's like torture!" Steph giggled.

"I forgot how bubbly you are." Steven said, joining in with her laughter.

"You know each other too?" Amy asked innocently, trying not to let on how much she cared about his answer.

"I used to live with Lee and his Mum for a while back in the day." Steven explained.

"And I was always coming over." Steph said.

"Wait, so you guys had a thing?" Amy asked, glancing between Steven and Steph.

"No, never." Steven said quickly.

"I had a fling with Lee though, but that was a long time ago." Steph told her.

"Oh god, I remember that. I was so nervous." Lee chuckled.

"You had nothing to worry about, you did good." Steph laughed, patting his knee playfully.

lipstick stain on the rim of the glass. Before she could stop herself, she picked up the glass and threw it into the sink, watching as it shattered into fragments. Chloe slowly rolled up her sleeve, gazing at the glass fragments in the sink, almost like she was in a trance that she couldn't break out of. Before she could stop herself she picked up a broken fragment and held it against the skin on her forearm, not even reacting as she applied pressure and slowly ran it across her arm. She sighed in relief as she watched the warm blood rolling down her arm and dripping into the sink, the pain in her heart slowly dissipating with every drop.

"Chloe." she heard Lee's voice from behind her.

"What?" she said shortly, quickly flinging the fragment of glass into the sink.

"Why are you upset?" he asked her.

"I'm not, I'm fine." she replied, beginning to panic as she glanced at her arm and saw that a trail of blood was still flowing down it. She closed her eyes for a moment, desperately hoping that if she kept her back to Lee he wouldn't notice what she'd done, the last thing she wanted was fake sympathy.

"Oh this again." he said quietly, sighing in frustration.

"Can you just leave me alone please?" she asked.

"But..." he tried, not entirely sure what to say.

"Leave me alone!" she exclaimed.

"Fine." he said shortly, quickly leaving the room. As soon as his footsteps left the room, Chloe clapped her hand over her mouth, the full realisation of what she'd done finally hitting her. She quickly picked up the fragments of glass and disposed of them in the bin.

"I'm sorry Mum." she whispered, quickly switching on the tap, to wash her blood down the sink before anyone could notice what she'd done.

"In a time of stress you'll always revert to your default setting, which for you is to hurt yourself." she whispered, remembering her therapist's words when she'd sat in her office all those years ago after her Mother passed away.

"Wait, you were his first time?" Chloe asked, swallowing the bile that was rising in her throat.

"Yep." Steph beamed.

"So you have me to thank for him being so good in bed." she added, bursting out laughing when Lee's cheeks coloured. Chloe fell silent, her stomach churning as she swallowed the vomit that was rising in her throat. Even though she knew that unlike her, Lee had a past, that didn't make it any easier for her to stomach, particularly now that the person he'd given his virginity too was back in his life and staying in his house. Suddenly all the laughter and flirtatious comments made sense. The two of them had a lot of history together and a special connection, since she was Lee's first time. Her eyes filled with tears as she sat in silence, feeling completely alone, despite being in a room full of people.

"Actually I have perfected my technique over the years." Lee winked.

"Do you remember how just after that, you boys were flying out to Australia and I was with you in the airport?" Steph grinned.

"Is that the time that I forgot I was holding your hand at the check in desk and tried to take you through to the departure lounge?" he checked.

"Yeah and I had to remind you that I wasn't flying out with you." Steph giggled.

"You wouldn't have got very far without a passport would you?" Lee laughed. Steph shook her head, unable to control her laughter. Chloe took deep breaths and shook her head slowly, trying to clear the images of the thought of Lee sleeping with the woman that was sitting beside him, laughing and joking with him. Everyone in the group turned to face her when a small sob escaped her lips, when she couldn't hold it in any longer.

"I think I need to go to bed." Chloe said, quickly standing up and hurrying out of the room, determined not to break down in tears in front of them. As soon as she reached the kitchen she placed her hands against the kitchen sink and hung her head, allowing the tears that she'd been fighting to flow down her cheeks. She sobbed quietly to herself, wrapping her arms across her chest, trying to find a way to shut out all of the pain that she was feeling. Her head swirled with a mist of thoughts, despite the fact that she wasn't sure how she was feeling about Lee or what was going on with her, she couldn't escape the deep hurt and fear that she was feeling. In all of her life, she'd never felt more alone than she did right at that moment. Her eyes flickered to the wine glass in the sink, a deep surge of anger building inside of her when she noticed Steph's

Chapter Seventy Five

"Chloe." a voice whispered in the darkness.

"What?" Chloe mumbled as she slowly opened her eyes, frowning when she noticed Amy squatting in front of her.

"You need to get up." Amy told her.

"What for?" Chloe frowned in confusion.

"Because you've barely left your room the past couple of days. Ever since Steph got here." Amy pointed out.

"I've been really tired. The baby has been keeping me up at night." Chloe said quietly, trying to hide how alone she was feeling. And how desperately she wanted to curl up in a ball and never wake up.

"That's what you told Nathan yesterday when he tried to get you up, but I'm not buying it." Amy said quickly.

"Budge up a bit." she continued. Chloe shook her head slowly, not quite able to bring herself to shuffle over to Lee's side of the bed.

"Why don't you come downstairs?" Amy suggested.

"Because I don't want too." Chloe whispered, her stomach churning at the thought of returning to the living room and being faced with the constant flirting under her nose. It was bad enough that she could hear the sounds of their laughter travelling upstairs almost constantly, but she couldn't quite bring herself to sit and watch it first-hand.

"I could run you a bath?" Amy offered, sighing sadly to herself when Chloe shook her head slowly.

"C'mon, come downstairs for a bit, you need to get some food anyway." she insisted.

"Lee is out anyway." she continued.

"Really?" Chloe frowned.

"Yeah he took Steph out to show her the studio." Amy explained. Chloe nodded slowly, her eyes filling with tears.

"He didn't even say goodbye." she whispered sadly.

"He came up too, but you were asleep." Amy told her.

"Honestly." she insisted when Chloe raised her eyebrow sceptically.

"Now come on, I'm not taking no for an answer." Amy beamed, grasping the duvet and quickly pulling it off Chloe. Chloe sighed and quickly stood up, following Amy downstairs before she could talk herself out of it.

"I also think we need to talk." Amy said, glancing at Chloe when she perched at the breakfast bar.

"But first, what do you want to eat?" she continued.

"Just a sandwich or something." Chloe said despondently, no longer having the energy to fight to get through each day.

"You can't just have a sandwich for dinner." Amy tried.

"I don't fancy a big meal." Chloe replied, quickly looking away from Amy's intense gaze.

"Anyway, I want to talk to you about Steven." Amy said tentatively.

"Yes I think I owe you an apology." Chloe sighed, slowly tracing small circles on the kitchen counter.

"I didn't mean to get so angry, I just want to protect you." she continued.

"I know and I love you for it, but just because you want to live your life a certain way, doesn't mean that I want to do the same." Amy pointed out.

"I'm sorry." Chloe whispered.

"You don't need to keep apologising." Amy smiled.

"Just promise me that you'll be careful. I don't want you getting hurt. Men aren't all they are cracked up to be." Chloe said sadly, placing her elbows on the counter and resting her chin on her hands, sighing deeply to herself.

"Yeah I noticed that Lee's been spending a lot of time with that woman." Amy said quietly.

"And they are very flirty." she continued thoughtfully.

"I'm glad I'm not the only one that noticed." Chloe sighed.

"Do you think it's because she was his first?" Amy said thoughtfully.

"I don't know, but I really don't want to talk about it." Chloe said quickly.

"You shouldn't bottle up your feelings." Amy pointed out.

"Only until the baby is born, then I'll figure everything out." she replied thoughtfully.

The two of them fell silent as the front door opened and closed.

"Oh for god sake." Chloe muttered under her breath, when she heard Steph laughing loudly about something.

"Oh hi Chloe, are you feeling better now?" Steph asked as she walked into the kitchen, closely followed by Lee.

"Yes thanks." Chloe said shortly, locking eyes with Amy across the kitchen. Amy shot her a small smile and quickly slid the sandwich along the counter.

"I'm not hungry." Chloe whispered, suddenly losing her appetite as Steph sat beside her at the kitchen island.

"Are you both okay?" Lee asked Chloe, gently wrapping his arm around Chloe's shoulders. Chloe nodded slowly. She gasped in pain, wincing slightly as Freyja kicked her.

"Is she kicking again?" Lee asked, sighing sadly when he noticed her face grimacing in pain.

"She likes to move about." Chloe said quietly, placing her hand on her sore abdomen and carefully rubbing it.

"I need to have a word with our baby when she is born. Tell her not to keep beating up her mother." Lee said quietly. Chloe's eyes snapped up when Steph leant over to touch her bump.

"Back off." Chloe warned, quickly moving out of her range before she could touch her baby.

"Alright, there's no need to get so defensive." Steph snapped.

"You have no right to touch my baby." Chloe told her sternly.

"Especially when she is inside me." she added.

"Okay whatever." Steph said, holding up her hands in defence.

"How long are you staying for?" Chloe asked, her temper finally starting to fray.

"Chloe." Lee said, before Steph had a chance to respond.

"It's a legitimate question." Chloe insisted.

"I think we need to give them a chance to talk." Amy piped up, quickly linking arms with Steph and leading her into the living room.

"Why are you being like this Chloe?" Lee asked as soon as they were alone.

"She hasn't done anything wrong." he added, before Chloe had a chance to respond.

"Apart from trying to touch my baby." she pointed out.

"You mean our baby." he pointed out.

"Besides she wasn't to know that you're very protective and only let me touch her." he continued, sighing deeply when Chloe slowly shook her head.

"Of course you would take her side. Who even is she and what the hell is she even doing here. Just turning up out of the blue!" Chloe exclaimed, the frustration that she was feeling finally bubbling over.

"She's my friend." he said shortly.

"You mean your ex." she said quickly.

"No she's not my ex. I told you before, you're the only person that I've dated." he sighed, trying to control the anger that was swirling in the pit of his stomach. Chloe had been pushing him away for the past few weeks and now she was trying to push him away from his friend. A small part of him couldn't help but feel that even though she didn't want him, she didn't want him to have anyone else in his life either.

"You had a fling with her then whatever!" Chloe snapped.

"Yeah when I was sixteen!" he exclaimed, no longer able to control the anger that was swirling in his stomach.

"You didn't tell me about her though did you." Chloe said angrily.

"That's because I didn't think it was a big deal!" he exclaimed.

"Oh c'mon, not only is she someone you had a fling with but she was your first. How do you think that's going to make me feel?!" she cried.

"Well, I'm sorry I have a past and I'm not a monk, but what do you want me to do about it?!" he said angrily.

"Not have her staying in the bloody house and spend all your time with her being flirty." Chloe pointed out.

"It's called having fun, maybe you should try it." he said shortly.

"Oh sorry, I'll try and be more like her for you." she snapped.

"Oh grow up Chloe." he replied, quickly walking out of the room. Chloe sighed angrily and ran her hand through her hair, hitting her hand against the kitchen counter as she tried to release the frustration that she was feeling. She slowly pushed the sandwich away along the counter, no longer able to stomach the idea of eating. Her heart sunk as she heard the sound of Lee's laughter, filling the living room. She couldn't help but feel like he would be happier if she was no longer around, and he wasn't the only one. Ever since the evening that she'd walked in on them playing on the games console and the atmosphere had completely changed, she couldn't escape the feeling that nobody wanted her around.

"At least you still need me Freyja." she whispered, her eyes filling with tears as she gazed down at her bump.

"For another couple of months anyway." she added, sniffing quietly to herself.

"Who are you talking too?" Amy asked as she walked back into the room.

"Nobody." Chloe replied, carefully standing up.

"You haven't eaten your sandwich!" Amy called after Chloe as she walked out of the room.

"I'm not hungry anymore." she called back, hesitating for a moment in the hallway before slowly climbing the stairs.

As soon as Chloe reached the bathroom, she switched on the bath tap and quickly locked the bathroom door behind herself. Her heart plummeted as she slowly removed her pyjamas and stared in silence at her reflection, no longer able to stop the warm tears from rolling down her cheeks as she stared at her hideous body.

"Life would have been so much easier if I'd died in the park." she whispered sadly, trailing her fingers along the scar on her abdomen.

"It's not like anyone needs me anyway." she continued thoughtfully, quickly climbing into the bath and curling into a ball, gently resting her arm against the side of the tub to keep her plaster cast dry.

"I'm so glad you haven't abandoned me little baby, you're the only one that hasn't." she sighed, her eyes flickering to the cut on her forearm that she'd made a couple of nights ago. She stared at it, completely transfixed, sighing to herself when she remembered the deep sense of relief that she'd felt when she'd hurt herself, how some of the anxiety had finally started to dissipate. Before she could stop herself she began to frantically scratch at the wound, desperately trying to open it back up so that it would bleed. She sighed in relief when the wound finally opened and a steady trickle of blood flowed down her arm, dripping into the bath water. Chloe stared in silence as she watched the droplets of her own blood swirling around the bath water. She sighed deeply, finally closing her eyes as she eventually started to relax.

Chapter Seventy Six

Chloe jumped and sat bolt upright on the sofa when she heard the front door open and close loudly. She rubbed the sleep out of her eyes, frowning as Nathan walked into the room.

"What are you doing here?" she frowned.

"I came over to check on everyone." he replied, perching on the end of the sofa, frowning to himself when he noticed that Chloe was still in her pyjamas.

"Have they gone out again?" he asked, sighing in frustration.

"No, they are still sleeping I think." she replied, tentatively sitting up and picking up a cushion and hugging it tightly against her frame, trying not to let on how desperately she longed for some comfort from someone. Despite the fact that she'd been pushing Lee away, she suddenly found herself craving the feel of being in his arms, for him to whisper in her ear and tell her that everything was going to be okay between the two of them and that he would never abandon her. But the last few days had made it clear to Chloe that he didn't care about her and their baby as much as he'd led her to believe. She'd barely seen him since Steph had arrived.

"But it's gone lunchtime." Nathan frowned, snapping Chloe out of her thoughts.

"They were having a party in the pool room until the early hours." she explained, placing her hands on her lap and picking her fingernails.

"He wasn't drinking was he?" he asked, his stomach churning nervously. Chloe nodded slowly.

"Judging by the noise and the amount of empty bottles, I'm going to say yes." she sighed, trying to hide how disappointed she was in Lee's behaviour. Her mind wandered back to all those months ago when he'd promised on their baby's grave that he wouldn't return to his drinking ways.

"She's really not a good influence on him is she." he said thoughtfully.

"But she's fun apparently." she muttered bitterly.

"I just don't get why she's here. She's been here nearly a week." she added thoughtfully.

"She always was a loose cannon." he said quietly, his heart breaking a little as he stared at Chloe. He couldn't help but notice that every time he saw her, she seemed more and more miserable, like a small part of her was dying inside with every day that passed.

"You know her from before too?" she asked.

"No, but I was talking to Steven about her the other night." he told her. Chloe raised her eyebrow and waited for him to continue.

"She basically just does whatever she wants and says whatever comes into her head. Goes through life on impulses and without thinking about the consequences." he explained.

"I kind of figured." she muttered, still not quite able to understand how someone could constantly flirt with a man, even though Steph knew that Lee was engaged and the two of them were expecting a baby.

"She has the morals of an alley cat." she said quietly, an edge of bitterness present in her voice.

"But apparently she's more fun and interesting than I am." she added, biting her lip as her eyes filled with tears.

"And definitely more beautiful." she added thoughtfully.

"I don't think that's true." he said quietly, sighing in frustration that once again Lee had no idea how much he was hurting the woman that he loved. Nathan had hoped the times had gone when Lee had acted like an idiot, and that he had matured, but clearly he was wrong.

"I guess I might have stood a chance if I still had my figure." she whispered. Nathan watched as she slowly fell sideways onto the sofa and curled into a ball, still holding onto the cushion tightly. A small sob escaped her lips as she dug her fingernails into the cushion. Nathan's eyes flickered to Chloe's sleeve when he suddenly noticed some blood that was seeping through.

"Chloe, you're bleeding." he said quickly. She followed his eyeline, nodding slowly, not really caring that she'd accidentally opened the fresh wound that she'd made last night.

"I'm fine." she said quickly.

"Let me check your arm." he insisted, quickly reaching over to her arm. Chloe moved her arm out of reach, before he could touch her.

"I can take care of myself." she said shortly, not quite able to bring herself to open up to anyone. Nathan sighed slowly, deciding not to press her. Even though it was clear to him that she was hurting herself, he had no idea how to handle the situation. His heart sunk when his mind wandered back to the conversation when she'd told them about her history of self-harming. The idea that she felt so helpless that she needed to hurt herself again, made him feel sick to his stomach. He couldn't help but feel a surge of anger towards Lee for the way that he was treating Chloe, ignoring her and causing her to feel so alone that she felt an overwhelming need to hurt herself.

"You don't need to hurt yourself Chlo Bo." he whispered, sighing to himself when she blinked

"But it helps. It's my reset button." she said quietly.

"I just feel so alone." she muttered.

"And it's even worse since Steph got here." she continued.

"Because you feel threatened?" he prompted her.

"Yes I guess so." she said sadly.

"I'll have a word with Lee." he said firmly, an edge of anger present in his voice.

"No, you can't!" she said quickly, her head snapping up.

"You can't tell him anything!" she continued, beginning to panic slightly at the idea of Lee finding out just how much he was slowly breaking her heart.

"But he's slowly destroying you!" Nathan said angrily, his temper flaring a little.

"I'll never forgive you Nathan." she said quietly, completely ignoring the steady stream of tears that were still rolling down her cheeks.

"Fine, I promise." he said reluctantly, still trying to suppress the anger that he was feeling towards Lee. He watched Chloe closely, his heart breaking that Lee could slowly destroy the kindest and purest person that they'd ever met. It was more than obvious how much Chloe was struggling, and Lee should be taking care of her, rather than spending all of his spare time with Steph. Nathan shuffled along the sofa, so that he was beside her.

Chloe nodded and curled back up on the sofa again.

"You're not alone Chlo Bo." he whispered, gently stroking her hair, in a desperate attempt to provide her with some comfort.

"I'm your big brother remember. I'll always be here for you." he continued, sighing sadly when she nodded slowly and gently wiped away her tears. He quickly picked up one of the blankets and placed it over her frame when he noticed that she was shivering.

"Promise me that you won't hurt yourself anymore." he muttered, his heart still hurting at the thought of it.

"I can't promise that, sometimes I need to do it." she admitted.

"At least call me if that happens, I can distract you or something." he pointed out. Chloe opened her mouth to respond, her stomach churning as she heard footsteps walking downstairs. She quickly sat up and wiped away her tears, safely tucking her arm underneath the blanket so that they wouldn't notice the blood stain on her shirt.

Lee froze as he walked into the room, frowning to himself when he noticed Nathan glaring at him angrily. He raised his eyebrow questioningly, frowning when Nathan slowly shook his head and looked away from him.

"What's your problem?" Lee asked, when he couldn't stand it any longer.

"You're my problem." Nathan said shortly, trying to resist the urge to lay into Lee.

"All you do is follow that tart around like a love struck puppy, when you have a fiancée and a baby on the way." he continued. Lee opened his mouth to respond, quickly closing it again when Steph walked into the room and handed him a coffee.

"Did you sleep down here Chloe?" Lee asked, finally noticing the collection of blankets on the sofa.

"I slept a little bit in front of the TV." she said quietly.

"Why?" he asked.

"Because the two of you were making so much noise that I couldn't sleep, so I came down to watch TV." Chloe explained.

"We were just having a little party." Steph giggled.

"She needs to get her rest though, you should be more mindful." Nathan piped up.

"He doesn't care anymore." Chloe said quietly.

"Are you kidding me?" Lee snapped, an edge of anger present in his voice.

"You clearly don't. So much for all that crap about you would do anything for me and the baby and you don't even care if I get enough rest. I guess I'm just an incubator to you." Chloe snapped, her temper finally fraying.

"That's complete bullshit and you know it!" Lee said angrily. Chloe scoffed sceptically, slowly shaking her head.

"That's not true at all Chloe." Steph piped up leaping to Lee's defence.

"He barely stops talking about Freyja." she continued.

"Excuse me?!" Chloe spluttered.

"How the hell do you know about my baby's name?!" she continued, her stomach churning as she glanced between her and Lee.

"It was meant to be a secret between the two of us, we weren't going to tell anyone!" she shouted, her temper growing when Nathan placed her hand on his knee to comfort her and she suddenly remembered that he was still in the room. Not only was Steph aware of the name that they'd chosen for their baby, but now Nathan was too. The secret bond and agreement between the two of them was fractured for good.

"It slipped out one day when I'd had a couple of beers." Lee replied, his stomach churning with guilt that he'd accidentally broken his promise to her. It hadn't been his intention to reveal their baby's name and he wished that he could take it back.

"You mean the beers that you're not supposed to be drinking." Chloe said bitterly.

"Don't worry Chloe, I'm not going to tell anyone." Steph said, shooting Chloe a small smile.

"That's not the bloody point. We weren't going to tell anyone!" Chloe said angrily.

"Least of all someone like you. You're not even family!" she continued.

"In fact, you're nothing to the baby!" she ranted, not quite able to control the deep anger that she was feeling.

"It's really not a big deal." Steph said, a small smirk playing on the corner of her lips. Chloe quickly looked away from her, taking deep breaths to try and control her temper.

"I am sorry Chloe, it was an accident." Lee said quietly.

"Yeah you said." she said shortly, not even able to bring herself to look at him.

"C'mon, let's go and make breakfast." Lee stated, quickly grasping Steph's wrist and pulling her into the kitchen with him, sensing that Chloe needed some time to calm down.

Chapter Seventy Seven

As soon as Steph and Lee left the room, Chloe angrily flung the cushion across the room, desperately trying to find a way to release some of the deep anger that she was feeling. She couldn't believe that he had revealed the name of their baby to someone, especially someone that wasn't even part of their family.

"You need to calm down Chloe." Nathan said gently.

"I'm not being unreasonable though am I?!" she exclaimed, still not quite able to suppress her temper.

"No you're not. He's completely out of line." he agreed.

"We haven't even told Sheila who is her grandmother and he goes and tells her." she said, her voice dripping with disdain as she couldn't even bring herself to say Steph's name.

"It doesn't excuse what he's done, but I do think it genuinely was an accident." he pointed out. Chloe fell silent, her temper flaring again when she heard the sound of hushed voices coming from the kitchen, she couldn't make out what they were saying, but her gut was screaming at her that Steph and Lee were speaking about her.

"He's so loyal to her, it's like he's forgotten about me and the baby." Chloe said, sighing quietly. Her ears pricked up when she heard Steph laughing from the kitchen.

"Oh I remember that when you were at that show and you didn't want to get your hair wet walking to the car so you asked to borrow my umbrella!" Steph giggled.

"And then they took a photograph of us and everyone thought you were my girlfriend." he laughed back.

"They are at it again." Chloe muttered sadly.

"I actually want to kick his arse for the way he's treating you." Nathan muttered angrily.

"You shouldn't get involved. You have the band to think about." she pointed out.

"And the tour in January." she added. The two of them fell silent as Steph and Lee walked into the room, each of them carrying a plate of toast.

"Don't worry, we didn't want any." Nathan said sarcastically, glaring at them both as they sat on the sofa.

"Nobody else matters anymore." Chloe muttered under her breath.

"Chloe, I would really like to clear the air. I promise that I will keep it to myself about Freyja's name." Steph piped up nervously. Chloe remained silent, not quite able to bring herself to look at either of them.

"Her name is actually really beautiful." Steph tried.

"It's the norse goddess of love." Lee explained.

"Ironic." Chloe muttered under her breath, so low that only Nathan heard her.

"I assume her middle name is going to be Private?" Nathan teased, chuckling to herself when a small smile appeared on Chloe's lips.

"You're obsessed." she smiled, elbowing him in the ribs.

"I still think it should be her first name, it's just too perfect." Nathan beamed.

"She's Freyja Emilia." Chloe told him.

"After my Mum." she added, her eyes glistening with tears as her thoughts wandered to her mother and how desperately she wanted her around, now more than ever.

"That's really nice." Nathan smiled.

"What about her surname?" Steph asked, glancing between the two of them.

"We haven't really spoken about it have we?" Lee said quietly, turning to face Chloe, his heart breaking a little, like it did every time that he looked at her and he was reminded that she didn't want him around. Chloe shook her head slowly, not really in the mood to talk to him about their baby.

"Well surely if you're getting married, you'll go for Knight won't you?" Steph prompted them.

"Yeah well that's a joke in itself!" Chloe said angrily, glancing at Lee when he coughed on his mouthful of toast.

"Why are you so interested anyway, it's none of your business?" Chloe rounded on Steph, trying to ignore Lee's gaze that she could feel burning a hole in her head.

"I'm just really pleased for you both." Steph smiled.

"And I can't believe this one is going to be a Dad." she added, beaming at Lee. Lee nodded slowly, swallowing the dry lump that was rising in his throat as Chloe's words swirled around his head. Even though he knew that she was pushing him away, for some unknown reason, he'd never for one moment considered the possibility that she wouldn't want to marry him as she seemed to be suggesting.

"And I can't wait to have a cuddle with her when she is born, I love babies." Steph smiled.

"I think I need some fresh air." Lee said, quickly standing up, trying to leave the house before he revealed how much Chloe's words had ripped into his heart.

"Are you coming?" he asked Steph. She nodded and quickly followed him.

"We'll be late back as we're going to the pub later!" he called to them, before leaving the house and slamming the front door behind them.

"She is such a bitch." Chloe muttered angrily, her stomach still swirling with anger that Lee had revealed their baby's name.

"Yeah I know, he is like putty in her hands." Nathan agreed.

"I don't understand why she seems to have so much influence over him." she said thoughtfully.

"Me neither, he's so different since she came back into his life." he replied, sighing sadly to himself, his eyes flickering to Chloe as she slowly stood up.

"He really doesn't care about me anymore." she muttered, her eyes misting with tears as she thought about all the times over the past few months that he'd told her how much he loved and cared about her. That he would always cherish her. She couldn't help but wonder if he'd meant a single one of those words that he'd uttered.

"I don't know what's gotten into him, he needs his arse kicked." he said quickly, his stomach churning with anger. He couldn't help but remember how Lee had made a promise to never hurt Chloe again after he'd spent the best part of a year bullying her, and how not only had he broken that promise, but he'd broken the promise to keep the name of their baby a secret.

"And why is she so interested in my baby." she frowned, snapping him out of his thoughts.

"She keeps asking questions all the time." she continued, her heart pounding against her chest as she began to pace, not quite able to escape the feeling in her gut that something wasn't right.

"She's probably just trying to suck up to Lee." he said angrily.

"But what was she talking about when she said she can't wait to hold her. Surely she's not still going to be here two months from now when the baby is born?!" she exclaimed, beginning to panic that Steph would never be out of their lives. Nathan frowned at her words, suddenly realising that she was correct.

"Oh my god." she whispered, her feet freezing to the spot as she finally stopped pacing.

"What?" he asked, watching her closely.

"What if she wants to take my baby from me?" she mumbled, gazing down at her bump as she rested her hand against it protectively.

"She won't." he quickly reassured her.

"But what if she tries too?!" she exclaimed.

"What if that's her plan, she wants to take Lee from me and then the two of them will raise Freyja together?!" she continued, her eyes wide with panic as she began to pace once again, her eyes darting around frantically.

"She can't take my baby!" she exclaimed, taking deep breaths as she continued to pace, trying to control the intense anxiety that she was feeling.

"Lee wouldn't let her do that." he pointed out, trying to find a way of calming her down.

"Really, he always takes her side!" she pointed out.

"Not over you and the baby he wouldn't." he reassured her, not entirely sure if Lee could be relied upon to stand up for Chloe, but choosing not to mention it.

"Besides, I wouldn't let her anyway." he added, shooting her a small smile when she took a final deep breath and eventually stopped pacing.

"I'll fight until my last breath for my baby girl anyway." she said firmly.

Chapter Seventy Eight

"I think maybe you should get an early night Chlo Bo." Nathan chuckled when she yawned for the fourth time in the past few minutes.

"It's not even nine yet though." she protested.

"You didn't get very much sleep last night though did you and you have to listen to your body." he argued, smiling slightly when she raised her eyebrow defiantly.

"Plus we have to finish the film." she pointed out stubbornly. Before Chloe could react, Nathan picked up the remote and quickly switched off the television.

"We can finish watching it tomorrow." he insisted.

"You need to get some sleep." he continued, smiling when she yawned once again. Chloe sighed in defeat when she suddenly realised that she was struggling to stay awake. She curled into a ball on the sofa, snuggling under the blankets.

"Aren't you going up to bed?" he asked her, frowning in confusion.

"I prefer sleeping down here on my own." she admitted, her cheeks colouring slightly when she felt Nathan watching her closely. He sighed sadly to himself, his heart breaking as he suddenly realised just how lost and alone Chloe was feeling. How she would rather sleep on the sofa alone than have to face the man who was hurting her on a daily basis.

"What are you doing?" she frowned when Nathan shuffled along the sofa and laid down beside her.

"I'll stay with you until the others get back." he told her.

"They'll be ages, they have late night parties remember." she pointed out, sighing sadly to herself.

"And Amy is staying at Steven's." she added.

"It's fine Chlo Bo, I don't want you to be alone." he said quietly, not quite able to bring himself to leave her completely alone in the house, particularly when she had been harming herself again. Chloe nodded slowly, sighing in relief that she still had one person in the world that cared about her.

"I'm so sorry for everything." she whispered, slowly wiping away the tears that were filling her eyes and snuggling against a cushion.

"Why are you apologising?" he frowned, not entirely sure what she was talking about. She remained silent.

"Just close your eyes Chlo Bo." he said softly.

"Don't carry on watching the film without me." she said quietly, a small sob escaping her lips when she chuckled. Nathan sighed to himself as he watched her crying herself to sleep, wishing that he knew what to do to make her feel better. He couldn't help but wonder if she cried herself to sleep every night, secretly suffering alone. His heart broke further when she sniffed quietly and wiped away her tears, crying out in pain when she accidentally twisted her broken wrist, forgetting in her anguish that she was still wearing her cast.

"It's okay Chloe, you're not alone." he said softly, trying to help her to relax. She nodded slowly as she closed her eyes, no longer able to fight the exhaustion that she was feeling. He breathed a small smile of relief when she eventually fell asleep, her chest slowly rising and falling. His eyes flickered to her arm, his stomach churning when he noticed the blood stain that was still present on her pyjama sleeve. Before he could stop himself, he slowly leaned over, glancing at Chloe nervously when she fidgeted in her sleep, fearful that he would wake her.

He gently rolled up her sleeve, feeling slightly guilty that he was going against her wishes, but not quite able to fight the need to check on her wound and to know that she was okay. He gasped, his heart plummeting when he laid eyes on several deep slices on her forearm. Nathan shook his head slowly, trying to control the deep anger that was swirling in his stomach.

"I'm sorry Chlo Bo. I was the one that encouraged the two of you to get together." he whispered, gently stroking the wounds with his thumb, not quite able to stomach the idea of his little sister harming herself deliberately.

"I thought he would make you happy." he sighed, leaning forward and placing a soft kiss on her forehead. He jumped, quickly rolling her sleeve back down as she fidgeted in her sleep. He sighed deeply when he heard the front door close with a bang, shaking his head slowly when Chloe bolted awake and slowly sat up, resting her elbow of the back of the sofa and placing her forehead onto her hand, still not fully awake.

"Put your arm down Chlo Bo." Nathan said quickly, his eyes flickering to the blood stain on her sleeve. Chloe gasped as she heard footsteps approaching the living room, quickly tucking her arm out of sight under the blanket. Her heart sunk when Lee and Steph entered the room, both of them glancing between Chloe and Nathan nervously when they noticed the tense atmosphere.

"What's going on?" Lee asked.

"Nothing." Nathan replied shortly, not even able to bring himself to look Lee in the eyes. He knew that if he looked at Lee, he would no longer be able to control the intense anger that he was feeling towards him and the last thing he wanted to do was cause Chloe any more suffering.

"There's obviously something." Lee insisted, glancing between the two of them, not quite able to shake the feeling in his gut that something was going on.

"I've only just woken up." Chloe muttered, her cheeks colouring as she glanced at Nathan and he shot her a small smile.

"Yeah but why are you sleeping down here?" Lee asked, his confusion growing when he noticed the collection of blankets on the sofa.

"Especially when you said that you needed to get rest." he added, slightly confused as to why she was sleeping downstairs, when she'd had a go at him for keeping her awake at night. Chloe shook her head slowly, trying to hold back the tears that had filled her eyes. In all the years that she'd known Lee, she'd never known him to be so unreasonable. He seemed to have no idea how she was feeling, either that or he didn't care enough to try and find out. She'd barely seen him all day, ever since he left after Chloe found out that he'd revealed the name of their baby. His apology had been thin veiled at best and then he'd spent the entire day with Steph, not even bothering to call or message her, yet here he was questioning her, almost like she'd done something wrong.

"Besides it's warmer upstairs." Lee tried again, trying to prompt her into responding.

"She slept down here, because I didn't want her to be alone." Nathan said shortly.

"Why?" Lee asked quickly.

"What's with all the questions, have you suddenly decided to care?!" Nathan said angrily, no longer able to suppress the anger that he was feeling.

"What's that supposed to mean?!" Lee snapped defensively. Nathan opened his mouth to respond, quickly closing it again when he locked eyes with Chloe and noticed the look of pleading in Chloe's eyes.

"On that note, I'm going to bed." Chloe said, quickly wrapping the blanket around her frame and standing up.

"Is this because I accidentally revealed the baby's name?" Lee asked incredulously, not entirely sure why he was getting such dirty looks from the two of them.

"I said I'm going to bed." she said shortly.

"Thank you for staying with me." she said quietly, shooting Nathan a small smile.

"Will you be alright if I head off?" he asked her, still not entirely sure if he should remain by her side or not. Chloe nodded slowly, hurrying to leave the room before Lee could ask her any more questions that she didn't want to answer.

Chapter Seventy Nine

Lee ran his hand through his hair in frustration, frowning to himself as Nathan walked away, slamming the front door behind himself. Nathan was one of his oldest friends, he couldn't understand why he refused to speak to him and seemed to be pushing him away in the same way as Chloe. Even though he knew that he hadn't spent much time with Chloe recently, that was a result of her not wanting him around. There was only so much hitting his head against a brick wall that he could take. He'd tried and tried to reach her, but she pushed him away each time, his heart breaking more and more when she did. To this day, he still had no idea what he was supposed to have done to make her hate him so much. His eyes wandered to the stairs as he found himself longing to follow Chloe and hold her tightly in his arms, but he knew that she wouldn't allow him too. It felt like his heart was being ripped out of his chest whenever she rejected him or recoiled from his touch, almost like she was disgusted by him. He couldn't help but wonder if she still wanted a future with him or if he was slowly losing her and their baby for good.

"Hey, you know what you need!" Steph piped up excitedly, snapping him out of his thoughts.

"My little Chlo back." he mumbled thoughtfully, biting the inside of his lip to prevent himself from crying.

"You need one of these bad boys." she grinned, handing him a beer. Lee sighed quietly as he took the bottle that she handed him, his eyes flickering once again to the stairs as he hesitated.

"Oh what the hell." he muttered, finally deciding that it was easier to drown his sorrows than face Chloe's constant disdain.

Chloe blinked slowly, carefully reaching out to switch on the bedroom lamp, frowning to herself for a moment as she gazed at the unfamiliar surroundings. Her heart plummeted when she suddenly remembered that she was sleeping in the spare room in an attempt to avoid Lee's presence. Chloe's eyes misted with tears that she'd woken up from her dream where the two of them had been happy and playing with their baby. She couldn't help but wish that she could return to her dream, since it was better than her current reality.

She sighed to herself as she heard the sounds of joyous laughter coming from downstairs. Chloe glanced at the clock, rolling her eyes when she realised that it was almost one am. She snuggled under the covers, trying to ignore the constant commotion from downstairs. Her stomach swirled with anger when she heard Lee singing along to a song on the radio. Without even laying eyes on him, she knew that he had been drinking, his singing voice sounding more hoarse than usual. Despite the fact that she knew that he didn't care about her, she couldn't help but feel disappointed that he didn't seem to care about his unborn baby. He needed to grow up and be a good father, not spend his time drinking and messing about with Steph.

Before Chloe could stop herself she threw off the covers and angrily marched downstairs, no longer able to stand the constant noise. She followed the sounds of their voices, shaking her head slowly when she realised that they were coming from the pool room. Her stomach churned with anger as she stood in the hallway, peering in the window to the pool room, not quite able to tear her eyes away from them as they messed around together, both of their faces lighting up in happiness. A lump rose in her throat when she realised that she'd been right all along....he truly was happier when he wasn't with her. Her eyes flickered over to Steph when she wrapped her arms around Lee's neck, gazing into his eyes, hesitating for a moment before placing a soft kiss on his lips. Lee placed his hands on her waist, a stunned expression on his face for a brief moment before he closed his eyes and kissed her back, craving the comfort of human contact that he'd been deprived. Chloe placed her hand on the door handle, curling it into her fist as she gripped it tightly, feeling the need to grasp something as she tried to process what she'd seen. She dropped to her knees, no longer having the strength to support her own weight. It felt like the rug had been ripped from under her feet, the full realisation hitting her that she had lost Lee for good, like she'd begun to sense. He truly did prefer to be around Steph and was clearly more attracted to her, so much so that he was prepared to cheat on the person that he claimed to love with all of his heart. Her eyes filled with tears as she gazed down at the engagement ring that was still in place on her finger. She quickly tore her eyes away from it, resting the back of her head against the door as she stared at the ceiling, trying to process what she'd just witnessed. Chloe closed her eyes, a small sob escaping her lips when she saw the image of Lee kissing another woman swirling around her head. In that moment she knew that he had truly forsaken her and there was nothing that she could do about it.

"I'm sorry little baby, but I can't stay here anymore." she whispered, gently resting her hand against her bump as she carefully stood up, slightly afraid that she was going to fall over as a result of the shock at what she'd just witnessed. She hurried upstairs, holding tightly to the banister as she walked, fearful that her legs would buckle from under her. The baby was now the only person that she had left, the only one that hadn't abandoned her for someone else. Chloe had always known that she was worthless but now she had the final proof. As soon as she reached the bedroom, she pulled her suitcase from under the bed, flinging open the wardrobe as she stared at her clothes that were hanging inside. Tears filled her eyes as she angrily ripped her clothes from the hangers, flinging them into the suitcase. She frantically hurried around the room, picking up her clothing and throwing them into the suitcase, desperate to leave the house as soon as possible. Her breath caught in her throat as she pulled her memory box out of the cupboard and stared at the contents. She staggered backwards, quickly perching on the end of the bed, her gaze fixed on the box. Her hands shook as she slowly removed her photo album. Before she could stop herself she turned to the last few pages, staring at the picture of Lee with her mother. A small sob escaped her lips as she brushed her finger against the picture of her mother.

"Why does everyone always abandon me." she whispered to herself, not quite able to process that she'd been cheated on once again. She'd thought that her heart had broken when Andy had admitted to her what he'd done, but the pain that she was felt was nothing compared to how she was feeling right now. She loved Lee with all of her heart, the way that she felt for him, she'd never felt for anyone, and she knew that she never would again. Her hands shook as she carefully picked up the baby grow that Lee had given to her when he'd asked her to become his wife. She closed her eyes for a moment, her brain swirling with memories for when she'd stood at the top of the tower, gazing down at the landscape and the man that had stolen her heart proposed to her. Her eyes snapped open as she quickly picked up her phone from the bedside cabinet and phoned Nathan.

"Hello." he said sleepily.

"Nathan!" she exclaimed, breathing a sigh of relief when he eventually picked up the phone. She frowned to herself when she realised how sleepy he sounded, her stomach churning with guilt when she glanced at the clock and realised how late it was. With everything that had happened, she'd completely forgotten that it was the early hours of the morning.

"Sorry, I didn't mean to wake you." she whispered, swallowing the lump that was rising in her throat.

"It's okay Chlo Bo, what's wrong?" Nathan asked, groaning quietly as he sat up in bed.

"You haven't hurt yourself again have you?!" he asked quickly, before she had a chance to respond.

"No." she said shortly.

"Can you come over and pick me up please?" she pleaded, her voice breaking slightly.

"I know it's late and I'm sorry to ask, but Amy won't be back until the morning and I can't stay here." she sobbed, no longer able to hold back the emotions that she was fighting.

"What's happened?!" Nathan asked quickly, climbing out of bed when he heard the distress in Chloe's voice.

"I'll tell you when you're over, please hurry Nathan." she replied, her heart pounding against her chest nervously at the thought of having to speak to Lee. To be face to face with the man who claimed to love her but clearly didn't care about her at all.

"I'll be right over." Nathan stated, snapping Chloe out of her thoughts. Chloe nodded slowly, flinging her phone onto the bed when she heard the dial tone. She stood up slowly, almost like she was in a daze, the tears still flowing freely down her cheeks as she quickly dressed, briefly glancing at her reflection in the mirror, before quickly turning away in disgust. Her heart pounded against her chest as her thoughts wandered to Steph and her slender frame. Chloe quickly picked up her photo album and hugged it tightly against her chest, slowly falling sideways onto the bed. She sniffed sadly to herself as she curled into a ball, closing her eyes, a small part of her wishing that she could fall asleep and never wake up, to escape from the pain.

Chapter Eighty

Nathan sighed sadly to himself as he climbed into his car, quickly making his way to Lee's house. His brain was swirling with a mist of his thoughts as he tried to figure out what could possibly have happened for Chloe to be so upset that she would call him in the early hours of the morning. He knew how independent she was, and how much she hated to feel like a burden to people, so he couldn't help but think that it was something bad. That she felt so alone and powerless, that she didn't know where else to turn.

As soon as he pulled into Lee's driveway, he quickly switched off the ignition and hurried into the house, still not quite able to escape the fear that Chloe might have done something to hurt herself, despite the fact that she said she hadn't. He quickly opened Lee's front door and removed his shoes in the hallway, sighing to himself as he heard the sounds of Lee and Steph talking to each other, their voices gradually getting closer to him. Nathan frowned to himself as he heard them place a cup onto the kitchen counter.

"I keep telling you how cute you are." Steph beamed at Lee, bursting out laughing when his cheeks coloured.

"Like that time a few years ago when the fans were waiting outside to see you and it was freezing cold so you brought them a hot chocolate to warm them up." she continued, smiling proudly at Lee.

"I think you made the fans day." she added.

"I only did what anyone else would have done." he smiled at her.

"A lot of people wouldn't." she insisted. Nathan sighed as Lee walked past the doorway and locked eyes with him, frowning in confusion.

"I thought you went home?" Lee frowned.

"Apparently not." Nathan said shortly.

"Oh hi Nathan." Steph said sweetly, quickly standing beside Lee. Nathan shook his head slowly, his temper slowly simmering.

"I am so sick of hearing about your trips down memory lane and so are the rest of us." Nathan said shortly.

"It's actually ridiculous." he added.

"What's your problem?" Lee snapped defensively.

"Maybe it's his time of the month or something." Steph said, giggling quietly to herself.

"Or maybe you've out stayed your welcome." Nathan snapped. Steph rolled her eyes at him, a small smirk playing on the corner of her lips as she maintained eye contact with him, staring him down. Nathan shook his head slowly, quickly turning his back on them and hurrying upstairs.

Chloe's eyes flickered up as the bedroom door opened and Nathan strode into the room, hurrying over to her as soon as he noticed her curled up on the bed. She carefully sat up and swung her legs over the bed, gazing down at her feet, still not entirely sure how to process what had happened.

"What's going on Chlo Bo?" he asked, quickly squatting down in front of her and taking her hands in his when he noticed that she was shaking. Chloe shook her head slowly, not quite able to bring herself to say the words aloud.

"Chloe?" he tried, softly wiping away her tears with his thumb.

"I saw them...." she started, trailing off when her voice began to break.

"Saw what?" he prompted her, his stomach churning nervously.

"They kissed." she muttered, angrily wiping away the tears that were flowing down her cheeks.

"I'm such an idiot Nathan." she added thoughtfully.

"You haven't done anything wrong." he said through gritted teeth, trying to control the intense anger that was swirling in his stomach.

"I always knew that I wasn't enough for him, I should have walked away when I had the chance." she muttered, carefully climbing off the bed and stuffing the photo album into her suitcase.

"Then he wouldn't have been able to cheat on me." she continued, kneeling down next to her suitcase, her eyes fixed on it, the realisation of exactly what had happened, finally dawning on her. Nathan watched in horror as Chloe placed her head in her hands and began to cry, her breath coming out in loud sobs.

"I'm going to kick his arse." Nathan said angrily, quickly standing up, no longer able to listen to her sobs that were so full of anguish, he could feel his heart slowly breaking for her.

"No don't!" she called after him, beginning to panic slightly.

"I just want to leave without a fuss." she added quickly. Nathan sighed to himself, keeping his back to her as he took deep breaths, trying to suppress the deep anger that he was feeling.

"Nathan please." she pleaded.

"Have you got everything?" he said quickly, trying to keep himself occupied so that he was able to resist the temptation to lay into the two people who had broken the heart of the person that he loved like a little sister.

"I think so." she said quietly, staggering as she slowly stood up. Nathan quickly reached out and placed his hand on her elbow, carefully steadying her.

"Do you want to come and stay at mine for a while?" he offered.

"Just for tonight." she said quietly, slowly wiping away the tears that were still flowing down her cheeks.

"When Amy is back from Steven's, I'll go back to Nottingham with her." she said matter of factly, quickly brushing her hair out of her face.

"You're really done with him?" he whispered.

"He cheated on me Nathan, I have no reason to stick around." she pointed out. He nodded slowly, sighing sadly to himself as he slowly zipped up her suitcase. Chloe sniffed quietly to herself as she slowly picked up her corset from the memory box, her heart pounding against her chest as she remembered the day of the photoshoot. A small smile played on the corner of her lips as she recalled the fond memories of how confident and empowered she felt when she'd finally conquered her fear of wearing something revealing in public. She would never forget how much Lee had struggled to resist her the whole day of the shoot and how Jonny had been unable to tear his eyes from her. She gently brushed the material with her thumb, trying to hold back the tears that were once again filling her eyes.

Nathan's head snapped towards her when she quickly stood up and picked up her suitcase, her jaw set in anger.

"I'll take that." he offered, holding his hand out for the suitcase. Chloe smiled her thanks and silently handed it to him, before taking one last look at the corset that she was still holding in her hand. She strode out of the room, taking deep breaths to try and suppress the anger that was slowly building inside of her. Nathan hurried after her, frowning to himself as she walked into the kitchen. He breathed a small sigh of relief when he realised that Steph and Lee were no longer in the room. The last thing he wanted to do was to face them, particularly when he was trying to respect Chloe's wishes to not give them a piece of his mind.

"Isn't that the corset from the photoshoot?" he frowned, finally glancing at what Chloe was carrying. She nodded slowly, her eyes fixed on it as she stood in front of the bin, hesitating for a moment.

"What are you doing?" he frowned as she flung it into the bin, angrily slamming the lid closed.

"It's not like I'm ever going to fit into it again!" she said angrily.

"Besides if he wants to fish it out of the bin, I'm sure Steph will wear it for him." she continued, an edge of bitterness present in her voice.

"You look beautiful in it though Chlo Bo." he pointed out, sighing sadly to himself when Chloe staggered slightly, quickly leaning against the kitchen counter for support. He watched as she placed her back against the counter, slowly sliding down the cupboards as she dropped to her knees.

"I can't believe it's come to this." she whispered thoughtfully.

"Me neither." he agreed, not entirely sure what to say to her.

"I'm just so tried of everything." she whispered, resting her elbow on her knee and slowly rolling up her sleeve, sighing sadly to herself as she gazed at the wounds on her forearm.

"You need rest in your condition, not all of this stress." he said angrily. He gasped to himself as she fell silent, absentmindedly picking at her wounds. Her head snapped up as he quickly crossed the room and squatted in front of her, taking her hands in his, to stop her from harming herself.

"Don't Chloe." he told her firmly.

"He's not worth it." he continued, carefully rolling her sleeve down so that her wounds were safely covered.

"C'mon, we need to get you to mine." he added, glanced around nervously, fearful that Lee or Steph would appear before they were able to leave the house. He couldn't help but feel that Chloe wasn't strong enough to face them after everything that she'd been through.

"I need to get my medication from the hospital." she said quietly, suddenly remembering that she hadn't packed her Iron tablets.

"Where are they?" he asked her, watching closely as she carefully rose to her feet. She remained silent and opened the kitchen drawer, her hands shaking as she picked up the tablets and placed them in her jacket pocket.

"I think I have everything." she mumbled.

"Anything that you don't have, we can ask Amy to pick up for you tomorrow." he told her. She nodded slowly, glancing down at his outstretched hand and quickly taking it, shooting him a small smile when he squeezed her hand reassuringly.

Chapter Eighty One

Chloe glanced at Nathan as they reached the hallway, her eyes widening when she suddenly remembered that her laptop was still in the living room.

"What's wrong?" he asked, instantly noticing the change in her body language.

"I've left my laptop in the living room." she said quietly, glancing nervously in the direction of the living room, her stomach churning when she heard Lee and Steph's voices travelling along the hallway.

"I'll go and get it for you." he said quickly, instantly realising that she didn't want to have to face the two people who had broken her heart. She shot him a small smile, before perching on her suitcase and silently picking her fingernails, still not quite able to process what had happened.

Nathan hurried into the room, throwing the door open with so much force that it clattered against the wall.

"What's gotten into you?" Steph frowned, glancing between him and Lee. Nathan remained silent, quickly swiping the laptop off the coffee table.

"Is this Chloe's laptop?" he checked, not quite able to bring himself to make eye contact with Lee.

"What's going on?" Lee asked nervously, instantly sensing that Nathan was furious about something.

"I asked you a question." Nathan replied shortly.

"Yeah it's Chloe's." Lee replied, still not quite able to shake the feeling that something was wrong.

"Why does she need it at this hour, I thought she was sleeping?" he continued.

"Don't even speak to me." Nathan snapped, tucking the laptop under his arm and hurrying out of the room. He sighed to himself as he walked back into the hallway and noticed Chloe quickly wiping the tears from her cheeks, clearly hoping that he wouldn't notice. She carefully stood up, watching Nathan closely as he unzipped her suitcase and placed the laptop inside.

Lee frowned to himself, his stomach churning nervously as Nathan walked away from him. No matter how hard he tried, he couldn't shake the feeling that something was going on that he wasn't being told about. He glanced at Steph when he felt her watching him closely, sighing as she shrugged in response, clearly just as confused by the whole situation as he was. Before he could talk himself out of it, he stood up and followed Nathan into the hallway, his heart plummeting when he noticed Chloe standing in silence, her gaze fixed on the floor, as Nathan quickly zipped up her suitcase.

"Are you going somewhere?!" he blurted, slightly afraid of her answer. She nodded slowly, not quite able to bring herself to look at him.

"Where are you going?" he asked, his heart pounding against his chest.

"Anywhere that isn't here." she said shortly, her gaze still fixed on the ground as she tried to hold back the tears that were filling her eyes. As soon as she'd heard his voice, it felt like someone had ripped her heart out of her chest, almost as if he had her heart in his hand and was slowly crushed it in his fist.

"Why?" he asked quickly, frowning to himself when Chloe scoffed in response, slowly shaking her head.

"Chlo?" he tried, taking a step towards her.

"Don't!" she exclaimed, quickly holding up her finger, her temper fraying.

"You've lost your right to call me that!" she continued angrily.

"What is it that I've meant to have done now?" he sighed.

"I think you know exactly what you have done." Nathan piped up.

"Enlighten me." Lee snapped.

"Surely you're not that drunk that you don't remember sticking your tongue down someone else's throat?" Chloe said bitterly. Lee swallowed the lump that was rising in his throat, finally falling silent as Chloe finally locked eyes with him, raising her eyebrow at him, almost like she was challenging him to deny it.

"I saw you." she added, trying to prompt him into a response.

"It was an accident." he muttered, his stomach churning with guilt.

"I'm sure it was, I always accidentally kiss people." she said sarcastically.

"I am sorry for it, I think it was the alcohol." he said quietly.

"I don't care what it was, you cheated on me!" she shouted, no longer able to control her temper.

"That's a bit dramatic, nothing is going on." he snapped defensively.

"And technically she kissed me." he added.

"Are you seriously trying to justify what you did?!" she exclaimed.

"You kissed someone else, that's cheating." she continued, slowly shaking her head, not entirely sure what was going on with him. It almost seemed like he didn't care about her and their relationship at all.

"How would you feel if I did that to you?!" she cried, still not quite able to suppress the anger that she was feeling. Lee opened his mouth to respond, quickly closing it again as he tried to process her words. He sighed deeply to himself, suddenly realising that she was right. Even though he hadn't intended for the kiss to happen, he wished that he could take it back and deeply regretted the hurt that he'd accidentally caused her.

"The worst part is that you traded in someone who is kind and pure for someone with no morals." Nathan piped up.

"She does have morals." Lee argued.

"Of course that's what you took from that." Chloe scoffed.

"Someone with morals doesn't kiss someone who they know is engaged!" Nathan snapped.

"Anyway that's not the worst part......the worst part is that you didn't even tell me." Chloe said quietly.

"If that was me, I would have been straight upstairs, on my knees, begging for your forgiveness, but you really don't give a shit." she said sadly, angrily wiping away the tears that were rolling down her cheeks as she finally realised that the man standing before her was a million miles away from the kind and caring man that she'd fallen in love with. Chloe stared at him as he finally fell silent, not even caring enough to fight for her.

"We should go." she muttered, turning to face Nathan. Nathan nodded slowly, quickly picking up her suitcase and opening the front door for her.

"Oh, and you can tell your little tart that I've left a present for her in the bin." she said shortly, hesitating in the doorway for a moment, before quickly slamming the front door closed behind her.

Lee slowly opened his eyes, squinting in the bright sunlight that was streaming in the bedroom window. He winced at the intense throbbing in his head, instantly regretting that he'd drunk so much and was now suffering the consequences. He slowly turned over in bed, trying to keep the noise down so that he wouldn't wake Chloe. His brow furrowed in confusion when he realised that her side of the bed was empty, the covers and pillows perfectly straight as if it hadn't been slept in. He bolted upright in bed as the events from last night suddenly came flooding back to him. Lee ran his hand through his hair in frustration as he thought about what he'd done. It had never been his attention to kiss Steph, but the alcohol had clouded his judgement. He knew in his heart that he should have pushed her away instantly rather than kissing her back. He'd have given anything to be able to take back his actions and save Chloe the hurt that he'd accidentally caused her. Before he could stop himself he swiped his phone from the bedside cabinet and quickly called Chloe, sighing sadly to himself when it went straight to voicemail.

He threw back the covers and quickly climbed out of bed, his stomach churning with guilt as he hurried downstairs, suddenly remembering that she'd told him that she'd left something in the bin. As soon as he reached the kitchen, he opened the bin nervously, not entirely sure what he was going to discover. His stomach churned as he stared at the corset, his hands shaking as he slowly lifted it out of the bin, his gaze fixed on it.

"What's that?" Steph piped up as she walked into the room, frowning at him as he stared down at his hands.

"It's Chloe's." he muttered, gently stroking the material with his thumb. He swallowed the lump that was rising in his throat as he thought about the woman that he loved with all his heart and how worthless he'd managed to make her feel. So much so that she was convinced that he would rather be with Steph than her.

"I'm such a fucking idiot!" he said angrily.

"You haven't done anything wrong." she sighed.

"She's the one who has been pushing you away for the past few weeks." she continued.

"That's not the point, I shouldn't have cheated on her." he said quickly, still wishing in his heart that he knew what he'd done to make Chloe hate him so much in the first place.

"I miss her so much." he whispered, his eyes filling with tears as he stared at the corset, still not able to tear his eyes away from it.

"Even though she's been checked out for a while, it feels different now that she isn't here." he continued thoughtfully, trying to suppress the panic that she was slowly slipping through his fingertips.

"Don't worry about it, she'll come back. She probably just needs a couple of days to clear her head." she pointed out, trying to reassure him. Steph sighed sadly to herself when he nodded slowly, his eyes brimming with tears.

"I am really sorry." she added, her stomach churning nervously that he was never going to forgive her for driving a wedge between him and Chloe.

"Sorry for what?" he frowned.

"I shouldn't have kissed you, I'd had too much to drink and you looked so handsome last night, I know I shouldn't have done it though." she explained.

Lee nodded slowly and quickly left the room, walking in a trance, not entirely sure where he was going, but suddenly feeling the intense need to be alone with his thoughts. He couldn't help but feel a pang of fear that Chloe would never forgive his actions. She'd always told him that she would never forgive infidelity and despite the fact that it was only a kiss, he had still cheated on her. He wandered into the nursery room, gazing at the surroundings as he placed his back against the wall and slowly slid down it, his legs finally buckling from underneath him. He gazed down at the corset that was still in his hands, slowly leaning forward and resting his head against it, sighing quietly when he inhaled her familiar scent.

"I'm so sorry Chlo." he whispered, wishing that he could turn the clock back to the way things used to be between the two of them. He placed the back of his head against the wall, no longer able to fight the tears that were filling his eyes, his gut somehow screaming at him that he'd lost Chloe for good. He sniffed quietly, angrily wiping away his tears as he gazed around the room, his heart pounding against his chest when he remembered how excited they had been to meet their baby and to finally become a family. His brow furrowed in confusion when he suddenly noticed that the drawers were open, the counters completely empty of all of the blankets that they'd been collecting in preparation.

"Steph?!" he called, quickly standing up as the panic started to set in. He began to pace frantically, glancing up as Steph walked into the room.

"What's wrong?" she asked, instantly sensing that something had happened.

"All of the baby's things have gone!" he exclaimed, his heart pounding against his chest as he opened the remaining drawers and noticed that they were all empty.

"She only had one suitcase last night though?!" he exclaimed.

"It was probably Amy and Steven." she replied, finally joining the dots in her head.

"What?" he frowned, quickly turning to face her.

"They were here earlier when you were still asleep." she explained.

"I just assumed they were taking Amy's things, but they had a lot of stuff so they must have collected the baby's things too." she continued thoughtfully.

"Oh my god." he whispered, taking deep breaths, his eyes darting around as he tried to process what was happening.

"She's not coming back is she?!" he exclaimed, running his hand through his hair as he began to pace, not entirely sure what to do. Steph opened her mouth to respond, quickly closing it again when she realised that she had no idea what to say to him. She jumped as Lee flung the corset onto the counter and hurried out of the room.

"Where are you going?!" Steph called as she hurried after him.

"She'll have gone to Nottingham with Amy." he said quickly, jumping the last few steps and pulling on his jacket.

"Wait!" she exclaimed. Lee turned to face her, raising his eyebrow as he waited for her to continue.

"Maybe you should let her calm down first." she suggested.

"Otherwise she won't want to talk to you if she's still angry." she continued. Lee sighed deeply to himself, quickly realising that she was right. Despite his better judgement, he knew that if he stood a chance of fixing things with Chloe, he needed to allow her to calm down.

"I need some air." he whispered, quickly closing the front door behind himself.

Chapter Eighty Two

"Right come on!" Amy exclaimed, gripping onto Chloe's arm and attempting to pull her off the sofa.

"No, I don't want too, I'm fine here!" Chloe protested, not quite having the mental or physical strength to stand up.

"You've been moping on the sofa for the past two days." Amy pointed out.

"I'm taking you for a walk or something." she added, sighing quietly when Chloe rolled her eyes.

"I don't want to go out. Leave me alone." Chloe said firmly.

"But the atmosphere here is horrible." Amy said in hushed tones, glancing nervously at the doorway, in case her Mother walked into the room.

"That's because she doesn't want me here." Chloe said sadly.

"Yet another person that doesn't want me around." she muttered under her breath.

"I really need to get my own place." she continued, sighing sadly to herself.

"It's difficult though isn't it, because you can't exactly get a job at the moment." Amy pointed out, her stomach sinking when Chloe nodded slowly and huddled under the blanket, her eyes full of a deep sadness that she was clearly trying to hide.

"It's a shame Kyle is still away at Uni, otherwise you could have got a place with him. I can't exactly afford to rent anywhere on my tiny wages." Amy said thoughtfully.

"I'm going to be a burden to anyone that I live with anyway, especially when the baby arrives." Chloe said quietly, her eyes filling with tears as she thought about her hopeless situation.

"Your Mum is right, I've made all of the wrong life choices." she added, sighing quietly to herself. The two of them jumped, glancing at Amy's phone as it began to ring. Amy sighed to herself when she saw that Steven was calling her.

"Aren't you going to answer it?" Chloe asked.

"I can't speak to him here." Amy muttered glancing nervously at the doorway as she quickly cancelled the call.

"Besides, I don't know if I want to see him anymore." she continued quietly. Chloe raised her eyebrow questioningly.

"Guys are just dicks, Dad cheated on my Mum, you've been cheated on by both of your boyfriends, what's the point of even trying." Amy explained, sighing despondently.

"Steven is a good guy though." Chloe pointed out, feeling slightly sorry for Amy when she realised how much she liked Steven.

"Yeah we thought that about Lee." she argued, angrily throwing herself on the sofa beside Chloe.

"I'm done with it." she added. Chloe sighed sadly to herself, gently wrapping her arms around Amy's shoulders and placing her head on her shoulder.

"Please don't live your life based on my bad experiences." Chloe muttered, no longer able to hold back her tears. Amy sighed quietly, gently resting her head against Chloe's, desperately wishing that she could do something to take away the terrible hurt that she knew Chloe was feeling. Her stomach churned with anger as she thought about Lee and how perfect he'd seemed when he stayed with them, how he clearly idolised and adored Chloe. How things had changed. Amy had looked up to him, admired how committed he was to Chloe and how much he loved her, but now she couldn't even bring herself to think about his despicable actions.

"Does he still keep calling you?" Amy asked, not quite able to bring herself to say Lee's name. Chloe nodded slowly.

"So does Nathan." she told her, trying to steer the conversation away from the man that had broken her heart.

"Have you spoken to him?" Amy asked.

"No, I don't want to speak to anyone." she whispered, gently wiping away the tears that were rolling down her cheeks. Amy nodded slowly, her heart breaking a little when she realised that Chloe was crying.

"You're sleeping in my bed with me tonight." Amy stated.

"No, it's fine. I don't sleep much, so I quite like being in front of the TV." Chloe argued, not quite able to bring herself to admit that she would rather be alone.

"The baby likes to move a lot at night." she continued, smiling slightly as she placed her hand on her bump. The two of them jumped, glancing at each other as the doorbell rang.

"I'll go." Amy sighed, quickly standing up to answer it. She gasped, her feet freezing to the spot as she stood face to face with Lee.

"I've just come to talk to her." he said quickly, when he noticed Amy's eyes narrowing angrily.

"She doesn't want to talk to you." she said shortly.

"Please Amy, I've just driven four hours." he pointed out, sighing sadly to himself when he realised how much everyone hated him. First Chloe, then Nathan and now Amy.

"I don't care. My loyalty is to Chloe, I owe you nothing." she said, an edge of bitterness present in her voice. Lee sighed to himself, hesitating for a moment before gently pushing past her.

"Wait!" Amy called after him, quickly slamming the front door closed and hurrying after him.

"What are you doing here?!" Chloe exclaimed as soon as she laid eyes on him.

"I came to see you." he said softly, his heart pounding against his chest as soon as he looked at her, the intense love that he felt for her on a daily basis suddenly overwhelming him. His heart broke a little as he stared at her tear stained cheeks and the dark circles under her eyes.

"What for?" she said dismissively, snapping him out of his thoughts.

"I have nothing to say to you anymore." she added, not quite able to bring herself to look at him.

"I'm so sorry Chloe, I never wanted this to happen." he whispered, squatting in front of her as he tried to get her to look at him.

"So you keep saying, but that doesn't change the fact that it did!" she snapped.

"You promised that you would never cheat on me!" she added angrily.

"But then saying that, you also promised to keep the baby's name a secret!" she continued, her stomach swirling with anger.

"Both of which were an accident." he said quickly, swallowing the lump that was rising in his throat as he thought about his actions and how he'd managed to tear his family apart.

"Bullshit!" she exclaimed.

"I wouldn't even be surprised if what I saw wasn't the tip of the iceberg!" she continued angrily.

"What are you talking about?" he frowned.

"You've been hanging out with Steph all of the time, I wouldn't be surprised if more didn't happen!" she ranted.

"It didn't Chloe, I swear." he said quickly.

"It doesn't matter anymore anyway." she said quickly.

"Please, can we talk about things so that we can work them out?" he pleaded with her, his heart slowly starting to break when he realised that she wasn't listening to anything that he was saying to her.

"There's nothing to work out, it's finished. There's no coming back from this." she said quietly, uttering the words that Lee had been dreading.

"You don't mean that." he whispered, biting his lip to fight the tears that were filling his eyes.

"I know I've really hurt you and I'm so sorry." he continued, trying to get her to respond to him. Chloe remained silent, not quite having the energy to argue with him any longer. She glanced down at her hands that were resting in her lap, quickly pulling them away from him when he reached to take her hand.

"Don't touch me!" she told him firmly.

"Please Chloe, we've been through too much to throw it all away." he pleaded, a note of desperation present in his voice.

"You should have thought of that before you kissed someone else." she said shortly. Before Chloe could talk herself out of it, she quickly reached behind her head, her hands shaking as she carefully removed her necklace, wincing slightly at the pain in her broken wrist.

"Chlo don't." he begged her, watching closely as she worked her engagement ring off her finger.

"I can't lose you." he said, his voice breaking with emotion.

"I love you." he whispered, glancing down at his hand as Chloe quickly placed her necklace and ring into his hand.

"I don't love you anymore, you've broken my heart." she admitted, her eyes filling with tears as she uttered the words that she'd been afraid of for some time.

"Chlo...." he started, trailing off as a small sob escaped his lips. He stared at the woman that he loved, desperately trying to resist the urge to touch her and hold her in his arms. His stomach churned as he tried to process her words, the realisation finally hitting him that he'd lost her for good, like he'd feared. He wiped away his tears, trying to fight the anger that he was feeling at himself for ruining their relationship for good.

"What about the baby?" he whispered, when he suddenly realised that not only had he lost Chloe, but that he might lose his daughter too.

"I won't keep her from you." she said dismissively. Lee nodded, slowly standing up, his eyes still fixed on Chloe, his feet frozen to the spot. Despite the fact that he knew she didn't want him around, he couldn't quite bring himself to leave the house.

"I'll get someone to call you when she is born." she said dismissively, quickly standing up and walking out of the room, without even looking back.

Printed in Great Britain
by Amazon